Nine Days
in
Rome

JULIAN GOULD

Illustration credit to Francesco Santosuosso:

for the portrait of author, Julian Gould

ISBN 978-1-63735-011-9 (pbk)

ISBN 978-1-63735-019-5 (ebook)

Library of Congress Control Number: 2023903166

PRAISE

A tremendous achievement for a first-time author. Julian Gould's *Nine Days in Rome* digs into the emotional depths of its characters—an unemployed executive chaperoning a tour of Rome and the teachers and students on the trip—while also deftly describing the wonders of the Eternal City. The book links the crises stemming from the teenagers' behavior to poor parenting, shining a light on how the complexities of modern life can make it difficult for young people to thrive. Part travelogue, part emotional thriller, the book makes for a gripping read.

Shawn Johal | CEO, Elevation Leaders

Growing up in the modern world isn't easy, and in *Nine Days in Rome,* a trip to the Eternal City sets off a series of incidents that test to the utmost the problem-solving ability of Atticus Winterle, the book's narrator. Both moving and a brilliant critique of the ramifications of bad parenting on the youth of today, the book details how Winterle, an unemployed corporate executive, handles the immensely challenging task of chaperoning the group of Atlanta high school students and their teachers. With little experience of teenagers, Winterle quickly discovers that he must use all his tact, interpersonal skill, and a little muscle to defuse a series of difficult situations caused by the troubles the students have brought with them from home.

Tamara Nall | CEO and founder, The Leading Niche

A thoroughly enjoyable and highly eventful account of a tour of the Eternal City of Rome by a group of students and teachers from Atlanta, Georgia, and their harried but resourceful chaperone Atticus Winterle, a senior executive based in Italy. He takes the role when between jobs and finds that it is both more thanhe bargained, and to his surprise, he finds himself bonding with both students and teachers as he does his best to keep the students out of trouble and the tour on schedule.

Eric Wentz | author of *Zero Two Hundred Hours*

A compulsively readable book that tells the unlikely tale of an unemployed senior executive who takes on the role of chaperoning a trip to Rome by a group of sixteen high school students and their three teachers from Atlanta, Georgia. From a fish-out-of-water story, the book quickly transitions into a psychological drama that contrasts the majesty of the ancient Italian capital with the turbulent lives of the students visiting the Eternal City.

**Dr. Kathy Humel | CEO,
senior consultant, RxKHumel, LLC**

DIVE INTO THE
ENCHANTING WORLD
OF ROME!

GOT A COMMENT,
PLANNING A ROMAN
GETAWAY, OR
CRAVING A TASTE OF
ITALY?

SEND YOUR QUERIES
TO
9DAYSINROME@GMAIL.
COM

To my three children, Rebecca, Flaminia, and Davide.
That they may be guided
through their lives by numerous, flawless choices.
And to my beloved wife,
Susanna, who has stood by me during the entire
realization of this book.

CONTENTS

Friday, April 30, Day Four

Saturday, May 1, Day Five

Sunday, May 2, Day Six

Monday, May 3, Day Seven

CHAPTER 1

"Mr. Winterle? May I take your tray?"

"Oh yes, please. I'm finished."

"We shall be serving a variety of teas and coffee, including a French press, shortly. In the meantime, may I offer you a hot towel for your hands?"

"Thank you."

"A splash more of Moët?"

"Absolutely…"

"Cathay Pacific would like to thank you for flying regularly with us Mr. Winterle. Please let me know if there is anything else I can bring you to make your flight more comfortable."

I was sitting in my very comfortable Poltrona Frau armchair and had dozed off just long enough to have this vivid memory projected somewhere in the recesses of my brain. Not unusual, I thought, that this particular recollection would come to mind considering the existing predicament I found myself in. Reminiscing about the glory days, either awake or dreaming, provided some temporary comfort. Those little hot towels, at forty-thousand feet in the stratosphere, were part and parcel of a world that I had come to take for granted for almost fifteen years—flights in first or business class; chauffeurs awaiting my arrival at airports in cities such as Hong Kong, Tokyo, London, and New York; five-star hotels;

membership at some of the best spas and athletic clubs; as well as exquisite cuisine in Michelin-rated restaurants.

On the rare occasions when I was not on a plane, I would drive to my spacious office in the center of Milan, Italy, in my company car—a Mercedes E350 AMG sedan—which was always at my disposal. While I was light-years away from being a Jack Welch or a Sergio Marchionne, I was very much at ease in my role as country manager in Italy for a manufacturer of a multimillion fashion accessories company. I had a great salary, a generous bonus potential, a lucrative stock option plan, and a comfortable retirement scenario. I was on top of the world. But just like Leonardo DiCaprio on the *Titanic*, feeling like you're "on top of the world" can have disastrous consequences.

In juxtaposition, I had a well below-average marriage, which ended up crashing to the ground in flames. The causes, according to my ex-wife, were the excessive travel, long working hours, and my general apathy when in her company. Apart from this last observation, which was accurate, I had a completely different opinion as to why our union dissolved— reasons that seemed important to me but not to anyone else. So be it.

Then again, in these modern times, wasn't this scenario a predictable outcome for marriage? For one reason or another, remaining legally or religiously bound to one another for even five or six years (if that long) has become a rarity of sorts. My wife and I were just another checkmark in the column for failed marriage statistics. Our brief union, however, had brought two beautiful children into the world, a boy and a girl who made life worth living. I had the money to spoil them and made sure to do so, especially when I left home to live in a much smaller apartment nearby.

The children were with me on those weekends when I wasn't traveling for work, and the time I spent with them was priceless. We would go to the movies, kick a soccer ball around in the park, do a little shopping, always find time for a gelato, and then come home and play board games until they fell asleep. There was never a boring moment. I had my career and quality time with my children. I considered myself fortunate and blessed.

Then came that fateful day when I lost my job, and everything took a turn for the worse. For no apparent reason, my ex-wife started limiting the number of weekends I could have with the children, while my new companion began suggesting, then insisting, that we spend more time on our own. Decisions were being made with little, if any, regard to what I felt or wanted.

This all seemed very long ago, but a glance at the free-standing calendar on my nearby desk showed that little more than a year had passed since I had been laid off. Not even the blink of an eye in the larger sweep of time, but a never-ending, torturous state of limbo for me. *Screw you, Lehman Brothers! Go to hell, AIG! And up yours, Fanny Mae, along with your subprime mortgages!* These conglomerates and the avarice of those at their command were the direct cause of me being graciously told to leave the company where I had worked for five years.

The ensuing worldwide panic, sparked by the collapse of this financial house of cards, took a stranglehold on consumers, lenders of credit, importers, exporters, and businesses of all sizes, bringing on a tidal wave of spending cuts that placed the heads of millions of employees on the chopping block. How ironic and, in fact, prescient that one usually speaks of the *head* count in an organization, and not the number of *people* (individuals).

My spacious office, the Mercedes, the international travel, the chauffeurs, the five-star hotels, the Michelin-starred restaurants—all became pleasantries of the past, along with those little hot towels on Cathay Pacific. And even though it matters a great deal whether you diligently save money for hard times (which, you can rest assured, will manifest sooner or later), the real trauma comes from that all-enveloping sense of impotence that starts the day you walk out of your office, carrying framed photos of your children in a plain cardboard box.

In a nutshell, you have been unceremoniously told that your contribution to the working world is no longer required. *Don't you understand that you're out of the picture?* Your input is neither vital nor sought after. No more board meetings, no more three-to-five-year business plans, no more decisions on yearly budgets, production timetables, supply chain issues, ex-factory/wholesale/retail margins, retail pricing, marketing plans, media/ad spend, distribution agreements, contractual obligations, account receivables, and end-of-month reporting. Gone are those periods of the year where you spend sixteen hours a day in the office bitching about everything, including not being able to find decent sushi at two o'clock in the morning. All history! You have become a nuisance.

"Wow, let's slow down here," I said out loud, addressing the air. My heart was galloping, and my palms were sweating. I sat up and realized I was again approaching the "black hole," as I called it—that dark, deep pit in my subconscious where I could see, feel, and hear nothing, except for a harsh, menacing, critical voice continually berating me. Here, time and space meshed into one dimension, and extraterrestrial forces glued me to my armchair. *Welcome to the Twilight Zone.* Cue eerie music.

This was a place where all my fears took over my thoughts, a place where I began to believe that I was indeed a failure. A failure in my career, to my children, to myself, a failure at living up to my responsibilities. This was a dark, foreboding gorge that I tumbled into far too easily and climbed out only with great difficulty. I had plummeted into this frightening state of mind over the past months much too frequently, and sometimes I remained there for days. I had to thank Francesca, my live-in companion, for pulling me out of these dark holes with sympathetic remarks:

"Get up and stop feeling so damn sorry for yourself!"

"I can't take this situation anymore!"

"Get out there and do something with yourself for Christ's sake!"

Yes, she could really be a bitch at times, but it worked. Francesca wasn't here now, though, so I had to get my act together and avoid falling over that precipice. I poured myself a second glass of a pretty decent 2005 Chianti into the wine goblet that stood on a beaten-up English drop-leaf table I had purchased at a flea market in Heidelberg many moons ago. I took a large gulp and attempted to focus my mind more constructively on the interminable emergency at hand—the need for a job, *any* job!

Since September 2009, I had been in touch with over twenty-five executive search firms from Milan to Hong Kong, and London to New York. I had beefed up my *LinkedIn* account, joined the *A Small World* and *Naymz* networking domains. All this had landed me several interviews with various companies that seemed willing to get to know me better and, possibly, make me an offer. However, due to "the current worldwide economic downturn, an "unexpected" budget freeze, "internal advancement," or a "change in strategic planning," the offers did not materialize.

I was also aware, strange as it may seem, that my name was a bit of a handicap when looking for employment, especially in a foreign country. My mother had fallen in love with the book *To Kill a Mockingbird* when she was pregnant and, yes, if you've read it, you can guess what happened—she named me Atticus. Atticus Winterle. My mother wanted a unique first name, something other than the ubiquitous Joe, Bob, Jim, or Billy. Well, she found what she was looking for. Would it have been better if she had been reading some other literary work? I doubt it. Had it been *Moby Dick*, I have no doubt she would have called me Ishmael. Or maybe Moby.

***

What unnerved me the most about job hunting was repeatedly getting the comment "Yes, we find your resume very interesting, but we were looking for someone a bit younger." The fact was, in Italy, as well as in most other European countries, "age-centric" discrimination was still commonplace, along with being denied a position due to physical appearance. Fine. I could understand that my fifty-four years on this earth didn't put me in the spring chicken category, but damn it, I had the know-how! To put somebody recently out of college in a middle to high position of seniority, with loaded guns of responsibility in their face ten to twelve hours a day, was just asking for trouble. Along with the pressure, fear, ignorance, and lack of on-the-job experience, as well as a total absence of people-management skills, it was inevitable that the result would be an array of very unsound business decisions. I certainly wasn't aware of any first-year medical students performing quadruple bypasses. Why should it be different in the business world?

These rookies can have so much gray matter that it oozes out of their left ear, but *experience* equals the amount of *time* in a work environment and the number of instances that one's head has, figuratively speaking, slammed against the wall after making a wrong decision. That is what tempers a person to take on those tough choices in the business world. Sure, you can pay these newcomers less, maybe even eliminate the bonus, and give them a Fiat instead of an Audi A4, with the promise of a corporate credit card after three years of employment. But where is your company going to end up if you eliminate your experienced staff, replacing it with youngsters who until yesterday were reading volume 1 of Philip Kotler's *Marketing Management?*

"Okay, Atticus," I muttered. "Get a grip on yourself. This isn't an appropriate way to approach the problem."

I was angry and frustrated, but I knew that these negative thoughts weren't going to get me anywhere. *What's done is done.* I just needed to keep communicating with every serious executive search firm I could find, continuing to get my resume in front of them—and fast. Luckily, I had put some money away for a rainy day. Unfortunately, the day in question turned out to be over a year, and with alimony payments, monthly rent, and all the smaller day-to-day expenses, my resources were drying up. What was it that the inimitable John Barrymore said? "You never realize how short a month is until you pay alimony."

Francesca's job for the time being seemed airtight, given that she was head of the general affairs department of a large consumer goods company. It was her job to implement those spending cuts, so fervently introduced in this new, high-anxiety corporate reality. Once it was decided which heads were on the chopping block, she had to handle all the legal issues with the lawyers and the unions—no simple matter in a country like Italy. I didn't believe for a moment that she was enjoying doing this to her fellow employees, but if she in the end was going to be axed, it wasn't going to happen anytime soon. With her salary, we weren't going to starve, but clearly, the situation had to change, and fast, if only to restore stability to my very fragile state of mind.

On top of everything else I had to deal with, yet another situation had arisen that I had to confront sooner rather than later. The very thought of it made me apprehensive and uneasy. Outlandish as it might seem, I did have a transitory job waiting for me (if anyone in their right mind could call it a "job"). I didn't want to even consider it, let alone accept it. I had tried every excuse imaginable with my friend Marco, who had gone out of his way to offer me this "opportunity," as he called it. Mind you, I had sound reasons for steering clear of Marco's proposal. First of all, it was going to take precious time away from searching for a real job. Second, and more importantly, I had no experience in this line of work, nor did I want to have anything to do with the target audience.

In the end, however, mainly because of Marco's concern for me and his maniacal insistence, I regretfully accepted. It certainly wasn't for the money—seventy-five euros a day wasn't going to put me on Forbes's list of the richest men in the world, even with the expenses covered. But a little extra cash in this particular period wasn't going to hurt. Also, I wouldn't be seeing the children for the next two weekends since they were with their mother visiting friends in Switzerland. After my divorce four years earlier, my Saturdays and Sundays with the children had become as close to an addiction as I had ever experienced. Not seeing them for fourteen days was going to be particularly hard on me. Francesca was also going to be away for almost three weeks. She was on a job-rotation program and had switched places for a month with her counterpart across the pond in their New Jersey office, where I guessed she would learn how to fire people the American way. *Sadly amusing*, I thought, finding this unintended oxymoron quite appropriate.

Settling back into my armchair, I accepted that I had no respectable way to reject Marco's offer, especially at this late stage. I reassured myself that the experience I was about to embark on was not going to be the nightmare I fully expected it to be.

"Rome is like playing in my backyard," I said. "Sure, I left seven years ago, but the twelve years I lived there count for something. There are going to be three other adults in the group, so I don't have to shoulder all the responsibility. All the travel arrangements have been made, the hotel and restaurants have been booked in advance, and we'll have a bus at our disposal the entire time. So what's the big deal?"

As I talked to myself, I realized I had an attentive audience: Cleo and Mao Mao, both of whom I found as kittens four years ago, abandoned on the hot asphalt under a dilapidated, municipal garbage bin. Cleo, a jet-black cross between a Siamese and a gray tabby, sat like a statue on the bookshelf, looking at me with an expression in her emerald-green eyes that, when translated from cat-*olese* to "humanese" meant "I shall miss you while you're away, and I shall be feverishly waiting for your return." In temperament, Cleo was more like a faithful dog than a cat. By contrast, Mao Mao's demeanor as he watched me from his cherished throw pillow was more feline in character and, therefore, much more to the point: "Who the hell is going to feed us, change our drinking water, and clean the litter box while you're traipsing around Rome for the next two weeks?!"

I finished my third and rather large goblet of dark-red Chianti. I had not eaten, and I was feeling slightly inebriated. So I continued with my one-man show. "No panicking, please. Rosanna and her husband from next door have the key to the apartment and shall be coming every day to feed you and change your water. But don't expect them to go and buy fresh fish and chicken livers at the market. It's going to be canned and dried food for you both until I get back."

Nobody has ever been able to convince me that cats don't understand humans—when they want to, of course. As soon as they heard "canned" and "dried food," Cleo and Mao Mao jumped off their respective perches and bolted out of the room.

"Spoiled brats," I muttered as I went into the kitchen with the empty wineglass to find something to nibble on. Living just a block away from a very well-furnished outdoor food market had not only lifted the bar for Francesca's and my culinary choices but also contributed greatly to our cats' absolute refusal to go near anything in a box or hermetically sealed container. Rummaging in the pantry, it dawned on me that I had not gone out food shopping in almost a week. I found a canister of rosemary-flavored crackers and a half-empty bag of stale pretzels, both of which Francesca had brought back from a business trip to Switzerland. Pouring the last contents of the bottle into my glass, I contemplated opening another. I glanced at the wall clock. It was almost ten o'clock.

I had to meet Marco at Rome's Fiumicino airport at fifteen past eleven in the morning. Over the past few weeks, he had repeatedly phoned me to try and give me detailed briefings regarding the who, how, where, and when of the "job." The thought of this encouraged me to go ahead and uncork another bottle of wine, this time a 2006 Barbera d'Alba from the Barolo region of Italy. Glass in hand, I walked out of the kitchen onto the balcony. The night was warm and balmy as was common for the month of May in Milan. I sat on a cushioned, wrought-iron rocker that I had picked up at a garden center a few miles away. The view was more breathtaking than usual, as were the delicious scents wafting from the family-run restaurant, La Pineta, next door, where they were cooking a variety of meats on two large open-air grills. The soupy smoke reached all the way up to the third floor. Occasionally, a very light breeze whirled around the apartment and blew away the strong smell of charred pork sausages, *lombata di vitello* (the Italian rendition of veal chops), and roasted chicken. Even if the haze from La Pineta ("pine forest" in English) obscured my view, there was nothing much to look at from here, least of all, a forest.

My apartment block was one of many that had sprung up on the outskirts of Milan since the late 1980s. These nondescript structures reflected the sad demise of most residential areas on the outskirts of European cities. The buildings' architecture held no charm, comprising a congestion of four-, six-, and eight-story light-gray cement structures with narrow potholed roads coiled around them like a mass of freshwater eels. They were an eyesore, a showcase for graffiti terrorists, and a nightmare for parking if you didn't have a garage (which I fortunately did).

Nonetheless, I wasn't opposed to living here. My children loved it because they each had their own room when they were with me on the weekends. The apartment had over 2,300 square feet of living space. An apartment that size anywhere else in the city of Milan would have been unaffordable. Francesca only supported the idea of living here because the place was big enough for her to have one room totally for herself and her hobby—painting.

Even so, she had wanted to move farther out of the city center, to a small town called Lodi, about twenty-five miles southwest of Milan. She persisted to the point where I gave in, and we went to see a townhouse that she loved (and that I barely approved of). We were just about to make an offer when doomsday hit, and I found out that I wouldn't be seeing another monthly paycheck for quite some time. Francesca reluctantly accepted the situation for now, so we were going to have to stay in our spacious yet drab abode.

My thoughts were interrupted by another eddy of sausage smoke from La Pineta. Glancing at my watch, I saw that it was almost eleven o'clock. That allowed me six hours of sleep before I had to get up, shower, shave, and jump into a cab for the airport. I pulled myself out of the rocker, swallowed a last mouthful of wine, threw the stale pretzels in the small outdoor trash can, and went back into the kitchen. It was too late to eat anything substantial, so I just had a slice of bread with some fresh parmigiano cheese.

The cats followed my example and finished off the last pieces of calf liver in their baby-blue ceramic bowls. After a quick visit to the bathroom, I went to the bedroom. The bed was almost hidden by piles of not-so-clean clothes, magazines, and books that I had heaped on it since Francesca's departure. It was like a detonation area for unearthed land mines. Our sleeping quarters were one of the biggest issues that Francesca and I had had to contend with when we decided to move in together a year and a half ago. We both had previous live-in arrangements and marriages punctuated by rather long periods of being single, so we needed to adjust to each other's habits of orderliness, or lack thereof.

My pet peeve was the kitchen, where absolute cleanliness and order are of the utmost importance (unless, of course, one is preparing a particularly difficult recipe). Olive oil, vinegar bottles, and those small look-alike spice jars need to be positioned on the right-hand side of the burners, and the cooking knives and various kitchen utensils placed upright in their granite, cylindrical containers on the left, hence leaving ample space on the marble countertop for dicing, cutting, and chopping. The pots and pans must be neatly stored in the ample cupboard space, the Le Creuset cast-iron cocottes in a straight line on the counter, and plates and cutlery stored in the appropriate drawers.

The living and dining room areas must be free of excessive clutter, but a bit of dust on the many bookshelves was acceptable. As far as the bedrooms and bathrooms were concerned, I only become slightly annoyed when nocturnal insect-like creatures begin to crawl on the night tables, vanity, and the bathroom sink. Francesca, however, had an altogether different point of view regarding the above-average square meter space we called home.

For her, the bathrooms and bedrooms needed to be perfectly tidy, always ready to undergo the white glove test. Floors and ceramic tiled walls in the bathroom had to be glistening, towels always in the correct place on their holders and folded so that the corners met exactly, and toothbrushes standing bristles up in their Murano glass holders. Even the first tissue popping out of the crochet-covered Kleenex box had to be puffed up just right.

In the bedroom, not a piece of clothing was to be lying around, having all been folded and placed in their cubicles. The bed was to be made to marine-corps standards. All the items on the dresser were to be spaced with mathematical precision. The living and dining room areas took a back seat to the bedroom for Francesca and could be orderly or disheveled.

Finally, there was the kitchen—a place where my Francesca took an enormous amount of pleasure in spilling various sticky substances on the floor or the counters, where dirty dishes could gather in the sink until they formed a towering, multicolored mass resembling something out of a Wes Craven horror flick and where, even worse, the olive oil and vinegar bottles remained on the *left*-hand side of the burners.

It's difficult to imagine that a loving and respectful relationship between two people could come to a screeching halt in front of a pile of dirty dishes and bathroom mold. But at times, the nasty temper tantrums that erupted over such trivial matters could last hours. In hindsight, this should have set off alarm bells. It was rare that Francesca and I would end these moments of tension with a good laugh.

Even though the windows in the bedroom were open because of the very warm evening air, there was no discernible breeze, just heat leaping off the asphalt below, with an occasional whiff of sausage smoke.

CHAPTER 2

After clearing the bed of books, magazines, and newspaper clippings, I sat on the side of the mattress, took off my shorts, and launched them toward the corner chair, missing it completely. I propped up three pillows behind my back and pushed the sheets to the other side of the bed with my feet. I was starting to imagine what the next couple of weeks were going to be like. What I really needed to do was to unfold those sheets of paper, which, not by chance, were buried underneath the pile of books on the bedside table and review the unavoidable: the names of the participants, schedules, the brochure of the hotel, various vouchers, and more importantly, the list of my duties and responsibilities. Marco had suggested that I go through the documentation carefully before arriving in Rome, but even though he had sent it to me via courier over a week ago, I still had not gotten up the courage to read a single word.

I took hold of the papers and pulled gently, attempting to keep the pile of reading material in its place, but Peter Drucker, Wilkie Collins, and Fyodor Dostoevsky nonetheless tumbled unceremoniously to the floor. This slightly annoying incident reminded me that I had not yet selected any books to carry on this ill-fated Rome excursion. Since my teen years, I had always found it difficult to fall asleep without reading at least a few pages, no matter what the hour, no matter the genre. I usually had a stack of books leaning on one side on my bedside table like the Tower of Pisa. Fortunately, I had been able to take all my books when I left my ex-wife without any reprisals from her. That was about all I got, besides two Persian rugs and the cats, which she barely tolerated.

I put the papers back on the bedside table and once again avoided looking at them by turning my attention to the books scattered on the floor. I was in the middle of Drucker's *The Effective Executive*, which was published in 1967 and had not aged. Along with Philip Kotler's *Marketing Essentials*, I was thoroughly convinced that these were two works that every business professional, present or future, must read. I decided that Drucker would accompany me to Rome. I picked up Collins's *The Woman in White* and wondered whether I should carry it with me or not. I was in the middle of the third reading of this great Victorian mystery thriller full of colorful characters, suspense, and plot twists. After a few moments' thought, I opted for another of Collins's works, *The Moonstone*, which I had read many years ago. The only problem was finding it.

Lastly, I retrieved Dostoevsky's *Demons* from under the bed. I had only recently begun rereading this masterpiece, but I wasn't going to bring it on the trip. Such a work required more concentration than I would be allowed in the days to come. I thought about how I had struggled through *Demons* and *Crime and Punishment* in college. At seventeen, I was unable to grasp the depth of Dostoevsky's portrayal of pathological states of mind and how humiliation and depression can lead to suicide, and madness, to say nothing of the sheer evil that a man can exercise against his own kind. I had often wondered how many college students, who had in their curricula a lengthy list of classics, were able to come away with even a vague understanding of the books they read. In my opinion, authors like Dostoyevsky, Tolstoy, Dickens, Hesse, Kafka, Melville, Proust, and Balzac, to name very few, could only be fully appreciated by readers of a certain age with a suite of life experiences behind them.

At seventeen going on eighteen, I had been busy studying only what was strictly necessary. I was also working part-time jobs to pay my tuition, chasing after girls, listening to

Black Sabbath and the Sex Pistols at stun-grenade volume, and trying to remember where I was every Saturday and Sunday morning after coming out of my drunken or stoned stupor. Reading such authors at a young age certainly wasn't useless, but I was firmly convinced that a true appreciation of their works could only manifest when one became more mature and life savvy. With Peter and Wilkie chosen for this tumultuous romp around Rome, and with Fyodor staying at home, I still needed two or three more companions to complete my literary baggage. I jumped from the bed, threw on the bottom portion of a pair of pajamas that were balled up under the corner chair, and made my way down the dark hallway to the living room. With no warning whatsoever, two luminescent green balls shot up from the middle of the floor, and I barely managed to stop my foot from crashing down in the middle of a cat's rib cage.

"Cleo! How many times have I told you not to get comfortable where humans pass?" I switched on the light, and there she was with her paws stretched out like the Great Egyptian Sphinx of Giza. All I got was a loud *purrr* and a look in her eyes that said, "Am I not just exquisite?" I didn't know anything about dogs since I had never had one, but cats have this very bad habit of positioning themselves in the line of domestic pedestrian traffic, usually in the dark.

Having reached the living room without making a doughnut out of the cat, I gazed at the nine large bookcases where the bulk of my reading material was spread out. The books I had collected over the years were numerous, not even including the fifteen hundred or so volumes I had left behind in the States. Here in Milan, I had about seventeen hundred books, even though the number seemed to be steadily growing. I ran my eyes across the shelves and ascertained what I already knew quite well—the complete absence of order was enough to make me give up even trying to find what I was looking for.

Stephen King's *The Tommyknockers* was sitting neatly between Bocaccio's *Decameron* and *50 Tips for Clog Free Drains.* Solzhenitsyn's *Gulag Archipelago* was squeezed between Carroll's *Alice in Wonderland* and Hawthorne's *Selected Short Stories.* Daft's *Organization Theory and Design,* eighth edition, was wedged in between Plutarch's *Parallel Lives* and Volume 3 of a book on Chinese language grammar. After a good fifteen minutes of searching, I reached the fourth bookshelf where I found *The Moonstone,* as well as Gibran's *The Prophet.* The wisdom in this latter book was certainly going to provide valuable guidance in those moments, which I knew were going to be frequent on this trip, when I would lose my calm and composure. Hopefully, Gibran's soothing words would contribute to healing my shattered nerves.

With my reading material selected and satisfied with the choices, I went back to the bedroom. I placed the books in a pile on the floor next to all the clothes that I had thrown off the bed. Then I went to the bathroom to brush my teeth, then stripped down to my birthday suit again, and hopped back onto the bed. I was about to turn off the table lamp when an unexpected gust of sausage breeze blew the dreaded papers off the bedside table. The time had come to face the situation. I leaned over the mattress, picked up the sheets, took a deep breath, and began to read.

American Students Abroad (ASA)

Mission

The American Students Abroad Association strives every year to give a select group of students across the United States the opportunity to travel abroad at the end of their senior year of high school. This overseas experience in various Western European countries, as well as Russia, India, and China, allows students to experience new cultures, acquire new historical perspectives, and share in the customs of the country they visit. At the end of each trip, the participating students are asked to prepare a term paper of at least fifteen typewritten pages describing their stay. This paper is then submitted to the university or college that the student will be attending and may be taken into consideration for the overall grade point average of their first year at the discretion of the college or university involved.

Background

Each year, ASA selects over 150 high schools and invites them to participate in one of the many ASA overseas travel programs. ASA takes into consideration each senior student's application by carefully examining previous grade point averages, school attendance, extracurricular activities, as well as the student's conduct history. If a sufficient number of students apply and are accepted for a specific travel program, their school is notified by ASA and a series of meetings are scheduled with the principal and teachers to explain the ASA program, answer questions, and provide general information regarding the destination country and travel arrangements.

Students who are selected for a travel program but are unable to meet the financial requirements can ask for financial assistance through the ASA board.

Application Process

In the month of January of the students' senior year, ASA prepares letters and questionnaires which are delivered to over 150 high schools across the nation. These letters and questionnaires are distributed by selected teachers to all applicable students. If the student in question is interested in participating in one of the ASA trips scheduled for that particular year, he or she must fill out the questionnaire and have it signed by at least one teacher and one parent. Groups usually comprise between twelve to twenty students. Failure to obtain a minimum of twelve students does not automatically imply that the school is left out of the program. Two schools can join together to make up the require...

Her chest was so large that her bikini top was having difficulty covering even a couple of square centimeters of flesh. Her legs were long and symmetrical, with small ankles and beautifully manicured feet perfectly accentuated in a pair of décolleté six-inch pumps. A small teddy-bear tattoo was sensually situated right above her left ankle. These same legs blossomed into a round, endlessly curved, tightly stretched work of art that gently swayed from side to side to Stan Getz's "The Girl from Ipanema." It was as if I had 360-degree vision, for I was able to view her from all sides, top and bottom simultaneously. Her movements became more and more vigorous, which resulted in her breasts breaking free from their cruel, albeit limited, captivity. She placed her hands below and cupped them, emphasizing their already impressive size.

All my blood seemed to be rushing toward my groin area as if a Hoover vacuum cleaner had been suddenly switched on between my legs. That peculiar feeling of dizziness associated with uncensored lust was taking full control of my senses.

She turned and started walking slowly toward me, still running her hands between her cleavage. Suddenly, I realized that my feet were wet and that the room I was in with this Las Vegas striptease artist was slowly filling with water. She seemed not to care and kept coming closer to me, moving her hands playfully over her entire body and toward the most feminine portion of her anatomy.

By now, the room was rapidly filling with water. As it reached above our knees, I was overcome by an uncontrollable desire to urinate. "Not now!" I pleaded as her fingertips reached my chest. Her touch was more than just warm and exciting—it was absolutely riveting. However, my need to urinate was coming close to the red alert signal before a nuclear detonation. But I just needed to wait for one more second to have her chest brushing up against mine, just one more second, just one more—

Suddenly, as if a coiled spring had been released behind me, I was sitting up. But a bright light shining on my face kept me from opening my eyes. Worst of all, everything was fading quickly out of view, disappearing from my short-term memory. I threw myself back onto the mattress, having understood at once that she was a figment of my imagination taking part in an X-rated dream that was ending too soon (obviously, Francesca had already been away too long). While hoping that I would fall back into the middle of it all, stopping the action from rewinding into oblivion, I was also fully aware that the sensation of wetness was still very much with me.

Then reality set in with all its unparalleled cruelty. The neural circuits in my brain were sending marching orders to my bladder. The two-word command was, "Urinate now!" I leaped to my feet, grabbed my genitals, and ran to the bathroom. I stood at the toilet emptying was seemed to be the Mediterranean and only then began to realize that there was, in fact, an exceptional amount of light streaming in through the bathroom window at this very early hour of the morning. Except that the amount of sunshine showed that the hour was not, in fact, early.

I quickly began to enter the mental state of "You are late!" where panic, due to increased adrenaline and complete disorientation, became one's only guide. I stumbled out of the bathroom looking for the nearest available device that displayed time. Almost as if turning to face an execution squad, I swung my head toward the wall clock in the kitchen— it was 8:05 am.

Once you realize that, yes, you are, in fact, late for work— or an important appointment like your best friend's wedding and your children's first school recital —another set of actions takes over. Your arms and legs are going each in their own direction—picking things up from the floor, kicking doors open and shut, washing, rubbing, spraying, brushing, drying, grabbing, dressing, and shoeing. Simultaneously, the brain begins to consider all the possible consequences that being late will bring and what excuse hasn't already been used all over the world by millions of individuals young and old:

"The cat vomited a hairball on my shirt." This excuse requires that you have a cat or quickly find one. Having two, this always worked for me.

"The toaster oven caught on fire and set off the sprinkler system in the apartment." This requires a sprinkler system.

"I had car trouble." This is unimaginative and overused.

And the most famous of all, "I set the alarm last night as always, but the damn thing didn't go off this morning." I hadn't even set the alarm clock, hence the mess I now found myself in. Luckily for me, I was not late for officiating the unveiling of a newly discovered Rembrandt nor, unfortunately, would my tardiness make me miss the signing of a multimillion-dollar IPO.

No, I was just going to be late meeting up with a group of tired, cranky, loudmouthed, apathetic, and probably rude high-school seniors and their three boring teachers from Atlanta, Georgia, who were waiting for me to escort them on a nine-day tour around Rome. Voilà! That was the reality of it all. The thought of having to deal with a group of people who were, on average, thirty-three years younger than me temporarily made me forget that I was now extremely late.

Standing in a daze, half-dressed and semi-washed, I heard my cell phone ringing in the bedroom. This was most definitely Marco calling from the airport in Rome, panicking at the prospect that I wasn't going to show up. A fiendish idea began to creep across that portion of my brain that controls the choices we make. What if I didn't answer? Marco wouldn't leave the group stranded in the middle of the airport. The phone was already on its fifth ring, and I knew that a decision had to be made fast. How tempting just to get back into bed, sleep late, and use my time more diligently in search of serious employment.

In the end, doing the right thing conquered this devilish temptation, and I grabbed the phone off the table.

"*Si, pronto!*" I bellowed out my hello.

"Atticus, *dove sei?!*" It was Marco asking me where I was.

"I'm about to catch a cab." Not really true, but there was no use making a bad situation worse.

"*Ma che cazzo fai ancora a casa?!*" Marco's tone of voice and choice of words communicated both frustration and panic.

"Yes, I'm sorry, Marco, I know I'm late, but the cat threw up all over my shirt as I was about to leave."

"That's a good one, Atticus! What an imagination! Your plane to Rome leaves at ten o'clock! You're going to be late!"

"Yes, I know, I know! I'll be there. Listen Marco, remember every once in a while that I'm the one doing you a huge favor." This was neither fair nor accurate, given that he was fully aware of my unemployment and was trying to give me a hand. It's true that he needed someone to substitute for him on this tour, but he could have picked from a number of his colleagues. Instead, he had persuaded his boss to allow me to take his place so I could make some extra cash. Marco really had my best interests at heart.

"I'll grab a cab and be at the airport in thirty minutes," I said, in a more conciliatory tone of voice.

"Did you go over all the material? Is it all clear? We won't have time to go over all the details by the time you get here."

"Yes, yes! I went over everything last night, no issues." Telling Marco that I had fallen asleep before the end of page 2 would have just added salt to the wound. And I could tell that he was beginning to relax a bit.

"*Sei proprio un cazzone...dai, che quando arrivi ti offro un buon caffè.*" Marco, offering me an espresso when I arrived at the airport made it clear that he was once again at peace with the world. The coffee ritual is of great importance to Italians. Offering an espresso to another person usually means "everything is cool," even though this is just one among many connotations. Marco's use of the Italian word for penis, *cazzo,* and then referring to me as a large penis, *cazzone,* didn't faze me in the least, given that most Italians used such words as part of their normal vocabulary. *Cazzo* was equivalent to exclamations in English such as "What!," "How!," "Oh my!," "Oh no!," "Damn!," and so forth. To state that someone is clumsy, foolish, stupid, and awkward and so on can be expressed with the superlative *cazzone.* Of course, this is not by any stretch considered an elegant or correct way of speaking. My daughter had once received a sound slap on the cheek for using the word, but the sad truth of the matter is that this is now considered a normal form of expression by most Italians.

I went back into the bedroom and sat on the corner of the bed to organize my thoughts. The dream was still fresh in my mind. How strange. I recognized that the body of this imaginary adult entertainment actress bore no resemblance to Francesca. This fantasy woman was endowed with very large breasts, long and sculptured legs, delicate ankles, and a derriere that could have been sitting in a museum. The body didn't have a face or a real head to speak of. I had taken the choice parts of the female anatomy and put them all together, with no thought about who "she" was. Where was Freud when you needed him?

Knowing that Marco felt reassured that I would actually arrive at the airport on time put me at ease about the rest of the dressing and packing that I had to do. For short business trips, I usually traveled with my trusty black Samsonite carry-on, but this was just too small for an almost two-week excursion. Francesca's midsize, dark-blue suitcase, which she had lent me, was already half full of variously colored long- and short-sleeved linen shirts, polo jerseys, and loose-fitting cotton pants that had been scattered on the floor. I pulled out the top dresser drawer and grabbed a handful of gym and dress socks, along with all the clean underwear I could find. Scooping up two belts, some shorts, and a bunch of T-shirts from the floor, I shoved everything into the Delsey suitcase and, with some difficulty, managed to shut it.

I certainly wasn't going to need a tie on this trip, but I felt uncomfortable not packing at least one. I examined my Hermès collection and picked one of the older designs. How true is the adage that once you wear a Hermès tie, you never go back to another brand. I pulled open the doors to the large wall closet to find a specific pair of pants and saw all my dress suits lined up: Canali, Zegna, Brioni, Versace. They were all there in their suit bags, like battle armors each awaiting the next campaign. Below, my five pairs of Berluti dress shoes were lined up in their blue velvet dust covers.

These were the uniforms I once wore, and it pained me to have no reason to don them. I grabbed the pants and the Pal Zileri jacket I was looking for and quickly shut the closet door. I decided to wear my very old, but still very comfortable, dark-brown Sperry Top-Siders but also threw in a pair of Florsheim loafers for the evenings. Now all I needed was my shaving kit, the books I had selected, and Marco's documents to review.

The books, my Moleskine notebook, city guides, and Marco's papers and vouchers hastily ended up in a leather briefcase I had purchased a few years back in Florence, along with some ballpoint pens, two pads of paper, a calculator, my Dell laptop with its Vodafone internet key, my cell phone, my passport, wallet, a small box of Italian Toscanello cigars, and a 1:100.000 scale map of Rome. Slipping on the Patek Nautilus that I had diligently saved up for over four years, I was ready to go.

April 27, 2010
Tuesday, Day One

CHAPTER 3

Cleo and Mao Mao looked at me suspiciously as I quickly went around closing and locking the windows. I went out onto the front balcony and filled their bowls to the brim with dried cat food, then changed the water in their chipped Limoges soup dishes. I left one of the balcony doors wedged open for easy access.

"Listen up," I said sternly. "I don't want the two of you hissing at Rosanna or scratching her ankles like you did last summer. Otherwise, you may just end up without food and water for the next two weeks. And try not to scratch the furniture or climb up the drapes, please." It was, of course, useless for me to go on like this because cats just do as they please, especially when you leave them alone for any period. I placed my bags near the front door and made one more inspection around the apartment to check if the stove burners were off, the gas intake valve was closed, the refrigerator was on low setting, the TVs and stereo unplugged, the faucets tightly shut, and all lights were off.

Satisfied that everything was in order, I finally called for a cab. After listening to approximately three minutes of Sinatra singing "New York, New York," an operator came on the line to say that my ride would be there in nine minutes. The wait was a bit frustrating, given how close I was coming to missing my flight to Rome, but on the plus side, I still had time for one of my favorite events of the day: *colazione*.

This Italian word technically means "breakfast," but it is a far cry from the American meal—typically, eggs and bacon, pancakes, waffles, cereal, muesli, yogurt, with a mug of coffee and a large glass of orange juice. Dad is usually running through the morning paper while sipping his drip-brew coffee from his favorite mug while Mom is barking orders at the little ones who are propping up their droopy heads over the cereal bowls.

If you are single or living together or married without children, an American breakfast usually means a visit to Starbucks or some other coffee and pastry shop. If late, you grab a coffee to go with a small paper bag containing a softball-sized brownie or blueberry muffin. On the rare occasion that time is ample, you can sit and take a glance at the paper while biting into the softball.

These and other American breakfast scenes in millions of households across the United States are light-years from colazione. Even if the average Italian family has a quick pastry, called brioche or cornetto, and a cappuccino or espresso at home, the real meaning of breakfast is embodied at the *bar.* Not the bar that we Americans go to for TGIF, to see the game, or to just get hammered. The Italian bar is a combination of a pastry shop, delicatessen, café, bistro (some, but not all, serve hot meals), pub (serving both alcoholic and nonalcoholic drinks), tobacco emporium, and candy store. But more importantly, it is a shrine where one gets the latest dirt about events in the neighborhood, where Sunday's soccer scores are discussed and argued over, as well as the latest international and Italian news so that when you read the paper, you are already 75 percent informed.

I had just a few minutes to get a cappuccino and a cornetto (a horn-shaped pastry) at just such a place, Filippo's, which was just around the corner.

I opened the door to the apartment, set my bags outside, and said goodbye to Cleo, who had come to the door almost as if to say farewell. She had such a sad look in her eyes that I had to bend down and pick her up a moment to console her. Mao Mao was probably under the bed thinking about Rosanna's ankles.

***

"So you're going to be a single man for the next two weeks, huh!?"

Filippo bellowed out the news as soon as I entered so that all the patrons could hear.

"Ah yes," I rebutted, "as single as one can be with thirteen teenagers running around you constantly." I had informed Filippo, the owner of the self-named establishment, a few days before about my upcoming role as a chaperone, hoping that he would dissuade me. Not a chance.

What mattered to Filippo was that *la Donna* ("the Woman"—in this case, Francesca) would not be with me. I had learned over the years that in Italy, one's girlfriend, fiancée, live-in, or wife can all be indicated by the words *tua donna*—"your woman"—and sometimes, less flatteringly, *la vecchia*—"the old lady." Furthermore, I had come to understand that if tua donna is on vacation, at her mother's, visiting friends, or anywhere that is sufficiently far away, the boyfriend, fiancé, live-in, or husband becomes, for all practical intents and purposes, a single man free to enjoy another female's company to any extent ("sufficiently far away" could sometimes mean visiting the neighbors). This, of course, was the Italian male's point of view.

"There is always the night, my friend, a walk around a romantic Roman square, a good bottle of wine, a beautiful girl, and you're set!" Filippo was gloating over what he deemed my good fortune.

At the cash register, Filippo's wife, a rather stout woman in her early sixties with a noticeable double chin, was less amused, shooting back that I would never do such a thing to Francesca. "Atticus *è fedele e anche un gentiluomo.*" Being described as "faithful" and "a gentleman" brought a sly smile to Filippo's face.

"*Ma si…*our Atticus is *very* faithful. But opportunity makes a man a thief. You want another cappuccino, thief?" Before I could answer, Filippo was already at the Cimbali grinding the aromatic coffee beans into a fine powder and loading the espresso machine.

Cimbali is a famous Italian brand of espresso machines that you can find in bars and restaurants across the globe. The large ones look like a cross between the front end of a Studebaker and a 1950s jukebox. But what comes out of those little spouts from these "made in heaven" appliances is absolutely exquisite if you enjoy real coffee.

I was annoyed that the taxi had still not arrived, and I was beginning to wonder if I needed to call again. Filippo was now steaming the milk with the aid of a narrow pipe attached to the Cimbali that delivered high-pressure steam through a series of small holes, creating a fine, creamy lather, which he then gently poured into the coffee cup along with the espresso gurgling out of the machine's spout. Filippo always said that the secret of a good cappuccino lay in slowly pouring the milk into the cup along with the coffee as it seeped out of the filter.

I took another pastry from the tray on the counter and bit into its creamy center. Filippo and his wife, and probably every customer of the bar, knew that I had been laid off from my job a year before. Going from a regular patron at seven fifteen every morning to not showing up before nine after that fateful day clearly indicated that I was out of work. However, in all these mornings, I had never received the slightest glance of pity or embarrassment, and I appreciated it. I felt quite at ease here when carrying out the Italian ritual of colazione.

I watched as the usual customers came in and out for their morning cappuccino or espresso—Salvatore, the butcher, from across the street; Claudio from the news kiosk; a couple of employees from the bank around the corner; and

Stefania, who ran a small dry-cleaning establishment right next door. The discussions amongst the clientele usually revolved around something seen on the news the night before, comments regarding one of the popular reality shows, or the results of the soccer games (during soccer season, the majority of the regular season games are played on Sunday). This morning, however, the big news was my trip to Rome without la Donna.

"Atticus, I think your taxi is here!" Filippo's wife yelled to me over the noisy conversations flowing from one group of individuals to the next. As I nudged my way toward her to pay for the pastries and cappuccino, everyone patted me on the back or shoulders, wishing me the best of luck as if I were leaving for a climbing expedition up Mount Everest. Stefania gave me a big kiss on both cheeks and pressed her rather scantily clad breasts against my chest. For a moment, I felt as though I was back in my X-rated dream.

"You behave yourself and do not pay attention to all of these *maiali*," she said, still keeping her breasts tightly pressed against me. Her referring to the men in the bar as "pigs" made everyone break out in laughter.

"Hey, Stefania!" Filippo yelled. "You keep squeezing him like that and either he's going to suffocate, or your tits are going to explode!" The customers let out a roar of applause. Stefania looked over at Filippo and gave him a wink that spoke a thousand words. She then turned back to me with a big smile, gave me another pair of kisses on my cheeks, and then released me. As I reached for my wallet, she said that the colazione was on her. "You have a good time and come back to us safe and sound."

"*Grazie*, and thanks to all of you for your good wishes." I waved to everyone, pointing at Filippo, who gave me an all-American thumbs-up.

Outside, the taxi driver helped me put my suitcase in the trunk of the car, then opened the door for me to get in. As I settled in the back seat, trying to remember if I had forgotten anything important, I saw Filippo, his wife, Salvatore, and Stefania standing outside the door waving. I rolled down the window and blew them all a kiss.

"*Fattene una per me!*" Filippo yelled as the taxi drove off. This literally translated into "Do one for me," which, with a little imagination and knowing that the indefinite article *una* refers to a female, expressed the idea. My last glimpse as the taxi pulled off was Filippo's wife slapping her husband over the head.

I rolled down the window a crack as we sped down the Via Cassanese, hoping that the taxi driver did not want to chat. I was beginning to get a little nervous, oddly, at the thought of missing my flight and leaving Marco in a difficult situation. He certainly didn't deserve it, even though I was thoroughly convinced that I was getting myself into a no-win situation. After what seemed to be just a few seconds, however, the taxi driver started cursing at the car in front of him: "Come on, move your ass, we're not going to a funeral!"

I pretended not to understand his Milanese dialect, but I could tell by the way he kept glancing at me in the rearview mirror that he was looking for some sort of approval for his judgement call. Darting a quick glimpse at the driver of the car in question, I realized that it was a woman behind the wheel of a brand-new BMW X5 SUV. This made things so much easier.

"What do you expect from a woman behind the wheel of a car like that?"

He smiled broadly into the mirror.

"You know," he said proudly, "I have been a taxi driver for almost nineteen years now, and it never fails to surprise me. A woman driver is as dangerous as a loaded gun, and the bigger the car she drives, the bigger the caliber of the bullet!"

This was a rather clever analogy, considering that the guy had probably just squeezed through junior high school. My own opinion regarding Italian females at the wheel of an automobile was certainly not as extreme, even though I knew very well that many of the close calls I had had driving in Milan were almost always due to women in SUVs and mindless "I'm immortal!" teenagers on motor scooters. I couldn't let the driver, whose taxi badge ID said that his name was Antonio, just hang there after this last comment, so I decided to play along, finding this early morning "Let's abuse someone" banter rather amusing after all.

"You've got to be very careful of men wearing hats as well," I said. "I've had two or three nasty experiences with those drivers."

Antonio was ecstatic. "Signor! How right you are! They're even more dangerous than women. I've had only one major accident in my driving career, and it was because of a cazzone with a hat who ran right through a stop sign. He didn't look left or right, didn't even have the courtesy to slow down."

In Italy, it's said that a middle-aged male driver wearing a hat is someone who usually walks, takes the bus or tram, or rides a bike. This explains the hat, which he doesn't remove the few times he gets into a car, hence the odds of an accident being relatively high.

Besides, hardly anyone in Italy does a full stop at the red octagon, nor at the stoplights for that matter, and the YIELD signs are seen as street decorations. Usually, Italian drivers slow down a little, do a quick glance to the left and right, and shoot through. In fact, Antonio's gripe, in this case, was with the driver's not *even* slowing down.

We turned on to the *Tangenziale* (the Milan beltway) and immediately encountered a wall of rush-hour traffic. I took the opportunity to reach into my leather briefcase to retrieve Marco's papers while Antonio was fiddling with his cell phone. I quickly reviewed the first page and skimmed through the second, which listed the various itineraries. I wanted to fully understand was what I was going to be up against for the next couple weeks. Page 4 answered my question:

Participating School:	Bradford High School
	Atlanta, Georgia
Class:	Senior
Teacher Chaperons:	Mr. John Seeward
	Mrs. Cynthia Ramsey
	Mrs. Barbara Cornwall
Student Participants:	13
Males	*Age*
Jeremy Nolan	18
Mark Hampton	18
Wayne Little	18
Bishop Horn	18
Anthony Carter	18
James Fingerton	18
Raymond Katzman	17 (March 15th)
Females	
Mary Lopez	18
Darlene Williams	18
Sabrina Hamlin	18
Vanessa Guy	18
Michelle Thompson	17 (February 27th)
Evelyn Farling	18

Medical Notes:	
Jeremy Nolan:	left arm amputee – prosthetic arm.
Notes (confidential):	
Evelyn Farling:	parents recently divorced.
Sabrina Hamlin:	younger brother recently deceased.
James Fingerton:	frequent states of depression.

Nothing terribly out of the ordinary here. Evelyn and Sabrina had some family trauma, and this James individual was battling depression. The teachers were obviously aware of all of this. If these three were on this trip, it meant that there were no specific concerns. Just fine with me.

As we inched along, I could hear Antonio continually cursing at the drivers in front of him, but I was too far lost in my thoughts to pay any attention.

I was on my way to the airport to take on this job against my better judgment. I was going to be paid, and therefore, Marco, as well as the Rome ASA office, expected me to take this responsibility seriously. This was legit. It was essential for me to be professional and use any know-how I had at my disposal. But what the hell did I really know about teenagers? And American ones at that.

I began to consider what my approach was going to be with this motley crew. Was it judicious to have a strict demeanor and show these kids who was boss from the start? Or was it more fitting to be Mr. Nice Guy and try to be chummy with everyone? Both methods had their positive and negative aspects. By acting like the boss, I would immediately lay down the law and at least have a slight chance of getting my directions followed—in other words, I would adopt the role of the marine drill sergeant. This, however, wouldn't fit my generally good-natured character, and I didn't care to fake it for the next two weeks.

The other more familiar approach, however, left me open to not being taken seriously, which would, in turn, leave the door wide open for the group to run roughshod over me.

My thoughts were suddenly pulled back to the taxi as Antonio stopped suddenly behind a young man on a Vespa motor scooter.

"Ma perché non guardi dove vai, stronzo!"

Apparently, the Vespa had swerved in front of Antonio, causing him to jerk the steering wheel to avoid hitting the scooter's rear wheel. This time, my driver referred to the culprit as *stronzo* instead of cazzone.

Stronzo literally means "excrement," if we are being civil, and "piece of shit," if we are not. Usually, Italians do not intend the civil meaning when using the word in anger. It is a term frequently utilized by most Italians and can refer to a fool, an idiot, or an enemy. However, it is also often used amongst friends or acquaintances to chide one another. In this case, Antonio was not chiding.

The taxi veered off onto the Viale Forlanini exit ramp, heading in the opposite direction to Milan's Linate Airport. This is one of three airports serving the Milano area, the others being Malpensa (for international flights) and Orio al Serio near the town of Bergamo that, like Linate, handled national and low-cost flights, along with some nearby European destinations.

Linate Airport's actual name is the Enrico Forlanini Airport, after the Italian scientist who developed an early steam-powered helicopter and some of the first hydrofoils in the late nineteenth century. He died in 1930. I suspected that very few Italians probably knew that Linate was not the proper name of the airport, which came from the village where the airport was built back in the 1930s.

"We'll be there in a second," Antonio said, smiling. I noticed the needle on the speedometer was closing in at 120 kilometers an hour. This was about 75 miles an hour, which, considering that we were on a four-lane city road, was not terribly unusual. Speed limits supposedly exist in Milan, as well as the rest of Italy, but I had rarely, if ever, seen a police car stopping anyone for driving too fast. There were street radar setups on most major roads and even more on the various beltways and highways that intersect Italy, but I had a strong suspicion that most of them were decoys and didn't even function. I had only met a handful of people who had actually received speeding tickets in the mail generated by one of these traps.

When I had my company Mercedes, I usually drove between 130 and 160 kph (81 to 100 mph) on the highway, but I was constantly moving out of the faster left lane to the center lane to get out of the way of oncoming vehicles. Italians have a love affair with speed. No wonder that Ferrari, Maserati, Lamborghini, Bugatti, Alfa Romeo, and Ducati are all Italian born.

As we banked off the exit ramp, which led to the departure area of the airport, Antonio was obliged to drop his speed to about 80 kph (50 mph), much to his dismay. Here we ran into an extremely congested area where taxis, city buses, tour buses, and private limos were fighting for each available square meter of space.

Amidst this confusion, the *Vigili* (soft "g") *Urbani,* or the municipal traffic cops, were attempting to keep some kind of order by frantically waving on drivers to move ahead and stop in the authorized areas, as if there were any available. Antonio took no notice of the confusion and skillfully maneuvered his car into a space the size of a sardine can between two large tour buses.

The meter read 14.75 euros, about 18 American dollars. I gave Antonio twenty euros, telling him to keep the change since he had gotten me to my destination in record time. He stepped out of the car, opened the trunk, handed me my travel bag, and as masterfully as he had nuzzled the taxi between those two buses, he wriggled himself out and shot off like a rocket. I looked at my watch: 9:20 am. I had to move.

Passing through the automatic glass doors, nostalgia hit me like a tidal wave. How many times had I been here in the last five years? Countless.

The line of people with their suitcases waiting to get checked in was terribly long, and I knew I wasn't going to make my flight if I joined the queue. I decided to attempt a little trick that had almost always worked to my advantage. I went over to the left side of the ticket counter area to the check-in desk for passengers with only carry-on bags, which had much fewer people in line. My Florentine leather briefcase was stuffed like a Thanksgiving turkey and counted as one piece of carry-on luggage, the maximum allowed, but I also had the Delsey, which was actually a bit larger and certainly heavier than your average carry-on. The trick was to keep the leather briefcase well within sight of the young woman at the desk and very nonchalantly drag the small suitcase directly behind my legs. To see it, she would have to stand up and look over the counter.

Luckily, when my turn came, the attendant, who was very attractive indeed, motioned me to come forward but was immediately distracted by a ringing phone. This allowed me to get right up against the counter with the Delsey literally standing on the back of my heels. Then I swung the briefcase up on the counter to retrieve my electronic ticket confirmation, passport, and Alitalia Freccia Alata mileage card. The young lady was still on the phone as she was typing away on the keyboard. Observing my U.S. passport, she asked in English whether I wanted an aisle or window seat.

"*Corridoio, per favore.*" I preferred answering in Italian. She put the phone down, smiled, and asked me in Italian this time, "Solo *un bagaglio?*" Just one piece of luggage?

"*Si, si. Solo uno.*"

In most European cities, I usually got away with declaring that I just had one piece of luggage instead of two by following the same tactical approach up to the counter. Except for that time in Barcelona when this suspicious and very evil-looking check-in attendant stood up suddenly and saw my suitcase nestled behind me. One would have thought I was trying to bring a grenade launcher on board. What a ruckus she had made! I had almost missed the flight by having to go and check that bag in at the regular ticket counters.

The young woman serving me now entered my mileage card number into the computer, placed her hand below the desk, and waited for the machine to eject the boarding pass and flight receipt. "Your gate number is number 21, 15A is your seat number, and you board…um, right now."

"Thank you very much." I gave her a smile and moved to my left along the counter, sliding the Delsey behind me with my right leg. I slowly placed my wallet back into my briefcase and waited until she was fully absorbed with the next traveler, who was already making a fuss about how long he had to wait in line. I then turned and pushed the Delsey in front of me until I was around the corner and well out of sight.

CHAPTER 4

It was 9:35 am. If the line at the metal detector wasn't too long, I still had a chance to grab a few newspapers before dashing to the gate.

Back when I had an office, the *Financial Times*, the *Frankfurter Allgemeine*, *Le Monde*, the *Herald Tribune*, and various Italian newspapers were always waiting for me each morning on my desk. I truly enjoyed seeing the stack upon my arrival, but after glancing at the headlines and putting them in my briefcase, I never ended up reading any of them from the first to the last page. What a waste of paper day in and day out, I had often thought. But it was another small ritual that made me feel part of it all, just like those little hot towels on Cathay Pacific. I had to admit, all this made me feel essential.

The anaconda-shaped line that always formed in front of the X-ray machines was almost nonexistent today. I had missed a flight or two before because of this line, not having the nerve to butt in toward the front, shouting about why I was late for my flight. And I was continually amazed at the number of people who did not hesitate to barge to the front, explaining to a sucker like me, who had been waiting for more than fifteen minutes, that they were late and that just *had* to get in front of me. For some of my Italian colleagues, this was standard behavior. For me, it just demonstrated a general lack of respect and total disregard for others.

I flashed my boarding card and passport to the security attendant standing next to the small conveyor belt. The stack of empty trays was piled to the side, waiting to be filled with personal belongings. I proceeded with the strip-down routine: my phone, belt, shoes, jacket, the Montegrappa

fountain pen I always carried in the inner pocket of my
jacket, loose coins, and my treasured Patek Philippe Nautilus
were all placed into one tray. The PC and its power pack went
in a second tray, then my turkey-sized briefcase and Delsey
followed on the conveyor.

After receiving an okay from another very bored-looking
attendant, I put back all my items on my person, then rushed
across the hall to the bookstore. I picked up the *Le Monde* and
Frankfurter Allgemeine newspapers to keep up with my French
and German, along with the *Il Sole 24 Ore*, which is the Italian
version of the *Wall Street Journal.* I would have enough time
ahead of me to actually read them this time, or so I thought.

Having incredibly crammed the papers into my briefcase,
I walked rapidly to Gate 21. Three people were already in
the line, but I saw through the large framed windows that
the shuttle bus to the plane was packed. As I was fumbling
for my boarding card and passport, I looked up to see the
attractive young woman from the check-in counter. And here
I was with my nice big Delsey right in front of me. She looked
quizzically at me and the blue suitcase.

"*Solo un bagaglio, signore, giusto?*" she asked with a grin.
Just *one* piece of luggage?

"Well, actually, one and *a half,*" I said, sheepishly. She let
out a small laugh and let me pass. She wasn't only attractive,
but a good sport as well.

I was the last person to board the very crowded shuttle bus,
finding myself in the back which, as anyone knows who has
traveled frequently, is the worst place to be. This is because,
as soon as those automatic doors slide shut, even people
who aren't prone to the condition become claustrophobic.
This particular bus was full of passengers, so I couldn't even
lower the handle of the carry-on without leaning heavily onto
another individual.

The second worst thing that can happen is when the bus
just sits there instead of driving to the plane. And that was

exactly what happened—the bus was neither moving nor its engine running, which meant no air-conditioning. Why did they shut the doors if the bus wasn't ready to go?

It was already about twenty-four degrees Celsius (approximately seventy-four degrees Fahrenheit) and extremely humid. I began to feel the first droplets of perspiration trickling down my face. I remembered a trip to Karachi, Pakistan, many years back when the bus actually remained shut and still on the tarmac for about fifteen minutes at over a hundred degrees Fahrenheit outside. I smiled now thinking about that experience, but I certainly did not find the situation humorous back then.

Luckily, this delay only lasted five minutes, which was tolerable, before the bus driver boarded, turned on the engine and air-conditioning, and drove off.

Even so, it took an interminably long time zigzagging around the airport service roads before we finally stopped at the side of the plane. An airline attendant gave the thumbs-up signal to the driver to open the doors, then the third worst thing happened: the side doors of the bus facing the plane opened, but the other doors remained closed. This is standard procedure, but if you are in the very back of the bus, you usually end up being one of the last to board. This is no problem if you just have a briefcase or a small carry-on, but it's an entirely different situation if you are loaded down the way I was.

In fact, as soon as I managed to get off the bus, I saw that there were already lines forming at the bottom of the front and back stair ramps. This meant that when I got onboard, the overhead bins were all going to be jammed full. However, the airplane was an Airbus 320, so I hoped I would find some space for my suitcase.

By the time I reached the top of the stairs, everybody, except for eight to ten people in front of me, was already seated. At least my seat was in the *corridoio*, or aisle—I never liked sitting in the middle or the window seat. I reached Row 11 and plopped the rotund briefcase on my seat. Then with a silent prayer, I scrutinized all the open overhead bins. They were all completely chock-full with suit bags, appropriately sized carry-ons, and briefcases. Looking down the aisle of the plane, I could see that practically all the passengers were sitting down. I could tell that most of them were businessmen, who are typically quick to store their items and take their seats.

So here I was, standing alone, holding this clearly oversized cabin bag, with about seventy-five pairs of eyes watching me with pity and disgust. I could almost hear their thoughts: *What a loser, probably his first time on a plane, doesn't even know the basics about carry-ons.* I was feeling as though I had belched loudly in front of the president of the United States or let off gas during a dinner with the Queen of England. A bleached blonde stewardess, seeing that my distress and enjoying it, walked up to me and, in a purposely loud voice, said, "That bag is *too large* to be considered carry-on, *sir.*"

I wasn't going to be humiliated any further, so I snapped back, "I believe you are correct. But I am here, and this bag is here, and I don't think that either of us wants to delay this flight any further for all these paying customers because of a slightly larger than permitted carry-on."

Now all eyes shifted to the hostess, and I felt that I had gained a few points, with her upper lip curled back from her perfectly straight pearly white teeth. She took the bag from my hand and growled, "You shall find it directly behind the last row!" She knew that this would inconvenience me upon our arrival since I would have to wait for everyone to get off first before I could retrieve it. But I wasn't fazed.

I pushed and shoved my leather satchel under the seat with great difficulty, sat down, loosened my jacket, and buckled the seat belt. All the overhead bins were closed, and the hostesses went through the in-case-of-an-emergency routine. I glanced through the Alitalia in-flight magazine and saw that there was a long article on where to dine out when in Paris. I decided to take the magazine with me.

The pilot came on over the PA system, but I wasn't listening. Being on an airplane had me thinking about how many things had changed in just eleven months.

My last business flight before leaving the company had been to London. It was a British Airways flight from Linate. I was decked out in my Canali suit and Berluti shoes, driven to the airport by the company driver, arriving at the Frequent Travelers lounge one hour before departure. This gave me the time for refreshments at the bar, a quick scan of the daily papers, and a look at the many emails on my Blackberry. For an overnight stay, I always had my trusty standard carry-on dimension Samsonite and therefore no problems with checking in. I was always one of the first to get on the shuttle bus and one of the first to board the plane, and I only got pleasant smiles from the hostesses as they handed me my glass of orange juice in the spacious business-class seat. What a difference from today!

We taxied down the service runway, and from what I could see through the next row window, we had two or three planes ahead of us. I was tempted to take out those newspapers and have a good read, but I knew that I had to look at Marco's documents.

Other than knowing that I had to chaperone this group of students and their teachers around Rome for what seemed to be an endless sequence of days, I really had no idea what my responsibilities were. Marco had told me that for all the important visits to the primary sites of Rome—the Colosseum, the Roman Forum, St. Peter's Square, the Spanish Steps, the Pantheon, etc.—we would have a tour guide whom I only needed to give the proper voucher. It was up to me, Marco added, to eventually take the group out for a walk around town in their free time. I fervently hoped there would not be much free time.

The plane slowly lurched forward and made that sharp hairpin turn that comes just before the pilot announces that take off is imminent. I reached down, opened the leather flap on the briefcase, and pulled out the sheets of paper. As I sat back in my seat, the plane began barreling down the runway.

It never ceased to amaze me: a long, wide steel tube with two flat, semi-triangular protrusions, weighing well over 150 thousand pounds, accomplishing the phenomenon of flight. I understood the basic principles of propulsion, lift, and thrust from the basic physics course I had taken in college. I was also well aware that you were safer in a plane than in your car. But when the nose lifted and I felt the shuddering of the wheels as they rose off the ground and folded in under the plane, I always thought of the old adage which said that if the good Lord had wanted man to fly, he would have given him wings.

All that tonnage of steel, aluminum, plastic, wiring, paneling, seats, nuts, and bolts, not to mention the two or four massive engines moving through the air at twenty, thirty, forty, fifty thousand feet at the command of a pilot and copilot, astonished me with every flight.

The plane was close to cruising altitude when I stopped wasting time daydreaming and finally looked at the papers clenched in my hands. I wasn't especially interested in the mission or objectives of the ASA, so I went directly to the page about my duties and responsibilities. I was supposed to read this, sign it, and give it back to Marco when he arrived in Rome.

I was also going to get €750 from Marco, about US$1,050, for the first ten days, with the balance for the remaining six days to be paid at the end of the group's stay. I flipped through the first five pages and found what I was looking for.

ASA Travel Chaperone Duties and Responsibilities

As the chaperone of an ASA travel group, you will have the opportunity to meet promising young students who are on the road to discovering countries, cultures, and languages different from their own.

You have been selected by the ASA local office in your country to be responsible for a group of students who will be traveling to a major city, or cities, where your expertise is vital. You have been chosen for your language skills, your knowledge of the area, and your ability to help solve any logistical, booking, health, or law enforcement issues. Direct responsibility for the well-being of the students is in the hands of the teachers who have been selected by ASA headquarters in Atlanta and who have signed their own set of rules and regulations regarding their obligations.

Please find attached two copies of a list of duties and responsibilities that we specifically ask of all our country chaperones. Print and sign your name below and return one copy to the local ASA office. You will not be able to begin your chaperoning duties until the local ASA office has received a signed copy of the Duties and Responsibilities list.

Duties and Responsibilities (ASA Chaperones)

1. Thorough understanding of all the information provided by ASA concerning the Group in question;
2. If possible, a preliminary inspection of the hotel(s) and restaurants where the Group will be staying/dining;
3. A meeting with the teachers traveling with the Group on the first day of arrival in order to become better acquainted with them, gather information regarding the

students, and review specific situations that may apply to one or more of the student participants;

4. Offer assistance to the teachers in regard to student curfews, overall behavior, any reprimands, and any assistance required if emergency contact is necessary with the U.S. embassy or consulate or with any of the parents in the United States;

5. Be punctual when meeting the Group at the airport of destination, with strict attention given to the scheduling of bus transfers, tours, breakfast and dining hours, and all other events on the Group's program;

6. Any form of coercion on behalf of the chaperone regarding how and where the Group spends its money for food or gifts/souvenirs/etc. shall not be tolerated and shall result in immediate dismissal of same;

7. Unacceptable behavior on behalf of any chaperone (excessive use of alcohol, any form of drug abuse, unruly conduct) communicated (with elements of proof or witnesses) to any ASA local office on behalf of teacher(s) or student(s) shall result in the immediate dismissal without pay of the chaperone in question;

8. Any form of physical or mental molestation of any of the students by any chaperone shall result in immediate dismissal without pay of the chaperone in question, as well as possible legal and criminal proceedings.

Please print your name and sign/date. If you have any questions pertaining to these responsibilities, contact your local ASA office for further information.

Name (Print): _____

Signature: _____

I had no problems with any of the requirements. I was going to be weak on the first point since I had no clue about young people in general, let alone those in the group, and the second was obviously impossible since I didn't intend to become a restaurant and hotel critic. But everything else seemed acceptable and for good reason. I lowered the fold-down tray, retrieved my pen, and signed the two sheets.

Part of the first requirement on the list of duties was actually in one of the several documents that Marco had given me. This was a set of papers stapled together that I now realized was a compilation "Who Am I" questionnaires for each of the students participating on the trip. Each page had the name of the student, their age, hobbies, the reason they wanted to be part of an ASA Group, likes and dislikes in food, music, sports, and a general comment on the bottom. I could have cared less what these students were all about, let alone what they thought of themselves, but I knew that sooner or later I was going to have to go through these papers to see if there was any intelligible information (which I strongly doubted) that would come in handy. I stuffed the papers back into the bag.

The questionnaires reminded me of the times when I had to decide whether to hire a new employee. I never looked at the candidate's résumé until after I had met them. The personnel department would choose which three or four candidates I should see after an initial meeting with the human resources manager. The candidates would then be given an appointment to meet with me. I always met them alone, never in my office but at the bar area of a nearby five-star hotel, with the meeting location given to them just a few hours before.

I conducted my interviews this way because I wanted to see how a possible future employee behaved in an environment that was full of distractions—hotel guests coming and going, the gurgling of the Japanese garden fountain, soft piano music, and the constant motion of waiters and waitresses. Would the candidate order a drink, especially if I ordered something alcoholic? It hardly ever happened. I also observed how the candidate sat in the chair: shifting about or perfectly still, legs crossed or two feet firmly planted on the ground, hands in the lap or arms folded. You can understand so much about people by just taking some time to look at them, especially when the individual in front of you knows that they are not in control of the situation, but you are. Realizing that their behavior will decide whether that final interview is successful or not brings out the best and worst in an individual.

How many interviews had I observed and then conducted over the years? Hundreds? Almost certainly.

I was off again dreaming about the past when the stewardess asked me a second time if I wanted something to drink. The food and beverage cart was practically touching my shoulder, and I hadn't even noticed.

"Just some mineral water please with a slice of lemon." She plopped a small drink napkin and a significantly smaller packet of dry breakfast biscuits on my tray table, and while her partner behind the drink cart was pouring my water into a plastic glass, she was already handling the drink requests from the two passengers seated next to me. I took my water, immediately drank half of it, then nibbled on the high-fiber cookies, which tasted like compressed wood chippings. This certainly wasn't business class.

Before placing the ASA papers and the in-flight magazine back in my briefcase and taking out a newspaper, I thought it would be best to become familiar with the names of the students who had medical and family issues.

"Let's see now, Jeremy Nolan has a prosthetic arm, okay, and Sabrina lost her brother recently. Got it. And Evelyn…" I was mumbling all of this to myself when the plane began shaking without warning and then stopped just as suddenly.

Despite all my years flying around the world, I had never grown accustomed to turbulence. And being so susceptible to silent yet painful manifestations of panic when a plane encountered air pockets, I had become quite an expert in predicting how long and hard the plane was going to be thrown around the stratosphere when encountering these roller-coaster rides at thirty thousand feet. The brief jolt we had felt I had just felt with nothing more afterward was not reassuring. If my experience was any guide, we were going to experience another jolt very shortly with prolonged bouncing commencing immediately afterward.

Bam! There it was, the second kick.

The PA system came on, and the pilot pleasantly informed us that due to bad weather over Florence and Pisa, which we were just beginning to fly over, there would be a "bit of bumpiness." How sweet! The passengers were requested, as usual, to stay seated and fasten their seatbelts.

There was a big difference between "wiggling," as I called it, which was the kind of turbulence that gives you the sensation of being on top of a large blob of Jell-O and which is pretty harmless, and the "jolting" kind that throws you side to side in your seat, which I considered borderline terrifying.

This was the jolting kind.

The plane began to shake continuously and then veer left and right, making us feel as though we were in a rowboat passing over ten-foot waves. I put my head back against the seat, closed my eyes, clenched the armrests until my knuckles were white. I also began reviewing all the sins I had committed, promising the Almighty that I would change my ways if He were to let the plane land safely. Given the strength of this clear air turbulence and its sudden onset, I felt that the plane would return to steady flight pretty quickly, but that didn't stop me going over the Ten Commandments to see where I wasn't up to par. Boy, was that a mistake!

We rocked and rolled for what seemed an eternity while the circles of perspiration under my armpits spread.

Then nothing.

In an instant, the jerking stopped, and the plane began cruising smoothly once again. I breathed a sigh of relief, but kept my hands firmly clenched on the armrests for a little longer. I had tended to forget the many promises I had made to the One on High as soon as the plane I was on landed safely. Sometimes I wondered if this would come back to haunt me.

I must have dozed off since the next thing I heard was the hostess saying place my seat in the upright position for landing. Sure enough, it was already 9:05 am, and the plane had started its approach to Rome's Fiumicino Airport.

CHAPTER 5

The landing went off without a hitch, and we were fortunate to taxi up to a finger instead of waiting out on the tarmac for another of those shuttle buses to take us to the terminal. I'd had enough of being a canned sardine for the day.

As expected, I had to wait for all the passengers to disembark before walking back to the end of the plane to retrieve my Delsey. The stewardess who had taken my bag gave me a sarcastic little smile as I walked by. I was strongly tempted to inform her that if trivial events like this amused her so much, she must have an awfully empty life. I decided, however, to keep my mouth shut and just walk past her.

I strolled out of the plane, walked down the finger that led into the national arrivals area, and made my way toward the international flight terminal of the airport.

Rome's international airport was actually named Leonardo da Vinci but, like Linate, was better known by the name of the small town where it was built on the west side of Rome facing the Tyrrhenian Sea—Fiumicino. The airport had undergone extensive modernization over the past five years, and the area I was walking through was totally new to me.

When I arrived at Terminal A, national arrivals, I observed the signs leading to the international departures, Terminal B. A series of very long *tapis roulant* quickened the pace to the terminal. At the end of this interminable walkway, decorated on both sides with ads from blue-chip companies, I was finally in the departures area of the international terminal.

The check-in counters were lined with passengers of every possible nationality. Rome is not only the capital of Italy but also one of the most visited tourist destinations worldwide. Thus, Fiumicino airport is always busy. This part of the airport complex had seen only minor changes since I had left Rome, so I was able to get my bearings quickly.

I entered an elevator near the middle of the terminal that took me to the international arrivals area directly below. As I stepped out of the elevator and my rendezvous point with Marco, my cell phone began to ring. Marco panicking once again at my absence, I thought.

"*Calmati,* Marco, *sono qua!*" I practically yelled at Marco to be calm and that I was already in the airport terminal.

"But I *am* calm," a rather startled voice said at the other end of the phone. It was Francesca. I hadn't looked at the number before answering.

"*Scusami amore, che bello sentirti.*" We usually spoke in Italian, switching to English every once in a while so she could keep in practice. Francesca's English was actually quite sound, though she needed some help with phrasal verbs. "But it's almost three thirty in the morning there. What are you doing up at this hour?"

"I couldn't sleep, and I wanted to make sure that you had taken up Marco's offer. You know he cares about you, and that a little extra money certainly can't hurt us right now."

In fact, Marco had been worried about me since Day One of my being laid off. He himself had gone from job to job over the years, never really finding something that he truly enjoyed and could excel at, so he had made it his personal mission to find something small for me to do until a big opportunity came along.

"Yes, yes, I know. As you probably understood when I answered the phone, I've just arrived in Rome. I'll see him in just a few minutes."

"Try to be patient with these students. Don't treat them as if they are your employees. Support the situation as best you can. And when you meet them for the first time, try not to go into one of your dissertations on how the teenagers of today are the ruin of the generations to come. And remember that in less than fourteen days, it will all be over. I shall be waiting for you when you return. Let's try to avoid taking the children the first weekend you're back, please, so that we can have some time on our own. It's something to look forward to, isn't it?"

I had no intention of getting into a discussion with her over the phone about my children. Francesca still hadn't figured out that my time with her was important, but my time with my children was inviolable. I knew that I would have to confront Francesca about this very soon.

"Well, yes, I mean, we'll see. I've got to run now. I'll try to behave myself and shall attempt to enjoy Rome, considering the circumstances. Walk as much as you can in Manhattan. It's the best way to soak in the city and remember to take in a few shows if you have time." She had never been to New York.

"The calendar is quite full, in fact. My colleagues have booked every evening for me during my stay. They're very sweet. I'm going to try to get some sleep now. Ciao, Atticus."

"Ciao, ciao."

The line went dead. I stood there a moment, feeling as if a trapdoor had been opened under my feet. What was I feeling, if anything? She obviously wasn't pleased with my elusive answer regarding the weekend together without the children. I would confront her head-on about this situation once and for all when I got back to Milan. Hopefully, she would come round to my point of view.

I was now in front of three sets of large sliding doors that intermittently opened and closed, disgorging human beings from all over the world. The Illy coffee bar, named after a famous brand of Italian coffee, was still there, directly across from the arrivals area. I walked up to the counter and ordered a cappuccino and some mineral water.

As I stood there sipping my coffee-and-foamed-milk combination, I thought about the number of times that Marco had called me this past week to give me a detailed briefing on what was expected of me. I usually had an excuse why I couldn't speak with him, which drove him crazy. I was chuckling to myself when I heard fast-paced steps coming toward me and my name being bellowed out in the terminal. I turned and found Marco coming at me like a freight train.

"*Sei qui finalmente, meno male!*" Marco yelled. "You're finally here!"

"Ciao, Marco. Yes, I'm here, you, see?" We gave each other a quick hug and kiss on the cheek, as customary among friends in Italy.

"Good to see you, Atticus! I was actually beginning to wonder if you would show up." I didn't dare acknowledge how close he was to the truth. Marco ordered a double espresso while fidgeting with his briefcase. "We don't have much time. The flight lands in ten minutes, and we still need to go over several things."

"I'm all ears."

"Did you read everything? Did you go over the Duties and Responsibilities form? Did you review the student questionnaires? Do you understand how the voucher system works? Are you motivated to do this?" I kept repeating "*Si, si*" ("yes") to everything without paying much attention.

How many times had Marco mentioned in one of his numerous phone calls that amongst the documentation, I would find a set of three-page questionnaires filled out by each student? From their age, hobbies, the reason why they wanted to be part of an ASA Group, the college they would be attending, etc. Of course, I hadn't even glanced at them.

He reached into his jacket pocket and took out a thick, crumpled envelope. "Here's the advance for the week. Seven hundred and fifty euros. You'll get the other half at the end of the trip. Give me the D&R form you signed before we forget."

"The D and *what* form?"

Marco looked at me and rolled his eyes. "The Duties and Responsibilities form, Atticus."

"Oh that…have it right here." I reached into my briefcase, found the form. and handed it to him.

"You have the second copy, correct? Read it every once in a while. ASA is very strict about these rules. A colleague of mine was fired during a trip in Spain for having taken a cut from a souvenir store where his group had been shopping."

The barman placed our coffees on the counter, and we reached for the small sugar packets in a tacky-looking imitation brass bowl resembling a Roman funeral urn.

"I think I should have you hanged, drawn, and quartered for getting me involved in this fiasco." Marco sipped his coffee, looking a bit embarrassed.

Three years before, Marco had read an article about me in one of the Italian financial magazines. He had sent me a letter along with a clipping of the article, saying he wanted work for me and the company I represented. I was flattered by the letter, but soon forgot all about it. Marco, however, being quite a professional in the field of marketing and PR, continued contacting me, and we ended up meeting one day for lunch. This began a steadfast friendship, which I was thankful for. I had come to fully respect his work ethic and his reluctance to complain when times were hard. He had been in charge of the PR departments for Hertz, the Italian motorcycle manufacturing company Moto Guzzi, and most recently, for General Motors when they launched the Cadillac and Hummer brands in Italy. This last position had been abruptly terminated in January 2009 when GM began its slide into controlled bankruptcy. At forty-six, going on forty-seven, Marco was now employed by the regional ASA office in Rome, and as a sideline, he wrote soccer articles for the *Corriere dello Sport* newspaper.

"You know, Atticus, I've chaperoned over forty groups, and it hasn't been all that bad. You meet some interesting people and get to see many important historical sites."

I favored him with my most skeptical smile. I expected to take nothing away from this experience except frayed nerves.

After paying for our coffees, we walked over to the arrivals' monitors, which were situated at the side of glass doors that ceaselessly opened and closed as people passed through. We looked for the Alitalia flight from Atlanta. It had landed ten minutes ago. We glanced around but didn't see a group of Americans congregated anywhere. "Thank goodness," said Marco, "they must still be at passport control or getting their bags." He began fiddling around in his backpack and took out two A4 plastic cards with ASA printed on them.

"Here, take one and hold it so that the people exiting those doors can see it." I felt foolish but did as he said. I was just hoping that nobody I had done business with over the years would walk through those doors and see me standing there with this oversized name tag. Flights from New York, Miami, and Rio de Janeiro had landed at the same time as the Atlanta flight. The glass doors continued opening and closing as travelers exited with baggage carts filled with an array of multicolored, multi-shaped luggage.

Occasionally, I saw myself coming through those sliding doors—donning an expensive suit and shined dress shoes, walking with a black professional carry-on and leather suit bag, and already on the phone and gazing through the crowd for the chauffeur or hotel limousine driver. One of these clones of me looked my way, trying to see what was written on the card, which I immediately hid under my jacket.

"What are you doing? Hold it up high so people can see it!" Marco pulled my arm upwards so that the card was in full view. My clone gave me what could be best described as a sarcastic grin.

"Lord, help me get through this," I muttered to myself.

We stood there side by side with those glossy name tags in our hands, watching the flow of humanity coming through those doors. I could tell when the passengers from Rio were coming out because the Italian and English speech switched to Portuguese. Soon, however, the Portuguese became intertwined with Southern-drawl English.

I had spent many summers with my grandparents in Tallahassee, Florida, and my grandfather was originally from Georgia. I knew that our group was going to exit soon. It must have been hot in Atlanta—flip-flops, shorts, skirts, tube tops, halter tops, T-shirts, and polos were the outfit of the day. At one point, two women passed the sliding doors with loaded luggage carts. They were looking left and right, their facial expressions saying a 'What do we do now?' demeanor. Were they the teachers? Question answered—both waved as soon as their eyes landed on the ASA tag that Marco was holding.

"Are you ready, Atticus? They're here."

Taking a deep breath, I followed him through the labyrinth of people who were standing and waiting for their party to arrive, bumping into a few with my suitcase and carry-on.

"Welcome to Rome! Now one of you is Barbara, one of you is Cynthia, correct?" Marco was at his most charming. Even though his English was mediocre, his friendliness immediately put the two teachers at ease.

"My name is Marco Iddino. I work for ASA Rome, and it is great pleasure for me to meet you. I, unfortunately, will not be with you on your tour, but I leave you in the very good care of Mr. Atticus Winterle. He is the chaperone for you."

"Hello, nice to meet you," I said." Did you have a good flight?" A rather obvious thing to ask, I thought, but I had to say something. The two teachers stared at me quizzically. They were wondering where they had heard that unusual name before. I was used to it.

The woman on the left replied first. "Well, hello. Yes, that's correct, I'm Barbara Cornwall, and this is Cynthia Ramsey. James Seeward, the other teacher, should be joining us any moment."

We were beginning to cause a traffic jam by standing and talking in front of the glass doors, so Marco suggested that we move off to one side.

Cynthia Ramsey answered my polite query: "The flight was never ending," she said, speaking in a monotone. "The farthest I had flown up until now was Phoenix, and I thought *that* was long." She was as thin as a thread, with a sharp, narrow face, who looked to be in her mid-to-late fifties, with a timid manner. Barbara Cornwall, by contrast, was a very attractive woman, probably about fifty.

"Here they come." Barbara pointed to a bald man with a solid build. Behind him was the line of students with whom I would be sharing the next nine days with. Being burnt at the stake seemed a better option.

Yes, I was inclined to be prejudiced against today's teenagers, especially Americans. What I saw every day in the press, on the internet, and glancing at the trash on TV led me to believe that for the average sixteen or seventeen-year-old, glorification of the superficial had conquered respect for substance. In 2010, ten years into the twenty-first century, all their clothes had to have a brand name, or it wasn't worth wearing; hanging out at the mall or the video arcade was cool; your MP4 had to have at least 16MB, or it was trash; your cell phone (preferably one of those new iPhones or a Samsung Galaxy) had to have a five-pixel camera, Bluetooth, and the capability to upload on Windows Messenger and email; you had to be into Twitter, Yahoo Messenger, AOL Instant Messenger, Skype, Facebook, eBuddy, etc. If you were using your father's old desktop COMPAQ for chatting and gaming, you were from the Middle Ages; and if you had an iMac, it must have at least a 17" screen with 2.93GHz and an ATI Radeon HD 4850 graphics processor with 512MB of GDDR3 memory.

Books were archaic and cumbersome, museums and art galleries were useless and a frightful bore, the *Encyclopedia Britannica* was an antique of no value, and Homer, Socrates, Plato, Pliny, Cicero, Ovid, and St. Augustine were probably casting names for vampires in the sequel to the *Twilight* movie.

I was fully aware that every generation had its teenagers since the beginning of time, even though in past centuries, a seventeen-year-old male was already considered middle-aged, and a woman of the same age was almost over the hill. And let's not forget that up until the end of the Second World War, fifteen- and sixteen-year-olds and even younger boys were going off to war.

The elders of yesteryear probably thought that the youths were incorrigible, much as the parents of today are dismayed by the behavior of their teenage children. But something had happened over the last forty years that had drastically changed the values of today's young people. Values that were tangible and important one day disappeared the next. How many times had Francesca and I discussed this phenomenon without arriving at a satisfactory explanation? She blamed the rapid advancement of technology, while I singled out the sexual revolution of the 1960s and the consequent breakdown of the family unit.

The solidly built, bald man came up to us. I cast a wary eye on the students behind him.

"Hello," he said. "My name is John Seeward, and this is our group."

Marco went into his spiel. "Hello, everyone. My name is Marco Iddino. I am very happy to meet you. I work for ASA Rome, but I will not be your chaperone this trip. I introduce to you Atticus Winterle who will be accompanying you."

I said hello and got back some "Morning," "Hey," and "Hi." Somebody whispered, "What kind of friggin' name is *Atticus?*"

Most of the students sat down on the floor, opened their backpacks, and reached for their cell phones. They were stretching, yawning, and scratching. I understood that they had just come off a nine-hour flight, but they resembled nothing so much as a new two-legged breed of cattle. Their behavior didn't faze Marco or the teachers in the least, but it irritated me.

"Okay, okay," said Marco. "Maybe you like to go to bathroom before we go downstairs to waiting bus?"

There was an effusive "Yes!" from the teachers and a strident "Yeah!" from the farm animals.

"Okay, okay. You leave bags here with me and Atticus and go over there to the left and you see boy and girl rooms. Thank you." Nearly everyone in the group trudged off toward the restrooms. Marco turned to me and switched back into Italian.

"Well, here you are, my friend. They don't look so bad. Try to keep on the good side of the teachers, and you'll see that everything will fall into place. As soon as they're all back, we'll go down together and meet your driver. The bus will be available for most of the excursions, but, for those near the hotel, you'll need to walk or take the metro to meet your tour guide."

I had mistakenly thought that the bus was going to be at our disposal at *all* times. Luckily, if I remembered correctly, the hotel was practically a stone's throw from the Trevi Fountain, which was about as central in Rome as you could get.

"Marco, Atticus, excuse me, but do you happen to know if our hotel is in a Wi-Fi hot spot? The kids will probably want to hook up their devices as soon as they get to their rooms."

Thank goodness Marco was still there because my facial expression was quite clear in saying, "How am I supposed to know?"

Marco waved his hands reassuringly. "No problem, no problem, all rooms in the hotel have internet access, also in the lobby and TV area."

I had not even perused the hotel brochure, obviously. I just stood there staring at Cynthia as if I had been instantly freeze-dried. Marco gave me a glance that revealed his thoughts as clear as telepathy: *You didn't look at any of the information I sent you, did you?* I felt like a child being scolded for spilling the milk. The situation was already aggravating me, and we hadn't even left the airport.

"Is the hotel far?" John asked.

Marco glared at me, but now I was able to supply an answer.

"No, no, not really," I said. "We are close to the Trevi Fountain, which is in central Rome. If the traffic isn't too horrible, we should be there in about forty-five minutes."

Most of the kids were back from the restroom when Barbara asked, "Can we get something to eat as soon we get to the hotel?"

I hesitated. *Think, Atticus, think. Try to come up with a plausible answer. ASA has probably worked with this hotel before. What would a group of people, especially teenagers, usually want to do after a nine-hour flight? Shower, change, and eat!*

Marco was about to give up on me when I blurted out, "Of course! You'll have time to shower and change before the buffet lunch in the dining area." Marco looked at me approvingly, even though I had completely invented the buffet.

"Okay then," Marco interjected. "If we are all here, let's go and find our bus." The group followed Marco as I stayed back to ensure there weren't any stragglers.

"Wayne, Bishop, come on, let's move." John snapped at two tall, well-built boys who were watching a group of flight attendants walking by. I could just imagine the testosterone-loaded remarks that they were whispering to each other.

"Evelyn, James, please unclasp yourselves and join the group," Cynthia ordered. I turned to see two students gazing deeply into each other's eyes. James was tall and thin. Evelyn, by contrast, was short and, to put it delicately, had some weight challenges in the other direction. *Wait a minute*, I remembered, *Evelyn Farling. Her parents had just recently divorced. And James, wasn't he the one with frequent bouts of depression? What a couple. Misery loves company.*

We were going toward a downward sloping moving walkway. Marco was at the front while Cynthia and I brought up the rear.

"How strange to be in a place where you don't understand what anybody is saying," she said. "Did I mention that the furthest I've been from Atlanta is Phoenix, Arizona?"

"Yes, yes you did." I was able to stop myself from rolling my eyes.

"How long have you been doing this kind of work, Atticus?" I knew this question was going to come up, but I wasn't expecting it so soon.

"Ah, well, actually this is my first assignment." What possessed me to blurt out the truth like that? Cynthia looked at me with a worried expression that made her emaciated face look even more skull-like.

I quickly added, "But I've lived in Rome for almost twelve years, so I know the city like the back of my hand. Plus, in my last job, I was in a management position, so I have experience in supervising people."

Cynthia still didn't seem terribly impressed.

We reached the end of the walkway and followed Marco out of the airport terminal. It was almost 11:45 am, and the sun's rays were beating down on us.

"Come, come please, this way." Marco was ably leading the group through the crowd of passengers entering and leaving the terminal, the endless carts of luggage, people waiting for taxis, and scattered police officers. Of course, there were also the "black market vultures," as I called them, to contend with. These were characters who pretended to be taxi drivers to charge five times or more than the normal fare to the city center. They usually had large, comfortable sedans and elaborate but forged identification that would impress a first-time visitor to Rome. Even though signs were everywhere indicating where the official taxi stands were, it was amazing how many tourists were ripped off on a daily basis by these shady characters.

"Taxi, taxi, don't you need taxi, beautiful ladies?" One of them was homing in a couple of students behind me.

"*No, non serve, gira alla larga.*" He frowned, not appreciating my telling him that the girls didn't need a taxi and to buzz off.

"*Ma guarda questo, che coglione!*" he snarled. That was another word near and dear to the modern Italian's heart—*coglione*, literally "testicle." The chap calling me this was small and ugly. I stood at six foot three inches and would have loved to continue the discussion with a little shove here and there, but this would have attracted the attention of the other vultures, and it just wasn't worth the risk, especially in the presence of the group.

Marco stopped at the side of a large metallic gray Mercedes tour bus that looked like it had just come out of the showroom. The luggage doors on the side were open, and a short, plump individual, who I assumed was the driver, was helping the students put their suitcases into the compartment.

"Well, at least ASA does things in style," I whispered to Marco.

"This is the Mercedes Benz Travego High Deck. Probably the best tour bus on the market today. It took the place of the Mercedes Benz O404. There's more room for the driver and tour guide, or chaperone in your case. It has a Euro 4 engine, 428 horsepower, fifteen rows of seats, it's 1,214 meters in length, has electronic braking and proximity control systems, acceleration skid control, two flat screen monitors, DVD player, small refrigerator, and adjustable footrests. There's more, but I have a hard time remembering all the specifications."

Anybody else would have been impressed, but I knew Marco always studied all the details pertaining to his job.

"How many square meters of luggage space there are between the front and back axle?" I asked him. I could see he was trying to remember. I gave him a slap on the shoulder and laughed.

"Marco, you are incredible. I should have hired you when I had the chance." He blushed again, beet red this time, as he took a notepad out of his satchel.

"Here, this is for you. It's a day-to-day agenda with all the information you need. Keep tabs on the timing. Tour guides don't wait for more than ten minutes. If you're late, they leave, and ASA has to pay them just the same. Remember to only take the vouchers you need for the specific day with you. Stolen or lost vouchers don't sit well with ASA. In the back of the notebook, you'll find all the phone numbers you might need, including my home number. I think that's it. Oh, one last thing, since you probably don't remember, the hotel arrangements are six double rooms and one single for the students, and four singles for you and the teachers."

"All right, I'll do the best I can." Talk about stretching the truth.

"You better. I told ASA that when you lived in the States, you did this for a living." Was this the reason for Cynthia's quizzical look at me when I told her this was my first time chaperoning? I would find out shortly.

Before I could reply, Marco trotted up the stairs of the bus. "Okay, okay, I leave you now," he said to the group. "You be in good hands with Mr. Atticus and with Mr. Riccardo, your bus driver. They both know Rome very, very well. Enjoy this beautiful city and have good time, goodbye."

As Marco descended the steps, you could hear a few *ciaos*, goodbyes, and some clapping.

"They're all yours, my friend. I'm going to email my ASA contact in Atlanta as soon as I get home and let him know that the group has arrived safely. By the way, as you heard, the bus driver's name is Riccardo. He's from Norcia, a small town in the Umbria region. He's married, has two kids, lives on the outskirts of Rome, and has been driving buses since he was eighteen. However, he's thinking about retiring after this assignment."

"Is that all? You mean you don't know what his mother's maiden name is or if his father wears dentures?"

Laughing, Marco gave me a quick embrace, and as we parted, he promised to get me an exceptionally good espresso when I returned the group to Fiumicino airport for their journey back to Atlanta.

So here I was, briefcase in hand, my Delsey in the luggage compartment of the bus, and a group of sixteen individuals under my care in one of the most beautiful, but also one of the busiest, cities in the world. I went up the bus steps. The doors hissed shut behind me.

CHAPTER 6

Once inside the bus, I shook the driver's hand. We exchanged names, and he asked me if we were ready to go. The three teachers were sitting in the front row; I asked them if everyone was accounted for.

"All here and ready for a hot shower!" said Barbara.

"Okay, then," I said to Riccardo." We're off."

I settled into the tour guide's seat, which was the only seat other than the driver's that is set lower than the rest.

"Air-conditioning, please!" came a yell from the back of the bus.

I didn't think that Riccardo spoke or understood very much English, but before I could translate, he pressed some buttons and turned a knob on his space-shuttle dashboard, and a blast of cool air blew from the ceiling vents that ran the length of the bus. So quiet was the engine in this metal beast that it seemed as though we were gliding on magnetic cushions.

We rounded a long, smooth curve that veered to the left and joined the main traffic artery out of the national arrivals area. Shortly afterward, the bus banked to the right and entered the Fiumicino-Roma autostrada, or highway. This would take us into the Quartiere Portuense, the eleventh district of Rome in the south of the city. From there, traffic permitting, it would take thirty to forty minutes to arrive at the hotel.

Most of the young men and women in front of me were chatting, and from what I could overhear, they were talking about the flight and discussing what they were going to do as soon as they got to the hotel. However, the teachers, directly behind me, were cemetery silent. I could feel their stares drilling into the back of my head, presumably expecting me to say something, like a formal greeting, maybe tell them a little bit about myself, anything to break the ice. It had to be done. I took the wireless microphone from its slot, found the small on/off switch on the side, and turned it on. Ricardo began to fiddle with a dial near the radio, and I realized that he was attempting to adjust the volume.

"Well, hello, and welcome to Rome!" My voice boomed out through the speakers, startling everyone.

"Wow, turn that friggin' thing down!" somebody immediately shouted out.

Riccardo was on top of it and turned a few more dials.

"Okay, better? Well, welcome to Rome," I repeated, getting some bored looks from the students.

"First of all, I want to eliminate any possible questions you may have regarding my first name, Atticus. For those of you who have read or seen the movie *To Kill a Mockingbird*, you may remember that the protagonist's name was Atticus Finch. My mother was reading that book when she was pregnant and obviously loved it." I paused a moment expecting some sort of reaction. Instead, you could have heard a pin drop. I cleared my throat. "Can you imagine if she had been reading *Moby Dick*? She would have probably called me Ishmael. Or Moby. Or Moby Ishmael." Not a sound. Was I speaking a foreign language?

The teachers must have read the book or seen the movie since they all nodded their heads. The students, who probably had never even heard of the book or movie, merely gave me the "Why would anyone call their child Atticus?" look. I was accustomed to it.

I tried a different tack. "I bet you're all tired, want to wash up a bit, and get something to eat."

"Yeah, and a couple of cold beers would be a good start!" came a loud reply, which generated some hand clapping.

"Can we stop this motor home somewhere and grab a six-pack of Bud?"

"Mark, cut the wisecracks please," Cynthia snapped from the front.

"My Dad told me that in Italy there isn't a legal drinking age, Mrs. Ramsey."

Cynthia was about to unleash more words in Mark's direction when I spoke. "Well, your dad is right and wrong." This got everybody's attention. "The age limit in Italy for purchasing and consuming hard liquor is eighteen. However, beer and wine can be consumed from sixteen and up, in a restaurant, for example."

This unsolicited piece of news generated a series of hurrahs and cheers from the boys and a few smiles and nods of approval from the girls. However, when I looked at the teachers, I only saw what could be best described as that look of horror displayed in Edward Munch's painting—*The Scream*—sketched on their faces.

Nevertheless, what I had said, whether the teachers liked it or not, was perfectly true. The company I had worked for up until eleven months ago had entered into a co-op promotion with a national beer producer to promote one of our jewelry lines. Our target audience was teenagers to young adults, from sixteen to twenty-two years of age. I had insisted that the marketing department research every detail about this specific cohort and brief me before I signed off on the project.

Besides, Italy's relationship with alcohol, as well as most other European countries, is much less restrictive than the "Thou shalt not drink" commandment pronounced on teenagers in the United States. Obviously, the teachers thought it extremely unwise that the first information the students should receive from their chaperone was that teenagers could order glasses of wine and mugs of beer. The damage was done, though, and I could hear the boys whispering happily to one another. I had visions of cases of beer flowing from one room to another in the hotel with students passed out in the hallways.

"Hey, calm down!" I said in a more authoritative voice, which immediately shut everyone up. "Italy and the rest of Europe may have different laws regarding the consumption of alcohol than the U.S., but penalties are severe for an establishment that serves liquor to anybody under the age of eighteen, and the Italian police are much stricter than Georgia state troopers." This was stretching the truth to left field, but it quieted a few students down and brought some color back to John's and Cynthia's cheeks.

I swung back and sat in my seat with the microphone still in hand. We were still on the bus, and I was already in hot water. What a start! This wasn't where I needed or wanted to be. For a moment, I seriously thought about calling Marco and telling him that I had already put my foot in it with the teachers. Someone better suited for this kind of work needed to be here. Certainly not me.

"Mr. Winterle?" a velvety voice spoke out from the middle of the bus.

"Yes?" I said, standing up and clumsily knocking the microphone against the armrest, which made a loud scraping sound over the speakers.

"Could you tell us something about the dos and don'ts while we're here in Rome? I mean, it's like I've never been outside of the United States before except Canada, which is like the States. I mean, in Europe, it's probably, I mean, different, right?" How in the world did this girl manage to stuff so many "I mean" in just a couple of sentences?

"Well, that's a very good question. What's your name, first of all?"

"My name is Darlene, Darlene Williams."

I decided to put my stubbornness aside for a moment. Like it or not, I had to create some sort of rapport with the group.

"Okay, great, Darlene. I'll try to remember your name."

I could see some eye rolls and heads shaking. Someone whispered, "That won't be difficult once he gets a look at her boobs." This remark came from one of the girls sitting at the front of the bus. I was stunned, to say the least. None of the teachers seemed to have heard the explicit comment, but I certainly had.

Darlene had a Marilyn Monroe head of hair, rosy cheeks, big doe eyes, and full lips. That was all I could ascertain from my vantage point.

"First of all, let me say that I would prefer you call me Atticus. Secondly, and before answering your question, Darlene, which is an important one, I don't think it would be a bad idea if we started by introducing ourselves. I would appreciate it if all of you could kindly tell me your names one by one so that I can begin to match a name to a face. Let's start with the two of you all the way in the back." There was a rather lengthy pause.

"James Fingerton."

"Speak up a bit. I didn't quite hear you."

"I said, James Fingerton!"

"Okay, I heard you that time, thanks." Wasn't this the student with frequent bouts of depression? Add a little pent-up anger to the list, judging by the tone of his response.

"Next please."

"Evelyn Farling." It was abundantly clear by her laconic response that she, just like James, wasn't going to add anything else. She was practically sitting on top of him. These two were probably going to be super-glued together for the best part of this trip.

"Okay, thank you. Next row up, please?"

"Yeah, hey, I'm Wayne Little." The student next to Wayne didn't say anything until he received a sound slap on the back of the head from Wayne.

"Oh yeah, sure, I'm Bishop, Bishop Horn." These were the two jocks who had been making appreciative comments to the airline employees at the airport.

"Are the two of you involved in sports? By the height and build, I'd say you're on the basketball team."

"Cool, that's right. I'm a forward, and Bishop here is a guard."

"Like two peas in a pod," someone murmured loud enough for everyone to hear. This drew a lot of laughter, especially from the girls.

"Cut the crap, cyborg hacker, or it'll cost you a carton of Marlboro!"

"Cool it, Wayne. You're getting off on the wrong foot," John Seeward said.

Cyborg hacker? Who was Wayne referring to? It then dawned on me that the cyborg reference must have been directed to the student with the prosthetic arm. What was his name? Richard? Jeremy? I could tell by the mild reprimand from John, and the lack of response from Richard or Jeremy or whatever his name was, that the cyborg comment was not considered offensive or mean-spirited.

"Okay, let's calm down and continue, please. At this rate, we'll be at the hotel before I hear all your names and get to Darlene's very good question. Next?"

"Sabrina Hamlin." This name I remembered. She had lost her brother in a car accident.

"Vanessa Guy." Vanessa looked extremely tired. She had dark circles under her eyes that not even her makeup could hide.

"Get any sleep on the plane, Vanessa?" I asked.

"Not a wink. Didn't sleep the other night either."

"Well, you'll be in the hotel soon, and you can get some shut-eye."

"Yeah, sure." She sounded unconvinced. I was certain after listening to Vanessa's tone that she had made the comment about Darlene Williams.

"Okay then, next row up, please."

"Anthony Carter." Interestingly, although Anthony was wearing a denim jacket, he had on a white shirt and tie underneath. He had round spectacles à la John Lennon and short, neatly cut hair. He looked as though he was on his way to a job interview. "Is this your first time to Europe, Anthony?"

"No, sir, and in a way, yes, sir."

Bishop Horn piped in before I could respond. "What the hell is that supposed to mean, Carter? Stop being such a wingnut." I had no idea what a wingnut was, but obviously it wasn't an expression of praise.

Wayne also chimed in, "Yeah, Carter, spare us all your lies for once."

In a flash, Cynthia was on her feet, with a finger pointed at both boys. "Mr. Horn and Mr. Little, I am warning you officially in front of everyone on this bus that if your insolent comments do not cease, you will be back on the next plane leaving for Atlanta. I hope I have made myself clear!"

Bishop and Wayne sank back in their seats, mumbling, "Yeah, okay, okay," which just goes to show you that you should never judge a book by its cover. This little, dried-up woman in the snap of a whip had transformed herself into Wonder Woman, minus the looks. I suspected that Carter was one of her favorite students and that her protective instincts were the cause of this metamorphosis. I tapped the microphone a few times to regain the students' attention.

"Okay. Anthony, you were saying?"

"What I meant to say is that I spent two summers with some relatives in a Swiss town named Bern." I could see that many students were openly shaking their heads in disbelief while Anthony was speaking, "But since Switzerland is not part of the EU, I guess that the correct answer to your question is no, sir."

"Excuse me, Mr. Winterle, what's the EU?"

This was Darlene Williams again. She had taken off her windbreaker and put her hair up in a bun with a large hair grabber. She was wearing a sheer light-blue tube top that, unfortunately at her age, clung to a pair of breasts that could have easily competed with Pamela Anderson's after the implants. Darlene was sitting ramrod straight in the high-backed seat as though she wanted me to notice her attributes. This set off alarm bells in my mind. Acting as though nothing was out of the ordinary, I replied, "The EU is short for European Union, which Switzerland is not part of. Therefore, Anthony's answer is correct. Switzerland is within the European continent, but it is not part of Europe, politically speaking."

It was Barbara Cornwall's turn to say something: "Darlene, you remember when we studied this earlier this year don't you? All of you wrote a paper on the foundation of the European Union. The Treaty of Maastricht, remember?"

Darlene shrugged her shoulders. "I must have been absent that day, Mrs. Cornwall." She looked straight at me with those big doe eyes and giggled. Barbara sighed and turned to me with a resigned expression.

I would have liked to discuss Anthony's time in Switzerland since I knew the Neuchatel Lausanne area quite well and had passed through Bern many times on the train. But there would be time for that later in the trip.

"Let's move on, then—yes, yes I know who *you* are now." This generated a laugh as I pointed my finger at Mark Hampton, who had made the remark about beers.

"And next to you?"

"Good morning," said the boy seated with Mark. "I'm Raymond Katzman."

I felt as though I had just been greeted by an aspiring politician. Raymond radiated self-confidence. He was wearing a faded dark-blue linen jacket and a tie loosely fitted around his neck.

"Is this your first time to Europe, Raymond?"

"Yes, it is, Mr. Winterle. I've spent a few summers in Tel Aviv with my extended family. I wanted to go back this summer, but my mom suggested that I come here. I enjoy history and government studies, so I guess Rome isn't a bad place to visit. It's where it all began, along with Greece, right?"

This generated a few smirks and exaggerated sighs from the other students, but less than I would have expected (especially from Wayne, Bishop, and Mark). Raymond may not have been particularly popular, but he seemed to be respected.

"Amongst plenty of other things, but if politics is something you enjoy, and I sense that it is, you couldn't have come to a better place. Greece can be the next trip." He sat back and gave me a thumbs-up.

Before I could get to the next row, I was thrown off balance as the bus swerved to the right. We had exited the Fiumicino-Roma highway and were now on the Viadotto della Magliana, which was a treacherous, crater-filled road that connected the highway to one of the main arteries of Rome, the Cristoforo Colombo Avenue. Even though this Mercedes Benz bus surely had the latest independent air-pressured suspension system, the cutting-edge technology was no match for the potholes it was presently encountering.

"Right," I continued once I had regained my footing." Where were we? I see we have a whole row of young ladies now."

"Hi, my name's Mary Lopez, and I've never been to Europe before. My dad's from Panama. I've been there a few times."

"Thank you, Mary. Who's next?"

"I'm Michelle Thompson, Mr. Winterle." Michelle had golden blonde hair and a wide smile. I noticed that as she began to speak, Raymond sat up and beamed at her.

"I've never been outside of the U.S., Mr. Winterle. I hope that doesn't put me in the dunce category."

"Not at all, you're here now, aren't you?"

"Yes, sir, and I'm thrilled."

Michelle struck me as the most genuine of all the students. She had a homegrown, well-disciplined, and good-humored country-girl disposition. She was not especially beautiful, but her smile was captivating.

"And you, sir, have the honor of being the last to introduce yourself."

"I'm Jeremy Nolan, alias cyborg." As he mentioned cyborg, he lifted his left arm and clenched his fist a few times. "No sweat, Mr. Winterle. I'm used to this hardware by now. It doesn't faze me anymore." At first, I didn't understand what Jeremy was talking about. I knew that he was the student with the amputated left arm, but I was seeing a human hand that opened and closed. Jeremy saw my confused expression.

"PVC—polyvinyl chloride, in other words—and polyurethane foam, Mr. Winterle. They work wonders. But if I slide off this fake skin, it's just titanium, aluminum, plastic, and fancy wiring. McG wanted to offer me the part of Marcus in *Terminator: Salvation,* but I told him I was off to Rome!" This received a few nervous laughs from the students and a look from the teachers that told me they would explain all this later.

"Well, it fooled me, Jeremy. Incredible craftsmanship. By the way, who is McG?" This query drew a few groans of the "old people are so ignorant" variety from the students, but Jeremy was quick to answer:

"Have you seen the *Terminator* movies? The first three?"

"Yes, the John Connor, destruction of mankind series, right?"

"Spot on. Well, *Terminator: Salvation* is the fourth and Joseph McGinty Nichol is the director, McG for short. He's going to probably direct the fifth and last installment as well."

"I see you have an interest in movies."

"It's one of my hobbies, especially the ones that deal with futuristic, high-tech plots. It's part of me, literally." Jeremy paused and glanced out the window.

"Hey, Mr. Winterle, what's that?"

I looked over to his left and saw that we were going past the Basilica of San Paolo fuori le Mura (literally "Saint Paul outside of the Walls"). The bus had already traversed the short stretch of the Via Cristoforo Colombo Avenue and gotten off on the Via Guglielmo Marconi, named after the Italian physicist whose work led to the invention of the radio. Riccardo had now turned right onto the Via di San Paolo, which passed right by this architectural marvel. Luckily, I had taken some guests of mine to this important religious structure a year or so before, so I remembered a few details about its history.

"That's one of the four major ancient basilicas of Rome. It's called 'St. Paul outside of the Walls.' The first construction goes back to the Roman emperor, Constantine, around AD 300. Various Popes made additions to the edifice throughout the centuries, but unfortunately in 1823, almost the entire basilica burned to the ground. So what you see today is a replica of what once was." I now had the full attention of the teachers and felt that any doubts that may have arisen because of the earlier liquor faux pas had been erased.

"Did you study up before picking us up Mr. Winterle?" Mary Lopez asked. "How do you remember all that stuff?"

"I lived in Rome for almost twelve years. I'm just picking my brain, remembering a few things here and there."

"Atticus, what's the difference between a basilica and a regular church?" asked Sabrina Hamlin. She was the first person to address me by my first name, as if we had known each other for some time. Losing her brother, the year before, must have been a tragic but maturing experience.

"Don't quote me on this, Sabrina, but the word *basilica*, which comes from the ancient Greek word *basilike*, signifies a large church consecrated by the pope. That wasn't the original meaning, however. Before Rome became Christian, a basilica was a public building that had various functions. We'll have to Wikipedia this one, however, since I am not one hundred percent certain." I had a feeling I was going to be a constant user of the online encyclopedia over the next fourteen days.

"Mr. Winterle, uh, excuse me, the word *basilica* does come from Greek." Jeremy was holding a small laptop in his right hand. "It refers to a public building, like some sort of courthouse, like you said, in the center of the city. The Romans then stretched the meaning to all public structures that were within the Roman Forum and all the forums in the cities that were under their control. The word has an architectural, as well as a religious, meaning."

"Well, that's *very* impressive, thank you," I answered, momentarily taken aback.

The teachers were all grinning at me.

"I'm online, Mr. Winterle." Jeremy had obviously taken his laptop out very discreetly and, with the help of an internet key, was already in the virtual world.

"Jeremy's not only a movie trivia whiz kid but also our computer expert, Atticus," John explained. "If he knocks you off your feet with any *other* kind of knowledge, it's probably because he's just read it off a computer screen."

This generated laughter from some of the students as well as a few articles of clothing thrown in Jeremy's direction. He was smiling shyly, and his cheeks had gone tomato red. I felt, however, that John's comment was slightly off-color, and I suspected that Jeremy had been hurt by it. I needed to take more mental notes.

"Just a few insights, everybody, now that I think about it, regarding Italian vocabulary. You are going to be hearing me, as well as the tour guides, use a series of Italian words denoting landmarks. Once you get the hang of it, you won't need to ask for a translation every time. Jeremy, open Excel on your laptop." He fidgeted for a few moments with his prosthetic arm.

"Got it."

"Write these down and then send an email to the group. *V-i-a* means road, *c-o-r-s-o* means main street, *v-i-a-l-e* means boulevard, *p-i-a-z-z-a* means square, *p-o-n-t-e* means bridge, *c-o-l-o-n-n-a* means column, *p-a-l-a-z-z-o* means building and, in some cases, palace, *s-a-n* is short for *santo* and means saint, *f-o-n-t-a-n-a* means fountain and *c-h-i-e-s-a* means church. Try to remember them. And keep in mind that in the Italian language, you pronounce what you see. It's really a simple language in this respect. The grammar is another story. That's enough for now. Thanks, Jeremy."

Most of the students had become quiet, some dozing off. I put down the microphone and turned to the teachers.

"I understand that the students have already been paired for their rooms. We have seven doubles and three singles, all with bathrooms, of course."

Cynthia shook her head.

"There should be six doubles and four singles, Atticus," she said. "Jeremy has a single room due to his arm. It was specifically asked for."

Well, there went my looking as though I had everything under control. Marco had, in fact, mentioned something about another single room before we left the airport.

"I am certain the hotel has arranged the rooms as was requested. I take it that everyone knows with whom they are sharing a room?"

"Yes, they're all set." Barbara was looking straight at me. The intensity of her stare marked her as a strong, determined woman. I noticed the few wrinkles at the corners of her eyes and on her forehead. She looked battle fatigued. I remembered the saying that the eyes are the mirror of the soul. This face, these eyes, I had seen them before—not hers, obviously, but someone who could have been her twin sister. Who was it? The memory eluded me.

"We'll get them set in their rooms. Atticus, and then have lunch," said John. "When they're finished, we can give them an hour or two to hook up their laptops or take a nap, then we can sit together and go over a few things. What do you think Barbara, Cynthia?"

Both women nodded.

"Mr. Winterle?"

"Please, call me Atticus."

"Oh yeah, sorry. Atticus, what's a large pyramid doing in the middle of the street? I thought we were in Rome, not Egypt."

Some of the snoozing students woke up at the word *pyramid.*

The bus had entered the Piazzale Ostiense, a large open area with the Ostiense train station on the right and the Gaius Cestius Pyramid on the left, along with the only Protestant cemetery in the entire city of Rome.

"That pyramid is actually a tomb for a Roman magistrate, whose full name was…, Jeremy?"

"Ah, yeah, hold on. Okay, his full name was Gaius Cestius Epulo." Other than his horrible pronunciation of the magistrate's name, Jeremy didn't let me down.

"And when was it built?"

"Between 18 and 12 BC."

"And how big is it?"

"Ahh, let's see, okay, about two hundred thirty-seven square feet at the base and about eighty-nine feet high."

"Thank you, Jeremy." I gave him a thumbs-up.

This little performance received a warm round of applause from both the students and teachers.

Mary's curiosity was still not satisfied, however. "But why a pyramid? Did this guy have a thing for the Egyptians?"

"It's a good question. What I can tell you is that after the Roman conquest of Egypt around 30 BC, the citizens of Rome became fascinated with Egyptian culture. You must remember that a couple thousand years before the Romans came on the scene, the Egyptians constructed architectural marvels such as the pyramids, colossal statues to the gods, as well as towering obelisks. You could equate the Romans' fascination of the pyramids with Apple's launch of the iPhone but on a much, much grander scale." This generated a few chuckles. "In fact, you are going to see numerous obelisks situated throughout this city, which gives further credence to this Egyptian love affair."

There was another area of interest practically adjacent to this pyramid that didn't get much mention in the guidebooks to Rome. I thought I'd have a little fun with it.

"By the way, there's a Protestant cemetery next to this tomb, which goes by the name of the 'Englishmen's Cemetery' due to the high occupancy of defunct British citizens. Who's the English literature buff on this bus?"

The girl with the beautiful smile, Michelle, timidly raised her hand.

"Well, here comes an extremely difficult question—and I mean difficult. Do you know the names of the English poets who are buried in this cemetery? Jeremy, keep quiet this time." He was typing away madly on the keyboard.

"John Keats, I believe, but I don't know of any others," Michelle said.

I was blown away. "Excellent! Does anybody want to try for the second name?" Cynthia's hand shot up.

"Percy Shelley, one of my favorites!" she almost shouted. "*Prometheus Unbound* takes up a good portion of our English literature curricula."

"Good, really very good!" Well, knock me on the head with a two by four, *never* would I have expected that a high school student and teacher from the United States would have known anything about these two great English poets, let alone that they were buried in this small, nondescript cemetery on the outskirts of Rome. Most Italians didn't know that this burial place even existed. This was a surprise to me, as had been most of this brief trip from the airport to the city center. Except for the two jocks, these kids seemed bright, interested, and respectful. I was frankly astonished.

While the students who participated in these ASA programs were probably the cream of the crop, I had thirteen of them here with me, not just two or three, and so far, I had not a bone to pick with any of them. It was obviously much too early to come to any sort of conclusion, but perhaps—just perhaps—I was going to have to rethink my teenager calamity theory.

No one was asking any more questions. Cynthia and Barbara were beginning to nod off. It was about 6:00 am Atlanta time. Jet lag was catching up with everyone.

CHAPTER 7

As Riccardo gingerly turned off of the Viale Aventino, we entered what might be described as the largest open-air museum in the world: the city center of Rome.

The bus was presently on the Via del Circo Massimo, named after the Circus Maximus, which runs the entire length of the road measuring well over two thousand feet. Only the skeleton of this palatial arena remains today, with sloped boundaries on either side where thousands of spectators once sat on stone bleachers. The imposing construction was dedicated to horse and chariot races from the 300 BC to AD 500. It is still used by Italians today for concerts or political gatherings. Behind the Circus Maximus stood the Palatine Hill with the majestic remains of the imperial palaces that were once the glory of Rome. The extensive Roman Forum was directly behind this outcrop of ruins while to the left, but not visible from the bus, was the Colosseum—one of the most famous historical monuments worldwide.

This is the blessing and curse of any tourist coming to Rome—there is just too much to see. I lived in Rome for a little more than twelve years, but it was safe to say that I had only seen 30 to 40 percent of the wonders of this architectural goldmine. Travelers who came for just a few days were just skimming the surface of a multifaceted city that could trace its history back to well before 600 BC.

From our present location, in front of the Circus Maximus, where the infamous chariot races were held—I remembered how much I had enjoyed *Ben Hur* as a kid—to the Trevi Fountain, which was a stone's throw from our hotel, one could visit a plethora of monuments, squares, palaces, museums, churches, temples, statues, and obelisks. This group had two weeks to soak in over two-and a-half millennia of history.

Riccardo was driving toward the Via della Grecia, from where we would turn right onto Via Petroselli. All the students began turning their heads from left to right, almost as if they were watching the finals tennis match at the Italian Open, to drink in the architectural marvels spanning over two thousand years: the Church St. Maria in Cosmedin, the Temple of Vesta, the Temple of Portunus, the Temple of Hercules Victor, the Arch of Janus, the Forum Boarium, the Temple of the Vestal Virgins, the Church of St. George in Velabro, the House of the Crescentii, the Theater of Marcellus, the Church of St. Nicholas in Prison. And this was just four hundred feet down this historical thoroughfare.

Barbara and Cynthia, unfortunately for them, were still fast asleep. John, however, was wide-awake and seemed to be taking everything in with hungry eyes.

"First time in Italy, John?" I asked.

"Yes, it is. It seems so strange to actually be looking at what I've only seen in history or art books or in documentaries on the Discovery channel. All the centuries that have passed leaving visible remnants, one on top of the other, here in one place. Amazing." John was certainly taken by what he was witnessing. His comment was articulate and genuine.

"So, John, Cynthia teaches English literature and has a particular liking for English poets. Barbara probably teaches history or a political science class, given her comment on the EU. But I don't know what you teach."

"You're right on the money about Barbara. She teaches a course in modern history, starting from the twentieth century. As for me, I teach a course called Business and Entrepreneurship. It sounds a lot more important than it actually is. We study case histories of companies that have emerged throughout the last fifty years and those that have failed. It's a course that's supposed to prepare those students who want to pursue a business management or economics curricula in college." He paused and looked out the window. "What's that on the right, Atticus?"

I turned to see that we were passing by two long stairways, both leading up to the Capitoline Hill. To the right, a set of gently sloping stairs led up to the Piazza del Campidoglio, designed by Michelangelo, while to the left, the steeper staircase led up to the Basilica of St. Mary of the Altar of Heaven.

"That's the Capitoline Hill John and that's the—"

But John was already looking elsewhere. "And what is this large building?" The bus had entered Piazza Venezia, where one of the most controversial monuments in all of Europe stood—the Monument to Vittorio Emanuele II, who was king of Italy from 1861 to 1878.

"An eyesore," I said. I chose the most neutral epithet that critics had used to describe the white marble structure since its unveiling in the early 1920s: "the wedding cake," "the typewriter," and "the monument to dentures" were some of the more popular barbs.

John looked at me in puzzlement.

"I'll explain later. We're close to the hotel so we should start waking everyone up."

As I said this, however, the bus braked hard and swerved to the right.

"*Li mortacci tua! Ma dove cazzo vai, stronzo!*" Riccardo outdid himself by stuffing four expletives in a sentence of eight words. I didn't see what happened, but I figured a scooter or automobile had cut in front of him. I switched on the microphone.

"Everything's okay, folks. We just had a little traffic incident, but our driver managed to avoid an accident. Driving in Rome, ladies and gentlemen, takes particular skill."

"Are we close to the hotel?" Raymond asked.

"Close, just a few more minutes."

Riccardo tapped my shoulder. "Signor Atticus, I'm going to stop in that clearing up ahead in front of that building. I can't go down Via Lucchesi with this mastodon."

Riccardo entered a small semioval area for parking and turned the bus so that it faced the direction in which our hotel was located.

"Okay, everyone, we've arrived. We need to walk a little way since the bus has to stop here." The students, tired and sleepy, groaned. Cynthia asked me for the microphone and stood facing the students.

"Listen up, please. Gather your belongings and exit the bus. Pick up your suitcases, and let's follow Atticus to the hotel, and no more complaining, please! The quicker we move, the faster you'll be in your rooms."

Moving in slow motion, the students gathered their belongings and started filing out of the bus. Riccardo was already outside hoisting up the luggage container doors and putting the suitcases, backpacks, and other items on the narrow sidewalk. I quickly looked through the notebook that Marco had given me before leaving and found Riccardo's cell phone number in the back with all the other numbers I might need.

"Your phone number ends in 7818, correct?"

"Yes, Signor Atticus, but there are two others."

"You have three cell numbers? Why, if you don't mind me asking?"

"Well, one is for work. The second is for my family, and the third, well, the third is for *le amiche*." He winked and smiled. *Amiche* translates into "female friends." Need one say more?

"Give me the phone number for le amiche," I said. "That way, I know that you'll answer if I need you." He laughed and gave me the number.

"We meet here tomorrow morning at nine o'clock and go to Piazza San Pietro," he said.

"Ah, yes, of course," I replied. "We'll be here at nine on the dot."

I couldn't admit to Riccardo that I hadn't even looked at the program and had no idea what we were going to do the next day.

"Wait one moment, please." He skipped up the stairs of the bus and went down the aisle. He bent down and disappeared for a second between the seats, then came back out. He had a leather-bound notebook, which he handed to me.

"They always leave something on the bus."

"Thank you, Riccardo. See you tomorrow."

I walked back to the group and held up the notebook, which was actually a 2010 diary. "Whose is this please? Our bus driver found it under a seat in the bus."

At first, no one said anything. Then the depressed girl, Evelyn, who was stuck like glue to the tall, skinny boy, walked quickly up to me and yanked what was probably a record of her innermost secrets from my hands. "It's mine." She walked back over to the boy, James. I was already starting to remember their names.

"Well, I'm glad the bus driver found it, Evelyn. Be careful next time, however, this goes for all of you. Try to keep tabs on your personal belongings."

"It won't happen again," Evelyn said tersely.

"Okay. This way, please. Let's try to stay in a single file and keep your eyes open for cars and motorbikes. The street is very narrow." I was in front of the line with Barbara at my side, Cynthia was seven or eight students down, and John was at the back of the line. All the suitcases had rollers. What an invention to put those two or four little wheels, not only on carry-on bags, but large suitcases as well. I had always wondered who had come up with such a simple yet revolutionary idea.

Everybody was struggling, however, because not even those wonderful little wheels were a match for the *sanpietrini*—small square blocks of black porphyry, a very strong rock originating from molten lava, which is used on most of the roads in the center of Rome, especially the pedestrian areas. This material has its advantages when used as a pavement; however, the irregularities in the spacing between the stones widen over time. Those little luggage wheels were now bumping into and getting snagged in those spaces.

I knew the hotel's name was the Te'Rovami, and that it was somewhere along the Via dei Lucchesi, but I didn't know how far up. Despite the narrowness of the road and the presence of pedestrians, cars and motor scooters were whizzing past at high speed. But this was Italy. Everyone thinks they are a NASCAR driver even behind the wheel of an old, beaten-up Fiat.

"Atticus, how long have you lived here in Rome?" Barbara asked.

"Close to twelve years, but not continuously."

"Have you enjoyed it?"

"Every minute. The traffic is horrible, the pollution can be very bad if a strong wind doesn't come off the sea to disperse it, there's graffiti on everything that stands still for more than an hour, the bureaucracy is a nightmare compared to most other European cities, and the noise of scooters, ambulances, buses, and cars is continuous."

Barbara looked puzzled. "Your definition of the word *enjoy* seems very different from mine."

I laughed.

"Let me put it this way. Rome is *alive* twenty-four hours a day, and you are living on layers of history that go as far back as 500 BC. Everywhere you look, there is something to marvel at. This road, for example. The buildings on each side could be two to three centuries old, but they are built on top or have been incorporated into previous structures that probably go back to Roman times. It's like a multilayered cake. The Trevi Fountain, which is farther up this road, was finished in the 1760s. It's practically a brand-new construction if we consider the age of this city. Just think of the architects, engineers, painters, sculptors, writers, musicians, historians, philosophers, politicians, as well as the emperors, royal families, and popes that have made contributions to this city. Rome is truly *caput mundi*, the center of the world."

Barbara raised her eyebrows and smiled at me. "You make it sound fascinating, Atticus. I think this will be a very exciting nine days." I smiled back. My antennae were picking up a weak signal, but a signal nonetheless. Possibly, just possibly, I was going to enjoy her company.

I noticed a blue light from a neon sign about one hundred feet ahead of us. People were entering and exiting, some with suitcases. I increased the pace a bit and finally made out the words *Te'Rovami Hotel* with three stars underneath. The name of the hotel was a rather dismal attempt at being creative. It was formed by combining the two words *Trevi* and *Roma* to obtain a third meaning *trovami*, which means "find me" in Italian, even though the "e" isn't part of the spelling.

"We're here," I announced to the group.

We entered a large, neat lobby with couches and coffee tables to the left and a wide Sony flat-screen television set on top of what looked like an original roman pedestal. John and Barbara maneuvered the students to this area while Cynthia, passports in hand, went with me to the front desk where a young lady greeted us with an eager smile.

"*Buongiorno*, and welcome to the Te'Rovami hotel."

"*Buongiorno, parla Inglese?*" I asked her quite ingenuously if she spoke English. The name on her lapel tag read "Ludovica Antonelli."

"Of course. I presume that you are the ASA group that we were expecting."

"Yes, that's correct. My name is Atticus Winterle, and I'ɪɪ the chaperone."

"Excellent. What I need, Mr. Winterle, is the hotel voucher and the passports of everyone in the group. I will be keeping the voucher, and the passports will be returned to you this afternoon. Or if you prefer, we can keep the passports in our safe and give you a photocopy of each one."

I turned to Cynthia. "That's not a bad idea," I suggested. "The students can carry a copy for identification purposes. They shouldn't go walking around with their passports. Too many pickpockets."

Cynthia agreed. We gave the young lady the students' thirteen passports, plus the three belonging to the teachers. I flipped my briefcase open, found mine, and the hotel voucher.

"Here you are."

Ludovica had already selected the room keys and was placing them on the counter. "Rooms 8, 9, 10, 14, 15, and 16. These are the double rooms for the students. They are all on the same floor. Room 19 is the single requested for the special-needs student." I was relieved that the hotel had been properly informed.

"Rooms 3, 5, and 6 are also single rooms for Mrs. Ramsey, Mrs. Cornwall, and Mr. Seeward. Mr. Winterle, you are on the third floor, room number 38." A little distance between me and the group was a positive. My privacy was important to me.

"If you wish, you can leave the suitcases here, and we shall bring them up to the rooms. The breakfast, lunch, and dinner area are through the doors at the bottom of this hallway after the elevators." Ludovica pointed to her right.

"Opposite the elevators, you will find the stairs. There is a buffet lunch waiting for the group. The restaurant closes at 3:00 pm. This is a floor plan of the entire hotel showing the emergency exits, which are here, here, and here." She highlighted the emergency exits with a green STABILO marker. "This is a list of useful phone numbers for restaurants, shopping, and events in Rome for the month of June. This is my card. My name is Ludovica, and you can reach me twenty-four seven on this cell phone number for whatever questions you may have."

"You've been very helpful," I said. "You obviously have worked with groups for a long time."

Ludovica nodded. "We have been working with ASA for the last six years, and I believe that they are pleased with us. That's our aim."

The students were told to be down in the restaurant at one thirty and that no one was allowed to go outside until after lunch. Some students were already going up the stairs to their rooms with their carry-on bags and room keys. A few others opted for the elevator. Barbara went up with them to supervise the settling in process.

John and Cynthia came over and gave Ludovica a list of the room arrangements. She immediately made four copies, one for me and one for each of the teachers.

"Okay then," Cynthia said. "I guess we'll see each other at one thirty."

"I'll come down a bit earlier to make sure nobody has the temptation to go outside on an exploratory excursion," I said.

Cynthia nodded in approval. I felt as if she was getting more comfortable with me. Time would tell.

CHAPTER 8

I took my key, the room list, my Delsey, and briefcase, thanked Ludovica once again, and headed toward the stairs. As I passed the first-floor landing and the open hallway that led to the rooms, I overheard Barbara yelping out commands, trying to get everyone settled in as quickly as possible.

I reached the third floor and headed down the corridor to Room 38, my home for the next nine days. A large window at the end of the corridor provided a view of a steeple and the rooftop of a church. Rome has more than nine hundred churches, so in any direction you go from the center, you will inevitably encounter many of these historical buildings. However, getting into them is a trying endeavor, since they all have their own specific, and often quirky, opening and closing hours. Knowing how to manage your time in Rome (and in Italy as a whole) when sightseeing is quite an art in itself.

My room was almost the last one on the left before the window. As I put the key in the lock, I grinned and tried to think of the last time I had seen a *real* hotel room key. In all my travels to various countries around the world, I always got keycards in a small foldable leaflet with the hotel's information printed on the back. Even though these were more convenient than a metal key, on more than one occasion, I had found myself on the twentieth floor of a hotel only to discover that the little green LED refused to glow when I swiped my card in the electronic lock's slot. Instead, I would get the stubborn red light that meant "Entry Denied." That led to having to find a service phone, usually on a table near the elevators, or, if there was no phone, going back down to the front desk for a new pass. It was nice to see a real key again.

This particular one was attached, by way of a short chain, to a thick brass plaque with the room number printed on it. This was obviously meant to deter the guests from taking the keys out of the hotel instead of leaving them at the desk. I opened the door and walked in, not knowing what kind of accommodation I would find.

My quick inspection found a relatively comfortable room, albeit lacking the perks that I had grown accustomed to during my international travels. There was a queen-sized bed with dainty bedside tables at the sides. Two modern wall lamps protruded from the wall above, serving as reading lights. The wall closet was on the bed's right with a small desk and chair on the left. A more economical TV—meaning a shoebox-sized version of the Sony flat-screen television in the lobby—hung on the wall in front of the bed. A small couch and table were near the window on the far side of the room. The bathroom was to the right as you entered, and as with almost all Italian hotel bathrooms, it was very constricted in size.

Given the sheer volume of guest accommodations that are required for tourists, religious pilgrims, and businesspeople, hotel rooms in the center of Rome are tiny compared to American ones. I knew this was going to be a shock for the students who were probably accustomed to the Holiday Inn, Best Western, Hilton hotels back in the States: big rooms, beds and bathrooms, ice machines in the corridors, and vending machines galore.

More than likely, they were going to be especially puzzled by the plumbing fixture next to the toilet: the bidet. This was a low-set sink that you straddle like a horse to wash the area between your legs. In fact, *bidet* in French means "pony."

When I had first come to Rome in 1982, I had found this piece of bathroom equipment puzzling, but today I really couldn't have a bathroom without it. I believed that by now, in 2010, most people were aware of this French invention, which dates back to the early eighteenth century, even though many probably have never actually seen one. I had thought many a time that for women, it must seem a godsend once experienced.

I unloaded the contents of my briefcase on the bed—papers, documents, wallet, cigars, and books tumbled out. I then arranged everything in some order, putting whatever I was supposed to read on the bedside table: the student questionnaires, Marco's day-to-day planning, and the room arrangements copy. Before plopping down on the bed, I plugged in the PC and connected the internet key, which dialed up the service provider.

I then kicked my shoes off, sat on the bed, and looked at the room arrangements.

BOYS	ROOM
Wayne Little	8
Bishop Horn	
James Fingerton	9
Anthony Carter	
Mark Hampton	10
Raymond Katzman	
Jeremy Nolan	19

GIRLS	ROOM
Evelyn Farling	14
Michelle Thompson	
Vanessa Guy	15
Sabrina Hamlin	
Darlene Williams	16
Mary Lopez	

TEACHERS	ROOM
Barbara Cornwall	3
Cynthia Ramsey	5
John Seeward	7

CHAPERONE	
Atticus Winterle	38

I wondered if the teachers had decided on these room pairings or if the students had made the final call. With the little knowledge that I had accumulated about these kids in the past few hours, I thought I could discern a pattern in how they were matched. Then again, it was too soon to draw conclusions.

I retrieved my Montegrappa fountain pen from my jacket pocket, opened the notebook to a blank page, and began jotting down some notes. This had been a habit of mine since entering the workforce back in 1983. I found that writing down notes with a pen, as opposed to typing them into some electronic device, made it easier for me to recall important details.

✓ Wayne and Bishop: the two basketball players were together but right across the hall from John. Troublemakers? Comments on the bus / bullies?

✓ Jeremy: with a handicap / specific interests in movies and computers / independent / not the trouble making kind.

✓ James and Anthony: James depressed / Anthony = Cynthia's pet student?

✓ Mark and Raymond: Mark = really interested in drinking or just a joker? / Raymond = clean-cut, *intelligent, looks like a politician. Raymond paired with Mark for a specific reason?*

✓ *Evelyn and Michelle: Complete opposites...Evelyn has issues, Michelle seems problem free.*

✓ *Vanessa and Sabrina: Vanessa does not look well. Just tired? / No info on Sabrina.*

✓ *Darlene and Mary: Darlene = young version of Jane Mansfield/must watch carefully when out on the streets/Mary seems bright and sharp /she may need to keep tabs on Darlene.*

I picked up Marco's agenda and looked at Day One and Day Two. Today counted as Day One, but nothing was planned. I had, however, already reluctantly accepted that the group would, in all likelihood, want to get out and do some sight-seeing before dinner.

I suddenly had the urge for a cold glass of water and looked for the minibar. Where was it? Was there even a minibar? I opened the closet doors and found it discretely positioned in the corner. The cabinet work was done so that the minibar looked like part of the dresser drawers. I recalled the many times I had almost given up looking for that small fridge in hotels around the world. I had come to the conclusion that the more luxurious the room, the more difficult it was to find the minibar. Was it in the closet? Under the television cabinet? In the mirrored hallway? Under the desk? Behind that Renoir imitation? Once found, however, the selection of spirits, champagne, wine, and soft drinks, not forgetting the omnipresent Toblerone chocolate bar, cans of pistachios, and mixed nuts was impressive and laughably expensive. This wasn't the case in the Te'Rovami hotel, though.

The fridge had two bottles of natural mineral water, two bottles of sparkling mineral water, two Cokes, two Fanta orange, and four small Tetra Pak fruit juice cartons. No Rémy Martin cognac or demi-liter bottles or Moët & Chandon. I unscrewed the sparkling water and downed half the bottle. What time was it, 12:45 am? I still had time to look through Day Two's itinerary.

Riccardo was right. We had to be at the bus at 9:00 am. The meeting with our tour guide was in Piazza San Pietro, St. Peter's Square, at 9:45 am. The excursion would take us in and around St. Peter's and the Vatican Museums to the Sistine Chapel and was scheduled to be over at 1:45 pm. Lunch was going to be at a restaurant not far from the Vatican at 2:00 pm, and I was hoping that ASA hadn't chosen any of those strictly-for-tourists-type eateries that were infamous for butchering Italian cuisine and foreigners' wallets. These so-called restaurants were usually in clusters close to major tourist attractions such as the Colosseum, Piazza Navona, and, of course, St. Peter's. The first hint that you were at one of these rip-offs, con artist places was the little American, and other countries', flags on the tables. Another warning sign was waiters hovering like vultures outside and coaxing you in. You were guaranteed to eat something out of a can or frozen ziplock bag and pay an exorbitant price for it. I had always felt that one should eat as the locals do when visiting a different country. The best place to do this in Rome, or any other European city for that matter, is in a restaurant where the customers are indigenous. You may or may not enjoy the food, but you begin to understand the culinary habits of the country that you are visiting, which always reflects quite a lot about its culture.

After lunch, Riccardo would pick us up at 4:00 pm at the same point he dropped us off, and we would return to the hotel. The rest of the day was free time, and I suspected that ASA had planned it this way, given that many of the students would certainly still be feeling the effects of jet lag. Dinner was again scheduled for 7:30 pm. I would decide tomorrow whether to take the students somewhere after their meal or let them venture out on their own. Some after-dinner walks, preferably unaccompanied, were something to look forward to.

Having a grip now on what was happening over the next twenty-four hours, I washed up, put on some fresh clothes, and headed downstairs. When I reached the hotel lobby, I walked up to the desk where Ludovica was typing away busily on the computer. As I put my key on the counter, she caught sight of me.

"Mr. Winterle, just one moment please." She turned to the desk in front of her and handed me the photocopies of all the passports. She was not only efficient, but quick as well.

"Grazie, Ludovica."

I sat down on one of the couches in the lobby and picked up an Italian fashion magazine from the table. After a few minutes, I heard some American voices. I looked up and saw Darlene and Mary leaving their keys at the desk. They turned, noticed me, and came in my direction.

"Hi, Mr. Winterle."

"Atticus, please, Darlene, Atticus."

"Yeah, okay, sorry." Darlene giggled and sat down, Mary plopping down next to her. They both wore tight jeans. Mary had on a light-blue blouse while Darlene was dressed in a sheer black tube top under a white button-down shirt. It took a herculean effort to look into Darlene's eyes. She was obviously aware of this and enjoyed the attention. I found the situation unsettling.

"So, Atticus, are you going to always be with us on this tour?"

"Yes. From today until all of you head back home.

Darlene clapped her hands and bounced up and down. This was distracting, to say the least.

"That's great Mr. Winterle! I told Mary I liked you as soon as we got on the bus."

I swallowed hard, hoping that other students would come down in the lobby quickly. My prayers were answered. I heard footsteps, and in came Jeremy, with Wayne and Bishop just behind him. They waved but went straight for the sliding glass doors.

"Wow, hold on, where are you headed?" I called out.

"Just outside for a smoke," Wayne answered. "Mr. Hacker here owes me a Marlboro." He gave Jeremy a punch on his good arm.

"Okay. But I want all of you on those steps and no farther. We eat in five minutes."

I watched them as they walked out and took cigarettes from a packet of Marlboro reds that Jeremy had in his pocket.

"Oooh, I just hate smoking! It makes your skin and hair stink." Darlene looked at me with her big doe eyes and pursed her cherry-red lips together.

I needed to get up. As I did, Barbara and John walked in, followed by most of the remaining students. "Three of the boys are out on the steps smoking," I informed the teachers, with a little embarrassment. In Italy, it's fairly common for young people to smoke and drink, but I realized too late that maybe the teachers had taken a "No Smoking" stance with the students on this trip. This would have come as no surprise to me, considering that the United States had declared war against smokers some years back.

"It's amazing that they lasted this long without a cigarette," Barbara commented.

James, Evelyn, and Cynthia came in. Evelyn's eyes looked red. She was arm in arm with James.

"What a sorry piece of humanity, fat bitch," Sabrina murmured. She spoke loud enough for me to hear, whether knowingly or not I couldn't tell. I wasn't so much struck at the harsh words as I was by the spite in her voice. There certainly wasn't any love lost between those two. Maybe the teachers would enlighten me during our meeting.

Cynthia went out to get the boys while John and Barbara herded the rest of the group toward the restaurant area. It was time to eat.

The dining area was large, organized, and well lit. A series of long tables covered with white linen tablecloths were in front of us, laden with an array of serving trays chock-full of Italian fare. At the end of the tables stood a gentleman in a white apron and chef's hat serving from three large, flame-warmed bain-marie.

Two waiters came out of the kitchen and guided us to our tables. Each one sat four to five and had a small ASA tag in the middle. I saw that Barbara, Cynthia, and John were seated together, so, presumably, the fourth remaining chair was for me. As soon as everyone was seated, one of the waiters came back out through the kitchen doors pushing a cart filled with bottles of water, Coca-Cola, Fanta, and uncorked bottles of red and white wine.

An alarm bell went off in my head. I signaled to the waiter.

He came over and automatically put a bottle of white and red on the table and was about to roll away to another when I gently took hold of his arm. I looked at the threesome in front of me. "Remember what I said on the bus. There isn't a specific drinking age in Italy for wine, which is more common than tap water. If we don't decide how to handle this quickly, there are going to be wine bottles on all four tables."

John calmly placed our bottles back on the cart. "I propose that we have water or a soft drink and that the waiter make the wine disappear for now." This was a wise decision. After a few words with our server, the cart went back in and out of the kitchen with only nonalcoholic beverages. The students hadn't noticed anything, so we were spared any useless protesting.

"Please, feel free to help yourselves," the waiter pointed toward the food-laden tables. Everyone got up and went to the left side of the buffet where stacks of white dishes and cutlery were at our disposal.

The variety was commendable for a three-star hotel. There were the classic *bruschetta al pomodoro*, stuffed zucchini, onions gratin, sautéed red and yellow peppers, spinach with garlic, roast potatoes, and artichokes *alla romana,* "in the Roman manner," which means stuffed with a mixture of parsley, lesser calamint—called *mentuccia* in Rome, and garlic. There were small mozzarella balls, the Italian variety of quiche Lorraine, rice salad with vegetables, assorted sliced meats, and, probably more in line with the taste of the group, two large trays filled with French fries and a stack of hamburgers. The two bains-marie had warm mashed potatoes, plain white rice, pasta with a Bolognese meat sauce and sliced roast beef. The hotel had cleverly mixed some standard Italian dishes with hearty all-American favorites.

Most of the students just looked skeptically at everything unfamiliar while rapidly emptying the trays of the French fries and mashed potatoes. I noticed that even the teachers were hesitant. I coaxed them into at least trying the stuffed zucchini and artichokes *alla romana.* Obviously, I was going to have to educate these people in the art of Italian cooking.

I took a few slices of the bruschetta, which is nothing more than grilled Italian bread rubbed down with a clove of garlic and topped with extra virgin olive oil and salt.

It was extraordinary how a mixture of such ordinary ingredients could ignite the senses—bread, garlic, olive oil, and salt. How much simpler does it get than that? But put these flavors together and boom! As Remy in the movie *Ratatouille* would say, you have an incredibly new taste experience. My satisfied expression spurred Barbara and John to get up from the table, saying, "We need to try some of that!" Cynthia, on the other hand, had only taken some carrot sticks, celery, and a few French fries.

"Not very hungry, Cynthia, or wasn't there anything that tempted you?" I asked.

"I don't eat very much, Atticus. Food just doesn't interest me that much. I just eat because I have to."

That was truly unfortunate, especially when you're in Italy. This just isn't the right country where anyone should pick at their food. Given that I didn't think I had ever met any foreigner who wasn't at first skeptical, then tempted, and eventually hooked on the thousands of Italian recipes from Sicily to the Austrian border, it was frustrating for me to watch Cynthia sit and nibble on carrot sticks.

In the meantime, John and Barbara had come back to the table with much more on their plates than just bruschetta.

"How would you like to plan the rest of the day?" I asked, diving into my zucchini.

"The students can go back to their rooms until we conclude our meeting," Barbara replied. "Atticus, can we plan a walk before dinner, say, around five o'clock?"

I was less than enthusiastic about this but knew that it was in the cards. I simply nodded in approval.

The waiters were going around the tables adding soft drinks, exchanging dirty plates for clean ones, and replacing cutlery. A third waiter came out from the kitchen wheeling a dessert cart that caught everyone's attention. There were some delightful items to behold and, even more delightfully, to taste: profiterole, *millefoglie*, strawberry *bavarese*, apricot *crostata*, pine nut cake, dark chocolate cake, a fruit *macedonia*, and goblets filled with an assortment of raspberries, blackberries, and blueberries. Even though most of these were unknown to the students and teachers, plates filled with small and large portions were flying off of the cart at the speed of light. But I had seen this all before. Unfamiliar dishes comprising vegetables, meat, fish, rice, or pasta would bring looks of suspicion from a virgin palate, especially if American. A dessert cart, however, despite having equally novel recipes and ingredients, never gave the slightest pause to those same palates. The waiters were now clearing away the practically untouched trays of artichokes, spinach, and onions. The trays on the dessert cart were already empty.

John stood up. "Listen up, please," he said to the students. "The four of us need to meet for about an hour down here, so we kindly ask you to go back to your rooms when you're done with your food, finish unpacking, hook up your laptops, email or Skype your parents, or whatever else you need to do. We'll meet up in the lobby at five o'clock for a walk before dinner."

The students got up and shuffled out of the restaurant. They all looked as if they needed a good nap. I saw the very tired girl walk by—Vanessa was her name, if I remembered correctly. "Try to get some shut-eye," I suggested.

She smiled, but weakly. "I'll try."

As soon as the students had cleared out, John took out some papers from his satchel and cleared his throat. I was about to be briefed.

CHAPTER 9

"I guess we can start. We should begin by telling you, Atticus, that ASA in Atlanta briefed us completely regarding the organization of the trip and explained to us what the chaperone's, that is, *your* responsibilities are. Therefore, I think we can begin by talking a little bit about the three of us and more about the students, so you have a better understanding of some specific issues that you need to be aware of."

"Fine with me. I'd also like to know more about those who are under the confidential notes column—Evelyn and Sabrina I believe."

"Absolutely," Barbara interjected. "We need to speak about them and each student so that you are aware of potential problems."

I raised an eyebrow at her choice of words.

John began by giving me a three-minute autobiography. He was fifty-two, had been teaching business-related courses at Bradford High for fifteen years after a short and, from what I could discern, unsuccessful business venture. This was his first time in Italy, as I already knew from our brief conversation on the bus. He had traveled to Australia and New Zealand and had stopped a couple of days in Frankfurt, Germany, on his way back to the States. That was the extent of his European experience. He didn't mention anything about his personal life—whether he was married, divorced, or had children. I found that significant.

From Cynthia, I learned that she had been teaching English literature for almost twenty-five years, the last three at Bradford High. The years had not passed without leaving their mark, I thought to myself. She closed by saying that she was a widow and didn't have any children.

"My turn, I guess," said Barbara. "I've been a modern history teacher, Atticus, since 1988, twenty-two years this November, and I have always taught at Bradford. Can't believe I've lasted this long. I'm married, and I have two children. They're grown, in twenties, actually."

She glanced at me, and I said, "So you got married very young, then?"

She shrugged, smiling at my implied compliment, and continued, "This is my first time in Italy. I've been to Amsterdam and France, but that was over thirty years ago. I've been looking forward to this trip and hope to get as much out of it as I possibly can."

Barbara was an attractive woman. I was still racking my brains trying to remember who she reminded me of. She had a full-bodied figure, and her few extra pounds only accentuated her curves. But as I had noticed before, there was a shadow of defeat in her eyes. Many stories were in this woman's past, and not all were good.

"And you, Atticus?" she asked. "We know all about your responsibilities as a chaperone but, come to think of it, we know very little about you because the bio info we received was about Marco Iddino. We were only informed at the airport in Atlanta that there was going to be a change."

Marco had obviously not confirmed my participation to ASA until the very last moment, knowing that I might have skipped out on him. He understood me very well.

"We really don't know who you are." John gave out a short laugh, but I felt three pairs of eyes focusing intently on me.

"Well, I'm fifty-four years old, and I've lived in Europe and China for the past thirty years. I started my European experience in 1983 when I worked at the American embassy here in Rome for the Federal Bureau of Investigation, and then—"

"The FBI?" John said, cutting me off.

"Yes. From '83 to '89. I was supposed to go back to the States for more training at the end of '89, but I fell in love with Rome and didn't want to leave. So I handed in my resignation, did six months of debriefing back in Washington, and then came back here."

This was the official story, but it was far from the truth.

"And then what?" Barbara asked, staring at me.

"Well, it was difficult to find a steady job, given that I had no business experience. I also couldn't talk about my last job due to secrecy constraints. One day, I met the personnel manager for American Express. He took a chance and had me hired as a junior product manager. I owe my career to that man. From Amex in Rome, I was assigned to the Paris office soon after. A few years later, I went to Berlin to work for a German wholesaler of fashion accessories, then on to Shanghai and Hong Kong where I lived for almost seven years. Then I was offered the position of country manager for a manufacturer of fashion accessories back here in Italy, Milan this time. I use the past tense because I was laid off a year ago due to cost cutting and a scale down in manufacturing." This was difficult for me to put into words, and I was surprised I had done so to strangers.

"So the aftershocks of the Bear Stearns, Lehman Brothers saga has hit this side of the Atlantic as well," John commented wryly.

"I don't think that any part of the world was spared. It was rough, and we're not out of the storm yet."

"Therefore, you took this job as a filler while you look for new employment?" Cynthia asked rather abruptly.

"I hope we can count on you, Atticus," John said. "In many ways, we are in *your* hands." He and Barbara seemed slightly embarrassed by Cynthia's question, but I appreciated her raising the issue. She sounded like a supervisor looking after the well-being of her team.

"I understand your concern, Cynthia," I said. "It's true I didn't really want to fill in for Marco. But I did take on the task, and I want to assure you that since I have made that commitment, I will do everything in my power to make the next two weeks as enjoyable and as safe as possible. Also, I must say that I am happy to have met you, and I feel that I've already established a certain rapport with some of the students."

"A few of the students have already mentioned to us that they think you're okay," said Barbara. "That's a big compliment coming from these kids, given that they've just met you."

"We need to bring you up to speed on them," John said. "Let's start with Sabrina and Evelyn."

"I think we should begin with Darlene," Barbara said, looking at me and raising her eyebrows. "You probably noticed that she's, shall we say, flamboyant. She likes to be looked at and, let's be blunt, desired."

"Yes, that's rather apparent," I said.

"Darlene's mother is one of those, in my opinion, sick women who put their daughters in every beauty pageant imaginable. I think Darlene's first was at the age of four. She's grown up in a world where cosmetics, hair products, clothes, and shoes reign supreme. By the time she was fifteen, she already looked like a young woman in her early twenties. And as you might have noticed, she likes to display her attributes by the way she dresses."

"What about her father?" I asked, given that a child's behavior is usually influenced by the good and bad behavior of both parents.

"Her father left home when Darlene was very young, I'm told," said Barbara "He lives in Mobile, Alabama, and is the editor of some sleazy biker magazine with content that I understand is borderline pornography. That certainly hasn't helped Darlene get her priorities straight."

"She plays up to older men, Atticus," John interjected. "She's approached me and other male teachers at school, not too obviously, and she has been reprimanded and suspended twice this past year. She likes flirting, but she doesn't realize that many men aren't going to stop at just talk. I think she's looking for a father figure of sorts."

"She's still a child in a *Playboy* centerfold body," said Barbara. I could see the concern on her face as she spoke about Darlene. "She's insecure and hungry for genuine parental love."

Cynthia, however, had a different take. "All complete nonsense!" she broke in. "The problem is that our school doesn't do more to stop this kind of behavior. Darlene should have been expelled for the way she dresses and acts. All this father figure talk is sheer foolishness. If she had been my daughter, I would have—"

Barbara interrupted Cynthia's tirade, "But you're *not* her mother, Cynthia, neither am I, nor John her father. We're her teachers. It was our responsibility to guide her. That's our goal. Whatever happens after she leaves Bradford is her responsibility, but for now, we must still support her." Cynthia was about to reply, but John cut in:

"Darlene isn't the only student on this trip. Let's move on. Atticus, you mentioned Sabrina. She lost her brother in a car accident last year."

I nodded.

"It's a tragedy right out of a movie. Her brother, Derek, was a junior at Bradford. He was a varsity football star and, in his spare time, an assistant coach at the elementary school down the road from us. He had excellent grades, surprisingly, for a football player. He helped prepare the annual yearbook. He was in the music club and the press club. He was popular and good-looking—a carbon copy of Troy Bolton from *High School Musical*, if you've seen that movie. Sabrina and he were very close."

"What happened?" I asked, preparing myself for something obviously unpleasant.

"He was on his way home after school on his mountain bike. It seems that he swerved into oncoming traffic to avoid a construction crew that was blocking his side of the road. He rode that bike like a professional, but he took risks. A tractor-trailer was coming in the other direction, and Derek ended up under the truck. The parents are still in mourning, and Sabrina has the double weight of grieving for her brother and trying to comfort her parents. It almost makes it harder because there's nobody to blame. The driver was sober and under the speed limit, the truck was in perfect working order, the street was dry, and even Derek himself wasn't drunk or high. The parents are obsessing over why this happened. Sabrina has her hands full."

"He was one of my best students," said Cynthia. I saw that her eyes had become wet. "Funny, isn't it? A football player who enjoyed reading and discussing James Joyce."

"Sabrina doesn't get along with Evelyn, does she?" I decided to ask some uncomfortable questions.

"Did you notice that from your FBI training?" Barbara said, with a half-smile.

I didn't tell her that the "fat bitch" comment was a dead giveaway.

"Sabrina absolutely hates her," Barbara acknowledged "Evelyn's parents had a messy divorce last year. Her father's the pastor of an Episcopal church on the west side of the city. He came home unexpectedly one day and found his wife in bed with another woman. Another kind of man might have tried to jump in—"

"Barbara, don't be so vulgar!" Cynthia protested.

"Oh, come on Cynthia, that's just the way it is. Instead, Evelyn's father went on a religious verbal rampage with his daughter and then with his congregation, saying his wife was a sexual pervert possessed by Satan. So the entire city heard their business. I know Evelyn's mother. She isn't a lesbian. She was just bored and frustrated because she hadn't had had a satisfying physical relationship with her husband for years. Now thanks to him, she's become an accidental icon in the gay community of Atlanta, but she likes the attention."

Cynthia shifted uncomfortably in her chair. She was obviously ill at ease with all this sex talk.

John chimed in with his two cents: "Evelyn got support from the school, but you can imagine the hell that broke loose on Facebook, Twitter, and other social media. Actually, there were thousands of tweets from people all over the country who came to her mother's defense, but there was also a good share of hate mail directed toward Evelyn. Barbara and I believe that Sabrina was involved in some of these anonymous online attacks."

"Why?" I asked.

"We think that all the media hype around what happened with Evelyn's mother must have gotten under Sabrina's skin in some way," Barbara replied. "Remember, all this happened just a few weeks after her brother died. Suddenly, people were only talking about was Evelyn's mom. What happened to Sabrina's brother just wasn't important anymore. Sabrina suddenly became hostile if Evelyn even approached her in the hallway, insulting her in the worst ways."

"And Evelyn? How is she coping with all of this?" I looked directly at Cynthia wanting her feedback.

"She's become a compulsive eater since this thing exploded in her face, and she's put on about twenty-five pounds. Her grades have dropped a lot this past semester, and she's become a recluse."

"Given all that, I wouldn't have thought either girl would be on a trip like this," I said. "So how come they're both here?"

Cynthia, Barbara, and John glanced at one another. Clearly, none of them wanted to field this one.

After a long pause, John took the lead. "That's a good question, Atticus," he said. "Both mothers believed that getting their respective daughters out of Atlanta would be a good distraction for them. I don't think that either of them realized how much pent-up hatred there was between the two girls."

"And you can bet your bottom dollar that since James was going, there was no way that Evelyn was going to opt out of the trip," Barbara added.

"Evelyn seems to be stuck to him with super glue," I remarked. "She hasn't left his side since they got on the bus at the airport."

Cynthia nodded. "James himself shouldn't be here." She looked ominously at Barbara and John. "Can we at least agree on that?" The other two shrugged. Cynthia continued:

"He's been depressed since he came to Bradford, but he really went off the deep end last year. He's got low self-esteem, no interest in extracurricular activities, and no friends to speak of, except possibly Jeremy. We're actually surprised that he hasn't attempted to do something foolish."

There was an uncomfortable pause.

"However, having said that, I must admit that he has decent grades. I don't think he even opened a textbook, and yet he managed to get Bs and Cs this past year and his junior year.

"So why is he on this trip?" I asked. "Did his parents also think sightseeing would be good therapy?" My sarcasm was shining through.

John nodded. "Sort of. We were reluctant, but his parents actually begged us and ASA to let him go. They thought that it might help him snap out of this lethargic state he's been in. They're at their wits' end. I personally don't think James cares one way or the other if he's here in Rome or sitting in his room back home. But he does seem genuinely interested in Evelyn. So that's a good sign. Maybe he just found someone who accepts him the way he is or there may be more serious feelings are at play."

"Is he on any kind of medication?" I asked.

"Yes," Cynthia answered. "He's on a pretty heavy dosage of protriptyline hydrochloride, and I make sure he takes his pill every evening."

" Is this drug some sort of antidepressant?"

"It's what they call a tricyclic antidepressant. The list of side effects is as long as your arm, but it seems to be helping him."

"Have any of these side effects manifested themselves since you left Atlanta?"

"He's been irritable, and on the plane, he said he felt weak and restless. Those are two of about twenty possible side effects," Cynthia added.

There were so many more questions I wanted to ask regarding James, but I would do so later. I needed to return to Evelyn. "By the way, what was the deal with the diary? Did you notice how Evelyn acted?" Her almost violent reaction when she saw me holding the pages of her innermost secrets had stuck in my mind.

"I guess there's something in that diary that she doesn't want anyone to see," said John. "That's natural for a girl her age. Maybe it was just an overreaction."

I wasn't completely satisfied by John's answer, but I decided not to push the issue for now. "We've only discussed four students, and I feel as if we could write a book about them. What about that girl Vanessa? Any issues? She looked so tired on the bus and at lunch, as if she were sleepwalking."

"No, nothing important," said Cynthia." Overall, she's one of my better students, although her grades have dropped this last semester." She pursed her lips. "There were a few going-away parties the night before we left. She may have had too much to drink."

This seemed all too plausible.

"Who else is on the girls list? I asked. "Mary, correct?"

"Yes, indeed. She's an A-student with me and with Barbara," John said.

"She had a B average in my class," said Cynthia, "but she could have done better."

"What can you tell me about Michelle? I had a very good first impression."

"There goes your FBI training again, Atticus." Barbara chuckled. "Michelle's the shining star of the senior class, probably one of the most respected students in the whole school. She's grade A across the board, scored a 5 on her AP exams in history and math and—"

I raised my hand, cutting Barbara off. "Excuse me, but I'm too old to know what an AP exam is."

"They're college-level exams. Students can take them to gain college credit before graduating from high school. Other than Michelle, who scored 5 on both exams she took, the highest grade possible, Anthony, Jeremy, Mary, and Vanessa took part at the end of their junior year."

"That's clear, thanks. Getting back to Michelle?"

"What else can I say? She spends practically all of her free time doing volunteer work at a geriatric center clear across town from where she lives. If a freshman or a newcomer to Bradford has a problem, she's the first in line to lend a hand. I've never seen her pouting or in a bad mood. It's remarkable. She's the first student from Bradford who's going to Harvard. We're all very proud of her."

This was all very impressive, but I doubted this girl could be so perfect. It would be interesting to get to know Michelle a little better.

"What can you tell me about that boy who mentioned Switzerland on the bus? Anthony, I think."

Cynthia piped up at once. "He's my...I mean, *our* Michelle, but the male version." Cynthia tried to cover her Freudian slip, without success. "He likes good literature and is an excellent student."

"He could do much better in my class" was John's less-than-enthusiastic comment.

"And mine," Barbara agreed.

"Oh, John, he's not cut out to be a businessman. His direction is literature, either as a writer or as a teacher. It's so clear." Cynthia was obviously taken by this student, but John and Barbara clearly didn't share her enthusiasm. I decided not to dwell on this and went to the next student.

"Jeremy is the computer whiz kid, right? Any issues regarding his prosthetic arm that I should be aware of?"

"He's a borderline hacker, Wayne was right on that one, and he'll go far. He scored a 5 on his computer science AP exam, the highest possible mark, and finished it in under an hour—a record. He's already received some interesting job offers from some local area software companies, as well as scholarships from a few prominent tech universities. We don't think he's made up his mind yet on what he wants to do when he gets back to Atlanta. His arm had to be surgically removed after a motor-cross accident two years ago. He was trying to copy some stunt from a *Mission: Impossible* movie, and it went horribly wrong. Don't get him started on movies, by the way, he'll talk your ear off."

"You mentioned Wayne—" I started to say but was cut off.

"Wayne and Bishop live in their own little, insignificant world," Cynthia said. Her face was grim. "All they know is basketball with no interest in anything else except beer, partying, and girls, of course. Jeremy was right when he said they're like two peas in a pod—where you see one, the other is right behind. They're inseparable fools."

It was amazing how these two students could incur Cynthia's wrath.

John nodded. "On that, Atticus, Barbara and I tend to agree with Cynthia. Wayne Little's father is a very rich businessman with a lot of clout in Atlanta. Wayne is an only child and has always gotten what he wanted."

"What about his mom?"

Barbara shifted a bit in her chair. "Messy divorce about three years ago. Wayne's father has a weakness for younger women and married a thirty-something-year-old blonde bombshell about a year and a half ago. One of those weddings that all the gossip magazines write about." Barbara continued, "Bishop Horn, on the other hand, comes from a much more modest family. He adores Wayne and sticks to him like glue, as you said. They squeaked by in every class this year with low and high Cs, but they would graduate even if they had straight Fs, given Wayne's father and his pull."

"Why would they want to come to Rome, then?"

"Probably just bored," John replied. "After Wayne's dad made a very large contribution to the school last year, there wasn't any rebuttal from the school board when Wayne and Bishop decided to take this trip."

"They are also under the impression that alcohol and girls are easy to get in Rome," Cynthia said. "That idea probably came from Wayne's father."

"What about Mark? Is there anything else I should know about him?"

"Mark is an average-to-good student," said Barbara, "but we're worried about his drinking. His father works for the Coca-Cola Company, and his mom either sits around the house or goes shopping. They seem to get along, but when Mark's father is home, which is rare, they end up drinking themselves to sleep. This is what I've gathered from a few people who know Mark's parents well."

Barbara seemed uncannily well-informed, but I supposed that was part of being an effective teacher.

"I don't condone Mark's parents' behavior," Cynthia added, "but this doesn't change the fact that he can be a bad influence on others. He usually joins in on Wayne's and Bishop's shenanigans. Needless to say, your candor on the bus about Italy not having a drinking age isn't going to help."

I knew this would come up and that Cynthia would be the one mentioning it.

"I believe that as an introductory statement to the group, the information was inappropriate. I see that now, and I apologize. Even so, I think they would have discovered it, anyway, once they began going out on their own. Alcohol tempts American teenagers, especially because they're constantly told that they have to stay away from it until they're twenty-one. It's not the same with European teens. When you prohibit something at their age, you raise the bar on the temptation gauge."

"And when did you get the time to become such an expert on adolescent behavior?" Cynthia's sarcasm was less than subtle.

Barbara cut in before I could raise the sarcasm stakes with some comment about childless women. "Hey, let's move on," she said, hastily. "We don't have much time left."

"What about Raymond? He seems to have a lot of a self-assurance And I got the impression that he's an exceptionally bright young man. Also, if I remember correctly, he's the only student, along with Michelle, who's still seventeen."

John nodded. "Michelle turned seventeen in February, and Raymond in March. They both skipped their sophomore year. They're our brightest students. We do have some concerns about Raymond, though."

"I was surprised. "Why? What's wrong with him?"

"You may have picked up that Raymond is Jewish?"

"It crossed my mind when I saw his surname—Katzman is Jewish."

"Correct. And as you as you probably gathered from his comments on the bus, he's very interested in politics."

"Yes. And?" I wanted John to get to the point.

"Because of his politics, he's apparently decided he doesn't want to go to college in the States, even though he could get into any Ivy League school. Instead, he wants to go to Israel and work for a right-wing Zionist political party called The Jewish Home. He plans to go to the Hebrew University of Jerusalem, but says he wants to devote himself to 'the cause,' as he calls it."

"The *cause*?" I looked at the three faces around me.

"The Jewish Home is a very small political party that does not recognize a Palestinian state or the Palestinians for that matter. Raymond's teachers are worried because when he speaks to us about 'the Israeli cause,' he becomes another person—an extremist advocating the use of violence as a means to an end."

"I didn't see him wearing a kippah," I said, "which is odd considering what you're telling me."

"You'll see him with it on Saturday. Other than that, he isn't the least bit ostentatious in his dress or his habits. I don't think he even bothers if food is kosher or not. He's dead serious, however, when talking about the State of Israel."

"What about his parents?" One always has to go back to the source.

"I know them rather well," said Cynthia. "His father was a professional musician. Raymond's mother does a lot of fundraising for Hebrew-language training centers in the Atlanta area, as well as study-abroad programs in Israel for Jewish students from Georgia. She's done a lot for the Jewish community." This I learned from Cynthia.

"One important note," said. "Raymond's uncle was killed in suicide bomb attack on a Tel Aviv bus. They were very close. This was about two years ago, and his death obviously had a great impact on Raymond."

I was silent for a few moments, thinking about everything that I had just heard.

"Thank you for sharing all this with me. Raymond's issues will obviously affect his future choices. But I don't see how it's relevant for this trip. The other students do have issues that may cause some difficulties over the next few days. I don't see Raymond as a potential problem."

"We thought you should know about his views, Atticus, just so you didn't get blindside by him. Make no mistake, he *will* confront you on these matters, I guarantee it. Let me tell you, before I met Raymond, I couldn't pinpoint Jerusalem on a map. Now I probably know more about the Israeli government than I do about ours. Raymond loves to share his ideals, and he looks for support wherever he can find it. We've had so many discussions that I feel like I'm being brainwashed."

This was just great, I thought. Not only did I have to be cautious about a sexually confused Lolita, a potentially suicidal manic-depressive young man, a drinking trio, and two girls with tragic family traumas, but I was also going to have to confront a seventeen-year-old political zealot. This chaperone job was turning out to be more complicated than I had bargained for.

The teachers fell silent. I looked at my watch. It was almost 4:00 pm.

"Darlene asked a very good question on the bus that I never got around to answer. It was about the dos and don'ts here in Rome. I need to answer that question for her benefit and the benefit of the ones who have never been to Italy, which means all of you."

They all straightened up, giving me their undivided attention. Now I felt like the teacher.

"First of all, passports and important documents should stay in the hotel, preferably in the front desk's safe deposit box. Cynthia, here are the photocopies of the passports." I slid them across the table. "Second, the boys must never put their wallets in their back pockets. If the girls don't have a money belt, they need to keep their purses or bags in sight and their hands on the clasps or flaps or what have you. The pickpockets in this city are true artists. They should only walk with small amounts of cash, just what they might need for the day, and leave the rest in their suitcases and keep their suitcases locked. Gypsies are a scourge in the city, both adults and children. They'll come up to you in groups of three or four asking for a handout, and before you know it, they've robbed you blind. When you see them coming, just keep walking and keep your hands on your valuables. Third—and this should be obvious, but I want you to tell them anyway— the girls must *never* accept a ride from anybody or go a house or an apartment. I suppose that once they've been here a few days, the students will want to go out on their own in groups."

"Might be a few hours," John said wryly.

I smiled. "Last but not least, if they want to go out dancing or to a club, they should be escorted. Ecstasy, methamphetamines, and other pleasant powders are sometimes put into the drinks of foreigners to rob them. Or worse."

Barbara, Cynthia, and John were looking at me as if they had landed in Dante's Hell instead of Rome. I chuckled at their naiveté.

"Why are all of you looking so appalled? If an Italian that knew no English landed at Hartsfield airport for the first time, and you had to tell them what to watch out for in Atlanta, wouldn't the list be similar? Suppose the same Italian were to land in Chicago or Detroit for the first time. Rome is just like any other very large city. You just have to use a little common sense." I turned to Cynthia. "Can you pass on what I said to the students, preferably before we go out this afternoon?"

"I'll do that as soon as we're done here."

"We'll also need to set curfews if they're going to be out without adult supervision. By the way, do the students have euros?"

"Most of them changed one hundred dollars at the airport," Barbara responded.

"That won't get them very far at the current rate of exchange. At any rate—no pun intended—when they change their dollars, they must do it in a bank, never on the street. They will get a better exchange rate, but they'll also get counterfeit bills." I looked at my watch. "I think that'll do for now."

"Yes, we've gone over quite a bit," John agreed.

After confirming that we would meet in the lobby at 5:00 pm for our brief excursion, the four of us walked out of the restaurant and headed for the front desk to retrieve our room keys. As I passed by the lobby, I noticed that a section of what I had thought was a wood-paneled wall had been removed. There was now a small but well-equipped bar in its place. The bartender was busy wiping down glasses and preparing bowls of nuts and chips. This was a clever form of camouflage.

"That's going to be trouble," Cynthia remarked as she looked at the bottles on the shelves. After what I had heard over the past two hours, I felt I needed a double bourbon, preferably without my usual soda.

CHAPTER 10

Back in my room, I threw myself on the bed and began to digest the information I had just been fed.

What I had gathered from the teachers only reinforced what I believed ever since my daughter and son came into my life: children are like buildings, who rise floor by floor. As they develop through the years, they become taller physically and emotionally. But the maximum height of any building is determined by the depth and materials of its foundation. Reinforced rebar concrete is worthless unless the correct proportion of cement, fly ash, gravel, and water are mixed together properly.

By way of analogy, if the parents' proportion of love, caring, attention, discipline, and the ability to listen are flawed, the child mirrors these deficiencies much as a defective building will bend to one side, forming large fractures in its walls. But our parents were also once children, and had parents of their own, and so on and so on for generations. Where should we place the blame for a behavioral problem? In the child? In the parents? In the grandparents? The great-grandparents? There are times that I had wanted to strangle, lovingly, of course, my fourteen-year-old daughter and ten-year-old son. And Lord knows they have received their share of warnings and punishments when necessary. But in those cases where they truly misbehave, who's at fault? My children? Or did their mother and I not give them that correct proportion of materials that would allow another floor of their skyscraper to be solidly built?

Look at Darlene's mother, the child pageant queen torturer. Was she put through a similar kind of misery by her parents and brainwashed into believing that it truly mattered whether she participated or not in those perverse exhibitions of the very young and innocent?

Or take Wayne. His father had spared no expense for the building materials and furnishings of the skyscraper, but he had spent nothing on the foundation. This shiny glass and aluminum structure was going to hit the ground one day.

At this point, I shook my head. "These aren't my problems," I said to myself. "I just need to make sure that the group gets to the bus on time, have their tours, go to the restaurants, and come back to the hotel in one piece. The teachers need to handle the rest. It's not my ball game."

This was now settled. In any case, I had more pressing matters to think about.

I walked over to the desk and switched on the computer, clicking on the Internet Explorer icon. There were two new messages from job search engines that I had activated months ago, but nothing about possible new employment.

There were still two hours before I had to go downstairs. I took my time bouncing between executive search web pages and Wikipedia, using the latter to memorize some basic information about the Trevi Fountain, which we would most certainly run into later this afternoon. After almost an hour, I began to see double. I lay down on the bed, intending to shut my eyes for just a few minutes.

That was a mistake…

I was running as fast as possible through the dark, rain-swept streets of a large, unknown city. Men and women in ankle-length black leather coats followed me, brandishing guns. Wayne's father? I knew somehow that it was him, even though we had never met. He was aiming and firing an M16 at me. And there was Darlene's mother, pumping away on a 12-gauge shotgun. Evelyn's father was on horseback, holding a crucifix in one hand and a mini Uzi 9mm in the other, howling that my soul would burn in hell for eternity. There were others. I didn't know who they were or why they were all shooting at me.

A phone, I needed to get to that ringing phone! It heard it ringing loudly, but where was it? I turned left into a long, trash-strewn alley with that bloodthirsty gang right behind me. The phone booth was about one hundred feet ahead of me. I ran as fast as I could and then heard the roar of an engine. Headlights came on and pointed in the direction of the booth with that engine constantly revving up. The ringing of the phone was so clear it was as if it were sitting on my head. I had to get to it before that vehicle obliterated it. Tires screeched and the smell of burnt rubber entered my nostrils, but I was at the doors of the booth. I swung them open, grabbed the receiver, and watched as those headlights plowed right into me...

Where was I? This wasn't my bed. And where is that annoying ringing sound coming from?

And then it hit me. No, this wasn't a *Matrix* remake. I had fallen fast asleep. What time was it? I looked at my watch: 5:25 pm.

Damn! That ringing sound was coming from the bedside phone. I grabbed it.

"Yes"

"Atticus, we're all down here and ready to go. Do you need much more time?" It was Cynthia, and even though her tone was very polite, I could tell that I was being reprimanded.

"I'll be right down, sorry. I was on the Internet and lost track of time. Just two minutes."

Granted that I didn't particularly care, but how pitiful I must have seemed—late for the first outing on the very first day.

I hung up and rushed to the bathroom. I rinsed my face, gargled some Listerine, and combed my hair. The vanity mirror unkindly displayed my groggy expression. I slapped my cheeks trying to bring some color to the surface. I then ripped off my wrinkled shirt and put on the first one I grabbed from the drawer. Snatching up the room key, I locked the door behind me and scrambled down the stairs.

The entire group was waiting for me in the lobby.

"Here I am, apologies for the delay. I take it we're ready?"

"Yes, and we had time to go over those dos and don'ts that Darlene asked you about on the bus." It was good to see Cynthia giving Darlene some positive feedback.

"Okay then, let's go. As soon as we go out of the doors, we shall be turning right and head down the rest of Via Lucchesi, which shall lead us directly to the Trevi Fountain."

We all exited the hotel, with Ludovica wishing us a good walk. The students seemed to be in a good mood now that they had eaten, showered, and rested. The heat slapped us as we walked out of the air-conditioned hall. It must have been at least ninety degrees Fahrenheit. As we set off, I asked, "In Europe, we use the Celsius scale, not Fahrenheit. How hot does it feel to you in Fahrenheit?"

"This has got to be around eighty-eight to ninety degrees, I figure," said Jeremy.

"And how do we get from Fahrenheit to Celsius?"

Jeremy answered without a pause, "You take the Fahrenheit temperature, subtract thirty-two, and multiply by five-ninths, or point fifty-six, so it's about thirty-one degrees Celsius if ninety is the correct Fahrenheit temperature." Everyone looked at him trying to figure out where his laptop was.

He noticed the stares and blurted out, "What? What's up?"

"Where's your computer, Jeremy?" John said, raising his eyebrows.

"What computer? It's in my room. I just knew the answer."

I decided to put him to the test: "How do you change a Celsius temperature back into a Fahrenheit?"

"You take the Celsius temperature multiply by nine-fifths, or one point eight, and add thirty-two."

"Very good, that's right."

Jeremy had gained some points from his fellow students and a few looks of disbelief from his teachers, especially John. Good for him.

I looked at the other students. "How are the rooms? Did you manage to get some sleep?" I was expecting some unfavorable comments.

"Small."

"The mattress is hard."

"Raymond snores."

"There's no beer in the refrigerator." This was Mark.

"I'm going to miss the next episodes of *Candy Girls and Kendra*!" This was Darlene's main concern.

"What's that thing in the bathroom next to the toilet, Atticus?" Jeremy asked. I smiled. I had expected that query at some point.

"It's a bidet. You sit on it, turn on the water, and wash." I didn't think it necessary to add details. I could see that the girls were considering the benefits of this, especially during a few specific days each month. Most of the boys just looked disgusted.

We were passing the Via della Dataria, which led up to the Palazzo Quirinale, the president's residence, named after the hill it stood on, the Quirinal.

"The city of Rome was built on how many hills?" I asked. "Does anyone know?"

"Seven or ten, Mr. Winterle," Michelle answered right off the bat. "There were seven hills within the ancient walls, but there are ten hills in reality. The other three are located outside the walls."

I pulled down the corners of my mouth, impressed. "That's really excellent."

"Encyclopedias go a long way, Mr. Winterle."

"Atticus, please."

"Atticus, sorry." What shocked me even more than Michelle's correct answer, however, was that she referred to the encyclopedia and not Google or YouTube or even Wikipedia. *Amazing*, I thought.

"In fact, the Pincian Hill, the Janiculum Hill, and the more famous Vatican Hill were part of the original city, but they were located outside of the walls that circled ancient Rome." This bit of information went right over the group's heads.

We were passing souvenirs shops, small takeaway pizzerias, and a few of those dreadful food traps with a waiter at the door saying hello in five different languages and attempting to usher the unwary tourist inside. The students were beginning to straggle, looking at the various types of bric-a-brac and curios in the small shops.

"Go ahead," I said. "Take ten minutes to look around. Just watch your change and remember that today, one euro equals approximately a dollar thirty-seven cents."

Cynthia and John were already checking out the goods on display, but Barbara stood on the small sidewalk soaking in the history and the beauty of the place.

"We haven't even been out here fifteen minutes, and I think I am already in love with this city," she told me as I stood next to her "It's amazing how fast the Rome bug bites."

I nodded. "This city has cast spells on many eminent visitors: Goethe, Keats, Shelley, Charles Dickens, Thomas Jefferson, Theodore Roosevelt. And of course, Atticus Winterle."

Barbara laughed.

"Seriously, though, the list goes on and on. It doesn't matter how much you read about Rome or what you see on

TV documentaries. It's only when you walk the city's streets that you experience its magic. It's like those people who try to tell you what being a mother or father is like for the first time. You think you understand, but it's only when *your* baby is placed in *your* arms that you realize that you knew absolutely nothing and what they really meant when they told you your world would change forever."

Barbara smiled at me. I looked at her. She raised her hand as if she wanted to touch my cheek, but then abruptly turned and walked away. Had I seen tears welling up in her eyes? Was she so moved by what I had said?

"Atticus, could you come over here a moment please?" Mary called.

I went over to where she and Vanessa were standing near a souvenir booth. A young man was holding out a white, poly-resin version of the Trevi Fountain in one hand and a Trevi fountain refrigerator magnet in the other.

"Yes, how can I help?"

"I like these," Mary said, "but he wants eighteen euros for the fountain and eight euros for the magnate. Is it too much?"

I turned to the young man. "*Posso vederli un attimo?*" I asked him if I could see them more closely. Even though "Made in Italy" was scratched on the bottom of the small fountain, I was certain that it was actually made in China or Vietnam or in a sweatshop somewhere in the Naples area. At least the magnet, which was about four by three inches, looked hand-painted.

"I would go for the magnet, Mary. These are shops, not open-air market stalls, so I don't think you'll be able to bargain. Eight euros are a little over eleven dollars." By this time, some of the other students had come over to see what was happening.

"Okay, I'll take this one," Mary told the salesclerk.

"I want one, too," one of the other students piped in.

"Yeah, so do I," said Vanessa. "My mom collects this kind of stuff." I noticed that her eyes were still tired and bloodshot. I was about to say something. but then thought doing so might be unwise. There would be another opportunity.

A little farther down, James and Evelyn were standing hand in hand in front of a small shop that was selling slices of pizza. They seemed indecisive. I felt as if I needed to get these two more involved on their first outing. I went over to them. "Hey, James, Evelyn, are you hungry?"

"Um, well, kind of," James actually said something. Other than when he said his name on the bus, I hadn't heard his voice at all.

I pointed at the slices on display. "You've got to understand that pizza over here is a bit different than in the States. Italian pizzas come out in large trays from wood-burning ovens and have a variety of toppings. The first one you see there on the left is the basic mozzarella cheese and tomatoes. The next is ham, mushrooms, and mozzarella, and so on. You decide how big a slice you want, and they cut it into rectangles. Would you like to try some?"

They both ordered the basic mozzarella and tomato pizza, which was called *Margherita*. One slice was about the size of a car license plate, so they divided it between them. I paid for the slice, and they walked away without a saying a word. I figured all this interaction with a stranger was probably too much for them in one day.

We continued walking, and after we had gone about three hundred feet, we arrived at the Piazza Trevi where the Trevi Fountain took the stage front and center.

"Can I have everyone's attention for just a moment please?" I called out. "Stand here by me for a few minutes, and then you can go off and take your pictures. You may all know that the ancient Romans were famous, amongst other things, for their aqueducts. They found sources of fresh water far from Rome and managed to channel them into the city using tunnels, galleries, and bridges. One of these aqueducts, the Aqua Virgo, which means 'virgin water,' still supplies water to this site today. However, we have to jump all the way to the year 1732, when the construction on the fountain you see here began. It was completed thirty years later, in 1762. The entire project was undertaken by an Italian architect named Nicola Salvi." I was rather pleased with myself for remembering this much from my hasty online research.

I continued by explaining that Pope Urban VIII had initially commissioned Gian Lorenzo Bernini, a renowned Italian sculptor, to undertake the Trevi project. When the pope died, however, everything came to a screeching halt. Bernini had at least managed to move the original Roman fountain, which Urban VIII found inadequate, from across the square to where it now stood so that it could be admired from the Quirinal Palace, which was the summer residence of the popes until 1870."

Barbara, Cynthia, and John were still a captive audience, but all the students except Michelle and Raymond were looking around, already snapping photos and clearly impatient to be cut free.

"One last thing," I said. "Tradition says that if you throw a coin over your left shoulder and into the water, you will come back to Rome." This initiated a search for loose coins and a rush to the border of the fountain.

"My mom made me watch a movie where there was a scene with this fountain." This was Darlene.

I nodded. "There's a famous Italian movie called *La Dolce Vita* where two of the protagonists embrace in this fountain, but that was way before your time." If I remembered correctly, *La Dolce Vita* was released in 1960.

"Was there a blonde woman with large boobs?" Darlene said.

I almost choked. "Um, yes, Anita Ekberg."

"Anita Ekberg! My mom loved her. She made me look at that scene over and over again from when I was about five. She always told me she hoped I would turn out like her. Or like Elizabeth Taylor. I must have seen *Cleopatra* a thousand times." For a moment, Darlene had an inward expression on her face that I couldn't quite interpret. She had traveled back in time, reliving a part of her childhood, but then returned to the present abruptly. I was tempted to tell her that there wasn't much of a difference between her and Anita, or Elizabeth for that matter, but that would have been inappropriate.

Already, men of all ages had gathered around us staring at or trying to get a better look at Darlene. If eyes were mouths, she would have been eaten alive. I looked over to where Barbara was standing and surreptitiously gestured toward Darlene and a group of men who were standing rather too close. Barbara immediately understood. She came over and threw her arm around Darlene and dragged her to one of the fashion boutiques opposite the fountain.

So, I thought, Darlene's mother made her watch Anita Ekberg again and again with her DD-cup breasts shaking loosely in a black satin evening dress in the Trevi Fountain. That certainly must have been educational.

Noticing Wayne, Bishop, and Mark sitting on a granite bench, I went over to them.

"So what do you think?" I said motioning toward the fountain.

"Yeah, it's all right," Bishop answered. He paused. "Are there dance clubs around here?"

Wayne interjected, "Or strip bars or, even better, lap dance bars? Can you tell us where they are?"

Mark added his main concern. "Are highballs expensive here? Where can you buy liquor?"

"Do you go to lap dance bars in Atlanta? Don't you need to be twenty-one?" All three boys raised their eyebrows at me as though I had said something pretty stupid.

"I just turned eighteen, Atticus," Wayne said, "but I've had IDs that say I'm twenty-two for the last two years. So do Bishop and Mark. Sometimes, my dad takes us to a few strip bars outside of town. That's pretty cool." Although this kind of boast would usually be expressed in a cocky manner, the expression on Wayne's face was just as vacant as Darlene's had been. It was rather odd.

"Yeah, Wayne's dad is really a trip," Bishop said, but I couldn't tell if he was praising or criticizing.

"Did you know that lap dancing and drunken orgies were pretty common in ancient Rome?" I asked.

That got the attention of the trio. "The Romans had a rule that a lot of people still follow today—work hard, play hard. There was a twist, though. At festivals or large banquets, important discussions were held before the fun began. Politics, war strategies, philosophical debates, reciting poetry, arguing over the favored gladiator to win at the Colosseum —all these were core topics at these gatherings." Maybe I was stretching the truth here to some extent, but I felt that it was worth bending the facts if I could talk to these boys and show them a perspective on life that went beyond basketball, girls, beer, and lap dancing.

"Those gladiators sound pretty cool. What other sports were these Romans into?"

"The Romans were very fit, Wayne. They did a lot of wrestling, swimming, hunting, and chariot racing. They played a form of handball and enjoyed running. They had weight rooms as well, usually located at the public baths. You could compare them to Gold's Gym."

"Hey, we've got a few of those in Atlanta! One's on Peachtree Street," Bishop exclaimed.

"Well, you see, Romans developed quite a few things that we tend to take for granted today. If you don't mind me sounding like one of your teachers, I would suggest that you use these next few days to learn something about ancient Rome and the people who once lived here. You may not have this opportunity again." I paused. "Here's what, I'll make a deal with the three of you if you promise to keep it to yourselves."

Now I had them *really* intrigued. All three were watching me intently.

I said, "Surprise me—and I mean really surprise me—with some of your own research on Rome, and before you head back to Atlanta, I'll take you to a place that you'll never forget."

Wayne, Bishop, and Mark looked at each other.

"Better than a lap dance bar?"

"This place will make a lap dance bar look like Snow White's cottage."

"You're on!" said Wayne. The other two nodded enthusiastically.

I put up my hand, and they all high-fived me. The ice was well broken.

I turned and walked over to Cynthia and John, who had been watching us curiously.

"That's probably the longest those three have spoken to an adult who wasn't their coach or a bartender," John remarked. "You must have been telling them how to sneak cases of liquor into the hotel."

Cynthia said nothing, but her expression was cynical.

"They're part of the group, aren't they? I need to treat them as I would any other student."

I had made the boys a risky promise, but they had to deliver the goods to close the deal. I would decide how to handle it later on.

Mary and Sabrina came up to us.

"Atticus, can we go into that church?" asked Mary.

They pointed at a building that stood at the three-way intersection of the Via della Stamperia, the Via del Lavatore, and the Via dei Lucchesi. I had no idea what the name of the church was, but as I was trying to remember it, I saw a tour guide enter with a group of elderly tourists who were English or Australian from the accent I caught.

"Sure, but listen up, let me teach you a trick. You see that group going in? I think they're English-speaking. Try to stay as close as you can to the guide without being noticed. Guides are paid and don't like people listening in for free. Go, go! And be sure to fill me in afterward." They ran off, excited about the little scheme.

The Piazza Trevi is not a huge space, but there are always many people due to the fountain's international fame. I had managed to lose track of some members of the group. I saw Barbara coming out of a shoe shop with Darlene, Mary, and Vanessa. Evelyn and James were sitting on a stone bench to the left of the fountain, still eating their pizza. I walked to the right, passed the entrance to Via delle Muratte, and saw Raymond and Anthony. Raymond was sitting on the broken portion of a fluted stone column that was probably once part of a temple. His legs were crossed, and he was jotting something down in his notebook. Anthony was speaking to him, but it seemed more like a monologue than a conversation.

I went up to them. "What's up, guys? Enjoying what you see?"

Raymond smiled. "It's pretty cool. I saw a picture once of this fountain at night with the lights on. Can we come back tonight and take a look at it?"

"No problem. After dinner, we can go get some genuine Italian ice cream just down the road from here."

Anthony was still wearing his windbreaker and the same tie, although he had changed his shirt. "You know, Anthony, it's really a small world," I said.

"Why's that?" he asked.

"When I was living and working in Germany, I used to go often to Lausanne in Switzerland to follow the development of some new wristwatch designs. Sometimes I flew back to Paris from Bern. It's an enchanting city. When were you there?"

"Um, before I came to Bradford High, but I wasn't there very long." He got up abruptly. "Um, I've gotta ask Mrs. Ramsey something." He walked off. Raymond, who was busy writing in his notebook, didn't notice him leave. I found it odd how Anthony seemed suddenly uncomfortable when I mentioned Switzerland. Hadn't he mentioned on the bus that he had visited relatives there? I shrugged and switched my attention to Raymond.

"You seem to be deep in concentration."

"I'm just jotting down some notes to myself. I don't know if the teachers told you that I'm moving to Tel Aviv after graduation."

"No, I wasn't aware." Better to play dumb.

"I'm interested in politics, and I want to be more proactive. I've signed up to be a junior member of the Jewish Home Party. I want to support the cause any way I can. Are you interested in Israeli politics, Mr. Winterle?"

"Well, it's difficult not to be, or at least take notice of what Israel says or does. The Middle East is pretty volatile, after all."

"If the Palestinians and Hamas would just clear out of the Gaza Strip, the volatility would diminish!" Raymond's demeanor had changed just as abruptly as Anthony's leaving. In place of the smiling face of a seventeen-year-old was a sudden mask of hatred that sent a shiver down my spine.

"Do you agree with me, Mr. Winterle, *or don't you?*"

I felt like I was walking on eggshells. I didn't want to close the door with Raymond so soon, but I knew that if I had answered no, he would probably avoid me for the rest of the trip. On the other hand, I didn't want to agree with him, since I didn't believe that expulsion was the solution to the problem. As always, the truth was somewhere in the middle.

"Tell you what, Raymond, since you're a man of politics and have a such an in-depth knowledge of the State of Israel, let's discuss this issue further before the trip is done, maybe over a beer. How does that sound?"

Raymond was not expecting this answer. He seemed suddenly off-balance.

"Well, sure, that sounds good. I'd like that."

"Okay, then. Let's set some time aside one day this week."

I looked at my watch It was already six thirty. Dinner was in an hour. If I was going to show the students the magnificent view from the Quirinal Hill, I needed to herd them up quickly.

"Raymond, can you give me a hand rounding everyone up," I asked.

"Sure, no problem, Mr. Winterle."

He put away his notebook and scurried off, soon returning with the rest of the students. I counted the heads and came to thirteen plus three. I noticed that Evelyn was speaking with Sabrina and that James was saying a few words to Bishop. The super-glue Evelyn must have been loosening up a bit.

"Mr. Winterle!" It was Mary tugging at my shirtsleeve. "We did what you said and stayed close to that tour guide. I learned so much! I can't even remember everything. The name of the church is Saint Vincent and Anastasius. It's eerie, though! I'm not sure if I heard correctly, but I think the guide said that the lungs, heart, and other organs of twenty-five popes are preserved in there. Is that possible?" Mary didn't even let me attempt an answer but went on breathlessly: "It was the church that the popes used until the 1820s because the palace they stayed in is up there." She pointed in the direction we were about to go. "It was their summer residence. Cool, huh? I didn't know popes were rich! Oh, and we found out that Pope John Paul II gave this church to the Bulgarian Orthodox Church in 2002. How do you *give away* a church?"

I paused to make sure she was waiting for a response, then said, "I think it was more a symbolic gesture, since the church isn't moving anywhere soon. More than likely, Bulgarian Orthodox services are held there for the Bulgarians living in Rome." This was the best answer I could give her. Then I had an idea. "Mary, what I want you to do for me, and you can tell Sabrina later, is to carry out a little more research on this church. Try to find out why some of the pope's innards are stored there. Then we can tell the group as well."

Mary beamed. "Yeah, sure thing Mr. Winterle."

"Atticus."

"Okay. Atticus. We'll look into it."

"Good. Are we all here?" I counted the heads again, coming to thirteen plus three.

"Okay, everyone, listen up. I'd like you to experience a special view of the city from the Quirinal Hill before we head back to the hotel. Follow me, please."

We took one of the many side streets from the Trevi Fountain, reached the end of the Via della Dataria, which curved sharply to the right into the Salita di Montecavallo.

Jeremy came up next to me. "Mr. Winterle, by chance, do you know of any recent movies that were filmed in Rome?"

"Well, off the top of my head, I would say the *Da Vinci Code* and *Angels and Demons.*"

He shook his head. "No. Everyone assumes that, but the *Da Vinci Code* was filmed in France and the UK and in movie studios. The exterior shots of *Angels and Demons* were taken in Rome. but the Vatican didn't allow them to film in the

Vatican or its churches. All the sets were built at the Sony Pictures Studio in LA. But they were able to use the Caserta Palace near Naples for some of the Vatican scenes. I'd like to see that palace. They filmed parts of the first and second episodes of the *Star Wars* saga and *Mission: Impossible III* there as well."

"You're a walking movie encyclopedia," I said, laughing. "Do you know anything else about the Caserta Palace other than it being a good movie location?"

"No, not really."

"Okay. Then I'm giving you an assignment. By Thursday evening, which gives you four whole days, I want you tell me everything you can learn and remember about the palace. If I'm satisfied, I'll buy you a couple of beers."

Jeremy grinned. "You're on!"

"Good."

In one of my very first jobs where I had to manage a team of people, I had insisted that any further research on any aspect of a marketing or sales plan be the responsibility of the team. Other than collecting all the necessary information required to make sound decisions regarding the project at hand, I observed that the employees' interest in the task at hand was greater if they took ownership of their analysis.

We had reached the end of the Via della Dataria, which curved sharply to the right into the Salita di Montecavallo. Three long sets of stairs took us to the gigantic square in front of the Quirinal Palace. The palace had been the residence of thirty popes since 1583, the official residence of the kings of Italy since 1870, and then the post–World War II presidents of the Italian Republic.

Once in the square, I pointed westward to the stunning view of the cupola of St. Peter's Cathedral in the distance. As everyone was snapping photos with their phones, I turned my gaze on two huge statues, an obelisk, and a fountain in the shape of a bird bath, facing the entrance to the palace.

After a momentary mental struggle, I recalled that the two statues were the Greek mythological figures Castor and Pollux. One of them was the son of Zeus, and the other was the son of Tyndareus, a Spartan king. I didn't know anything about the obelisk nor the fountain, but I knew how to obtain the information now that I had gotten Mary to research the church and Jeremy the Caserta Palace.

"Evelyn, Vanessa!" They were standing together at the border of the piazza, still taking pictures of the breathtaking scenery. I motioned to them to come over.

"Everything okay, Atticus?" Vanessa asked. Evelyn, as usual, was silent.

"Yes. I need you to do something for me. You see the statues, the obelisk, and that huge fountain?"

"Kind of hard to miss them," said Vanessa.

"What I need is the two of you to do some research so that you can tell me and the group what they are and why they are here."

"No problem. I can Wiki it," said Vanessa.

Evelyn, however, paled white as a sheet. "No!" she said, shaking her head almost violently. "I'm not good with this, and I'm damn sure not presenting anything to anyone!" She turned and walked away, heading straight for James.

Vanessa turned to me with a rueful expression. "Don't worry, Atticus, she'll be all right. She's just a little strange sometimes. I'll work on her."

She trotted back to the parapet to take a few more pictures. She still looked very pale and unwell to me. I looked at my watch once again. It was already seven twenty-five. We were going to be late for dinner.

"Hey, everyone, we have to go!" I called out.

John, Cynthia, and Barbara immediately brought everyone together. We walked down the same series of steps and backtracked to the hotel. The first outing had gone better than I had hoped.

CHAPTER 11

The group was hungry, thirsty, and interested in the dinner menu. As we entered the hotel, I told everyone that that they had just five minutes to go to their rooms, freshen up, and come back downstairs. Ludovica was still at the front desk and had our keys waiting on the counter as we arrived.

"I heard you coming," she said as she handed me my key.

"You're absolutely incredible, Ludovica," I replied with a smile. "Thank you."

Once in my room, I put on a clean shirt and placed my Toscanello cigars in my shirt pocket. I was looking forward to a good smoke at an outdoor café while admiring the Trevi Fountain at night.

When I arrived downstairs, the three teachers were waiting for me at the restaurant doors. Barbara seemed slightly anxious. "The kids are all inside, Atticus," she said, "but we need to discuss something before we go in."

"Okay. What's the problem?" I asked.

"The wine. We would really like a glass of wine with dinner, but we need to say something to the students. Cynthia's opinion is that we are the adults, and we can do as we please. John agrees, but I think that we need to tell them something. What's your view?"

I nodded. "Listen, you probably won't like what I'm going to say. But I believe it's the best way to handle the matter if we don't want trouble up the road." The three of them stared at me. I continued: "In Italy, drinking wine at the dinner table is as normal as drinking iced tea in Georgia. Sixteen- and seventeen-year-olds drink a beer or some wine, and there's nothing odd about it. I say we put a bottle of wine on each table and explain that we want to see if they can be trusted.

Let them get into what it means to be an Italian. Learning about a country's culture isn't only learning about its history. It's also about understanding and appreciating the present. Now if our trust turns out to be misplaced, we'll crack the whip. That's what I suggest."

There was a pensive silence.

Cynthia spoke first, "This could lead to trouble, especially with a few elements in the group. You know who I mean."

"I realize it's a risk, but I think it's worth a shot. Barbara, John?"

John was nodding. "We're in Italy," he said. "We need to understand how things work over here."

"I think it's worth a try," said Barbara. "I agree with you." She shot a sideways glance at Cynthia. "And thanks, Atticus, for having some faith in these students."

The restaurant was full, mostly with hotel guests from various parts of the world. I heard some German and Japanese as I walked to our table. As soon as the overly efficient waiter saw the four of us, the breadbasket and drinks cart began wheeling in our direction. As he placed the wine and water bottles on our table, I told him to wait until I had said a few words to the students before he went to their tables.

"Listen up, please," I said, going to the middle of the four tables. "Your teachers are trustworthy people." All the students looked over at John, Barbara, and Cynthia. "I'm sure you remember our discussion on the bus this morning about drinking habits in Italy as compared to the States. Here, drinking wine or a beer with dinner is normal from the age of sixteen. Since this trip is not only about learning facts about the beautiful places you'll visit, your teachers agree that you should also take part in the customs of this great country. Therefore, as is the tradition in Italy, you'll have a bottle of white wine and red wine on your table that you can enjoy with your dinner."

The students started clapping, and some cheered.

I grinned and raised my hands. "All right, settle down, please. Just keep one thing in mind. You've been offered a pleasurable addition to your meals. Don't let me or your teachers catch any of you abusing this privilege, or we'll lay down some stiff rules that will make us very unpopular. Enjoy your dinner and the wine."

More applause.

"One last thing. Do yourselves a favor and at least try a little of all the things you see on these serving trays behind me. The food in this country is fabulous, and it would be shame to leave here having only eaten hamburgers and mashed potatoes. Thanks." I went back to our table and sat down.

"Well done, Atticus," John said while lifting his glass in a toasting gesture. I lifted my glass of red wine and clinked it against John's.

"*Prosit,*" I said, touching Barbara's and Cynthia's glass as well. I received a puzzled look from Cynthia.

"That's a Latin expression, which comes from the verb *prodesse,* which means 'to be advantageous.' So let's toast to the *advantageous* outcome of this trip."

We all took a big swallow of wine, and John, rather quickly, I thought, took up the bottle and refilled our glasses.

"Let's see what they've prepared for us tonight," I said. I led the way to the buffet. There were some dishes that had been present at lunch, but the majority of the trays had new delicacies that made my mouth water, such as fried calamari, stuffed sardines, breaded veal cutlets, chicken *alla cacciatora,* various grilled vegetables, *polpette,* the Italian rendition of meatballs, saffron rice, and stuffed tomatoes. In the bain-marie at the end of the table, the waiter stood ready to dish out a risotto with mushrooms, spaghetti with *vongole* (clams), beef stew with vegetables, and fried chicken. These last two trays were certainly intended for the ASA group and any other American guests. But I saw that some of the students had taken my advice and were venturing into unexplored culinary territory. A few of them, however, once they saw the beef stew, just couldn't resist. When we were seated once again, I noticed that Barbara was truly enjoying her chicken.

"This is just exquisite," she raved. "I need to ask them for the recipe," she said between mouthfuls.

"It's really quite simple, Barbara," I said. "You need six to eight pieces of chicken, a large white onion, some sweet bacon, some garlic, olive oil, a large glass or red wine, some mushrooms, and a can or two of peeled tomatoes. I also add two tablespoons of flour once the chicken has a nice gold color." I got some wide-eyed stares.

"I enjoy cooking," I explained. "It's one of my few hobbies. And the only place better than Italy, perhaps, for enjoying this hobby is France. I believe Julia Child would agree with me on this one."

"You're full of surprises, Atticus," said John. "I have trouble boiling eggs."

"Cynthia is quite a cook," Barbara said, with a smile. I had the feeling that the wine was beginning to loosen the tension between the two of them.

"Oh, no. I can put a few things together, but I'm no cook," Cynthia demurred.

"What are you saying, Cynthia? Your chicken and rice, fried corn, and buttermilk biscuits are unbeatable."

Hearing these dishes mentioned, my childhood memories of Tallahassee, Florida, came rushing back to me. I could see my grandmother at the stove carefully and lovingly turning that fried corn in the skillet while the chicken and rice simmered in an iron pot. My olfactory system was actually deciphering the smell of these recipes that I had not tasted in thirty-two years. What messages were those receptor neurons in my nose sending to my brain but, more importantly, how? This was all a mystery to me. Smell is, I believe, the most overwhelming of our five senses.

"If it's as good as they say, Cynthia, I'm inviting myself over to your place on my next trip to Atlanta," I said. "I especially adore fried corn. I've tried making it many times, but it never comes out like my grandmother's."

"Not a problem," Cynthia replied, smiling. "Just give a few days' notice so I that I can get my hands on some organically grown sweet corn."

We toasted again, and I noted that the red wine was already finished.

By this time, almost everyone's plate was empty, and nobody was getting up for seconds or thirds. We were all waiting for the dinner plates to be removed so that we could have dessert.

"Maybe one of you go around the tables and just check in and see how things are," I suggested. "Try to throw an eye on the levels of wine in the bottles to see if somebody has over imbibed."

"Good idea, Atticus. I'll go." John got up and walked over to the table next to us, placing his hands on Michelle's and Vanessa's shoulders.

"Atticus, you surprise me," Barbara exclaimed. "This is the first time you've chaperoned a group of students and their teachers, but it's like you've been doing this for years."

I remembered with a smile that Marco had told the ASA offices in Atlanta that I had done this as a living. Luckily, ASA hadn't said anything to the teachers, so I could honestly accept Barbara's compliment.

"Thank you, Barbara, but let's wait until we're at least halfway into the trip before making any judgments."

The waiter passed by our table, saw that the red wine bottle was empty, and exchanged it with a full one.

"We need to talk a little about tonight. I promised Raymond some gelato and a look at the Trevi Fountain all lit up. I'll take whoever wants to go with me. I don't think any of them should go out without an adult present."

"I don't think any of them are going to last too much longer," Cynthia said, her words slurring a little. "They'll want some sleep after the trip." In addition to the wine, the fatigue after our long day was catching up to her. John came back to the table and sat down.

"Well, I think you'll all be pleasantly surprised," he said. "Most of the bottles I saw were more than half full. And the biggest surprise of all, Wayne, Bishop, Jeremy and Mark didn't finish the red wine and left the white untouched."

"That's good news," Cynthia said, then added, "but the evening isn't over yet."

I was wondering if anybody had noticed that at *our* table, the bottles of red and white were empty and a second bottle of red was already half consumed.

"Well, so far, the situation looks promising," said John. He turned to me. "Atticus, any plans for this evening? I think I'm already getting over my jet lag." I brought John up to speed. Barbara made the announcement as the students were devouring their dessert.

"Can I have your attention please?" she said, speaking rather loudly. But most of the other hotel guests had vacated their tables, so Barbara's wine-induced volume didn't bother anybody.

"Atticus has kindly offered to take us out for ice cream. No wandering off on your own tonight, ladies and gentlemen, and we want you back in your rooms no later than, say, eleven pm." Barbara turned and looked at me. I gave her a thumbs-up. She then asked for a show of hands from those who were calling it a day. James, Anthony, and Jeremy put their hands up. Vanessa, Sabrina, and Mary also opted to stay in the hotel. Evelyn's hand remained down, but then James looked at her with a questioning expression, and she quickly raised it.

"I'm staying in the hotel," Cynthia said. "I'm tired, and I have to make sure you-know-who takes his medication."

"Okay, then, downstairs in ten minutes for those going out," Barbara called out.

"Hold on, sorry, my mistake. We didn't say anything about tomorrow." I got up and clapped my hands to get the students' attention.

"Listen up, please. We need to be at the bus at nine o'clock sharp tomorrow. We're going to see St. Peter's and the Vatican Museums. I would suggest you set your alarms for eight o'clock so that you have time for breakfast. We won't be back at the hotel until four or five, so bring what you need for the day. Good night to those who are hitting the hay."

We all walked out of the restaurant. I already had my cigars and wallet in my pocket, so I didn't need to go back to my room. But in the lobby, I realized that I didn't have my cigar lighter with me. I had left it behind because of the flight restrictions. Luckily, the front desk had a jay filled with matchbooks. The name of the hotel, address, and phone number were on the front flap, and there was a thumb-sized photo of the Trevi Fountain on the back. Tacky, but informative. This gave me an idea. I dug my hand back into the jar and pulled out a handful of those matchbooks. I then sat down on the couch and waited for the others.

Michelle, Raymond, and Mark were the first to arrive, then Darlene and Sabrina right behind them. Darlene had managed to change once again, but this time, she was wearing a soft yellow button-down shirt and a pair of black jeans. She sat down next to me, and I noticed that she had on a pair of four-inch-high-heel sandals.

"Darlene, those are beautiful shoes, but you saw what the pavement is like out there didn't you? I don't want you to break an ankle."

"Oh, that's so sweet of you to think about that, Atticus, but I'm a pro on heels. You should see my six-inch pumps. They make these look like house slippers."

Barbara and John entered the lobby, and I was momentarily stunned by Barbara's metamorphosis. She had put on a low-cut, spaghetti-strap tank top, which accentuated her nicely sized breasts, with an emerald-green cotton sweater draped across her shoulders and a pair of cream linen pants with open-toed sandals on her feet. She was already an attractive woman, but now she bordered on soft-porn sexy.

The two jocks were right behind John. Wayne had Bishop in a playful headlock, and Bishop was clearly enjoying the tussle.

"Okay, everyone. This afternoon, I promised Raymond some Italian ice cream. I know a little place just off to left of the fountain that's quite good. After that, I'm going to sit in the Piazza Trevi and enjoy a cigar. By the way, I want each of you to take one of these." I gave everyone a matchbook from the bowl. "Keep this with you just in case you get lost. The address and phone number of the hotel are on the front. I would be very grateful if this first evening, you didn't go wandering off on your own. Everyone set? Then let's go."

We set off, the students clearly eager for this nighttime adventure.

CHAPTER 12

We soon reached the Piazza Trevi, and although we had seen it earlier that day, the spectacle in front of us now was jaw-dropping. The piazza was the same, the boutiques, small cafés and newsstands were the same, the thundering noise of the water cascading down from the fountain was the same—but the fountain was *not* the same.

Everyone stopped in their tracks as though simultaneously entranced by a sorcerer's spell. The magic spouted right before their eyes. Inside the fountain's vast basin, the water was aglow, shifting from sparkling emerald to luminous blue to translucent turquoise. The brightly lit backdrop showed the god Oceanus, standing on his shell chariot, pulled by Tritons harnessing wild winged horses, seemingly ready to break free from the jagged rocks to which he was fastened. The stone of the monument glowed gold from the lighting and exuded a soft, cotton-textured color, which was in juxtaposition with the brilliant alternating illumination of the water, creating an unforgettable visual experience.

"It's stunning, Atticus, just stunning." Barbara was standing next to me, her body almost touching mine. The wine had her more than a little unsteady. She had put a few drops of perfume on her neck, and the Roman breeze wafted this delightful scent to my nostrils. She turned and looked at me, bringing our faces even closer. She didn't move back, however.

I remembered what Filippo had told me in the bar about beautiful women, a bottle of wine, and romantic Rome. How absurd his words had been, I had thought at the time. Now he seemed wiser by the second.

With execrable timing, John came up to us. "I'm looking forward to a good ice cream cone. I think everyone would like one, so lead the way, Atticus."

John seemed slightly tense, and I began to wonder if Barbara's proximity to me had him annoyed. As the rest of the group began to gather around us, I led everyone to the left of the fountain, following its elaborate border. Many people were out—couples hand in hand, tourists, and a few men in business suits, probably on their way home after a busy day at the office. That had been me not so long ago.

We veered left into the Via dei Crociferi. At the end of this rather narrow street, before the Via dei Sabini, there was a small, unpretentious ice cream parlor that had some of the best homemade ice cream I had ever tasted. I saw a gathering of people up ahead in front of a bright light. The *gelateria*, as ice cream parlors are called in Italy, was still there and seemed to be doing a brisk business. Everyone gathered behind the small crowd in front of the glass display case.

"Let me tell you what you'll see once we get to the counter," I said to the group "There will be a series of buckets with an array of flavors. The Italian favorites are *amarena* or black cherry, *fior di latte* or cream, cappuccino, pistachio, wild berries, strawberry, passion fruit, lemon, coconut, chocolate, melon—"

"Hey, Atticus, no sweat," Mark interjected. "We've got these kinds of places in Atlanta. Morelli's and Bruster's. They're all over the place."

"Thanks for the update, Mark. I have no doubt that Atlanta is filled with ice cream parlors, but get a taste of *this* ice cream and then tell me if it's the same as Morelli's and Bruster's and those other places in Atlanta."

We had reached the counter and the students, fascinated by the colors and textures before their eyes, weren't listening to me anymore. Cones ranged in price from €1.50 to €2.50 to €3.50. Almost everyone went for two to three scoops, walking away with large blobs of ice cream on precariously thin cones. When I got up to the counter, I ordered a €2.50 cone with one scoop of wild cherry and a whipped cream topping. It was as good as I remembered. Given the *oohs* and *mmms* behind me, the others seemed to be enjoying their selections.

"So, Mark, what do you think?" I inquired.

"It's good stuff," he answered, trying to keep the ice cream from falling off its wafer support.

"Not only is it good, ladies and gentlemen, but look around you and appreciate the surroundings in which you are enjoying your ice cream. It's not every day that you can say you had a gelato while roaming around the Trevi Fountain." I wanted these kids to soak in the atmosphere down to their bones.

I began looking for a nice outdoor café where I could smoke my long-awaited cigar. I turned and saw Darlene still working on her ice cream. I was amazed at how she was strutting with those heels on the small and sometimes slippery cobblestones.

"I'm impressed, Darlene," I said. "I thought by now you'd be barefoot and carrying those heels in your hand."

"It's all a matter of what you're used to, Mr. Winterle, I mean Atticus." She released one of those alluring smiles. "But, you know, it's also sexy to walk barefoot, don't you think?" She winked at me, and my innards began to churn.

We were passing by a small café with people sitting at small tables outside. Only one table was unoccupied. I quickly chewed up the rest of my ice cream cone.

"Ladies and gentlemen, I'm stopping here," I announced. "If you would like to join me, feel free. If you want to take a walk around, please stay in groups. Remember that curfew is set at eleven o'clock."

"We're going to check out what's going on farther up," said Wayne, walking away with Bishop, Mark, and Michelle. I was sure that Cynthia would have a cow had she known these boys were going off on their own. Michelle, however, was with them. I decided to take a calculated risk that she would keep them in line.

John and Raymond said they would take a quick walk behind the fountain and then join me. That left Barbara and Darlene, who did not seem to have any intention of going off on their own.

"Can we join you, Atticus?" Barbara asked.

"It would be my pleasure."

A waiter came out and saw the three of us. After pushing his eyes back into their sockets from seeing Darlene's chest, he vanished inside for a few moments, then came back out with two folding chairs. The table was very small, and the space available under the awning was microscopic. When we sat down, my knees were pressed against Barbara's linen-enclosed thighs while Darlene's legs were thrust under my chair. I needed a drink, quickly.

The waiter came back out, placed a very large scented candle on our very tiny table, and asked us what we would like.

"Barbara, what would you like?"

"I would love a Black Russian, a bit heavy on the Kahlúa, please."

"Darlene, do you have a preference?"

"Can I get a Cuba Libre? I have them all time in Atlanta."

I looked at Barbara. What was the teachers' mandate on hard liquor on this trip? Darlene was eighteen, and she was sitting with two adults at an Italian bar. Were it up to me, she could order whatever she wanted.

"Okay, Darlene, but just one," Barbara said.

The waiter managed to peel his eyes off Darlene and looked at me. "I would like a Remy Martin in a warm brandy snifter, if possible." As if reading my mind, he placed an ashtray on the table before heading back inside to get our drinks.

"Do you smoke, Barbara?" I asked.

"I quit about five years ago. However, there are still moments, like this one, where I would gladly take a puff."

"Oh no, Mrs. Cornwall, what are you saying?" Darlene almost wailed. "Cigarettes are *sooo* gross. They make your hair smell bad and are horrible for your complexion. It's really good that you quit. Mr. Winterle, you should stop smoking, too—"

I cut her off by raising my hand.

"Darlene, I smoke one of these maybe once a week or twice a month. And I don't intend to stop."

She sat back in her chair and pouted.

"I just hope that the smoke from my cigar doesn't bother you." Luckily, there was a slight breeze that was blowing directly toward me, which would keep the smoke out of their faces.

"What exactly is that, Atticus?" Barbara was looking at the awkwardly shaped clump of tobacco leaves I had taken out of the box.

"It's a Toscanello, which translated literally means 'small Tuscan cigar.' The tobacco for this cigar comes from the Tuscany region of Italy, hence the name. It was originally considered a cigar for the less well-off, but it became popular among rich landowners shortly after it was first made in 1818. It has a strong, peat moss aroma. It's not a connoisseur's cigar, but I enjoy it more than its Cuban counterpart."

The waiter brought the drinks as we were speaking, and I was surprised at the large glasses. We toasted to the end of our first day. Barbara downed half of her black Russian in one gulp as I lighted my cigar from a packet of matches supplied by the waiter.

I caught sight of John and Raymond out of the corner of my eye. They came up to the café but had to stand in front of our table due to the lack of space.

"We went up a wide street behind the fountain, but decided to turn back," Raymond said. "It just kept going and going."

"Probably the Via del Tritone. Beautiful street, but yes, it's a long one."

John was listening to me but gazing intently at Barbara. In fact, he was almost glowering. Barbara sitting virtually on top of me seemed to be annoying him.

"Raymond, did you enjoy the ice cream?" I blurted out, trying to distract from John's staring.

"It was better than any ice cream in Atlanta, even better than Tel Aviv. I'm going back to the hotel now. I'm really tired."

"We'll be coming up shortly as soon as I finish off this cigar."

"Any sign of Wayne and the others?" John interjected rather aggressively.

"No, but it's ten thirty, so they still have a little time. When we get back to the hotel, if they're not in yet, I'll go and look for them."

"Let me know, and I'll come out with you. Good night." John gave Barbara one more reproachful glance, then turned and went off with Raymond toward the hotel.

Barbara looked at me and shook her head slightly. I took that to mean she would explain John's attitude to me later, but it was hard to tell since her head was beginning to sway from one side to the next. Darlene was oblivious to the situation. She was enjoying her drink and eyeing the men who were passing by and stopping to get a second look.

"Shalimar, right?" I queried. The name of this French perfume had suddenly come back to me.

Barbara looked surprised.

"Now, how did you guess that, Atticus? Have you been in my beauty case?"

"It's one of my favorite perfumes. Not many women can wear it with the right effect."

She smiled. I wondered what I was doing. I had just met this woman, and I was already getting myself into trouble, maybe deep trouble.

"And am *I* a Shalimar woman?" Barbara asked as she leaned toward me, showing her impressive cleavage.

"Yes, you most certainly are, Barbara."

Darlene was now looking at the two of us, puzzled. I came back down to earth in a hurry, looked her way, and blurted out a piece of advice.

"Do me a favor, Darlene. Tomorrow, wear a comfortable pair of shoes. The Vatican is a huge place, and you'll be doing a lot of walking."

Barbara sat back in her chair and finished the rest of her Black Russian.

The waiter brought me the bill. Barbara and Darlene insisted on paying for the drinks and attempted to snatch it from my hand. I threatened both with a bath in the fountain, fully clothed, if they persisted. I found out quickly that my warning had backfired.

"I'm ready!" was Darlene's response.

"You can throw me in that fountain anytime!" was Barbara's.

They were both past the giddy stage, laughing and having a hard time getting up out of their folding chairs. Barbara was clumsier than Darlene. I paid the waiter and gave him a nice tip. I was planning to come back.

My cigar was only half consumed, but it was time to put it out and concentrate on getting these two women to their respective rooms, and fast.

Darlene wasn't quite steady on her feet anymore. She took off her heels, lifted them over her head, and began to giggle. This sparked the attention of a number of Italian men in our vicinity. No time to think about that, as I just managed to catch

Barbara after she tripped over one of the table's legs. This caused her to swing back toward me. We ended up embracing involuntarily with her lips a few inches from mine.

"Oh, Atticus, after only one drink? How naughty you are."

"Barbara, we need to get Darlene to the hotel." I was dead serious. She took hold of herself in a split second.

"I'm sorry, I'm…I think I've had too much to drink. The wine, it was the wine." That bottomless Kahlúa and vodka mixture didn't help either, I thought to myself.

"No worries, Barbara. We just need to get *you-know-who* back to the hotel."

Darlene was chatting with four young guys. This girl had such seductive power over men, like a one-ton magnet on a bag of nails. Barbara immediately walked over to her and pulled her back to where I was standing. I took Darlene's shoes in my right hand.

We walked toward our hotel. I admired how Barbara had sobered up in such a hurry and had taken control of the situation. I was still thinking about that embrace.

"I'm fine, really. My head is just, it's just spinning a bit, but I'm…okay," Darlene blurted out. "I like it when you put your arm around me, Atticus." She turned her head, and again had a pair of lips zooming in on me. If I had been a different kind of person, I probably would have had a great deal of fun taking advantage of this situation with Barbara and/or Darlene that night. I grinned, imagining Filippo.

"Okay, Darlene, here we are. Let's get those shoes on before we enter." I thought that she felt miffed that I hadn't at least attempted a kiss.

"I'm fine now," she said. "I can get to my room on my own."

"What's your room number, Darlene?" Barbara was quizzing her.

"Room 16. Good night." She gave me a hurt look and walked through the glass doors.

Barbara didn't go in right away.

"I'm sorry, Atticus, for the way I acted. I don't know what came over me. I…I just feel so comfortable in your company. I don't make a fool out of myself like this with men I meet for the first time, at least not lately." What did *that* mean?

"No apologies required, Barbara," I said. "We're tired, and we had a little too much to drink. If I may say so, however, you are an attractive and fun person to spend time with. Your husband is a very fortunate man."

"My husband?" She bellowed out a laugh that came right from the gut. "Oh, my dear Atticus, you're a chaperone, a cook, and a comedian as well! We'll have to have another drink together, and soon. I'd like to tell you a thing or two about my so-called husband." With that, she got up, chuckling to herself, and went through the sliding glass doors. I watched as she retrieved her room key and headed for the stairs.

I sat on the outside steps for a moment, attempting to wrap my head around Barbara's strange reaction when I brought up her husband. I had a feeling there was some dirty laundry hidden in her closet.

As I was about to get up and enter the hotel, I heard hurried footsteps. At first, I thought it was some of Darlene's admirers who were charging the hotel. That would have been easier to handle, as it turned out.

"Mr. Winterle, thank God you're here! We need your help!" Michelle was sweating, her voice full of apprehension. Behind her were Wayne and Bishop, holding up a swaying Mark between them.

"Okay, calm down, what happened?" I tried to act cool and collected, but it wasn't working.

"We were all having a few beers at a bar down the road. Mark said he was going to look at one of the souvenir shops, and he left."

"But he didn't come back," Wayne cut in.

"We left the bar and started looking for him, but he wasn't in any of those tourist shops," Bishop said. "We finally found him in another bar farther down the road with about ten empty shot glasses in front of him!"

"We had to give the bartender eighty dollars before he would let us leave," Michelle said, as she wiped the sweat off her brow. "Luckily, Mark had five twenties in his pocket."

I had already figured out something of the sort as soon as I saw Mark's condition. He was pale, with vomit all over his mouth, face, and clothes, but at least he was conscious. My mind was going faster than a Cray XMT supercomputer. I was thankful that the other two boys seemed perfectly sober. That was a huge help.

"Listen," I said, "we've got to work like a team, or Mark is up to his neck in shit and so am I."

My voice had dropped a couple octaves. I wanted the three of them to understand that we had a colossal problem on our hands. I would handle the situation at the bar on my terms, but that would be attended to later.

"We're going to go in. Get your room keys, and the two of you are going to bring Mark up to my room, Room 38, okay?" Everyone nodded.

"Michelle, I need you to go back to your room and act as if nothing happened. Not a word to Evelyn or anybody else. If you run into Mr. Seeward, act as naturally as possible. Wayne, Bishop, keep your mouths shut about this. This could easily get Mark sent back to Atlanta on the next flight out."

I took a used tissue out of my pocket, which was better than nothing, and tried to clean Mark's face as best I could.

Mark started talking. "Hey! Atticus...Atticus, that's a screwy name...I've told you, did you know my dad, yeah, he told, me that I...can drink, did you *know that*—"

"Yes, Mark, you told me. Now let's get you to bed."

We walked up the three steps. The sliding glass doors opened, and I walked ahead toward the desk to get my room key. The boys tried to place Mark's feet on the ground so that he looked as if he were standing. The night clerk, whom I had not seen before, looked at me, the boys, at Michelle, and then looked down at his computer. He asked, "Is there anything you need, Mr. Winterle? Some hot tea, coffee, a few extra towels, aspirin?"

I was a bit startled that he knew my name, but it wasn't the time for questions. His voice, which was deep and calm, reminded me of Mr. Spock from *Star Trek*. But his hair was white, his face creased with age—he looked like the ideal grandfather, both authoritative and kind.

"A pot of hot tea, some aspirin, and a large bottle of water would be helpful."

"Room 38, correct? I take it that the young man will be in your room for some time?" he asked, as though confirming the solution to an equation.

"*Lo tengo con me finché non si riprende.*" Mark was going to stay with me until he felt better.

"I'll have everything brought right up."

"May I use the phone, please?" I had to call John to tell him that everyone was back in the hotel. Spock handed me the receiver, and I dialed John's room number.

"Yes, hello?" John was very much awake, unfortunately.

"John, it's Atticus. I just wanted to let you know that everyone is accounted for."

"Did everyone make it back sober?"

"Everyone is just fine."

"Barbara back as well? Need me to come down for a room check?"

"No! I mean, that won't be necessary. Everyone is in their rooms, including Barbara. Good night, John. We have a long day tomorrow."

"Good night, Atticus."

I breathed a quick sigh of relief. "Let's go,"

Michelle told me that if I needed anything, I could call anytime. Wayne and Bishop dragged Mark between them to the elevator. I scampered up the stairs to my room. I heard the elevator doors open as I was unlocking my room door.

I cleared the bed of papers, books, and everything else that I had thrown on it. Wayne and Bishop stumbled in with Mark and gently placed him on the bed. Mark was chuckling, then laughing, and then he began to cry. This was a good sign. He was just hammered. When I first saw his condition, I thought that I was going to have to take him to the hospital, which would have spelt the end of Mark's Rome experience and my very brief position as a chaperone.

"Okay, then, everything's clear, right? This never happened. Go get some sleep, it's late. Thanks for getting him back here." The two boys left.

I shut the door behind them and began to consider what I should do next. Should I tell Barbara? John? Cynthia? No, definitely not Cynthia. She would have loved the opportunity to make an example out of Mark. John, too, had a similar view of Mark. Besides, I had just called him to say that everything was fine. No, the two of them needed to be kept out of the picture. That left Barbara, who was probably fast asleep by now. I needed to handle this on my own.

Mark was sharing his room with Raymond. It was almost midnight. But I had to call and tell him that Mark was with me. Raymond seemed trustworthy. I searched for the room arrangements and found the number: 12. Okay. The phone rang five times before he answered, his voice sleepy.

"Raymond, it's Atticus, sorry about waking you. Can you hear me?"

"Yes, yes, what time is it? Is something wrong?"

"Listen to me. Mark is with me in my room."

"*In your room?*"

"Yes. He had a little too much to drink, and I'm going to keep an eye on him."

176

"A little too much or way too much?"

"Let's say he overdid it. I'm going to bring him back to the room at about six thirty this morning so nothing will look suspicious. You realize that if the teachers get wind of this, Mark's trip is over?"

"Mrs. Ramsey would love it."

"You've hit the nail right on the head. Now get some sleep. I'll get a second key from the front desk to get into your room."

"If you need anything, call me."

"Thanks, Raymond. I'll handle it. Not a word to anyone. Good night."

Now I needed to think about Mark. He had rolled over to one side and was mumbling in his drunken stupor. As I began to take Mark's shoes off, I heard a light knock on the door. Who was it? Then I remembered Spock. I looked through the peephole and saw him standing outside. I opened the door, and he wheeled in a cart with hot tea, a stack of towels, a laundry bag, a bucket, a box of aspirin, and two boxes of Kleenex. He had thought of everything.

"Please give me a call downstairs if you require anything else."

"May I ask your name?"

"Giovanni."

"You are extremely efficient, Giovanni. Thank you."

"I've worked in this hotel for fifteen years and with student groups for eleven, Mr. Winterle. This is far from unusual. And remember, *Plures crapula quam gladius*. Good night."

Giovanni left as silently as he had arrived. His Latin proverb, which says that drunkenness kills more than the sword, didn't do much to ease my mind.

I got Mark's shoes and socks off, then pulled off his trousers, which were stained with regurgitated tequila—at least, that's what it smelled like, along with beef stew and urine. Luckily, he was wearing an extra-large T-shirt that was easy to get off.

I put his clothes, including socks, in the laundry bag. Now I needed to get some warm tea down his throat. This was obviously going to make him regurgitate, and I understood why Giovanni had included a bucket on the cart. He wasn't kidding when he said that he had seen situations like this before.

I took a few newspapers out of my carry-on and spread them out on the floor between the bed and the entrance to the bathroom. I had enough to cover most of the wall-to-wall carpet. I then went back over to Mark, placed two pillows behind his head, and pulled him up in a semi-sitting position.

"Whaaa, what's going, going…. on? Where am I? Mr. Winderr…lee?"

"Keep cool, Mark. Everything's going to be fine. Just drink some tea for me now."

"No, no, I'm…I'm going to throw up…I don't want to drink any, drink anymore…"

"Open your mouth, Mark, and take small sips."

After an initial sip, Mark relaxed and drank the tea down quickly. It didn't matter—it was all going to come up, anyway. Within moments, he was leaning over with me trying to aim the bucket at the jet stream coming out of his mouth. The smell was so overwhelming that I had to open the large window on the opposite side of the room. This allowed for a rapid exchange of fresh air. I wasn't fast enough, however, to get back to the bucket, and Mark's next spew landed all over the newspaper.

I put my mind at ease, fully aware that this was going to be the routine for at least the next few hours and that this was how my first day with the ASA group from Atlanta was going to end.

Wednesday
April 28, Day Two

CHAPTER 13

I came downstairs the next morning at minutes to seven o'clock. Ludovica was behind the front desk.

"I hope you didn't have too much trouble last night, Signor Winterle."

I wasn't surprised that she knew what had happened.

"Well, everything is under control now. Giovanni was a big help. Please thank him again for me when you see him."

"I most certainly will."

I went to the restaurant. Other than a couple of elderly Japanese tourists, I was the only person there, but there was already a vast selection of fruit and chocolate-filled pastries laid out. There were also various juices, yoghurts, and cereals to choose from. They had scrambled eggs, sausages, bacon strips, and an Italian version of hash browns, The students would certainly find something that they would like. Except, perhaps, Mark.

I grabbed a plate and walked over to the bain-marie containers. I took a few sausages, but when I looked at the scrambled eggs, I was reminded of what Mark had spewed on the newspapers, so I passed on that. As I sat at my table and started eating, I went over the events of the last few hours to see if all my tracks had been covered.

Mark had continued vomiting until about four. I kept filling him with slightly sugared tea to clean out his stomach. The bucket was in full use until about three, after which Mark was able to get to the bathroom on his own two feet. We had spoken a bit, but I didn't bring up his foolish behavior nor did he. At four thirty, he fell asleep. I set the alarm for six fifteen, which gave him time to rest but still let me get him back to his room before anybody else was up and about. I lay next to Mark and tried to get some sleep myself. But it took about half an hour before I finally managed to doze off.

When the alarm did go off, it sounded like a symphony of jackhammers. Mark didn't stir, however, and I let him doze for a little while longer.

Rummaging through the drawers, I found a T-shirt of mine that he could wear. I didn't have any trousers that would fit him, so I retrieved a large bath towel from the bathroom. Surprisingly, when I nudged him, he woke up almost instantly, and other than the Atlanta Braves' batting practice session that was taking place in his head, he seemed almost functional. He had no memory of what had happened, nor did he understand why he was in my room. I explained everything to him in the fewest words possible, speaking softly, so as to not aggravate his monstrous headache. Most importantly, I assured him that other than Wayne, Bishop, Michelle, and Raymond, nobody knew anything—and it had to stay that way. Mark nodded awkwardly.

As he struggled to put on my T-shirt, I went down to the front desk to ask for the master key. Luckily, Giovanni was still behind the counter.

"I need it back immediately, Mr. Winterle," he said. "That key is only for the staff."

"I'll be back in five minutes. Thanks, Giovanni. And where do I put the laundry bag? As you can probably imagine, it's full."

"Just set it outside the door. The clothes shall be returned to you tomorrow evening."

I ran back up to my room to find Mark standing but swaying precariously. We slowly went down the hallway, and then took the stairs. I did not want to chance meeting anyone in the elevator. Mark's arm was around my waist when we arrived on his floor. I checked to see that the corridor was clear, and we proceeded to his room.

I gently slid the key into the keyhole and turned the doorknob. Raymond was sleeping soundly and didn't stir. Mark went in, gave me a thumbs-up, and mouthed, "Thank you." I shut the door and hoped for the best.

I immediately took the pass key back down to Giovanni, then went back to my room. I placed the laundry bag outside the door, rolled up, and threw away the scattered pages of newspaper that were on the carpet, then showered and dressed. And here I was, sipping my espresso as if nothing had happened. I actually felt rather perky, considering I only got one hour of sleep.

Only one thing was bothering me, almost more than Mark's stupidity. Weren't the real bad boys supposed to be Wayne and Bishop? Hadn't I practically been told to expect them to get drunk, put their hands up women's skirts, and cause general havoc? I should have expected them to be in the same state as Mark last night, if not worse. I was missing something here.

A few daily Italian newspapers were on the table, and I quickly glanced at the headlines. Iran and the fraudulent elections were still taking top spot. Italian Prime Minister Silvio Berlusconi, was being attacked, again, by the leftist parties about his private life. Benjamin Netanyahu stated that he could foresee a Palestinian state, but with a set of uncompromising restrictions. I thought about Raymond and what he would say about this. Wounds were so deep on both sides of the Israeli-Palestinian issue that I didn't see a plausible solution in the foreseeable future. I was looking forward to picking Raymond's brain, once the conversation was confined to a constructive exchange of opinions.

I was lost in thought when I looked up and saw James and Jeremy.

"Well, good morning!" I exclaimed. "Two early birds, I see." James was plugged into an MP3 player, and Jeremy was carrying his laptop.

"Yeah, we couldn't sleep," Jeremy said. "It's not even one in Atlanta. I never go to bed before one or two. Can we sit here?"

"Please." I was a little surprised. I thought that they would have preferred their own table. "Go get some food," I suggested. "I think you'll find a few things to your liking."

They both came back a few minutes later. Jeremy had done the Denny's breakfast combo: eggs, bacon, sausages, and hash browns. The only thing missing was a side order of pancakes. James, however, had opted for the Weight Watchers diet: yoghurt, fruit, and a croissant. No wonder he was so thin. He also didn't seem terribly alert. I wondered if the medication he was taking was actually doing him more harm than good. Jeremy put down his plate, went over to the drinks table, and came back with two glasses of orange juice. It just amazed me how naturally he was holding one of the glasses with his prosthetic hand. Just as nonchalantly as his real one.

"What are you listening to, James?" He had the volume so loud that he didn't hear me. Jeremy nudged him, and James looked up.

"Yeah…what?"

"I said, 'What are you listening to?'"

"Nothing you would know," he replied.

"Try me," I rebutted.

"*RATM.*" He spelled out the letters in a slightly supercilious tone.

"Which album?" I asked. "*The Battle of Los Angeles? Renegades? Evil Empire?* Or *Live and Rare?*" Jeremy looked up from his computer, looked at James, and then looked at me.

"Fuckin'-A! I mean, sorry, but that's awesome, Mr. Winterle!"

"So which is it, James?" It was my turn to be a little patronizing.

"*The Battle of Los Angeles,*" James said, with a delightfully stunned look on his face.

"Good choice. You can't beat 'Calm Like a Bomb' or 'Maria' or 'Born of a Broken Man,' for that matter."

James didn't put his earplugs back in.

"How do *you* know about Rage Against the Machine?"

"Where is it written that someone in their fifties can't enjoy alternative metal or funk rock?"

"Who else are you into?" James's curiosity switch had gone from off to on.

"Let's see, Marilyn Manson, Nine Inch Nails, Korn, Slayer, Cypress Hill, Rob Zombie, and on a more commercial level, Lynyrd Skynyrd, AC/DC, and Slipknot."

As I went down the list, Jeremy's lower jaw was progressively inching its way down toward the tabletop.

"And then there are a few bands that are way before your time: Black Sabbath, Led Zeppelin, Yes, Deep Purple, Def Leppard, The Reds, the Psychedelic Furs, Rammstein—the list goes on. Oh, by the way, I'm in love with Avril Lavigne."

Attempting to regain some advantage, James blurted out, "The only one I don't know on that list are The Reds. And you didn't even mention one of my favorites, The Dead Kennedys." James was putting me to the test.

"Never cared for them. That 1950s rock 'n' roll sound mixed in with some pseudo-punk guitar thrashing doesn't do anything for me. Maybe *Holiday in Cambodia* and *California Über Alles* can make the cut, but that's about all."

James just stared at me as if he had overdosed on his medication.

"Jeremy, you should be able to find some songs from The Reds in that PC of yours," I said.

"I've already got The Reds website up. I'll see if I can download something on James's iPod."

"Good. Download 'Victims,' 'Joey,' and 'Whatcha' Doin' to Me'. Now, James, don't let your food just sit there. Nothing worse than cold scrambled eggs." I drank some of my juice, rather pleased with myself.

"Good morning, Atticus." Vanessa had walked in with Sabrina.

"Well, well, we've got some more early birds. Did you have a good sleep?"

"Yeah, but we've been up since five. I never get out of bed before seven at home, but this morning, I woke up and just couldn't fall back asleep." Vanessa looked somewhat better and had some color in her cheeks.

"You're on the same wavelength as Jeremy and James here, Vanessa. What all of you are experiencing is jet lag. Your biological clock in Atlanta is fighting with the actual time here in Rome. It'll wear off in a few days. Go get some food, then come and sit with us. Grab a chair for Sabrina from another table. We can seat five here."

I knew that Sabrina intensely disliked Evelyn, and consequently, she probably felt less than amicable toward James. She hesitated, in fact, but when she saw that Vanessa had sat down with us, she took a chair from the next table and placed it between Jeremy and me. I got up and went to get some grapefruit juice.

Although I didn't take long to return to the table, James had already informed the others about my impressive knowledge of songs and bands.

"You really listen to Marilyn Manson? He's such a weirdo," said Sabrina.

I sipped my juice. "He may be weird, but he produces some exceptional music. *The Golden Age of Grotesque* is a masterpiece. 'mOBSCENE,' 'Spade,' and 'Better of Two Evils' are incredibly forceful compositions."

Jeremy was beyond surprised. "Really fuckin' awesome, Mr. Winterle, you're blowing' my mind!"

"Watch the language, Jeremy," Vanessa said.

"Yeah, yeah, okay, sorry for the language, but Atticus is really shock and awe!"

"'mOBSCENE' was Derek's favorite song," James said.

There was a sudden chill at the table. I could have sworn that the temperature in the room had fallen twenty degrees.

"What did you say?" Sabrina said very slowly.

"It was his favorite song," James repeated, either ignoring or oblivious to the daggers in Sabrina's eyes. I quickly put two and two together—John had mentioned Sabrina's dead brother at lunch the day before.

"What the hell do you know about my brother?" Tears were welling up in Sabrina's eyes. Everyone was frozen.

"We were both Manson fans. He was one of the few people I knew who really got into that kind of music." James was speaking at his plate, quietly.

"My brother didn't listen to that kind of crap, and he certainly wouldn't have listened to anything with a loser like you!"

Before I could say anything, Sabrina got up and headed for the exit. Vanessa went after her. Jeremy and I looked at James, who just kept staring at the plate in front of him. He slowly put his earphones back in and turned up the volume.

As they were leaving, Cynthia came into the restaurant, accompanied by Anthony. She must not have noticed anything strange in Sabrina's demeanor because she looked over at me with a refreshed morning smile. This was for the best. I didn't want to start explaining a situation to her that wasn't even clear to me.

It was close to 8:00 am. Raymond arrived, with Evelyn and Michelle close behind. I stared at him, hoping to get his attention. Raymond turned and gave me a small nod. I took that to mean that Mark was still alive.

"Good morning, Mr. Winterle. Did you *sleep* well?" Michelle's stress on the word *sleep* told me what she was really asking. She sat down next to me.

"Fine, Michelle, just fine. Better than expected." I leaned over slightly and whispered, "I'll feel better when I see Mark, Wayne, and Bishop in here, though."

"Good morning." It was Barbara, with John at her side.

"Good morning," I answered. "How are you?"

"Refreshed. I slept like a rock."

"And you, John?"

"Just fine, thanks." He looked around the room.

"Who's missing? Wayne and Bishop, which figures, Mark naturally. Darlene, Mary? No, there they are."

Darlene had just walked in behind Mary. She looked as if she had just gotten off a yacht. She had on blue linen trousers, a light-blue-and-white button-down blouse with a scarf around her neck bearing her initials and a pair of Gucci sunglasses propped on her head. I looked at her feet. She had taken my advice and was wearing a pair of faded denim and white Converse All-Stars. She went over to sit with Cynthia and Anthony.

"Hi, Atticus!" Darlene said. "Look at the shoes."

"Perfect! You'll be comfortable with those. Go get some breakfast. We don't have that much time left."

She had probably forgotten all about the night before. She was radiant and as friendly with me as she had been before my rejection of her drunken advances.

I heard new voices behind me and turned. Wayne, Bishop, and Mark entered the restaurant, laughing at some joke they were sharing.

"Good morning, Atticus. Hey, Michelle, Jeremy." Wayne seemed to be in a great mood.

"Good morning to the three of you. Get any sleep?" I was looking directly at Mark.

"Yeah, great," said Wayne cheerfully. "Mark's got a head-ache, jerk can't handle a beer…" Wayne was quite the actor.

"Shut up, fool. I'm fine." Mark looked at me and gave me a forced smile. He was very pale, and there were dark circles under his eyes, but he was walking and talking. That was good enough for me.

"How about you, Bishop?" I asked.

Wayne cut in again. "Bishop always sleeps well. Problem is that he snores like an ox." Wayne put his arm around Bishop's neck. Bishop just beamed an embarrassing smile.

"Go eat something. You've got five minutes," I said.

They sauntered off and sat together at the fourth table. The door to the restaurant reopened, and Sabrina and Vanessa came back in. They walked directly to the buffet tables without looking at anyone. Good enough for now.

The waiter passed by, and I asked him for another espresso. Michelle, who was sitting next to me, was eating a bowl full of Muesli cereal. James was lost in his world of music. Jeremy was still working on his full breakfast plate. He looked up at me. "I'm ready to be grilled on the Caserta Palace, Atticus."

"Already? I only gave you that assignment yesterday afternoon."

"I've been up since four thirty am. I looked at my watch which was still on Atlanta time, and it was ten thirty pm. I couldn't sleep after that."

"I'll throw you some questions regarding the palace later, and I may need you to present your findings to the group." Before he could respond, I glanced at the time and saw that it was 8:30 am. We had to move. Riccardo had made it quite clear that we had to be on the bus at 9:00 am sharp. I rose to my feet and knocked a spoon against the water glass.

"Listen up, please! I hope all of you slept well, even though I bet that most of you were up very early." Everyone nodded. "As you may know, it's called jet lag. The official time for you right now is Rome time, and it's eight thirty-five in the morning. Your body clock, however, is telling you that it's two thirty-five, which is the time in Atlanta. Today is going to be difficult, considering the six-hour difference.

However, as your body gets accustomed to Rome time, you'll feel less drowsy during the day." Even as I was speaking, I was wondering how I was going to make it through the day with one hour's sleep.

"Okay, you've got ten minutes—and I mean ten—to get what you need and meet in the lobby. The bus is waiting for us. Let's move, please."

I walked over to Cynthia, who had joined John and Barbara. "How was your evening, Cynthia?"

"Quiet, Atticus, quiet. I read a bit, gave James his medication, and fell asleep early. Our troublemakers seem to be good spirits. Mark looks like a train hit him, and I wouldn't be surprised if he overdid it last night right behind our backs."

What you don't know won't hurt you, Cynthia, I thought.

"We can't look over their shoulders the entire day now, can we? Everyone was in by curfew, and that's a good beginning. In five minutes, we meet in the lobby." I left, not wanting to bicker with Cynthia.

I arrived in the hall with everything that I needed for the day. As Marco had suggested, I only took the two vouchers for the tour guides and the restaurant voucher for that day, leaving the rest in my room. Michelle, Mark, Wayne, and Bishop were already sitting on the couch in the lobby. As soon as Mark saw me, he got up and hesitantly came in my direction. "Mr. Winterle, I just wanted…I just wanted to say thanks, I mean, for what you did."

I looked at him seriously.

"I'll accept your thanks after you've explained to me what you wanted to prove with that stunt. You were an inch away from going to the hospital to get your stomach pumped and two inches away from heading back to Atlanta this morning. Furthermore, you could have placed Wayne, Bishop, Michelle, and me in a very embarrassing predicament."

I was being deliberately hard on him. Mark had to realize that he had really gone overboard. He looked hurt. I was about to say something to lighten up the situation when my phone rang. It was Marco. I backed away from Mark and answered.

"Ciao, Atticus! How are things?"

"Ciao. Remind me to wring your neck next time we see each other."

"Why, what's wrong?"

"In a few words, Marco, this isn't your everyday normal bunch of students." I was speaking in Italian but kept my voice low. "You know those Spanish soap operas that are so famous with Italian housewives? Take a few of those, sprinkle in some *Dallas* and *Dynasty* and top everything off with a few of those revolting reality shows, and that's what I've got on my hands. It's only the beginning of Day Two, and I feel like I've been with these people for a month."

There was a pause at the other end of the line.

"Makes everything more exciting, doesn't it?" Marco said. I thought I heard him trying to suppress a laugh.

"*Exciting?*"

"Well, sure. Never a dull moment, right? I'm sure you're handling everything as if you were back in your old job, running the show and managing the situation, that is. How's Mark Hampton doing?" I looked at the phone incredulously and placed it back to my ear.

"What do you mean?"

"Did he get over his drinking binge?"

"What? How did you—"

"Atticus, Atticus," said Marco. "Giovanni and Ludovica keep me informed about everything that's going on, just in case you need an extra hand."

"You're incredible, Marco. I'll tell you the truth. You couldn't have two better informers. Ludovica is as efficient as a Swiss bank, and Giovanni is clairvoyant. He knows what you need before you even ask!"

"I like working with the best. You need to go now. Riccardo is waiting for you. Remember, the name of your tour guide at the St. Peter's is Rosanna. She'll have an ASA card with her at the bus stop, so you can find her easily."

"Got it, thanks. By the way, is anything else going to happen tonight that I should be aware of?"

"No, but it's already comforting to know that something will probably happen, isn't it? I know you'll be able to handle anything these kids throw at you. That's why I picked you. Ciao, *bello*."

Marco hung up.

Somebody tapped me on the shoulder. It was Barbara. "Are you all right?" she asked, speaking almost in a whisper. "Why didn't you call me last night?"

I was confused. Had she expected me to invite her to my room last night? Talk about moving fast. She noticed my puzzlement.

"I came up to your room last night after we left each other at the entrance of the hotel," she said. "I wanted to explain why I laughed at you like that. But when I entered the hallway, I saw…" She lowered her voice even further. "I saw the boys carrying Mark to your room. I remembered that Michelle was with them, so I found her and asked her what was going on. She trusts me and told me everything out in the hall. I went back to my room, hoping you would call me. I've been up all night."

"We're all here and ready to go!" Cynthia said. She and John had come up behind us. Barbara and I both jumped a bit. They both looked at us curiously. But I was quick to respond.

"Yes, um, yes, we can go. I was telling Barbara confidentially that we need to keep our eyes open with Darlene. Last night, she attracted too much attention. She's never to go out alone. We can talk about this later."

I walked over to the glass doors and cleared my throat. "Okay, everybody! Keys on the front desk. Let's roll."

"Have a good morning, Mr. Winterle," Ludovica said.

"Wish me a good evening as well. I suspect I'll need it."

Ludovica smiled as I walked out of the hotel with the group behind me.

CHAPTER 14

We went to the left and headed down the Via Lucchesi. We passed the Pontifical Biblical Institute on our left and Piazza Pilotta on our right. Motor scooters were zipping back and forth, and the streets were full of pedestrians. The students seemed to have gotten the hang of walking on the narrow streets and stayed in single file. We passed under the same archway we had the previous day and then, to our left, found Riccardo leaning on his Mercedes bus exactly where he had dropped us off before.

"Ciao, Riccardo! *Come va?*" I greeted Riccardo and asked him how he was.

"*Sto benissimo grazie. Una serata memorabile.*" He was well and told me that his evening was memorable. I wanted to tell him that mine was as well, but more than likely for diametrically opposed reasons. The students boarded the bus saying "ciao" as they passed Riccardo.

"We're on time, right?"

"Absolutely, Signor Atticus. You are perfectly on time, but you know that everything now depends on the traffic."

In fact, the traffic in Rome was known for being more chaotic and congested than just about anywhere else in the world. For example, a one-lane road meant something totally different to an Italian living in Rome as compared to an American driver in the United States. Usually, a "one-lane road" means one car at a time, each behind the other. In Rome, however, it means at least two cars side by side, along with several motor scooters and motorcycles. Not a square foot of space goes unobserved in a Roman traffic jam, and any sort of vehicle is bound to maneuver its way into it one inch at a time. Of course, this kind of undisciplined driving generates a constant cacophony of horn honking that can drive you crazy if you're not accustomed to it.

Everybody had quickly boarded the bus by now, and I had the impression that the students had positioned themselves in the same seats they occupied in their drive from the airport into town. Barbara, Cynthia, and John were in the front seats, Riccardo was at the command center, and I was standing on the front steps with the microphone in hand.

"Good day, everyone!" The sound level was just right this time. "As I said last night, we have a full day today, and I hope that your eyes and ears will be wide open. While I speak to you now, please keep your eyes peeled and look around you. We shall be cutting through the center of Rome, passing some very important architectural points of interest with historical significance. I can assure you that if we had to acquire an in-depth knowledge of the buildings, monuments, and piazzas — you remember what piazza means?— and ruins between where we are now and St. Peter's Square, it would take us a couple of months to go three miles."

The bus moved off down the Via 4 Novembre, which became Via Cesare Battisti.

"Okay, we're coming up on the Piazza Venezia. I want you to look at the building on your right, which is called the Palazzo Venezia, as well as that very large white marble monument in front of us."

Riccardo must have picked up on what I was saying, given that he could have gone straight down Via del Plebiscito, which would have shortened the ride to the Vatican. Instead, he turned the bus to the left and stopped in proximity to the two structures which I had mentioned to the group.

"Riccardo has kindly paused for a moment. I can only give you bullet-point information so if you want more, you'll need to get on your PCs when you get back to the hotel. This building here next to us was built around 1460 by a cardinal—I forgot his name—who then became a pope, and it served as a papal residence. Much of the material that was used to build this building came from the Colosseum, believe it or not. Unfortunately, builders back then tended to use the stone and iron reinforcement bars from Roman monuments to build palaces and other buildings in the fifteenth and sixteenth centuries. You see that balcony up there directly above the entrance? That's where Benito Mussolini, Italy's Prime Minister in 1922 and the founder of Italian Fascism, addressed the crowds before and during World War II. Enough said. Look in front of you now." Riccardo budged the bus forward about one hundred yards.

"John, you were asking me about this on the way in from the airport. It's the Vittorio Emanuele II monument, and it marks the unification of Italy under the reign of, you guessed it, King Vittorio Emanuele II. It was built at the beginning of the twentieth century and is considered an eyesore for most Italians, given its pompousness and mix of architectural styles. The Tomb of the Unknown Soldier is located halfway up the monument."

"It looks like my mom's wedding cake," Mary remarked.

I laughed. "That's perfect! That's actually one of the nicknames it has acquired over the years—the Roman wedding cake. We'll be back to see it on one of our tours, I'm sure."

The bus was now passing the church San Pietro della Valle. I only knew that Act I of Giacomo Puccini's opera *Tosca* takes place inside it. Not of interest, I assumed, to anyone on the bus except me.

It was now nine twenty, and the traffic, as expected, was becoming heavier. We were about to cross the Tiber River and enter the Via della Conciliazione. This was the grand avenue that blossomed into one of the most important squares on earth, ecclesiastically as well as artistically—St. Peter's Square.

"Ladies and gentlemen, we are crossing the Tiber River, which cuts through the city of Rome and was crucial through the centuries as a means of transportation and commerce. If you look to your left, you can see the Castel Sant'Angelo. We'll discuss this grand fortress on the day we go there for a tour." (I was guessing here.) "Now I need you to focus on the Vatican."

Most of the students were now up on their feet, looking straight ahead through the large front window of the bus at the majestic dome of St. Peter's towering in front of them. The buildings that lined this pathway to the city of the popes were practically all seminaries, religious universities, and biblical study centers. As we slowly approached the Piazza San Pietro, I saw a large horde of tour buses up ahead already parked or looking for a parking space. Riccardo was already eyeing where he could stop. I was looking for Rosanna, our tour guide, who would be displaying ASA identification. Riccardo smoothly veered to the right and inserted the bus between two others with masterful ease.

A bustling stream of human bodies flowed down the sidewalk, all going toward St. Peter's Square. At a certain point, there was a break in the crowd, and I caught sight of Rosanna. She was standing next to the entrance of a small coffee bar, a large ASA card held across her chest.

"All right, ladies, and gentlemen, we've arrived. Our tour guide's name is Rosanna, and she's right outside the bus. We're in her hands until approximately a quarter to two. I kindly ask you to pay attention and retain as much information as you can. I think you'll enjoy what you see and hear."

"Hey, Atticus, are you going to be with us for the entire time?"

"That's the plan."

"Cool." It was Wayne. Needless to say, I was pleasantly surprised.

198

Riccardo told to me that he would be back at four o'clock to pick us up. The doors of the bus hissed open, and everyone filed out.

"Signora Rosanna?"

"Yes?"

"Hello. My name is Atticus Winterle, and this is the ASA group. I believe you were expecting us."

"Buongiorno. I am Rosanna Marangoni.It's a pleasure to meet you."

"Likewise. We have six girls and seven boys in this group, with three teachers—Mrs. Cornwall, Mr. Seeward, and Ms. Ramsey."

Rosanna was in her mid-fifties, rather short and on the heavy side. After greetings were exchanged, she assumed her tour guide role.

"Good morning to all of you, and welcome to the Eternal City, Rome. We shall actually be leaving Rome very shortly and be entering the smallest country in the world, Vatican City."

This brought forth confused looks on the students' faces.

"We shall continue down this road, called the Via della Conciliazione, on foot until we arrive in Saint Peter's Square. I will be holding up this small flag when we are walking so that you shall know where I am at any given moment. Not necessary now, but important when we find ourselves amidst the crowds. If we are all ready, I kindly ask all of you to follow me."

Rosanna had a strong Italian accent, but her English was flawless. I saw that the little flag she was referring to was the Tibetan Flag and ventured to guess that she was a supporter of the exiled Tibetan government and therefore opposed to China, which claimed authority over the land of Tibet. The students lined up behind Rosanna and started walking. Strangely enough, Evelyn and Michelle were directly behind me while James was farther up talking to Jeremy and Anthony."

"Did you sleep well, Evelyn?" I inquired.

"All right, I guess. Michelle was really jumpy. She kept getting out of bed and moving around. I think she even left the room at about midnight, but maybe I was just dreaming."

I thought of Barbara, who had gone to speak with Michelle about Mark.

Evelyn continued, "You know, Mr. Winterle, you really blew James's mind this morning. He said you know your stuff in music."

"Well, we do have some of the same tastes."

"He told me that the only other person that possibly knew more than you was Derek. But he's dead now."

"Yes, I was told that he died last year. A tragedy." I was too curious to let this conversation stop here. "Were Derek and James friends?"

"They were tight and enjoyed the same bands, but they kept it to themselves. Derek was 'Mr. Popular.' Best at everything. My James isn't popular. Everyone treats him like crap. He only has me."

She stopped abruptly, biting her lip. This was the most Evelyn had spoken in my presence since we had met, and it was in stark contrast with what Sabrina had shouted at James this morning at breakfast. We still had some ways to go before getting to the Piazza San Pietro, so I ventured one more question:

"Why then, Evelyn, does Sabrina seem to dislike James so much?"

Evelyn turned and looked at me. "Because she's a fuckin' bitch, that's why!" With that, she walked faster and made her way to James's side. The soap opera was thickening with even more drama.

We had come to the last Italian piazza before Vatican City territory, Piazza Pio XII, named after the 216th pope, whose papacy covered World War II. Here, Rosanna stopped in her tracks and asked everyone to come around her.

"Are we all here? Good. When we cross this road, we shall be in another country, the Vatican City State, the headquarters of the Catholic Church, its most important Christian temple, and the end point of pilgrimages for centuries. Maybe you are not aware of the Lateran Treaty, which was signed in 1929 between Benito Mussolini on behalf of the king of Italy and the Vatican secretary of state on behalf of Pope Pius XI, which officially recognized the Vatican as an independent, neutral country or city-state."

Barbara was looking at her students as though waiting for one of them to display their knowledge about this topic.

"What does *Lateran* mean?" asked Mary.

"Good question. The treaty took the name *Lateran* because it was signed in the Lateran Palace, one of the many properties of the Roman Lateranus family. It became the residence of the popes during the fourth century. Maybe you'll see it before you go back home." Rosanna paused a moment before resuming.

"Needless to say, the Vatican is one of the best-known tourist attractions in Italy and the rest of the world. It is home to one of the largest art collections on the planet, and the buildings in which they are located are architectural marvels in and of themselves, spanning the last five hundred years. Do you know that before the first century BC, this entire area was a mosquito-ridden swamp? The Roman emperor Caligula, who reigned from AD 37 to 41, cleaned things up and built a circus here before being murdered. This was not the circus we know today, even though the origins begin here, but a place for chariot racing, gladiator battles, mock warfare between armed men, the slaughtering of Christians, and other bloody attractions. Under the reign of the emperor Nero, Saint Peter was crucified head down in this circus. After the Edict of Milan, signed by the first

Christian Emperor Constantine in AD 313, which forbade the religious persecution of Christians, Constantine initiated the construction of the first Basilica of St. Peter's on the site where he was martyred. The old Basilica lasted up until the fifteenth century but was torn down by Pope Julius II. This led to the construction of the largest church in the world, which you see in front of you."

I was listening to what Rosanna was saying but found myself wandering within my own thoughts.

I accepted this job because Marco had insisted so much. I had no desire to do it, and I remembered how, just the morning before, I almost hadn't answered Marco's phone call. But in just twenty-four hours, something had changed. Willingly or not, I was beginning to get involved in the lives of these students and their teachers. They had begun opening up to me, and I found that I was enjoying getting to know them. More importantly, I was quickly coming to the conclusion that these young people needed someone to listen to what they had to say. In a way, this chaperoning experience was turning out to be similar to some of my past managerial roles in large companies. There was a team of people, schedules and rules to adhere to, and an objective to reach: a fifteen-page research paper to complete at the end of the trip. But as with all teams of human beings in a large or small organization, there are differences of opinion, likes, and dislikes amongst colleagues, covert and overt prejudice regarding the race, the physical appearance, and the religious affiliation of those you must work with. And of course, there was that hard, addictive desire to push out in front of the team and exclaim "I did it. I know it. It was *my* idea!" instead of "*We* did it. *We* came up with the solution." How much difficulty I always had explaining to my employees that we were all working for one objective, that we were all on the same side. The enemy was the competition on the outside of our office building, not on the inside. Why waste precious time competing amongst ourselves?

I would always present my employees, new and old, a copy of Abraham Lincoln's "House Divided" address, which he gave in Springfield, Illinois, before becoming the sixteenth president of the United States. I had Lincoln's source for this illuminating speech framed on my office wall:

"And knowing their thoughts he said unto them, 'Every kingdom divided against itself is brought to desolation; and every city or house divided against itself shall not stand.'" (Matthew 12:25)

Such a powerful truth, encapsulated in just a few words. How many wars, destruction of lives, and downfall of countries were the result of "houses divided against themselves"? On a lesser scale, how many companies, communities, and families had also fallen due to this division?

I gradually tuned in back to what Rosanna was saying. She was describing the pope's exile to Avignon in the south of France in 1309, during the papacy of Clement V. She was a virtual fountain of information: names, dates, cities, even using a few Latin phrases here and there. But I could see that she was losing the attention of some of the students. They had already begun to whisper amongst themselves, take pictures, and distance themselves from Rosanna. I needed to come up with something, or within a half an hour, Rosanna would be talking to herself.

"Rosanna, excuse me just a moment, please," I said. "Other than deciding to stay in Avignon, I believe Pope Clement V was famous for having persecuted and suppressed the Knights Templar. Anybody here ever played Assassin's Creed?"

"Sure thing," Jeremy responded.

"Good gaming," Mark commented. "The third installment is called 'Brotherhood.' It's going to be released in November."

Raymond joined in, "It's better on Xbox 360 than PS3."

"You don't know what the hell you're talking about, Raymond." This was James. "It's the same thing on Xbox or PS3."

"Better graphics on Xbox," Raymond shot back.

"Okay, okay." I nipped this budding debate in the bud. "What I wanted to point out is that the game picks up on the subject of the Knights Templar and the Crusades. Listen up, please. Evelyn, Vanessa, you know we need some information regarding the Quirinal Hill, remember? The obelisk and that large bird fountain? Mary, you're looking into that church at the Trevi Fountain, and Jeremy, you've Palace. Now I need somebody to give me some feedback on the Knights Templar. Mark? Can I count on you for this?"

"I'll handle it, Mr. Winterle. Just give me a few days, please." Mark was still pale with dark semicircles under his eyes.

"Take all the time you need, Mark." I gave him an approving nod. "Excuse me once again, Rosanna. Please, continue."

I got a smile and a wink. She had picked up immediately that the information she was offering needed to be lightened up a bit if she didn't want to lose her audience.

Rosanna raised her Tibetan flag, and we crossed the Via Paolo VI named after Pope number 262, whose papacy lasted from 1963 to 1978. The group moved straight ahead toward the obelisk that stood in the center of the ellipse.

"Ladies and gentlemen, you are now standing between the arms of the Mother Church, as Gian Lorenzo Bernini, the architect who created this masterpiece, described it. What you see here around you was built between 1506 and 1626. You can see on both sides of the famous colonnade, which is composed of a series of four columns, two hundred and eighty-four in all, that surround this ellipse we are standing on. On top of the colonnade, there are one hundred and forty statues of saints sculpted by various artists between the years 1662 and 1703. In front of us, you see that these 'arms' straighten out to form a trapezoid. This gives more impact to the majestic façade of St. Peter's. Originally, there was only one fountain in this area, the one that you see over there, but when Bernini finished his work, he added the one you see to the left of this obelisk to balance the effect of the ellipse. Now about this obelisk which we are standing under: it is actually Egyptian and dates back to the thirteenth century before Christ. It arrived in Rome in AD 37 but was in the circus that I mentioned before, the one that Caligula had built. In 1586, it was moved to where it stands now. It is the only obelisk in Rome that remains standing from the beginning of the Roman Empire. It was said that a bronze ball on the top of the obelisk held Julius Caesar's ashes, but this has never been proven. That bronze ball now sits in a museum."

Very good, Rosanna, I thought. This was the kind of information that the students enjoyed, as shown by how silent everyone had suddenly become. I was hoping that she would continue to sprinkle the necessary pedantic information with small highlights that the students could relate to.

"We could go on and on, but there is still so much to see, and it is already ten thirty. Let's go inside St. Peter's. This way, please."

We began walking toward the façade of St. Peter's, which gives the impression of being adjacent as one exits the ellipse and enters the trapezoidal space that Rosanna had spoken about. The imposing staircase into the main entrance of the basilica by way of a vaulted atrium seems almost a stone's throw away. However, the three sets of steps leading up to the atrium are, in fact, quite distant, which I believe is the optical illusion that Bernini was striving to attain.

We reached the bottom of the stairs that led to the entrance, and our guide stopped us for a moment. "From here, you can't even see the dome of the Basilica, which is four hundred and thirty-five feet high. Pope Paul V, who held the papacy from 1605 to 1621, commissioned the architect Carlo Maderno to design this façade. The window that you see above us, right under the triangular pediment, is where the name of the new pope is pronounced by the College of Cardinals. By the way, do you see the two clocks on the far sides of the façade? They were added in the nineteenth century. Personally, I think they are an ugly addition." This got a few chuckles.

Rosanna led us up the stairs to the grandiosely decorated portico, under the watchful eye of police officers. I was expecting to see metal detectors, but there was only an occasional check of bags, purses, and money belts. I found that this level of security was dangerously insufficient and, at best, foolishly naïve. But that was the Atticus of the past brewing inside the Atticus of the present.

I had read various Italian and English guidebooks about St. Peter's over the years and found that most were all in agreement that because of the balanced proportions of the interior of the basilica, one did not feel dwarfed by its sheer enormity.

Hogwash.

I could tell in an instant that at least sixteen people with me agreed with my assessment. As we entered, everyone just stopped in their tracks for a moment looking up.

"Wow, baby!"

"This is bigger than the Georgia Dome!"

"Where does this thing end?!"

"Awesome!"

These were just some of the comments that I overheard from the students. Barbara was standing still and shaking her head. John seemed to be in a trance while Cynthia just seemed dumbfounded. Rosanna let everyone take it all in for a few minutes.

As she was waiting, I approached her and suggested that after she had said a few words about the popes, the architects and the sculptors who contributed to the building of this basilica, she should immediately take the group over to the first small chapel to the right where Michelangelo's *Pietà* was located. Time was flying, and I told her that I wanted the students to have at thirty minutes to walk around on their own before we left for the Vatican Museums. One could spend weeks in St. Peter's and still not be fully informed about its history, its construction, all the structural variations made through the centuries, let alone the religious and political context in which this basilica became one of the most important symbols of Christendom. And we didn't even have an hour.

Rosanna lifted her flag in the air and made her away up the center of the nave. Everyone was gathered around her. She began by explaining that St. Peter's was the largest Christian church in the world, able to hold up to sixty thousand people.

"Just like I said, it's as big as the Georgia Dome," Bishop said loudly enough for everyone to hear. Rosanna then listed the most significant moments in the realization of this architectural marvel. As she did so, I went and stood next to Barbara. She gave me a little smile, and I could see that her eyes were moist.

"It's absolutely overwhelming," she whispered. "This place makes me feel so small and fragile, and at the same time so serene."

"You're only forty feet from the entrance. There are still six hundred and ninety feet to see. When you go down the nave, you'll see the largest churches in the world marked off on the floor. Even the Notre Dame in Paris and the Cologne Cathedral are puny by comparison. You have to stroll around the inside of this building to understand it, in my opinion. The historic and artistic facts and figures are of great interest, but you can read all that in a book or on Google and Wikipedia. What you get from a contemplative walk in this place goes beyond just information and becomes a truly personal experience."

Barbara looked at me with shining eyes. She leaned closer and put her mouth up to my ear. "I'm going to take in as much as I can," she whispered.

I could smell the residue of Shalimar on her skin. As I was enjoying the Barbara's closeness, I noticed Rosanna and the group going in the direction of Michelangelo's *Pietà*, the marble sculpture that portrays the body of Jesus lying on the lap of his mother, Mary, after she had taken him down from the cross. I really wanted the group to see this statue, which is a pinnacle of Renaissance art. Rosanna began by noting that Michelangelo was just twenty-two years old when he was commissioned to sculpt the piece in 1497.

"I'm eighteen, and I can't even draw a stick figure," Vanessa said.

"Is the statue wet?" Mary said.

I understood why she asked. Parts of the sculpture, such as Christ's arms and chest and Mary's robes, had a glossy sheen. This was the genius of Michelangelo. He had taken a block of marble and chiseled and polished it to what millions of people see today. I had once seen a documentary about Michelangelo's life and art. He said that he could see the statue inside a block of stone, and all he did was remove the superfluous rock. Remarkable.

"She looks kind of young to be Jesus's mother," Mark observed.

"That's a very good point," Rosanna responded in a very animated manner. "In fact, Michelangelo was criticized for portraying Mary at such a tender age, for making her so beautiful, and for showing her completely resigned to the fate of her son. I believe, however, that this is what Michelangelo wanted to express—Mary's innocent beauty and her subdued, noble grief. These were the outward manifestations of a profound and unblemished spirit. Through the death of her son and her never-ending faith in God, she personifies the apex of human suffering, as well as the eternal celestial joy one obtains when in the presence of God."

A hush fell across the group. "That was sweet, way over my head, but sweet," Bishop remarked, drawing a few giggles from the other students. Rosanna wagged a stern forefinger at him, but she was smiling.

"Something's written on that sash across Mary's chest," Darlene observed. "What's that all about?"

"Another very good question," Rosanna said. "The story goes that one day he overheard some people saying that the *Pietà* was the work of another sculptor. This upset him so much that he sneaked in during the night and carved the words you see there, which from Latin translate to 'Michelangelo Buonarroti, Florentine, made this.'"

The only person who seemed uninterested in the *Pietà* was Sabrina, who had split off from the group and stood leaning against a balustrade with her arms folded. I thought I knew why and went over to her.

"What's up, Sabrina? Something troubling you about that statue?" I asked.

"Yeah, I've got a problem with it." She had tears in her eyes.

"Does it remind you of your brother's passing and your mother's grief?"

"It reminds me of my brother. That's it."

This was an unexpected and intriguing response.

I was tempted to speak to Sabrina about someone who had helped me through a very difficult time, but I hadn't yet built up a sufficient rapport with her for that kind of conversation. She would have thought I was completely out of my mind. Instead, I said, "I'm always available if you want to talk about it."

She shook her head. "No, I'm good." Wiping the tears from her face, she walked back to the others.

Rosanna was telling everyone that they had exactly twenty minutes to look around before meeting back at the *Pietà* at 11:30 am sharp. "I shall be walking up and down the center nave, so if you have any questions, you can find me and ask. Just be sure that you stand under the dome and remember that it was built back in 1546, designed by Michelangelo, and is four hundred thirty-five feet high."

As the students scattered, Rosanna called after them, "Oh, and don't forget to look closely at the papal altar above the tomb of St. Peter. Look down at the two short, curved stairwells, and you will see a gilded coffer where St. Peter's remains are stored. This is also one of the entrances to the underground crypt where small portions of the old basilica built by the emperor Constantine can be seen and where various popes have been buried." But she was speaking to the wind since all of them had hurried off to explore.

I noticed that Cynthia was still looking intently at the *Pietà*. I went over to her.

"Much better in real life than in the pages of an art history book, right?"

"It's amazing," she said, not taking her eyes off the statue. "All that grief, but her expression is one of peace and calm." Her face suddenly contorted. "What wouldn't I do to attain even half that level of tranquility!"

I had no idea how to respond to Cynthia's sudden baring of her soul. Still looking at the statue, she said, "Let's just say, Atticus, that my married life was well below par. My husband, while in the navy, had the opportunity to come to Rome. This was before we were unfortunately married. I was so jealous and waited anxiously for any news about his visit to the beautiful city. But there was no news, not even a postcard. He had come to Rome with his buddies for other reasons I found out much later.

"Now I'm here, in Rome, in this marvelous church looking at a masterpiece, and I keep asking myself how my husband could have been so stupid, so ignorant. As I look at Mary's face, I can see that she must have suffered much more than I did, having to witness the death of her son. And yet she seems to have peace of mind. Peace of mind…I don't think I've ever known what that means." She kept staring at the statue, placed her hand in mine, squeezed, then let it go. She looked at me straight in the eyes. "I'm, I…I'm so sorry, Atticus, I didn't mean to bother you with my troublesome past."

"It's no problem, Cynthia. I appreciate you telling me." There was obviously more to this story, but for now, Cynthia was stopping there. It was time for me to make a short, strategic retreat so that she could reflect. In fact, she had already turned back toward the statue.

I began walking to the front of St. Peter's, passing works of art that have enthralled generations. At a certain point, I veered to the left to look at one of my favorite sights in the basilica—the monument to Pope Alexander III. This was the pope who had commissioned Bernini to construct the enormous colonnade on St. Peter's Square. What I particularly liked about this monument was the personification of Death as a skeleton holding an hourglass from under a heavy drape of marble, the message being that the hourglass runs out of sand for everyone, the poor and the unknown, as well as the rich, famous, and powerful.

I finally reached the main altar area and found myself under St. Peter's dome. Light was shining directly through four of the sixteen windows at its base, giving the sensation that this enormous structure was floating above you like the UFO in Steven Spielberg's *Close Encounters of the Third Kind*. Architects today are still scratching their heads over this feat of engineering.

Maybe forty-five minutes had passed since we had entered St. Peter's, and my head was already spinning. No matter where you rested your eyes in the basilica, you saw something that reflected important historical, architectural, artistic, political, and religious events spanning the past six hundred years. I was hoping that the students would take in the atmosphere of the place and eventually study up on an aspect of the basilica that truly interested them.

Gradually, I started back toward the entrance. Raymond was walking slightly ahead of me, and I quickened my pace to catch up with him.

"So what do you think, Raymond?"

He shrugged. "Artistically and architecturally, it's very impressive. I just can't get terribly enthusiastic about a building that glorifies a religion that has a lot to answer to for what it's done, or let happen, over the centuries."

I remembered what John had told me at lunch the day before. This kid just couldn't resist a debate. But I nodded in agreement.

"Well, there's no doubt that the horrible behavior of many popes, the Inquisition from the Middle Ages onward, and the more recent scandals involving the Vatican Bank and indictments of pedophilia against certain priests haven't been good publicity for the church as a whole."

Raymond looked at me with an exasperated expression.

"And what about the church's culpability in the treatment of Jews? What about the Holocaust? It was the Catholic Church's centuries of preaching against the Jews and depicting them as Christ killers that aided and abetted the persecution of Jews all over the world. That led to one of the largest genocides of human beings in history. The Catholic Church has apologized for the Inquisition, but they have done practically nothing to important questions relating to Judaism."

Raymond stopped talking, expecting some kind of rebuttal. I felt as if I had been hit by a verbal tidal wave.

"Well, Raymond, I said yesterday that I wanted to have a chat with you about your future plans. I think we've started that discussion with the questions and assertions you just made. The trouble is now we're a little late already for the Vatican Museums. How about we continue our discussion in the next few days?"

"I'll be ready when you are." There was no doubt about that.

We were now back at the *Pietà*. Rosanna was standing with Jeremy, Mark, Mary, and Vanessa. They were all engaged in what looked like a very animated chat. The students were sending rapid-fire questions to Rosanna, and I was delighted to see that she was ricocheting answers just as fast. Wayne, Bishop, and Michelle arrived from across the nave. I found it curious that Michelle, the "good" girl, seemed to be always hanging out with the "bad boys."

I did a quick head count and realized that we were missing James and Evelyn. Rosanna had her flag up above her head. I turned toward the main entrance and saw the two of them walking in.

"We were looking for the two of you," I said. "Was outside more interesting than inside?"

"Sort of," James answered. "I wanted to get a better look at those two large statues out there." This was hardly informative, considering that most of the statues outside St. Peter's were at least two meters high.

"Which statues, specifically?"

"The one of Charlemagne and the one of Constantine."

I frowned, puzzled. Charlemagne was the first emperor to be crowned in the old St. Peter's Basilica on Christmas Eve in the year 800, but I wasn't aware of any statue of him in St. Peter's.

Rosanna and the rest of the group came up to the exit. I reached over and tapped Rosanna on the shoulder, whispering in Italian, "Is there a statue of Charlemagne outside somewhere?"

She nodded. "It's in the atrium to the left."

"And let me guess, on the far right?

She nodded again. "There's a statue of Constantine."

I was flabbergasted. I had been here many times and never noticed these two statues. I went back over to James and Evelyn.

"Well, James, I learned something from you today. I didn't even know those statues existed, and I think it's safe to say that I've been here at least fifteen times."

He grinned. "Evelyn and I were just standing close to another group, and I got the lowdown on Charlemagne. I didn't know who he was before the guide spoke about him."

I turned to Evelyn. "Did you like what you saw today?"

"It's all right," she answered. "I'm just not into churches or religion." With that, she walked off and joined the group. I could imagine that with a father like hers, religion was probably the least important facet of her life. I considered for a moment at how difficult it must be for her. The fallout from her mother's one-off sexual experience, so unfairly publicized by her zealot father, must have been unbearably humiliating. I could understand why she had found comfort in James. An unassuming, shy, introverted boy who lived in his own world was probably the perfect medicine for Evelyn. It was going to be a challenge making any inroads with these two. Twenty-four hours earlier, I could have cared less. But now I was willing to take on the challenge. I looked back at James and decided to get a few more points in the music category.

"Hey, James, what do you think about the band Disturbed?" He looked at me realizing that he was being put to the test.

"*Ten Thousand Fists* and *Indestructible* are okay."

"What? Come off it, after *The Sickness*, they became way too commercial. That was their first CD, and I don't think they've done anything better since."

"Seriously? The only good songs on that album are 'Stupify' and 'Down with the Sickness.'"

I shook my head. "No way, James. 'Numb,' 'Conflict,' and 'Droppin Plates' are clear winners. You saw *Dawn of the Dead*, didn't you?"

"Yeah, so?"

"What was one of the title tracks of the movie?"

"'Down with the Sickness,'" James answered thoughtfully.

"See? They got into movie music. They come out with their first album and immediately go commercial. I prefer it when bands don't sell themselves off to Hollywood. You know what I mean?"

I gave him a playful slap on the shoulders, and for the first time, I saw James smile.

CHAPTER 15

We all followed Rosanna and exited the basilica. When we reached the bottom of the stairs that led up to the portico, Rosanna stopped and turned to the group.

"Ladies and gentlemen, take a look at that building directly in front of us." She pointed at a building that was part of the Vatican complex abutting St. Peter's Square. "Look at the first row of windows from the top," she continued. "That's where the pope addresses the crowds on Sunday."

"I remember seeing that on some news channel back home," said Mary. "He stands at that window with thousands of people standing down here looking up at him."

"Is it safe?" asked Anthony "I mean, standing there at that window like that? Someone down here, up on one of those columns or on the rooftop of any of those buildings over there, could take him out with a .338 Lapua single-bolt rifle or even a .308. The pistol grips on those things make for incredible precision. Of course, if the shooter was on top of a building on the other side of the colonnade, he'd probably need a Barska SWAT series scope and a Hyskore rifle sled."

Anthony seemed to be measuring the distance between the pope's window and the building opposite us in his mind. Nobody said anything. A slight chill ran through my veins. Anthony realized that a sudden silence had engulfed the group.

"What?" he said. "Look, it's possible, okay? I mean, I hope the pope has some protection up there because it would be so simple to land a 250-grain bullet right between his eyes."

"Anthony! I think that's more than enough." It was Cynthia, and she was looking at him in disbelief. Anthony turned beet red and looked down at his shoes. Rosanna observed the sudden tension and maneuvered us past the obelisk in the direction of the Vatican Museums.

"That guy's got a screw loose somewhere," I heard Mark say.

"He's got Columbine on his mind," James noted, hand in hand with Evelyn.

Anthony certainly seemed to know a lot about guns, but James's Columbine remark certainly wasn't reassuring. I felt I should dig deeper into Anthony's background in an attempt to understand where he was coming from. I also wanted to talk to Cynthia about him since she most likely knew more about Anthony than either Barbara or John.

By now the sun was doing its dance on the top of our heads. Some of the students had walked with their bottles of water, but most had not.

So, as we were heading down the Via Angelica, which ran along one of the many Vatican walls towering obliquely above our heads, I asked Rosanna if we could cross over to the other side of the street to one of the many coffee bars that were strewn between countless souvenir shops.

She gladly agreed. "I'm dying for an espresso myself." The two of us made our way to the front of the group and over to a series of broad white stripes that were painted from one sidewalk to the next, which indicated where pedestrians were permitted to cross the road. The students must have thought that once they were on these zebra stripes, vehicles would stop to let them pass. How far from the truth! Nobody in Italy stops for pedestrians. That is rule number one to remember when walking in any Italian city.

Thus, the students crowded behind me and Rosanna, pushing us across the road. We both had to turn and yell at them as a large white van whizzed past, missing Rosanna by no more than three inches. Cars, scooters, motorcycles, all types of utility vehicles, and small trucks just kept speeding by. The trick is to start *easing* your way out into the middle of the road and stare hard at the oncoming drivers. Only then do they start to slow down and let you pass. We asked the others to stay close together. Eighteen people advancing together across a street tends to slow down traffic. As soon as there was room to maneuver, however, drivers rocketed off like stock car racers at the Daytona 500.

Having managed to cross the road, we entered a rather large establishment that had a generous bar counter area with three attendants handling orders. I asked everybody what they wanted, telling them that it was on me.

"Can I have a beer, Mrs. Ramsey?" said Wayne. I was afraid that his feeble attempt at being funny was going to fail.

"Don't you already have a six-pack strapped on that money belt, Wayne?" Cynthia shot back. John looked at her with a stunned expression, as did Barbara. Wayne was speechless. I looked over at Cynthia. She gave me a quick wink. Her moment alone with the *Pietà* must have done her some good.

In Italy, you usually pay at the cashier first and then take your receipt to the bar to get your order. On this occasion, however, the bartender took my order, given the large number of our party and the multiple orders for water, Cokes, some takeaway cappuccinos and espressos for Rosanna and me. As I was paying, John, who was with a few of the students, signaled me.

"We're just going next door for some postcards," he said.

"No problem, just be quick," I replied.

As the cashier was handing me my change from a fifty-euro note, Barbara came up to me. "The kids said to tell you thanks for the drinks," she said.

"No problem." I glanced around. We were momentarily away from everyone else, so I decided to get her take on Anthony's comments.

"Interesting how Anthony calculated how easily a sniper could kill the pope. I've also had my doubts over the years at how secure that man is standing at that window without bulletproof glass in front of him, especially after the attempt on Pope John Paul II's life in 1981."

"The attacker was a Turk, if I remember correctly," Barbara answered.

"Yes, exactly. Ali Agca was his name. I'm sure you noticed how nonchalant Anthony was running off that list of guns and accessories for a headshot."

"I worry about Anthony, as does John. Cynthia sides with him all the time, though. That's actually become an issue since Cynthia came to Bradford three years ago. I'm glad that they won't be around each other once we're back in Atlanta. It's not a healthy teacher-student relationship, in my opinion."

"I want to pick your brain about a few of the others one of these nights. Maybe with another white Russian?"

"Gladly," Barbara said, smiling.

I was beginning to be taken by this woman, absurd as it seemed. After all, we had just met and under a set of circumstances that were not congenial to a romantic interlude. And I was troubled that Francesca hadn't even crossed my mind these past twenty-four hours. What was I to make of that?

From outside the bar, Rosanna called out to the group. Her little flag up over her head. It was time to go.

John and the others joined us with their small purchases, and we managed to cross back over the Via Angelica without anybody getting run over. We then proceeded to the Piazza del Risorgimento, which was named after Italy's unification in 1871. How strange that such a historical territory had only become a nation-state a mere 140 years earlier. The United States of America was, in fact, officially "older" than Italy by 85 years.

Over the last fifteen centuries, everyone from the Greeks, the Ostrogoths, the Lombards, the Moors, the Germans,

Spanish, Portuguese, and the French had made parts of Italy their sovereign territory. Most had come and gone, but many had decided to stay. This is what made Italy such a varied place. People from Milan were as different from people from Palermo as a Texan is from a Filipino. This variety occurs within an area of just 116,000 square miles, putting Italy seventy-first on the global country size scale. These differences are also Italy's curse, given the deep-rooted animosity, distrust, and even hatred evident from one town to the next.

We continued our walk along the Viale dei Bastioni di Michelangelo until we came to the Viale Vaticano, where we made a sharp left. We continued along the high, thick walls of the Vatican City. The students didn't seem to mind the walk but were quickly emptying the bottles of water that I had purchased at the bar.

"I suggest that you finish your drinks and any snacks you may have before we enter the museum," I called out. "They don't allow food or drinks inside."

Rosanna was walking ahead of us. A line of people was blocking us, presumably waiting to purchase tickets to the Vatican Museums. Rosanna stepped to the right and signaled to us to follow her. We were now close to the entrance of the museum. Overhead, a sculpture of the coat-of-arms of Pope Pius XI was represented between the statues of Michelangelo and Rafael. Rosanna asked us to wait for a few moments. She went over to some of the attendants near the entrance. They must have known one another since they exchanged the traditional kiss on the left and right cheeks. I saw her point to us and then at her watch. Whatever she said or did must have worked because she waved for us to come over.

As we entered, we encountered a spiral (more precisely, a helicoid) staircase, which had been designed by a famous Italian architect named Giuseppe Momo in 1932. I had always enjoyed walking up and down this cylinder-like structure, which made one feel like you were inside an oversized corkscrew. At the top of this staircase, which was over three stories high, Rosanna went to the ticket counters and did her magic once again, displaying various papers and pointing to us. She concluded her business and came back to the group.

"Okay, I need a few minutes of your undivided attention. First of all, take one of these entrance tickets and keep it until we leave the museum. Secondly, we would never be able to see all the artwork here unless we intend to stay for at least a few months. Pope Julius II, whose papacy lasted from 1503 to 1513, is considered to be the founder of this magnificent collection of art. He set up these museums with a few statues that were unearthed during his papacy, which he decided to display to the public. You will see these statues here. Since Pope Julius II, each pope has added, demolished, and rebuilt the buildings that make up the Vatican Museums, and many popes added more works of art to the collection. It would be safe to say that the works of art here comprise one of the most important—if not *the* most important—collections in the world today. The one masterpiece that we shall spend some time looking at closely is the Sistine Chapel. I shall be giving you as much information as I can about the beautiful statues and paintings you'll see as we proceed to the chapel, but I shall be very brief due to time constraints. This way, please."

I decided to take a short break from the tour. I wanted to jot down a few notes on what had transpired over these last twenty-four hours. As Rosanna started walking off, I caught up with her and said that I would be breaking away from the group for ten minutes and would meet them in the Sistine Chapel. I sat down on a long white marble bench near the entrance to the ladies' room, trying not to bump against some Japanese tourists who were fiddling with their digital cameras. Reaching into my back pocket, I took out my Moleskine notebook to add a few more notes to the ones I had written yesterday. I found the size and format of these little notebooks extremely convenient. I was told when buying one the first time that Vincent van Gogh had used them to make rough sketches and that Hemingway never traveled without them. I don't know how much truth there was to this, but I certainly was hooked. I took my fountain pen from my jacket pocket and began to write:

✓ Barbara: need to understand much more about this woman. Is there something in the air?

✓ John: special interest in Barbara? What's his story?

✓ Cynthia: horrible marriage/loosening up a bit? Doting on Anthony?

✓ Wayne and Bishop: contradictory...sold as big troublemakers—no sign yet / why always together? Why almost always with Michelle? Remember promise made...

✓ Mark: got away with it. Handling himself well. Keep an eye on him.

✓ Raymond: Friday night discussion. Visit Rome synagogue with him?

✓ James: Music freak / Sabrina's brother's (Derek) friend? Have we started to melt the ice?

✓ Anthony: gun fanatic? Switzerland situation? What's this kid's story?

✓ Evelyn: At war with Sabrina. Stuck to James;

- ✓ Sabrina: still upset over brother's death. Link between him and James?

- ✓ Darlene: try talking to her without looking at her cleavage / need to keep a vigilant watch on her.

- ✓ Vanessa: she always looks so tired? Just my imagination?

- ✓ Mary: No issues. Don't know much about her.

- ✓ Michelle: Miss Perfect it seems...

These were the situations that I needed to be aware of. Lord knows it was more than enough to think of after only a day and a half into the trip.

I looked at my Patek wristwatch. It was time for me to meet up with the group.

CHAPTER 16

As I followed the arrows pointing me to my destination, I felt as though I was in a time machine. Wherever I looked, there were works that spanned the ages from classical antiquity, Etruscan, early Christian, and medieval times up to the Renaissance and the nineteenth century. I arrived at the entrance to the Sistine Chapel, named after Pope Sixtus IV for the extensive restoration he ordered in 1478. Security here was particularly tight, with the personnel conducting a thorough examination of visitors' personal belongings. This was quite understandable, given the frescoes that covered every single inch of the walls and ceiling.

Once inside, I marveled at Michelangelo's work, including the best-known image of God with His extended forefinger almost touching the hand of a languid Adam. How many times had this one panel of the Sistine Chapel ceiling been reproduced on everything from T-shirts to shopping bags to coffee mugs? I shifted my gaze to *The Last Judgment*, which Michelangelo had painted on the altar wall. The souls of evil men being cast down to the pits of Hell at Christ's Second Coming was as powerful a message today as it must have been shortly after its completion.

Almost as impressive were the wall paintings below the ceiling that covered both sides of the chapel along with the portraits of various popes at the sides of the large window arches. Between 1481 and 1485, artists such as Perugino, Pinturicchio, Botticelli, and Piero di Cosimo had been commissioned by the same Pope Sixtus IV to represent the life of Moses and important key events in the life of Christ.

Along with the masterfully marble-inlaid floor, this entire space was an explosion of color, especially after the very controversial restoration begun in 1980. Centuries of soot, candle smoke, dust, and mold from water infiltration were carefully cleaned away to reveal what scholars say were "Michelangelo's true colors." However, skeptics and critics hold that the cleaning process removed the darker colors that according to them, Michelangelo was famous for.

Looking at the Sistine Chapel today, you get the impression that it was painted recently rather than five centuries ago. The overall visual effect, however, is unsurpassed—a veritable celebration of Renaissance art.

I looked around to see where my "flock" was amongst the crowd of visitors. I immediately saw Rosanna, who was pointing at various scenes on the ceiling and giving explanations to John and a few other students. I turned to the left and found Barbara, who was with Darlene and Mary. In a corner near the altar, I saw Wayne, Bishop, and Michelle. It looked as though Michelle was lecturing the two.

Raymond was off to one side studying a particular fresco. Near the marble screen that separates the area designated for the clergy from that of the lay congregation, I saw Cynthia speaking to Anthony. His hands were in his pockets, and I suspected that he was being scolded, probably for his sniper comments.

Rosanna turned and saw me. She excused herself from her small group and came over in my direction. Speaking in Italian, she told me that we were at the end of our tour.

"I hope they didn't give you any trouble," I said.

"No, none at all. It's normal that in a group, there are those who lose interest faster than others. I was actually surprised at the kinds of questions that they asked. Where is she—ah, yes, that girl over there." She pointed at Michelle. "She was so interested in what she was seeing, and you could tell that she had studied up before coming here." This didn't surprise me. "And there was a boy..." Now she pointed at Wayne. "That boy was really hungry for information. He asked me a lot of questions, but only when we were alone or when only a few others were around. As soon as more people came closer, he started acting as if he were barely interested. Strange, no?"

I found this puzzling, but then remembered my promise to Wayne, Bishop, and Mark about the "hot spot" I would take them if they dazzled me with some research. I figured Wayne was sucking up to Rosanna for free information. That displayed a certain initiative. Good for him.

Rosanna continued, "Oh, Mr. Winterle, if I might add. It is really none of my business, but that young lady over there." Rosanna shifted her eyes in Darlene's direction. "You are aware that this girl needs some, let's say, extra care?"

"Extra care?"

"She's looks to be quite a *woman,* but she is, what, seventeen, eighteen years old?"

"Just turned eighteen, I think."

"You understand what I mean, don't you? I know all the security guards in this place, and almost all of them asked me to tell them where she is staying. Can you imagine? Please, Mr. Winterle, keep extra close eye on her. I would not want her to get into any trouble that could spoil her Rome experience."

With that, Rosanna glanced at her watch and informed me that she had to meet a group of Hungarian tourists at the entrance of museum. She then raised her Tibetan flag in the air one last time to gather us all together.

We made our way back through and out of the museum, moving rather quickly. Rosanna exchanged goodbyes and thank-yous with the students and teachers. She gave me her business card, and we promised to keep in touch.

I glanced at the time. It was a little past two o'clock. Time for lunch. "Can I have your attention, please?" I said, clapping my hands a few times. "We should already be at the restaurant, so we've got to move fast. It's not far from the bar we stopped at on the way over here." This news elicited a few moans and complaints of thirst, heat, sore feet, etc.

"Well, then, the quicker we move, the better off you'll be. Doesn't anybody walk in the United States anymore?"

"Why walk when you can drive?" was Wayne's immediate response. I didn't feel like rebutting.

"I don't have a small flag, but try to keep up with me, please." With that, I turned and started down the Viale Vaticano. I had peeked at the restaurant voucher while sitting on the bench jotting down my notes and had recognized the street address—Via Plauto, 32 Borgo Vittorio.

The Borgo district is a residential area outside the city's walls, where one could live well and affordably. In 2000, the Holy Year, and in 2005, in preparation for the millions of pilgrims coming to Rome for the memorial services of Pope John Paul II, certain parts of the old Borgo were transformed into a series of fast-food joints and cheap souvenir shops. If I remembered correctly, however, Via Plauto was a little bit off the beaten track, and I was hoping that ASA had done its homework, picking a place that exuded true Rome ambiance.

We were back in the Piazza del Risorgimento and hooked a right that would take us to the Via Porta Angelica. We then went across the road at the same zebra stripes from that morning. I could tell that the group was slowly getting the hang of crossing busy city streets in Rome without getting flattened.

After leaving the Vatican perimeter with its majestic walls, we passed small shops selling religious items, a few bars, a small Catholic bookstore, an antique furniture repair shop, and a small Persian carpet boutique. We turned left into Via della Grazia and then immediately right onto the Via del Mascherino, then once again onto the Borgo Vittorio. We passed a McDonald's, and some of the students cheered as they saw it. As we kept making our way toward the Via Plauto where we would find our restaurant, I thought about all the main areas in Rome, in Italy, and in the world where you could find a McDonald's. It was an unimaginable success story: the right product, at the right price, in the right place, and constantly promoted. Kotler, who literally wrote the book on marketing, had a McDonald's case study in it. That sameness was the secret of McDonald's globally successful business model: every customer was assured they were getting the same taste and quality and price no matter where in the world the fast-food outlet was. Moreover, the company knew exactly how to pinpoint the best locations in all the major cities on the five continents. And whether their outlets were in Shanghai or Moscow or Johannesburg or Amsterdam or London or Rome or any other city I had visited, they always had customers no matter what time of day or night. And the beauty of it all was that the McDonald's golden arches in Shanghai looked exactly like the ones in Zurich, which looked exactly like the ones in New York, and so on. I had the same experience entering any McDonald's in any country in the world as I had when I was in an American Embassy in a foreign land, as though I was in United States territory. I would have loved to work for McDonald's international franchising department.

We were now at an intersection with the Via Plauto directly in front of us. Now we needed to look for number 32, or La Trattoria di Plauto, which was the name of the restaurant. The small corner grocery store was number 12, so we were on the right side of the road.

As we moved along, I saw, after just a minute or two, the entrance to our restaurant. From the outside, it seemed to have all the ingredients of a typical Roman trattoria. The exterior was very simple, with nothing but a rather decrepit wrought-iron lantern by the door. The name of the restaurant was in large wooden letters above the entrance with the *r* in *Borgo* hanging to one side. But you should never be fooled by the external appearance of an eating establishment in Rome or in any other Italian city. Sometimes the best food and the best prices can be found in exactly these kinds of restaurants.

"Hey, Atticus, what does *trattoria* mean?" Mary asked.

"A trattoria is a level below a *ristorante*, or restaurant. The recipes are local, the prices are lower, and the décor is simple—but nine times out of ten, the food is excellent. Let's go inside and see what they've cooked up for us."

I walked in first to scope out the premises. A few tables were set out to the right of the entrance after a small counter that served as a pseudo reception area. To the left, there was a bigger room with four round tables, all with an ASA identification card in the middle. In the corner of the room, there was a smaller table occupied by a gentleman who could have been the owner of this trattoria, a rather stout fellow dressed in grease-smudged cook's white pants and apron, and a third man in a waiter's waistcoat. All three were smoking while talking vivaciously. I looked at the teachers, who were visibly apprehensive. I, on the other hand, was utterly enthusiastic, given that this place had that homegrown look and feel, which usually meant exceptional food, rich in fat, olive oil, herbs, and spices. We could expect a lunch that would be indifferent to our cholesterol levels, but extremely gratifying to our taste buds.

"Nice!" said Mark, watching the two men. "Can we smoke in here too?"

As soon as the men caught sight of us, the owner put out his cigarette and came over to greet us.

"Buongiorno!" he said with welcoming effusiveness.

"Buongiorno," I replied.

"You must be the group we were waiting for. ASA, yes?"

"That's right. Sorry to be late." It was almost two thirty. "We were tied up at the Vatican a bit longer than expected."

"Absolutely no problem! My name is Pino, and I am the owner. Please make yourselves at home. Your tables are over here. The bathrooms are on the other side through that door on the left."

The students went over to the tables to get a seat. I stopped the teachers and suggested that we split up this time and sit amongst the students. Cynthia didn't seem too enthusiastic about this idea, but John and Barbara nodded in approval.

By this time, the waiter and cook had finished their cigarettes and disappeared into the kitchen. Some students were still deciding where to sit when John took the last chair at Mary's and Sabrina's table. They looked around, puzzled. Barbara, who had already sat down, called out to Darlene, Vanessa, and Jeremy to come sit with her. Cynthia, unsurprisingly, seated herself next to Anthony, with Evelyn and James taking the other two chairs. Mark and Raymond had already seated themselves at one of the smaller tables, which left me with Michelle, Wayne, and Bishop. An opportune combination.

After everyone had chosen their seats, some of the students got back up to go to the restrooms.

Pino came over to me and gave me a rundown on what had been prepared for lunch. It was music to my ears. *"Oggi abbiamo spaghetti all'amatriciana con sugo rosso, abbacchio e pollo arrosto con patate al forno, spinaci all'agro con aglio e peperoncino, fagioli con cipolle, formaggi misti e dolci vari."* These were all typical Roman dishes, from the spaghetti with slab bacon and mushrooms to the roasted lamb and chicken, the spinach with butter and hot peppers, steamed beans with parsley and finely chopped onions, plus a variety of cheese and desserts. This was as good as it got.

As soon as everyone was seated once again, one of Pino's waiters, speaking in heavily accented English, told us what he was about to serve. Everyone looked lost.

I stood up and said, "I suggest you at least *try* everything that comes out of those kitchen doors. Be sure to taste the roasted lamb, along with the chicken. It's a traditional plate here in Rome. And easy on the wine, please. The day isn't over yet, and I need you alert for this afternoon."

This wasn't really true, considering that we were free after lunch, but a warning seemed appropriate.

Wayne sat down next to me, looking completely perplexed. "Atticus, what's the deal with the bathrooms in this place?" he said, sounding quite vehement.

I had a feeling everyone had been surprised, if not shocked.

"Instead of a toilet, did you by any chance find a hole in the ground with an elevated footrest on either side?" I asked.

"That's right! Not a problem if you have to take a piss, but what do you do if you have to take a crap? And how do *women* handle it?"

"Well, Wayne, Michelle is right here. Maybe she can explain it to you."

"It's certainly different. I felt like I was a kid again on a camping trip with my parents." Michelle seemed unfazed, but Wayne was still in shock. The topic of conversation for the next five minutes at all the tables was the bathroom experience.

These *Gabinetti alla Turca*, or squat toilets as they are called in English, are common in more modest-eating establishments in Italy, Spain, and southern France. They are the main type in Turkey, Greece, the Balkans, and in the former Soviet republics. A doctor friend of mine had told me many years ago that this squatting position is actually more conducive to liberating your lower intestine and colon. However, it's of the upmost importance, as Wayne had noted, that your aim be precise.

I poured wine for Bishop and Wayne, but only half-filled their glasses. Michelle wanted a Coke instead. I was glad to be at this table with her and the two boys, hoping I could get a handle on some things about this trio that didn't seem to gel.

The waiter brought loaves of fresh bread and baskets of bread sticks, which the students attacked like a pack of ravenous wolves. Pino and another waiter followed with large ceramic serving trays that they gracefully maneuvered from one plate to the next, placing a hefty portion of spaghetti all'amatriciana on each.

"Atticus, what kind of spaghetti sauce is this?" Wayne asked. "It looks and smells completely different from what I get at home."

Bishop and Michelle had already started eating and seemed quite satisfied with their culinary encounter with a new spaghetti sauce. Wayne forked up a mouthful and nodded in appreciation.

"It's called all'amatriciana," I answered. "The main ingredients are tomatoes, smoked slab bacon, a white onion, red pepper, olive oil, and Pecorino cheese. Some will tell you that it's a traditional Roman recipe, others say that it's from a town called Amatrice, about one hundred miles northeast from here. It all depends on who you speak to."

I lowered my voice and looked at the three of them. "Listen, I wanted to thank you for getting Mark back to the hotel last night."

Michelle wiped her mouth with her cloth napkin. "It's the three of us, plus Mark, that need to thank *you* for all that you did. If Mrs. Ramsey or Mr. Seeward had found out what happened, Mark wouldn't be here right now."

"That's true. But you've got to tell me honestly…" I lowered my voice even further. "Is he going to pull this stunt again?"

The three of them glanced at one another. By some sort of unspoken vote, Bishop answered, "Yeah, he probably will."

I sighed. "You seem pretty sure about that, Bishop,"

"I am. The three of us have seen this before. He goes for weeks drinking normally and then, wham! He downs a bottle of gin or vodka or tequila, just like he did last night."

Wayne and Michelle kept eating their spaghetti while looking down at their plates. Bishop wiped up the last vestiges of sauce from his plate with a piece of bread and popped it into his mouth.

"He's had his stomach pumped twice already this year," he said.

Michelle and Wayne stopped eating, staring at Bishop.

"Hey, it's all right," I said, noting the sudden tension. "It's much better that I know these things. But if he does this again and we're not in the vicinity, he could find himself in real trouble."

Wayne relaxed a bit, as did Michelle.

The plates were gathered up and replaced with fresh ones. From what I could see, all the retrieved plates seemed empty, or nearly so, which meant that the first course was a success. Pino came back out of the kitchen, this time with his four-wheeled cart. On top, he had a large platter with roasted *abbacchio* (lamb), and chicken. On the bottom were two trays of baked potatoes with rosemary and black pepper.

As portions of lamb, chicken, and potatoes were being dished out, I looked at Wayne and Bishop.

"Something's been bugging me about that incident with Mark," I said, "and I was hoping you two could set my mind at ease."

"Shoot, Atticus," said Bishop.

"Why were the two of you so *fortunately* sober last night? Yesterday, you only asked me questions about bars and booze, and honestly speaking, your teachers didn't paint a pretty picture about your alcohol-related habits."

Instead of answering, Wayne and Bishop stared at Michelle. They were obviously waiting for her to say something. She looked at them and said, "It's going to be fine. Atticus is on our side. Maybe not now, but later, he'll understand."

Understand what? I was at a total loss. Then as I was about to speak, someone grasped my shoulder. I looked around—it was John.

"How's it going over here?" he said. "Everybody is enjoying the meal, Atticus. ASA couldn't have picked a better place."

"I'm glad. I was afraid that the first impression may have turned some of you off."

"Yes, we had a few doubts at first. But the food has completely put them to rest." John patted me on the shoulder and made his way to the men's room.

"Excuse me just a moment." I got up and walked around to the other tables. Darlene was digging into her roast potatoes while Vanessa's plate was already empty.

"How's everything?" I asked.

"The food is awesome, Atticus," said Darlene, "but if I keep eating like this, I'm not going to fit into my clothes."

"With all the walking you'll be doing these next few days, I don't think that'll be a problem whatsoever." I turned to the other students at the table. "Raymond, Vanessa, everything okay?"

"Just fine, these potatoes are awesome," Raymond said indistinctly as he continued eating.

"Some vegetables are coming out now. Try them. It's amazing what Italians can do with spinach and beans."

I walked over to the next table where Cynthia and Anthony were sitting with James and Evelyn. I put my hand on James's shoulder, which made him jump.

"Sorry," I said. "I didn't mean to startle you. I just wanted to see how the meal was coming along."

"Wonderful, Atticus, just wonderful," Cynthia replied. "I always stay away from fatty foods, but that lamb was just too much of a temptation. And the spinach, I've never tasted anything like it before!"

"It was probably freshly picked this morning, and that makes a big difference. Enjoy."

I then went over to Barbara's table, where Jeremy, Mark, and Sabrina were sitting. "Everything okay?" I asked.

"Yeah, fine, just gorging ourselves here," Jeremy replied.

"It doesn't get much better than this," said Sabrina, giving me a thumbs-up.

"Mark, everything all right?" I inquired. He was still pale, and I could see he wasn't eating much of anything.

"Just tired and thirsty," he replied. No surprise considering that he had vomited out eighty percent of his bodily fluids the night before.

"Take it easy. You'll be back in the hotel within the next two hours." I gave him a wink, and he attempted a smile in return.

I then leaned down close to Barbara's ear and whispered, "I finally figured out who you remind me of. I'll tell you later."

"I'm very curious," she said, giving me a wink.

That feathery feeling you get when you're truly interested in someone kicked in. When was the last time I had had this sensation? I couldn't remember.

A variety of hard and soft cheese selections were being served up to the students, and I thought it was an appropriate moment to do a bit of food education.

"Listen up, please. Don't think me off-the-wall or a stickler for unimportant details, but this, my friends, is real Parmigiano." I held a piece of this particular cheese up for everyone to see.

"In America, we call this Parmesan cheese, thinking that we are eating genuine Italian cheese. I don't have anything against grated Parmesan cheese, but Parmesan and Parmigiano are like beer and champagne, two distinctly different things."

"I prefer Kraft-grated Parmesan," Anthony said.

"You're nuts, Anthony! This is a hundred times better," Mary exclaimed.

"It tastes like a completely different kind of cheese," John added.

"Exactly! This is the real thing, just like the consistency of the spaghetti that you ate today. Didn't anybody notice that it almost seemed slightly under cooked?"

"Yeah, I thought they made a mistake in the kitchen," said Sabrina.

"No, the mistake is in how pasta is cooked in the US. We cook it until it becomes like glue, nice and mushy. Now that may be how most Americans like their pasta, but in Italy, pasta must always be slightly al dente, which literally means cooked 'to the tooth' or slightly hard. So that's your food lesson for today. Try the other cheeses, and don't forget to dig into the desserts as well." I actually received a short round of applause as I took my seat.

The tables were cleared, and two dessert carts were rolled out of the kitchen, loaded with an incredible choice of pastries, cakes, and fruit combinations. As in the hotel the night before, the trays quickly emptied, with only a few mixed fruit bowls left untouched.

"Atticus?"

"Yes, Wayne?"

It was obvious that he was having difficulty in getting the next words out.

"Maybe one of these nights we can meet up again, I mean, the three of us with you. There are a few things we'd like to get off our chest."

Wayne was struggling, Bishop looked nervous, and Michelle's eyes were watering. What the hell was going on?

"No problem, whenever the three of you want." I decided to take this a step further. "Let's be clear, however, I am not your parents, I am not your teachers, and I am not your parish priest. I'm just a chaperone. But I know how to listen. And I shall certainly listen carefully to anything you may want to tell me. I don't pass judgment, but I can attempt to give some advice, hopefully useful, since I've been around thirty-plus more years than any of you. You may see me flinch if you tell me that you're all serial killers, but other than that, I'll be as calm as a cucumber. Is that clear?"

"Yes, crystal clear, Atticus," said Wayne. "Thanks. After seeing how you handled Mark's situation, we have a feeling we can trust you."

For a moment, Wayne's usual expression of arrogant superiority changed to one of serenity and peace. Then he looked up, and I could tell from his stiffening that someone was coming our way. The Wayne of only seconds before vanished.

"Hey, got a cigarette, Wayne?" It was Jeremy.

"Yeah, but where the hell are yours? You're full of it if you think I'm going to be your pusher on this trip."

"Atticus, mind if we go out and have a smoke?" said Jeremy.

"I think if you ask Pino, he'll let you smoke in that other room if there aren't any other customers."

And so it was. Pino showed Mark, Wayne, and Jeremy to a table and lit up himself. I was left alone with Michelle and was about to ask her a question when Vanessa and Mary came over and sat down.

"Can we have a cappuccino, Atticus?"

"No problem. Let's see who else wants one." I asked for a show of hands for cappuccinos and espressos. Almost everyone opted for a cappuccino while only John and me asked for an espresso.

"Can I have a latte instead, Atticus?"

"Sure, if you tell me first of all what a latte *is*…"

I knew that a latte referred to *caffè latte*, or coffee with milk, but I wanted to have a little fun.

"What? You don't know what a latte is and you live in Italy?"

"I'm pulling your leg, Vanessa. Here in Italy, if you order a latte at the bar, they're going to serve you a cold glass of milk." I told Pino what Vanessa wanted.

"Atticus, is the rest of the afternoon free?" Mary inquired.

"Yes, it is, until dinner at seven thirty."

"So we can go out a little on our own when we get back?"

"It's absolutely fine with me as long as your teachers agree. I would just like to have a general idea where you are heading."

"We're big girls now, Atticus. We won't get lost. You really can't with Google Maps."

"Yes, you are big girls, and Google Maps is great, but you are in a new city where you don't know the language. I need to take care of my flock."

"Like a shepherd, you mean? I've never had a shepherd before…I've never even had a sheep dog." Mary burst out laughing, as did Vanessa. I could tell Michelle was trying to keep it in, probably in deference to me, but she wasn't doing a good job.

"Ha, ha, ha. All right already," I said. "Can't a person even use figurative speech anymore?" But this only prompted more hilarity.

"Fi-gu-rative spe-eech?" Mary could hardly get the words out because she was laughing so hard. "You just called us a bunch of sheep!" I just sat there while this tidal wave of jocularity rolled over everyone in the group. Vanessa, Mary, and Michelle started making bleating sounds, as did some of the boys. I wasn't getting any support from the teachers, who were laughing like the others. I just sat there and stewed.

Thankfully, Pino came out of the kitchen holding a large tray with many long, slender glasses filled halfway with a fluorescent-green liquid. This got everyone's attention.

Pino proudly beamed a smile as he informed us that this was on the house and that he had made it. The waiter was placing the concoction in front of everyone before I could tell them what it was exactly. A strong smell of lemon immediately hit everyone's nostrils.

"It's an after-dinner digestive called *limoncello*, made from lemon peels, sugar, and pure grain alcohol," I explained. "It's a bit strong, but very pleasant, especially if fresh out of the freezer like this is. Sheep are particularly fond of it." This just prompted more bleating, laughter, and napkins thrown in my direction.

John and Barbara didn't seem concerned any longer with more alcohol accompanying Italian meals. I couldn't tell what was going through Cynthia's mind, though. I myself was a little more hesitant because of Mark, but luckily, he was still feeling the effects from the night before.

Everyone sipped at their green elixir, and there was a general sensation of surprise and satisfaction. The boys in the other room were finishing up their cigarettes and were halfway through their digestive.

Sabrina turned to me. "Do you have any teenage children, Atticus?"

I gathered that Sabrina thought me old enough to have children in their late teens.

"Not yet, *fortunately*. My two children are nine and thirteen. I still have some slack with my nine-year-old son, but my girl is beginning to, shall we say, grow up."

"Has she had her period yet?" Mary asked very matter-of-factly.

"Uh, yes. Seven or eight months ago. I'm divorced from my wife and only see them on the weekends, so it's hard to keep up with everything that happens in their lives on a day-to-day basis."

"She'll start getting into boys within the next year, Atticus, then you've got your work cut out for you," Mary said with a chuckle.

"Come off it, Mary," Sabrina interjected. "Boys only get really interesting when you're fifteen or sixteen. They're just a bunch of Mamma's goofballs before that." Sabrina seemed very sure of herself.

"I just hope there are more interesting specimens in college. If I have to put up with the Waynes, Bishops, and Marks of this world much longer, I'm going to become a nun."

I tried to keep my surprise off my face. Michelle glanced at me, and I read in her eyes that I would understand *later*.

"Now that's a bunch of crap, Michelle. You're always hanging around them. Even today, you're at their table." There wasn't any ill will in Sabrina's comment; she was just stating the facts.

"You know I've got a mission to save the world, Sabrina, so what better place to start than with those three clowns?"

Sabrina and Mary laughed and began sugaring their cappuccinos, which had just arrived. The waiter placed my demitasse of espresso in front of me. My head was spinning with the conversation over the last hour and a half, but the aroma wafting from that small coffee cup relaxed me almost immediately.

Michelle looked at me and then at the minute portion of dark liquid. "What exactly *is* an espresso, Atticus? Is it different over here than at Starbucks?"

"I would say that it all depends on the coffee beans and how Starbucks roasts them. Once you have the blend of beans that you want, you grind them down into a fine powder, and the espresso machine does the rest. Water is pressured through the coffee, which produces a much thicker and darker liquid than what you get from a regular drip coffee machine. It packs a punch as well. More than three of these a day, and the caffeine level in your blood skyrockets."

"I think I'll stick to my cappuccino and *caffè* latte," Michelle said, smiling.

I looked at my watch. It was almost four o'clock, and we needed to meet up with Ricardo. It was already past our deadline.

"Okay, everyone, let's get ready to go. Riccardo is waiting for us at the bus." This announcement drew a series of *boos.*

"Can't we stay a little longer, Atticus?" said Darlene. "It's kind of cool sitting around the table like this, sipping limoncello and chewing on these hard biscuits, you know what I mean?"

I hadn't noticed that someone had put baskets of *cantucci* (hard dried biscuits with almond shards and pine nuts) on each of the tables. Italians usually dipped these into sweet wine as a dessert.

"Fine, Darlene, a few more minutes then." I took out my cell phone and sent Riccardo a text message informing him that we were running late.

It was quite satisfying to see that everyone was so at ease here. This really wasn't out of the ordinary. Sitting at the table in Italy, whether in a restaurant, a trattoria such as this one or an osteria, which is a further step down in the eating hierarchy, can go on for hours. The many dishes to try, the wine, the desserts, the coffee, and the digestive ritual all lend to a pleasurable, unrushed atmosphere.

After another ten minutes, I got up out of my chair and went over to Pino to give him the voucher and thirty euros as a tip. He had been very hospitable.

I had a harder time getting Barbara, John, and Cynthia out of their chairs than the students. They were jabbering away a mile a minute about colleagues, next year's curriculum, and the graduation ceremony. Michelle was whispering something to Mark, probably giving him the heads-up on what we had discussed earlier. Darlene was leaning against the wall, attempting to converse with one of the waiters. A profusion of "Grazie, grazie" were exchanged with everyone grabbing a name card of the trattoria as they headed out.

Overall, the group was stuffed, tipsy, and tired. It wasn't a long walk to the bus, but I made sure to be more careful when shepherding them across the busy roads. Nobody seemed too terribly alert.

CHAPTER 17

We exited the restaurant and turned left, following Via Plauto all the way down to Via dei Corridori. From there, another street would take us straight onto the Via della Conciliazione where all the tour buses parked. We had gone about two hundred yards and had successfully crossed two intersections when the road we were on turned into Vicolo delle Palline. I was glad that nobody asked me what *Palline* meant because I would have had to answer, "small balls," and this would have paved the way for a great deal of silly laughter and joking.

A *vicolo* is a very narrow road usually allowing for only one direction of traffic. But in Rome, "one-way" holds little, if any, significance. Scooters and motorbikes were tearing up the road in both directions.

When we got to the end of the "little balls" road, we encountered the Il Passetto, which is a long, elevated wall that starts within Vatican City and goes all the way to the Castel Sant'Angelo, the fortress for the popes for many centuries. It had fallen into disrepair since the 1700s but was restored during the Holy Year in 2000. As we were walking through an archway in this imposing wall, I explained to the group that Pope Urban VIII had used this escape route on May 6, 1527, when Charles V, the ruler of the Holy Roman Empire, sacked Rome. Nobody was paying attention, however, not even asking why the ruler of the Holy *Roman* Empire would want to sack *Rome*. The fatigue from yesterday's trip, the hot day today, all the walking, and the *limoncello* had done them all in.

We were on the Via della Conciliazione now, and I immediately spotted our silver-metallic Mercedes Travego and waved to Riccardo. He opened the doors for us, and we tumbled, sighing with satisfaction at the air-conditioned coolness.

"Apologies, Riccardo, there were long lines at the Vatican Museums," I said.

Some tactful lying seemed necessary. Giovanni's Latin proverb the night before made me think of another one from the Roman orator Quintilian who, almost two thousand years ago, said, "*Mendacem memorem esse oportet*," or "Liars must have good memories." How very true.

Riccardo maneuvered out of his parking space and headed for the hotel. Most of the students began to doze off. I turned to the teachers.

"It's almost five o'clock, and dinner is at seven thirty. What are your thoughts about after dinner? Do we cut them loose?"

Cynthia replied immediately, "I think they've had enough for one day. The visit to the Vatican and the lunch were fabulous, Atticus, but the wine and the little green drink was probably a bit more than they can handle. You saw how carefree they all were on the way back to the bus, didn't you?"

"You seemed rather *carefree* yourself, Cynthia. I haven't seen you eat that much since you arrived, and I believe you were washing it all down with that nice dry white wine."

"That has nothing to do with what we're discussing, John. The four of us are adults and are responsible for our actions. Those back there, if you need to be reminded, are our students and are under our care until we get back to the States. We'd all be in jail if we were in Atlanta for aiding and abetting liquor consumption to minors."

Considering what Cynthia had "confessed" to me in St. Peter's, I tried to be understanding, but wasn't it much better to let the kids have a glass of wine, a beer, and an occasional limoncello with their meals instead of forbidding all alcoholic beverages? Wouldn't this just provoke them to go out on their own raiding all the bars in town?

"Cynthia, we've already discussed this," said Barbara. "We can't control them twenty-four hours a day. Is anything going to change if we start restricting their movements over here? I think we'll just create frustration and resentment. So far, they've all acted responsibly, and I think they appreciate the trust we've placed in them." *All except Mark,* I thought to myself.

Cynthia obviously did not care to be lectured by Barbara. She smacked her lips and said, "All right. What do you two enlightened, progressive-thinking teachers intend to do?"

The sarcasm detector was glowing red. I broke in before John, who was beginning to lose his temper, could respond.

"I believe it's rather simple. If they go out without one of us, they have to be in groups of at least three, and we set the curfew at eleven pm. John, you and I will make the rounds at that hour, okay?"

"Fine by me," John murmured. I looked at Barbara, who was nodding in approval, and at Cynthia, who was frowning. By this time, Riccardo was almost at our drop-off point.

Most of the students had dozed off, but at the back of the bus, I noticed Vanessa chewing her nails. She was very pale. I was about to go down the aisle of the bus to see what was wrong when the bus swerved to the left and came to a rather abrupt stop.

"*Siamo qui,*" Riccardo announced that we had arrived. I took the microphone out of its slot and switched it on.

"Okay, sleepyheads, we've arrived. Time to wake up and get back to the hotel."

It was quite a task, but we finally managed to get everyone up and out of the bus. Cynthia, Barbara, and John started herding the students along the road back to the hotel while I stayed behind to talk about the next day with Riccardo.

"Do we see each other tomorrow, same time?' I asked him.

"We don't meet until Wednesday. I have another group that I must take to Tivoli tomorrow. I think your schedule is for the Pantheon and Piazza Navona, which are very close."

It was useless to act as if I had a clue about tomorrow. I hadn't bothered to look.

"Thank you, Riccardo. We'll see each other Wednesday."

The group hadn't gone too far, so I quickened my pace to catch up with them. When we entered the lobby of our hotel, Ludovica was at the desk putting our room keys on the counter.

She cleared her voice and held up eight fingers. "Dinner is at eight o'clock. This gives you thirty extra minutes to rest up."

We all trudged up the stairs. I was exhausted. I had been awake for more or less the last forty hours. As I approached my room, I saw something hanging from the doorknob. A white plastic sack was covering what looked like a series of clothes hangers—Mark's laundered T-shirt, pants, and socks from the night before. I opened the door, hung the bag in my closet, kicked off my shoes, and threw myself on the bed. Before fading into the land of dreams, I reached for my cell phone and set the alarm for 7:45 pm. That was the last thing I remembered.

I opened my eyes after the third ring of the alarm, immediately wide-awake. I had slept for almost two hours, but it seemed as though I had only fallen asleep two minutes before. I couldn't remember the last time I had slept so soundly and awakened so energetically. If this was the effect, I needed to get my hands on a case of Pino's limoncello.

I washed up quickly and changed my shirt and pants. I decided to have a look at the itinerary for tomorrow before going downstairs. Riccardo was right. No bus was required for tomorrow. We were to meet the tour guide at the Pantheon at nine thirty. From there, we would go to the Piazza Navona.

No official lunch was scheduled, and the students were free for the entire afternoon. I left the room and went downstairs.

I wasn't surprised to see that only a few students, along with Cynthia, were in the downstairs lobby. I was almost certain that most of the group was going to be late, even though Ludovica had graciously bumped dinner forward by thirty minutes.

Cynthia came up to me.

"I wanted…I just wanted to apologize for my behavior on the bus this afternoon. I know I treat the students as if they were still thirteen-year-olds. It's just that they grow up so fast, and there are so many dangers lurking around every corner. I guess I'm just being overprotective."

"This certainly isn't a fault, Cynthia. I would prefer that my children had an overprotective teacher rather than one that just counts off the minutes until class is over." I paused a moment before continuing.

"I'll be flat-out honest with you, Cynthia. I wasn't too terribly excited, to put it mildly, to chaperone this group around Rome for any amount of time. But in just thirty-six hours, I've come to be very happy to be here. I was prejudiced, and still am to a certain degree, against today's teenagers and what they stand for. But I see this group of students, like all of us, as a product of the environment they were born in. We're all a reflection of the family that nurtured us, the friends we associate with, and all of the influences, good and bad, that we encounter every day of our lives. There are thirteen good people here, Cynthia, and I am getting a feeling that they've already been through their fair share of tough times for their age. These next seven days should become a memory that they treasure for the rest of their lives. I think that we have an obligation to make this happen. Within limits, of course."

Cynthia was listening attentively. I continued, "I have a favor to ask you."

"Sure. If I can do it, I will."

"Try to get a bit closer to Darlene, Wayne, Bishop, and Mark during this trip. I know you're not too taken with their attitude and behavior. But I've found that what they project and who they actually are aren't the same in some respects."

Cynthia pursed her lips.

"I'll try, Atticus. It won't be easy. You've seen them for what? Not even two days, but I've been with them since I arrived at Bradford three years ago."

"Oh, I fully understand that Cynthia, and it could very well be that they have managed to pull the wool over my eyes. My gut, however, is telling me something different."

"Okay, Atticus, I'll do this for you...and for me." With that, we joined the others in the dining area.

A quick head count found that Sabrina, Vanessa, and Mark were missing. Raymond came over to the adults to say that Mark wanted to sleep in and would see us tomorrow morning at breakfast.

"That's fine," I said. "Today was a long day."

In fact, looking around the room, several students still looked groggy or tired. Only Mary, Michelle, and Jeremy seemed well-rested. I was about to say a few words to Barbara when Sabrina came through the restaurant doors and headed straight for our table.

"Hey, all! Vanessa won't be coming down to dinner," she said.

I immediately remembered how deathly pale Vanessa had looked on the bus that afternoon. "She's in bed, and I'm a little worried. She goes from being really cranky to crying about nothing. I think she's sleeping now, but she's been acting postal."

"I'll go up and see what's going on," Barbara volunteered. "Give me your room key, Sabrina, so I can go in without waking her."

Sabrina handed over her key and left. I turned to Barbara. "Excuse my ignorance of modern-day American vocabulary, but what does 'acting postal' mean?"

"It means that you're acting in a bizarre fashion, as if you were out of your mind."

Well, that wasn't promising. It worried me, in fact, that Vanessa, who really hadn't looked well ever since her arrival in Rome, was being described by that phrase.

"She's been acting strange these last few weeks," John added.

"I agree," Cynthia said. "Her grades have fallen this past quarter as well, which is unusual for her. She's told me over and over that she's just tired and worried about college."

"Where's she going?" I asked.

"The University of Maryland. She wants to study astronomy, and Maryland has a strong program in that field."

As we spoke, the waiters placed the usual bread baskets, wine, and water bottles on the tables. Some of the students went to get some food, but nobody seemed particularly hungry. We waited for Barbara to come back. After five minutes, she came in and informed us that Vanessa was just exhausted and had asked to be left alone until morning. But even as Barbara was saying this, she glanced sideways at me. There was something more going on.

We got up from the table and went to the buffet. After Barbara returned the room key to Sabrina, she joined me in the buffet line. I only wanted some steamed vegetables and a bit of risotto with mushrooms.

"What's that dish you're having, Atticus?" Barbara said, speaking a bit more loudly than was necessary. When Cynthia and John came up behind us, she murmured so only I could hear, "I need to speak to you urgently after dinner."

"This is a rice dish with mushrooms," I said, also speaking rather loudly. "Very good if not left on the burner for too long.

It tends to overcook if you're not careful." We moved away from Cynthia and John, who were deciding on the dishes.

"I'll call you when I'm back in my room," I said quietly.

We went back to our tables and started eating. The risotto was not bad, although the rice had been, in fact, overcooked, probably to satisfy a more American taste.

"Atticus…"

"Yes, Wayne?"

"Can we come down to this room after they've cleaned up and play cards or do some emailing?"

"I'm not sure. Let me find out."

I called over one of the waiters and asked him if the room was available. He said he would check and left the restaurant, presumably to go to the front desk. He came back almost at once and told me that as long as we left it the way we found it, we could use the room until midnight. I turned to Wayne.

"It's all yours. Be sure to clean up after yourselves, or it'll be the last time you use it."

"No problem. Thanks, Atticus."

"A show of hands please of those who are going out." John had taken out a small pad of paper and pen from his shirt pocket. Mary, Michelle, Evelyn, Raymond, Anthony, and James raised their hands.

"Curfew is at eleven. We want everybody back in their rooms by that hour. Stay in groups of threes if you're not with me or another adult. Is that clear?"

"I'm coming as well but just for thirty minutes," Cynthia said. "I'd like to see the Trevi Fountain lit up again."

"Barbara?" asked John.

"No, I'm calling it a night."

John seemed put out by this. Before he could turn to me, I got up and told the group that I would remain at the hotel. "I have to finish some paperwork, but I'll be doing the rounds with John at eleven. Also, we meet in here for breakfast at eight forty-five. Have a good walk for those who are going out." Everybody got up and started heading out of the restaurant.

"Atticus," Bishop piped up. "Is it okay if we order a few beers from the bar and bring them in here while we play cards?"

"I don't have any problem with that as long as you drink in moderation. I don't want to see thirty beer cans in there or stashed in some trash container somewhere. And don't think I won't go around and check!" I threatened.

Bishop laughed. "That's fly, Atticus," he said. "I promise we'll keep things under control."

I guessed that "fly" meant "cool" or something along those lines.

Barbara had already gone up to her room. I decided to wait in the lobby until Cynthia, John, and the others had left the hotel. As I was waiting, Wayne, Bishop, and Jeremy came downstairs with their laptops. Darlene and Sabrina soon followed with the playing cards, pens, and postcards. Finally, Cynthia and John came down with the others who were going out.

"I'll be back in time to make sure James takes his medication, Atticus."

"That's fine, Cynthia. John, at eleven down here for a room check, okay?"

"For sure. See you later."

I was finally able to go to my room and call Barbara. She picked up immediately.

"Is the coast clear?" she asked.

"I think so. I'm the only one from the group on this floor."

"I'll be right up."

CHAPTER 18

I put the receiver down and got up to open the door a crack. In what seemed no time at all, Barbara appeared. She had changed into a white blouse with a beige knee-length skirt. A silk Pierre Cardin scarf around her neck completed her ensemble.

"Come on in," I said, taking my appreciative eyes off her outfit and peering down the corridor to make sure nobody from our group suddenly appeared.

Only when she entered did I notice that she had two small bottles of red wine and two wine glasses. The worried expression on her face, however, dictated that we would only get to the wine after we discussed what was concerning her. She put the bottles and glasses on the desk and sat on the corner of my bed.

"Atticus, we have a problem."

"You mean *another* problem?" I was thinking about Mark and his binge-drinking.

"Yes, another one, but this more serious. It's Vanessa."

I knew it. My gut had told me there was something wrong with her from Day One.

"I went up to the girls' room and let myself in with Sabrina's key. I knocked first, but there was no answer. Vanessa was in bed. She was sweating and mumbling, but she was out cold. I looked around the room, and then something told me to go into the bathroom and do some snooping around. On the sink I found a large jar of extra-strength Tylenol, 290 gelcaps, unopened. And in Vanessa's beauty case under the sink, I found another one."

"Stupid question, but how do you know it was Vanessa's beauty case?"

"Her initials were on it. But there was a big *X* drawn on the lid in black permanent marker. Why would she do that? I realize that both she and Sabrina could have brought their own supply of Tylenol, but if Vanessa had marked her jar with an *X* to differentiate it, why was it sitting in her beauty case under the sink? The jar's safety seal was already broken, so I opened the container. Look what I found inside."

She reached into her pocket and took out a handful of colored pills in different shapes and sizes.

"Not Tylenol, Atticus."

"No, it certainly isn't."

I hadn't seen a dose of Tylenol in years, but these small, candy like pills were not for headaches. There was something particularly sinister about them. "These are Valium. I've taken a few in my life, and I recognize the shape and the cut in the center of the pill." Barbara picked two tablets from her hand and placed them on the bed.

"This one has a name on it. The writing is very small, but I was able to make it out. It says Halcion. I googled it. It's a brand name for Triazolam, which is a very strong sedative banned in some countries, but not the U.S."

"Could Vanessa possibly be on some medication that we are not aware of?"

"Not likely. All the parents had to sign an ASA document that stated whether their child had a medical condition which called for special attention. Only James's parents filled out that part for his depression. I checked her before I left the room. She didn't have a fever, and there were no signs of vomiting, so I came back downstairs with these in my pocket."

"Are you thinking that she may have overdosed on this stuff?"

"No, I don't think so. At Bradford, teachers take CPR classes as well as basic drug abuse classes so we can identify the most prevalent illegal drugs are and how to spot a kid who's under the influence. You wouldn't believe what these kids are swallowing, snorting, inhaling, and injecting. The big thing now is prescription drugs, especially any kind of painkiller."

"You mean these kids are raiding their parents' drug cabinet to get a high?"

"Their parents', their grandparents', anyone who's taking prescription medication. It's simple and cheap. The other benefit is that they can hide these pills in over-the-counter drug containers like a big Tylenol jar."

"So think she might be addicted to sedatives?"

"It could very well be. The problem is, the more you take them, the more you want them, and when you take too many, they start to have the opposite effect. You get restless, your nerves are on end, you can't sleep, and you begin to lose your appetite. All symptoms that we're seeing in Vanessa."

"Hasn't she been eating?" I had not noticed.

"Today, at lunch, she had a little spinach, maybe a few potatoes, and she was in a sour mood. I tried to make her eat some of those fabulous desserts that were on that cart, but she didn't want to even look at them."

I drummed my fingers on my thigh.

"What do you think we should do?" I asked.

"I don't know if it's possible, but we need to know exactly what she's been taking before we can confront her about it. If we were in Atlanta, I'd immediately go to Grady Memorial Hospital, but over here, I haven't a clue."

I realized that we did have someone who could help—Marco.

"Let me make a phone call."

I looked at the time. It was almost ten o'clock, not too late. He would certainly still be awake. He picked up on the second ring.

"Good evening, my friend. Do we have another problem? One of your student's in *Rebibbia* by chance?"

"No, Marco, I'm fine, and no one is in jail, yet." Marco had alluded to Rome's maximum-security prison. "But we do need your help."

"What's up?" Marco stopped his joking, realizing that something was up.

"I need a lab test run on a few pills we found in one of the student's bathrooms. Mrs. Cornwall and I think they are sedatives, but we don't know how strong they are and what the side effects could be."

Marco fell silent for a moment.

"I understand, Atticus. Here's what we will do. Put those pills in an envelope, seal it, write my name on it, and give it to Giovanni or Ludovica. I'll stop by early tomorrow morning and pick it up. My brother-in-law is a pharmacist. I should be able to let you know something by midafternoon."

"You're an angel. For now, only Mrs. Cornwall and I know about this. I would like to save this girl from an immediate trip back to Atlanta, if possible."

"I understand that, Atticus, and it is interesting that you are so concerned about this group, considering that two days ago you could have cared less—"

"Marco, please, not now."

"Okay, okay. But remember, if those pills turn out to be something dangerous or not prescription drugs made out to this girl's name, ASA could be sued by the parents for negligent conduct. The teachers that are with you could also face criminal charges for attempting to hide illegal substance usage. Keep this in mind, please."

Marco was as cool as a cucumber, simply stating the facts clearly and succinctly.

"I understand, and I agree with you, but let's first see what exactly these pills are, okay?"

"Fine. I'll call you tomorrow, Atticus, as soon as I have the results."

I wished him a good night and ended the call. I then explained to Barbara what the plan was.

"Now what about tonight? If Vanessa wakes up and decides to take more pills, that could be very dangerous."

"That crossed my mind. I'll tell Sabrina to keep me updated on Vanessa every hour on the hour. I have a good rapport with Sabrina. I won't tell her anything specific, but I'll hint that it's a medical issue. That's about all we can do for now."

"You realize that we haven't even taken into consideration that Sabrina may be taking these things as well."

"It's a possibility. She hasn't buried her brother in her head yet, so I could see her popping a few of these. But it's only Vanessa who's displaying signs of drug abuse. I think we need to concentrate on her for now."

"I think Sabrina is downstairs with the others in the restaurant," I said.

"I'll go down and check. I'll be right back."

"I'll go to the front desk and drop off these pills for Marco."

I let Barbara go out first and followed her after counting to twenty. Downstairs, I found Giovanni at the front desk.

"Good evening, Signor Winterle, I assume you require one of these?" he said, staring at the monitor in front of him. He slid a yellow A4 envelope in my direction. The envelope already had a white label stuck on the front with Marco's name on it. Inside the envelope, I found a small ziplock plastic bag. How terribly efficient.

With the pills safely inside, I sealed the envelope and slid it back toward Giovanni.

"I hope, Mr. Winterle, that you shall be able to get some sleep tonight."

"So do I, Giovanni, so do I. Thank you again for all your help."

"*In omnia paratur.* Good night, sir." With that, Giovanni turned and went through the service door in the back. My Latin was rusty, but I was able to catch the meaning: "Always be prepared for all things."

I got back to my room. It was almost ten thirty. There was a soft knock at the door. I got up and let Barbara in.

"I spoke with Sabrina," she said. "I told her that Vanessa was feverish and to please keep an eye on her and to call me if she felt it was necessary. She was going up to the room in about ten minutes."

"Fine, that should help us for tonight. I took the pills downstairs."

Barbara relaxed a bit. She sat down on the bed and kicked off her sandals and leaned back on the pillow. Her toenails were perfectly pedicured and painted in a clay-colored polish. Darlene was right, feet could be sexy.

"You should see them all down there. They're having a good time sending emails, playing cards, and writing postcards, and there were only four beer cans on one of the tables." She inclined her head to the desk. "I was hoping that we could have that wine together, Atticus, but it's already past ten thirty. You need to be downstairs in thirty minutes."

"Yes, I know. If you don't mind, I'll keep it here, and we can try another night. When, by the way, did you get that wine? You were up here in a flash after I called you."

"I bought it at the bar this afternoon. Let's say that I was looking forward to our next meeting. Unfortunately, we'll have to take a rain check. I'm so exhausted. We've been here two days, and these kids are driving us to the nuthouse. And you—you must be a complete train wreck."

"I can't say I'm as fresh as a rose, nor do I smell like one, to be honest." I really needed a shower. "Barbara, can I ask you a question?"

She sat up. "Certainly."

"It's none of my business, but am I getting in the way between you and John? It's as plain as the nose on my face that he's not appreciating my presence where you're concerned. I'm sure you've noticed it as well."

Barbara laughed gently and shook her head.

"John has had a crush on me for the last, oh, maybe eight months. He's a considerate and kind person, and he'll probably be a very decent family man one day, but he isn't my type, and he's having a hard time accepting that."

"Has he ever been married?"

"No, never. He told me once that he had gotten a girl pregnant when he was eighteen. The girl had just turned seventeen. They were both kicked out of their respective homes, can you imagine? They stayed together for about six months in a little apartment on the south side of Atlanta that he could barely afford with the money he got flipping hamburgers at McDonald's. One day, he came home, and she had disappeared with the baby. He has no idea what happened to her or the child. I think it hit him hard. John is into trekking, mountain climbing, the whole great outdoors experience. I think he's just trying to run away from his past and all that open space gives him some peace of mind. Did you ever see *Into the Wild*, that film by Sean Penn?"

"Yes. I enjoyed it."

"It's John's bible. He lives by that film." She paused and looked at the clock radio beside the bed. "I'd love for us to keep talking, but it's nearly eleven already. I'm afraid John will come up here looking for you soon."

"You're right. Promise me that we'll pick up where we left off."

"Oh, we will." She got up, stood in front of me, and said, "May I?"

"Yes, you may."

She took my face between her hands and kissed me on the lips. It wasn't "Frenching," just a nice warm lip on lips kiss.

"I hope we'll pick this up as well," I said.

"So do I." She put her sandals back on.

"I hope you get some sleep."

"You too, Atticus. You are a lovely person."

She turned and left.

I waited a little while before leaving the room myself. As I walked down the stairs, I thought of Barbara's last words: *You are a lovely person.* I didn't remember the last time I had received such a heartfelt compliment, not even from Francesca.

When I arrived downstairs, John was sitting at the lobby bar and sipping on a clear liquid from a highball glass with a few ice cubes.

"Hey, John, how was the outing?"

"Atticus. Hi. All good. We had a nice walk." I sat at the bar next to him. The bartender asked me if I wanted anything.

"Do I have time for whatever you're having?" I asked John.

"Sure, we can give them an extra ten minutes. Everyone who went out with me is already accounted for. I'm having a Cointreau."

"That's fine." I turned to the barman. "*Un* Cointreau *per me, liscio per favore.*"

"What does *liscio* mean?" John asked.

"It means without ice or straight up. How is it that you drink Cointreau? Not a very common beverage back home, or have I been away from the States too long?"

"It's quite popular in the bars in Atlanta. I like it on ice, but friends of mine use it when making margaritas. They say it adds an extra 'orangey' punch."

The barman turned and placed a liqueur glass in front of me. I took a sip and immediately tasted the strong citrus flavor that is the trademark of this French triple sec.

"So where did you go this evening?"

"We went back in the direction of that big white construction. What was it, the 'wedding cake,' I think you called it?"

"The Vittorio Emanuele II monument."

"But then we stayed to the left of it and ran into a very wide road that, from what we could tell, was surrounded by Roman ruins. I think we caught a glimpse of the Colosseum lit up at the end of the road."

"Was there a large column near the beginning of these ruins with a statue of Saint Peter on the top?"

"Yes, I don't know if it was Saint Peter, but there was a tall white column all lit up, in fact."

"You were looking at Trajan's Column in Trajan's Forum. The large road you were referring to is the Via Fori Imperiali. It does go to the Colosseum. We'll most certainly have a tour in that area, given that it's the heart of Imperial Rome. Did the students remain with you and Cynthia, or did they go off on their own?"

"No, surprisingly, we all stayed together. I don't think they feel confident enough yet to go out on their own."

He took a swallow of his drink. "And you, Atticus? Did you get to that paperwork?" There was a hint of suspicion to his question.

"Not as much as I would have liked," I answered, trying to avoid his inquisitive stare.

"That's too bad." John took the last sip of his drink. It was embarrassingly evident that John believed me as far as he could throw me.

"I think we need to get moving," he said. "There are still a few vagrants in the back."

"I'm right behind you," I said as John kindly paid for my Cointreau.

We got up and walked to the dining area. "Ladies and gentlemen, time to start packing it up," John announced as we entered. The five students in the room got up and started putting their things together. The room was perfectly in order, with just a few beers and Coke cans on the tables. We were amidst model adolescents, it seemed. John and I exited the way we came in and headed upstairs. Everyone who wasn't downstairs was in their respective rooms. Then John remarked, "Atticus, we missed a room—Vanessa's!"

I had this horrible flash of John and I walking into that room and seeing Vanessa suffocating on her vomit with pills all over the floor. We reached Room 15. John knocked on the door. There was no answer. He knocked again. No answer. I began to perspire.

"Vanessa, Sabrina?" John said softly at first, then with a raised voice. He knocked harder on the door. We heard a creaking mattress spring. The door opened. It was Sabrina.

"Hey, Mr. Seeward. Hey, Atticus."

"Hi!" came from inside the room. It was Vanessa. She was on the bed, with playing cards spread out in front of her, along with an array of candies and chocolate bars.

"Couldn't you hear us knocking on the door?" John said, slightly annoyed.

"Sorry, Mr. Seeward, it's kind of hard hearing anything else when you've got Lady Gaga full max in your ears." Vanessa and Sabrina held up two pairs of earphones. They were both plugged into the same music player.

"Everything okay?" I ventured.

"Yeah, we're fine, Atticus," said Vanessa. "I missed dinner, sorry, but I was really tired. I've got the munchies now, and I've been going through Sabrina's supply of goodies."

She seemed to be another girl entirely and in good spirits. Still a bit pale, but far from her previous deathly shade of gray.

"Okay then, have a good night. We'll see each other in the morning," I said.

I was at a loss. Wasn't this the girl who had been sweating and murmuring in her sleep, not eating, and in a wretched mood, with a pusher's collection of pills in her Tylenol jar? I was interrupted by the sound of footsteps coming up behind me. The group we had left downstairs was coming down the hallway.

"We're all here," said Wayne. "They've locked up downstairs."

"Thanks, Wayne," I replied. "All of you get some sleep, and we'll see each other in the morning."

I thanked John again for the nightcap and went up one flight of stairs to my room. Once inside, I sat on the corner of the bed and reached for the phone. I wanted to call Barbara and give her the good news about Vanessa. I dialed her number. She picked up after the second ring.

"Yes?"

"Barbara, sorry, were you already asleep?"

"No, Atticus. I just got out of the shower. Talk to me, anything new?"

I didn't answer. The thought of her naked and wet on the bathroom rug distracted me.

"Atticus?"

"Oh yes, sorry, I just wanted to let you know that we did our room check, and we saw Vanessa and Sabrina."

"And?"

"Well, you wouldn't believe it. She was playing cards with Sabrina and eating candy bars. She looked rather well and seemed calm."

"I don't understand, Atticus."

"Neither do I. Could it be that we overreacted?"

"We may have, a little, but this doesn't hide the fact that there is a large quantity of sedatives in her bathroom."

"That's true." I paused a moment. "Let's see what Marco tells us tomorrow. Try to get some sleep now."

"You too, Atticus. By the way, I'm looking forward to that wine."

"So am I."

I ended the call and headed for the bathroom.

I had a nice, long, warm shower, as well, which I found very relaxing. Once in bed, I set the alarm on my cell phone for 6:00 am so I could start reading those autobiographical notes the kids had written before leaving Atlanta. Maybe I would pick up some clues about Mark's and Vanessa's bad habits.

What I wanted to read now, though, was something that would take my mind off everything that had happened in the last twenty-four hours. I picked up Wilkie Collins's *The Moonstone* and started where I had left off a few weeks ago.

Thursday
April 29, Day Three

CHAPTER 19

My neck was sore. There was something papery between my fingers, and a light was on somewhere. It took me just an instant to realize that I had fallen asleep while reading. I reached over to the bedside table for my watch—it was 5:35 am.

I would have liked to roll over and continue sleeping until 6:00 am. But as soon as my eyes opened, my mind ran to Mark, Vanessa, Barbara, Cynthia, and so on. I got up and went to the bathroom to brush my teeth and splash some warm water on my face. I then headed over to the desk to boot up my Dell. I picked up the stack of student bios that were sitting on the chair and began flipping through them, suppressing a yawn. I took a quick glance at the questions first.

Hobbies:

*Favorite subject(s) in school:
Favorite sport(s):
Favorite music:
Favorite foods:

*University: Major and Minor you want to pursue?
Why did you choose to go on this particular trip?
Have you already made some career plans?
*Do you have any medical matters of concern?
*Parents' situation (D, S, W)?
Brothers / Sisters?
*In case of an emergency, who would you like us to contact first?

The asterisks highlighted the questions where an answer was mandatory. Michelle's bio was the first on the stack. Her penmanship was, unsurprisingly, neat and clear.

She liked gardening and reading, especially poetry, and she enjoyed all kinds of music but with a penchant for jazz and country. Under "favorite foods," she had written that she had a particular liking for everything her parents grew on their farm. She didn't mention anything about her social work, to which she seemed to devote a great deal of time, according to her teachers. Her favorite subjects in school were history, English literature, and math.

Her one-paragraph answer as to why she wanted to go to on this particular trip was notably straightforward. She had studied Italy and, more specifically, Rome, especially the Imperial and the Renaissance periods. and found them fascinating. She added as a footnote that as her first trip out of the States, she couldn't have thought of a better place to go.

The "Career Plans" question was curiously blank, even though I was quite certain that she must have had a general idea about what she wanted to do.

She had an older brother, but she didn't mention his age. In case of any kind of emergency, she wrote that her parents should be informed. I was still looking for something that was out of place or not quite right in Michelle's background but hadn't found anything yet.

I heard two short beeping sounds. I looked up and saw the brightly colored butterfly that my daughter had created as my PC screensaver. Mail had arrived. Logging into my email provider, I saw that there were three new messages. Two were spam, but the third was from a certain Signora Visconti from Bailey & Courtney, an executive search firm I had sent my resume in March.

I clicked on it.

Lo and behold, it appeared to be something interesting. Mrs. Visconti wanted to inform me that she had a client in the luxury market segment who was looking for a general manager, with special emphasis on international sales and greenfield operations. She suggested, if I were interested, an initial telephone conversation at my earliest possible convenience. I clicked "respond" and began typing feverishly. I informed her that I was available that same day, preferably in the afternoon, around 4:00 pm. I didn't think that we would be back at the hotel before then. I thanked Mrs. Visconti for the opportunity, reread what I had written ten times, and then hit "send."

I sat back in the chair and began wondering what product group the company in question covered, the roles and responsibilities of the position, what the organizational structure looked like, where they were located and whether it was a family-run operation or a corporation. All standard questions that anyone in my shoes would have asked. But then I slipped off into the more personal aspects of the job, daydreaming about what the salary would be, the bonus, the benefits, the car? Very natural, I suppose, but how fruitless! None of this fantasizing had brought me anything except bitterness this past year. I fought the temptation to just sit there and dwell on all of this. I had had too many negative outcomes to be optimistic this time, but hope is always the last to die.

Before shutting off the computer, I googled through an infinitesimal portion of the mounds of information I found on the Piazza della Rotonda where the Pantheon was located, as well as the Piazza Navona. I went on Google Maps and reviewed the most important monuments, piazzas, and the like that we would encounter on our way over there. I soon stopped. As always, there was just too much to absorb. I would do the best I could with what I remembered and had read during my years living in the city.

I switched off the Dell and plopped down on the bed. It was nearly six forty-five. Breakfast was served at seven. I decided to use the fifteen minutes looking at the next student bio. It was Darlene's. This was going to be enlightening.

In the "Hobbies" section, she had, not surprisingly, written "Beauty pageants" and nothing else. Her favorite subject in school was business and entrepreneurship, the class that John taught. Was this because she had taken a liking to him? Under "University," she had written "Westwood Community College." The reason she wanted to come on this trip was to get a sense of fashion trends in Italy. *More to buy up the fashion trends in Italy*, I thought. Under "Career Plans," she had listed beauty pageant queen, model, or a job on the *Entertainment* channel. She left the medical section blank and circled "divorced" in regard to her parents' marital status. No brothers and sisters were mentioned.

I truly felt sorry for Darlene and the many other teenage girls out there who had D or DD cups attached to an attractive body and a pretty face. It was a cross to bear instead of a fortunate combination of chromosomes. Meeting a girl like Darlene for the first time would lower the gaze of even the most well-mannered and irreproachable heterosexual human male. There was just no way to get around it. For a large percentage of men (and some women), the main goal after meeting Darlene would be to get her clothes off. Full stop. Girls like Darlene usually become well aware of this "weapon" shortly after their bodies blossom. Using their physical attractiveness to gain advantage quickly obliterates a young girl's innocence. My hope was that Darlene would bond with people who liked her for who she was an individual, and not because she looked like an inflatable sex doll.

Enough of that. It was five past seven, and I was hungry. I put on a pair of dark-blue slacks, a black polo shirt, and my old Sperry Top-Siders, and out the door I went.

As I expected, I was alone again in the restaurant, except for the same Japanese couple from yesterday. The waiter brought me an espresso with some cold milk on the side. I went to get some pastries and jam. As I got back to my table, I was bewildered but pleased to see Mark walking in. He looked much better. Only a residue of dark circles around his eyes remained, and his complexion looked much better.

"Good morning, Mark," I said.

"Morning. Is it okay if I sit here?" He pointed to the empty chairs at my table.

"Make yourself comfortable. But go get something to eat first. You must be famished after skipping dinner last night."

"Yeah, I'm starving."

He went over to the buffet table. My pleasure at seeing how much better Mark was made me think of how well Vanessa had looked last night. Maybe things were looking up. Mark came back with his plate heaped full of scrambled eggs, sausages, thinly sliced roasted potatoes, bread, a few slices of cheese, and strips of baked ham. In his other hand, he skillfully carried two glasses of fruit juice. Sitting down, he dug right in.

"Did you get up early this morning?" I asked.

"At five o'clock. I think I conked out around seven thirty last night. So I've been out cold for about ten hours. I feel good this morning."

"Great, because we have another long day ahead of us."

"I studied up on the Knights Templar. Pretty neat stuff. We can talk about them when you want."

"Good for you. I'd like to get those of you that have small research projects to tell us what you learned. Maybe after dinner one of these nights."

Mark might have been listening to me, but most of his attention was focused on devouring everything in front of him.

"Any news from back home?" I asked.

"Nothing special. My parents are gone somewhere, golfing, maybe in the Bahamas. That's where they always go. I sent them an email to tell them that I got here in one piece, but no answer. I'm not surprised." I found this comment interesting since it aligned with what Barbara had told me about Mark's parents' general apathy in his regard.

"I take it you didn't write her about your little exploit the other evening?"

"No, not a word. I don't think it would have made a difference but no use rubbing it in, right?" He paused a moment, then said, "She won't ever know what happened, right, Atticus?" He suddenly looked ill at ease.

"Pull that stunt again, and I'll call her personally," I shot back, catching him off guard. I shook my head. "Your parents won't know anything about what happened from me, and I doubt from anybody else who knows. You've got three very good friends. You know that, don't you?"

"I know. Misha's cool and keeps me in line." He was obviously referring to Michelle. "Wayne and Bishop are like brothers. They're a little off the wall, but we cover…I mean, we look after each other." He turned beet red after that possible faux pas. What did these three have to "cover up?" Was this in reference to what Bishop had told me about Mark's stomach being pumped twice this year? Could it be that Mark's parents were unaware of this? I found that hard to believe. I was tempted to investigate a bit further, but instead pretended that I hadn't picked up on the Freudian slip.

"And your dad, any news?"

"No, but that's normal. He's never around. He works for an international division of Coca-Cola, so he's always overseas—in Europe, the Middle East, and Africa. I think his title is EMEA director or something like that." This was correct, given that EMEA is a business acronym for Europe-Middle East-Africa.

So what Barbara had told me about Mark's parents matched what Mark was divulging to me now to a T. He made no mention, however, of their questionable drinking habits.

Mark finished one of the glasses of orange juice in one go. "I got an email from my older sister this morning. She's a lawyer in Sacramento. A few months ago, she invited me to come and stay with her this summer for a few weeks before I go to college. That would be awesome. We've always been really close, although she's eleven years older than me." A rather lengthy span between kids, I thought to myself.

"Sounds like a good time," I said.

"Yeah, I can't wait."

"Are you going to college after the summer break?"

"University of Georgia. It's about seventy miles from Atlanta, in Athens. It'll be good to get out of the house and into a dorm."

"Any idea what you'd like to major in?"

"I kind of like journalism. My dad went there and said it was a great school, but he majored in economics. I guess I'm sort of following his footsteps, like it or not." Mark's tone of voice dropped when he uttered this last sentence, and I was about to ask him another question when I received an unexpected tap on the shoulder. I turned to see one of the waiters standing next to me.

"Signor Winterle, *mi scusi. Hanno bisogno di lei al ricevimento. E' urgente.*" My presence was requested at the front desk for what seemed to be an emergency. I wasn't terribly concerned, expecting that it was probably Marco who had come to pick up those pills.

"Excuse me, Mark, I'll be back in a moment."

"Sure," he said, chewing on his sausage.

I went out the door, down the hallway, and to the front desk. Ludovica was standing there with the telephone receiver in her hand. Marco was nowhere around. Alarm bells went off in my head.

"Mr. Winterle, please dial seven and then room number 15." Whose room was this? I quickly dialed the three numbers and waited.

"Hello?" A soft but agitated voice answered on the other side of the line.

"It's Atticus, who's—"

"Atticus, it's Barbara." She continued whispering, "I'm calling you from Vanessa's room. We very much still have that problem on our hands. Can you come up to my room in a couple of minutes, please? It's urgent."

"No problem, I'll be up at once."

"Thank you." She hung up.

I gave the receiver back to Ludovica. She already understood that there was some more trouble.

"If you need anything, Mr. Winterle, please do not hesitate to call me. By the way, Mr. Iddino came by this morning and picked up the envelope."

"Thank you very much, Ludovica."

I went back to the restaurant to tell Mark that something had come up. As I opened the restaurant door, I saw him at the buffet table loading up again. Raymond was with him. I decided against saying anything to them, turned around, and went upstairs. I peeked around the corner and looked down the corridor. The coast was clear. I walked down to Barbara's room. The door was opened just a crack. I knocked softly and let myself in.

Sabrina was in Barbara's bed, and it was clear that she had just woken up. Barbara was sitting opposite her on the only chair in the room.

"Good morning, Atticus," Barbara said.

A subdued "Hey" came from Sabrina.

I sat at the foot of the bed. "Tell me what's happened."

Sabrina and Barbara exchanged glances.

"I'll start," Barbara said. "Sabrina called me at about four this morning. She told me that Vanessa was in bed one moment, then sitting up the next, then walking around, and then back in bed, continuously. Correct, Sabrina?"

"Yeah, that's about it. I managed to call Mrs. Cornwall because she went to the bathroom for a few minutes. Atticus, you saw us about eleven last night, right?"

"Yes."

"Well, we continued playing cards, and Vanessa kept eating all my candy bars. She seemed okay, but boy, did she have a lot of energy. She kept fidgeting, she just couldn't keep still. At about twelve thirty, I was dead tired and wanted to get some sleep, but she begged me to keep playing. We played a few more hands, but then I said enough is enough. Then she got angry with me and started cursing me out. It's only because she's been a friend of mine since seventh grade that I didn't slap her across the face."

"Then what happened, Sabrina?"

"I turned off my light and tried to get some sleep. She started crying, saying that she didn't have any friends and that nobody gave a flying 'eff' about her. I tried to calm her down, but it didn't help much. The last thing I remember before I fell asleep is that she went into the bathroom and took some more Tylenol."

My conspicuous reaction must have been transparent because Barbara gave me a warning glare. I cleared my throat and said, "Just to be clear, Sabrina, how do you know what she was doing in the bathroom? You were in bed, right?"

"Yeah, but I saw everything from the reflection in the mirror. Vanessa turned on the light, but she left the door open. You know, I've told her already more than a few times to cut it out with those Tylenol pills. She was already taking three or four at Hartsfield before we got on the flight. She's popping them just like my mom was taking uppers and downers after my brother died."

Suddenly, the light switch tripped on in the recesses of my brain.

I looked at Barbara. I knew that she had come to the same conclusion. Vanessa was taking sedatives to mellow out and then some other kind of pill to rev her back up. That's why there were different sizes and colors of pills in that jar. Up and down, up and down. She was on a continuous narcotic roller-coaster ride.

"I called Mrs. Cornwall at about four when she got up and locked herself in the bathroom. She was all sweaty and completely out of it."

Barbara picked up where Vanessa had left off: "I came right over, of course, and told Sabrina to come to my room and get some sleep. I stayed with Vanessa, putting cold towels on her forehead. She was extremely dizzy and thirsty, so I gave her a couple of bottles of water from the fridge. I had to help get to the bathroom twice. She couldn't get out of bed by herself. At around six o'clock, she finally fell asleep."

"You should have called me earlier, Barbara."

She didn't answer immediately, looking uncomfortable. "It would have just caused an unnecessary commotion, Atticus, and I remembered that you had told me that you hadn't slept the night before." We stared at each other as we tried to adjust ourselves to the situation at hand. "I really didn't know what to do, Atticus."

"Excuse me," Sabrina interrupted, "but something's telling me that the two of you know more about what's going on than I do."

I looked at her and made a decision. Then I looked at Barbara, who gave me a slight nod.

"You're right, Sabrina. In fact, you need to know something that Mrs. Cornwall and I are very worried about. But you have to keep it to yourself. Can we trust you on this?"

Sabrina sat up, adjusting her oversized Hello Kitty T-shirt. "Yes. I won't say anything to anyone if you don't want me to."

"We don't think Vanessa has any Tylenol in her Tylenol jar. We think that it's filled with other kinds of pills, like Valium, which we found, and uppers and so on."

"I knew it!" Vanessa yelled, clenching a victory fist as if she had won the lottery.

"Shhhh!" Barbara warned, nudging the mattress with her foot.

"Sorry, sorry, but I just knew that there was something really weird going on. She put that big X on the lid and was always looking for a new place to hide her jar."

"We've sent some of the pills to a lab to find out what she's taking," I said.

"Other than Valium, I bet she's popping Percocet or Dilaudid to go down and probably Ritalin or Dexedrine, fifteen- or thirty-milligram doses to give her a buzz."

She looked as thoughtful as Anthony had while scoping the distance between the pope and his would-be assassin.

"You seem very well informed, Sabrina," I said dryly.

Sabrina nodded. "Because of my mom, Atticus. She takes pills for breakfast, lunch, and dinner. And every sorry-ass doctor she goes to is just so happy to prescribe her a more powerful trip." Sabrina was now pulling at the bottom of her T-shirt nervously. "I've taken a few more than once too—uppers, I mean. Friends have asked me to lift pills from my mom, so I did and took a few myself. I could have taken a hundred, and she wouldn't know, considering the truckload she has. Our entire neighborhood knows that we have a makeshift pharmacy in our house. Everyone starts busting open their parents' medicine cabinet sooner or later, right, Mrs. Cornwall?"

Barbara and I just looked at each other helplessly. I would have liked to ask Sabrina some questions, but there just wasn't any time. It was already eight twenty, and almost everyone was certainly downstairs at breakfast by now. Then I had a flash. We needed to take advantage of Sabrina's know-how.

"I think you can help us, Sabrina. You have much more hands-on experience than we do in this area, sadly. What's the best thing we can do right now to get Vanessa off this garbage? I want to avoid calling a doctor. That would mean informing Mr. Seeward and Mrs. Ramsey, which means she would be back on the first flight home, with other problems to follow."

"The best thing to do," she said very matter-of-factly, "is to throw that garbage away, make her drink a lot of warm tea, no sugar, as well as lots of water. She needs to pee, I mean, go to the bathroom as much as possible to flush that stuff out of her system. She'll be a real bitch the first few days. She has to eat something more substantial than a bunch of candy bars."

"Okay, that's a good start. Now we need a game plan for today. Barbara, you need to stay with Vanessa, if you don't mind."

"That's a given."

"Make her drink as much as Sabrina suggested and call Ludovica at the front desk for anything you need brought up here. Sabrina, go back to your room, change, and then go downstairs. It's probably best that you inform Mrs. Ramsey and Mr. Seeward that Vanessa isn't feeling well and that Mrs. Cornwall will be staying with her."

"All set, Atticus. Mrs. Cornwall told me to bring a set of clothes and everything I needed for the day with me before I left my room this morning."

I gave Barbara an approving smile. "Good forward thinking. All right, then, I'm going downstairs first. I'll inform Ludovica that you'll be calling for some tea and food later on."

Before leaving the room, I wrote my cell phone number down on a piece of paper for Barbara and asked her to call me every so often to let me know how things were going. Then I left the room, already planning what to do for the next few hours.

Chapter 20

There was nobody in the hallway. Everyone was probably still at breakfast. I quickly went down the steps and told Ludovica that one of the girls wasn't feeling well and that a teacher, Mrs. Cornwall, would stay with her this afternoon. Ludovica promised that she would personally take care of any requests from Room 15. I then went to the restaurant.

As I had expected, almost all the students were downstairs. Cynthia and John, strangely enough, were at the same table as Evelyn and James. I received quite a few "good mornings" from the students, most of them using my first name, which I found quite gratifying. I waved to everyone and went over to the beverage cart, trying to seem as casual as possible. I poured myself a glass of pineapple juice and went over to John's table.

"Good morning, everyone."

"Morning, Atticus."

I pulled up a chair and sat between Cynthia and James.

"Slept well, Evelyn, James?"

"Yeah, I guess," was all Evelyn could muster.

"You look well rested, Cynthia. Did you get a good night's sleep?"

"I slept very well, Atticus, like a rock. And you?"

"Very well indeed, all the way to—"

Before I could finish answering, I saw Sabrina enter the restaurant and come our way. I stopped speaking abruptly and took a sip of my fruit juice, pretending to be distracted by a fly that no one else could see.

"Good morning, Mrs. Ramsey, Mr. Seeward, Atticus."

She didn't acknowledge James or Evelyn.

"I just wanted to let you know that Vanessa didn't get much sleep last night, and she's not feeling very well this morning. I told Mrs. Cornwall. She's with Vanessa now. She told me to let you know that she's going to stay in with Vanessa this morning. They won't be coming with us today, Atticus."

"She must be quite sick. Otherwise, Barbara wouldn't feel the need to stay with her," said John. "Did Vanessa eat anything last night other than candy?"

"Some chocolate bars, but that's about it," Sabrina answered, with a sideways glance that called on me to say something, quick.

"Thank you, Sabrina," I said. "I'll tell the front desk to take up some breakfast for the two of them. Vanessa probably just has the stomach flu."

I thought this was a believable response, but Cynthia looked at me skeptically. She was sharper than I thought.

"When we finish breakfast, we'll stop in and see what the situation is," she said. "Go get something to eat, Sabrina, thank you."

Cynthia was clearly suspicious. As for John, he appeared more concerned with Barbara's absence than Vanessa's health.

"We haven't seen Mark this morning, Atticus," Cynthia remarked, looking around the room.

"He was here with me earlier," I answered without thinking. "I mean...I was up quite early, and I came down before to get something to eat. Mark and Raymond were down at about seven thirty. They must have gone back to their rooms."

Now both John and Cynthia were looking at me suspiciously. I glanced at my watch hastily and said, "I'd better tell the students what we're doing today."

I stood up and moved to the center of the room.

"Good morning again, everyone. Listen up, please. It's nine o'clock, and we need to be out of the hotel in ten minutes. No bus today. We're walking. It's going to be another hot day, so if you want to change into something cooler, do it now, please."

There were a few moans and groans at the thought of walking, but not as many as I expected. I caught sight of Darlene, who was wearing her comfortable Converse All-Stars but not much else. She had on a short white tennis skirt that looked as if it had been spray-painted onto her hips and a blue low-cut corset top. I considered telling her to change into something a bit less revealing, but I decided that would be futile. Anything she wore would probably have the same effect.

"In the hall in ten minutes, please," I finished.

I returned to the table but didn't sit down. Evelyn and James had left.

"I'm going to go up to my room and get my guidebook," I said to James and Cynthia. See you soon." All I got were two curious looks.

I bolted to my room as soon as I was out of the restaurant. Once inside, I went immediately to the phone and called Vanessa's room. Barbara picked up after the first ring.

"Yes?"

"Barbara, it's me. Is Vanessa sleeping?"

"Yes, thank goodness. She's sweating a lot, but her forehead is cool, so I don't think she has any fever. Thanks for the breakfast, Atticus."

I was about to ask, "What breakfast?" Then I remembered Ludovica. She was already in control of the situation.

"No problem. But John and Cynthia are on their way up to Vanessa's room."

"I thought as much. Thanks for—" I heard knocking in the background.

"Got to go. Big kiss!" she whispered before hanging up. I only hoped that Cynthia and John would not prolong their stay.

When I arrived downstairs, all the students were already there. Sabrina was speaking with Mary and Michelle. I was relying on her discretion regarding her roommate.

"Is something wrong with Vanessa, Atticus?" Wayne asked.

"Nothing serious, Wayne. I think she has some stomach trouble this morning. She didn't eat anything last night and didn't sleep well. Mrs. Cornwall will be staying with her today." By this time Mark, Jeremy, and Bishop had come over to us and were listening closely.

"She's been acting kind of crazy lately," Bishop remarked. "Real nervous one moment and then completely out of it the next. It's not like her." He sounded perplexed.

"When we get back, let's go and see how she's feeling," Wayne suggested. "We can sing her that song she digs so much. That'll either get her back on her feet or make her puke!" This got a few thumbs-up from the boys. I didn't know what song they were referring to, but I found it interesting that it was Wayne who was suggesting how to cheer up Vanessa. I still hadn't seen any sign of that rude, arrogant, alcoholic jock that the teachers had told me about. The pieces of the puzzle weren't creating the expected visual.

Cynthia and John turned the corner into the lobby. I went over to them. "Well? How is she?" I asked, fervently feigning ignorance.

"Probably just what you thought, Atticus," Cynthia said. "A bad stomach flu. She isn't feverish, but she seems very weak and very tired." Cynthia seemed satisfied with her diagnosis.

"Can we call a doctor this afternoon, if we need it?" John asked. "We'll need to report this to her parents if she isn't better by tonight."

This was my greatest concern. "Of course," I said, trying to sound as nonchalant as possible.

I walked over to the glass doors, apprehensive about what this day would bring. "Okay, everyone, we've got to make a move. We have a lot of ground to cover today. Please follow me."

I waved to Ludovica, mouthed grazie, and exited the hotel with the group behind me.

The sun was already beating the pavement mercilessly. There was a slight breeze, and the sky was cobalt blue. There wasn't a cloud to be seen. It was a marvelous day to explore almost twenty centuries of civilization.

I took the group back to the Trevi Fountain, where we then hooked a left onto the Via dei Crociferi and went past the ice cream parlor we had visited Sunday night. We successfully crossed the Via del Corso, dodging a few cars and motor scooters, and entered a large open space named Piazza Colonna. To our right and in front of us were two majestic buildings. The one standing to our right had a significant role in Italian politics.

"That looks like an important building, Atticus," John said. "What is it, exactly?" I was about to answer when another voice arose from the group. "Look, there's another column with little men wrapped all around it, just like the one we saw last night. What is it, Atticus?" It was Mary.

I opened my mouth, but Michelle was already throwing out another question. "What's this building Atticus? It's got *Il T-e-m-p-o* written on the front."

I stopped in my tracks, turned around, and put my hands up as if surrendering to the inevitable.

"Ladies and gentlemen, before you fire off any more questions, let's make a few things crystal clear. Rome, as most of you have realized by now, is an open-air museum. The city is filled with buildings and monuments and statues and fountains and all sorts of structures that have historical, religious, and artistic significance. Every building that we have passed since leaving the hotel has something of importance to tell us. The Pantheon, which you shall see shortly, has a story to tell, which is nineteen centuries old.

But we need to meet our guide so that you can find out why this particular structure is so important. For now, suffice to say that the column we just passed is called the Column of Marcus Aurelius, and yes, it's very similar to the column that some of you saw last night, which is dedicated to the Roman emperor Trajan. Those little men that you mentioned, Mary, are actually representations of two important battles that Marcus Aurelius won during his reign. The statue on top of this column, however, is St. Paul, while statue on Trajan's column is St. Peter. I want one of you to tell me about Marcus Aurelius before this week is over. Plus, I want to know what two battles are presented on that column and against whom they were fought." I paused, but nobody volunteered, so I continued my mini lecture. "John, this building on our right that you asked about is called Palazzo Chigi, and you're right—it is important. It's the headquarters of the Italian Prime Minister and his cabinet. Can somebody tell me who the Italian prime minister is?"

"Silvio Berlusconi," Jeremy pronounced the name rather well, even assuming a slight Italian accent. "He's all over the web. Seems like he's quite a character, and he chases after good-looking young ladies. Nothing wrong with that, I guess."

"Well, yes, he's quite a colorful individual, but he's done more for this country in his terms as prime minister than the forty years of destructive mismanagement of the center-left Socialist coalition. We can discuss this one day as well if you wish. This building to our left that we are passing now, Michelle, is called Palazzo Wedekind. I'm not sure who this Wedekind was—a rich banker, I believe. What I do know is that it is now the headquarters of one of the national newspapers, *Il Tempo*, or The Time."

We walked a bit farther and entered another very large square.

"This building to our right, Raymond, is called Palazzo Montecitorio, the Italian House of Parliament. That's why you're seeing so much security around it. Italy has 635 parliamentarians, believe it or not. A boatload for such a small country. This is where they meet. I'll show you the headquarters of the Italian Senate this afternoon."

It was nine thirty, and I kept remembering what Marco had told me about being on time for the tour guides. I was also thinking about Barbara and Vanessa and Marco's report about the pills, plus my telephone appointment with Baine & Courtney at later at four. It was going to be a very long day.

I picked up the pace a bit, but before getting to Via Aquiro, where we had to turn left, out came another question, this time from James:

"Is that another Egyptian obelisk, Atticus? These Romans must have had a thing with these Egyptians."

I saw that my astonishment that James had asked a question was mirrored by Cynthia and John.

"You're right, James," I replied. "The Romans were fascinated by Egyptian culture. This obelisk dates to at least to the fifth century BC. I can't tell you much more about it than that. *Maybe* you could do a little more research for us on it?"

He nodded. That was good enough for me.

We had gone down Via Aquiro, entered a small square, passed the umpteenth church, then made a right onto Via degli Orfani. This street's name literally translated into "Road of the Orphans." I had no idea why, unless there had been an orphanage located here in the distant past. As we walked, the heady aroma of brewed coffee wafted over to us. In the present day, the street of orphans was now famous for a coffee shop where you could sip some of the best espressos in Italy and taste a large array of blends. The smell was intoxicating, but the clock was ticking.

After zigzagging on small, history-drenched side streets, we finally entered Piazza della Rotonda—literally, the "square which is round," referring to the shape of the world-famous monument in front of us.

There it stood in all its majesty, as it had for the last nineteen hundred years—the Pantheon. Originating from the ancient Greek, this word translates into "the totality of the gods." This was the temple of all the gods—and what a temple it was! In the center of the square, in front of the Pantheon's grand entrance, stood a fountain with yet another obelisk in the middle. I looked over at James and pointed to the fountain. He raised his eyebrows in disbelief, smiling.

I began scouring the square for a man with an ASA identification card. I had read in Marco's notebook that his name was Angelo Simeone. We were about twelve minutes late, and I was hoping that he hadn't already deserted us. After a rapid glance of the eight enormous columns that hold up the triangular gable of the Pantheon's portico, I noticed a small, nondescript man holding something to his chest, but I couldn't tell what it was. I walked in his direction, asking the group to wait for me. Sure enough, this little man was holding a very little card with three small letters typed on the front: ASA.

"Good morning, are you Mr. Simeone?" He looked at me as if I had just landed from a distant universe.

"Yes, I am. Is the group ready?"

"Yes." I pointed to the students and waved them over.

"May I suggest that you make a bigger *ASA* sign next time? The one you have can only be seen with a microscope."

My attempt at humor failed. He just looked at his watch and said, "You are fifteen minutes late. Please, this way." With that, he turned, crossed the portico, and entered the Pantheon, everyone trotting behind him. I would have preferred to start the tour outside of the Pantheon so that the group grasp this extraordinarily well-preserved temple with their heart and mind.

Since the seventh century, under the papacy of Boniface IV, the Pantheon had been turned into a church called Santa Maria dei Martiri, or "Saint Mary and the Martyrs." Luckily, this did not bring about any irreparable changes to the building other than two small, unrelated bell towers that were placed on the sides of the portico in 1626. These were then torn down, fortunately, in the early nineteenth century.

The emperor Marcus Vipsanius Agrippa had originally built a temple here, rectangular it seems, in 27 BC. A tremendous fire in AD 80, however, destroyed just about everything in the Campus Martius, which in Latin means the "Field of Mars." This was an area of public land, about 1.2 square miles, that had initially been used for military training and therefore been named after Mars, the Roman god of war. Within the AD 100, many important buildings were constructed within this area, including the Baths of Agrippa, the Pantheon, the Temple of Neptune, and the Saepta Julia. This last building was used initially for the casting of votes by the assembly of Roman citizens but, shortly afterward, was turned into a theatre for cultural and sporting events. Scholars are of the opinion that the front portico of the Pantheon was one of the few structures left standing after this devastating fire. I had once read that it was the emperor Hadrian who had rebuilt the Pantheon as it is today. Recently, however, I learned that emperor Trajan and his architects may have had more to do with the actual design of the rebuilt temple after a second fire in the year AD 110. This seemed odd to me, given that this round structure was synonymous with the Greek architectural aesthetic, which Hadrian was fond of, more than the classic rectangular design of Roman architects. What seems certain is that what we observe today was built between AD 118 and 125. It was better to leave all the bickering about who did what and when to the historians and archaeologists. It suited me just fine to know that what I was beholding now was just about the exact same thing that every day Romans saw and probably took for granted so many centuries ago.

I stood for a moment in the center of the portico amidst sixteen enormous gray-granite, forty-three-feet-high columns, and gazed up at the vaulted ceiling. I was certain that the guide would tell the group a little something about this particular portion of the Pantheon upon exiting the building.

I entered the circular structure behind the group. There was only one opening in this fully enclosed area—a round twenty-six-foot aperture in the center of the domed ceiling, the single source of natural illumination. The rays of sunlight were streaming through this opening, striking the miniscule dust particles in the air. This had the effect of projecting a cone-shaped formation of tiny golden sparkles that ended in a larger circle of light on the opulent marble floor.

I started walking to my right, around this structure, which was 142 feet in diameter. A cloud formation must have shrouded the sun for a brief moment since it suddenly became dark. This was the magic of the place. There was a communion between Mother Earth, the heavens, and this structure. Apollo, the god of the sun and its light; Jupiter, the god of thunder, lightning, and the creator of clouds; Luna, the goddess of the moon and its eerie brilliance; Aquilo, Favonius, Auster, and Eurus, the gods of the four winds; and Aurora, the goddess of the dawn—all entered the Pantheon, making it part of their terrestrial residence. It was truly the home of all the gods, as its Greek name signified.

The genius behind the construction of the dome, one of the largest in the history of architecture, was the positioning of five circular bands of twenty-eight square recesses that got smaller in size as they reached the opening in the center. This allowed much less weight for the semisphere and so less thrust against the circular supporting walls. Truly an architectural stroke of genius! I was admiring this feat of engineering when I felt a few sudden taps on my shoulder. It was the tour guide, Angelo.

"*Abbiamo finito qui. Seguitemi per andare a* Piazza Navona."

Informing me rather rudely that he had finished what he had to say about the Pantheon and that we were to follow him to the Piazza Navona, Angelo turned and walked toward the exterior of the building without even looking back to see if we were following him. I looked at the students' faces, as well as John and Cynthia, and saw that everyone was looking put out.

"The guy's a jerk, Atticus!" Wayne, surprisingly, was the first to offer up his opinion.

"He wouldn't even let us ask questions!" Mary chimed in.

"He only spoke about how long, how wide, how thick everything was and the distance between the ceiling, the floor, the walls, the columns and everything in meters and centimeters," Sabrina complained.

"He kept saying that we were late. I guess we slowed you up a bit." It was Raymond, and he was almost apologetic.

"Is that a coffin, Atticus?" Wayne was pointing at Vittorio Emanuele II's tomb.

"What's that altar doing over there, Atticus?" Bishop said. "Is this a church?"

I didn't know what the guide had told the group these last twenty minutes, but obviously, there was a vacuum of pertinent and interesting information.

"Stay put." I went after the guide, who had already exited the building and was waiting by the fountain with the obelisk, his arms crossed in apparent disgust. I went up to him, and in a more serious tone than I usually adopted, I asked him what he did when he wasn't conducting tours.

"I am studying for what you Americans call a PhD in architectural engineering."

"Ah, I see. And how long have you been working with ASA?"

"I don't see what business it is of yours, but if you must know, almost a year, on and off."

I took a deep breath and let loose, "Well, Mr. Simeone, rest assured that this is the last group of visitors you shall be in charge of for ASA. You obviously don't have the slightest clue on how to conduct a tour, nor do you know what to say about the Pantheon or how to say it. It is obvious that you derive no pleasure in doing this job and that you probably only enjoy hearing yourself speak. If you think that escorting foreigners around this city is like preparing for an engineering exam, you are sorely mistaken. You may possibly know quite a bit about the technical specifications of this magnificent construction behind us, but you don't even know how to communicate this rather boring information that anybody could easily find in a textbook. Furthermore, you are totally unaware, purposely or not, of the magic this building encompasses, of the influence it has had on so many great people throughout the centuries. For Christ's sake, you don't even seem to know that Raffaello is buried in there! Now, buzz off and go back to your books on engineering. Good day!"

With that, I turned and went back to the group. I knew that I had taken a calculated risk by dismissing Mr. Simeone. ASA might not find it terribly amusing that its first-time chaperone had taken it upon himself to fire a guide. I needed to let Marco know as soon as possible.

CHAPTER 21

When I got back to the group, I apologized and told them what I had done, which got me an unexpected round of applause. I then took the group back inside the Pantheon and began telling them everything I knew about it.

There were seven niches, if I remembered correctly, alternately semicircular and rectangular as well as exquisite frescoes and statues to admire, but I particularly wanted the group to see the tomb of King Vittorio Emanuele II and his son, King Umberto I, who reigned from 1878 to until he was assassinated on July 29, 1900. Most of all, however, I wanted the students to see the tomb of Raffaello Sanzio, better known as Raphael, one of my favorite Italian Renaissance painters, who was so very prolific during his brief thirty-seven years on this earth.

"I don't know how many of you are knowledgeable of the painter and architect Raffaello." I did not receive any discernable reaction this time, not even from Cynthia or Michelle, who had previously surprised me when we had passed by the English cemetery on the way to the hotel. "His work is right up there with Michelangelo's and Leonardo da Vinci's. Google him when you get back to the hotel. I am bringing him up because here he lies." I pointed to an ancient sarcophagus under a low arch. "That's a bust of him to the left of the Madonna and child." I pointed to the statue of the *Madonna del Sasso*, or the *Madonna of the Rock*, that Raphael commissioned to one of his students, Lorenzetto Lotti, and which now stood above Raphael's sarcophagus. "To the right of the Madonna is the resting place of Maria Bibbiena, Raffaello's fiancée, who he never married. She was the niece of a powerful and rich cardinal who also commissioned many works to Raffaello."

"Why didn't he?" Darlene asked. "Seems like he could have married into a lot of money."

"Well, let's just say that there was another woman, Darlene, a baker's daughter, Margherita Luti, who, by some accounts, absolutely dominated Raffaello, if you catch my drift."

"You mean they had the hots for each other?" Wayne chimed in."

"Yup, you can say that again."

"Cool. We certainly didn't hear any of this from that dork tour guide." Mary added.

"What happened to Maria?" John asked. "Well, I really don't know, but other than not marrying Raffaello, she certainly could not have asked for a more illustrious burial site. Come on now, there are a few more things to see."

Approximately twenty minutes later, upon exiting, I asked everyone to look up at the portico ceiling.

"Doesn't it look incomplete as if something were missing?"

"Looks like someone ripped off the ceiling," Evelyn observed.

"You don't know how right you are, Evelyn. That's exactly what Pope Urban did in 1625. He stripped all the bronze paneling to make a large number of canons for the Castel Sant'Angelo, which we passed on our way to the Vatican yesterday. Do you remember the high altar in St. Peter's where those four twisted columns hold up the canopy?" Everyone nodded. I said, "Well, take a guess at what those four columns are made of?"

"You mean a pope stripped the Pantheon down to build an altar in a church?" asked Michelle.

"That's the story, Michelle. There's an old Latin saying that was coined by the Romans that goes *Quod non fecerunt Barbari, fecerunt Barberini*, which means, 'What the barbarians didn't do (to Rome), the Barberini family did.' But let's be clear. Pope Urban VIII, who was part of the Barberini dynasty, was the patron of many artists and architects in his time. Unfortunately, he also used the marble that covered the Colosseum to embellish many of the buildings he commissioned. Sadly, the Colosseum and other Roman temples were used as a rock quarry. Don't forget that before Emperor Constantine, Rome was pagan, not Christian. All these temples and palaces built to worship the gods were of no importance to Pope Urban. Therefore, he used all the materials he could get his hands on to build works of art that glorified the Christian God. Put yourselves in Pope Urban's shoes for a moment, and you can probably understand his point of view. It's all a matter of perspective."

The students seemed to be giving all this some thought until Raymond spoke up:

"That's nice, Atticus, but can we stop somewhere and get something to drink? It's hotter than hell out here."

"No problem." I looked around the square and saw that all the outdoor cafés and restaurants had their large umbrellas open.

"Go take advantage of the shade under those patio umbrellas and order something to drink or eat. Let's meet up again at twelve thirty right at that fountain, and then we'll head off to Piazza Navona."

This suggestion was enthusiastically accepted by the students since it meant they would be on their own for a bit. Only Cynthia and John remained with me.

"How about we get a nice cold beer?" I suggested.

"That's a very good idea, Atticus," John agreed.

"If it's okay with the two of you, I'm going to walk around a bit more and just absorb the history," Cynthia said.

I recognized her rapt expression from the previous day. I think she was making up for lost time and, even more, lost dreams.

"If you need anything, John and I will be sitting right over there." I pointed to the first cafe on the right-hand side of the square.

"Fine, see you a little later, then."

She walked away, but it was as though she drifted off.

John and I seated ourselves outside the Rotonda bar. I ordered two bottles of Peroni Chill Lemon, which was a beer with a refreshing citrus taste and just two percent alcohol. We just sat for a while observing the Pantheon. If that circular structure could speak, what would it say about all it had witnessed throughout the centuries? Would it praise the acts of man, or would it weep at man's stupidity? Probably more of the latter, I suspected.

"So, Atticus, what do you think about the trip so far?" John asked. "A bit different than managing a company, I presume."

"John, I told Cynthia yesterday that I didn't want to chaperone this group."

John looked at me with raised eyebrows.

"Marco, the guy you met at the airport, thought he was doing me a favor offering me this job. I thought it was going to be a waste of time. That's until we were all on the bus Sunday morning. Then something changed. Tell you what, ask me the same question in a week's time. Then I'll give you my answer." We clicked our glasses together.

There was a brief, content silence. This was the right time to get to know more about John. A stunning woman in high heels and a business tailleur (suit) displaying abundant cleavage passed directly in front of us. The sight of her gave me an idea.

John was peeling the clothes off this brunette stunner with his eyes. "I believe that a large percentage of the most beautiful women in the world live in Italy," he remarked.

I nodded. "Makes it difficult being married, at times. I'm divorced, so I have a few liberties. Are you married, John?" There was a lengthy pause before John answered.

"No, I'm not. I have a child, but I'm single." John's tone of voice made it clear that he would have preferred to get off the subject, but the sadist in me continued regardless:

"It's not easy being a single parent. Boy or girl?"

"A girl. But she doesn't live with me. I haven't seen her in years." John was now fidgeting with the sugar packets on the table, his jaw tightening. He cleared his throat and threw a question at me. "Do you have children, Atticus?"

"Two," I replied. "A nine-year-old boy and a thirteen-year-old girl. They live with their mother, and I don't get to see them as much I would like."

"Well, at least you get to see them. You know where they are, you know if they're sick, if they need something. You can follow their progress in school, take them to the park or to the movies." It was as if John were speaking to himself. I wasn't about to interrupt. "I presume you get to spend some time with them on their birthdays, Christmas, other holidays. You can discuss their dreams and hopes, share special moments. Do you understand where I'm going with this, Atticus? You could be in my situation." John stared hard at me. I suddenly had the urge to find a corner to sit there with my dunce cap on. In comparison with his situation, I was a lucky man.

"We're on a subject which strikes a nerve with me, Atticus. Sorry if I seemed to take you task."

"No apology required."

John grinned and patted me on the back. As he did so, a cell phone close to us began to ring. It took me a moment to realize that it was my phone. I reached in my back pocket, pulled it out, and looked at the display: I didn't recognize the number, but there was a *06* in the beginning of the number, Rome's area code.

"*Pronto*," I answered.

"Mr. Winterle? It's Ludovica from the hotel." I excused myself from John a moment and went into the bar.

"Yes, Ludovica. What is it?"

"Just one moment please, I shall connect you to Room 15." I waited a few seconds and heard a phone ringing. The pickup was immediate.

"Atticus?"

"Yes, Barbara, it's me. How's it going?"

"Some bad and some good." I could hear someone weeping in the background.

"Is that Vanessa crying?"

"Yes, she's been like this since she woke up. She wants to take more of that trash…"

I heard Vanessa start to snivel. "It isn't trash, goddamn it! I just need a couple Demerol, please!"

"Vanessa, do you want me to call your parents!? Do you want to get packed back to the States tomorrow? How about missing graduation!? And a police record before college!? We've been through this a thousand times already!"

Barbara was yelling at Vanessa, and I could tell that the situation was explosive.

"You're just a bitch, Mrs. Cornwall! You have no idea what I'm going through!"

I said, "Barbara, listen to me, you don't have to put up with this. Just blow the whistle, and we'll take her to the hospital. ASA and her parents will take care of the rest."

"I'm tempted, Atticus, really tempted, to call her parents right now and tell them that their sweet little angel is a pathetic little drug addict!"

Barbara was clearly saying this for Vanessa rather than me.

"No! No! Don't call them, please, please don't do that!!" Vanessa was panicking.

"Well then, pull yourself together!" Barbara said sternly.

As Vanessa continued sobbing, Barbara told me that on a positive note, she had eaten lunch and kept it down. She was also drinking a lot of tea and water and going to the bathroom. Barbara then whispered, "I still think we can pull her through. I'm going to keep trying. I have to go now."

The phone went dead. I walked back to the table thinking about how useless I was in this situation.

I couldn't leave the group, but at the same time, I wanted to get back to the hotel as soon as I could. I sat down trying to look at ease.

"What's up, Atticus? Nothing serious, I hope." Clearly, my poker face wasn't as good as I hoped. "No, no, not at all," I said. "Just some personal matters I need to straighten out." I looked up to see a slightly breathless Cynthia approaching our table.

"Oh, Atticus, it's just amazing! I went down this street." She pointed to her right to the Via Minerva that led to the Pantheon. "There's a church a little way down, very plain on the outside with an adorable statue of a small elephant with an obelisk on his back. I went inside and had to sit down to catch my breath. It's just so beautiful, and the ceiling…you feel as if you're looking at a starlit night sky. But get this, there's a statue by Michelangelo in there as well. I overheard a guide say it. Can you imagine? A *Michelangelo* statue just standing there, like one of those plaster of Paris statues we have in our parish church. It's just mind-boggling! And, Atticus, there's the cast of a body of a woman, I think, under the altar, but I didn't understand who it is. Do you know, by any chance?"

Cynthia had by this time sat down, and John had ordered her a bottle of cold water. I smiled to myself, remembering how, ten years ago when I had started living in Rome, I had gone on a group tour with two nuns as our guides. The church that Cynthia was speaking about was one of the first buildings we saw.

"It's called Santa Maria sopra Minerva, or 'Saint Mary above Minerva'—above the *temple* of Minerva, to be more exact. Minerva was the Roman goddess of wisdom, music, and poetry, amongst other things. This church was built on top of the remains of her temple, but I believe there are opposing views on this. The statue that you saw inside was, in fact, sculpted by Michelangelo. The body under the altar is that of Saint Catherine of Siena. She was born in the fourteenth century in a town called Siena, north of Rome, near Florence. She was proclaimed a saint under the papacy of Pope Pius II, but don't ask me when."

"Well, that's certainly more information than I'll remember, Atticus. Thank you."

I drank the last bit of my beer and looked over at the fountain where a group of boys and girls were having fun splashing themselves with water from the basin. Then I realized that it was *our* group of students doing the splashing.

"What time is it, John?"

"Oh my, it's twelve fifty." The three of us laughed at our lack of punctuality. I paid the waiter, and we walked over to the fountain.

Mark looked up, grinning. "Twenty minutes late, Mrs. Ramsey! What kind of example is that for us?"

"I'm your teacher, Mr. Hampton. I have privileges you don't."

With that, she punched Mark in the arm and smiled. The group was stunned, and Mark was dumbfounded. You could tell, however, that he was secretly pleased about this unexpected attention from Cynthia. She seemed to be softening up a bit.

"So what have you been up to this past hour?" I asked.

"Most of us sat at that bar over there, Atticus and had ice cream," Mary said. "It wasn't as good as what we had the other night, though."

"If it wasn't so good, why did you eat half of my banana split?" Mark said.

"I only ate the bananas you left behind, jerk." She gave him a shove.

"Any news about Vanessa, Atticus?" Sabrina asked hesitantly. "Is she getting over her stomach flu?"

"I haven't heard anything from Mrs. Cornwall yet. I don't want to call because Vanessa may be sleeping." *Liar, liar, pants on fire...*

"What's on the agenda now, Atticus?"

"The Piazza Navona Raymond. We're actually very close. First, I want to take you around the exterior of the Pantheon to see how well-preserved it is after nineteen centuries. It has resisted earthquakes, floods, civil wars, plundering by various armies—"

"As well as a few *popes*," Darlene interjected.

"Excellent observation, Darlene! Okay then, let's head this way, down Via Minerva. By the way, what does *Via* mean?"

"Street!" a number of voices yelled.

"Very good. Follow me, please."

As we headed down the crowded street, I showed the group the remains of temples built by Emperor Agrippa and the church that Cynthia was so taken with in Piazza Minerva. I explained to them that the statue of the small elephant in the middle of the square was designed by Gian Lorenzo Bernini, the same sculptor who had done so much work inside and outside of St. Peter's.

"Another obelisk, Atticus," James observed. This was the obelisk on the back of the elephant that Cynthia had seen. "I gotta check this out on the web."

"You do that, James, and give us that update." It was good to see that James was becoming actively interested in the history of Rome.

Some of the students broke away from the main group and went inside St. Mary above Minerva, even though I would have liked to move on because of the situation back at the hotel. When we were all back together again, we made a left onto Via della Palombella. Here we passed more ruins, this time of the Temple of Neptune, the god of the rivers and seas. Agrippa, when he was general of the Roman army, had won various important battles at sea and decided to give thanks to this god by constructing a place of worship in his honor. Via Palomebella veered gently to the left where we passed in front of an interesting church named San Eustachio, or Saint Eustace.

"Does anybody here know who Saint Eustace was?" Silence fell over the group. "Not to worry, I didn't have a clue until I entered this church many years back. He was a Roman soldier back in the AD second century. Legend has it that while on a hunting trip, he ran into a large male deer with huge antlers, and between the antlers, Eustace saw Christ on the Crucifix. Long story short, he converted to Christianity and was martyred along with his family sometime after. If you look at the top of this church, on top of the triangular gable, you'll see a stag's head with antlers in commemoration of the saint."

"How old is the church, Atticus?" Michelle inquired.

"Probably eighth or ninth century," I said, taking a wild guess.

"And we tend to get excited in the States over buildings that aren't even a hundred years old," John said, shaking his head. "What a difference from over here!"

"What's up with the spray paint in this city, Atticus?" Wayne asked. "Seems like everything that doesn't move is covered with it."

"That's a very good observation, Wayne, because it opens a large can of worms. For those of you who have seen, for example, the Liberty Bell in Philadelphia, the Statue of Liberty in New York, the Capitol building in Washington D.C., or the Tullie Smith house in Atlanta—"

"You know about the Tullie House, Atticus?" Evelyn cut across.

"I usually drove through the Atlanta on I-75 when I would go to Florida. I always tried to catch a few sights on these long road trips. The Tullie House was on my list."

"Did you know that it's haunted?" said Anthony.

Sabrina threw up her hands. "Get off it, Anthony, that's just a bunch of crap!"

"I've heard that old man Smith still walks around the place at night," Anthony replied. "I know someone who snuck in a few years back and saw Smith with a hatchet in his hand."

I noticed that Cynthia was looking at Anthony with a despairing expression.

"You're just not happy, Anthony, if you're not making up stupid stories twenty-four seven, are you?" Sabrina responded angrily. "You've been telling lies ever since you were born!"

I tried to ease the sudden tension. "Hey, hey, the Tullie House isn't the issue. Let me get back to what I was saying. My point is, you'll never see graffiti sprawl and trash around those buildings or monuments that I mentioned. Now just take a degree look around you here, right here where we're standing. What do you see? Spray-painted writing and drawings on the walls almost everywhere, pieces of old posters that have been glued to anything that doesn't move, which is against the law. Look at that writing on the first column of this church. Do you know how hard it is to clean off that paint without damaging the column underneath? Now, look at how the cars are parked and the motor scooters. Some are up on the curbs, on sidewalks. That scooter over there is leaning against that broken column that could be well over fifteen centuries old. The inhabitants of this city are living in an area that is unique to the world. I think that's clear to all of you by now. But they treat Rome as if they were living in the worst neighborhood of an American city."

"And why is that, Atticus?" Raymond asked.

"Well, I've heard all kinds of theories on that question, Raymond. Some blame it on the fact that Rome isn't a city but a museum so they can't 'live' it as they would a proper city. I find that a pitiful excuse. They're arguing that if Rome was more like Atlanta or Miami, there wouldn't be any issue with writing on the walls or throwing trash on the ground. Which is just ridiculous."

"Maybe it's the tourists who are dirtying up the place," Darlene suggested.

"That's another fairy tale I've heard many times from people living here, Darlene. But do you have an overwhelming desire to go and buy a can of spray paint and write something on the exterior of the Pantheon or this church in front of us or one of the many fountains we've seen these past few days? Do *any* of you?"

Darlene and the others shook their heads.

"The majority of the tourists that come to this city are like all of you—they are literally blown away by what it has to offer historically and artistically, and they come away from Rome respecting it, loving it. No, ladies and gentlemen, unfortunately, the damage done to this city center is by the hands of its inhabitants. That's the sad truth."

I stopped pontificating about this deplorable situation, which probably didn't greatly interest anyone. The students realized that I was worked up about this and remained silent. Personally, I had nothing but contempt for people who took it upon themselves to be "creative" by spray-painting their moronic messages and meaningless designs over monuments and buildings that had withstood centuries upon centuries of time, only to be corroded by pressurized paint. I had once suggested once to an Italian policeman friend of mine that after a first warning, the second time a person was caught spray-painting a building, the penalty should be having a finger amputated. He thought it a bit extreme. I didn't.

"Enough about all of this. Let's go this way." Up ahead, if I remembered correctly, before we got to the Corso del Rinascimento, there was an entertaining little fountain called the Fontanella dei Libri, or the Small Fountain of Books.

"Anybody still thirsty?" I inquired.

"Yes!" everyone responded immediately.

"Here's a very interesting fountain that you can drink from or fill your water bottles with."

"This water is really drinkable?" Mary looked a bit uncertain.

"One of the many wonderful aspects of this city, ladies and gentlemen, is that you can drink directly from just about any fountain you find in the center of Rome. Only if you see a sign which reads, *Acqua Non Potabile*, which means 'non-drinkable water,' do you need to avoid it."

The fountain was made up of four large stone books, two on each side of a stag's head, resting on two small tables, reminding us that we were in the district of Rome named after St. Eustace.

Wayne was puzzled. "What's the deal with the books, Atticus?"

I looked around. "Who has an answer to Wayne's question?"

Bishop took a wild guess. "Is there a bookstore or a library on the other side of this wall?"

"You're closer than you think, Bishop. What does a library make you think of?"

"Homework, unfortunately."

"And therefore?" I edged him on.

James cut in before Bishop could answer, "There's got to be a school of some sort on the other side of this wall."

"Bravo, James! Good for you. We are standing actually in a place that's renowned for its learning. Here, on the side of the fountain, we have the first university of Rome, and across the street, we have the Italian Senate. We saw the Chamber of

Deputies when we were in front of the Palazzo Montecitorio, remember? Let's go now to a little further on and turn to our left to take a look inside the university."

CHAPTER 22

We walked around the corner and surprisingly found the gates open. Once inside the rectangular courtyard, we were surrounded by a building with a two-level colonnaded portico and the Church of Saint Yves in front of us. A plexiglass panel at the entrance provided a brief history of the building in Italian, English, and German.

Pope Boniface VIII founded the university in 1303. It was called Studium Urbis, or "The city's place of study." The church was built in 1640. It remained the University of Rome all the way up until 1935, when a new university with the name La Sapienza was built on the east side of Rome with various faculties spread around the city. This building presently housed the National Archives.

"What's the oldest university in the States?" I asked. I myself did not know that answer.

"It's a fight between the University of Pennsylvania and Harvard," Michelle replied. "But it seems that Harvard is considered the first institution of higher learning in America, even by its rivals." She spoke rather diffidently, and I had a feeling that she didn't want to bring more attention to the fact that she was going to Harvard since her school had already made such a production about it. Other than being an accomplished young person, she was apparently also humble.

"Hey, Atticus, look on top of the church," said Evelyn. "Doesn't it look like a miniature Tower of Babel?"

I looked up. Evelyn was spot-on. I had no idea why the end of the church tower had this particular shape.

"You're right," I said. "How did you know?"

"Genesis, chapter eleven, verse four: 'And they said,'" "Come, let us make a city and a tower, the top whereof may reach to heaven; and let us make our name famous before we be scattered abroad into all the lands...'" and so on and so on. I guess I have to thank my warped dad for this."

An awkward silence fell over the group. It was the first time Evelyn had referred to her immediate family, and in public. James rushed in with a question:

"The Tower of Babel, Atticus. What does it make you think of?"

I was about to answer "Pieter Brueghel," the Flemish artist who in the sixteenth century had painted two variations of the Babel scene when I realized James was testing me. I said, "Track two of Elton John's *Captain Fantastic* album."

"When was the album released?" he challenged.

"1975."

"Was it his eighth, ninth, or tenth studio album?" James asked, smiling mischievously.

I was stumped.

"Don't know, do you?" James was getting a big kick out of this.

"No, I don't. But how do you know so much about Elton John? A bit before your time, isn't he?"

"Who says that an eighteen-year-old can't be interested in music from the past? I guess it's like a fifty-year-old who's interested in music from the present. Get my drift, Atticus?"

"Touché, James. You just scored a few points."

"By the way, it was his ninth album. But you passed by the skin of your teeth."

James raised his hand, and I immediately raised mine for him to high-five me. It was a gratifying moment.

"Fuckin' awesome," Jeremy said, loud enough for everyone to hear.

"Jeremy Nolan, please watch the language," Cynthia warned, but she was smiling.

"Let's move on. How do you say 'square' in Italian?"

"Pizza!" Mark yelled, getting a few laughs.

"Not pizza, Mark, piazza. You must still be hungry."

"Starving."

"Well, you'll find your heart's content of pizza and other food on the Piazza Navona."

We exited the building, turned right, crossed the Via dei Staderari and found ourselves in front of *Palazzo Madama*. There wasn't much to see other than the façade of this Renaissance building, which was first built in the late fifteenth century and completed in 1505. For nearly two hundred years, it belonged to the Medicis, probably one of the most influential Italian families, along with the Barberini. Other than having "produced" three popes and two queens of France, Catherine de' Medici and Marie de' Medici, the family did probably more than any other to promote banking, the arts, literature, and science. I gave the group a brief overview of the Medici family and its influence.

"The building you see was named after Margaret of Austria, who married into the Medici family. She enjoyed being called *Madama*, or 'Madam' in English, so she named this palace accordingly. Her husband was killed, and she married into another very important Italian family called the Farnese. You must understand that powerful and very rich families all over Europe were attempting to marry off their children to other influential families or, better yet, to royalty. If this wasn't possible, the sons were usually made archbishops or cardinals of the church or, best of all, the pope. The goal was always to obtain more authority and clout. Pope Paul III, for example, was from the Farnese family."

We were interrupted by the sound of a siren and an impressive motorcade that passed us and raced down the

Corso del Rinascimento. It may have been the prime minister Berlusconi leaving the senate from behind Palazzo Madama.

"Three hundred and fifteen members make up the Italian Senate, and this is where they meet. How many senators do we have in the United States?"

"One hundred, two for every State. A senator's term lasts six years," Raymond rattled this off quickly and precisely.

"Good. Now, doesn't it seem odd to you that a country with a surface area as big as the state of Arizona should have three times the number of senators and...Raymond, how many members in the U.S. House of Representatives?"

"Four hundred and thirty-five, plus five nonvoting members." Raymond knew his stuff.

"Therefore, almost two hundred more members in Italy's Chamber of Deputies than the United States House of Representatives. Incredible, isn't it?"

Raymond looked puzzled and asked, "What's Italy's population, Atticus?"

"Just under sixty million compared to over three hundred million in the U.S."

"Sounds like somebody's got their hand in the jelly bean jar, if you know what I mean," John said.

"You don't know how right you are, John," I replied. "Italian politics, that's a place where you *don't* want to go." We crossed the Corso del Rinascimento and headed down a very short street whose only purpose was to separate two buildings. As soon we were clear, we found ourselves in Piazza Navona.

It was obvious that the students were overwhelmed as we entered one of the most beautiful squares of any city in the entire world.

Originally this piazza, which is 902 feet long and 348 feet wide, was an equestrian stadium built by the emperor Domitian toward the end of the first century AD. The buildings and churches that now surround this long and rather narrow stadium were built on top of what we would call today the "bleachers" that surrounded this arena. How many chariot races, gladiators, ferocious animals, and martyred Christians had this space seen? How many gallons of blood had been spilled on these stones?

The main attractions of this piazza were its three fountains, with the most noteworthy at the center. There was another obelisk in the middle of this fountain, but it wasn't an original. Then there was the Church of Sant'Agnese in Agone by Borromini and the Villa Pamphilj that housed the Brazilian embassy since the early twentieth century.

The most important feature of the Piazza Navona, however, was its location as an always open center of live entertainment for citizens and visitors, twenty-four-hour days, seven days a week. This piazza hosted a nonstop festival of street artisans, magicians, fortune tellers, and circus acts. When I lived in Rome, there was always some form of entertainment taking place no matter what time of day or night I crossed the piazza. I always enjoyed the street artists, as well as the Christmas and Easter markets with their kaleidoscope of handcrafted, colorful items. Piazza Navona personified the spirit of this city.

I was especially pleased to see a long line of caricature painters set up with their easels between the Fountain of the Four Rivers in the center of the Piazza and the *Fontana del Nettuno,* or the Fountain of Neptune, to the north. This would be an enjoyable experience for the students.

"Let's go to the front of that church directly ahead of us, and I'll fill you in on a few pieces of information before cutting you loose," I told them.

We crossed the Piazza Navona and stood at the gated entrance of Sant'Agnese in Agone. I explained that the church had been built in the 1650s in commemoration of Saint Agnes, a thirteen-year-old girl who was martyred here during Emperor Diocletian's reign. The "in Agone" referred to the Greek words αγον ο, meaning a place of struggle or competition, which is what this arena had been. The skull of Saint Agnes was located in this church.

> *"She danced along with vague, regardless eyes*
> *Anxious her lips, her breathing quick and short:*
> *The hallowed hour was near at hand: she sighs*
> *Amid the timbrels, and the thronged resort*
> *Of whisperers in anger, or in sport..."*

Michelle recited these words with a clear and delicate voice that captivated everyone. She paused, and Cynthia picked up where she had left off:

> *"Mid looks of love, defiance, hate, and scorn,*
> *Hoodwinked with faery fancy; all amort,*
> *Save to St. Agnes and her lambs unshorn,*
> *And all the bliss to be before tomorrow morn."*

Cynthia looked at me and smiled. I clapped my hands and was joined by the others. "That was beautiful," I said. "But I must confess I don't know what it was."

"'The Eve of Saint Agnes,' a poem by John Keats," Michelle explained." He's buried in that cemetery near the pyramid. It's my favorite. That was the eighth verse."

"That was truly moving. Thank you, Michelle, Cynthia." I was in awe. This group was continually surprising me. After a few seconds, I continued to explain that Pope Innocent X came from another powerful Italian family—named the Pamphili—and that he wanted this church to be the chapel for the family palace next door, the Palazzo Pamphili. After discussing some of the aesthetic elements of the architect Borromini's design of the façade of the church, as well as the two fountains on either side of the piazza, we moved over to the center fountain, the Fountain of the Rivers.

"The four male statues you see on the fountain each represent an important river—remember, we're in the year 1651: The Nile in Africa, the Rio de la Plata in South America, the Danube in Europe, and the Ganges in Asia. Near the figure that represents the Ganges, you can see, at the bottom of the obelisk, the coat of arms of Innocent X who commissioned this work of art. Legend has it that Gian Lorenzo Bernini, who sculpted this fountain, placed the Rio de la Plata statue with his arm extended, and his hand opened in the direction of the church, as if horrified by the vision in front of him."

"It almost looks as if he's sickened by its presence," Cynthia said, studying the statue.

"In fact, it was well-known that Bernini and Borromini, the architect of Sant'Agnese, were archrivals. Even though the church was built several years after the fountain's completion, you really come away with a feeling that Bernini knew that Borromini was going to build something monumental across the way."

I looked at my watch. It was almost two.

"All right, everyone. Take some time now to visit this incredible place, get something to eat, then we'll meet back here at three o'clock. After that, we'll go back to the hotel, and you can then go off on your own. How does that sound?"

Everybody murmured their agreement to the plan.

"By the way, if you go down to the north end of this piazza, you'll enter a small street that leads into a square called Piazza Tor Sanguigna. When you get to the corner, you'll see how Rome is layered just like a chocolate cake, one stratum on top of another. Take a look."

I really wanted to head back to the hotel and see what was up with Barbara and Vanessa. I told everyone that I needed to go to the ASA office for some paperwork and that I would be back shortly.

As soon as everyone was out of sight, I began to run in the direction of the hotel. Although I was in good shape physically, after two days or not enough sleep and too much food, I was straining just to trot at a fast pace.

Luckily, I was able to shorten the distance from the Piazza Navona by taking a few small side streets. Even so, by the time I had reached the Trevi Fountain, I was covered in sweat. It was coming up on two twenty as I rounded the corner at the far end of the Piazza Trevi. The hotel was a stone's throw away.

I entered the lobby and saw Ludovica at the desk. "Things seem to be quiet in Room 15, Mr. Winterle," she said as she handed me my room key.

"Thank you, Ludovica, really, for everything."

"No problem at all, Mr. Winterle."

I walked up one floor, catching my breath and cooling down. By the time I reached in front of Vanessa's door, I was back to normal, though still perspiring. I knocked softly. I heard chair legs scraping and soft footsteps. The door opened. Barbara looked very surprised. She entered the hallway and closed the door gently behind her. She then turned and did something unexpected but very satisfying. She embraced me, looked me in the eyes, and gave me a warm peck on my lips.

"Mr. Winterle, how wonderful to see you again. Did you fall into a fountain on your way over here, or are you just excited to see me?"

"Both, Mrs. Cornwall. I think I need a shower."

"What a wonderful idea. I need one as well." Standing in the middle of the hallway *embraced* was not the best of ideas. We reluctantly let go of each other.

"So how are things now?" I asked.

"Much better. She's sleeping soundly, and her breathing is regular. After I hung up, we went at it for another fifteen minutes before she began to get hold of herself. When she settled down, a stream of information came out of her

314

mouth that I wasn't at all aware of. I really feel sorry for her. These kids, Atticus, they have such a burden to carry on their shoulders." She shook her head. "Promise me that tonight we'll have that wine together. I would like to share a few things with you, that is, if you don't mind."

"Not at all. I'm looking forward to it." I glanced nervously at my watch. It was already two thirty-five. "I need to run in a minute, Barbara. I've already managed to fire a tour guide this morning, and I don't want to be late with the group."

"Fired the tour guide? That sounds rather authoritative of you, Mr. Winterle."

"The guy was a total jerk."

"So you're the chaperone and guide today?"

"Yes, indeed. We're having a good time. Are you okay for food and drink?"

"Ludovica has been fantastic. We have all we need."

"Okay, good to hear. By the way, I'm cutting the group loose at about four o'clock. I don't know who will be coming back to the hotel and who'll be taking a walk. I think the boys want to come and see how she is and, if I'm not mistaken, sing her a *song?*"

Barbara let out a small laugh.

"That must be Wayne's idea. I'll explain tonight. I'm going to stay with Vanessa until Sabrina gets back. She may be well enough tonight to come down for a bite at dinner. Any news from your friend, Marco?"

"Not yet, but he's bound to call."

"She practically told me everything that was in that Tylenol jar, so I don't think I'll be surprised, but you may be. You better get going now."

She gave me a wink, kissed, and hugged me again, and was about to go back inside the room when I took her arm.

"Angie Dickinson."

"Excuse me, Atticus?"

"Angie Dickinson, that's who you remind me of. Remember the show *Police Woman?* It was on the air in the mid-seventies. Boy, did I ever have a crush on her from the first episode."

"I do remember that show. Pepper was her name, and she played the part of a detective. I shall take that as a compliment, Atticus. She was a very attractive woman."

"She most certainly was. And so are you."

We kissed again quickly before she closed the door.

I went up one more flight of stairs to my room. As soon as I entered, I went to the bathroom and washed up the best I could. I couldn't change shirts since this would have raised some eyebrows. I opened up the mini bar and downed a small bottle of mineral water. There wasn't any more time to lose. I needed to walk back to Piazza Navona and try to look as dry as possible. I combed my hair, slapped some Acqua di Parma cologne, and left the room. As I walked down the two flights of stairs, my phone rang. I saw Marco's cell phone number shining on the small screen.

"Ciao, you must have ESP. We were just talking about you."

"Ciao, Atticus. Let me get straight to the point." He was as serious as I had ever heard him. "Your young lady there has quite a cocktail of pills in her possession. Even my pharmacist brother-in-law was shocked. You've got a piece of paper and something to write with?" I arrived in the lobby and went to the front desk. I asked Ludovica if she could give me some paper and a pen.

"Shoot, I'm ready."

"The *appetizer* is a series of amphetamines including Ritalin, twenty-milligram doses; Dexedrine, 15-milligram doses; Vyvanse; and Adderall. This is what was making her fly high. To come down, she was on a first course of Valium, Halcion with Xanax, and Percocet as dessert. These are all prescription drugs, Atticus, to be handled carefully. Too much mixing, and you risk heart failure. What in God's name is this girl doing with all this *merda?*" Marco's use of the Italian word for "shit" on this occasion was more than appropriate.

"I wish I knew. All I can say now is, thank you. One of the teachers has been with her all day in her room, and it's been tough. We think that we've gotten over the worst of it, though. She's flushed her system, and we're keeping our fingers crossed."

"This is serious, Atticus. I believe you are aware of that. Something goes wrong here, and we will all be in a great deal of trouble."

"Yes, Marco, I read you loud and clear."

"Let me know if I can be of any more assistance. By the way, try not to fire anybody else over the next few days."

For a second, I didn't understand what he was talking about, then I chuckled. "Sorry, Marco. I should have informed you earlier. But take my word for it, the guy has no business being a tour guide. The entire group will vouch for me."

"You actually did ASA a favor, Atticus. They were trying to find a delicate way to eliminate him from the roster of guides, and now you've resolved the problem. You'll find a form tomorrow morning at the front desk to fill out describing what happened. If you could have the teachers sign it as well, it would assist ASA greatly."

"Will do. Thanks once again for all your help. I'll need to offer you something stronger than an espresso next time we see each other."

"I'm looking forward to it. Ciao, Atticus." The line went dead.

It was 2:52 pm. I had eight minutes to get back to the group. I took the same route I had taken to get to the hotel. I was moving at a good pace now that I was warmed up and a refreshing breeze was making my jog back much easier. When I arrived on the south side of the Piazza Navona, I slowed down, tucked my shirt in, and attempted to neaten my hair. I then walked back to the Fountain of the Four Rivers and sat on a granite bench. It was 3:05 pm, and nobody was there yet. Good. This time, they were late.

CHAPTER 23

I looked from one end of the piazza to the other. The three gushing fountains glimmered in the afternoon sun. The restaurants with their outdoor sun umbrellas were filled with customers. Some were eating, some were having a chilled bottle of white wine, and others were just sipping an espresso as they leafed through the newspaper. I observed an elderly couple at a corner table, either German or Swiss, since the man was wearing ornate suspenders, and they both had matching brown leather sandals. They were holding hands, smiling at each other, and every once and a while toasting with their wineglasses. For all I knew, they could have met yesterday, but I enjoyed imagining that they had married young, had gone through the roller-coaster ride of life with its ups and downs, side by side as inseparable companions, and now they were topping it all off with a good bottle of wine under a beautiful summer sun in one of the most romantic places in the world. Would I be so lucky one day?

"Hey, Atticus, mind if I sit down?" I turned to see Raymond standing behind me.

"Have a seat. See anything that interested you?"

"A group of us went to the far end over there." Raymond pointed to the northern end of the piazza. "We had some pizza and then just looked around."

"Was Michelle with you?" I ventured.

Raymond nodded, blushing a bit. I had seen Raymond admiring Michelle on more than one occasion. I wanted to stick my nose in something that wasn't my business.

"If I may ask, Raymond, have you ever asked Michelle out on a date?" Raymond's eyes opened so wide I almost feared they would fall out of his head.

"What? A date? Well…no, not really. Why would you ask me that, Atticus?"

"Because I think you like her more than as a friend."

Raymond got up and started to pace. Why is it that people start walking back and forth when they're nervous?

"Well, yeah. I've always liked Michelle. But I don't think she likes me like that. She's always real nice to me, but I think it stops there."

"Hey, Atticus!"

I looked up. It was Mark. The Michelle discussion would stop here for now. Suddenly, it started to rain. I was immediately soaked.

But how was that possible? The sun was shining! Then the uproarious laughter made me realize that I had just been targeted by the water brigade. I turned slowly and saw the entire group, including Cynthia and John, doubled over. Darlene, Sabrina, Mary, Wayne, and Bishop were holding empty water bottles in their hands. This was war! I got up and began running after the culprits. My intention was to grab one of them and get close enough to the fountain to splash him or her as they had done me. As soon as Darlene saw me coming, she slowed down, probably waiting for me to grab her. I was tempted to but thought it highly unwise. I darted off in the direction of Mary and caught up with her instead. I picked her up and hauled her over to the fountain kicking and screaming. At that point, everyone began splashing everybody else. Darlene looked disappointed.

"Well, that was certainly unexpected!" I said, catching my breath. I was absolutely drenched. "And thanks, Mark, for distracting me like that. I guess you were the bait."

"Well, someone had to do it. You should have seen your face!"

"At least we're all cooled off now," said Cynthia, still grinning.

In fact, everyone was laughing or smiling. I felt as if we were beginning to build a real team here. I just needed to get Vanessa back in the group now.

"So what did all of you do besides plan this terrorist attack?" I asked.

"Some of us had our caricatures done." Mark walked over to John who had a thick roll of paper safely tucked in the back of his backpack. He began unraveling the A3 sheets on a stone bench. They were done quite well.

"They wanted twenty-five euros, but we got them down to twenty. How's that for bargaining?" Bishop seemed proud. I gave him a thumbs-up. I didn't tell him that he could have easily negotiated down to ten.

"We went down to the end of the piazza, Atticus, as you suggested, and saw part of the old arena that was under a three-story building," said Michelle. She indicated Cynthia, Raymond, Anthony, and Mary. "They left an opening on the side so that you can see it."

Raymond was staring at Michelle, smiling idiotically, and you could tell he was hooked. I was happy for him. He couldn't have picked a better girl. I was wondering if Mary had taken a liking to Anthony, who seemed to have alienated everybody before and during this trip, since she had teamed up to go along with him. It would have been better had Cynthia not joined them, I thought. This boy needed some breathing room and support from his peers, not from an overbearing teacher. The group had been hard on Anthony these last few days, but this was understandable. Whenever Anthony opened his mouth, the most bizarre remarks came tumbling out. Hopefully, Cynthia would shed some objective light on this individual one of these days.

"Did all of you get something to eat?" I asked.

"Pizza, Atticus," Jeremy answered. "Lots of pizza in big rectangular slices. Really good stuff." He seemed particularly satisfied.

"Good. I'm going to show all of you one more place you may want to explore. Then you'll be on your own until dinnertime. This way."

We walked south, passed the third fountain of the Piazza Navona, and made a left down a short, narrow side street. We then turned right and passed directly in front of the Church of Sant'Pietro della Valle, which we had seen on the way to the Vatican the day before. The first response I got when I told the group the name of this late baroque masterpiece had me stunned.

"Is this where the first act of *Tosca* by Giacomo Puccini takes place?" asked Mary.

Everyone watched her in puzzlement. I looked at her in awe and said, "Quite correct, Mary. This is the church where Puccini set the stage for Angelotti, Cavadarossi, and Tosca to meet."

Now everyone was looking at me as if I were speaking Cantonese.

"How do you know about these operas?" I asked.

"My parents are opera freaks," she explained. "I've heard them all over and over again since I was born: *Tosca, Madame Butterfly, Othello, The Barber of Seville, Turandot, La Bohème, La Traviata, Tannhäuser…*Shall I go on?"

"No, I'm impressed enough as it is."

We had safely crossed the busy intersection and were standing in front of the church. Strangely enough, it was open.

"Go inside and take a peek at the dome. It's the third highest in Rome, after St. Peter's and another church outside the city center."

Everybody walked in. I stayed outside, lost in thought. I had only become interested in opera when I was in my late thirties, and I hardly knew anyone my age who had any particular liking for this art form. Yet here was Mary Esposito, barely eighteen years old, who not only knew *Tosca* but was also aware that the first act took place in this church that she had never seen before. Mind-boggling.

Approximately ten minutes went by before everyone was back outside.

"There's some serious artwork on that dome," Jeremy remarked, "but it's so high you can't make anything out."

Jeremy was spot-on. Giovanni Lanfranco painted this magnificent fresco in the middle of the seventeenth century, depicting angels, heavenly vistas, and the souls of those who had arrived in Paradise. The problem was that the dome was so high that the fresco might as well have been in Heaven.

When everyone had regrouped, I led them to the right, following the exterior wall of the church until we came upon a statue that I wanted the group to see: *l'Abate Luigi.*

"You remember, ladies and gentlemen, that when we were back at the Pantheon looking at the portico ceiling, we discussed how some popes stripped the old Roman ruins for materials in order to construct other monuments?"

Everyone nodded.

"Well, if someone was overheard criticizing the pope or other influential figures in the fifteenth or sixteenth century, they would have been imprisoned or even executed."

"What?" Mark exclaimed. "Executed for *criticizing* someone? Whatever happened to freedom of speech?" Mark protested.

"Things were very different back then."

"Come on, Mark," Raymond interjected. "There are places in the world even today where criticizing the regime can get you thrown in jail, tortured, or hanged—Burma, Iran, North Korea, Cuba, to name a few."

"Very true," I said. "I think we Americans sometimes forget how lucky we are to live in a country where we can express ourselves in speech without restrictions, even though we abuse this privilege at times, in my opinion. We must make sure that it stays that way. Never let anyone trample on your First Amendment rights. Anyhow, getting back to our statue friend here, to avoid being caught, the citizens of Rome would write their criticisms and complaints on wooden boards and hang them around the neck of this statue and five others around Rome. I guess you could say that these statues were the precursor to the modern-day blog."

"Nice!" Jeremy said. "Do these statues have a name?"

"Yes, indeed. This statue's name is Abbate Luigi, or Abbot Luigi. Legend has it that it was named after a priest from a nearby church, but nobody knows who the statue represents. Supposedly, this priest looked a lot like our friend here. By the way, the head has been stolen several times. The one you see here is a copy of the original. More than likely, we shall see the most famous of these "speaking statues" before you head back to Atlanta."

I looked at my watch. It was almost 4:10 pm. The phone call from Baines & Courtney was bound to come any moment now if they hadn't called already. My phone was turned off, and in any case, I certainly wasn't prepared to handle a telephone interview in this moment.

"I promised all of you that I would give you some time on your own. If you go this way"—I pointed to my left—"you'll run into another piazza called Campo dei Fiori. They used to hold public executions there." This got a rise out of the boys. "If you go in the other direction, you'll go along some interesting little streets and end up at that large white monument dedicated to Vittorio Emanuele. Try to stay in small groups, please, and be back by seven fifteen so you can wash up before dinner. Do you still have those matchbooks that I gave you the other night with the address and phone number of the hotel?" Some of the students said yes, but others no longer had them.

"Okay then, take out your cell phones and write this address and phone number down," I instructed and dictated the information so everyone had it registered.

Cynthia was looking discomfited. "Are you sure about this, Atticus?" she asked. "We haven't been in this part of town before."

"We all have access to Google Maps, Mrs. Ramsey," Wayne cut in before I could reply. "We won't get lost. We're big boys and girls now."

"Big in body but, I fear, small in good sense," Cynthia came right back at Wayne with a weary look on her face.

"You've been schooled, my man!" Mark said, slapping Wayne on the back.

"Mr. Hampton, I include you first of all in this category," Cynthia added, drawing more laughter."

John chimed in, "Be careful crossing the roads and watch your belongings, please."

"And please be back at the hotel in time for dinner," Cynthia chirped in at the end.

They all walked off together, but I could tell that soon they would split up into their own little batches.

"Cynthia and I are going to stay behind them as much as we can," John said. "What are you going to do, Atticus?"

"Same with me, John. I'll keep track of some of them. I just need to make a call to ASA for some paperwork I need to fill out."

I had to turn my phone back on fast now that there was a break in the tour.

"Okay then, if we lose you, we'll meet up in the lobby," Cynthia added.

"Great, see you there."

They all began heading off in the direction we had come in that morning. Curiously, I was almost despondent to see them go off without me. How foolish.

I promptly turned on my phone, hoping that I hadn't missed any calls. But as the phone activated, a series of beeps sounded, the message showing I had lost one incoming call. Damn it! The number was listed as private, so I couldn't call back. It was now close to four thirty, and I began to worry that Baines & Courtney was the kind of executive search firm that took offense to missed appointments.

I began walking after the group, wondering once again about what the future had in store for me when the phone began ringing. Two words were flashing on the phone: "private number." This had to be Baines & Courtney calling back. *Okay, calm now, composure is of the essence*, I thought. *Make up a good one, Atticus, as to why you didn't answer before.* I pressed "answer."

"Pronto!" I said, full of energy like the very busy man I was.

"Pronto, Signor Winterle?" The voice on the other end of the line was velvety smooth and professional.

"Yes, speaking."

"This is Baine & Courtney calling. Hold the line please while I switch you over to Ms. Silvestri. Thank you." There was a hardly perceptible clicking sound, and after just a few seconds, another voice was on the line:

"Pronto, Signor Winterle?"

"*Si, sono io,*" I acknowledged once again that it was me.

"Hello, Mr. Winterle, this is Dottoressa Silvestri. Is this a good time for you?"

Her introducing herself as Dottoressa informed me that she was a college graduate. *Dottore*, or *Dottoressa* for a woman, means "doctor" in English as well as in Italian, but it also serves to communicate that you have at least obtained a bachelor's degree. I remembered how confusing it was for me when I first arrived in Italy. I was of the impression that more than half of the Italian population had graduated in medicine.

"The time could not be better, Dottoressa Silvestri. I must apologize for not having been available at the specified hour. I was still under the dentist's weapons of mass destruction at four."

This got me a chuckle, which relieved my concern about missing the first call.

"No problem at all, Mr. Winterle. I hope that it is nothing terribly painful."

"No, just a good cleaning and some poking and probing. I'm fine now." Lying was not only terribly convenient at times but also terribly hazardous.

"Well, then, let me start by explaining to you the reason for my email and this telephone call."

Ms. Silvestri was handling an international company with its headquarters in the Liguria region of Italy. They were in the luxury business, and their products ranged in price from €700,000 to €14 million. She couldn't tell me the client's name, but I had a strong feeling that we were speaking about luxury yachts. I was even more certain when she told me that there would be frequent travel around the world for trade fair purposes. She went on to tell me that the company in question had been in its line of business for the last forty-five years and had been profitable up until four years ago. It was an Italian blue-chip firm, but stock prices had been in decline for the past two years, given shareholders' unhappiness with the bottom line.

"The company has had trouble retaining specialized personnel, and the overall quality of the product has come under scrutiny," Ms. Silvestri explained. "Customer complaints have risen, and there is a lack of proper after-sales support, which is vital for a premium brand such as this one. All of this is worrisome, considering the average sales price. Furthermore, there was a large exposure to currency movements, and the earnings forecast for fiscal 2010 and 2011 are grim. In other words, there is a strong need for a company rehash."

"I understand," I said.

"So, you see, Mr. Winterle, we are looking for a strong personality with at least twenty years' experience who can put this company back to the forefront. The products are extravagant and luxurious, the company is known for its high quality, and they have a strong retail base in Hong Kong, Fort Lauderdale, Dubai, the south of France, and Cyprus." Fort Lauderdale? It had to be luxury yachts.

Mrs. Silvestri then began asking about my background. She obviously had my resumé in front of her since her questions were about my professional track record from 1984. As we spoke, I was walking back and forth along the Via degli Orfani in front of the coffee bar that we had passed on our way to the Pantheon. I was going to treat myself to a double espresso with a touch of whipped cream after the call. We spoke for about twenty minutes again before winding up.

"Well, Mr. Winterle, I seem to have all the information I need. At this point, I would propose that I submit your candidature to our client. Is this all right with you?"

"That's fine."

"Good. I have two other candidates that I shall be presenting along with you. My deadline is the end of next week. After the presentation, I believe that a decision shall be made on my client's behalf by the beginning of July. They would like to have their man on board before the summer holidays."

This meant before mid-August. I wondered if the terminology "on board" was a Freudian slip on her part. We ended the conversation with a promise to keep in touch. She promised to update me on any relevant news in the meantime.

I went into the coffee shop and had my espresso. It tasted even better than I had expected. That touch of freshly whipped cream gently spooned on the inside of the cup's rim made all the difference in the world.

I was jubilant over the prospect of a new challenge. What Ms. Silvestro had told me about the company in question did not bother me too much, given that I had been thrown into reengineering projects in the past. My only real concern, if I got the job, was the declining quality and servicing of the product. After-sales service was such a fundamental part of any product-based company, yet I had been continually flabbergasted over the years by just how little was budgeted for this in the organizations I had worked for. "Produce it, price it, promote it, sell it, and who cares about the rest" was the attitude of most companies. But brand damage caused by poor after-sales service can spread like wildfire, especially given the high-net-worth clientele that this company dealt with. This was going to be my main challenge if I was hired for the position.

However, I presently needed to address my immediate challenges and check on Vanessa and Barbara. I would relieve Barbara from her watch when returning to the hotel. Her day had certainly been a long one.

I paid for my coffee, drank some water, and was back on the street. When I arrived at the Via del Corso, I turned left and then almost immediately to my right onto Via Marco Minghetti, named after an Italian prime minister of the late nineteenth century. This street would lead me to another called Via dei Vergini, or "Street of the Virgins," which had the double advantage of being close to the hotel and hopefully still had what might be described as a boutique for smokers at the intersection with Via dell'Umiltà. I was looking for a particular Dupont cigarette lighter, gold-plated with a diamond point finish.

I found the shop, but strangely, it was closed. Shops in Rome often closed for lunch between one and three, but it was now nearly five o'clock. Well, at least the boutique was still in business.

When I arrived at the hotel, not a soul was in the lobby. It was comforting to see, however, that Ludovica was still at the front desk manning the ship.

"Good afternoon, Signor Winterle," she said.

"Good afternoon, Ludovica. How are *things?*" She understood my meaning at once.

"Everything has been very quiet since your visit earlier this afternoon. I had some more tea and soft drinks sent up to the room about fifteen minutes ago."

"Mrs. Cornwall informed me how helpful you have been. I can't tell you how much I appreciate it."

She blushed a bit and went back to what she was doing.

I retrieved my room key that she had placed on the desk, then headed directly to Vanessa's room.

When I knocked on the door, I got a rather cheerful "Come in!" I opened the door and was surprised to see Barbara and Vanessa playing backgammon.

"Hello, Atticus, all back from the tour?" said Barbara.

Vanessa said nothing, gazing at the backgammon board as though she were in a championship final.

"Yes, I'm back. The others are still out with John and Cynthia." I was speaking to Barbara but staring hard at Vanessa. She still didn't look up or say anything. I let the silence stretch out uncomfortably. Finally, Vanessa raised her head.

"Hello, Miss Guy," I said, speaking in my sternest tone. "It's good to see that you are sitting up, drinking tea, and still breathing. I presume that this is much better than being in the intensive care unit of a Roman hospital or lying on a cold slab in the city morgue. Or would you have preferred that?" Tears started rolling down her cheeks, splashing onto the game board. I ignored this. "I need to ask you a question before I decide to blow the whistle on you or not." I was dead serious. She looked at Barbara, who said nothing, then back at me.

"This is my question," I continued remorselessly. "If Mrs. Cornwall and I were to leave this room right now for ten minutes and that Tylenol jar was still in the bathroom filled with that vast assortment of junk, would you rush in and swallow a few? Answer me truthfully. Lying will only make things worse for you."

She just stared at me with a frightened expression on her face. She then took a deep breath, her shoulders shuddering as if suddenly experiencing a violent chill.

"Three hours ago, I would have said yes. Now, with Mrs. Cornwall's help, I think I can say no. But I'm not going to lie and say that the urge isn't still there."

I gave her points for admitting to not being out of the woods yet. I dropped my Darth Vader voice. "Very well, Miss Guy, I appreciate your honesty. That answer gives you some breathing room. For now—and let me emphasize, for *now*—I have no intention of informing anybody about this, including your parents."

Relief crossed her face.

"Are you hungry, thirsty?" I asked. "How do you feel now?"

"I go from hot to cold, from shaking like a leaf to feeling pretty well."

"Are you nauseated?"

"No, I've kept down everything that I've eaten, for now."

"Well, I'm not a doctor, but you're probably experiencing withdrawal symptoms. I don't know how long they'll last or if they'll get worse. Time will tell."

"Mrs. Cornwall told me that Sabrina knows what I did. Does anybody else know?"

I looked at her with a little more sympathy.

"No, just the two of us and Sabrina. Everybody else thinks you just have a bad stomach flu."

"Good," Vanessa murmured.

"I think that it's for the best if you stay in your room tonight for dinner," Barbara suggested. "We'll ask Sabrina to keep you company."

"Yeah, that's a good idea Mrs. Cornwall. I wouldn't want to get into one of those fits down there in front of everyone."

I looked at Barbara and asked, "Did you tell Vanessa that the boys wanted to check in on her and sing her a get-well song?" Barbara's and Vanessa's eyes opened wide, and they began to laugh.

"I think we owe you an explanation, Atticus," Barbara responded, putting her hand on my shoulder. "Vanessa? You want to fill him in?"

"This is all about Wayne, the jerk. He knows that I love the movie *Three Men and a Baby*. He's also convinced that I look just like the mother of the baby in the movie. He's so weird."

This was all new to me, given that I wasn't acquainted with the movie.

"And she does, Atticus," Barbara said. "I don't know the actress's name, but they're the spitting image of each other."

"At the last school dance, Wayne, Bishop, Mark, and Jeremy got up on stage with nothing but white shorts and head bonnets, and they sang one of the theme songs of the movie, 'Goodnight Sweetheart Goodnight.' It was *sooo* embarrassing!"

"Well, get ready, I think you're in for round two as soon as they get back. Remember you're getting over a nasty stomach flu—nothing else."

I looked at my watch. It was getting close to six forty-five, not even an hour before dinner.

"Barbara, I'm sure you would like to get back to your room, finally."

"For sure. I need a long hot shower and a fresh change of clothes."

Vanessa looked at her. "Mrs. Cornwall, I don't know what to say except thanks. Thanks a lot for what you did and what you had to put up with today."

Vanessa leaned over and let herself be hugged by Barbara.

"Vanessa, can we leave you alone until Sabrina gets back?" I asked, watching her intently.

"I'll be fine, Atticus."

"Okay then, we're going back to our rooms. I'll make sure that dinner is brought up for the two of you around seven forty-five."

I put my hands on her shoulders, and she looked at me with her swollen eyes.

"I'm really sorry. I screwed up, big time. It's just that I've been going through some rough stuff lately."

"You're more than halfway to solving the problem, Vanessa, by admitting that you made a mistake. I'm proud of you."

She gave me a weak smile.

Barbara and I got up, asked Vanessa to give us a call as soon as Sabrina arrived, and left the room.

Once out in the hallway, Barbara took my hand. "Glad to see you again, Mr. Winterle," she said.

"I hope you haven't changed your mind about that wine tonight."

"I'm counting the minutes." We arrived at the end of the hall and stopped a moment at the landing.

"Did we do the right thing leaving Vanessa alone?" I said. "Marco called me right after I left the room this afternoon. The concoction of pills in that jar is what we thought it was. Uppers and downers of the most dangerous kind, if taken like M&Ms." I listed what Marco's brother-in-law had found.

"My, my, the complete spectrum." Barbara was silent for a moment. "I think that she'll be fine, eventually if not right now. After a couple bouts of hysterics, she opened up to me. I think she talked her way out of swallowing any more of that junk. That's my impression, at least."

"You were really something to have gone through what you did today. I don't think that many other teachers would have put up with it."

"She's just a messed up, confused kid, Atticus, thanks to her parents. Maybe what we did last night and today and giving her a second chance can help her get back on track." Barbara paused a moment.

"Everything all right?" I asked.

"Oh yes, I'm just in desperate need of a bath. We'll see each other at dinner." She blew me a kiss and went into her room. I went up one more flight of stairs and was only too happy to take a shower myself. I smelled like a goat. I stripped down to my nothings, let the hot water run until the bathroom looked like a Turkish sauna, and went under the stream. How many movies over the years had shown the protagonists standing in the shower, their heads bent down to let the water run down their backs while deep in meditation? Well, there I was, rehearsing for that next shower scene.

The one thought that was doing laps around my brain was this group of people. Only three days had passed, yet I had become more involved, at various stages, in the lives of sixteen individuals who, under normal circumstances, I would never have met. And thirteen of them were high school students, an age group that I had previously held in low esteem. But here I was, deeply concerned about these adolescents and their three teachers. I was worried about Vanessa, Wayne, Bishop, James, Darlene, Evelyn, and the others. I felt pity for Cynthia and empathy for John. And then there was Barbara, who I was hoping to take to bed soon.

All in three days. What would the next six bring?

CHAPTER 24

Flash Back

The two individuals knew exactly where they were going, and the pitch-black darkness only aided them in their goal. The sky above was filled with murky, rain-threatening clouds, and the moon was hidden. Perfect conditions for a break-in.

Moreover, the targeted residence had all the blinds down and the curtains drawn on the first floor, which greatly facilitated the duo's secretive movements. There was only a perimeter of dim light glowing around the large window frames on the right side of the house. A rhythmic thumping of music combined with intermittent peaks of muffled laughter confirmed that people were inside. Maybe a party was going on?

Very good.

This would allow for a close encounter with those inside before the targets could even realize what was happening. So far, everything was proceeding even better than planned.

They had made their way to the back of the house and down seven concrete steps that led to the basement door. Once there, the younger of the two inadvertently let the large duffle bag on his shoulder slide off, hitting the ground with a noticeable thud.

"Careful, Steve," the older one hissed. "Do you want to ruin everything? That stuff is fragile!"

"Sorry, Joe…it slipped off." Steve did not like being treated like a fool, especially by his older brother. "Hey, you think they set the alarm?"

"I don't know, but it's kind of strange that the curtains are all shut."

"Couldn't have happened on a better night. I'm going to open the door now and trip the alarm if it's on."

"Do you have the code?"

Joe rolled his eyes at the foolish question, but just answered, "Yeah." It had been child's play to get a copy of the key as well as the alarm code.

The residents had decided to renovate the washroom area, to which this particular door gave access, just the week before. The day the new door was installed, the carpenter had left a small, transparent ziplock baggy on his toolbox containing two extra keys. All they had to do was take one of them.

But even better luck was on the side of the two young men. Inside that little ziplock bag, there was a small piece of paper folded in two. Lo and behold, a six-figure number was written on it. This could have meant anything except for the fact that someone had written "alarm" next to it. Obviously, the homeowners had total trust in the handyman.

Joe proceeded to slowly insert the key into the lock and then gently turned it to the right. Click. The door opened. Both young men entered the room quickly and shut the door behind them. A flashlight went on, and the perpetrators immediately located the alarm box, and Joe quickly entered the code. The only problem was whether the residents had changed the code in the past seven days. But as the last digit was punched in, the red LED stopped blinking. The alarm was off.

The rest would be easy. Steve unzipped the duffle bag, and Joe carefully took out the tools and the lighter. Steve then lifted out a large box.

There was no difficulty in getting to the stairs that led to the ground floor. A Waterford table lamp was on in the den, giving off a soft glow.

The door at the top of the stairs was open, and the music was still playing loudly. They heard laughter and inarticulate noises. At the top of the stairs, the box was silently opened, and the contents were removed. The lighter was flicked, and the tiny woven strips of cord were lit.

Showtime!

The young men burst into the living room.

***

I turned off the water, stepped out of the shower, and reached for the towel above the bidet. I wrapped it around me and was brushing my teeth when I heard my cell phone ring and saw Francesca's name flashing on the screen. I really hadn't thought about her since I had met the group. How very odd. I brought the phone to my ear.

"Hello? Francesca?"

"Hello, my love. How are you?" She sounded buoyant.

"I'm fine, just a bit tired."

"And the students? Are they putting up with you and your sour moods?" She was attempting to be humorous, but it wasn't working with me.

"Yes, yes. I think I've actually scored some points." I was trying to bring some enthusiasm into the conversation but wasn't quite making it. I said, "Tell me about New York."

This got her going on a nonstop description of all that she had done and seen since she had arrived in Manhattan. She rattled off names of restaurants, clubs, and discotheques that she and her colleagues had gone to. I threw in a "Nice" and "Really?" at the right points, but all the while she was talking, I was thinking, *This is the woman I've been living with for over a year now, and I'm not interested in anything she's saying.*

"And, Atticus, listen to this. The company has asked me if I would be interested in transferring to New York for a couple of years. Isn't that incredible? I can't believe it! You can easily find work here. The crisis isn't as bad as they say it is, and you have a solid resumé. They told me to think it over, but I'm sure that you are as excited about the possibility as I am, aren't you? Atticus? Are you there?"

"Ah, yes, I'm here. I'm sorry, what was that about staying in New York?" I was light years from this conversation.

Francesca's tone changed abruptly. "Are you alone, Atticus?"

"Of course I'm alone. The connection just isn't great."

"I was telling you about the offer they made me to stay in New York for a couple of years." She had turned ice cold.

"Well certainly, that sounds interesting, but it isn't something we can decide over the phone, right?"

"Of course, Atticus, might as well wait and let this opportunity slip through our hands. We'll talk about it some other time. Good night."

The line went dead. I knew I should call her back. I didn't.

What was Francesca thinking? A move to the Big Apple? How could she assume that I could decide to move to New York over the phone? The company she worked for was obviously satisfied with her performance, but there were so many other issues to consider as well. She knew that I had sent my resumé to the big-name executive search firms in the States and that the feedback had been lukewarm at best. This was mainly because the supply of senior managers far outstripped the current demand. How, then, could she tell me that the crisis *wasn't so bad*? And most importantly, she didn't say anything about the children. Not a word. Yet she knew that I lived for my weekends with them. So how could she think that I would just get up and go across the Atlantic?

I was looking through my pants and shirts and throwing them about the room, obviously releasing my frustration on these inert items. Once dressed, I sat on the corner of the bed, settled down, and regrouped my thoughts.

I was annoyed with Francesca, but then again, how was I to explain my behavior with Barbara since our arrival in Rome? Had I, in any form or fashion, attempted to stop the sentimental and physical liaison that was very rapidly taking shape? No. I was annoyed with Francesca's obvious insensibility, but how much worse would her reaction be if she found out about my romantic inclinations toward another woman?

The phone on the bedside table rang. It was Vanessa calling to tell me that Sabrina was back. I told her that I would have dinner sent up to the room shortly.

"Thanks, Atticus, for everything."

"We'll see each other later. Bye."

It was nearly seven thirty. Time to go downstairs. Before heading to the restaurant area, I stopped by the front desk. Giovanni informed me that Ludovica had left for the day. I briefly explained the situation in Room 15 and asked him if it was possible to send some dinner up to the girls. As usual, he answered me with his head down, eyes fixed on the PC monitor.

"Mr. Winterle, I was informed of the situation in Room 15 by Miss Ludovica. I shall see to it that dinner for two, plus beverages, is sent up to the young ladies at eight o'clock. Would chicken, mashed potatoes, and salad be to their liking?"

"Sounds like a winner."

"I take it, Mr. Winterle, that the young lady in question is feeling better?"

"Yes, much better. I hope it continues that way."

"*Si finis bonus est, totum bonum erit.*"

I smiled at him. All's well that ends well. Hopefully, Giovanni was right.

As I entered the brightly lit room, I saw that the ASA tables were filled, except for three vacant chairs—Sabrina's, Vanessa's, and mine. I was a bit surprised since I had expected that one or more from the group would have arrived late for dinner after the full day. I also noted that Cynthia and Barbara were sitting at the student tables. That was a good sign.

The students began calling out to me when they saw me at the entrance. "Hey, Atticus." "Hi, Atticus." "Come sit with us, Atticus." "Over here, Atticus." I was very pleased, even though I noticed that a table of Asian tourists was slightly annoyed at the sudden commotion. I waved to everyone, placing my index finger on my lips to tell the group to quiet down a bit.

The selection this evening seemed even more varied than the night before. What sparked my interest was the three different risotto dishes—one with saffron, one with Parmigiano-Reggiano, and the third with artichoke hearts. There was a tray of lasagna that was certainly going to go fast and a round serving dish of spaghetti *aglio, olio e peperoncino*. This was one of my favorites: spaghetti cooked al dente with olive oil, finely sliced garlic, dry red peppers, and a generous topping of freshly chopped parsley. At the end of the table, I saw a large baking pan filled with fried chicken, and on the side, large bowls filled with mashed potatoes and French fries.

Everyone must have been hungry because the plates were overflowing with food. Barbara was just leaving the buffet table with an assortment of fresh vegetables as I approached her. She looked ravishing. She had showered, done her hair, and been a bit more liberal with her lipstick and mascara.

"Hello, Atticus, did you have a good day?"

"Yes, Barbara, thanks. And you?"

"Could have been better, but I plan to make up for it tonight."

She winked at me and walked back to her table. I was beginning to get a hot flush right there between the pickled onions and the grilled zucchini.

Jeremy and Mark were sitting with Darlene, with an empty chair at their table.

"Mind if I sit here?" I asked.

"No problem, Atticus."

I took my seat. "How's the food tonight?"

"Awesome, as usual. The lasagna just blows your mind. I won't be able to eat it anymore when I get stateside." Mark was shoveling it in as he spoke.

"There's something that looks like rice up there, but it's yellow," said Darlene. "Isn't that weird?"

"It's rice with saffron, Darlene, a spice originally from India. Try it."

"I think I will." She got up from her chair. She was wearing a pair of jeans that had apparently gone through a washing machine cycle with a thousand razor blades. The rips in the garment revealed a great deal of skin. Never a boring moment with Darlene's attire.

"Hey, Mr. Winterle," said Jeremy. "I mean, Atticus...I'm good with the Caserta Palace when you are."

This was the second time that Jeremy had volunteered to share his research with me—and now in front of an audience. I began to understand that he was looking for a spotlight for himself and that he needed some camaraderie from his peers.

"Okay, Jeremy, I'm all ears. I think there may be a few others who are also interested in what you have to say." As I was waiting for Jeremy to finish up his dessert, I noticed that the students were moving their chairs closer to where I was sitting. This was becoming something of a town-hall meeting.

"Hey, I didn't think I was going to have a crowd," Jeremy said, hastily swallowing the last bit of his apple and walnut pie. This only egged those present on. John, Cynthia, and Barbara started chanting, "Je-re-my, Je-re-my!" and this soon caught on. Luckily, the Asian tourists had left, and the room was all ours.

"All right, all right already, let's keep it real, please." Jeremy stood up and took a piece of paper from his pocket, which he unfolded. I had to keep reminding myself that he only had one arm.

"I was given the *very* difficult task by Mr. Winterle, alias Atticus, to research the Caserta Palace near Naples—"

"We see you sweating, Jeremy," Darlene said.

"Let me start off by saying that this palace is really big—"

"Most palaces usually are, Jeremy," Mary interrupted.

"Well, I don't know about you, Mary, but I haven't heard of many palaces that have twelve hundred rooms and eighteen hundred windows."

This got their attention.

"This place is two hundred seventy yards long and two hundred yards wide. That's almost three football fields long, get it? Construction began in 1752 and finished in 1780, but they kept on adding and changing things until 1845. But what's really cool is that they used this place to film parts of *The Phantom Menace* and *Attack of the Clones*, Episodes One and Two, of *Star Wars*."

"That must have gotten you all hot and bothered, movie maniac," Wayne remarked.

"Not finished yet, bro…not only *Star Wars* but also the awesome scene in *Mission Impossible: III* where that Lamborghini gets blown to bits. Parts of *Angels and Demons* were filmed there too. That's awesome."

"Do you remember who wanted it built, Jeremy?" I asked.

"Yeah, Atticus, hang on, it's here somewhere. Yeah, here it is. Charles III, King of Naples."

"Good for you. One last question, and this is for anyone in the room except John, Cynthia, and Barbara…"

"That's discrimination," John interjected.

"Maybe, but I'm making the rules tonight. What other palace in Europe is similar in scope and size to the Caserta Palace?" I could tell that Michelle knew, but she decided to remain silent.

"Ah, Versailles?" Evelyn ventured.

"Very good! Versailles was the palace that all the royal families of Europe looked up to and admired. And where is Versailles?" I paused a moment and looked at Michelle.

"It's about twenty miles west of Paris, Atticus. It's been a dream of mine to go there. Maybe, just maybe, one day…"

Something in the way she said those last two words put me on edge. Full of hope and despair at the same time. But I couldn't linger on this now.

"Well, Jeremy, thank you. I believe that you deserve a round of applause." With that, everyone clapped their hands and gave Jeremy the acclaim I think he was hungering for.

"By the way, what did all of you do this afternoon with your first hours of liberty?" I inquired.

"Some of us went to that piazza you were talking about, Atticus," said Raymond. "Camp do Fo…"

"Campo de' Fiori. Did you see the statue of Giordano Bruno?"

"Yeah, the guy who was burned at the stake by the Inquisition. He must have gotten under some pope's skin."

"Indeed, he did. Pope Clement the XIII, to be exact." I didn't mention that this pope, in particular, was extremely harsh with the Jews living in Rome at the time. That would surely have gotten Raymond wound up.

"You know what's really cheap over here, Atticus?" Mark said, apparently bored by the Inquisition.

"What's that?"

"The pizza. We got a piece today as big as a manhole cover, and it cost us three euros. We would have paid at least twice that in Atlanta. Problem is, they screw you over on Coke. It's €2.50 for a can, that's almost US$3.50. I need to complain to my dad."

The price of food and items in general led to other discussions about what the students had done today. I sat back and enjoyed the back-and-forth.

"Hey, Mrs. Cornwall," Bishop called out. "What's up with Vanessa? Is she feeling better?"

"Yes, but we need to check in on her. Thanks for reminding me, Bishop."

"Atticus, can we have ten minutes on our own before you head up to see how she is?" Wayne said.

I looked at him. I didn't know what he was talking about.

"You know, that thing we want to do for Vanessa…"

"Oh sure, of course." I had forgotten all about whatever performance they had in store for her.

"We'll meet upstairs then in about fifteen minutes, okay?" I confirmed. "And listen, everyone, if we lose sight of each other, we meet tomorrow morning at eight forty-five for breakfast."

"That's cool." Wayne turned to the others and said, "Let's go."

All the boys and a few of the girls got up and followed Wayne out of the restaurant. I was at a loss, again.

"You said Vanessa was feeling better right, Mrs. Cornwall? She may wish she was still sick after what she's going to see in a few minutes." Mary was shaking her head and giggling to herself.

"Wayne should be an actor, not a basketball player," Evelyn added, her head resting on James's shoulder.

"He's too wrapped up in his macho world right now to think of anything creative, Evelyn," said John. "Maybe when he's older."

"Oh, what are you saying?" Cynthia rolled her eyes. "Wayne has about as much creativity inside of him as this chair. That young man just needs to understand that there is more to life than a basketball and a six-pack."

I noticed Evelyn staring at her with contempt. Michelle had her head down instead and was fiddling with the dessert knife. Darlene was nibbling on her bottom lip.

"Darlene? Did you want to say something by chance?" I asked.

"Well, Atticus, I mean…well, no, not really." It was crystal clear that she did have something on her mind, but I didn't insist.

After a few more minutes of random chatter, it was time to go upstairs. "I think it's time to go see what the boys have in store for Vanessa," I said. "Should be interesting."

I got up and headed for the exit. We all went up the one flight of stairs. On the first floor, we were stopped by Jeremy, who was now wearing one of the hotel's bathrobes.

"Atticus, we need you to go and knock on Vanessa's door," he said. "Just act as if everything is normal. We'll handle the rest.

I hoped that Vanessa was in good shape. If she was trembling, sweating, and pale, the kids might realize she didn't just have a stomach flu. I knocked. The door opened immediately. Sabrina stood there, smiling.

"Hey, Atticus, come in." I walked in and saw Vanessa propped up in bed with her laptop on her legs.

"Hi, Atticus."

"Hello to you both. How was dinner?" I didn't see any sign of plates, cutlery, or glasses. Had Giovanni forgotten?

"They came up here with a cart loaded with food. I don't think we're going to eat for the next two days. A waiter was here about ten minutes ago and cleared everything up for us. He was really sweet."

"That's good news, because I think you'll need a full stomach for what you're going to hear next."

I was very serious and played the part. I heard a noise outside the door and was hoping that the boys would do something fast since Vanessa was beginning to look nervous. She was probably thinking I had changed my mind and decided to inform her parents about what had happened. I was almost felt sorry for her when there was a loud knock on the door.

"Who is it?" Sabrina asked.

"It's Jeremy, Sabrina, open up, it's important."

"Go ahead, Sabrina, open the door," I said.

I tried to contain the smile that was fighting its way to my lips but failed. Vanessa realized something was up. As soon as the door opened, she put her hands over her face and shouted, "Oh no!"

Someone had turned on a CD player and a cadenced "Doh-doo-doh-doo-doo" was heard as Wayne, Bishop, Mark, and the rest of the boys piled into the room, some leaping onto Sabrina's bed wearing only gym shorts and towels around their heads. Wayne, Bishop, and Mark began to sing karaoke style while the others did back up with the "Doh-doo-doh-doo-doo."

> *Goodnight sweetheart, well, it's time to go!*
> *Goodnight sweetheart, well, it's time to go!*
> *I hate to leave you, but I really must say,*
> *Oh, goodnight sweetheart, goodnight!*

By this time, everyone was laughing and enjoying the performance. Wayne was most definitely a showman, leading the singing and the dance moves. The song went on for three more verses with the chorus in between. By this time, Vanessa was practically in tears with embarrassment. The boys began to leave the room with the last lines of the melody, blowing

Vanessa a kiss. Wayne and Bishop hugged her. Another display on their part that I wasn't expecting.

I left the room last and waited for Cynthia and John to be out of earshot before asking the girls to call me or Barbara if there were any problems.

"Don't worry, Atticus," said Sabrina. "Van and I have had a good long talk. I told her I'd slap her silly if she ever tried anything like that again."

Vanessa didn't say anything, still recovering from the performance.

"Good night, then. If you're up to it, Vanessa, we meet in the breakfast room at eight forty-five tomorrow morning."

"Yeah, I'm looking forward to it, Atticus. I'm a bit tired of being holed up in this room."

"I bet. Sleep well."

I closed the door behind me and found most of the group still in the hall discussing what to do that night. Wayne was back in his clothes and had his PC under his arm.

"We're going back to the restaurant like last night, Atticus," he said.

"Fine, Wayne. By the way, it was a great performance. Vanessa surely appreciated it."

"I hope so. I don't do that for just anyone."

He went off down the hall with the Bishop and Mark.

"Hey, Mr. Seeward, remember you promised us a hand of poker over a few beers?"

"I'll be down in just a bit, Mark."

"Can we go out a bit, Atticus?" It was Darlene.

"I have no problem as long as your teachers don't."

Cynthia and John reminded her that she needed to be in a group. We asked for a show of hands to accompany Darlene. The ever-reliable Michelle raised her hand, as well as James, Evelyn, Anthony, and Mary.

"Please be back by eleven thirty—no excuses," John warned. "Atticus, mind doing roll call with me?"

"No problem, John. We'll meet downstairs at the bar."

He disappeared inside his room, as did Cynthia just as Barbara was walking out of hers with a summer shawl around her shoulders.

"Atticus Winterle, it's a beautiful night tonight, and I was cheated out of some wonderful sites today. Would you mind taking me for a walk to see a few of them?"

"I'd be delighted. I'll join you downstairs in a moment."

I hurried off to my room, rather excited at the prospect of a romantic walk under a Rome moonlit sky. Needless to say, I was rapidly juggling a series of emotions that were accumulating inside of me. On the one hand, I felt as giddy as a schoolboy on his first date. On the other hand, I knew I was getting myself involved with someone to the point of no return. It would be impossible to resume a "things as normal" attitude with Francesca if I let this romantic interlude continue. Furthermore, I knew that our telephone conversation earlier in the evening was clouding my judgment. I was also worried that someone in the group might have gotten wind that there was something going on between Barbara and me. This would only embarrass me with the group and create a headache for Marco and ASA. I still had time to back out of all of this. It was as easy as calling Barbara down at the front desk informing her that this wasn't a good idea. But then I decided—to hell with it!

I was feeling better now than I had in more than a year. I grabbed my wallet and cigars and headed for the lobby.

CHAPTER 25

Giovanni was at the front desk, and Barbara was sitting in the lobby, looking at a magazine. I left the key on the desk, thanking him for the umpteenth time for all he had done, and walked over to Barbara. She looked up at me. In an instant, I could tell that she had been struggling with all of this, just as I had a few moments earlier.

"Atticus, I apologize. I don't know anything about your personal life, and I feel as if I made you rush into something that might make you uncomfortable." She had such a beautiful expression on her face. "I'm acting like a schoolgirl; I know I might cause some trouble for myself and the others if somebody puts two and two together."

I started to speak, but she raised her hand.

"But! But I don't care right now. I'm happy, and I haven't felt this good in years. I'm ready to have a romantic evening, if you wish."

We were definitely on the same wavelength.

"Rome is waiting for us, Barbara." I extended my right arm at a ninety-degree angle. She gave me a warm smile, hooked her arm into mine. As we walked out of the hotel, I saw Giovanni grinning to himself.

We could not have asked for a more beautiful evening. A warm, pleasant breeze blew gently, and the sky was painted with dark orange and maroon hues as the sun disappeared below the horizon.

I decided to go toward the Piazza della Rotonda, the same route I had taken with the group that morning. I pointed out a few things here and there but in a lackadaisical fashion. I was lost in the warm evening, the ambience of Rome, and in Barbara. I think we were both aware that walking so closely together was very unwise with some members of the group out and about, but it just didn't seem to matter to either of us.

When we reached the piazza, the Pantheon was shrouded in a velvety orange glow produced from the artificial lighting surrounding the structure. The massive bronze doors leading inside were shut for the night. I took Barbara underneath the columned portico and repeated most of my lecture to the students earlier in the day.

"I can't—and won't tell—you anything about the interior of the Pantheon until you see it with your own eyes. I know I've already used the analogy with you that it's like explaining what it means to be a parent for the first time without experiencing it."

Barbara nodded. "And you may remember that I was fighting back a few tears when you did."

I nodded.

"Let's go sit and have a drink, Atticus. I'd like to clear up a few things."

I led her to one of the small cafés, close to where John and I had sat earlier in the day. A waiter dressed in a white jacket and a black clip-on bow tie pointed to a free table.

"Would you care for some champagne, Barbara?"

"I'd love it."

"Please." As I ordered a bottle of Veuve Clicquot, well chilled, Barbara reached in her purse and took out a pack of Marlboro lights.

"I thought you told me the other night that you had quit smoking," I remarked.

"I did, but I need a cigarette tonight," she replied. Something was up.

The waiter came out with an ice bucket and two champagne flutes. He pulled out his corkscrew, applied it dexterously, and the cork popped that wonderful sound synonymous with festivity, celebration, and romance. The waiter poured the champagne and took his leave. Barbara and I lifted our glasses and looked into each other's eyes.

"To having met you, Barbara."

"And to having met *you*, Atticus."

The glasses clinked together, and we let that heavenly liquid that only the French can produce flow down our throats. I reached into my pocket and took out a pack of matches to light Barbara's cigarette and my cigar. We then just sat a moment, gazing before us.

"I don't know where to start, Atticus. Maybe with those tears that I was fighting back on Sunday."

"I'm your captive audience."

Barbara cleared her throat. "When you mentioned how special and how new the experience of being a parent really is, and that you don't understand it until they put your baby in your arms…well, that touched me deeply. I have two boys. Steve is twenty-six, and Joseph is twenty-eight. I felt exactly what you described when my boys were born, amazed at what Mother Nature was capable of. I was a relatively young mom, but I wouldn't have switched places with anyone else in the world."

She took a prolonged drag on her cigarette.

"We were a very comfortable family financially. We had a big house, we took vacations every summer and winter, and we had plenty disposable income. My husband is a dentist and has his own practice. The boys went to a private elementary school and then junior high school not far from Bradford High. They had good grades, and other than some typical teenage rebellion, they never gave us anything to worry about. What more was there to ask for, right?"

I simply nodded. Obviously, this was all a prelude to a calamity.

"The first bomb dropped at the beginning of Joseph's sophomore year in high school, around mid-1997. My husband came home one night from work and wanted to speak with me. He seemed very agitated, and I thought to myself, *Here we go, he's sleeping with his secretary*. If only…"

That didn't sound promising.

"This was a man that had always been there for me and the family. True, in bed there had already been a free fall for several years, but I managed things on my own when my hormones got out of control. I thought it was normal that husbands just conk out after almost sixteen years of marriage. Anyway, he sat there in front of me, Atticus, and told me that he had been bisexual for several years. That was the first wave of the tsunami, but the second was even more devastating. In a nutshell, he was hoping that I would agree to some evenings of wife swapping with some couples he had met."

I poured out the third glass of champagne, attempting to act as nonchalant as possible. Not that easy, given the circumstances. Barbara paused a moment and rubbed her forehead.

"I'm sorry, Atticus. Maybe I shouldn't be discussing all of this with you."

"I will listen to anything you want to tell me. If you want to stop, that's fine too."

Barbara took a deep breath, exhaled, and continued her story:

"You know what I find inexplicable, Atticus? I didn't fly off into a rage, start throwing plates, and tell him to get out of the house. He realized how deeply he was hurting me with his words and offered to leave the premises right then and there. We ended up sitting silently for what seemed an endless amount of time. I told him that I needed some privacy to collect my thoughts and that we would speak about all of this the next day when the kids were at school. I don't think either of us got any sleep that night. He stayed downstairs, and I just sat in the master bathroom all night long. Well, the next morning I prepared breakfast as usual while my husband was reading the paper. The kids went off to school, and I gave him my answer."

She hesitated a moment and downed the remaining champagne in her glass.

"I told him that I was willing to give his wife-swapping fantasy a try. You can just imagine how stunned he was. It was as if Santa Claus had just come down the chimney. No moving out, no messy divorce, no selling the house, no guilt wars with the kids, and on top of that, he would be free to experiment with his sexual desires with his wife. I don't think he was expecting that at all."

"May I ask why you agreed to this request?"

"I've been asking myself that question for almost thirteen years, every day of every week, of every month, of every year. I was probably too comfortable in that big house and just too attached to the material world. I was also terrified about what a divorce would do to the boys. But if I'm being completely honest, the years of physical loneliness and watching porn movies on my own had made me hungry for the touch of another man and, perhaps, for another woman. I had no idea what it was going to be like to be making out with another man while watching my husband on top of another woman."

I refilled her glass and mine. We both needed it.

"We first started this wife-swapping game with some white couples and then black. I was shocked at how many prominent Atlanta couples were into this—doctors, lawyers, politicians, the whole shebang. What went hand in hand with these games was the latex jumpsuits, the eight-inch clear plastic pumps, the vibrators of every size and form, the kinky lingerie, you name it. I went along with it, had my share of orgasms, and when my husband and I would get back home, we switched back into the normal family mode, as if nothing had happened. This went on for about a year. In the summer of 1999, Atticus, the end of July, my husband introduced me to a very handsome black couple. She was extremely attractive, and I remember that I was honestly hoping to make love to her more than to her husband. We scheduled a party at our house when the boys were going on a two-day fishing trip to Savannah, or so we thought."

"You *thought?*"

"Getting there, Atticus." She emptied her flute of champagne in one go, again.

"We invited this couple to dinner on a Friday at about eight o'clock, and by ten o'clock, all the sex toys were out, and we were one on top of each other."

Barbara's voice began choking up. Large tears were beginning to flow down her cheeks, and she took my hand and squeezed it tightly.

"You don't need to do this, Barbara."

"Oh, but I do, I do! I've never talked about this to anyone. It's been eating at me for so many years. We were in the living room. Of course, all the drapes had been drawn, the music was rather loud, and we were not speaking, as such. There was no way we could be seen or heard by the neighbors." Her next words left nothing to the imagination.

"I still remember as if it were yesterday. I had on a latex pair of knee-high boots, and I was having oral sex with this woman, Atticus, while watching my husband, dressed in my panties and silk stockings, getting sodomized by this large black man. We had been smoking some grass, and the gin tonics were flowing. At a certain point…at a certain…point, I looked up, and standing in front of me were my two boys, Atticus. My two boys! They were just standing there, in the living room, looking at us. That horrified expression on their faces is burned into my brain and it will remain there until I die."

She began sobbing silently, albeit uncontrollably, and placed her head on my shoulders. This went on for a few minutes. Barbara then sat up in her chair, wiped away the tears, took another long drink, and lit up another cigarette.

She let out a small, sarcastic laugh, and continued her astonishing story:

"They had come back from Savannah earlier than expected, Atticus, for my *birthday*, can you believe it? My birthday! They were both wearing 'Happy Birthday, Mom!' T-shirts, and Mark had a large cake with candles lit in his hands. My husband had locked and dead-bolted all the doors from the inside except for the basement door. It was a new door that we replaced when we did some work in the laundry room. It just had the standard key lock. The alarm was on, but we didn't know that the boys had somehow managed to get a copy of the code. That's how they managed to sneak in without any of us noticing. Needless to say, the cake ended up flung against the wall in an outburst of rage. The boys left the house in Joseph's car, and I only found out six months later that they had driven straight to Charleston, South Carolina, to stay with some friends. We didn't hear from them for over a month. We received a letter from Joseph a few days before the start of his senior year and Mark's junior year informing us that they had rented a small apartment on the outskirts of Atlanta and that they had no intention of coming home. He asked his father, my husband, to send eight hundred dollars a month to his bank account by wire transfer for the rent and food. He wrote that this was the least his degenerate father could do. He finished the letter by saying that they never wanted to see their slut mother or father ever again. They warned us that if they ever caught sight of us at their school, they would stop attending and disappear forever."

Barbara was staring at nothing in front of her as she said this. The screeching of a motor scooter snapped her out of the spell.

"What's the situation now between you and your husband?" I asked.

"You remember, Atticus, that I laughed when you mentioned how lucky my husband was the other night? Well, we're still together. That's right—together and going forward! After that pitiful scene, we sold the house and bought a smaller one on the northeast side of town. He still has his dentistry practice and still sleeps with men and women when he wants. We do gardening work together, but apart from that, we live in our respective worlds. He tries to stay close to me, and I know he's as devastated as I am by what happened, but it's all so difficult. Even if they are filled with rage and hatred, the boys have been discreet all these years, and nobody outside the family until now knows about any of this."

Barbara paused, but she wasn't finished.

"After high school, Joseph went to UCLA, and Mark won a scholarship to Stanford. I know this because one of their high school teachers, who knew something serious had happened between us, informed me. I also know that Joseph graduated in archeology with honors and is living in Sydney, Australia. Mark went into finance and is living in Hong Kong, as far as I know. A friend of theirs since elementary school, who is also aware that something happened between the four of us, tells me about these things in secrecy. They went as far away as they could from us but managed to stay relatively close to one another. They're the only family they have."

There was a long pause, and I knew that the story had now come to an end. I had no idea what to say. What I knew was that we had finished the bottle of champagne. We were not going to make it to the Piazza Navona, not this evening.

"You'll let me stay with you tonight, Atticus, won't you?"

"Of course, Barbara. We should start heading back. It's almost eleven, and I have to do the rounds with John at eleven thirty."

I got up and went inside to pay the waiter. When I came back, I approached Barbara from the back, put my hands on her shoulders, and kissed her on the cheek.

"It took an enormous amount of courage to tell me what you did tonight," I said.

"I feel a little better, Atticus. Nothing has been resolved, and I have lost my two children forever, but that load I've been carrying on my shoulders for these past thirteen years is now half the original size. I have you and Rome to thank for this."

She got up. Even though we had had quite a bit to drink, the conversation had been so sobering that we didn't feel any effects. We didn't say much on the way back to the hotel, except to comment on some of the magnificent buildings we passed along the way.

When we very close to the Trevi Fountain, I noticed a stunning woman with a full head of blonde hair, tight black pants, and high-heeled sandals leaning against a lamppost with a group of men and women. Then I suddenly realized that I was looking at Darlene.

I leaned over to Barbara and whispered, "The students are up ahead."

"Hey, Atticus, Mrs. Cornwall!" It was Michelle. The others all turned and started in on us: "*What have the two of you been doing? Where have the two of you been?*"

Barbara was right out of the starting gate, "Atticus was so kind to show me the Pantheon."

"Pretty great, right, Mrs. Cornwall?" said Michelle.

"Very much so, Michelle. I'd like to see the inside before we leave."

"We'll take you, Mrs. Cornwall, if Atticus doesn't find the time," Darlene said, with a slight bit of bitchiness in her tone.

"You've got a deal," Barbara replied, playing dumb.

"Who's your new friend, Darlene?" There was a young man standing very close to Darlene, with a beer in his hand.

"Oh, this is Gi-a-co-mo. He's from Florence but goes to the University of Rome."

"Hello, Giacomo," Barbara and I spoke at the same time.

"Hello. I very sorry, but my English not that good."

Darlene's eyes were all over Giacomo. "We met at a bar down this little street, Atticus. Giacomo is graduating this year. He's going to be a lawyer. Isn't that awesome?"

"Yes, indeed. Awesome." Somehow, I wasn't convinced.

Darlene leaned over to Barbara, saying, "Isn't he just *sooo cute?*"

I smelled trouble.

"We'll let you get on with whatever you're doing, ladies and gentlemen," I said. "You all need to be back in about fifteen minutes, though."

Barbara and I walked back to the hotel. She knew what I was concerned about.

"He seems like a decent guy, Atticus."

"I hope so."

We walked into the hotel and saw Giovanni behind the front desk. He had placed our room keys on the counter before even seeing us.

"Good night, Mr. Winterle, Mrs. Cornwall. *Si quaeris peninsulam amoenam circumspece.*"

We reached the stairs and started going up. "What did he just say, Atticus?" Barbara asked.

I smiled at Barbara, "It was a compliment, in Latin. I'll tell you later. My door will be unlocked. See you in a bit."

I left Barbara outside of her room and went to mine. I unlocked the door and then went back downstairs to wait for John at the bar. I ordered Cointreau for two, no ice, and glanced through an Italian newspaper. John rounded the corner and sat down next to me.

"Cointreau?" he asked

"Yup, but no ice this time, just a chilled glass. Are the boys still in the restaurant?"

"Yes. I won sixteen dollars and twenty-five cents at poker. The students get to keep their winnings, but I have to put mine into the pot for a going-away party on the last night we're here. Figures. Did you go out for a smoke?"

"I went out, but just for a walk." We sipped our Cointreau. My head was beginning to feel heavy, especially after all that champagne.

"I think Vanessa really got a kick out of that show the boys put on," I said. "I've got to hand it to Wayne. He doesn't seem at all like the reprobate the three of you described at lunch on Sunday, at least not on this trip."

I knew I was pushing my luck here by implying that he, Cynthia, and Barbara didn't, in fact, know very much about some of their students. John stared at his Cointreau and pursed his lips. The glass doors of the hotel opened behind us. The students had come back from the Trevi Fountain. Everyone went by, some calling good night to me and John, and walked up to their rooms. I glanced outside and saw Darlene with Giacomo. She noticed that both John and I were watching her, and she quickly kissed her friend on the cheek and came inside.

"Something we need to worry about, Atticus?" John murmured as Darlene waved and rushed toward the stairs.

"He seems okay, so far."

I explained to John that I had met Giacomo on the way back from the Pantheon. "We just need to be extra vigilant with Darlene," I said. "I don't want her going out on her own with that guy or any other."

"I'm with you on that." John finished the last few drops of Cointreau and looked at his watch. "I'm going to go round up the group in the restaurant. Everybody is in the hotel now, so I don't think we need to go knocking on doors. See you in the morning."

I said good night and went up quickly to my room. When I arrived, I found the door locked, as I had hoped. I knocked, and Barbara let me in.

CHAPTER 26

Barbara had switched on the TV, and one of the BBC's anchors was speaking about the continuing unrest in Iran. The two small wine bottles, uncorked, were on the desk along with the glasses.

"Everyone accounted for?" she asked.

"Yes, they're all in the hotel." I poured the wine and passed a glass to Barbara.

"Let's hope that we won't have any more surprises tonight," she said.

I raised my glass. "To us again."

"To us."

We sat down on the bed, our legs touching. The combination of champagne, Cointreau, and now wine was making my head spin.

"I checked in on Vanessa before coming to your room," Barbara said. "She was writing emails and seemed to be much better. Sabrina will keep an eye on her."

"Okay." I shook my head. "I never knew there could be so much drama with young people."

"You have no idea," she said, rolling her eyes. "Speaking of which, you never did tell me what happened with Mark other than the fact that he drank a bottle of tequila at light speed. At least, that's what Michelle told me."

I filled Barbara in on the details.

"His parents are in total denial about their own drinking problem," she said. "That first bourbon and soda turns into two, then three, and so on until the evening turns to night. I guess Mark is lucky that he isn't a full-fledged alcoholic himself, at least not yet."

"Bishop told me that he had his stomach pumped a few times this year."

Barbara stared at me in disbelief.

"I don't think any of his teachers know about that, if Bishop's telling the truth. I certainly didn't."

"Michelle and Wayne didn't deny it, so I would say that the information is correct."

"Is that what the four of you were whispering about over lunch yesterday?"

I smiled and gave her a kiss on the cheek. "You're quite a snoop, aren't you?"

"The four of you looked as if you were discussing state secrets."

I was tempted to tell her about Wayne and Bishop and how they wanted to speak to me about something important. I decided to wait.

"What about Mark's sister?" I asked. "He told me that she lives in Sacramento."

"I know very little about her. She didn't go to Bradford and left home at a young age. Mark worships her to the point of…" She broke off.

"To the point of?" I looked at Barbara inquisitively.

"No, nothing really. He just seems spellbound when he mentions her."

"Anthony is the other one who troubles me. There's something going on with that kid, but I can't put my finger on it."

"Well, you might have noticed that Anthony is Cynthia's pet."

"To put it mildly."

"John and I don't understand why she's taken him under her wing. He's not a troublemaker, but he's not an outstanding student, either. His grades are Cs and Ds. And then he's a compulsive liar. You've probably picked up on that."

I nodded. "And what was up with all that about sharpshooters over in St. Peter's square?"

"Anthony is a gun nut, Atticus. Handguns, rifles, machine-guns—you name a brand and model, and he'll tell you all about it. When he speaks about weapons, he becomes another person. He could have easily bumped Nicholas Cage out of the leading role in the movie *Lord of War*. We don't think he's got an arsenal at home, but he has raised some eyebrows amongst the faculty."

"So we have an insecure, academically poor student who lies twenty-four seven and loves guns. That's a reassuring picture. Doesn't Cynthia see any of this?"

"You can't talk to her about Anthony. If you begin criticizing him, she freezes up as if you were condemning Mother Theresa."

"She doesn't have any children, correct?"

"Nope."

"Do you know anything about Anthony's parents?" I ventured.

"Very little. I've only seen them on parent-teacher nights twice a year. They hear about Anthony's poor grades and go home. They're both rather young. The mother is a nurse. I don't know what his father does."

She paused a moment, gazing into her wineglass. "I feel I should be doing more for these kids, be more involved in their personal lives. If I could help one, just one, student to get out of a difficult situation maybe, just maybe, it would..." Her voice broke, and she paused again. "Maybe it would ease some of my own pain." She swallowed some wine and got hold of herself.

"The kids on this trip are just thirteen of the one hundred twenty students I had this year. I really thought I had a handle on them well before leaving Atlanta. Now I realize that I don't know them at all."

"Over one hundred students? That's a lot," I said, rather taken aback at the thought.

Barbara laughed ruefully. "You've been in Europe way too long, Mr. Winterle. We're considered an elite public high school because our student population is relatively small. Most high schools in the US have well over fifteen hundred students, with the senior class in the two hundred fifty to three hundred range."

I was dumbfounded. "How in the world can a teacher have any interaction with their students if they have to manage such a large number?"

"I have four classes of seniors, Atticus, about thirty to a class, and that's considered very unusual. But you're right. Most teachers just can't keep up with everyone. When you find one who's dedicated and makes that extra effort for those students who are in need, you've found a goldmine. But remember, the clerk at my local bank earns about as much as a first-year teacher. What does that tell you? There's so much talk about how teachers have the futures of our kids in their hands, but a starting salary of thirty thousand dollars a year isn't a calling card for the best talent out there now, is it? And don't get me started on what some people get paid for hitting a ball in a hole in the ground or throwing one through a hoop!"

A silence fell between us. She refilled her glass. I watched her, just taking her in. Then a thought occurred to me.

"Coming back to Vanessa, what if there's a problem, and she calls your room?" I asked.

"I plan to be in *my* room in a few hours," Barbara said. She saw my disappointment. "You know I can't stay here all night. It's just too risky."

She was right, but I had been looking forward to waking up next to her the following morning.

Barbara took a sip from her wineglass, then turned to look at me.

"Atticus, I'm tired of talking about all of this. May I use your bathroom?"

"Of course, it's all yours."

She got up, wobbling a little, and turned the TV off as she passed. I didn't know what to do exactly. Should I just remain where I was? Did I need to turn down the bed? A few minutes later, I had my answer.

Barbara came out of the bathroom wearing only her panties. Her breasts were large and firm for a woman over fifty, and the rest of her body was worth a second look, a third, a fourth…

"Atticus," she said politely.

"Yes, Barbara?"

"Please take your clothes off."

She lay on the bed and propped up a pillow behind her back. She was raping me with her eyes, and I found it terribly exciting. I proceeded to undo my shirt buttons and take off my trousers and underwear. I had never considered myself as especially well-endowed, but the erection I had now wasn't insignificant. I positioned myself next to her on the bed. The fingers of her left hand stroked my chest. I was about to explode.

"I haven't had sex with another person for longer than I can remember, Atticus," she whispered. "I never thought I would want too anymore. But you, and the magic of this city, have brought back that desire in me. I want to take advantage of it, to the fullest."

What happened after that would have made any X-rated film seem rather dull. We had no sex toys, no latex, no eight-inch plastic pumps, no handcuffs—just our bodies celebrating the pleasures of touching and being touched. Eventually, we returned to bed after having sat, crouched, laid, stood, and kneeled on every item of furniture in the room. If we had a harness, we would have done it hanging from the ceiling. We were drenched in sweat and breathing deeply.

"Oh my goodness, Atticus," Barbara sighed. "That was phenomenal. I don't even remember how many orgasms I had. I don't think I'll be able to do much walking tomorrow."

She nestled close to me. I was grateful for the silence that followed, given that I was lost in introspection. Did I feel bad about what had just happened? Did I feel guilty for having betrayed Francesca? Not in the least. I knew right then and there that as soon as she got back from New York, I would end our relationship. Barbara was the straw that broke the camel's back, and I was very pleased that the camel had become a paraplegic with no prognosis for recovery.

"Barbara?"

"Yes, Atticus?"

"How do you feel about what we just did?"

"I was just thinking about that. If you're wondering whether I have regrets, the answer is no. In fact," she added, smiling, "I hope that before I leave for Atlanta, we shall do it several times again."

"And your husband?"

"Well, I guess that any other woman, and probably most men, would find it very hard to believe that we are still living under the same roof. I've thought about this time in and time out. Jeff suffered and is suffering just as much as I am for the loss of our children. Believe it or not, I know he loves me. He's always been there for me and responsible, both emotionally and financially."

"A rather important part of the marriage equation, I would say."

"Absolutely, Atticus, absolutely! But this begs a question. Let's try not to consider for a moment that horrible night when the boys discovered our secret life. Up until then, if I want to be honest with myself, I wasn't put off by these acts that my husband asked me to be part of. Does that make me a sick woman? Do I have a sexual disorder? Or did I just put into practice fantasies that many women have but hide under layers of fear, embarrassment, or false modesty? Don't get me wrong. I'm not patting myself on the back or waving the victim flag. I could have put my foot down and pulled out of this marriage when Jeff revealed his inclinations to me." Barbara paused. "It's funny, Atticus. Jeff has never forgotten my birthday or our wedding anniversary. He still surprises me with bouquets of flowers, unexpected gifts, and love letters. He's extraordinary in that way, even though I'm sure I don't acknowledge these gestures the way he would want me to. I thought for some time that he was just trying to buy me off for the big day when he was going to ask me to join in on his sexual exploits, but it's not that way at all. He still does it because I mean the world to him, and I need to keep that in mind." She shook her head. "What about you, Atticus? I don't even know if you have a girlfriend, or if you're married."

I explained my situation, including a short recap about my ex-wife and two children. I also told her about Francesca and how a veil that had been covering my eyes for a little over a year had suddenly been lifted thanks to her.

"I don't know if I should feel too terribly proud about possibly putting an end to someone else's relationship."

"Barbara, I never had a true relationship with Francesca. She's satisfying in bed and very business savvy, which I like in a woman, but that's the extent of our relationship. I've been putting off what I should've done months ago."

"Are you in love with me, Atticus?"

This question took me completely by surprise. She laughed.

"Don't be frightened, Atticus. Let me make this a bit easier for you. Ask me the same question." I hesitated. "Go ahead."

"Are you in love with me, Barbara?"

"No, Atticus, I'm not. I'm still in love with my husband."

She stopped for a moment and then looked at me with watery eyes.

"You know who you are, Atticus? You are that special person that comes along during a lifetime if you're very lucky. For me, you signify tenderness, understanding, and passion. You have made me forget for a moment that immense hurt inside of me. No one has been able to do this—no one. You are my angel from Rome. Think about what I've just said, and then one of these days, you can tell me what's in your heart."

"All right, we have another date, then."

"More than one, I hope."

We kissed and both instinctively looked at the electronic clock on the bedside table. It was 2:23 am.

"I'll need to go back to my room soon," Barbara said, propping herself up on the pillow.

"I hope nobody called," I said.

"It was worth it," Barbara replied, stretching languidly.

"Stay another thirty more minutes, then," I said, "and I'll make it even more worth your while."

"Sounds like an offer I can't refuse," she said, reaching for me.

We ended making love again, and this time, I was beginning to feel a throbbing sensation between my legs.

"Oh, that hurt so good, Atticus," Barbara said. "But please, time out now!"

I stroked her hair, which was wet with perspiration.

"Is this how you thought it would be with Angie Dickinson?" she asked with a chuckle.

"Better," I replied.

We drank the last bottle of mineral water in the mini bar, but we were still thirsty. Barbara glanced at the clock again. I thought of a way to keep with me a little longer. "You were going to tell me something about Vanessa, remember?" I said.

"Oh, yes. That conversation was a real eye-opener, Atticus. I knew her mom was a dental hygienist and that her husband is not Vanessa's dad. Her stepfather has two children from a previous marriage, about five years younger than Vanessa. According to Vanessa, these two girls have managed to buddy up with her mom and have brought her to their side of the camp. What used to be a close relationship between Vanessa and her mother has gone sour. The stepfather doesn't like Vanessa, so that is part of the situation she's living with."

"Now we see why she started taking the pills."

"But that's not the end of it. Vanessa tells me that her old stepdad dabbles in cocaine and has gotten her mom to start."

"What about her real father? Any hope there?"

"Not really. He left home six years ago with the wife of a business colleague. Seems they live in Portland, Oregon. She told me she receives a card from him once a year around her birthday, which she throws away without even opening it."

I shook my head. "For Christ's sake, isn't there one normal, nonalcoholic, nonaddicted, nondeviant mother and father out there anywhere?"

This was a knee-jerk reaction, and I immediately realized that I had just kicked Barbara in the stomach. "I'm sorry, Barbara, I wasn't in any shape or form referring to you."

"I know you weren't, Atticus, but I'm in that category, unfortunately. What can I tell you? Ours is a rotten generation."

She seemed to have taken my insensitive comment in stride, but I knew that I had reawakened the pain. She pointed to the clock.

"My dear Atticus, I really need to go now."

She stood, got dressed, and went into the bathroom to straighten out her hair. I put on my vest and shorts.

When she came back out, I started to try and apologize. She put her finger on my lips. "Don't say anything, Atticus. It's good to see a person who could easily care less about these kids' problems actually feel something for them instead. I admire that about you."

We gave each other a long hug.

"What are we going to see this morning, Atticus?" she inquired. "I have some catching up to do in this city."

"The Colosseum and the Roman Forum."

"Sounds wonderful. Get some sleep now."

With that, she slowly opened the door, peered cautiously out at the hallway, and was about to slip out of the room when she stopped and turned toward me.

"You didn't tell me what Giovanni said when we entered the hotel."

"Ah, yes. *Sic quaeris peninsulam amoenam circumspece.* It translates into 'If you are looking for or seeking a beautiful peninsula, look around you.'"

Barbara smiled.

"How very lovely. Not terribly original, however."

I raised an eyebrow.

"It's the motto of the state of Michigan."

And with that, she exited, closing the door softly behind her.

I just stared at the closed door. The state motto of Michigan? How did she know that? I wasn't even aware that states had mottos.

I was now wide-awake even after a great deal of alcohol and a rather decent performance in sexual prowess. I tried not to think about the hurtful comment I had made and hoped that Barbara would not dwell on it. Getting back into bed, I decided to read a few more student bios. Anthony's was at the top. This I needed to see.

Just a few lines in, and something was already off. Under "Hobbies," Anthony listed music, sports, and studying human anatomy. This last entry was curious, to say the least. Also odd was what he had omitted firearms, even though Anthony's in-depth knowledge was no secret. His entry under "Sports" made me laugh out loud. Other than chess and backgammon, which were stretching the definition of the word *sport*, he had written "polo." Who was this kid trying to fool?

I wasn't surprised to see that he had put English literature as his preferred school subject, given his special relationship with Cynthia. He had left the space about college blank. Strange. Anthony's silence on where he would continue his education was juxtaposed by what I saw under "Career Plans": plastic surgeon. This was a bad script for an equally bad soap opera.

Beneath the question on why he had chosen this particular ASA destination, Anthony had typewritten his answer on a separate page, which was stapled to the questionnaire. After reading a few lines, I realized that Anthony had copied everything from a guidebook on Italy.

So apart from being a consummate liar, Anthony was also a plagiarizer. This young man had an insecurity complex as big as a Boeing 747. A part of me wanted to confront Cynthia about this boy, even though I had already gotten myself involved knee-deep in Mark's drinking and Vanessa's pill popping. Why should I have even the slightest concern about Anthony, anyway? Less than a week ago, I was dreading this trip and had absolutely no interest in meeting these individuals, let alone being their chaperone. Now I found myself curious about these kids' backgrounds and what made them tick. I genuinely didn't understand my change of heart.

Furthermore, the very rapid physical and emotional relationship that had bloomed between Barbara and me was mind-boggling as well. I had had my share of one-night stands when I was younger, neither more or less than any other red-blooded male, but what had grown so rapidly between Barbara and me was much more than just a brief physical intimacy. She had opened herself up to me, peeling back a hardened shell where some very ugly secrets had been festering.

I think that this is what I appreciated the most about Barbara, as well as with some of the students who had begun to see me as a platform where they could unload a lot of emotional baggage. It was silly, but I felt as if I were needed.

I smiled to myself and looked at the time. It was almost three thirty, and I was still wide-awake. I decided to take a last look at my emails. There were four. The first was from a job search engine that listed an endless number of positions in Italy, but no middle or senior management roles. The second mail was spam, an advertisement for a week's vacation at a beauty spa on the island of Capri. Not something that I could take advantage of for the moment. The third mail was from Mrs. Silvestri of Baine & Courtney. I opened it. She thanked me for our phone conversation, writing that she had found it very informative.

As soon as there was any news regarding her client and the search being conducted on their behalf, she promised to get in touch with me. I found this to be very professional. I was always amazed how many international search firms never even bothered to respond to a candidate's query for a certain position or to the registration of a resumé. I knew I was entering limbo every time I sent out an email with my CV attached. At least Ms. Silvestri had taken the time to keep me updated.

The last email was from Francesca. It was a page long, and from the very opening sentences, I knew that she was annoyed at my lack of enthusiasm about a possible transfer to New York. I logged off without even reading the rest. I wasn't in the mood to deal with this right now. I switched off the computer, got back into bed, and reached for Wilkie's *The Moonstone* on the night table. But then I took up Kahlil Gibran's *The Prophet* instead.

The words on page 24 caught my attention:

Then said a rich man, Speak to us of Giving. And he answered: You give but little when you give of your possessions. It is when you give of yourself that you truly give.

There are those who give little of the much which they have—and they give it for recognition and their hidden desire makes their gifts unwholesome. And there are those who have little and give it all.

These are the believers in life and the bounty of life, and their coffer is never empty.

It is well to give when asked, but it is better to give unasked, through understanding; And to the open-handed the search for one who shall receive is joy greater than giving. And is there aught you would withhold? All you have shall one day be given; Therefore, give now, that the season of giving may be yours and not your inheritors.

I thought about these words as I fell to sleep.

Friday
April 30, Day Four

CHAPTER 27

I was experiencing extreme discomfort. The vertebrae in the back of my neck had been nailed together. The stiffness was highly unpleasant.

Although I was adapting to the glaring light on my right, I still couldn't understand where that rapid thumping sound was coming from.

I had fallen asleep while reading, just as I had the night before. This was becoming a bad habit. My head had slumped down, and my neck muscles were now screaming for revenge.

There it was again—*thump, thump, thump*—but this time, I distinctly heard my name called out in a harsh whisper.

"Atticus, Atticus!"

What time was it? I looked at the bedside clock: 4:10 am.

If someone was knocking on my door at this hour, then something was definitely wrong. Wonderful.

"Coming," I called out.

I got up, threw on a pair of shorts and my polo shirt, then opened the door. Barbara and Michelle pushed their way in. I shut the door behind them.

Barbara was breathing somewhat heavily. "I'm so sorry, Atticus, but we have another problem on our hands." I didn't know whether to laugh or cry. Had Vanessa overdosed? No, it couldn't be that because Michelle was with Barbara, and Michelle didn't know anything about Vanessa. On the other hand, she knew about Mark. *That's it*, I thought groggily, *Mark stashed away a couple of bottles of bourbon, and he's now lying on the floor of his room in an alcohol-induced coma.*

"Atticus, it's Evelyn," said Barbara.

"Evelyn?" I said, still in a stupor.

Michelle was Evelyn's roommate. That made sense, but my immediate thought was whether I had the stomach to hear what had happened.

"Michelle, go ahead," Barbara said. "Tell Atticus what you saw."

Barbara motioned for Michelle to sit in the armchair. To think that only a few hours ago, Barbara and I had performed some of the most sexually extravagant aerobatics imaginable on that same piece of furniture made me want to smile, but I got a grip on myself. Barbara sat on the bed, and I leaned against the door.

Michelle said, "I felt I had to come to Mrs. Cornwall now, because I saw something that I found really worrying."

She took out her mobile phone from her night robe pocket. It was only then that I realized that both Michelle and Barbara were in their bedclothes. The silk and cotton robe that Barbara was wearing was generously open at the top. I could see more than just the upper slope of that wonderful cleavage. Barbara noticed me staring at her and my pleased expression. She cleared her throat and covered herself, giving me a warning look. I rapidly came back down to earth as Michelle handed me her phone.

"These are images of some pages from Evelyn's diary," she said.

I raised an interrogative eyebrow.

"I don't normally go looking through people's belongings," Michelle explained hastily, "let alone someone else's diary. But I felt I had to."

Barbara got up from the bed and gave Michelle an encouraging pat on the shoulder. "Tell Atticus why."

"Okay. I was having trouble sleeping so I decided to read. That was about three. I have one of those small reading lamps that you clip to the pages of your book. I used that to read so I wouldn't wake up Evelyn. Then I saw Evelyn's diary on the floor. I got out of bed to put it back on her night table, and when I picked it up, I saw that some of the pages had been ripped off." She paused, biting her lip.

"Michelle, it's okay," I reassured her. "You wouldn't have called Mrs. Cornwall if you weren't concerned about Evelyn, right?"

She took a deep breath and continued, "Yes. What I read frightened me. That's why I took pictures of them. When I finished, I put the diary back on the floor where I found it."

"Barbara, I take it that you've read this already?"

"Yes. And I think we need to take some sort of decision, fast. This time, we may have to involve Cynthia and John. We can't risk keeping this to ourselves."

I looked at the first image.

April 26, Monday

I wish J knew that it's only because I care for him so much that I agreed to go on this trip. Why couldn't we have just put everything behind us as we had originally planned?? Every minute on this useless planet is a waste of our time. I love him, and I want to be with him for eternity. We'll finally have some peace. We won't have to listen to anyone, discuss anything, put up with our parents' shit all the time. Sounds too good to be true. Got to go now. Have to throw a few rags in my suitcase before Mom comes up here and starts shooting off her mouth. Won't be able to write anything tomorrow night on the plane. See you Monday.

April 27, Tuesday

We've been here only one day, and I'm already bored shitless. The trip was sooo long. At least Jane sat next to me. We ended up playing cards for hours. J. fell asleep almost immediately. Must be his medication. Met our chaperone and get this, his name is Atticus.

> *Incredible. What kind of mother would name her kid like that?!*
> *He goes on and on telling us worthless crap about this dump of*
> *a city. Should have heard how he got all excited about a stupid*
> *piece of pizza J and I were ordering. He acts squeaky clean with*
> *everyone. He isn't gay because you can tell by the way he keeps*
> *eyeing Cornwall that he wants to get into her pants. Well, See-*
> *ward didn't have any luck, maybe this Atticus guy will.*

I stopped and looked at Barbara. She, of course, knew exactly what part I had reached.

"It gets even better as you read on," she informed me. I returned my gaze to the images, pressing the button to go to the next set of photos.

> *April 28, Wednesday*
>
> *Atticus shocked the hell out of J. and the rest of us this morning!*
> *Seems he's into RATM, Manson, Korn. Pretty frigging weird*
> *for a fifty-year-old. J made a big mistake telling him at the table*
> *that Derek was into Manson. You should have seen Sabrina. I*
> *think she practically shit in her pants. She's such a loser! Thinks*
> *she knows who her brother was when she doesn't have a fucking*
> *clue. I went ballistic when Atticus mentioned her name on our*
> *way to the Vatican. I probably overdid it but who gives a fuck?*
> *It's all going to be over soon, anyhow. Wouldn't it be great to*
> *see the expression on Ramsey's, Seeward's and Cornwall's faces*
> *when they find out? It's really strange but I feel a bit sorry for*
> *Atticus. He'll probably get a whole wagonload of crap poured on*
> *his head from our dear, loving parents (assholes). If he's any sort*
> *of man, he'll tell them to fuck off and that if they didn't want*
> *two screwed up kids they should have aborted or at least attempt-*
> *ed to do something right in these past seventeen years!!! Oh J…I*
> *love you soooo much! It's almost time my love.*

That was it. I looked at Michelle and then at Barbara. We just sat there without saying anything for what seemed an inordinate amount of time.

Finally, Barbara spoke, "Atticus? What do you think we should do first?"

Barbara was staring at me as if she expected me to come up with a brilliant plan. I didn't have one. As a senior manager, I had almost always encountered employees who came to me to get help with stressful personal situations. Some of them had even talked about suicide. But I was always able to hand them over to professional counselors provided by the company. I had no such option now, however.

I turned my attention to Michelle for a moment and attempted to put all the Agatha Christie novels I had read to good use.

"Michelle, you said that you found the diary on the floor. Near Evelyn's bed?"

"Yes, and not even that close to the bed. It was almost in the middle of the room."

"So she was either reading or writing something in it before she decided to start ripping some of the pages out. Then she dropped it on the floor. Did you by any chance notice a pen on the floor as well?"

Michelle shut her eyes for a moment. "No, I don't remember seeing anything except the diary."

"That's okay. If she had a pen or pencil in her hand when she fell asleep, presuming she fell asleep as she was writing in her diary, it could have remained on the bed."

I began to pace slowly in the small amount of space I had available.

"What are you thinking about, Atticus?" Barbara asked.

"I don't understand a few things. Bear with me for a moment. First of all, remember how Evelyn reacted when I held her diary in the air the other day outside of the bus? She seemed genuinely terrified that I had it. My first question is, how do you forget such a precious item on a bus? Why do you even take it out of your bag? She was all over James from the airport to the hotel."

"It may have just slipped out of her bag," Barbara hazarded.

"Maybe. But here's my other question—why didn't Evelyn put her diary away before falling asleep?"

Barbara frowned. "Maybe she just conked out, and it slipped off the bed?"

"Slipped off the bed and bounced almost to the middle of the room? If I'm reading or writing something in my diary in a room that I'm sharing with another person, I'd make damn sure that I put it away in a safe place before going to bed, especially if I'm writing about killing myself. And there's another problem. Why were some of the pages half-torn out? Did she have second thoughts about what she wrote? If so, why didn't she tear out the pages completely and get rid of them in the toilet, for example?"

Michelle rubbed her forehead. "Do you think that Evelyn put the diary on the floor hoping that I would see it and look through it?"

"Yes and no. I think that she may have done it accidentally but on purpose, if you follow me."

Barbara nodded. "You mean, subconsciously, she wants somebody to find out what she's planning so they can stop her?"

"Maybe," I said. I turned to Michelle. "Do you know Evelyn very well?"

Michelle shrugged. "I know she had her share of trouble, and she can be very unforgiving with other people."

"Like with Sabrina?" I said. "She seems to really hate her."

"Exactly. But I try to be close to her when she needs someone to talk to and when James isn't around."

"Does she trust you?"

"I think she trusts me. She complains to me about her parents and their behavior, but not much else."

'You didn't by any chance get to see what she wrote for Tuesday?"

"No. She started moving around in the bed as I finished taking a picture of Monday's entry, so I put the diary back on the floor. I didn't want to risk her waking up and seeing I had it."

"Why?"

"I was thinking about yesterday when we were at St. Yves. She mentioned that the top of the church looked like a miniature Tower of Babel and ran off a verse in the Bible, remember?"

"Sure. Then you and James got into an Elton John trivia contest."

"That's right. Remember how everyone was enjoying James and I prodding each other? Evelyn came up and hugged James afterward, and she looked happy. She didn't seem like someone who wants to commit suicide, at least not at that point."

Michelle nodded. "Evelyn has been in a better mood. She actually told me last night that she was beginning to like Rome."

"I think that's significant," I said. "She's obviously changed her opinion since Monday. We can't dismiss what she's written in her diary, but I don't believe she really wants to end it all."

Barbara shook her head almost violently. "I hope you're not suggesting that we just forget about all of this and hope for the best?" she said. "These two kids are walking on a high wire over the Grand Canyon, and if it snaps, we're going to find ourselves with two lifeless bodies on our hands!"

"I'm fully aware of the gravity of the situation, Barbara, really, I am. The problem, however, isn't Evelyn. It's James. If someone snaps, it'll be him, not Evelyn. Look at the facts for a moment: Evelyn has a sentimental attachment to James. She talks to Michelle occasionally, letting out her frustration about her parents. She has a diary in which she expresses her anger. She's let herself go physically, which is a tangible form of protest, and she makes it clear that she's pissed off at the entire world. In other words, she's venting, and she wants us to listen. The diary on the bus and now on the floor are to get our attention. Now let's consider James. Depressed, antisocial, and on strong medication. And yet a good student without even studying too much, interested in music, and a friend of the most popular guy in school. And what happens? This friend gets flattened by an eighteen-wheeler. It seems that nobody even knew that Derek and James were buddies, except for Evelyn. I haven't seen James socializing with anyone except Jeremy. From what I understand, his parents are at a loss as to what to do with him, so I don't expect that there is much of a meeting of the minds between them. I don't think he has a diary, so he doesn't express himself in writing. To top it all off, he has to listen to Evelyn griping about the world twenty-four seven. So who's the potential time bomb here, Evelyn or James? What did Cynthia say the other day at lunch? That she wouldn't be surprised if James committed suicide. Seems that I'm not the only one who has this nutty idea."

I picked up my phone and looked at the time. It was almost 5:15 am.

"What we need now is a game plan," I continued. "Michelle, you need to go back to your room. When Evelyn wakes up, just act normal. Try to be close to her without raising suspicions. I trust your judgment. If you need to communicate with Barbara or me about anything she says, I'm sure you'll find a way to do it. I'm going to home in on James today. I think I have a good way to reach him."

Michelle nodded, "I'll do my best," she said. She flashed one of the beautiful smiles and left the room. I turned and looked at Barbara. She was on her feet with her arms folded tightly across her chest.

"I don't know if we should be taking this on all by ourselves," she said.

"We have to be very careful how we handle this, Barbara. One mistake on our part could bring about disastrous consequences. If we tell John and Cynthia, and they fly off the handle, it may just push James closer to the brink."

"And Evelyn? You're certain that she's not about to kill herself?"

"I can't be one hundred percent certain. But I've had to deal sometimes with employees who wanted to call it quits, literally and otherwise. Evelyn doesn't fit the profile. Her actions aren't that of a person who wants to end it all. It's the quiet types, like James, who worry me."

She put her head on my shoulder and began crying. I was surprised, but then I realized she felt responsible. "Barbara, none of this has anything to do with you."

"In a way, it does. I've been James's and Evelyn's teachers for four years. Four years and I didn't see any of this happening. I didn't know about Mark having his stomach pumped, and I didn't have a clue about Vanessa...I feel like I've failed with these students, just like I failed with my children."

She took a few deep breaths. I hugged her and planted a soft kiss on her forehead.

"You know what really worries me about Evelyn's diary?" I said.

"What?" she asked, sniffling.

"That it was so obvious that I wanted to get into your pants." Barbara looked up at me abruptly, then laughed, as I had hoped. She wiped her eyes and nose with a tissue.

"Amazing, isn't it, she picked up on that immediately? She hit the nail on the head about John too."

"And you just know that if she figured out all of this, several other students have as well. These kids are much more on the ball than I thought."

"So, Atticus, what do you want me to do?"

"Well, we've got plenty on our plates. I don't know if Vanessa will be strong enough to come on today's tour. I was thinking about asking Sabrina to stay with her today. Can you try to arrange that this morning? We also need to look after Mark. I don't expect any drinking binges during the day, but the evenings are always risky. And to top it off, now we have Evelyn and James. If I see the situation getting out of hand, I promise I'll be the first to blow the whistle and inform John and Cynthia."

Barbara wasn't entirely convinced, but she nodded in agreement. "All right," she said. "I'd better get back to my room before we confirm the students' suspicions."

I laughed.

When she left, I sat on the bed, thinking. I was indeed taking a risk, and Barbara was right to be concerned. Just because I had had some luck in resolving and hiding Mark's foolish escapade and Vanessa's pharmaceutical joyride didn't mean that I had what it took to prevent two possible suicide attempts. I had absolutely no experience in adolescent psychology and no direct experience with teenagers. These were not managerial problems that required a business solution, but issues involving human beings at an extremely delicate age.

"Be sure of what you're doing, Atticus," I told myself.

I decided to shower, put on a fresh set of clothes, and take a walk around the hotel to clear my head. It wasn't even seven o'clock yet. There was an hour and a half before the group met for breakfast.

When I arrived down in the hall, Ludovica was already diligently at work in front of her computer terminal.

"Good morning, Ludovica."

"Good morning, Mr. Winterle. You are up early this morning."

"Yes, indeed. I take it Giovanni has already finished his shift?"

"He left about an hour ago. By the way, Mr. Winterle, I believe you were expecting this from Mr. Oddino."

She handed me a white vanilla envelope with my name on it. I tore open the top and peered inside. It was the document that I needed to fill out regarding the behavior of our guide at the Pantheon. I folded the envelope and put it in my pocket.

"Thanks, Ludovica. I'm going out for a little pre-breakfast walk."

"Be careful of the street cleaners, Mr. Winterle. They're going around the area in those little sweeping machines. They will not stop for your trousers."

"I'll keep my eyes open, Ludovica. Thanks again." I probably stared at her a little longer than I should have, judging from the way her cheeks became bright red. What a charming and graceful young lady she was.

As soon as I was outside of the hotel's sliding doors, I smelled the soapy, industrial scent that told me the street-cleaning machines had already passed by. I slowly made my way toward the direction of Piazza Trevi, being extra careful on the wet cobblestones. When I arrived at the fountain, I took in the sights and sounds of the early morning in this small corner of the Eternal City: elderly couples making their way to morning mass; a small group of partygoers who were finishing off their long night with an early morning cappuccino at a small outdoor kiosk; groggy-looking city sanitation workers cleaning up yesterday's trash around the fountain; and a few homeless people waking from a night on hard granite benches in one of the world's most picturesque settings.

The smell of fresh pastries from the various bakeries located near the Trevi Fountain was so overwhelming that

I decided I couldn't wait for breakfast back at the hotel. I entered a coffee bar that was right next to the small establishment where Barbara, Darlene, and I had had drinks on Sunday night. It was only three days ago, but it seemed more like three months with all that had happened since then.

The scene inside the bar was so very familiar. Patrons were exchanging heated opinions on yesterday's news events, a few elderly women were sharing neighborhood gossip, two well-dressed gentlemen were discussing a business deal, and the Cimbali coffee machine was spewing out espresso in a set of warm little cups. The only two things that were different from Filippo's bar was the view outside and the two German tourists who were attempting to ask the cashier for directions. I ordered a cappuccino and a cornetto filled with apricot jam and decided to sit at a table toward the end of the bar rather than consume my pre-breakfast treat standing at the counter. I bit into the warm pastry, then uncapped my fountain pen, and took out my trusty Moleskine notebook from my back pocket. As soon as the nib of the pen touched the empty page, it took off as if it had a life of its own:

1. What were we doing today? Colosseum, Roman Forum and then? / Need to check voucher for lunch location.
2. Keep watchful eye on Evelyn / Liaise with Michelle as much as possible / First sign of trouble blow the whistle?
3. Need to get Vanessa hooked up with Sabrina for the day / Barbara checking up on this.
4. Get more involved with James after today's tour go to Franco's CD store with him / Try to milk him for more info.
5. Watch out for Darlene's new friend / Seems innocent enough.

6. Is Mark out of the woods? / Keep an eye on him.
7. Wayne, Bishop, Michelle need to speak with me / About what?
8. Anthony + Cynthia / need to understand what's going on here.
9. Remember to give some time to Raymond / Promised him tomorrow night.
10. Remember to fill out ASA's questionnaire / Lousy guide.
11. Barbara? Tonight? Hopefully...
12. Check out the bar where Mark got smashed on tequila. Call Giorgio.

That seemed more than enough to chew on for now. I closed the notebook, finished the small amount of cappuccino left in my cup, and left the bar.

CHAPTER 28

The commotion around the Piazza Trevi was intensifying. There were already two large groups of tourists standing near the edge of the fountain, both led by flag-waving tour guides. One was carrying a small British flag, the other a Spanish one. How many times had Oceanus, standing erect in his chariot with the thundering sound of cascading water around him, looked down upon admiring eyes from all over the world? How many generations had he seen come and go and how many more would he see before becoming another architectural casualty of Father Time's inexorable passage?

I turned onto the Via Lucchesi in the direction of the hotel, stumbled on a cobblestone, and inadvertently bumped into a thin woman right in front of me. As I started apologizing, I saw to my great surprise that I had run into Cynthia.

"Well good morning, Atticus!" she said, having regained her balance. "You're up and about early this morning."

"Good morning to you as well, and apologies for having crashed into you. I lost my footing there for a moment."

"No harm done. Isn't it just a beautiful morning? I've been walking around since six."

"Did you have a cappuccino and a pastry? They're fresh out of the oven at this hour."

"No, but you're tempting me."

"Come on, then, I'll lead the way."

My invitation had an ulterior purpose. It was time to start digging into Anthony's background, and this was a perfect opportunity. I found a smaller coffee bar with a few tables outside. We sat down and ordered, and I waited until our coffee and pastries came, chatting aimlessly. Once they were before us, however, I stopped the pleasantries, bluntly raising my concern with her.

"Cynthia, I was wondering if you could help me. I've been asking myself some questions regarding our group."

"More than glad to help if I can."

"I had some trouble falling asleep last night, so I picked up those student questionnaires and went through a few in detail. You've read them, haven't you?"

"Oh, yes. John, Barbara, and I all have copies. Which students were you scrutinizing?"

"Actually, one in particular—Anthony."

She tried to look nonchalant as if my bringing up that particular student was no different from any other name. But her thin fingers picked nervously at her pastry.

"What about Anthony?" she asked, her tone already defensive.

"Everything, Cynthia, from his hobbies to his wanting to be a plastic surgeon. You remember some of things he wrote, don't you?"

Cynthia remained silent, biting into her brioche. I pressed on:

"And polo? Anthony doesn't strike me as being the polo-playing type at all. Then he has all this information and interest in firearms, but he left that out of his hobbies. And do you remember what he wrote about why he wanted to come on this trip? It's straight out of a guidebook, word for word."

Cynthia still said nothing, but she was looking distressed.

"He wants to be a plastic surgeon," I continued remorselessly, "yet he didn't mention where he's going to college, and I don't—"

Cynthia raised her hand abruptly, stopping me. "Why in the world does Anthony's questionnaire bother you so much, Atticus? Has he created any problems on this trip so far? Has he been misbehaving or rude? Aren't there others in the group who require more attention with their antics?"

She was right. There were others who did need more attention, but Cynthia didn't know that. And I wasn't about to tell her.

"Actually, no, Cynthia," I lied. "The other students have not been a concern. The troublemakers, according to you, are Wayne, Bishop, Mark, and, to some extent, Darlene. But all of them have been on their best behavior since they got here." The Holy Father himself could not have said this with greater sincerity. "But one student who can't tell the truth if his life depended upon it and who can give a detailed plan on how to shoot a pope between the eyes with a sniper rifle is Anthony."

If looks were daggers, I would have been sliced to pieces by Cynthia's piercing gaze. She rose abruptly, ready to walk off. I caught her arm. "Cynthia, I know you care about this boy," I said. "If you do, look at Anthony's questionnaire again. Then let's talk about it. I think he needs help, and I think you might be the best person to give him that help."

She didn't answer me, and I let go of her arm. I paid for our breakfast, then we walked back the short distance to the hotel in silence. As we entered the lobby, Cynthia excused herself and said that she would be down at nine o'clock to catch the bus. I went to the restaurant.

Nearly everyone from the group was already there, filling their plates at the buffet table or polishing off what they had already taken. Barbara, Mary, Sabrina, and Vanessa were at their table, so I went across to them before going to get my own breakfast.

"Good morning," I said. I turned to Vanessa. "I'm surprised to see you down here. How are you feeling?"

"Much better, Atticus," she replied. "I woke up starving. Sabrina and I came down at a quarter to eight. I know everyone wants me to rest, but I want to come on the tour today. If I get tired, Sabrina and Mrs. Cornwall said they would come back to the hotel with me."

I looked at Barbara, who nodded.

"Okay, it'll be good to have you with us."

I walked over to the breakfast items but only took a jelly-filled *ciambella*, the Italian rendition of a donut, and a glass of grapefruit juice before heading to the table where Anthony and Raymond were sitting.

We exchanged good mornings, and Raymond immediately asked me if there were any synagogues nearby.

"Yes," I replied. "The Great Synagogue of Rome is not far, and if I remember correctly, there's a museum in there as well. Pope John Paul II visited that synagogue in 1986. A historic moment, considering that no pope had officially attended a synagogue in centuries."

I regretted my comment even as the words were leaving my mouth. I had once again opened myself to a religious rejoinder from this young man. And Raymond did not disappoint.

"I guess that John Paul thought he could wipe away hundreds of years of religious persecution against the Jews by showing up and patting the chief rabbi on the back. The Catholic Church must have gotten some good media coverage."

How much bitterness was in this boy?

"I don't think that it was the wrong thing to do, Raymond. John Paul's visit was probably a good start in warming relations between two of the most important religious faiths in the world." Raymond opened his mouth again, but I wasn't going to let him get one more word in edgewise. "Remember," I cut across, "we made a deal to meet up before you leave so that we can discuss all of this a bit more in depth."

"Yeah, I haven't forgotten."

I turned to Anthony, who was concentrating on his plate.

"Anthony, I saw on your student bio that you're into polo."

This was hitting below the belt, but I was determined to get him to tell the truth for once. Even Raymond looked at Anthony suspiciously.

"Oh, you read that?" he said, stabbing at his scrambled eggs nervously. "Well, yeah. I guess I am. I mean, it's okay." He may have been a bad liar in writing, but he was even worse once his mouth opened.

"Good. There's a polo field not too far from here. I believe they let anybody join in on a game. Do you prefer arena polo or regular outdoors?"

"No real preference. Arena or outdoor, it's all the same to me."

Wrong answer Anthony. I was digging a hole for him, and he was ready to fall in.

There's a big difference between the two variants. If you played arena polo, which requires a much shorter field and three players, you were not likely to be comfortable in regular polo, where the field could be up to three hundred yards long and required four players to a team.

"Do you play defense or offense?" I asked.

I was staring at him unblinkingly. Sweat started to form on his temples.

"I, um, prefer defense…" He almost stuttered.

"Ah. So, if I remember correctly, letters A and B are the offensive players and C and D the defensive ones. Do you play C or D?"

In fact, the four players on a polo team are numbered 1 through 4, the first two being offence and the last two defense.

"Sometimes A, sometimes B."

With this second answer, Anthony was at the bottom of the hole with no chance of climbing out. He obviously knew nothing about polo. I had enough to confirm this for now, so I stopped my grilling and looked at the time.

"We need to be out of here in ten minutes. Finish up, and I'll meet you in the hall." Anthony was only too relieved to see me get up and leave the table.

I clapped my hands. "Can I have everyone's attention please?" I said. "We've got ten minutes before we meet in the hall. The bus is waiting for us."

I left the restaurant area and went back to my room to collect the vouchers, my wallet, and my guidebook. I descended the steps by twos to the reception area. When I arrived, the only other person there was Cynthia. As soon as she saw me, she got up and came toward me.

"Atticus, I want to apologize once again for my behavior. I know there's a problem with Anthony, but I…I just have a hard time admitting it." This was certainly unexpected. "I don't need to read Anthony's bio to know where the pitfalls lie. I know Anthony very, very well." She paused and looked over my shoulder. We were still alone.

"If we can find some time to discuss this, I would appreciate it. It felt so natural telling you about my husband that I'm certain I'll feel better after telling you about my concerns about Anthony."

This sounded almost ominous. I had the feeling that instead of just discovering the bad habits of an insecure young man, I was about to enter a much larger emotional orbit.

"I'd like to get your input, Cynthia. I'm not trying to poke into people's lives here, but I am worried about Anthony."

"I believe you are, Atticus," she said. "That means a lot to me."

With that, she gently squeezed my hand and released it just as the students came walking in.

Back to the role of chaperone. I stepped forward. "Okay then, ladies and gentlemen, if you have everything you need for the day, we can head out." I did a quick head count. Everyone was accounted for.

The students made their way through sliding doors and took a left up the long narrow street to where the Mercedes bus was parked. I waited for James to pass before making my way into the line. I had to find an excuse to spend some time with him alone and had come up with what I believed was a clever scheme—I would invite him to do some music shopping with me at an old hangout. The stumbling block was that Evelyn and Jeremy were stuck to James like glue. Well, it was now or never.

"James." I tapped him on the shoulder.

All three stopped and turned. "Hey, Atticus," James said.

"I need to go get some CDs I've been meaning to buy. How about coming with me later on to a music store not far from the hotel?"

Before James could answer, Jeremy cut in, "No problem, Atticus. I'd like to see what's on the charts over here."

"It's all right with me." Evelyn chimed in. Although my focus was on James, I took it as a good sign that Evelyn wanted to be involved. James himself finally answered:

"Yeah, sounds good."

"Great," I said. "We'll meet up then when we get back to the hotel."

We made good progress getting to the bus. The students were really getting the hang of avoiding cars, motor scooters, and other pedestrians on the narrow Roman streets. Riccardo was smoking a cigarette and talking vehemently on his cell phone. When he saw us, he waved and moved off to the side. I could tell by the way he kept gesticulating that he was very upset with the person at the other end of the line.

As the group entered the bus, I realized that Riccardo was speaking—more accurately, pleading—with his wife. He was desperately attempting to reassure her that he hadn't been in somebody else's company the night before and that she was insulting him by even thinking such a thing.

We were all comfortably seated when Riccardo finished his phone call, entered the bus, and settled into the driver's seat. He was mumbling expletives to himself.

"Everything okay, Riccardo?" I asked diffidently.

"My old lady, she's always on my back, always complaining, always checking in on me. She never believes anything I say!"

I could have pointed out that his wife had some basis for not believing him, but I suspected he wouldn't have understood.

Italian men make a distinction between their wives and their mistresses. The wife is to be respected, revered, and placed on a pedestal, especially if also a mother. Sexual excitement, however, tends to dissipate when the initial passion becomes the monotony of day-to-day routine. It's the "I can't do *that* with her anymore" syndrome even if, in most cases, the wife has no problem continuing to do *that*. Plenty of other women are available to fulfill those sexual fantasies that the husband no longer cares to do with his wife. This approach to intimacy probably isn't much different from the way many married men around the world view the lifespan of sexual activity with their wives. I thought for a moment about Barbara, who was sitting right behind me. The bus bounced as it hit a crater in the road, shaking me out of my thoughts, and I realized that I had left Riccardo hanging.

"You need to cover your tracks, my friend," I said hastily. "Your wife obviously knows you well."

He grumbled a bit. Evidently, he wasn't going to change his ways, but he probably didn't want to upset his wife more than absolutely necessary. "I'll bring her some flowers tonight. That should calm things down a bit."

I grinned to myself. How much time would pass before the next heated phone call?

"Atticus, where are we heading to this morning?" asked Mary.

I took the microphone from its holder and switched it on. "We have another full day ahead of us and it starts with the Colosseum. What does word *Colosseum* bring to your minds?"

"Gladiators!"

"The thumbs-up and thumbs-down routine!"

"Christians being torn apart by lions!"

"Russell Crowe!" I didn't have to turn my head to know it was Darlene who had come up with that analogy. At least she had been able to link the film *Gladiator* to the Colosseum, even though her interest was in Mr. Crowe.

"*Gotta Be Somebody*," said someone else.

This made me get out of my seat. I looked at James, who had a satisfied grin on his face. This was obviously another challenge. What was he referring to? I didn't have a clue. Everyone was looking at me, expecting an answer.

"I'm throwing in the towel on this one, James. Mind filling me in?"

Jeremy, Evelyn, and a few others were patting James on the back.

"You've heard of the band Nickelback, haven't you?"

"Sure, I've got a few of their CDs. *Silver Side Up* and *The Long Road.*"

"But you obviously stopped there. Haven't you heard their latest album, *Dark Horse?*"

I hadn't. I just stood there, watching James and the rest getting a kick out of my silence. Little did they know how pleased I was to see James and Evelyn smiling with the others. Michelle, who was sitting directly behind Evelyn, shot me another one of those contagious smiles.

"Haven't seen the music video for 'Gotta Be Somebody' either, have you?"

"I'm not into music videos," I answered.

"That's a pretty lame excuse, Atticus." James was in his glee. "For your information, the first part of the 'Gotta Be Somebody' music video takes place in the Colosseum."

"You obviously haven't seen *Transformers 2*, Atticus." Jeremy was out to get a piece of me as well.

"Actually, I have, but I didn't like it."

"Excuses, excuses. What's the theme song of that movie, Atticus? Or is it too *commercial* for you?" This additional jab from James received a series of *ooohs* and "Two points for James!" from the group.

"'Burn it to the Ground,' Atticus, also off of the *Dark Horse* album. You should listen to it and catch up a bit on your music trivia. You're a slacker."

I wasn't just going to sit back and take this. I decided to come back at James with something he could never know.

"Evanescence."

"What about them?" I had James's attention.

"What was their first album?"

"*Fallen*, 2004," James replied smugly.

"Nope, you have to go back to 1998." This was Mark surprising me now. "Evanescence EP, there are seven tracks by Amy Lee and Be Moody."

"Very good, Mark," I said.

"You're talking about my favorite band, Atticus," Mark rejoined.

"Okay. Well then, Mark, James—what's on the cover of that record?"

"An angel."

"Good, Mark, but I need more. James, not up on your Evanescence trivia, I see."

"I'm not really into them."

"Well, for your information, that angel is part of a tomb, and that tomb is in that cemetery near the large pyramid we passed coming in from the airport."

"You've got to be effing kidding me!" Mark exclaimed. "That's unreal. I've got to see that!"

"I highly recommend it, Mark. And, James, by the way, you've got a few more days in this town, my friend. I'll be waiting for you." With that, I brought my index and middle fingers up to my eyes and then turned them in James's direction, a gesture which I believe was still in vogue.

"Come at me whenever you want, Atticus," he said, grinning.

I felt a slight tug on my shirt—Riccardo was trying to get my attention. We were practically in front of the Colosseum, but the onboard "entertainment" had absorbed everyone's attention, and nobody had really noticed.

"*Tra poco mi fermo*, Signor Winterle," Riccardo informed me that very soon he was going to stop and let us off. We had already gone all the way down the Via dei Fori Imperiali, the road of the Imperial Forums, and had entered the Piazza del Colosseo. We swerved around to the right of the Colosseum on to the Via Celio Vibenna, a very short portion of wide road named after an Etruscan ruler who, along with his brother Aulo Vibenna, conquered Rome in the sixth century BC. This road then takes on the name of Via di San Gregorio, after Pope Gregory I, as soon as it straightens out heading southeast from the Colosseum.

There was a long line of tour buses on the Via di San Gregorio, and Riccardo was having difficulty finding a place large enough to fit ours. We were to meet our guide at the Arch of Constantine at 9:45 am, so we still had some time to spare. We were practically at the end of the road when Riccardo noticed a bus pulling out of its slot.

"*Eccoci!*" Riccardo's, "Here we are!" was synchronized by his skillful maneuvering of the Mercedes into the now available parking space.

"We've arrived, everyone. We need to get out of the bus and head back down this road toward the Colosseum. Take a look on your left as you do so, and you'll see a portion of the Palatine Hill, where many of the Roman emperors had their palaces."

As I was about to exit the front of the bus, I placed my hand on Riccardo's shoulder and told him to go easy on his wife this evening.

"*Si, si, è una brava donna, solo un pò rompi palle.*" He admitted to me that she was a "good woman" but that she tended to "break his balls." There was nothing else to add.

"We will meet here at three thirty, after your lunch, on this street," Riccardo reminded me.

"Ah, yes, that's right. See you then." Thank goodness he had mentioned the pickup time and lunch. I hadn't even looked at the voucher and neither had a clue as to where the restaurant was nor the time we had to be there.

As Riccardo drove off, I quickly opened my briefcase, fumbled through the papers, and found Marco's notebook. I looked up Day Four: today's restaurant was on Via Capo d'Africa and was called Al Foro—meaning "at the Forum." We had to be there at one forty-five. I knew that this was one of the roads that branched off from the east side of the Colosseum and ran parallel to Via San Giovanni in Laterano, but which one was it?

"Everything okay, Atticus?" asked Barbara, seeing me frowning.

"Absolutely, Barbara. Just getting my bearings for the day."

She winked at me and grinned, which helped put me at ease. I would worry about the road later.

CHAPTER 29

We started down the broad, tree-lined sidewalk in the direction of the Colosseum, which was partially visible from where we were. Our guide's name for the day was Massimo. According to Marco's notes, he would be waiting in front of the Arch of Constantine with a flag of some sort that we would easily recognize.

John and Cynthia were lagging behind, soaking in everything with greedy eyes. Barbara was up ahead, within earshot of Evelyn. She was probably not enjoying the sights as much as her two colleagues, given her worry over Evelyn. This was unfortunate. We were just one hundred yards away from the nerve center of one of mankind's greatest civilizations, and it was well worth absorbing as much of the atmosphere as possible. Each of the students was enthralled by the spectacle before them. Off to the right stood the Colosseum, a testament to the glory of Rome. The Arch of Constantine was now directly in front of us while to the left a large open area was filled with grandiose ruins—the heart of the Roman Forum.

Vanessa turned to me. "Hey, Atticus, I think that's our guide over there."

She pointed toward a rather young man wearing a pair of oversized feminine sunglasses. He had on dark-purple pants, pointed ankle-high boots, a white-and-purple striped shirt, and an off-white linen jacket. A bow tie with purple polka dots completed his attire. More than his flamboyant dress, however, what drew Vanessa's attention was the large Coca-Cola flag he was holding above his head—certainly a very noticeable and appropriate form of identification for our group. As soon he noticed us, he began waving his flag excitedly and called,

"Hello, everyone!" His voice was somewhat high-pitched, and I heard some giggling behind me.

"Massimo, I presume?" I stretched out my hand.

"Yes, yes, Massimo is my name, Massimo Angelini. You must be Atticus, Atticus Winterle, correct?" He shook my hand gently without gripping it.

"That's right. And this is the group from Atlanta, but I think you already know that." I pointed to the flag.

"Oh yes, yes! Atlanta, the home of Coca-Cola!"

He waved the flag a bit more in a joyous fashion, which generated some more giggling. I cut it short by loudly introducing John, Cynthia, and Barbara. The students had formed a circle around us and were scrutinizing Massimo from head to toe. He didn't take exception to this and just started chatting away. His English was excellent, with only a slight Italian accent.

"Beautiful, beautiful city, Atlanta. I had a marvelous time there. I enjoyed the High Museum of Art, Stone Mountain, the Atlanta Botanical Garden, and the Coca-Cola Museum, naturally! Unfortunately, I was only there three days, so I didn't see as much as I wanted to."

"I've lived in Atlanta all my life, and I didn't even know there was a botanical garden, and I've never been to the High Museum," Mary admitted.

"Oh, but you must go to both! Just the collection of orchids is enough to take your breath away! And after the gardens, it's just a hop, skip, and a jump to the High Museum. The modern art section is to die for!" Massimo probably realized that he was going off track and suddenly changed tone, bringing us all back to Rome:

"Enough, enough, we can speak about Atlanta some other time. We're here today to speak about all of *this*!" Massimo spread out his arms in homage to the monuments surrounding us. "I want all of you to look at this incredible structure right here next to us before we head over to the

Colosseum. This is the Arch of Constantine. Where can I begin? Look at the magnificence! Look at the details! Would anyone here like to tell us why this structure is called the Arch of Constantine and who Constantine was?"

"He was the emperor that stopped persecuting Christians. Isn't that what Rosanna told us at the Vatican, Atticus?"

I looked at Vanessa and nodded approvingly. She was still rather pale and had some residue circles under her eyes, but she was attentive.

"And he signed some sort of decree that made Christianity the official religion," Sabrina added.

"The Edict of Milan, signed in 313," said Raymond.

Massimo placed his hands on his heart. "Wonderful! Just wonderful. How very nice to have such a knowledgeable group! Just one correction, if I may: the Edict of Milan decreed religious toleration for Christians. It did not automatically make Christianity the official religion. It helped, of course, that Constantine converted to the Christian faith in 312 after the battle of the Milvian Bridge, which is not very far from where we are standing. Does this battle ring a bell with anyone?"

Everyone was silent. Massimo was about to explain when a voice piped up hesitantly from behind Evelyn and James. It was Michelle.

"Constantine wanted to put an end to the tetrarchy, the rule of the four emperors, that started around the year 300. He fought one of these emperors, Maxentius, at the Milvian Bridge. Constantine won the battle. Maxentius died in the Tiber River. This Arch was built to commemorate that battle."

Before Massimo could respond, someone behind me said: "There's a statue of Constantine at St. Peter's. Before you go in, to the right." It was James. I remembered that he had pointed this out to me when we were at the Vatican.

"I have no words!" Massimo gushed. "Maybe all of you need to take *me* around for a tour and not vice versa!"

He pointed at Michelle. "And you, young lady!" To be so knowledgeable about the Battle of the Milvian Bridge and Maxentius! Impressive, truly impressive." Massimo began applauding, and the rest of us joined in. Michelle blushed. I glanced over at Raymond who, once again, was looking at Michelle adoringly. I wondered if she knew about her admirer.

"Now, let's see if I can tell you a few things about this masterpiece that you *don't* know," Massimo continued. "I admit this may be difficult, but let's see." Massimo truly had a flare for rapidly engaging the students and teachers. This tour was going to be a success.

He began by going over the standard details regarding the height, length, and width of this three-entrance arch with its high central opening and lower side openings, as well as the general layout of this structure with its eight Corinthian columns, four on each side, the entablature, and the attic, which is the architectural term for the large, upper portion of an arch. Massimo reiterated the year of its completion, around AD 316, and that it was the Roman Senate that dedicated this arch to Constantine for winning the battle. He then began to meticulously point out the various friezes, reliefs, and statues that covered the arch, doing so in such an enthusiastic fashion that you were bound to listen.

The most surprising information we got from Massimo was that a large portion of what we were seeing had been recycled from existing monuments dedicated to other emperors such as Hadrian and Trajan, who ruled almost two hundred years before Constantine. Massimo went on to explain that there were various opinions regarding this use of existing statues and reliefs. One such theory was that since the Roman Empire was no longer in expansion but in a process of "downsizing," as it were, many architects' and sculptors' studios had closed for lack of work. Supply and demand—the times may change, but this golden rule of economics always holds true.

Another theory held that there just wasn't enough time to complete the arch, given its impossible deadline and that existing relief works had to be practically "glued" onto the exterior.

"If I was Emperor of Rome, I wouldn't want a rehashed monument," Anthony asserted.

"Very good point young man!" Massimo responded. "What is your name?"

"Anthony."

"Ahh, Anthony, which translates into *Antonius* in Latin. The great Marcus Antonius or Mark Anthony in the English language. His love affair with Cleopatra is legendary to this day."

Anthony blushed a bit and lowered his head.

"Well, Anthony, how right you are! Who in their right mind, and as Emperor, would want a secondhand pieced-together monument? Was the use of statues and reliefs from monuments dedicated to Hadrian and Trajan an insinuation that better times were a thing of the past? Or was the use of these sculptured elements an honor instead of an affront? Hadrian and Trajan were venerated as being good and just emperors who brought peace and long-overdue prosperity to Rome. Equating Constantine to these two individuals may have been a form of flattery. In my opinion, though, I believe Anthony is correct. There's something very odd about all of this."

"Is there anything on this arch that pertains to Constantine?" Cynthia asked.

"Yes, amazingly, there is! Look at the top of the two smaller arches right and left. You see that series of friezes there? They wrap around to the sides of the arch as well. Those are totally dedicated to Constantine."

He proceeded to speak about each one, even though it was rather difficult to differentiate what was happening given the sheer number of figures and objects that made up each panel. On the side of the arch facing away from the Colosseum, Massimo showed us the most important relief, according to him. This showed Constantine's soldiers on a makeshift wooden bridge fighting against Maxentius's men, who were drowning in the Tiber. The students were all straining to get a better look at the overwhelming battle, which had been chiseled onto such a small space of marble.

Massimo continued: "Another element totally dedicated to Constantine is the inscription that you see in the center of the attic, and which is repeated on each side of the Arch."

He began to read the inscription in perfect Latin in an oratorical tone of voice. When he finished, most of the students clapped, and he bowed flamboyantly. What a character!

"My friends, we could spend all day here examining and commenting on this structure, but we need to move on. Let me just close by saying that in the inscription I just read you, there is a phrase which says *quod instinctu divinitatis*, which means 'by divine inspiration.' In other words, by divine inspiration, Constantine 'delivered the state from the tyrant.' This refers to the legend that Constantine had a dream before the battle on the Milvian Bridge, where he was told to place the sign of the Latin Cross on the shields of his soldiers. This would ensure his victory over Maxentius. Constantine converted to Christianity shortly after this victory, and as one of you so correctly mentioned, he went on to sign the Edict of Milan in 313. Now I ask myself, does 'by divine inspiration' here on the inscription refer to Jesus Christ? Because, if you remember correctly, and this is what I find puzzling, we saw reliefs on the arch depicting sacrifices to the pagan gods— Apollo, god of the sun, and Diana, the goddess of the hunt, to name a few. What is all this telling us? My opinion is that there are still many unresolved mysteries wrapped around this monument, as well as Constantine's conversion to Christianity. So be it! We must be off now!"

And with this Massimo turned, lifted his head as though he were a Shakespearian actor, and set off toward the Colosseum.

He walked at a rapid pace, and most of the students had to trot to catch up with him. Cynthia and John lagged behind with me. I could immediately tell from their disapproving expressions that they were about to trash Massimo.

"Atticus, this guide," John began. "He knows his stuff, and he certainly has the group's attention…"

"But look at how he's dressed and how he acts," Cynthia chimed in. "It's completely inappropriate, if you ask me."

Barbara rolled her eyes. "Oh, Cynthia, please!" she said. "What does it matter as long as he does his job?"

John, probably realizing Barbara wasn't on the same page, attempted to backpedal with a joke. "Don't worry, Cynthia, Atticus and I will take him down if he touches one of the boys' butts."

Cynthia was indignant.

"Don't be so vulgar, John. I didn't mean *that*! One can't even express an opinion anymore."

"Don't worry, Cynthia. If perchance Massimo were to act in a way that embarrasses someone, I'll take care of it." She looked at me, and I could tell that what I had just said hadn't reassured her in the least. With that, Cynthia quickened her pace. Barbara, John, and I just grinned at one another.

We caught up with the rest of the group. Strangely, Massimo had passed the entrance I had always taken to go into the Colosseum and had instead gone farther up, stopping at a large patch of small trees located close to the Via Foro Imperiali, the grand avenue that ran along the entire Roman Forum.

"Ladies and gentlemen! Welcome to the Colosseum!" Massimo announced.

Massimo pointed to the low, unkempt knoll directly in front of him. The students looked at Massimo and began chuckling. He just stood there, smiling more and more broadly. I could feel Cynthia's apprehension.

"Nobody knows what in the world I'm talking about?" Massimo said, clapping his hands. "Oh, this is just fabulous!"

Massimo then cleared his throat, clasped his hands, and began speaking in a strong, clear voice, like a tenured history professor in a university class. It was almost uncanny how easily he shifted from silly to savant.

"This is where a large statue of the emperor Nero, well over one hundred twenty feet high, was located after being moved from his incredibly luxurious palace, the Domus Aurea, which covered portions of the Palatine Hill behind us, the Esquiline Hill in front of us and to the left, and the Caelian Hill farther back. More than a palace, it was more like a small town, twice as large as your Perimeter Shopping Mall back home."

"That's where I get my hair done!" Darlene almost squealed.

The students were clearly impressed by Massimo's detailed knowledge of their home city.

Massimo continued: "This statue was known as the *Colossus Neronis*, the *Colossus of Nero*. Where you now see the *Amphiteatrum Flavia*, or 'Flavian's Amphitheater' in English"—he pointed to what we all believed to be the Colosseum—"there was an artificial lake that was part of Nero's magnificent living quarters. So, you see, ladies and gentlemen, the Colosseum, as the world knows it today, is named incorrectly. The Colosseum referred *only* to Nero's statue, which stood here *before* the construction of the amphitheater and well into the Middle Ages."

"There must be an explanation for this change of names, I presume?" John inquired.

"Well, yes, there is, if we listen to what various historians, philosophers, and religious authorities have told us over the centuries. But it almost seems too simple to believe. We know that Saint Bede, the English monk who lived from the late seventh to the early eighth century, mentions the *Colossus* in one of his works, stating that as long as it stood, Rome would stand. Given that he was referring to the statue of Nero, we know that it was still standing in the eighth century. It is argued that before the year 1000, the statue was torn down for its bronze. From that point on, the statue was practically forgotten, and the name *Colossus* was inherited, shall we say, by the amphitheater. This seems to be the explanation. Who's the poet in the group?"

For a moment the students, who had been listening intently, were confused by this sudden question. I looked at Michelle and Cynthia to see if they would acknowledge their poetic inclinations. After a few seconds, Cynthia raised her hand.

"Good! Can you tell me, my dear, something about George Gordon Byron, better known as Lord Byron?"

Cynthia frowned, but I couldn't tell whether it was because she was trying to remember what she knew about Byron or whether she was offended by Massimo calling her "dear."

"He was one of the finest English poets who ever lived, a true romantic," she began. "He produced his best work in the first twenty years of the nineteenth century, led an unruly personal life in England, and spent his last years in Italy and in Greece where he died at the age of thirty-six fighting in the Greek War of Independence."

"Marvelous! Do you study any of his works in class?"

"Only a few, unfortunately. *The Corsair*, a few cantos of *Don Juan*, but that's about it."

"What about Childe Harold's Pilgrimage?" Massimo asked.

"No, unfortunately."

"Truly unfortunate." Massimo kicked a stone with his pointed ankle boot. He then spread out his arms. We were about to get another performance.

"While stands the Coliseum, Rome shall stand; When falls the Coliseum, Rome shall fall; And when Rome falls—The World. From our own land, Thus spake the Pilgrims o'er this mighty wall, In Saxon times, which we are wont to call Ancient; and these three mortal things are still On their foundations, and unalter'd all; Rome and her Ruin past Redemption's skill, The world, the same wide den—of thieves or what ye will."

Massimo stopped and slowly brought his hands down to his side, bowing his head as would an actor on stage. Another round of applause rose up from the group.

"Thank you, thank you, my friends. *Childe Harold's Pilgrimage* is by far my favorite epic poem and the fourth canto, verse 145, fits just beautifully with what we were saying about the Colosseum. Byron was referring here in this verse to the amphitheater and not to the *Colossus of Nero.* He may not even have known that such a statue existed. Enough now! Let's go off to see the gladiators!"

Massimo again began strolling quickly, this time in the direction of the entrance of one of the most well-known monuments in the world. Once again, the students were scampering behind him, with Cynthia, John, Barbara, and me attempting to keep pace.

"Well, he certainly knows his poetry, as well as the city of Atlanta."

Massimo had started to make a favorable impression on Cynthia.

"He's just great," said Barbara. "Look at how the students are all flocking around him.,"

"Him, or *her?*" John said.

"Oh, John, cut it out," Barbara replied. "That sounds like something Wayne would say."

I found it interesting that Barbara had specifically mentioned our basketball jock. Since we had joined Massimo, I had observed that the students who I most expected to poke fun at his flamboyant dress and manner were, instead, quite respectful. Wayne, Bishop, and Mark were, in fact, sticking closest to Massimo's side as he went from one place to the other. *Curious,* I thought.

As we approached the entrance of the Colosseum, the crowd of people around us tripled. As with the Vatican, there was a line for groups and for individuals. Massimo adroitly made his way through the throng to one of the makeshift counters. He waved to a young man sitting behind a large pane of glass, who was evidently selling entrance tickets. As soon as he noticed Massimo, the young man got up out of his seat, leaving the people in line just standing there, and came up with a broad smile to Massimo. There were effusive salutations.

Massimo handed him some paperwork. They chatted a few more minutes, and I overheard the young man say that there was extensive restoration going on throughout the Colosseum and that we would only be able to go to the front portico area. Massimo took it all in stride. They kissed each other on the cheek and hugged before the young man went back behind the glass-paned counter to wait on what had become a very impatient line of visitors. Massimo raised his Coca-Cola flag and yelled, "Follow me!"

We made our way down the corridor, turning at the black and yellow detour signs that were up everywhere. There was a little pushing and shoving with all the tourists who were coming and going, but we finally made it to the inner portion of the Colosseum.

The students were mesmerized by the spectacle in front of them. We were on the east side of the Colosseum. The enormity of the ellipse before us reflected the Romans' impressive architectural skills.

With its 617-foot length, 156-foot width along its transverse axis, and its approximately 164 feet in height, the Colosseum to this day still manifested its past glory. Massimo had propped himself up on a large stone protruding from below the railing.

"*Senatus Popolusque Romanus*!" Massimo addressed us as the "Senate and People of Rome." He lifted his arms, his head thrown back. "Look before you and marvel! Marvel at the power and glory which was Rome! '*I see before me the gladiator lie: he leans upon his hand – his manly brow consents to death, but conquers agony and his droop'd head sinks gradually low and through his side the last drops, ebbing slow From the red gash, fall heavy, one by one, Like the first of a thunder shower; and now the arena swims around him—he is gone, ere ceased the inhumane shout which hail'd the wretch who won.*'"

Massimo dropped his head forward, as though exhausted from his speech. Then he looked at us. "How fitting this verse from *Childe Harold's Pilgrimage*, don't you think?"

The group, surrounded now by visitors from all over the world, was a bit subdued in their applause. Massimo didn't take offense and kept going.

Look down there my friends, below what were wooden planks that made up the floor of this fascinating theatre. You can still hear the wild animals that were chained to those cubicles, the gladiators arming themselves, the soon-to-be slaughtered Christians moaning and begging for mercy, the pulleys and chains in constant motion hoisting up the next participants of a usually violent and bloody battle ending in excruciating pain and death."

"Kind of like a modern-day sports arena," commented Bishop.

"Exactly, my friend! Exactly. This is the ancient ancestor of the Georgia Dome home to your Atlanta Falcons." With that, Massimo won over even the few skeptics in the group. "Forty-one to thirty-eight against the Pittsburgh Steelers, week seven of the 2006 NFL season. A field goal in the last minutes of the game made the difference—I was there."

Wayne was amazed. "I went to that game with my dad! You were *there*, Massimo?"

"I surely was. It was during my three-day visit to Atlanta I told you about."

The students and teachers were still reeling from this unexpected revelation when Massimo summoned us to attention. He then proceeded to give us an informative description of the Colosseum, from its beginnings under Emperor Vespasian in the year AD 72 to its inauguration in AD 80 under Emperor Titus, all the way to its demise in the early Middle Ages. Massimo eloquently provided the group with interesting tidbits of information, keeping everyone attentive. He used layman's terms to describe the architectural brilliance behind the Colosseum's construction. This building had withstood wars, fires, earthquakes and, most damaging of all, the continual pilfering of marble, granite, and bronze up to the eighteenth century. Yet here it was, a good portion of it still erect, still defiant in the face of age, negligence, and exploitation.

Finally, Massimo stopped talking. "I'm thirsty!" he announced. "How about we go and get something to drink? Maybe a *Coke*?" He giggled at his impromptu wit. Nobody demurred, so we all got behind him and headed out the way we came. Darlene was a few steps ahead of me, so I quickened my pace until I caught up.

"So how do you find it, Darlene?" I asked.

She smiled. "It's neat so far—I mean, interesting. Massimo's a real trip, isn't he?"

"Well, he's certainly entertaining and knowledgeable."

"He acts just like my hairdresser, Danny, back home. I think being gay is such a waste. You should see Danny. He's got a dream body, but if I show him these"—she cupped her breasts, "he says they do nothing for him." She gazed down pensively. "They're not so bad, are they, Atticus?"

"Darlene, you're a beautiful young lady even without those." I saw a look of disappointment in her eyes. Darlene wasn't expecting that response. I was pleased about that.

"Come on now, we're losing the group." We made our way through the crowds.

Massimo had stopped in front of one of the many street vendors who were out in front of the Colosseum selling everything from cheap, plastic miniatures of the monuments surrounding us to postcards to food and drinks. Before I could do or say anything, he was taking orders from the group, and a slew of Coke cans and water bottles showed up on the small aluminum counter. I reached for my wallet, but Massimo beat me to it and paid for everything. Working myself through the thirsty bunch, I tapped Massimo on the shoulder, handing him thirty euros. He turned and shook his head.

"Please, Mr. Winterle, it's an honor for me to offer something to drink to such an attentive and intelligent audience."

"But, Massimo, I can get this reimbursed."

He shook his head again. "Atticus...may I call you Atticus?"

"Absolutely."

"*To Kill a Mockingbird*, one of my favorite films." Before I could respond to this throwaway remark, Massimo was already on another topic.

"Do you know how many groups I have each day, Atticus? Maybe three or four if it's slow, and up to seven or eight when the day is full."

He took my arm and gently walked me slightly out of earshot from the group.

"I usually lose people's attention after ten minutes. Furthermore, I have to hear regretful little comments regarding my dress, my gestures, or my way of speaking.

Many times, I get those looks as if I had some sort of disease. Being a *checca* is not easy, especially in Italy."

Massimo had used the Italian slang version of "homosexual." I was about to interject, but he held up his hand.

"A group like this, Atticus, is a rarity in my business. Yesterday, when I read that today's first encounter was going to be with a bunch of high school students from the southern part of the United States, I was preparing myself for a bad start to the day. Instead, this group goes to show you that you should never judge a book by its cover. They have been attentive, well-mannered, asking excellent questions and not one—and I mean none—comment about the rather eccentric way I do my job. The very least I can do is to offer them something to drink."

He paused a moment, adjusting his flamboyant sunglasses.

"You are lucky, Atticus. I have heard horror stories from other chaperones. I'm sure these students will surprise you, if they haven't already."

Massimo squeezed my shoulder. I looked at him and just nodded my head.

"Well, back to work," he said. "We have so many more architectural wonders to admire, and very little time left." With that, he turned and assumed professorial demeanor once again. "Ladies and gentlemen, please follow me. We still have much to see, and time is short. The Roman Forum awaits us!"

With that, Massimo picked up his usual stride and headed back in the direction of the Arch of Constantine. I was thinking about what he had just told me when Vanessa came up behind me and tapped my shoulder.

"Atticus, if it's okay with you, I think I'm going to grab a cab and go back to the hotel. I'm feeling a little weak. Guess I wasn't ready yet for a full day of sightseeing."

"No problem, Vanessa," I said. "But I need you to go back with a teacher."

I called out to Barbara, who was with Cynthia a little away from me. They both came up to us. "Vanessa is tired," I explained. "She needs to go back to the hotel and rest."

"Fine, just show us where we can—" Barbara began to say.

"No, Barbara," Cynthia interrupted. "You lost all day yesterday. I'll go back with Vanessa. Just tell me where we can find a cab, Atticus."

"But, Cynthia, you were especially looking forward to this tour," Barbara said.

"That's not a problem," Cynthia replied. "I'll have plenty of time to come back. Maybe Atticus will be so good as to bring me here again one afternoon?"

"Absolutely, Cynthia. We shall make time for it."

"It's settled, then. Atticus, point us to where we can go catch a taxi, please."

"No, no, I'll go and show you. Hang on one second so that I can tell Massimo."

I caught up with him and the rest of the group, explained the situation, and told him that I would catch up. I then went back to Barbara, Cynthia, and Vanessa and led them to the Via Fori Imperiali where a line of taxis stood waiting.

"Hope you feel better, Vanessa," I said. "I'll check in on you as soon as we get back."

"Don't worry, Atticus, I'll be fine." She looked at me intently to let me know that I had nothing to be worried about.

I went to the first cab in line and explained where he had to go, giving him ten euros. He seemed appreciative. Then I turned to Cynthia. "I've already paid for the ride," I told her. "Don't give him anything more when you arrive."

They got into the car and left.

CHAPTER 30

Barbara turned to me. "Vanessa didn't seem very happy going off with Cynthia, did she?" she observed.

I shrugged. "No. But to be honest, I'm glad you got to stay. I'm really enjoying this day."

Barbara smiled, looked around as though searching for a pickpocket, then gave me a quick and unexpected kiss on the lips.

"You're becoming rather audacious, Mrs. Cornwall." I grinned.

"Oh yes, Mr. Winterle. Carpe diem, that's my motto here in Rome."

I took a hold of her hand, and we ran back across the Via Fori Imperiali without incurring any bodily harm from the wannabe NASCAR drivers.

"Not too fast, Atticus," Barbara said. "I'm a bit sore between the legs. Maybe you forgot what you did to *her* last night…"

I laughed, rather pleased with myself.

As we passed the Colosseum, I asked Barbara if she had picked up any worrisome signals from Evelyn or James.

"None so far. They've been very attentive and seem to be interested in what they're seeing."

"Hard not to be with Massimo."

"Indeed. He's really an incredible guide. Do you think we'll be able to have him for other tours?"

This had already crossed my mind. I would give Marco a call to ask if we could have Massimo at least one more day before the group headed back to Atlanta.

Barbara returned to our main concern. "We need to keep our eyes and ears peeled in the evenings, I think. If Evelyn or

James plan to do something extreme, it's not going to be in the middle of the day in front of the other students."

I pursed my lips. While Barbara might have been right, it was simple to throw yourself into the middle of speeding Rome traffic or in front of a subway train. But I didn't want to think about that.

Barbara and I turned onto the Via Sacra, which was the avenue that cut straight across the Roman Forum since the times of Julius Caesar. To our right were the remains of the Temple of Venus and Rome, as well as the Church of San Francesca Romana. More ruins were on our left, but I didn't have an inkling about what had stood there so long ago.

As Barbara and I approached another grandiose arch, I saw Massimo holding forth from up on the side of a monument, having once again managed to perch himself up higher than the rest of the group. As he saw us approaching, he spread his arms as widely as he could and yelled, "All hail, here forth comes Emperor Atticus with the lovely Signora Cornwall by his side!" This drew a good deal of laughter from the students. John, on the other hand, looked somewhat put out. I felt a bit sorry for him. I also noticed that Evelyn was whispering something to James, probably commenting about how I wanted to "get into Barbara's pants."

Been there, done that, I thought.

"We were just finishing up here, my dear Atticus. Let me just quickly bring you and Mrs. Cornwall up to speed. We have just entered the Roman Forum by way of the Via Sacra, the Peachtree Street, if you will, of downtown Rome. This was the center of all activity in ancient Rome—legal, religious, and philosophical matters were discussed here, as well as commercial negotiations, politics, banking, you name it. It all happened where we are walking." Massimo's ability to refer to Atlanta's landmarks every now and then continued to hold his audience's attention. "And this second splendid arch we have been admiring is the Arch of Titus, dedicated to the emperor Titus by his brother, Domitian. It celebrates the sacking and destruction of Jerusalem in AD 70 on behalf of Titus when he was still a general. And as our friend Raymond here so correctly informed us, this was just the first of three wars between Rome and Jerusalem. And if I understood correctly, it has remained an important day of fasting in the Jewish calendar. Raymond, would you kindly tell Atticus and Signora Cornwall what you told us earlier?"

With absolutely no hesitation, Raymond spoke up:

"This first war between the Romans and the Jews is important because it was the second time that the temple was destroyed—the Temple on the Holy Mount, that is. The first temple was destroyed way back in the fifth or sixth century BC by the Babylonian emperor Nebuchadnezzar, and the second time by Titus in AD 70. However, it just so happens that the destruction of the temples took place on the same day, called Tisha B'Av, which means the 'ninth day of the month of Av' in the Hebrew calendar. This year, in the Gregorian calendar, we shall commemorate this event on the nineteenth and twentieth of July."

As Raymond finished, he glanced at Michelle as if seeking her approval. Everyone remained silent for a moment. I remembered that John had told me at lunch that Raymond wasn't terribly observant. That may have been the case, but he certainly seemed very knowledgeable regarding certain historical aspects of his religion.

"Thank you, Raymond, very informative indeed," said Massimo. "But now, my friends, let's keep moving!" Massimo jumped down and headed down a walkway that had been tread on by humans and animals for well over two thousand years.

It was almost twelve thirty, and I knew that everyone would soon be hungry. I believe that Massimo was also aware of this, given that he very briskly took us through the rest of the Roman Forum, pointing out the main attractions but keeping the explanations to the bare essentials.

We saw the meagre remains of the Temple of Venus and Rome, the Church of San Francesca commissioned by Pope Paul I in the ninth century, and the more imposing ruins of the Basilica of Maxentius, the same emperor who Constantine had defeated at the Battle of the Milvian Bridge. We walked past the Church of Cosmas and Damian where Massimo told us that the circular portion had been incorporated into the church under Pope Felix IV in the fifth century. What was now the back of this church had originally been constructed as a temple to Valerius Romulus, Emperor Maxentius's son.

"The same Maxentius that got his butt kicked at the Milvian Bridge, right?" Wayne asked.

"The very same, my friend. As the basilica that we just left behind us was being built to honor him in life—this was between AD 308 and 312—Maxentius was also building, around AD 309, this temple to honor his son in death. Life has many twists and turns, doesn't it?"

Massimo looked at me briefly and winked. After a few more steps, he stopped in his tracks.

"Ladies and gentlemen, we are in front of the Temple of Vesta and the adjoining House of the Vestal Virgins. The Vestal Virgins were high priestesses, six in all, who belonged to distinguished families. They entered the service of the goddess Vesta between the ages of six and ten and remained in service for thirty years. For this thirty-year period, they were sworn to a vow of chastity. Any of the priestesses who broke this vow were buried alive and the family shamed for all their days."

"Bradford wouldn't have any girls left if they took that vow," Wayne blurted out.

"Wayne!" John admonished.

"Not that you could tell the difference, Wayne," Darlene went on an unexpected attack.

Wayne smirked. "Just because you haven't been knocking boots in the last few days doesn't mean you wouldn't be the first to be buried up to your neck."

"Wayne, that's enough!" John said warningly.

Darlene drew herself up, with noticeable consequences. "At least nobody forgets my boots. None of the girls at Bradford seem to have even tried yours on for size. Probably because the size of your *boot* is size what? Small?"

"Darlene!" Barbara said.

Darlene became mute, but gave a quick, searing glance at Bishop before walking off.

Massimo jumped in before Wayne, who was now seething, could say anything. I was only thankful that Cynthia was not around to hear any of this.

"Oh my, oh my! We do have some frayed nerves in this crowd. Let's suffice it to say that to remain chaste for thirty years is quite a task. Not surprisingly, many of these young women while in the service of the goddess Vesta did not make it to the end of their period of duty."

Massimo looked at his watch. "It's very close to lunch time, my friends. With your teachers' permission, I would suggest giving you fifteen minutes to wander around a bit on your own. We shall all meet back here at Temple of Vesta at, let's say, one o'clock?"

This proposal, other than relieving the tension generated by Darlene and Wayne, was well received.

I saw Wayne, Bishop, Mark, and Michelle heading east toward another arch that, if I remembered correctly, was dedicated to the emperor Septimius Severus. They were talking intensely, and to my eyes, their body language seemed agitated. Evelyn, James, and Jeremy had gone off in the opposite direction. I lost sight of Darlene, Mary, Sabrina, and Anthony, but right now, I was more concerned with Wayne's and Darlene's exchange.

John was talking with Barbara, so I ended up standing there by the House of the Vestal Virgins with Massimo.

"It's a peculiar age, isn't it, Atticus?"

I didn't immediately understand if Massimo was referring to classical Rome or the students.

"Yes," I said, figuring that single word covered both.

Massimo took me very delicately by the arm and switched into Italian.

"You know, Atticus, we only met a few hours ago, and although I realize that I may seem presumptuous, I believe that I have a quite a knack at seeing through people, even if I am in their company for a very short time. Perhaps that is because we homosexuals are more fine-tuned to the innermost secrets of our fellow man. I'm not patting myself on the back, mind you. But it is a fact that we must defend ourselves from prejudice and hate more than a heterosexual does. Therefore, most of us develop a keener insight into the human heart and psyche, if only as a matter of self-preservation." He fell silent for a few moments. "Let's go this way, Atticus, toward the Curia." We walked in the direction of the building that had served as the meeting place of the Roman Senate.

"As I mentioned before, there are some special students in this group. But when someone demonstrates 'special' or 'unique' qualities, there usually lies hidden some form of eccentric behavior, conflicting passion, or an internal battle over right and wrong. You don't mind me talking to you about these things, do you, Atticus?"

"Not in the least," I replied sincerely.

"The young lady who just now was in that fight with the handsome young man…"

"Yes, Darlene."

"Darlene?" Massimo giggled. "Oh superb! The name fits just perfectly, doesn't it? Says a great deal about the mother of this young lady." "Our Darlene, Atticus, reminds me of some female friends of mine. They are so insecure about who they are that their bodies become their primary friend and focus. And when you have a body like Darlene's, the power you yield can be intoxicating. All their flirting and exposure of skin are just fruitless attempts to acquire comfort and warmth. What they get instead is a hard penis and a lesbian's full attention."

"Impressive, Massimo. That's exactly what I have on my hands—an eighteen-year-old Anita Ekberg ready to shed her clothes for anyone who will give her some attention."

"Obviously, the young man she was sparring with doesn't care to give her any of his attention. Very odd, don't you think, Atticus? A tall, handsome, well-built young man not having the slightest interest in our buxom Marilyn Monroe, who is obviously willing to let him partake in the attributes that God gave her?"

I could feel the blood draining from my face. I shook my head at Massimo. "I just don't think Wayne is attracted to Darlene. That probably hurts her ego, so she strikes out at him. According to the teachers, Wayne and Bishop are just two beer drinking jocks with their periscopes locked on to anything with a skirt."

"'Periscopes?' Was that a calculated metaphor, Atticus?"

"Well, the imagery is accurate."

"Well, I have made mistakes in the past, but I wonder if…" Massimo trailed off.

"If what? I hope you're not suggesting that Wayne might be, ah, *attracted to men*?" I unintentionally said these last three words in shocked tone, as though being gay was worse than being a serial killer.

"Oh, heaven forbid!" said Massimo, throwing his hands up in a gesture odd despair. "We might as well burn him at the stake if that's the case! How catastrophic that would be." Massimo chuckled, knowing that I hadn't intended to offend him. "I don't know for a fact that our boy Wayne likes men, or women, or both. Let's just say that his heightened curiosity in my person, some questions he asked me when not overheard, and the dominant role that he has with that other boy—"

"Bishop?" I blurted out.

"You see how quickly you answered me, Atticus? You as well have obviously noticed this young man's peculiar behavior."

It was true. I now realized that Wayne and Bishop had never been apart since their arrival in Rome.

"Well," Massimo continued, "all of this plus that final battle of words with our Atlanta Jane Mansfield tends to point to his, how shall I put it, 'lacking in sexual prowess' when it comes to women. Does this choice of words please you more than 'he may like men'?"

Massimo winked at me and said, "So you see, Atticus, this building that stands here in front of you is actually a reconstruction that took place after the ravaging fire of AD 283 under the reign of Diocletian." He had so naturally changed the subject that John and Barbara, who I hadn't even noticed coming up, had no clue what we had been discussing.

"Massimo, excuse me, but John and I were over there between those ruins." Barbara pointed behind her. "We could barely read a thing because some idiot spray-painted everything on the information totems. We don't have any idea what we were looking at."

"I would be honored to fill the two of you in. Atticus, I'll meet you back at the temple with the students in ten minutes. I can escort the group to the restaurant before I head off to meet my next group."

He turned and led Barbara and John to a wide-open area covered in white stumps of what once were towering columns.

I stayed back, motionless, with Massimo's words ringing in my head. Wayne and Bishop...*gay?* Had these two boys managed to fool *everyone?* Weren't these supposed to be hard-drinking, women-on-the-brain, lap-dance addicts that I had been introduced to? John and Barbara, not to mention Cynthia, all asserted that Wayne and Bishop were the troublemakers in the group and that they required extra supervision.

And then, all of a sudden, just like in a movie where the protagonist is overwhelmed by a series of revelatory flashbacks, I saw a different situation unfold before my mind's eye. At the airport, Wayne and Bishop ogling the airline attendants passing by, but they were predominantly *stewards* not stewardesses; at the Trevi Fountain when Wayne, Bishop, and Mark asked me where the lap-dance bars were in town, the noticeable indifference displayed by Wayne and Bishop; Mark being dragged back to the hotel falling down drunk, but with Wayne and Bishop perfectly sober. And *how about* Wayne's performance during the song and dance routine in Vanessa's room? Wasn't there something a bit too feminine in the way he moved his body during the lyrics of the song? Finally, Michelle telling Wayne and Bishop that I would *understand* what they had to tell me. Was this what she was referring to?

Enough, I told myself. I didn't want to dwell on this any longer. This was an unfolding situation, and I would confront it if and when there were further developments. It really wasn't any of my business, anyway.

Where our restaurant was located and what would the specialties of the day be were my primary concern right now.

CHAPTER 31

I looked up and saw Massimo in the distance with Barbara and John pointing to the Arch of Septimius Severus and vivaciously gesturing as he spoke to them. I looked at my watch—12:55 pm. the forum was now teeming with tourists, large groups with tour guides as well as smaller groups of three to five people with just guidebooks. I had made my way back to the meeting point. The students were slowly heading back in my direction. Massimo, Barbara, and John came up.

"We are ready to head to the restaurant," Massimo announced. "Everyone, follow me please." As Massimo backtracked the way we came into The Forum, the students practically wrapped themselves around him like bees on honey.

"I'm going to take James, Evelyn, and Jeremy to a music store when we get back to the hotel," I informed Barbara and John. "Maybe we should let the kids break out on their own until dinnertime, if that's all right with the two of you."

"Fine by me, Atticus," John answered. "I'd like to get out and about and take some photos." John glanced at Barbara. He was clearly hoping that she would tag along.

"Sounds good to me," Barbara said. "I think they're getting the hang of Rome, and as we've said, we can't be on their shoulders twenty-four hours a day."

Barbara didn't say how she was going to spend the afternoon, nor did she show any interest in John's plans. He was obviously discouraged, and I could appreciate why, especially now.

"Any idea regarding the restaurant we're off to, Atticus?" he asked. "I'm starving."

"I haven't a clue," I answered. "But I know that the location is a bit off the tourist track, so I'm hoping we eat as well as we did yesterday."

With Massimo leading the way I didn't have to worry where Via Capo d'Africa was, which was one less concern. I understood now why ASA had suggested that the chaperones acquaint themselves with the eating establishments before taking their respective groups. I was bothered that I hadn't done this with yesterday's restaurant nor the one we were about to visit. How very bizarre—I was really beginning to take this job seriously.

Massimo and the students had stopped at a crosswalk, waiting for the three of us to catch up. When we arrived, he lifted his Coca-Cola flag over his head with his right arm and put out his left arm at a ninety-degree angle to his body to signal to the drivers to come to a halt. We walked the three lanes of one-way traffic, reached a small cement island where Massimo switched hands, stopped the other three lanes of one-way traffic going in the other direction, and guided us across. None of the vehicles attempted to accelerate or swerve passed us—instead, they all stopped in an orderly and non-Italian fashion. Massimo was clearly a sorcerer, as well as an exceptional tour guide.

Slightly off to our right was the beginning of Via Capo d'Africa. We walked by the small workshops, boutiques, pizzerias, and a small theatre. After having passed a bad copy of an English pub, we found ourselves in front of the restaurant Al Foro, or The Forum. The two rather large shrubs in granite flowerpots on each side of the door looked like they hadn't been watered in days, if not weeks. The glass door had a dozen or so decals running up and down the left and right side, informing patrons which credit and debit cards were accepted. In the middle of the door, there was a small sign that read "We don't accept €200 notes" in three languages. The restaurant had obviously had their fill of counterfeiters. Massimo opened the door and went inside. The rest of us followed, but I lingered outside.

"John, Barbara, go ahead. I need to make a quick phone call."

I punched in Marco's number. After the second ring, he picked up.

"Ciao, Atticus. Is it bad or good news this time?"

"Actually, it's a question." I went on to explain how satisfied the group and I were with Massimo and that we wanted him back.

"I'm not surprised. You know how many groups get hooked on Massimo? He's a professional—flamboyant, as you no doubt saw, but very competent."

"*Flamboyant* is putting it mildly. One of the teachers found him, let's say, inappropriate."

"Let me guess. That skinny woman, Cynthia something—"

"That's her. She's back at the hotel now with our pill-popping student. By the way, I think that girl will be fine. We had a long talk, and I think she realizes the stupidity of her actions."

"That's good to hear, Atticus. Hopefully, she's not hooked on that crap. I was worried that this could have gotten us all into deep trouble."

Marco had taken a risk in not reporting Vanessa's drug use, and I appreciated that he had let me handle the situation my way. "Listen, I'll see what I can do with Massimo. Tomorrow is impossible, but maybe I can get you hooked up with him again on Friday or Saturday."

"Work your magic," I said and ended the call. My stomach was now rumbling, and I was more than ready to discover what the restaurant had to offer.

As soon as I opened the door, an aroma of rosemary, thyme, oregano, and cloves of garlic wafted into my avid nostrils.

Other than our group, there were tables filled with persons who, judging from their ease and familiarity with their surroundings, I suspected were regular customers. This was a sure sign that the food was going to be good. For our group, the waiters had set up the tables in horseshoe fashion so that we could all sit together. Everyone was seated except Massimo, who was conversing with a stout man whom I assumed to be the cook since he was wearing a food-stained smock.

"Atticus, there you are!" Massimo hailed. "Come here so that I can introduce you to Dario, one of the best-kept secrets of Rome." It turned out that Dario was both the chef and owner of Al Foro. He was describing the dishes of the day to Massimo, and from what I overheard, we were in for a treat.

As I was listening, Mary called out to me: "Can you get Massimo to stay and have lunch with us? He says he can't." Everyone started asking Massimo to remain with us. He had certainly worked his charm on these students. Before I could say anything, Massimo held up his hand, getting instant and obedient silence from the group.

"My dear friends, I am honored by your request and deeply moved. Alas, there is a group of Australians waiting for me in the exact location where we first met this morning. I must be off now to show our friends from down under the marvels that your eyes beheld earlier this morning."

The students were disappointed but stopped their protesting.

"However, if Atticus and your teachers were to be so kind as to invite me to dinner with all of you one of these evenings, I would be greatly pleased to see all of you once again." Thunderous cheers went up, with John and Barbara (and me) nodding in approval. Massimo went over to John and Barbara, kissing them on both cheeks—customary when leaving someone's company in Italy, but from their red faces, not the custom in Georgia. Massimo then came over to me, gave me a big hug, and told me that he would be overjoyed to have our group once again on a tour of the city. I told him that I had already sent a request to ASA via Marco.

As Massimo was heading to the door waving and sending kisses to everyone, he stopped abruptly and once again put his hands in the air for silence. I knew right away that we were in for another poem.

"*Farewell!*" Massimo declaimed. "*A word that must be, and hath been—a sound which makes us linger; yet—farewell! Ye! Who have traced the Pilgrim to the scene which is his last, if in your memories dwell, a thought which once was his, if on ye swell, a single recollection, not in vain—He wore his sandal-shoon, and scallop shell; Farewell! With him alone may rest the pain, if such there were—with you, the mortal of his strain.*"

With that, he turned and went out the door as our applause followed him.

I looked over at Michelle to see if she knew what we had just listened to. Our eyes crossed, and I could tell that she understood that I was waiting for some input. "I'm not sure, Atticus, but it sounded like a final verse out of *Childe Harold's Pilgrimage*. Massimo has been quoting it all morning."

"We'll drill Mrs. Ramsey on this when we get back to the hotel," I said.

Michelle gave me a thumbs-up as I found an empty chair and poured myself a glass of red wine. The off-white tablecloths were already bedecked with wine and water bottles, Cokes, a few Fantas, and the omnipresent straw baskets filled with freshly baked bread, breadsticks, and crackers. Everyone was chatting away. I couldn't see Barbara very well from where I was sitting, but I noticed that John was continually looking in her direction. Wayne and Bishop were sitting next to each other with James and Jeremy. They all seemed more interested in devouring breadsticks than speaking with one another.

Jeremy, who was in front of me, did not notice me examining, *again*, his prosthesis. I was once again amazed at the naturalness of that man-made object and the enormous strides that had taken place in the field of medicine. I remembered reading just a few weeks before about the first successful transplant of a complete face. Science fiction was swiftly leaping from the pages of paperback novels and into our everyday lives. My train of thought was broken by the sudden scent of basil leaves and fresh tomatoes.

As I took a long, satisfying swallow of wine, three waiters appeared, gracefully maneuvering large aluminum serving trays filled with pasta. Each tray was a different recipe, and I was pleased that the students would further appreciate that pasta wasn't just spaghetti and meatballs or ravioli out of a Chef Boyardee can.

What was there to say about this particular food with a history of over ten thousand years, when Neolithic man began crushing grain with large stones? From its primitive origins to the refined dishes served up in gourmet restaurants around the world today, "pasta" has become synonymous with "Italy." Other than China, where a millenary culinary tradition of noodles and *jiaozi* exists, no other country in the world has developed and refined so many recipes for this humble mixture of flour and water. You can easily find Italian cookbooks that have up to five thousand different recipes for pasta. Considering the sauces, toppings, and the variety of other foods that can be mixed with pasta, it has become the one-course meal par excellence on a global scale.

Some agnolotti *di carne* was delicately forked out onto my dish. This is a moon-shaped, soft pasta ravioli filled with a meat-and-ricotta cheese mixture, topped with a butter-and-cream sauce aromatized with sage. Before I could dig in, another waiter showed up to my right and gave me a generous portion of bucatini *al pomodoro e basilico*. Bucatini are a type of spaghetti, but it's hollow and much thicker. It is a veritable feast of aromas when seasoned with fresh tomatoes, cooked al dente, and sautéed in olive oil and basil leaf. A third waiter approached me from the left with another excellent choice—pappardelle *con panna, funghi, piselli e prosciutto.* Pappardelle are a rather broad egg noodle that is a perfect match for a mushroom, pea, ham, and cream sauce with a dash of nutmeg. The *tris di pasta,* or "three varieties of pasta," had now been served. We could all dig in.

"This is great stuff, Atticus," said Mary, who was sitting to my left. "Do Italians eat like every day?"

"Pasta in this country is like burgers and fries in the US. Your typical Italian family consumes a plate of pasta at least five or six times a week." Mary was rapidly maneuvering her fork between plate and mouth. I decided that this was a good time to probe her surprising knowledge of lyrical music.

"So, Mary, do you still listen to opera? Is there a particular one that you care for?"

"Yeah, most of the time. I listened to so much of it when I was younger that for a while there, I got sick of it. There's nothing worse than when your mom or dad wants to force you to like something they like. I had a real problem with them until I was about fifteen. I think that they finally figured out that I was going to choose what I wanted to believe in and what music I wanted to listen to, no matter how hard they tried to influence me."

Mary managed to divulge all this between a mouthful of agnolotti and *papardelle.* "An opera that I particularly enjoy is Giordano's *Andrea Chenier,*" she concluded in answer to my query.

Had she named the better-known *La Bohème, L'Aida,* or *Tosca,* I would have still been pleasantly surprised, but her alluding to a lesser-known work such as *Andrea Chenier* was quite unexpected. Noticing my stunned silence, Mary rather hesitantly asked me if I was familiar with this opera.

"Oh, yes. I just wasn't expecting you to mention it."

"I think I know it by heart. It's my dad's favorite. He swears by the Hungarian State Orchestra version with Jose

Carreras and Eva Marton, but I much prefer the rendition with Maria Callas and Mario del Monaco. Did you see the movie *Philadelphia?*"

"That was quite some time ago, but yes, I have."

"Do you remember when Tom Hanks is listening to that piece of music in his apartment and translates it from Italian to English for Denzel Washington?"

"Vaguely, yes."

"Well, that's Callas singing the aria *'La mamma morta'* from the third act. It makes me get goosebumps all over." Mary dived back into her *bucatini.*

I sat back in my chair, thinking about Mary's in-depth knowledge of opera and feeling ashamed, once again, over how wrong I had been about this group of students in general and my initial prejudice toward them. The waiters came and smoothly began taking away the empty plates and replacing them with clean ones.

Dario had definitely prepared for us, considering what the house served up next: *polpetta di tacchino con uova sode, involtini di sarde con carciofi, galletti farciti con pepperoni,* as well as large bowls of fresh green salad and an array of thinly sliced grilled vegetables with olive oil and shards of garlic. Other than the *involtini di sarde,* which are large stuffed sardines, the turkey loaf with eggs and the roasted *galletti* (small roosters) stole the show. Everyone seemed genuinely pleased with what they were eating, even though they were most likely tasting these dishes for the first time.

The wine was flowing rather freely amongst the students, but from what I could tell, no one was abusing the privilege. I had often thought that teenage alcoholism would be much lower in the United States if there were a culture of drinking wine and beer with meals from an adolescent age. I had been brought up this way. While my high school buddies were busy cutting and pasting together fake IDs to buy cases of Schlitz or Coors on Friday night, I was drinking Ginger

Ale or Schweppes tonic water and always ended up being the designated driver, dumping my classmates on their front lawns late into the night. I just didn't feel the need to belt down a six-pack at the speed of light, knowing that if I wanted a beer or a glass of wine, I just needed to go to the fridge at home and help myself. Needless to say, I was envied by more than just a few of my classmates.

Sabrina peered at me from the opposite table. "Atticus, I hope there isn't anything else coming out of that kitchen. I'm about to explode."

I shrugged. "I have a feeling it's not stopping here. Dario is probably going to wheel out some rather interesting desserts soon."

Wayne, Bishop, and Mark had gotten up and were heading toward the door. "We're going out for a quick smoke, Atticus," said Wayne.

Barbara had gotten up from her seat as well and walked behind me, heading to the restroom. As she did so, she gave me a quick caress on my neck. She must have had a little too much wine because what she believed was a secret gesture was seen by Evelyn, James, and John, who, in that instant, were staring straight at me. To make matters worse, I immediately turned Ferrari red, as was my wont when I am even slightly embarrassed. This only put the shade of guilt on what might have been construed as an innocent gesture on Barbara's behalf. Michelle and Mary, who were sitting in front of me, were now also staring at me as if I were ill.

"Is everything okay, Atticus?" Michelle asked.

"I'm fine Michelle, just fine. Something must have gone down my windpipe." I feigned an unconvincing cough. From the corner of my eye, I could see Evelyn and James smiling and shaking their heads. John had gotten up and gone outside. I felt bad for him, but there was nothing I could do about it. Barbara came back out of the restroom and was heading back to her seat. She must have detected the tension in the air because she steered away from me to go and sit down.

Luckily, two waiters burst through the kitchen doors with dessert carts laden with an ample selection of diet-bashing cakes, pies, and puddings. This redirected the attention from me and onto the goodies that were heading in our direction. John and the smokers had returned and gazed avidly at everything being served: *tiramisu, budino al cioccolato, millefoglie, semifreddo con fragole, crème brulèe, torta alle noci, sorbetto di limone e di fragola*, plus an assortment of fresh fruit.

"*Tutto fatto in casa*, Signor Atticus, *fresco, fresco.*"

Dario was indeed a well-kept secret, as Massimo had put it. This was not your standard trattoria fare. You could tell that Dario was passionate about cooking. He proudly informed me that everything was *fatto in casa*, or homemade.

A worshipful silence fell as everyone plunged their forks and spoons into a dark chocolate pudding, a thin multi-wafer cake layered with whip cream and strawberries, walnut and almond pie, a coffee and cream pudding with a crushed biscuit base, and fresh raspberry, blueberries, peaches with vanilla ice cream and sweet watermelon. Then the comments began:

"This is just awesome."

"Out of this world!"

"Friggin' fantastic!"

Moans of satisfaction arose from the tables to the point that someone passing by outside would have thought that an orgy was taking place. I knew that the eat fest wasn't finishing there, however. A cook and host such as Dario was certainly going to bring out the *limoncello* or some other Italian digestive to close this dining experience.

I looked at my watch. It was getting onto three o'clock. We still had thirty minutes. The swinging doors of the kitchen flew open—and lo and behold, there was one of Dario's waiters wheeling a cart loaded with bottles, all unlabeled.

I saw a bottle with that greenish-yellow liquid that spelled *limoncello,* which we had tasted after the Vatican visit. But there was also a bottle with a red liquid, and another that was deep purple. The third bottle had a clear fluid, more than likely a type of grappa, which was a liquor produced from the leftovers of grapes that have been pressed for wine. The alcoholic content of grappa can be anywhere from forty to eighty proof, so the students needed to act responsibly.

"Ladies and gentlemen," I announced, "we are about to close another delightful lunch with some digestives produced, I believe, by our host."

"*Tutta produzione nostra,* Signor Atticus, *limoncello, fragolino e mirtillo più una bottiglia di grappa, abbastanza forte di gradazione.*" Dario confirmed that everything on the cart was homemade: the limoncello made of lemon peels, *fragolino* produced from wild strawberries, *mirtillo* from blueberries, and the bottle of grappa that, Dario warned, had a high alcohol content.

"Give everything a try without going overboard," I said to the students. "You've all been very trustworthy so far."

I shot a glance at Mark, who lowered his head.

Two other waiters were placing four small shot glasses in front of each student, and a third was pouring a small amount from each bottle into each glass. Dario must have understood my concern because the waiters were pouring a miniscule measure in each glass.

The students started sipping and commenting.

"Wow, that's the most powerful strawberry juice I've ever had!"

"The lemon thing is even better than what we had the other day."

It was now creeping closer to three thirty. We needed to head back to the bus. I reached into my pocket and took out the restaurant voucher and thirty euros from my own pocket. Another well-deserved tip was in order.

I stood up and tapped a spoon against my water glass. "Attention, everyone, let's give a hand to Dario and his staff and get ready to go back to the bus, please."

There was a light spatter of applause, and Dario bowed, looking quite pleased. Everyone got up with noticeable lethargy and plodded out of the restaurant. There was no silly behavior and, most importantly, no staggering. Only Barbara seemed a little too giddy and carefree. I was happy for her, though. I was certain that her unloading her "dirty laundry" with me at the Pantheon had allowed her at least some serenity.

Outside the trattoria, we were greeted with intermittent sunshine and a cool breeze. The temperature had dropped two to three degrees with the sun playing hide-and-seek behind large cottony clouds. We retraced our steps to the Colosseum.

"Where to now, Atticus?" asked John, who was out in front. We had reached a large thoroughfare, which split into three different directions. The Colosseum was directly in front of us.

"Keep following the sidewalk, John. Our bus is ahead somewhere."

I looked down at the row of behemoths, trying to pinpoint ours. Mark saw it first.

"There's our Merc. That's one badass bus."

I could not have agreed more with Mark's colorful description. Our Mercedes Travego was certainly an impressive piece of machinery.

Darlene spoke up in a rather trepidant tone, "We're here, and our bus is over there, and there's a six-lane road between us, and no zebra stripes."

She was right. I had been lost in my thoughts, enjoying the breeze and the pleasant stroll. We should have crossed much earlier. The road in front of us was a straight line for about a mile, unleashing the dragster instinct in those behind the wheel of a car. From where we were, getting the group on the opposite side in one piece was practically impossible. Then as I was wondering whether we should walk back to a safer point, Riccardo came to our rescue.

Noticing us assembled on the other side of the road looking very uncertain as to what to do, he stepped off the sidewalk and came toward us with only his two hands held high against the oncoming traffic. That didn't work terribly well, however, since the vehicles just swerved around him as if he were a pile of debris. Riccardo then withdrew a red signal pallet from the back of his trousers, which the police use to wave off traffic when in pursuit of a vehicle. This got the drivers' attention. Cars and motorbikes began to slow down and even stop in front of him. With his pallet, sunglasses, dark trousers, and black polo shirt, he could have been mistaken for a plainclothes policeman.

He signaled to us to start moving in his direction. When we had all reached the sidewalk next to our bus safely, cheers and compliments went up from the entire group. He was as proud as a peacock, and rightly so.

Once the students and teachers were on board, I patted him on the back. "That was incredible," I said. "But tell me, where did you get that police pallet? Is there something I don't know?"

"No worries, Mr. Atticus. I have a few friends here and there, and they get me these things when I need them. They come in handy at times."

I wasn't going to debate that.

As Riccardo turned and boarded the bus, my cell phone began to ring. It was the hotel.

"Hello, Mr. Winterle? It's Ludovica on the phone. Mrs. Ramsey would like to speak with you. Let me connect you."

"Just one moment, Ludovica…before you put me through, and between you and me, is there something I should know?"

"Well, Mr. Winterle, I saw Mrs. Ramsey in the hotel lobby a few hours ago with one of the students who did not look well at all."

"Not well as in…"

"Very pale, jittery, perspiring heavily."

Vanessa. Questions began tumbling through my mind. Had she taken more pills? Or just spilled the beans? If so, what had been Cynthia's reaction?

"Mr. Winterle?"

"Yes, Ludovica, I'm here. Go ahead and put Mrs. Ramsey on the line."

As I waited for Cynthia to pick up, I saw Barbara looking down at me from her window with a concerned expression.

"Atticus?"

"Yes, Cynthia, it's me."

"Atticus, I really don't know what to do." Cynthia's voice was tense, but she was controlling herself. "Vanessa isn't at all well, and I think we need to take her to the hospital."

I attempted to remain calm, taking a few steps farther away from the bus to avoid being overheard.

"She seemed well when you left us at the Roman Forum, Cynthia, just a bit tired. Did something happen in the meantime?"

"The traffic was horrible, so our cab ride was about twenty minutes long. She started to fidget with her hair, her fingers, and then she broke out in a sweat. It got worse once we got back to the hotel. She was almost shouting at me for no reason, then looking totally spaced out. If I didn't know any better, I would say she was on some kind of drug. But how is that possible?"

Okay, good. At least Vanessa had controlled herself enough not to say anything about the pills. But would it last? I needed to get back to the hotel ASAP.

"Does she have a fever?" I asked.

"Not that I can tell. Her limbs are cool, and her forehead isn't at all warm. She was under the covers, saying she was feeling a bit chilly, though. She's been asleep for about an hour. I slipped out of the room to call you. Where are all of you right now?"

"On the bus in a minute and heading your way. Sit tight, Cynthia. As soon as I get there, we'll decide the best course of action."

"All right. Can you tell Barbara and John what the situation is?"

"Of course. We'll be there as fast as we can."

I boarded the bus, took the microphone out of its mount, and with difficulty, got back into my role.

"Listen up, please. When we get back to the hotel, all of you are free for the rest of the afternoon. James, Evelyn, Jeremy, if you're still interested in going to that music store with me, the invite is still on."

Jeremy gave me a thumbs-up while James and Evelyn, who were entwined in the back of the bus, just nodded.

I stood there for a moment in a daze. How stupid was I not to foresee that Vanessa wasn't out of the woods yet? How was I going to approach Cynthia not knowing what Vanessa might have told her?

I flipped down the tour guide seat and sat down, feeling something crunch up in my pocket. I reached in and pulled out the envelope with the complaint form that Marco had left at the front desk. I unfolded the sheet of paper and spread it out on the console in front of me. I needed to get my mind on something else.

There were a series of questions with tick boxes for the most appropriate answer and then a small space at the bottom to write a full explanation of what had transpired. I ticked off the most negative answers to the fifteen or so questions and wrote out my comments on the back of the page. I didn't try to be tactful or even polite. The individual in question had no business being a tour guide.

Once finished, I got up and went to John's seat. "Would you take a look at this and if you agree with my comments regarding that idiot at the Pantheon yesterday?"

"Sure." He went over it quickly and grinned. "You can be brutal, Atticus."

"Was he that bad?" Barbara asked.

"Worse than bad."

I took the paper back from John and stuck it in my pocket.

"Well, I guess you have to flex your muscle every once and a while." Barbara raised her eyebrows and gave me a mischievous smile. John, luckily, did not see this since he was putting his signature at the bottom of the paper. I went back to my seat, already beet red from Barbara's not-so-subtle humor.

Surprisingly, the traffic wasn't heavy, and Riccardo managed to make good time. Our bus was just a few blocks from our drop-off.

Jeremy waved his hand at me. "Can we have a few minutes before heading off to that music store?" he asked.

"Absolutely, we can meet in the lobby, let's say, at four thirty?"

"I'm good with that," he replied. "How about it, James?"

"Yeah, fine by me."

This worked out well, given that I was going to deal with Cynthia. As soon as we got out of the bus, I would corner John and Barbara and fill them in regarding Vanessa. Riccardo swung around the small parking area at the entrance of Via della Pilotta, the road that led straight to our hotel.

"Okay everyone, you are now on your own," I said. "I'll be in the lobby shortly."

We got off the bus, and the students headed off.

CHAPTER 32

Once all the students had vanished from sight, I took Barbara and John by the arms, pulling them to one side.

"Is there a problem, Atticus?" Barbara asked.

"There might be. I was speaking with Cynthia earlier. Vanessa isn't well." I hesitated. "Or maybe it's more accurate to say that she hasn't gotten better."

Barbara tapped her teeth with her forefinger, but that was the only sign of any turmoil. John, who had no clue about Vanessa's true condition, was not especially concerned.

"Well, she didn't look entirely well this morning," he said. "She must be fighting a bad flu or something like it. Was Cynthia worried?"

"She felt that Vanessa might have to go to the hospital."

Barbara remained as cool as a cucumber. "Well, Cynthia goes overboard sometimes," John said reassuringly. "Let's get back and see what the situation really is."

We went into the hotel and up to Vanessa's room. I knocked gently. Cynthia opened the door and stepped outside, closing it quietly behind her.

"Let's go to my room," she said. "Vanessa is asleep." Cynthia turned and headed for her room. She was graveyard serious. We followed her like scolded children.

Once in her room, she looked around at all of us, then focused on me. "Atticus, I don't know what is going on, but I have the feeling that you"—she paused and glanced at Barbara before returning her gimlet gaze to me—"and possibly others are hiding something." There was a perturbed expression in her eyes which did not agree with a mind at peace with itself.

"Hiding something?" I said, looking back at Cynthia straight in her eyes. "What on earth do you think we're hiding?"

I was standing my ground. Cynthia crossed her chest and took a step back, a well-known defensive move when someone is feeling insecure. She may have had a feeling that something was being covered up—and this was true—but did she have the facts to back it up?

"Vanessa's been acting strange ever since we got back to the hotel. When I tried to ask her some questions, she began barking at me like a wild dog. She just kept walking around her room like a caged animal. She was mumbling to herself saying things like, 'No, no, I promised, I can do it, I can make it, I promised…' Then she just sat on her bed saying over and over that she needed to see you or Barbara. Then she fell asleep. I want her to see a doctor right away. I want the opinion of a professional and then we"—she looked and pointed to John, Barbara, and herself carefully avoiding me—"the *teachers,* will decide whether she needs to go back home or if she can stay with the group for the rest of the trip."

The tension in the room was becoming cheesecake thick.

"Maybe she just has a high fever, Cynthia," said John. "People get delirious if they're burning up."

"Oh, she's delirious all right, but she has no fever. Her forehead is cool. As I told you over the phone, Atticus, if I didn't know any better, I would say that Vanessa overdosed on something. This, along with the fact she kept asking for you or Barbara, makes me think that she wanted to confess something to one of you that she didn't want me to know." She paused. "So what do the two of you know about this that I don't?"

Cynthia's arms were still crossed, but she was speaking more aggressively. She was building confidence. John had turned so he was almost side by side with her. He was obviously beginning to side with Cynthia's skepticism.

446

I had to make a decision. Either I told the truth, which would mean the end of Vanessa's trip and my chaperoning experience, or I came up with a good story, hoping that Barbara would follow my lead.

"Okay Cynthia, I will get a doctor over here as soon as possible. I think that's a good idea. As far as knowing something that you don't, you're right. Barbara and I do know something."

I didn't look at Barbara, but I felt, rather than heard, her quick intake of breath.

Cynthia sat down in the armchair and steepled her fingers. "I'm listening," she said.

"We think that Vanessa took too many Tylenol gelcaps."

"*What?*" Cynthia came to her feet. "Tylenol?"

"She's been feeling under the weather ever since she arrived in Rome. We've all noticed that. I brought it up with her yesterday, and she told me she was medicating with Tylenol, taking three or four at a time, but they weren't helping. I told Barbara, who had a talk with her."

Cynthia looked at me skeptically. "That sounds a bit far-fetched. Tylenol is just a mild acetaminophen."

Barbara picked up my lead. "Even so, all that Tylenol taken can't be healthy. And if she had any wine or beer along with them, some sort of side effect is going to show up."

Cynthia sat back down again, but this time, she rested back in the armchair. "Okay, that might be so. But I don't understand why you, Atticus, and especially you, Barbara, didn't tell John and me about this. Did you know, John?"

"Nope!" John was looking a bit sour now. That Barbara and I were sharing secrets was just another stab in the back for him.

I raised my hands. "Cynthia, I asked Barbara not to tell the two of you anything. She wanted to, but I didn't want to see Vanessa sent back to Atlanta for what I believe was a foolish but innocent mistake. I realize that I overstepped my boundaries and, if you would like to file a complaint, feel free to do so. My only objective was to avoid unnecessary alarm."

Cynthia opened her mouth to speak, but I interrupted her. "Marco's brother-in-law is a pharmacist, as well as a registered general practitioner." Since I was already lying, I figured I would go whole hog. "I'll call and see if he's available to come over and take a look at Vanessa. If he concludes that the gelcaps are the cause, the three of you can then decide on the next step. I only ask that you let Vanessa finish her Rome trip with her classmates."

Cynthia said nothing, seeming lost in thought. Then she asked a question that caught me off guard: "Does Sabrina know anything about this?"

Damn it! I hadn't even thought about Sabrina.

"I haven't spoken with her. Have you, Barbara?" I said.

Barbara shook her head. "She knows that Vanessa has been under the weather, but that's all."

Hopefully, Barbara understood that she had to get a hold of Sabrina before Cynthia or John did. She looked at her watch.

"Atticus, John, we need to get downstairs," she said. "Some of the students are waiting for us, remember?"

Good for you Barbara, let's break this up, I thought.

"That's right," I said. "Cynthia, why don't you and I go to Vanessa's room and see how she is? Then I'll call Marco. John, Barbara, go ahead and enjoy the afternoon. Do me a favor and tell James, Evelyn, and Jeremy that I'll be down shortly."

John and Barbara headed downstairs to the lobby while Cynthia and I went to Vanessa's room. I knocked gently on the door and opened it.

Vanessa was still under the covers, but her eyes were open. When she saw me standing behind Cynthia, she became agitated and started speaking incoherently. My well-orchestrated yarn was about to be torn to shreds by something she might blurt out.

"Atticus, I'm...o, I'm not sure...I tried, I really am trying..."

I gently pushed passed Cynthia and sat on the side of the bed, taking Vanessa's hands in mine. The next few minutes were going to be crucial if I wanted Cynthia to continue believing my deception.

"Vanessa, everything is going to be all right." I gently squeezed her wrists and gave her a hurried wink. "I told Mrs. Ramsey about the Tylenol." I squeezed Vanessa's wrists once again as I said this.

"The...the Tylenol?"

"That's right. She knows that you took way too many."

I could feel Cynthia right behind me, like an obsessed shadow, observing every move I made.

"Yeah...I guess...I guess I overdid it. I'm sorry. I wasn't feeling well..."

"Don't worry, Vanessa, everything is going to be fine. We're here to make sure you get on your feet as soon as possible and enjoy the remaining days here. We're going to call a doctor to visit you just to make sure that you're okay and that there won't be any other strange side effects." At the mention of a doctor, Vanessa's eyes widened. I immediately applied pressure on her wrist once again, and she understood that the situation was under control. There was a knock on the door. Cynthia turned and opened it. It was Sabrina.

"Hey there, I just wanted to check in with my roomie and see how she was doing."

"Hi, Sab...Thanks. I'm better, I think..."

Cynthia glanced at Sabrina. "Any idea what's causing Vanessa to feel so ill, Sabrina?"

"I think she caught a bug even before we came here," Sabrina replied with no hesitation.

Nice work, Barbara, I thought.

"Sabrina, can you sit with Vanessa until dinner?" I asked.

"No problem, Atticus."

"All right by you, Cynthia?" I asked assertively.

"Yes, of course. I shall speak with you later, Miss Guy. There shall be some disciplinary measures to take into consideration."

Vanessa just lowered her head on the pillow and rolled to one side. Cynthia and I left the room.

"Atticus, I have to think about all of this. Something just seems out of kilter. You realize that Vanessa's parents must be informed in the meantime?"

I took a deep breath and thought carefully before answering. "Cynthia, I'm going to ask you for a favor. I would like you to wait for Vanessa to recover and for the two of you to have a chat before we take any action. After that, and after we hear what the doctor says, then you, Barbara, and John can decide what to do. If this includes sending Vanessa back to Atlanta prematurely, you will also have to make an official request for a new chaperone since blame rests on my shoulders as well."

I didn't give Cynthia a chance to respond as I turned and headed for the stairs that led down to the lobby.

James, Jeremy, and Mark were sitting in the lobby waiting for me. Evelyn, who had earlier shown interest in going with us, was conspicuously absent.

"You're over thirty minutes late, Atticus," Jeremy said. "What kind of example are you setting for us?"

"I was with your teachers for a good cause, so cut me some slack, Mr. Wisenheimer."

"No worries if you're not up to this, Atticus," James said. It was apparent that he didn't think he was worth my time. I walked over to him. He was sitting with his head bowed, elbows on his knees, staring at the floor.

"Listen, James, I realize you don't want to look like a bonehead in front of your peers here, so if an hour in a music store where your limited knowledge of rock 'n' roll will be revealed, you can stay here and enjoy watching the carpet."

"Hey, James, better get your act together, bro," chided Jeremy.

James raised his head, and I almost saw a smile flicker on his lips. "You're on," he said.

He got up and headed for the exit.

Good. My presumed indifference was a nonissue.

"What about Evelyn?" I inquired. "I thought she was coming too."

"She decided to head out with Mrs. Cornwall," Mark said.

As James and Jeremy made their way to out of the hotel, I took Mark by the arm and whispered, "Show me that bar where you overdid it on the tequila if we pass it. Just stop in front of it for a few seconds so I'll know."

"Okay, yeah, I remember where it is."

It took just a few minutes to get to the Trevi Fountain, awash in its pomp and splendor. Mark looked at me discreetly inclining his head toward a side street.

"To the right, gentlemen." We had turned on to Via del Lavatore, a relatively short stretch of road chockfull of curio shops, small tourist-trap restaurants, bars, and just about every other kind of "Rip me off, I'm a tourist" business. The boys were still ten steps in front of me when Mark began to slow down. At a certain point, he stopped, glanced to his left, and pretended to adjust the laces on his tennis shoes. He then quickly moved on, catching up with the other two. I saw what I needed to see: Il Papagallo, or The Parrot. A small bar-cum-convenience store with a few outdoor tables that were currently filled with a group of Australians, guessing by the accent.

"Gentlemen, to the left up ahead." It would take us another ten minutes to get where we needed to go. I took advantage of the time I had to make two calls. The first to Marco and the second to my friend, Giorgio.

"Ciao, Atticus, more emergencies today?" Marco said.

"Actually, yes, there is one."

There was a brief silence at the other end of the line. "I'm afraid to ask, Atticus, what's happened?"

I explained everything that had happened from when Vanessa left the Forum to my conversation with Cynthia.

"So now my brother has been promoted to general practitioner? He'll love that."

"Marco, you can see that it's all for a good cause, can't you? He just has to visit the girl and tell her what to do to rid her system of the, um, Tylenol. I think we're already in a good place. She's been drinking water and warm tea for the last twenty-four hours. I just wasn't expecting another withdrawal, especially in Cynthia's company."

"So Mrs. Cornwall is in on all of this, I presume?"

"Yes, she knows as much as I do, and we are both very concerned."

"Listen to yourself, Atticus, 'concerned,' 'all for a good cause.' I think it would have been better for you to remain detached and uninterested as you were just seventy-two hours ago."

I wasn't sure if Marco was teasing me or reprimanding me.

"Okay, Atticus," he said. "I'll get my brother-in-law to do this for us. He owes me. Understand, however, that he shall be making some far-fetched statements to the teachers. I will inform him about everything so that he can judge what to say and what not to say. An excessive use of this Tylenol, which sounds to me like extra-strength aspirin, is a far cry from the dangerous combinations of pharmaceuticals that girl was taking. You'll owe me big for this, Atticus."

"I know. I'll make it up to you."

"I'll send you a text message and let you know when he can be there. We'll try for the morning."

Marco ended the call. I turned my attention back to the boys, who had paused at a fork in the road.

"Head to the right," I said.

I needed to make that second call. I scrolled down my cell phone address book and found Giorgio's number. I pressed the "send" button and hoped that the line wasn't busy as it almost always was. I had to try three times, but then I got a ringtone.

"Well, hello, my good friend! I thought you had forgotten about me."

"But, Giorgio, you know that is entirely impossible."

I had worked closely with Giorgio when I was with the FBI stationed at the American embassy in Rome. Giorgio was a lieutenant colonel of the Guardia di Finanza, which was the Italian version of the U.S. Customs Bureau, Drug Enforcement Administration, and Internal Revenue Service wrapped up in one key government entity. After I left the bureau, Giorgio was one of the very few work contacts I stayed in touch with. We would meet for lunch every so often, and he would practice his very poor English with me. He was an extraordinary professional at his job but had absolutely no aptitude for languages. I suspected this was a key reason he had never been promoted to a higher level in the GF.

"Giorgio, I'm calling you for a favor. I know how busy you are, but I believe that this could be right up your alley."

After I described what had happened and explained what I wanted him to do, he became enthusiastic.

"Wonderful, Atticus! A little bit like the old times, only fewer guns. Just tell me when and where."

I gave him the address and the name of the place. We arranged the exercise for Saturday at six o'clock.

"Thank you, Giorgio. I'll give you a call on Saturday to confirm."

I ended the phone call, feeling a little better. We had reached an important junction in the road, which split off into five different directions. "Wait up," I called to the boys. "We need to go down those stairs in front of you and cross to the other side." One of the roadways was the Via del Traforo, which was built back in 1902 and went underneath the length of the Quirinale Palace gardens, the residence of the president of Italy since 1946. Times had certainly changed. I could not fathom a four-lane public road beneath the White House grounds, under the Kremlin, or below 10 Downing Street in today's volatile geopolitical climate.

We headed down the staircase that led to an underground passage that exited on the other side of the street.

"This would have come in handy earlier today, Atticus. You looked like a little, lost puppy until Riccardo came to our rescue."

"Ha, ha, what a comedian." I gave Mark a slight shove to the back of the head.

We were now at the intersection of Via del Tritone and Via dei Due Macelli, the "Road of the Two Butchers," so called because slaughterhouses occupied this street up until the 1830s. We made a left, and after a few steps, we were at our destination.

"All right James, I hope you're up to this," I said.

He just looked at me with a challenging stare. The duel was on.

This particular store, Da Franco (literally, "At Franco's Place"), was unique in that it still had vinyl records, as well as CDs and music DVDs. It was one of those die-hard establishments that had yet been displaced by Amazon or by the large book and music chain stores that were springing up like mushrooms everywhere. I had not actually known whether it was still open or not. Franco, the owner, had told me that he would only close or sell upon his death. Presumably, he wasn't dead yet.

James and Jeremy headed over to the CD section and started flipping through the assortment. Mark went in the direction of the music DVDs. I had always enjoyed, when living here in Rome, perusing the store's large collection of new and used albums. I wondered if Franco was still running the place or if he had retired. Twenty years before, I used to come here regularly, and Franco was already in his late fifties.

Then it started. James started coming at me with a series of rapid-fire questions.

"What can you tell me about Anthrax? Know any of their stuff? Album titles?"

"I don't care for them," I answered just as quickly. "They remind me of KISS without the makeup. I had copies of *Stomp 442* and *The Threat Is Real*, but I gave them away a long time ago."

"That's awesome, Atticus," said Jeremy. "A point for you."

Apparently, he had appointed himself scorekeeper.

"My turn, James." I was thumbing through some old classic titles. "*Sabbath Bloody Sabbath*. Who, what, where, and when?"

"Black Sabbath is the band. It was their fifth studio album, recorded in the UK and released in 1973. Best song on the album, 'Killing Yourself to Live.'"

"I'll accept that, though I prefer 'Sabbra Cadabra.'"

"And one point for James. We're tied."

Jeremy was getting a kick out of this.

"What's your take on Alice in Chains, Atticus?"

"A poor copy of Nirvana, and I would say the same thing for Soundgarden."

"Ditto that, I'm with you for once," James said.

He was grinning, and I felt that a bond was beginning to form between us.

"The only good thing that came out of the Seattle movement, other than Nirvana, was Pearl Jam," I asserted.

"*No Code* and *Riot Act* are their two best albums," James returned.

"I'm with you on *Riot Act*, but I think that *Backspace* was their best effort by far."

"You guys should go on a rock 'n' roll quiz show. You're both epic, really epic!"

Jeremy was enjoying this battle.

Mark came up. "Hey, Atticus, mind if I head out? I need to grab some toothpaste and bottled water."

"No problem," I said. "You can get back to the hotel on your own, right? Do you still have that matchbook with the name and address of the hotel on it?"

"I've got it," he said, digging it out of his back pocket.

"Okay. See you at dinner. James and I still have some work to do here."

Mark headed out. This was fortunate. I wanted James alone. I just needed to find a way to get Jeremy out of here as well. My interest in James had already been fueled when he revealed that Derek, Sabrina's deceased brother, listened to Marilyn Manson with him, much to her incredulity and disgust. Additionally, Evelyn's diary entries made me want to get into this boy's head.

Our back and forth continued with Deep Purple, Blue Oyster Cult, Emerson, Lake & Palmer, Depeche Mode, Nazareth, Korn, Iron Maiden, Rob Zombie, Slayer, Judas Priest, Metallica, The Clash, Rammstein, and other bands. Finally, Jeremy got bored.

"Hey, you two aficionados, I'm heading back. Don't sweat it, Atticus, I can get back to the hotel blindfolded."

"Okay, Jeremy. We'll be back soon."

Now it was only James and me.

"What about Frank Marino and Mahogany Rush, James?" I asked.

"I don't know that much about them."

"And The Prodigy?"

"*Spitfire* and *Hotride,* two kick-ass tunes."

"I concur."

I was still flipping through records that were taking me down memory lane when I glanced up at James and noticed that he looked awkwardly rigid. He was staring at a CD that he was holding in his hands. He looked as if he had seen a ghost. I walked over to him.

"James, everything okay?"

He didn't seem to hear me. He just kept staring at the CD as if in a trance. It was from a group called Gorgoroth and the title of the CD was *Quantos Possunt ad Satanitatem Trahunt.* I knew a little more than average about this Norwegian band. They had ranked highly for a few years in the Satanic/death metal/black metal charts. However, I didn't care for their lyrics, which literally sang praises for anything demonic. If I remembered my Latin, the title of the album was something like "They drag as many as they can to Satan."

I touched James's shoulder, and he jumped back, startled.

"Easy there, James, it's just me."

"Sorry…I kinda lost it there for a moment."

I took the CD from him and put it back on the shelf.

"I'm going back to the hotel," he said abruptly.

He turned and went toward the door.

"Wait up, James, I'm coming with you."

He didn't answer and just kept walking. I wanted to speak to the man behind the counter and ask about Franco, but it was more important to stay close to James. I grabbed the store's business card on my way out.

James was walking so quickly that I found it difficult to keep pace with him, but once down the stairs that led us to the other side of Via del Tritone, he slowed down. I kept silent, not knowing what to say. But then he opened up:

"That was pretty girly of me," he said, smiling ruefully. "I just freaked out there for a moment. Must be my medication."

I suspected that he wanted to avoid talking about what really triggered him. But I wasn't going to let this opportunity to understand him better slip by.

"It looked to me like you were upset by that Gorgoroth CD. You were fine until you saw it."

"Well, it's some pretty creepy shit they sing about. Do you know them?"

"A few of their things—*Human Sacrifice* and *Rebirth*—but it's not my thing. And their music videos are just shock trash. Take 'Possessed by Satan' and 'Carving a Giant.' Either they really believe in all of that crap or they're just exploiting it to make a buck. Do you like their material?"

"No, not really. But…" He trailed off.

"But?"

His shoulder slumped. "But Derek was a big fan."

"I see. The two of you listened to Manson together, right?"

James stopped and turned to me. "It's not the same thing! You know music. Manson, Prodigy, Black Sabbath, and Slipknot…they're totally different from Gorgoroth."

"I agree. Gorgoroth's music pushes Satanic—"

"That's what I kept telling him!" James almost shouted, cutting me off. Some passersby glanced at the agitated young man. "He just wouldn't get off this Satan shit—he just kept at it! He really thought, he thought…" He didn't finish the sentence but paused and looked at me with tears welling up in his eyes. "It just ate him up, Atticus, it destroyed him." James dropped his head and began to cry like a small child.

What he said next, between sobs, sent a chill down my spine.

CHAPTER 33

It was almost half past two in the morning. Barbara and I were on our fourth mini bottle of red wine from the bar downstairs. She had come to my room around midnight. We had immediately begun hashing out the day's events.

Everyone had gone off on their own that afternoon while Michelle, who complained of a bad migraine, remained in the hotel. Barbara told me about the offhand remark that John had made after leaving Cynthia, about Barbara and me becoming so "chummy," sharing secrets about the students and who knew what else.

"I laughed and told him to blow it out of his ear, for lack of a better place," she said with a chuckle.

"That was a bit over the top, don't you think?" I remonstrated. "It's clear as day that he has a crush on you. Didn't you notice him pouting when you didn't offer to go out with him this afternoon?"

"I know. Maybe I shouldn't have been so hard on him. But Cynthia had already raised my blood pressure with her high-and-mighty show of authority. John's remark just sent me over the edge. Not to worry. I'll patch things up with him later."

"Anything unusual with Evelyn? I thought she was going to tag along with James to the record store."

"I think she would have, but when she saw that Mark and Jeremy were going, she backed out. She can put up with Jeremy, but not Mark. She seemed okay, though. Quiet as usual, but no signs of suicidal behavior. I'm beginning to think that you were right, Atticus. The potential time bomb here isn't Evelyn, but James."

I still had not told her anything about my one-on-one with James that afternoon, and I didn't bring it up now. Instead, I stayed on Evelyn: "That's why I told Michelle to try and get another look at Evelyn's diary."

"What?"

"It's the fastest way to understand if we are going to have to take action," I said. "Michelle's smart. She'll find a way."

"That's if she's up to it," Barbara cautioned. "She was still nursing that migraine at dinner and looked miserable. Anyhow, if she does find something important, I hope she doesn't come here right away. I haven't hidden under the bed since I was sixteen."

"No worries. I told her that whatever she found could wait until morning unless it was an emergency. And she'll call my room first in that event. But I must say, imagining you naked and under my bed is rather exciting."

Barbara grinned. "Forget imagining and just take a look at me naked *on* your bed."

She got on her knees and slid off her beige bathrobe. Over the next twenty or so minutes, I experienced the most ardent sexual pleasure a human body was capable of. Nothing on our two bodies was left unexplored. We were intertwined like two Slinkies after a head-on collision. We were loudly and carelessly satisfied.

Afterward, Barbara lay on her back, and I was on my stomach with my left arm draped across her chest. Both of us just lay there, exhausted and smiling.

"My, my, Mr. Winterle," said Barbara, sighing. "It just keeps getting better. I'm worn out!"

"You are amazing, Barbara, simply amazing," I returned. "I've never been to where you took me."

"*Idem*, Mr. Winterle, *idem*. You see, I know a little Latin too."

"I'm impressed."

After a quick shower, we threw our bathrobes back on, returned to bed, and opened the last bottle of wine. I passed a full glass to Barbara as she was drying her hair.

"Any idea what Cynthia did after roasting me this afternoon?" I asked.

"No clue," she replied. "When I got back to the hotel, she was sitting in the lobby with Anthony. I don't know if they had gone out together or just stayed in the hotel."

"There's something off-kilter about their interaction."

Barbara nodded. "The way she sides with him all the time is peculiar."

"How long has this been going on?"

"As long as I can remember. Anthony came to Bradford in eighth grade. Cynthia started teaching there a year later and was all over him like a mother hen."

"Well, Cynthia seems to be a bit of a loner, and Anthony has an insecurity complex the size of the Empire State Building. Maybe they're just made for each other."

"Or it may be that we're reading too much into all of this. Anthony is a perfect target for bullying, and he's always shied away from those who excel in sports and extracurricular activities. Since she's not up there on the list of most popular teachers, they probably just relate better to one another."

"Could be."

There was a brief silence. Barbara sipped her wine, put down the glass, then put her head on my chest. "You haven't told me a thing about your day," she murmured, "especially about the visit to the record store."

I sighed. "Where do I begin? Well, for one thing, I told Cynthia she would have to find a new chaperone if Vanessa was sent back to Atlanta early."

"Oh, come on now, Atticus, talk about over the top!" Barbara chuckled. She paused. "Ahh, now I understand... Cynthia asked John and me to meet with her privately after the doctor had visited Vanessa."

"Which will be tomorrow, or rather, *this* morning."

After I had returned with James from the record store, I found a message on my cell phone from Marco alerting me that his brother would come over around 8:00 am. I had informed Cynthia at dinner.

"They'll have to get a teacher to replace me as well if you go, Atticus. I won't go along with such a decision."

"Well, we're not there yet. Let's see how Cynthia reacts to the, ah, diagnosis."

"I take it you fully briefed Marco on the situation? Is his brother-in-law really a doctor?"

"He's a pharmacist."

"A pharmacist?" Barbara raised an eyebrow.

I nodded ruefully. "I may have pushed all this a bit too far with Marco. I'm asking his brother-in-law to blatantly lie about Vanessa's condition, which could get him in a serious amount of trouble if any of the truth were to come to the surface one day."

Barbara didn't answer immediately, and it was apparent that she was nurturing the same opinion. She sat up, placed her right hand under my chin, and looked straight at me.

"If it's all for Vanessa's good, then I think it's worth it. Nobody else would have gone to this trouble to help this girl. These kids are fortunate to have met you. And so am I."

She kissed me on the cheek. I flushed my customary cherry red. Then I cleared my throat and drew back.

"I have something to tell you about James and, believe it or not, Derek."

She pulled her bathrobe tighter around her and sat cross-legged.

I told her about the musical knowledge duel between James and me and how he seemed to be genuinely enjoying himself until he came across the Gorgoroth CD and what he had said about Derek's fascination with that band.

I told her as well about the scene after the record store when James, between tears, came right out and told me that Derek had committed suicide. "Then I found out why the CD upset James so much," I said. "He told me that Derek had killed himself because he followed the Satanic principles that band promotes."

***

We had been standing on the corner of Via del Tritone and Via della Panetteria when James broke down. I put my arm across his shoulders and steered him into an unassuming coffee bar, taking a table in the back where we had some privacy. I ordered two espressos while he regained some composure. As we drank, James told me about Derek—how he had been into the occult for a several years and was a registered member of the Church of Satan founded by one Anton LaVey. According to James, Derek was an avid reader of the Satanic Bible and attended black masses as well as other demonic meetings in the Atlanta area.

My conversation with James from that point on was laser-etched on my brain. I asked the obvious questions.

"Did Derek's parents or Sabrina have a clue about any of this before his death? It seems he was leading two lives, James. How was he able to hide his other self from everyone?"

James wiped his eyes with the heel of his palm. "There's a junkyard for old shipping containers about six miles from where Derek lived. Nobody ever goes there. He had found an old, rusted MAERSK unit way in the back and fixed it up. He had a desk, books on the occult, a kick-ass stereo system, a bed, some throw rugs an old couch, and even a small fridge. He put up soundproof panels all around the inside so you could pump up the volume and not hear a damn thing outside and installed an air conditioner running off a generator. You could've lived in that place. The only thing missing was a bathroom."

I frowned in puzzlement. "But Derek was Mister Popular. He was on the football team, had top grades. How does that square with worshipping Satan?"

James shook his head as though he was also confused. "He said it was all for Lucifer, all part of a bigger plan. He showed me a letter he was going to give to his parents before he did himself in. It was all planned—from the beginning. This guy was a fucking genius."

James didn't say this with any hero worship in his voice, just anguish.

"How did you get involved with Derek?" I asked. Sabrina had commented that her brother would never have hung around a loser like James.

"It was a few months before he died. He stopped me one day when I was walking home from school and gave me the directions to his hideout and a time to meet up. He didn't say anything else. He was in his new Camaro, and I remember thinking how that guy had *everything*. I almost didn't go. I figured that he and his football buddies wanted to dance all over my face somewhere in private, but I was still curious. I went to the junkyard early and found the MAERSK container. I hung around for about twenty minutes and didn't see or hear anything strange, so I jumped the fence and waited. A few minutes later, one of the doors of the container opened, and Derek came out and invited me in. There was no sign of anyone else hanging around, but for all I knew, his homies could have been hiding behind the other containers. I didn't particularly care anymore, so I just went in."

"This still doesn't explain why, James."

"I'm getting there, Atticus. What's the friggin' deal, anyway? The guy's dead and buried! Why are you so fucking pushy about all of this!"

What a dramatic split-second metamorphosis. In my eagerness to get answers, I had forgotten that it was James I was talking to—a troubled young man on potent antidepressants with no self-esteem. He had opened up to me more or less by chance. Now I was perilously close, with my careless insistence, to getting the door slammed in my face.

"You're right, James. It's not important. Derek is dead and gone, and we have to look forward, not backward. Want something else to drink, a sandwich or something?"

It was as if he hadn't even heard me. As if there had been a momentary warp in time, he just picked up where he had left off:

"I went in and sat down on the couch. He opened two Coors and sat opposite me. He said that he liked my 'Screw it all' attitude and the way I called a spade a spade. He actually apologized that he couldn't hang around me in public, but he said that I would soon understand why. He had found out from Jeremy that I had his same tastes in music. He showed me his CD collection. Mercyful Fate, King Diamond, Mayhem, Behemoth, Manson, Slipknot, Slayer, Ozzy…he must have had over five hundred CDs neatly lined up on these makeshift bookshelves in there. There were posters and pictures on the inside of the container, all with Satan and demons. When I asked him about it, he just said he liked the imagery. I didn't freak out about it because Derek was so natural and easygoing that I just relaxed and had another beer. I wasn't going to get my face kicked in after all."

James only found out later that Derek had only two goals in life: to worship Satan and punish all of those who believed in what he considered the ultimate hypocrisy—human love.

"He had the Nine Satanic Statements, the Eleven Satanic Rules on Earth, and the Nine Satanic Sins written in block letters across one side of the container. I read them so many times that I know them by heart. Derek would give me examples to prove that these were the true commandments. He even had me believing some of this shit after a while."

"Such as?"

"Well, a few of things that stuck with me were like 'Satan represents kindness to those who deserve it instead of love wasted on ingrates.' He always brought this up when he talked about his parents and Sabrina."

I was tempted to interrupt him once again and ask a few leading questions but decided against it.

"And some of those Eleven Rules on Earth...such as 'Do not harm small children.' Kind of screwy that this would fit in with anything having to do with Satan, don't you think? Another one that made sense to me was 'When walking in open territory, bother no one. If someone bothers you, ask them to stop. If he does not stop, destroy him.' Makes fucking good sense to me."

"So Derek killed himself in order to get back at his family?" I tried to be as casual as possible asking this explosive question.

"Listen, Atticus. Derek spent the last four years of his life being the best at everything he did. Everything! He would train in the middle of the night, study all weekend long, do part-time jobs to save up for clothes, books, CDs. The guy was on a constant energy buzz. He did all that because he had a cause. I thought it was screwy from the start, and I thought it was plain crazy after he died. But I admire, I don't know, his *focus*. He knew that killing himself would be like spitting in his parents' faces. He showed me a letter, ten freaking pages of the most badass shit I've ever read. He knew about his mom and dad's...habits, let's put it that way. He told me his mom would screw all the pool cleaners who came to their house, that his dad liked to hit up anything that was barely out of elementary school, preferably black or Mexican, that Sabrina's been fucking older black dudes since she was fifteen. He ripped his parents and sister to shreds.

After reading that stuff, I think that any one of them would have put a fucking bullet in their head. All part of the plan, Atticus. Derek wanted to dish out the most intense pain he could on his family, and he would do it on the chosen day, April 30."

I asked another obvious question.

"Yeah, it has something to do with a historical get-together of witches somewhere in Germany. Walpurgis Night, he called it. It was an important day for Derek."

The meetings in the container over the following two months were frequent and lengthy, with Derek doing most of the talking. They would drink beer, smoke some grass, and listen to Derek's CDs.

"I did most of the drinking and smoking because Derek couldn't risk showing up drunk or stoned in public. That would have completely fucked up four years of hard work."

James fell silent for a moment and looked at his clenched hands. Neither of us had touched our espressos.

"He told me one night that he couldn't be seen in public with me—that it would 'Raise eyebrows,' as he put it."

"Did that bother you?"

"Well, it would have been pretty cool rolling up with him in his Camaro to school just to see the dumbass expression on people's faces. But I understood him, Atticus. He couldn't be seen anywhere near the school with a loser. He needed to be in the spotlight right up until the end. No flaws, no screwups. Just perfection. And that's what he got."

James remembered that on one occasion, Derek had gotten rather drunk, which was out of the ordinary, given that he wanted to celebrate. Yale University had written and expressed interest in his academic as well as football accomplishments. His parents were overjoyed and so proud, calling all their friends and gloating over the news. This was going to make everything so much sweeter when he did himself in.

"So you knew when he was going to commit suicide," I said.

"Yeah, I knew it all, the whole plan. I knew when, and I knew how."

I watched him intently. His expression became defensive, almost embarrassed.

"And now you want to ask me why I didn't stop him, right? Go ahead, Atticus. Go right fuckin' ahead!" James had raised his voice, and the few patrons in the bar stopped what they were doing and looked our way.

"Well, the question does come up rather spontaneously, don't you think?" I was as cool as ice. James was expecting a different reaction. He lowered his head and went back to ripping his hands.

"No, I didn't try to stop him. I didn't do a damn thing to get in the way of his plans. I didn't tell anyone. I didn't say or do anything to try to change his mind. I didn't do shit, Atticus."

Tears were welling from his eyes and landing on the table. I remained silent, waiting to see if he was going to add anything else. As much as I would have gone on speaking with him for hours, it was getting late, and we needed to head back to the hotel. And then another metamorphosis: James regained his composure, looked at me, and spoke with absolutely no emotion.

"He was my friend. He trusted me. He let me into his world, shared everything with me. Nobody has ever given me any of their time. Nobody has ever given a shit about me. Only Derek. I wasn't going to be the one to destroy his project. It wasn't going to be me." James got up. "I wanna go back now, Atticus."

"Okay, James, let's go."

We were silent as we walked back to the hotel. James went straight to the restaurant. I went up to my room, splashed some cold water on my face, and headed to dinner.

***

With this, I stopped talking for the first time in the last fifteen minutes, a very long time when speaking without interruption. There was a deep silence in the room. Barbara had placed her glass on the bedside table, and she was just looking at some fixed point on the wall opposite her. Her arms hung loose by her sides. "Defeatism" was the only noun I could come up with when looking at her.

"Are you okay?" I asked.

"No, I'm not." Barbara wasn't in a good place. "What was it that Derek wrote in that letter to his parents? That his mom was whoring with the pool cleaners and that Sabrina has a special relationship with older black men? Doesn't a lot of this sound rather familiar to you, Atticus?"

I then brilliantly stuck my foot in my mouth.

"Why do you want to draw analogies between what was going on in Derek's family and with your past, Barbara?"

"Analogies? Is that the best you can do, Atticus?"

She got off the bed, closed her bathrobe tightly around her waist, and went to the window.

"The word *analogy* is a gross understatement, Atticus! Is there any difference at all between what my husband and I subjected our children to, a goddamn live porn show, and what Derek says his parents were up to?! I guess I should just drop down on my knees right here and now and thank the Lord that He didn't let my children get involved in the occult and have their brains splatter all over the front end of an oncoming semi!" Yelling was in fashion these last twenty-four hours. First, Cynthia, then James, and now Barbara. She turned and glared at me.

"It's all about the wrong choices, Atticus! I *chose* not to leave my husband for comfort's sake. I *chose* to have sex with men and women I had never met before because my orgasms were more important to me than my two children! I chose to think of me and me only! It seems that Derek's parents were also making all of the 'right' choices. We have no right to call ourselves parents, Atticus! No right!" Tears started to flow. "Derek was a good kid. He was every teacher's dream pupil. All of this shouldn't have happened, it just shouldn't have." She brought her hands to her face and now began to sob uncontrollably.

I got up and took her into my arms. The outpouring of tears lasted a few more minutes before she began to get hold of herself.

"I'm sorry, Atticus, it's just too much sometimes," she said, sniffling.

"You've been carrying a heavy burden on these beautiful shoulders for too many years," I said. "It's good for you to let it all out."

We went back to the bed and sat down. Barbara rested her head on my shoulder and started fiddling with the sash on her bathrobe. This was the perfect moment to attempt to say something meaningful. "Barbara," I said. "We're all outcomes of the choices we make in life. You just said it. That's what makes us human beings, not gods." I moved my hands from her back to her arms and legs. "This is all flesh, blood, and bone, and, as the saying goes, the flesh is weak. Our wants and desires are dictated by the here and now, not the future, which we cannot see. I know I sometimes come across as cynical and biased, but I truly believe that the majority of human beings do the best they can with the resources at their disposal. But we're all shaped by mistakes others have made, especially our parents' mistakes, and our children will also be impacted by the bad decisions we make now and in the future. Your children went on and made lives for themselves, successfully so, it seems. Derek chose—choices again—another path. Some of us have thicker skins and can put up with, excuse my French, bullshit. Others can't cope. We all have our personal baggage, filled with pluses and minuses. That's what makes us who we are. That's what makes us human."

Barbara gazed at me. "Thank you for that, Atticus."

"My pleasure."

She frowned. "I wonder if Derek's parents ever got that letter. Obviously, Sabrina didn't read it, the way she still worships her brother."

"Well, it's certainly something that I wouldn't share at the dinner table."

She hesitated a moment, wiping the last remnants of tears that were still clinging to her cheeks. "I would love to stay here until morning, Atticus, and ask you loads of questions, but we need to get some sleep."

"We won't get much, considering that it's half past four."

"Half past four? No way! It was two o'clock just a few minutes ago!"

Barbara dropped her bathrobe and took up her clothes from the armchair. As she stood there in the chiaroscuro lighting of the room, I thought to myself that Helmut Newton could not have wished for a better subject for his Hasselblad.

She dressed quickly, then went to the bathroom to inspect herself in the mirror. Here she was, about to go out into a deserted hallway at almost five in the morning, but still worried about her appearance. If she had had some makeup with her, I am sure she would have put it on. What was it that Mae West had once said? "It's better to be looked over than to be overlooked."

Barbara noticed me grinning to myself as she switched off the bathroom light.

"And may I ask what it so amusing, Mr. Winterle?"

"Oh nothing, it's just that I thought that a little more mascara and some Chanel nail polish, possibly number 475, were more appropriate for a two-minute walk down a dark hallway."

"You're just a laugh a minute, Atticus. Just remember, wise guy, that if I hadn't put any makeup on before getting off that plane, you wouldn't have even noticed me."

"I was taken by your demeanor and your mind. I wasn't paying much attention to the rest."

She dashed over and jumped on me, pushing me down onto the mattress. She placed her hand between my legs. "Well now, I didn't know that my *mind* had this effect on a man."

Before I could get my hands underneath her blouse, she pulled back and wagged her finger at me.

"Uh, uh, uh! Not now. If I take my clothes off again, we won't leave this room for hours." She patted down her hair once again. "Atticus, what time did you say our so-called doctor was coming?"

"Eight o'clock. I'm going to have a chat with him before he sees Vanessa."

"Okay. And what time do we need to be ready to go? I don't think we mentioned anything about today's itinerary."

Barbara was right. I hadn't said a word about it. "Marco moved the meeting time with the tour guide to ten thirty. If you bump into our kids, please tell them to be in the lobby no later than nine forty-five."

"Sounds good. See you later, my darling Atticus."

She kissed me softly on the lips and then silently opened the door, took a peek to make sure the coast was clear, and made her way out into the hallway.

Saturday
May 1 , Day Five

CHAPTER 34

I closed the door behind her and thought about what I should do next. It was now close to five. At seven thirty, I needed to be in the lobby to make sure that I cornered Marco's brother before Cynthia or John did. I set the alarm for seven since I wouldn't need more than a half an hour to get ready.

I didn't care to look at my emails, so I opted for something that really needed to be done—going through those student bios. I reached for the pile of papers on the corner of the desk, picked up the pillows that had been unceremoniously thrown to the floor during our lovemaking, and made myself comfortable on the unkempt bed.

Who was next in the pile? Maria Lopez, my opera enthusiast, whom everybody called "Mary." I remembered her telling me on the bus that her father was from Mexico and her mother from Panama, or was it Colombia?

I found out quickly that she was on the school soccer team and that she enjoyed a wide variety of music with a particular liking, needless to say, for opera. A few of the reasons she gave for wanting to participate in this trip were for the art and architecture, two fields she was interested in, to see St. Peter's, and to taste authentic Italian food.

Mary had left the medical matters column blank and had ticked "Married" under her parents' marital status.

I fought off the overwhelming urge to close my eyes and fall into a deep sleep. I wanted to get through this and at least one more bio.

Under "University," Mary had written "Marquette." All I knew about this particular university was that its hometown was Milwaukee, Wisconsin, and that it was a private school, if I remembered correctly. Mary had added that she was particularly interested in their liberal arts program and that...

It was suddenly so hot and humid. I was drenched in perspiration. I was also quite uncomfortable sitting on a hardwood chair with my arms behind my back and my hands shackled in cuffs of some sort. Where was I?

There was a darkness composed of dust and ash with just the glow of what seemed to be a series of bonfires ablaze off in the distance. What was that smell, so overpowering—a mix of sulfur, decaying flesh, and excrement.

"I hope you don't feel too ill at ease, Atticus." The words flowed out of the murkiness. I then heard soft but resolute steps approaching me accompanied by the grating sound of a metallic folding chair being dragged across the floor.

"Who are you?"

"Just someone you've never met in person but about whom you seem to have a good deal of information, thanks to a friend of mine." A strong beam of light was shone in my face. "I thought it would be a good idea to come and share a few things with you, things that you still don't grasp after your tête-à-tête with James."

It was Derek. But how was that possible? The light shining in my face suddenly went off, and a strong, cold, fluorescent glow illuminated the area around me. There he was, sitting about six feet away, a young, blond man dressed in his Sunday finest, gazing at me with ultimate satisfaction.

"So sorry about those cuffs around your wrists, Atticus, but it's required for later. Have patience."

"What is it you want from me, Derek?" I asked.

He laughed shrilly.

"My goodness, Atticus, how entertaining!" He coughed a bit and patted himself theatrically on the chest. "My dear Atticus, what in the world could I ever want or need from you? I am fully content, I have all that I need, and I am in a place where I have always wanted to be."

He spread out his arms and looked about him as if he were admiring the king's private apartments at Versailles. "As I said before, I'm just here to fill you in on a few things. I'm actually doing you a favor."

With that, he slowly got up from the chair and began tapping his forehead slowly with his index finger as if deep in thought.

"What was that you were saying a short while ago to that little whore of yours, Atticus? Something about 'choices'? Yes, that's it, choices. How fascinating." Before I could respond, he rapidly turned toward me, glaring with a hyena-like sneer.

"Choices!? You selfish, sadistic pieces of shit! You bring us into the world and then 'choose' how to deal with us? Is that how it is, Atticus?"

He started walking in circles around me, becoming more and more agitated. "I get it. It's all clear now. Tell me if I've got this right. Today, as a parent, I can choose to ignore you little Sally or Peter by drinking or drugging myself into oblivion, but tomorrow, I may choose to cop a feel between your legs, Sally, or to beat you silly, Peter, for having spilt that goddamned milk on the floor again! Have I got this down pat, Atticus?"

"Derek, what are you saying? Why are you—" He leaned down in my face now, just inches away. His breath was worse than the stench surrounding us.

"What am I saying? What I'm trying to describe to you, Atti-cus, are the joys of childhood! We are totally at your mercy—we look up to you, we love you, we adore you, our mommy, our daddy…and how are we rewarded? How?! Well, let's see…"

He straightened up and took a piece of paper out of his back pocket, except that the paper began to magically mushroom into a large folder composed of hundreds of pages.

"Oh, what a list! What a list of rewards for us, your chil-dren. How fortunate we are! Would you like to hear and see a few, just a few of the infinite number of prizes that are bestowed on us?"

Derek's tone of voice had not changed, but somehow, a metamorphosis was occurring, with Derek rapidly becoming younger, looking now more like a boy of seven or eight in-stead of a teenager of eighteen.

"Derek, I really don't understand, I just want to—"

"Shut up, Atticus, and enjoy the show!"

The lights went out, and three rows of large television moni-tors appeared in front of me.

They were all aglow with that white static you get when there is no video or audio signal. The air was suddenly clear of dust and ash, and the awful odor was gone. There were consoles, computers, and synthesizers with their bright LED lights shining in an array of colors. It could have been the Fox News nerve center. Shadows were darting here and there around all this audiovisual equipment, but only Derek was in full view in a spotlight shining on him from above.

"Atmosphere, we're missing atmosphere…music, please!"

At first, I could not make out what was coming over the loudspeakers, which were somewhere in this large makeshift control center. But then I figured it out—it was Wagner, Das Rheingold, the end of Scene Two. That hammering sound...a perfect fit for what I was experiencing.

Derek's voice was thundering across the room as he gave orders to the sinister apparitions. He now looked more like a boy of three or four years of age. The large notebook he held in his hands was as big as he was.

"Ready, Atticus? Let's take a look at some of these choices of yours. Row one, go!"

The white noise emanating from twenty or so flat-screen monitors was abruptly replaced by images of a variety of family homes seen from the outside. From modest abodes to luxurious villas. And then in a split second, we were inside these residences, and I saw families going about their daily business. But the 'business' they were going about began to turn ugly. The first screen showed a young child standing in its crib crying desperately while the mother, in what certainly was a drunken stupor, stumbled over herself with a cocktail glass in her hand. Another monitor showed two terrified toddlers embracing each other in a kitchen where a father was pushing and shoving his wife against the counter, raising a menacing fist close to her face. There were scenes of parents ripping up report cards and throwing them in their children's faces, school projects that were swept off the tables or kicked aside with shouts of "You're useless, what a disgrace, you're never going to achieve anything in life!" There was a father grabbing his golf bag, energetically pushing his wife to one side, with a small boy chasing after him, a softball and mitt in his hands that would never be shared with his dad. Every story on every screen was one that portrayed neglect, rebuke, ridicule, and humiliation.

"I feel, Atticus, that all of this is boring you just a bit…all pretty humdrum stuff, don't you think? Nothing out of the ordinary here…" Before I could answer, Derek continued, "But this is just the tip of the iceberg, Atticus. More choices, please! Row two, on!"

The second row of monitors replaced the white noise with the same start as the first row—a variety of family homes once again all shown from the outside, then we were taken inside. It quickly became an ugly sight.

Children were being slapped, whipped with belts, and hit on the face and body with an array of items from rulers to hockey sticks. One father was holding a football in his hands while fiercely taunting his young son who was standing in front of him with crooked shoulder pads and a ripped jersey. The father then threw the football so hard at the child's head that he fell and didn't get back up. The man just left the room, slamming the door behind him.

There was no discrimination here. There were straight as well as homosexual and lesbian parents, white, black, Latino, Asian, all basking in their moments of glory. The one common thread in all the videos was the physical and mental abuse that all the children were enduring.

"We're running out of time, Atticus, we need to beef this up a bit." Derek looked at the monitors and crossed his small arms across his chest. "This is still all minor league, isn't it? Let's see some major league action! Row three please, on!"

Same scenario. Homes on the outside, and then on the inside. I was praying that this would all be over soon…

The young girl, portrayed on the first monitor, possibly nine years of age, was standing in front of a full-length mirror in what appeared to be her bedroom. The only illumination in the room was coming from a Mickey Mouse night-light that was plugged in close to where the girl was standing, but I could make out a few stuffed teddy bears and a Barbie doll resting on the floor. She had pajamas on and was holding something in her right hand that glimmered in the low light. I couldn't make it out. Suddenly, a triangle of light appeared on the floor and then vanished just about as quickly as it had appeared. A door had opened and closed behind the girl who hadn't moved an inch. She was no longer alone. A tall male figure came into view from the rear. A chair was drawn, and the figure sat down.

"Hey there, honey. Gosh, you look beautiful this evening." The man was looking at the girl's reflection in the mirror. "We're just missing one thing…can you go ahead and put some on for your daddy?"

The little girl nodded her head mechanically, slowly raising her right hand. Now I could see that she had a shiny lipstick container between her fingers. She started smearing the stick across her lips the way a young child would. The figure behind her, in the meantime, was loosening his trousers. Rage was building up inside of me. I wanted to take my eyes off that monitor, but couldn't.

The young girl then turned toward the monster in the chair. The horrid lines of bright-red lip rouge covered with the tears streaming down her face was only a prelude of the grotesque act that was about to take place.

"Beautiful, just beautiful. Now my little dove, do what your daddy wants you to do."

"But I…I don't want, want to do it anymore, Daddy." How many times had this child been put through this?

The man's suave voice suddenly turned aggressive. "Do you want me to hurt your little sister again? Do you want me to hit Mommy again? Now get on your knees!"

The girl did as she was told.

I turned my head.

"Come, come, Atticus, weak stomach? You said it, not me. It's all about choices..."

"You're wrong, Derek! Dead wrong! This is sickness, perversion, evil, this is..." He cut me off with a loud bellow.

"Choice, Atticus! Choice! This father chose to do this to his daughter, he wants to do it, and he doesn't give a shit about the consequences! Lift your head, Atticus, and stop acting like a pathetic wimp! There's plenty more to see. Take a look at the creativity, the talent, the example that you so-called parents share with us!"

I did as he said, first looking at him with all the hatred I could muster, and then back at the monitors. The scenes displayed were of unspeakable violence and abuse.

Beatings and tortures such as the cigarette burns being inflicted on a young boy's arm flashed on one of the screens in front of me. More sexual abuse, a woman shaking her infant with homicidal fury before flinging it against the wall. My teeth were gritting, and I could feel tears welling up inside of me, but I wasn't going to give Derek the satisfaction of seeing me cry. I closed my eyes and took a deep breath. It was in that split-second that I noticed the stench once again. Opening my eyes, I was back to where this all had begun. The ash and dust were back in the air with the bonfires in the distance. The monitors and all the hi-tech equipment were gone, and Derek was once again a young man sitting in the folding chair in front of me. I thought I heard a siren of some sort far off in the distance but concentrated instead on what appeared to be a gas can on Derek's lap.

"Do you know what is truly absurd, Atticus? Do you know what the tragic irony of all of this is? No? Well, let me enlighten you. The true sickness of all of this is that we, the children, feel guilty. We feel as if it's our fault that our parents behave this way. We obviously deserve it! Do you understand the power that parents yield? The destructive power that can utterly crush another human being?" Derek was pointing with what looked more like a talon than a finger at me.

He stood up and walked in my direction. "It's time for me to go, Atticus, and for you to get back to your favorite pastime, which is fucking Mrs. Cornwall. That's all you've been thinking about lately, isn't? It would be decent of you to spend a little more of your precious time with the students on this trip. You've only begun to crack the ice with a few of them."

Derek opened the nozzle on the can and poured the contents over his head.

"What are you doing, Derek? Stop it!"

He took a cigarette lighter of his pocket and flicked it. He burst into flames. The siren in the background was getting louder. Derek began to scream, pointing his torched arm toward me. "It was my choice Atticus... my choice!" He gave out a ghastly laugh as blood began to roll out of his charred eye sockets. He then fell to his knees as the fire continued its deadly dance across the entirety of his body. The siren was very close to me now. I desperately wanted to release myself from the cuffs on my wrists.

That siren...so loud...so repetitive.

My hands were free! But I could not move about easily, what was getting in my way?! I couldn't see clearly...something soft, warm, enveloping...and that siren!

I opened my eyes. I was sitting up in bed, the pillow and bed-sheets all tangled up around me.

The siren? It was the clock alarm.

I leaned over and shut it off. I fell back onto the mattress, breathless and perspiring. A nightmare. Vivid, with every detail, including the stench that was etched in my mind and nostrils. Those horrible images broadcasted on those monitors—from what recesses in my brain had those sprouted from? Why had my subconscious punished me with these scenes of cruelty and perversion?

It was abundantly clear that what James had told me about Derek and my ensuing conversation with Barbara had left their mark on me. Even more surprising was how every detail of what I had just experienced had remained crystal clear. I hardly ever remembered any of my dreams once I was awake.

I rolled to one side and began to think about what I told Barbara regarding how we are shaped by the choices we make and, consequently, how these choices can have a positive or negative effect on our children. Had I been too glib? Too shallow? Was I also, as a parent, looking for an easy way out, blaming a poor outcome on the haphazard act of having chosen one course of action over another? I didn't remember having said anything to Barbara about responsibility and accountability regarding our children—two words that, as far as I was concerned, went hand in hand with parenting. Simple to say, but to put into practice? Perhaps, just perhaps, it was easier to have responsibility and accountability take a back seat and let "choice" do the driving. "I made the wrong choice" is more convenient for our peace of mind than "I wasn't responsible."

I spent the next fifteen minutes washing up and dressing, but I was miles away in thought. What was I trying to tell myself with Derek's last remark before he set himself on fire? *It would be nice if you would spend more of your precious time with the students* and that I had only begun to *crack the ice?* Was I telling myself that my only goal had become *fucking Mrs. Cornwall?* That nothing else really mattered? That the group, to be frank, wasn't at all important to me?

I thought about that evening, after James and I had gotten back from the music store. I had come down to dinner and noticed that he had gone to sit next to Evelyn and Jeremy. Evelyn was talking to James, but he wasn't answering. He was just sitting there lost in space. I sat down at the table with Raymond, Vanessa, and Sabrina. I saw that Cynthia and John were sitting together and that, other than a quick wave of their hands, they were doing their best to cold-shoulder me. Barbara was sitting at the table next to mine, and I did remember that I was overcome by an overwhelming urge to lean her over onto the table and take her from behind. My libido was running the mile in record breaking time.

After dinner, the group had split up and gone off in various directions, with only a few of them remaining in the hotel. Many of the students had asked me to go with them, but I had declined. I could tell that some of them were disappointed. My only objective was to get Barbara to my room ASAP. I wanted to share the day's events with her, but primarily, I wanted to *fuck Mrs. Cornwall.*

Okay, okay, so for one evening, I was a bit absent with the group and was thinking more with the head between my legs rather than the one on my shoulders. This certainly didn't warrant such a harsh accusation of indifference from my subconscious. What I had done and was doing to save Vanessa's ass from getting kicked off this trip was one example of how I had come to care about these kids!

I was annoyed and frustrated with myself. But now I needed to concentrate on the present. It was time to go downstairs to meet up with Marco's brother. I looked at the clock. It was getting on seven fifteen. I needed to go downstairs.

When I arrived in the main hall, I peeked into the restaurant but saw no one from our group. As I approached the front desk, Giovanni came out of the back office.

"Good morning, Signor Atticus."

"Hello, Giovanni. How are you?"

"I believe, if I may, more rested than you. This group is keeping you busy, no?"

He was speaking to me, once again, with his head down over some papers that he was scrutinizing, never locking eyes with me.

"Let's say that they are a handful. But no complaints. Believe it or not, I'm enjoying the challenge."

"This is good, Signor Atticus. *Labor voluptasque dissimillima natura, societate quadam inter se naturali sunt iuncta.* If you require my assistance, you know where to find me. I shall leave you now to your company. Good day to you." He turned and went into the back office. What "company?" Nobody had entered the hotel. I turned and was startled to see John standing quietly behind me.

"Didn't mean to frighten you, Atticus."

"No worries. I just didn't hear you coming in."

"Was that Latin that guy was speaking? I studied it a long time ago, and it sounded familiar."

"Sure was. He likes throwing Latin phrases my way to test me out." I think that John was waiting for me to translate, but I wasn't in the mood.

"Okay, um…I'm heading to breakfast, do you want to join?"

"Can't. I'm waiting for the doctor. You know, for Vanessa." My gut was telling me that John had already forgotten what the four of us had discussed just hours earlier.

"Oh! Right, Vanessa…Cynthia mentioned that he was coming by this morning."

"That's right, eight o'clock."

He hesitated. "I wanted to apologize for yesterday. Cynthia can go overboard at times."

"No bad feelings, I hope."

John's way of apologizing was to blame Cynthia. If he had stopped at "yesterday," I would have been fine with it.

I shrugged. "Let's see what the doctor says, and we'll take it from there."

"Okay, then. See you later." He turned and went in the direction of the breakfast area, a bit like a scolded puppy.

I looked up at the lobby clock and went over to sit on a red velvet couch in the lobby. I was mulling over what Giovanni had told me in Latin when Barbara and Cynthia appeared.

"Good morning, Atticus," said Barbara. "John told us you were in here waiting for the doctor."

"Yes."

Cynthia clasped her hands. "Barbara and I were thinking, Atticus, that it would be best if you and the doctor went up to see Vanessa alone. If we all go trouncing in her room together, she might become agitated."

Well, this was unexpected.

"In any case, if the doctor only speaks Italian, Barbara, John, and I wouldn't be of any use anyway, would we?" Cynthia seemed genuinely sheepish.

"All right, Cynthia, we'll do that," I said. "When we finish with Vanessa, we'll come down to the breakfast room so that the doctor can give you his evaluation. Okay?"

"Yes, yes. I think that would work just fine. Thank you, Atticus." She attempted a smile, turned, and headed off in the direction of the restaurant. Barbara gave me a wink and a thumbs-up before turning the corner.

What a change in attitude since yesterday afternoon! Had Barbara said something to her? I would quiz her later.

I was so lost in thought I hadn't even noticed the tall, well-dressed young man standing at the front desk and conversing with Giovanni, who had again appeared magically from the back office. I did, however, notice Giovanni pointing in my direction. The gentleman in question had obviously inquired about me.

"Buongiorno, you must be Atticus Winterle."

"Yes, I am, and you must be Marco's brother-in-law."

"That's right. I'm Stefano. We can speak in English if you wish." He was courteous enough, but it was clear that he was not at ease.

"I would prefer to continue in Italian. The teachers and the rest of the group are in the breakfast area just around the corner."

"I understand."

"Stefano, first and foremost, I want to apologize for all of this," I said in a hushed voice. "I realize that you have already gone out of your way to check on those pills and that—"

He cut me off by raising an open hand. "Just tell me how you want me to approach this situation. I can do all of the basic checks such as a heart rate measurement, blood pressure, check her pupils, temperature, ask her a few questions regarding her appetite, her mood, if she is having trouble sleeping, and so on. My degree as a pharmacist allows me to ask basic health-related questions, but I am not an MD, as you say in the United States."

Yup, he was most definitely not comfortable being here. I wondered what he owed Marco to do this for him.

"That's all we need, Stefano. Just the basics. You know the story I told the teachers…that is…about the Tylenol gelcaps?"

"Yes, I studied up on the brand last night." Well, at least he came prepared.

"When you're through, we can discuss the outcome together before we meet with the teachers. There is one in particular, Mrs. Ramsey, that is more than displeased and would love to cut this girl's trip short right now."

He was listening to me but kept silent. He could tell that I was trying to claw my way up a mirror, and I was beginning to think that he was enjoying it.

"I can't tell you what to say to the teachers, Stefano. I am fully aware that all of this could put you in a great deal of trouble, and I wouldn't try to stop you if decided to back out."

He pursed his lips and kept staring at me for what seemed an endless amount of time.

"You do realize, Atticus, that you have a most unusual name." I was thrown off by this sudden digression.

"Yes, it's not a common one."

"You may know that *Atticus* was a Christian martyr who was burned at the stake in Armenia in AD 310."

I shook my head. "No, this is news to me."

"I also did some research on the origins of your name, and when I learned that, other than a Roman philosopher, an archbishop of Constantinople, a Greek rhetorician, it was also the name of a martyr, I decided to help you out." Stefano gave me a smile, and I knew then that we had broken the ice. "But before we do anything, Atticus, we need a good espresso."

"I shall take care of it," I said, with a grin.

Giovanni, who apparently had the hearing of a bat, was already on the phone with the kitchen. The espressos arrived with a small container of warm and cold milk and a sugar bowl. Stefano told me that Marco had always spoken very highly of me. I was pleased and embarrassed at the same time. I made a promise to myself then and there that once I was back in a top management role, I would do everything in my power to get Marco on board with me.

We threw down the espressos in one go. It was time to get upstairs.

CHAPTER 35

I went to the desk and dialed Vanessa's room number.

"Hello?"

"Sabrina?"

"Yes?"

"Hi, it's Atticus. Is everything okay?"

"Oh, hi, Atticus. Yes, we both slept like rocks."

"Is Vanessa awake?"

"Yeah, she's here. Just a second."

"Morning, Atticus," said Vanessa.

"Vanessa, hi. I'm here with the doctor. We're about to come up."

"Are the others coming too?" Her voice had become tense.

"No, just me and the doctor…"

"Does he know the truth?"

"Yes, but he's also aware of our Tylenol story."

"I'm in my PJs, but I guess that's okay, if he's a doctor."

"No problem. He'll need to do some basic checks such as blood pressure and heart rate. Can we come up?"

"Yeah, sure."

"Okay." I handed the phone back to Giovanni and thanked him.

"All right, Stefano, we can go."

I led the way out of the lobby and to the stairs. The prospect of going to Vanessa's room unnoticed was instantly dashed. Almost all the students had decided to go down to breakfast at the same time as I was going up the stairs with Stefano. Greetings flew.

"Hey, Atticus!"

"Morning, Atticus."

"Already done with breakfast, Atticus?"

"Going to back out on us again tonight, Atticus?"

"Where'd you disappear to last night?"

"Who's your friend, Atticus?"

"Where are we going today?"

The last person that passed us was Michelle. I immediately observed that something wasn't right. She was very pale with dark circles under her eyes. Stefano looked at her questioningly. She appeared to be slightly off-balance and was holding on to the handrail. Michelle gave us both a brief, forced smile as she headed down the remaining stairs.

"Is that young lady all right?" he asked when Michelle was out of earshot.

"She's had a migraine headache these past twenty-four hours."

"I see."

We had arrived at Vanessa's room. I knocked. The door opened immediately, and Sabrina came out into the hallway.

"Hello, Atticus. I'm heading to breakfast."

"Okay, Sabrina," I replied. "Be in the lobby and ready to go at nine forty-five."

"Got it."

Stefano and I entered the room and found Vanessa sitting on the bed.

"Good morning, Vanessa, this is Doctor…" I didn't even know his last name.

"You can call me Stefano, Vanessa."

"Hi. You've got an interesting accent," said Vanessa.

It was only then that I noticed that Stefano's English had a British inflection.

"I studied in the UK for three years, near London, and I go back frequently."

"Cool. I've never been to London. Maybe one day."

Stefano put his bag on the desk and began to take out various devices.

"Vanessa, how old are you?" he asked.

"Eighteen next month."

"Atticus, given that Vanessa is still a minor, I cannot examine her without another adult in the room, a female. Is there someone, maybe one of the teachers that we call?"

"No!" Vanessa had tensed up. "I mean, is it necessary? I'm comfortable enough with Atticus here. I really don't want a teacher up here right now."

Stefano looked at Vanessa and then at me. "Okay, Vanessa, if this is workable for you, we can avoid having another person here. I will have to lift your T-shirt when measuring your heartbeat. Maybe I can ask you, Atticus, to step out in the hallway, leaving the door ajar? Is this acceptable for both of you?"

"No issues with me." I headed out the door.

"Good with me. No peeking, Atticus!"

"I'll keep my eyes closed."

Vanessa giggled, but I knew she was nervous.

"Keep calm, Vanessa," I called out. "Stefano is here to help."

"Yeah, I know. Thanks, Atticus."

I walked a few feet away, not wanting to eavesdrop.

Even so, I caught a few words and sentences here and there. Stefano was very thorough in explaining the checkup process as he went along. He was also asking Vanessa a series of questions, and I could make out bits and pieces of the answers: "Two years now, maybe more…," "Mostly uppers…," "at parties, they're all over the place…," "my parents don't know and don't care…," "dizziness, lots of vomiting…," "I get these urges…," "it's really hard, really hard…" Then for a few minutes, I could only hear bits and pieces of Stefano's voice. Afterward, silence fell.

"Atticus? Can you come in please?" Stefano called.

I entered the room and closed the door behind me. Vanessa was still sitting on the bed, but her eyes had watered up.

"Atticus, I've had a serious discussion with Vanessa. I have told her that I shall go along with this Tylenol fairy tale as long as she understands and does something about what I believe to be her addiction to pharmaceutical drugs, more precisely opioids."

I flinched at the word *addiction*.

"Yes, addiction," Stefano repeated. "I am not happy with her vitals. Her pulse is high, heartbeat erratic, little reflex in her joints, no appetite, and the list goes on. This stimulant abuse has been going on now for over two years, correct, Vanessa?"

"Yeah, that's about right. I started a little over two years ago. Mostly at parties, and at football games, and when my parents get all over me for nothing."

"And, and, and…let's just say, most of the time." Stefano was blunt.

"There's nothing much she can do from here from a clinical perspective, Atticus, if we do not wish to raise suspicion. For now, she must continue drinking fluids, eat fruit and vegetables, and start doing some exercise. But when she's back in the States, I want to her to check into a rehabilitation program."

Vanessa hung her head. Stefano turned to her.

"There aren't more of those drugs hidden anywhere, correct?"

"Promise. I got rid of everything, all gone. My roomie can vouch for me."

"And there are any classmates that you could 'borrow' from?" he asked.

Vanessa hesitated. "I thought Sabrina had brought some along, but I was wrong."

"Could anybody else have stashed a supply in their suitcase?" I asked.

Vanessa thought for a few moments. "Maybe Evelyn or Raymond. I know he takes uppers during exams."

Raymond? Mr. "I'm off to save Israel" himself?

"Mark may have some, maybe Darlene…"

Well, great, just great! I thought. Why bother going to a pharmacy for a prescription when you can just ask our friendly neighborhood teenage junkie? I could see from Stefano's expression that he was having similar thoughts.

"What should Atticus and I be thinking, Vanessa?" he said. "Are you going to go around asking for a refill?"

"I said no!" Vanessa snapped. "I could've asked some people already if I'd wanted to."

"All right, that's good news," I said. "I suggest you get dressed and come along with us this morning. A walk will do you some good."

"Yeah, I'm okay with all of that, Atticus. I asked Sab to bring me some orange juice and yoghurt from downstairs."

"That's good." I turned to Stefano. "You and I must get downstairs and meet with the teachers. I leave it up to you as to how you want to handle the discussion."

I looked at my watch: close to nine thirty.

"It was nice meeting you, Vanessa," said Stefano. "Look after yourself, and please take my advice—stay away from that stuff."

"I will. Thanks again for your help."

We left Vanessa's room and headed downstairs.

As with the staircase, a flood of students came out of the breakfast area just as we walked in.

"We're ready to go, Atticus, you?"

"Didn't see you at breakfast, Atticus…"

"Still busy with your friend?"

"Where are we going today?"

"Let's make some plans for tonight."

When the tidal wave was over, I led the way inside with Stefano behind me. Sabrina was walking out with a few things for Vanessa. I gave her a thumbs-up as she exited.

Cynthia, Barbara, and John were sitting at a table in the back of the room. They were nursing three empty cappuccino cups. John reached over and pulled up two additional chairs from the table next to theirs. I introduced Stefano and then signaled to the waiter to bring two espressos, three more cappuccinos, and some mineral water. The room was now empty of any students, with just a few guests seated around the dining room.

John took the lead: "Doctor, we appreciate you taking the time to visit with Vanessa. The parents have entrusted us with their children's well-being, and when problems come up, well, we have to do whatever we can to make things right."

Barbara chimed in, "We've got a good group of kids, but they are still kids even though most of them are nearly legal adults. At any rate, we have the authority to send any of them back home if they break the rules. But we want each student to get the most out of this trip and go back to Atlanta all together next week."

Cynthia spoke up, "I was the one who insisted with Atticus that a doctor come see Vanessa. I became alarmed when I noticed strange behavior on her part."

"Can you tell me what you found strange, unusual? Try to be as specific as possible, Cynthia. I may call you Cynthia, yes?" Stefano was turning on his Italian charm.

"Surely, Cynthia is just fine. Well, for instance, she was perspiring heavily, fidgety, and answering aggressively when I asked her a few questions. Then there were moments where she just fell silent, eyes closed and crying."

"A wide spectrum of behavioral manifestations, in other words."

"Yes. You can understand why I became anxious."

"Certainly. A responsible adult could only be concerned." Stefano sipped his coffee and looked pensive. Nobody said a word.

"As all of you are aware, I have just come down from visiting with Vanessa, and my evaluation is as follows." You could have heard a pin drop. "She has been quite foolish, but innocently so…" I was interested in where he was going with this.

"These Tylenol gelcaps that Vanessa has been consuming are quite harmless when taken in the correct dosage. However, when you start throwing them down like popcorn, thinking that the more you take, the faster the pain will go away, then you run into problems. Add some alcoholic beverages and the human body reacts. Depending on one's chemistry, there can be a wide range of side effects. In Vanessa's case, the symptoms, due to this high intake of acetaminophen, the active ingredient in Tylenol, have translated into the behavior which you observed, Cynthia. Had it been another student, you would have probably seen another kind of reaction. I measured her vital signs, and other than her pulse, which is a bit on the high side, there's nothing out of the ordinary."

Stefano was lying through his teeth. Cynthia, however, looked relieved, which was the goal of all this theater.

"She knows she must drink a lot of liquids, water preferably. Eat vegetables and fruit and do some light exercise, such as walking."

"In your opinion, could she have a relapse? I mean, is there the possibility that Vanessa could look for other pills to take?" Cynthia was spot-on.

"I can't give you a yes-or-no answer to that. What I can say is that she was experiencing some rather severe post-menstrual pain, and she didn't want this to ruin her trip. That's why she went overboard with the Tylenol. She's aware of her mistake and does not want to repeat it."

Give that man an Oscar, I thought.

Barbara interrupted, "Atticus, it's almost ten, we told the students to be ready at nine forty-five." She wanted to bring this discussion to an end, and so did I.

"Yes, we need to hit the road," I agreed.

Everyone thanked Stefano, who very generously offered his services in the future if they were required. I, for one, was hoping that it wouldn't be the case.

"*Io vado avanti. Mi sa che dovete fare due chiacchiere…*"

"Grazie, Stefano. *Ci sentiamo dopo.*"

Stefano knew that the teachers and I would want to discuss this matter amongst ourselves. I thanked him and said that I would speak to him later. I attempted not to look triumphant as he left, but I was getting a kick seeing Cynthia at a loss for words. I would have enjoyed sparring with her a bit, but we didn't have time.

"We can discuss all of this later," I said. "We're running late. By the way, Vanessa is coming with us."

"Is she feeling up to it?" Cynthia asked.

"Yes. She insisted," I lied. *Why stop now?* was my thought.

John was upbeat. "Good to hear. Some fresh air and the walk will do her good."

"Let's keep an eye on Michelle as well," said Barbara. "She told me this morning that she felt a little better, but she looks awful. That migraine is taking its toll."

Cynthia squeezed my shoulder. "Thank you for arranging everything, Atticus," she said. "I feel more at ease now about Vanessa."

"No bother at all, Cynthia," I said. I was not worried that Vanessa would be going home early or that there would be a chaperone change.

CHAPTER 36

When we appeared in the lobby, you would have thought that royalty had arrived.

"Wow! Here they are!"

"Make way, make way!"

"All rise!"

"It's the four musketeers!"

"Mark, there were three musketeers, not four," Mary corrected.

"No, Mary. Athos, Aramis, Porthos, and D'Artagnan—that makes four."

"D'Artagnan meets up with the *three* musketeers in Paris. Check it out on Wiki."

"Okay, whatever Miss Know-It-All."

I wouldn't have been able to name more than two of the musketeers on the spur of the moment. These kids were just sharp as tacks.

"Okay, listen up please!" I called out. "We're going to the Capitoline Hill today. There's going to be a lot to take in. Let's just hope we have decent tour guide."

"We're screwed if he's like the one we had at the Pantheon," Raymond said.

"Well, if they are, Raymond, I'll just have to take 'em down." I traced a line across my neck with my index finger, then high-fived with a few students, getting laughs from the others.

"Awesome!" Raymond said.

"By the way," I added, "you're going to be on your own for lunch today. I'll point out some good places after our guide leaves us. Dinner will be at seven thirty this evening.

Does everyone have what they need for the day? Everybody has some money with them?"

"Yup."

"We're cool."

"Ready to rock 'n' roll."

"Off we go, then. To the left, please, to where our bus usually parks."

Everyone filed out of the hotel. I saw that Michelle was waiting for the rest of the group to pass through the sliding doors. She wanted to tell me something.

"Hey, Michelle, how are you feeling? Would you like to stay here in the hotel today?"

"No, Atticus, thank you. Nothing is going to get in the way of this trip, not even these headaches. Don't worry. I feel better today, just a bit weak." She attempted one of those beautiful smiles, but it was forced, not spontaneous. She said, "I took some more pictures of Evelyn's diary. Really bizarre stuff. You and Mrs. Cornwall need to read it."

"Is there anything we need to worry about right now?"

"No, I don't think so. There wasn't really anything more about 'ending it all' or doing something stupid except for Thursday's entry, at the end. But I think it can wait."

She whispered the last few words. Wayne and Bishop were in front of us. They looked around.

"What's up, Em? Still got that sledgehammer knocking you on your head?" Wayne asked.

"Yeah, but better than yesterday. Can I hang on to the two of you?"

"That's what we're here for." She went between them, hooking her arms through the crook of their elbows. She had her two knights-errant.

I made my way to the front of the group as we headed down Via della Pilotta. I was very curious to see what Michelle had photographed from Evelyn's diary and wondered if it really could wait. I decided to trust Michelle's opinion.

I reached Vanessa, who was walking next to Barbara.

"Feeling up to this, Vanessa?" I asked.

"Yeah, I'm okay. If I get tired, I'll ask Michelle if I can borrow her crutches."

I chuckled and moved forward to James, who was holding hands with Evelyn.

"James, Evelyn, all good this morning?"

"Yeah, why?" James responded.

"Just asking." I hadn't spoken with him since we returned to the hotel yesterday. He seemed to be the same old James, which was what I wanted to see. I was now almost at the front when I bumped into Darlene.

"Sorry about that."

"No worries, Atticus. We can rub shoulders whenever you want."

It was then that I glimpsed Darlene's feet. She had on a pair of high-heeled sandals with a thin mesh of transparent plastic that covered the top of her feet, showing off her pedicured, cherry-red polished toenails.

"Darlene, you're not going to last very long in those."

She grinned and shook her head. "I've already told you. I'm a pro in these things. I think they look good on me, don't you?" She stretched out her left foot and flexed her toes, then winked at me. All kinds of warning signals started going off in my head again. I just laughed and moved away.

"Just don't break your ankle."

"Okay, Mr. Worrier."

Barbara called out, "Atticus, can we stop a moment? I want to take a few photos."

"Sure, Barbara, go right ahead."

It was actually a picture-perfect panorama. We had entered the Piazza Venezia with the monument to Vittorio Emanuele II in front of us. Cameras and cellphones were being pointed in all directions.

After a few minutes, I said, "If we're finished here, let's head over to that building in front of us."

We crossed Via del Corso, a straight one-mile road that stretches between Piazza Venezia and Piazza del Popolo, one of the largest urban squares in Rome. Shortly afterward, we made a ninety-degree turn crossing Via Del Plebiscito. We were now directly in front of the Palazzo Venezia.

John signaled to me. "That's the balcony you showed us the other day on the bus, right? Where Mussolini addressed the crowds?" He pointed above us.

"That's right," I replied.

Anthony, strangely enough, was the first student to comment: "I think I saw a video on the History Channel of him talking to these mobs of people."

"You probably did," I said, nodding. "Most World War II documentaries include the same footage of Mussolini speaking from that balcony to masses of people. They would stand shoulder to shoulder in this piazza to hear what he had to say. He was quite a captivating orator."

"Sounds like the Italians really dug this guy," Anthony said.

"Do us a favor, Anthony. Tell us something more about Mussolini and this building one of these nights. I don't think I've given you a project to work on yet."

Anthony suddenly became red in the face and began to stammer. "I don't, um, I don't think that's a-a good idea."

Cynthia suddenly appeared next to him as if by magic. "I'll help you Anthony," she said.

"Just a few pieces of information, Anthony, things you find interesting," I said encouragingly. "You can do it." This kid needed a massive dose of motivation.

"I-I'll try…"

"Good. Let me know when you're ready."

Mark called out to me, "Check it out, Atticus. There's a guy in front of that white monument over there with an Atlanta Falcons football jersey on. It's a small world."

I looked over to where Mark was pointing, along with some of the others, and saw a fellow with a black, red, and white football jersey, about two sizes too big.

"That's Michael Vick's jersey, number 7." Bishop was sure of himself.

"Atticus, that guy looks familiar," Sabrina said. She broke into a big smile. "It's Massimo!" she exclaimed.

I looked closer. Yes, indeed, it was! His hair was combed differently. He had a pair of biker sunglasses on, and other than the jersey, he was wearing black jeans and black running shoes. What a difference from when we first met at the Colosseum.

"Yeah, it's him! Hey, M-a-s-s-i-m-o-!" Wayne managed to get his attention by screaming across the heavy traffic between us and our favorite tour guide. Massimo, hearing his name, caught sight of us and threw both hands in the air, waving energetically. He then pointed proudly to his jersey with both index fingers while strutting around like a triumphant peacock.

"What an extravagant individual," Cynthia muttered, but with a grin on her face.

"Yes, indeed, but a top-notch guide," Barbara said. "So glad we have him again today."

"Well, the students are certainly enthusiastic," John noted.

All the students were yelling in Massimo's direction, cheering him on as he did his little dance on the sidewalk, oblivious to the stares from passersby.

Taking advantage of a rare break in the traffic, I was able to maneuver everyone across the busy intersection.

"Hello, hello, everyone!" How very nice to see all of you again!" Massimo was genuinely elated, as were the students.

"So very good to see *you* again so soon," I said, smiling. "Quite unexpected!"

"Well, Atticus, your friend Marco pulled some strings yesterday and managed to move me from an extremely boring group of Swiss senior citizens to the most exciting, upbeat, and inquisitive student group in Rome!"

Everyone laughed as Massimo bowed to them with his hands clasped in front of his head.

"Where'd you get this, Massimo?" Bishop asked, indicating the jersey.

"At the Georgia Dome, where else? I believe I told all of you that I went to see the Falcons against the Steelers in 2006. Do you think I could leave a game like that without a Michael Vick souvenir? A great quarterback—and one gorgeous man!"

Massimo brought his pinky up to his mouth in mock concern. "Oh dear! Should I have said that?" This only produced more laughter.

"Hey, Massimo, you know that Vick plays for the Philadelphia Eagles now?" Wayne said." "He was booted from the Falcons after he got caught running a dogfighting ring on his property."

"Oh, no! I didn't know. Well, looks like I'm going to have to get a new T-shirt."

"It's a football *jersey*, Massimo, not a *T-shirt*."

"A *jersey*? Like New *Jersey*? Like *Jersey* of the Channel Islands? How odd."

Raymond spoke up, "It could have something to do with the fact that *Jersey* of the Channel Islands was well-known for its knitted fabric during the Middle Ages..." Everyone, including me, looked at him as if he had grown an extra head.

"Well, I've certainly learned something today!" gushed Massimo. "Raymond, correct? Our Arch of Titus expert from the other day." Raymond just nodded.

"'Raymond,' from the Germanic name *Raginmund,* meaning 'a protector and giver of advice.' Seems to be a perfect fit for you, young man."

I wondered if Raymond was aware of the German origins of his name and if this troubled him in any way.

"All right, everyone!" Massimo switched to his professorial persona. We have much to see today!"

Everyone settled down and listened intently.

"Look around you," Massimo began. "We are at the nerve center of Rome. Look at the important roads leading in and out of this square. Directly in front of us we have the Via del Corso, which goes to the Piazza del Popolo, a must-see before you leave Rome. The road on my right goes to the Piazza della Repubblica. Take the left, and you will very soon cross the Tiber and arrive at Castel Sant'Angelo. Behind us is the Via dei Fori Imperiali, which leads straight to the Colosseum, while directly to our left, you can reach the Circus Maximus. This is the heart of Rome, my friends, with its major arteries stretching across the city. Look to our left—you can see the Palazzo Venezia, built between 1455 and 1467 by the future pope, Paul II. Would someone like to take a guess at what this building was mostly constructed with?"

"Pieces of the Pantheon?" Mary guessed.

"Very close!" Massimo said.

"The Colosseum, I bet!" shouted Sabrina.

Massimo clapped his hands. "Excellent! Rock was taken from the Colosseum as well as the Theater of Marcellus, which is just down the road from here to build a large portion of what you see standing today."

Jeremy turned to me. "What was that you told us over at the Pantheon, Atticus? Something about what the barbarians *didn't* do, some famous family *did?*"

"The Barberini family. Good memory, Jeremy." I gave him a thumbs-up.

Massimo leaned across to us. "In fact, Atticus, a little bird told me that you are quite a tour guide yourself."

"No, that's your job, Massimo. I just had to step up the other day."

The students weighed in at once:

"Step up? You rocked, Atticus!

"You wasted that fool. He was useless."

They explained to Massimo how I had fired our good-for-nothing tour guide at the Pantheon. I was delightfully embarrassed. Massimo looked at me and smiled.

"Yes. I can see how Atticus would have taken matters into his own hands. Bravo!" Massimo started clapping, and everyone followed suit.

"Okay, okay," I said, raising my hands. "Can we get back to where you left off?"

Massimo was enjoying himself at my expense. "All right, ladies and gentlemen," he said eventually, still smiling to himself. "This palazzo, other than being the residency of a few popes, serving as the Embassy of the Republic of Venice as well as the Austrian Embassy, became in 1929 the headquarters of Benito Mussolini, the prime minister of Italy and head of the National Fascist Party. From that balcony that you see there, Mussolini, in 1940, declared Italy's entrance into World War II to a massive crowd down below."

I was a little surprised to hear Vanessa ask a question. "That building on the right looks almost like the one on the left, Massimo. Same architect?" Her voice was weak, but I was very pleased to hear her participating.

"Good observation, very good observation, but you will be surprised to know that the building on the right was built in 1902."

"1902?" Raymond exclaimed in disbelief. "That's almost five hundred years later than the one on the left! Could have fooled me." Raymond was right. There was not a great deal of difference between the two structures at first glance.

"It's one of the headquarters of the Assicurazioni Generali, one of the top five insurance companies of the world. But the architect did deliberately design a building that resembled the Palazzo Venezia in order to provide a certain harmony to this large square."

The students nodded.

"Now, ladies and gentlemen," Massimo continued, "look in front of you. I believe you crossed the Via del Corso to get over here this morning." He pointed to the one-mile thoroughfare that exited Piazza Venezia leading to Piazza del Popolo. "Take a look at that building on the left. It was built in 1657 and passed through various hands before it became the property of one Maria Letizia Ramolino, who spent most of her time on that covered balcony you see there on the first floor. Who was this woman? Would someone like to take a wild guess?"

Nobody answered. Massimo was about to enlighten us when I heard a voice:

"Wasn't that the name of Napoleon's mother?"

Massimo turned to look at Michelle, his mouth hanging open.

"I am truly amazed, flabbergasted. Indeed, Maria Letizia Ramolino was Napoleon's mother. How did you know that? Miss Michelle, correct?"

"Yes. Well, I like history, and I suppose I just remembered that name from reading about Napoleon." Michelle was still being supported by Wayne and Bishop, and it didn't take Massimo a nanosecond to realize that she wasn't one hundred percent.

"I see that chivalry is not dead. Gentlemen, take good care of our scholar."

"She's in good hands," Wayne assured him.

"Indeed, she is, indeed, she is," Massimo replied, seeming a little distracted.

He turned and raised his hands. "Now, my friends, please turn around and behold this corpulent monument." The bizarre and unflattering use of the adjective *corpulent* and Massimo's less-than-enthusiastic expression suggested that he fell into the large category of people who immensely disliked this landmark.

"It's huge."

"It's really white."

"A wedding cake, like I said earlier," Darlene added.

"Oh marvelous, just marvelous." Massimo was getting a kick out of the students' spontaneous and apposite remarks about this enormous structure built in the honor of the first king of Italy, Vittorio Emanuele II.

"I could go on and on about this architectural behemoth dedicated to one of the kings of Italy, but I shall stick to the more salient points." After unloading more information than we could possibly remember, Cynthia pulled at Massimo's jersey.

"You don't care for this monument, do you?"

"Oh my, is it *that* evident, Miss Cynthia?"

"Yes, it is."

"I am *very* sorry. I am not doing my job. I am not creating any *emotion*, any *atmosphere*. But I cannot. Just look at this monstrosity!" Massimo was visibly upset. "Do you realize, ladies and gentlemen, how many Roman ruins and medieval buildings were destroyed to build this garish, tasteless thing? Can you see how it has nothing to do with our surroundings! Right behind this eyesore is the Roman Forum. Over there"— Massimo pointed to his right— "is Trajan's Forum and here, just here to our left, as we shall behold shortly, we have the Campidoglio, the Capitoline Hill, which was designed by Michelangelo."

Massimo reached for a handkerchief and dried his eyes. "Well, I guess no one can say that I am not passionate about my opinions."

"It's certainly more interesting listening to your heartfelt point of view than just getting a set of facts," said John.

"Can we go up the steps and go look around a bit?" Vanessa asked.

"Why, certainly. The only positive feature about this thing is that it's tall. In the back, there is an elevator that goes all the way to the top. The panorama from there is worth experiencing. Go, go, but please be back here in fifteen minutes."

Everyone went off in various directions. Massimo and I were now alone.

"My dear Atticus, I can't tell you how happy I am to be here," he trilled.

"So am I. You couldn't have made the group happier."

"Well, I could have avoided that last outburst. Had I been with the Austrian group this morning, I would have just kept giving them those boring facts that you can read out of any guidebook. With this group, I feel that I can be myself. Special people, really."

No doubt about that, I thought.

Massimo had switched to Italian to avoid any eavesdropping. "Have there been any interesting developments? I mean, since you and I spoke at the Forum?"

"More than a few. I'm getting more and more involved with these students—"

"And teachers," Massimo interjected.

I looked at him sideways.

"My dear Atticus, I do apologize." He glanced in Barbara's direction. "Perhaps I am reading more into it than I should, but that middle-aged beauty over there, when she looks at you, oh my! Let's just say that I've unfortunately never seen such an expression of admiration on any of my lovers' faces."

My cheeks were becoming red as a stoplight. Massimo grinned from ear to ear. "Lucky you, my friend, she certainly is voluptuous."

We were interrupted by yelling. Wayne, Bishop, and Michelle were well above us, waving and calling us by name. We waved back.

"So, our two boys up there, anything new?" Massimo asked.

"They asked to speak to me in private, along with Michelle. Whatever it is they want to tell me, it's a lot of stress."

Massimo pondered this for a moment. "I believe that the young lady is their confidant, Atticus. These boys have found someone they can trust. It shall be interesting to hear what they tell you. I think I already know, and I foresee nothing terribly pleasant."

I was about to ask him what he meant, but Massimo took hold of my arm. "Let's wait until they speak with you." A shadow had come over his face. "Then we shall talk."

He paused. "By the way, what is wrong with our Michelle? She looks frightfully pale."

"Bad migraine. She's been wrestling with it for a few days. She said that she was feeling better this morning."

"Quite a remarkable young lady. There are only a handful of adults I know that can recognize the name of Napoleon's mother without any historical context. I do hope that what is ailing her passes quickly."

"So do I."

"One last thing, Atticus. Did you see the shoes our Marilyn Monroe has on? You must have. I think every man that girl has passed today is thinking about those shoes and all the rest. I wish I could walk in those things, but it wasn't meant to be. Keep an eye on her, Atticus, even two. That girl exudes sexual magnetism."

I nodded.

Fifteen minutes passed, and Jeremy was first down the steps of the monument.

"I know you don't like it, Massimo," he said. "But it's awesome. It would make for a sweet movie set for a sci-fi flick."

"What an excellent suggestion!" scoffed Massimo. "Too bad it's not sitting in Cinecittà instead of the middle of Rome."

"*Cine* what?"

"Cinecittà is the Hollywood of Italy, Jeremy, and it's about a thirty-minute car ride from here. Hundreds of films were produced there, including *Ben Hur, The Ten Commandments,* Mel Gibson's *The Passion of Christ,* Scorsese's *Gangs of New York, Ocean's Twelve,* to name a few."

"That's pretty awesome." Jeremy was impressed.

"Don't take my word for it quite yet, but maybe, just maybe, I can get you into the Cinecittà Studios for a personal guided tour. Would this strike your fancy?"

"It would strike it fine!" said Jeremy. "Can you really try?"

"Let me see what I can do. I shall let you know soon."

By now everyone was back with us. Massimo once again took charge of the group. We headed to the left and followed a wide, curved sidewalk that formed the Vittorio Emanuele's monument perimeter. Barbara, who had been speaking with Darlene and Mary, broke away and walked over to me.

"All good, Atticus?"

"So far. You?"

"Same. I spoke with John. He was embarrassed about his behavior regarding Vanessa and even apologized."

"I received mine this morning," I told her with a grin. "Beat you to it."

"He likes you even if you are jumping in the hay with the woman of his dreams."

"Now that was cruel! Listen, Catwoman, what did you do to Cynthia to make her change her attitude? Threaten her with bodily harm?"

Barbara smiled mischievously. "Let's just say that I blackmailed her a bit."

"What?"

"Can't tell you now. It'll have to wait until tonight."

I nodded. "By the way, Michelle managed to photograph a few more pages."

Barbara raised worried eyebrows.

"No concerns for now," I reassured. "Michelle said there was nothing 'life-threatening,' if you catch my drift."

"All right. Let's catch up later."

We had unknowingly separated ourselves from the others and were beginning to stand out. Barbara walked toward Massimo, who was at the front of the group with me in tow.

We continued our walk around the gargantuan structure until we came upon a clump of ruins pinned between the side wall of the Vittorio Emanuele Monument and a long, sweeping staircase leading up to the Basilica of Santa Maria of the Altar of Heaven. Massimo had stopped in front of this three- to four-story accumulation of time-honored bricks and arches and turned to face us.

"Behold, ladies and gentlemen, an example of an *Insula Romana*, the literal translation being 'Roman island.' What was intended by 'island' back then in the AD second century, when all of this was built, was a Roman city block. Here you can get a sense of how and where your everyday Roman lived. Consider this as one of the first examples of the modern-day condominium, with small eating establishments and convenience stores on the ground floor and apartments from the first floor up."

The students, teachers, and I were so interested in what Massimo was so ably describing that I did not notice anything until I felt the palm of my hand closing over a rigid, square substance. Michelle had sidled up to me in the best spy-craft style and put something into my hand.

It was a tiny plastic square.

"It's my spare memory card. I transferred the photos onto it," Michelle said sotto voce. "I didn't know if you had internet on your phone, so just in case you want to take a look sooner than later…" She turned back to watch Massimo. Nobody noticed a thing. I slipped the memory card into my shirt pocket.

"So, you see, these ruins then became, in time, the lower levels of medieval city dwellings with new shops and eateries, and so on and so on up until the beginning of the twentieth century. All of Rome can be compared to one of those oversized pastrami sandwiches you can get at Reuben's Deli on Broad Street, just one layer after the other." Massimo grinned in anticipation of the students' reactions.

"Best cheesecake in town!" exclaimed Mary with a thumbs-up to Massimo.

"Did you go before or after the Falcons Steelers game, Massimo?" Wayne asked.

"Before, after, all the time. Fabulous sandwiches!" The way in which Massimo was able to continue to tie in some Atlanta nostalgia here and there cemented his relationship with the group more and more.

Then he once again became very serious, and I could tell we were in for another passionate outburst.

"Can you just imagine, these ruins, of which we see only a fraction, spanning over a period of some eighteen hundred years, covered this entire portion of the city until it was decided to tear everything down to make room for that hideous, inflated, pompous rock formation!?" The students and teachers had begun to take Massimo's flare-ups about the Vittorio Emanuele monument in stride.

"Hey, Massimo," said Bishop. "Where does this huge staircase go?" He and the others were already making their way to the first few steps that led to the Basilica of Santa Maria. I was certain that Massimo would have preferred to continue protesting about the sheer volume of the destruction that was carried out to make room for the Vittorio Emanuele Monument, but he wisely decided to get over it and move on.

"One hundred and twenty-four marble steps, ladies and gentlemen, all finished in the year 1348. Folklore has it that if you go all the way up on your knees, you will win the lottery."

"Even Fantasy 5 and Cash 4?" Mark asked, excitedly.

"Sorry, young man," Massimo responded. "The legend only includes the Italian lottery, not Georgia."

I didn't have a clue as to what Mark was referring to, but I was clearly the only one in the dark.

"So between going to Reuben's, the Falcon's game, Stone Mountain, the botanical garden, and other sights, you also managed to play the lottery," John noted.

"I most certainly did. It's the first thing I do whenever I visit a new country. I always find out what lotteries there are to play and bet some money. I actually won three hundred dollars on Cash 4."

"You'll have to teach us how to play the Italian lottery, Massimo." John's curiosity had been sparked.

"Consider it done!"

By this time, most of the boys, as well as Michelle, Darlene, and Mary, were going up the first few steps on their knees, with the others taking photos of them.

Massimo giggled. "All right, all of you martyrs for money, before attempting to get all the way to the top, let me tell you a few things about the exquisite work of art that you shall see once you arrive. First of all, who of you is going to tell me the difference between a basilica and a church?"

I looked for Jeremy, who had answered the same question on the bus coming in from the airport. Sure enough, he had already put his hand up.

"It's a Greek word, Massimo, and it means some large public building with lots of columns inside to divide up space. I think I remember reading that it was a place where people met to do business."

"Excellent, Mr....?"

"Jeremy."

"Very good, young man, you are correct. A basilica was a grand place indeed, usually an open space, surrounded by a *stoa*, which is another Greek word meaning 'a covered walkway lined with series of columns.' Two apses, which are nothing more than a large dome cut in half from to bottom, usually protruded at both ends. It was a place to go and debate over political matters, to conduct business transactions, and where one could resolve several bureaucratic issues. The word *basilica* only began to refer to a religious building in the fourth century, when—and let's see who was listening the other day when we were at the Arch of Constantine—something major occurred…"

"The Edict of Milan. 313, right?" Raymond had clearly been listening that day.

"Bingo, young man! The Edict of Milan, which stopped the persecution of Christians and permitted religious liberty, gave builders and architects of the day the opportunity to build basilicas for religious use as well. And one of the many basilicas in Rome and the rest of Italy is up there at the end of this stairwell, the Basilica of Saint Mary of the Altar of Heaven, built between 1250 and 1270. Now, before entering, take a good look at the very plain façade that you can even see from here. Then go inside and feast your eyes!"

Massimo was back to his old self, and his captivating theatrical description of the basilica sparked everyone's interest. "Go, go, go! I need to run up these other stairs"—Massimo pointed to the less angular stairwell that led up to the Campidoglio, or city hall— "and get our tickets for the museum. I shall be with all of you in the basilica shortly." He turned and scampered off.

Cynthia came up to me as Massimo left. She looked a little trepidant.

"Atticus?"

"Yes, Cynthia?"

"Guess I'm back a second time in three days to apologize for my behavior." She paused a moment, searching for her next words. "I was believing, or wanted to believe, in some sort of conspiracy theory between you, Barbara, and Vanessa, which just wasn't there."

Why is it that even when you get away with a lie, there is still a sense of defeat? I thought.

"These kids, Atticus, they've really taken a great liking to you, and in such a few days. I've been their teacher for years, and I haven't really made a dent with any of them. Maybe I'm just a little jealous…" Cynthia attempted a smile, but she was clearly hurting inside.

I shook my head. "I think that the duties, obligations, and accountability of a teacher don't necessarily fit with being on a student's list of the most popular people. I'm with this group for ten days, Cynthia, but then we go our separate ways. That allows me and the students to be more open to one another. There's no magic here. As for making a dent, I would say that Anthony really looks up to you and depends on you."

I could have avoided bringing up Anthony into the discussion, but I felt it was the right moment to do so. Cynthia bit her lower lip. Something was definitely on her mind.

"You owe me a walk through the Forum," she said rather abruptly.

"Um, yes. That's right."

" I think the time has finally come…finally."

She turned and headed up the stairs leading to the basilica. Now what was that all about?

"Atticus! Here I am!" I turned to see Massimo skipping down the Campidoglio staircase, waving tickets in his right hand and holding his left hand out as if to balance himself. The Atlanta Falcons jersey, dark pants, and aggressive sunglasses were in stark contrast to his baroque mannerisms.

"Oh my goodness, I'm out of breath! I'm just not in shape anymore."

"You look good to me Massimo. I'd like to know how you keep so slim."

"Atticus, loads and loads of sex! It's just amazing how many calories you can burn off."

He winked at me and started going up the basilica's staircase in the same manner he had come down the Campidoglio one.

"Meet you at the top, Atticus!"

"Okay, I'll be there shortly."

I took out my cell phone, ejected the memory card, then replaced it with the one Michelle had given me. I didn't want to wait until after the tour to do a read-through of Evelyn's new entries. I remembered distinctly that the last entry I had read was Wednesday, April 28, where, according to Evelyn, both she and James were about to end it all. This had put Michelle, Barbara, and I on high-alert status. I was still convinced, however, that James was the main concern, not Evelyn.

CHAPTER 37

I unlocked my phone screen, moved the cursor to the memory card folder icon, and clicked. There were four photos of four pages.

The first and second pages were dated Thursday, April 29. Good. Michelle had been able to pick up where she had left off a few days earlier. I glanced around. The coast was clear. I began to read:

April 29, Thursday

I thought that this was really going to be a crappy day when Ramsey and Seeward decided to sit down with me and J at breakfast, totally uninvited! Do they really think that we could give a rat's ass if they sit with us? Luckily, it took just a few minutes for them to stop asking us stupid questions and making even more stupid comments about this trip. Then Atticus decided to barge in and sit with us. He looked weird, hyper, like he popped one too many Ritalins or Adderalls. He's probably just pissed because he didn't get laid. Cornwall's a married mamma…she's gotta be careful! Ha-ha! Then things got really bad when that shank S came to our table to tell us that V was sick and wasn't coming with us. Lucky you, V! I should pretend to be sick so I could just stay in bed and think about when it's all going to be over.

We then had to walk almost a mile to go see some old build-ing with a huge hole in the ceiling. How stupid is that? We did have a super badass tour guide…this guy didn't give a shit about what he was telling us. I liked his style, his SCREW YOU! style… kick-ass! Then Atticus fired him right there on the spot and told him to beat it. Gotta say, Atticus has balls (bet that makes Cornwall happy!). But then we had to go back inside the building with the hole in it and get the grand tour. Like it or not, Atticus knows what he's talking about. He almost got me interested —ha! Fat chance!

I kinda blew Atticus's mind when I went off on my Genesis rep-ertoire. I should've kept my mouth shut, but this little Tower of Babel I saw sitting on some building (old university?) was totally cool.

Atticus cut us loose in the afternoon. J and I managed to walk back to the hotel even if we got lost a few times.

I had reached the top of the stairs. No one from the group was in sight. I was too engrossed to stop reading.

Wayne, Bishop, and the other screwballs put on a good show for Vanessa this evening. They all crammed into her bedroom and sang "Goodnight Sweetheart…" with just bath towels wrapped around them. For a basketball player, Wayne can actually dance pretty good. You should've seen Ramsey's face. Looked like she was gonna choke. Too bad she didn't. One less slime bag in the world. I hate the way she's always getting on Wayne's and Bishop's case. They're not so bad and certainly light years better than that lying son of a bitch Anthony. Touch a hair on that worthless kid's head, and Ramsey has a shit fit.

> *I think jocks are the scum of the earth, but Wayne's okay. He's always been cool with me even when the rest of the world decided that I was their toilet.*
>
> *Saw Atticus and Cornwall walking around the city tonight. Just like two sick lovebirds.*
>
> *Seeward must be shitting in his pants.*
>
> *M's asleep but she's—————————————————*

The last two lines were hidden. Michelle had used the Paint feature to black them out. Strange. Before I could go further, my phone rang. It was Marco's number.

"Atticus, ciao, *tutto bene?*" asked Marco.

"Yes, everything is fine. Thank you for the surprise today."

"You mean Massimo?"

"I certainly do."

"It was easy, Atticus. He insisted on having another tour with your group. All we had to do was switch him with your previously scheduled guide."

"Well, you couldn't have made the group happier. Oh, and I must also thank you for your brother-in-law. He was very convincing, which is what I needed."

There was a slight pause at the other end of the line.

"I understand, Atticus, that it's what *you* needed, but let me tell you, Stefano is very worried."

Marco was right. What I wanted may not have been in Vanessa's best interest.

"He didn't like what he saw and heard. He also thinks that she will try to find some more of those pills sooner or later. He says she needs some counseling, and fast."

"She's with us now. She had some breakfast this morning and looks better. I fully understand Stefano's concerns. Let him know that Barbara and I, as well as her roommate, are going to watch her like hawks."

I wasn't so naïve, however. I realized that if Vanessa wanted to go on another pill binge, she would find the way to do it.

"Stefano mentioned another girl, Atticus…"

"Another girl? Who?"

"One he said that he met going up the stairs to Vanessa's room."

"That must be Michelle he's referring to. What about her?"

"You told him that she was suffering from a bad migraine, but he's skeptical and thinks it was something else."

I was flabbergasted. "Why?"

"He became concerned when he saw her so off-balance and pale. He also noticed that some blood vessels around her temples were redder than normal."

"I don't know what to say. She's also with us today, even though she was feeling quite weak this morning. I used to suffer from migraines when I was younger, and I remember that when they were really bad, I couldn't even get out of bed."

I didn't mention that Michelle had needed physical support from Wayne and Bishop to get to Piazza Venezia.

"I understand, Atticus. My brother-in-law tends to want to play the doctor sometimes, especially with his family. He may have gotten a bit carried away with his role."

"No worries, Marco, and rest assured that we are also keeping an eye on Michelle."

"Very well. Enjoy the rest of the day with the group. Let's hope the day is quiet."

"That makes two of us."

The call ended and I entered the Basilica. Once inside, I immediately understood why Massimo had told the group to look closely at the very plain façade before going in. The very austere Gothic exterior was juxtaposed by a baroque celebration of the interior. Opening the main door of the basilica reminded me of the 1939 classic *The Wizard of Oz* when Dorothy exits her house after a fierce tornado has dropped it down on Munchkin land. The film up to that point was filmed in black and white. As Dorothy opens the door, however, everything goes to Technicolor.

The students were spread out around the area. Massimo was by the main altar with Barbara, Wayne, Bishop, and Michelle.

"It's really glitzy in here," remarked Mark, coming up behind me. "Look at all these chandeliers." At least fifty of these glittering ornaments hung from the many arches.

"It certainly is in stark contrast with the exterior," I said.

"Yeah, Massimo told us that there used to be mosaics on the outside, but that was a long time ago. He also said that each one of these columns is different from the other. They were all taken from Roman ruins around town. That's kinda mind-blowing."

I looked more closely at the columns nearest to me, which separated the central nave from the two aisles of the basilica, and it was true—you could see the differences from one column to the next.

Jeremy came up to us. "Atticus, remember what you were telling us about *Assassin's Creed* the other day at St. Peter's?"

"Yes, I do, its link to the Knights Templar."

"Well, another chapter is coming out this November— *Assassin's Creed Brotherhood*. I read in a gaming magazine that most of the story takes place here in Rome and that at one point, the apple from the Garden of Eden gets buried right underneath this church! I'll be gaming in November and seeing places on video where I've actually been standing. Now *that's* super cool!"

Jeremy had lost me with the "apple" and it being hidden underneath this basilica, but his enthusiasm was good enough for me. I had never been a videogame aficionado, but I was all for any youth-orientated entertainment that managed to use history and geography as a backdrop.

Mary, standing with Vanessa a little way off, called out to me, "Hey, Atticus, this is really over the top." She was pointing to the ceiling. "Massimo told us it was built in the sixteenth century. I don't think I'll ever see anything like that over my head again." Mary gazed upward in a state of wonderment. The wood-gilded paneled ceiling with its papal stems was stunning. But I knew she would soon discover that other ceilings and domes of churches in Rome would be equally, if not more, impressive.

"Massimo is like a walking art history book," Vanessa chimed in. "I don't know how he remembers all those dates, names, and stuff."

I was pleased that Vanessa was taking an active interest in the tour and that she hadn't asked to go back to the hotel.

"Are you feeling better, Vanessa?" I asked. "Can we say that your flu has passed?"

"Flu? Oh, right. Yes, much better, Atticus. I'm feeling stronger. I'm just really thirsty."

"We'll take care of that as soon as we get down those steps." I turned to take another look at the sheer grandeur of the basilica and saw Massimo coming our way, summoning the students who were still scattered around to follow him.

"My dear Atticus, I think we can say that we are finished here for now. Let's go and see what Michelangelo has in store for us." He headed out the main doors of the basilica with most of the students behind him.

As soon as I stepped outside, I could feel the warmth of the sun enveloping me. It was going to be a hot day. Luckily, there was a slight breeze coming off the sea, and the humidity level was low. I took a moment and looked at the students. I was enjoying spending time with them. I remembered what Giovanni had said to me in Latin that morning: *Labor voluptasque dissimillima natura, societate quadam inter se naturali sunt iu.* "Work and pleasure, though of dissimilar nature, have become joined together." How true in this case.

When I had reached the last of the 120-odd steps, I found the group in front of one of those food and beverage carts. Bottles of water, Fanta, and Coca-Cola were going from hand to hand. Mary and Vanessa were speaking with Sabrina and Darlene, who had removed her X-rated high heels and was barefoot. Evelyn, James, and Jeremy were sitting on the first wide step that led up to the Campidoglio. Wayne, Bishop, Mark, and Raymond were gathered around Massimo, who was obviously telling them something humorous given the amount of laughter generated by the four boys. John, Barbara, Michelle, Cynthia, and Anthony were taking pictures of the scenery as well as one another.

I was in awe at how events had changed so rapidly. Less than a week ago, I would have given an arm and a leg to get out of this chaperoning experience. Now I found myself really wanting to do whatever I could to right some of the wrongs in their lives. What I had read out of Evelyn's diary had only intensified my desire to try to help. But who was I fooling? I had to bear in mind that this trip would be over in a few days and that, more than likely, we would never see one another again. These nine days were just a drop in the ocean of life for these kids. We were all living in a parenthesis in time.

"Ladies and gentlemen!" Massimo called everyone to attention. "We are about to go up the delicate incline of this noble staircase to reach the Capitoline Hill, a place that humans have been lived in since the Bronze Age. That's over three thousand years ago." Massimo pointed to the very wide steps. "Before going up this rather peculiar staircase, can anyone tell me why Michelangelo designed it this way?"

"Looks much easier to go up and down this than that staircase over there," Evelyn said, pointing to the steep staircase that led up to the Basilica of St. Mary.

"You're half the way there, young lady. Good! Any other reasons?"

"Animals wouldn't have any problem getting up this thing," James suggested.

"Very good! Very good!" Massimo was in a flurry of excitement. "And most importantly, what *animal*—" Massimo was interrupted.

"Horses!" Raymond shouted excitedly. "People rode on horses back then!"

"Excellent! Horses, yes!" Massimo was thrilled. "Our modern-day automobile was a horse back in the days of Michelangelo. Nobility, businessmen, and soldiers needed to get to the top of this hill, and they certainly weren't going to walk if they could ride. What a group! What a group of very bright people I have!"

He raised his arms on both sides. "Now look to the right and left, my friends. Do you see these two exquisite Egyptian statues of lions?" Both sides of the staircase were flanked by these imposing, dark-colored sculptures. "These magnificent animals were found in the ruins of the Temple of Serapis and Isis, two Egyptian gods, which was located close to the Pantheon. They were like rock stars during the reign of the emperor Caligula."

"What is it with this Egyptian thing?" James inquired. "We saw a pyramid when we drove into town, and everywhere you go, you see obelisks and now Egyptian lions."

"You bring up a very good point. James, is it?"

"Uh, yeah, that's right." James was surprised that Massimo knew his name.

"If you would like my opinion as to why there was all this Egyptian fanfare at that time, I would say that it was all due to a woman."

This got everyone's attention.

"Yes, ladies and gentlemen, it is my absolute belief that Cleopatra, who I know you have heard of, had more to do with Rome's fascination of Egypt than any political, war maneuvering, conspiratorial activity that was taking place at the time."

"Elizabeth Taylor played Cleopatra," Darlene said, speaking rather glumly. "That's another movie I must have seen a million times. My mom swears by it just like that Trevi Fountain flick." There was no enthusiasm in Darlene's voice. She was just stating a fact.

"An excellent movie. Darlene, correct?"

"Yeah, that's me."

"Cleopatra was a great beauty, very cunning and powerful, so we are told by writers of that time. A woman with beauty, intelligence, and power is undoubtedly a force of nature."

The girls responded enthusiastically to Massimo's statement:

"Got that right!"

"That's sweet!"

"We've got them eating out of our hands, chumps!"

Then John decided to challenge Massimo.

"Massimo," he said with a sly grin, "why is it that since Cleopatra, the world has had beautiful women, intelligent women, and powerful women, but not all three traits in *one* woman?"

There was a moment of stunned silence.

"Mr. Seeward!"

"Did you say that?"

"How dare you!"

"What a chauvinist!"

John was amused by the reactions from the girls, who had surrounded him to unleash their fury. Naturally, the boys joined in the clamor, cheering John on.

Massimo approached me with a twinkle in his eye and murmured, "Should I tell them that she was Julius Caesar's lover and then Marc Antony's, and God only knows how many others in order to get her way?"

I grinned. "You know what they say, Massimo—*tira più un pelo di fica che un carro di buoi in salita…*" Massimo looked at me with feigned shock. Then we both laughed and decided it was best not to go into Cleopatra's carnal customs.

"Okay everyone, it's time to leave Mr. Seeward alone. We have plenty more to see and we are behind schedule."

As we all followed Massimo up the stairway, Barbara came up beside me.

"Can you believe what John just said? It's so unusual for him to show any kind of humor, and well, that was pretty funny. You and Massimo were certainly getting a good laugh out of it."

I smiled. "We were discussing whether he should bring up how Cleopatra used her foremost weapon of persuasion, if you know what I mean."

"Well, she certainly used it wisely, it seems. Good for her. That's all you men have on your minds, anyway." Barbara gave me a wink and a punch on the shoulder.

"There's an old Italian proverb that I shared with Massimo that says, 'The pubic hair of a woman is stronger than a loaded wagon pulled by a group of oxen.'"

Barbara looked at me with two wide eyes, but before she could say anything, we saw Massimo standing precariously on the balustrade halfway up the stairs.

"Look at this, my friends." He pointed to a statue of a hooded bronze individual set atop a large timeworn pedestal on a grassy knoll to the left of the staircase. "And listen to these impassioned words: '*The field of freedom, faction, fame and blood; Here a proud people's passions were exhaled, from the first hour of empire in the bud to what when further worlds to conquer failed; But long before had Freedom's face been veiled, and anarchy assumed her attributes; Tell every lawless soldier who assailed trod on the trembling senate's slavish mutes, or raised voice of baser prostitutes.'*"

Massimo paused, lowered his head, and pointed once again to the statue. At this point, several people had started gathering to see the performance of the tall, thin man in the oversized Atlanta Falcons football jersey. But Massimo wasn't finished.

"'Then turn we to her latest tribune's name, from her ten thousand tyrants turn to thee, redeemer of dark centuries of shame, the friend of Petrarch, hope of Italy, Rienzi! Last of Romans! While the tree of freedom's withered trunk puts forth a leaf, even for the thy tomb a garland let it be, The forum's champion and the people's chief, her new-born Numa thou, with reign, alas! Too brief.'"

Massimo jumped down from the pedestal to the applause of the crowd that had gathered around us.

"Let me introduce Cola di Rienzo, *Rienzi* in Roman dialect, to whom our beloved Byron dedicated these verses."

"*Childe Harold's Pilgrimage*, right, Massimo?" said Michelle.

"Absolutely, fourth canto."

"You quoted Byron when you left us at the restaurant the other day, *Farewell a word that must be...* Always the fourth canto, right?"

"Nothing gets by you, my lovely scholar." Michelle blushed.

"Who was this guy?" Raymond asked.

"Suffice it to say that he was a man with a vision, a vision of what Rome was during empire. He worked all his life to bring some of that glory and power back to Rome, which, in the early fourteenth century, had degenerated into a filthy, corrupt, disease-ridden city. He wasn't successful, unfortunately, and was brutally murdered in 1354 by a crowd of people who had lost faith in him."

"Well, at least Wagner liked him," Mary offered.

"Excuse me, Miss...?"

"I'm Mary. If Richard Wagner decided to write an opera about him, this Rienzi guy must have been pretty influential.

It's called *Rienzi, the Last of the Tribunes*, in five acts." Massimo looked dumbfounded.

"Mary is our opera aficionado, Massimo," I explained. "She's extremely knowledgeable on the subject, to put it mildly."

"I would say she is, Atticus. Young lady, I can assure you that I had no idea about this opera. I have learned something new today. Thank you."

"My pleasure, Massimo." Mary was beaming with satisfaction.

"She has beauty and brains, but no power," John interjected impishly. "Not quite a Cleopatra…"

"Mr. Seeward!" Mary shrieked.

"What did you say, John?" Cynthia said, rising to the occasion this time.

"Get him!" Sabrina led the charge, and the scene was repeated with John being deluged with verbal tirades by the girls.

Barbara came over and stood beside me. "What's with John today?"

"I don't know, but he seems to be enjoying himself." I took hold of Barbara's arm for one instant and leaned in closer to her.

"I read a few of the pages that Michelle gave me."

"And?"

"I haven't finished yet, but that girl certainly has an unhappy soul. She lashes out at everything. I'm going to try to finish the other pages when we're in the museum. I'll let you know if I find anything to be concerned about."

Barbara nodded. "Okay. I'm trusting you on all of this."

I didn't know if that was good or bad.

The group had come to order, with John looking a bit rumpled but otherwise pleased with himself. Massimo had led them to the top of the wide ramped staircase, with Barbara and I not too far behind.

When we arrived in the square at the top of the Capitoline Hill, we were greeted by an elegant ensemble of buildings centered around an equestrian statue. I had been here many times when living in Rome and, like many other inhabitants of the Eternal City, never took the time to research what I was observing. However, I did know that the large bronze figure on horseback was a Roman emperor.

"Does anyone have a fifty-euro coin?"

"Here's one." Anthony waved the coin in the air.

"Very good. Now take a look. On the front you can see the number *50*, the word *cent* below, and to the left, a map of the European Union States in 1992 at the signing of the Maastricht Treaty. Now look at the back."

"There's a man on a horse."

"Yes, that's right, and…?"

"There's some sort of geometrical design below the horse," Raymond said. He glanced down. "I think we're standing on it." Raymond looked again at the coin in Anthony's hand and then at the pattern, which extended across the entire square.

"Yes, indeed! Very good. And now you can see that very same man and that very same horse behind me. May I introduce you to Marcus Aurelius, the emperor of Rome from AD 161 to 180?"

"How old is it, Massimo?" Darlene asked. "The statue, I mean. It looks almost new to me."

"You have made an important observation, Darlene. The statue you see here is a copy of the original, which is now housed in the museum here to the right. You shall admire it when we go inside. This copy was produced in 1981. Extensive restoration had to be done on the original due to corrosion. So, Darlene, you are correct when you say that this statue looks *new*."

Our barefoot Lolita was pleased as punch.

"Now," Massimo continued, "would everyone turn around and look at the two statues that are on either side of the stairs that we just climbed." We all looked at the very large, practically nude male figures with a large horse alongside each of them.

"Any guess at who these two gentlemen could be?" asked Massimo.

There was a moment of silence before an unexpected voice broke through.

"With that stupid-looking cap they have on, which looks like the top portion of an eggshell, and the two horses," Evelyn said, "I would say it's got to be Castor and Pollux. There's also a copy of them standing over there at that palace we saw the first day, Atticus, near that large bird bath, that's what you called it."

"That's absolutely right, Evelyn," I said.

Massimo waved his hand tragically in the air. "That's it," he wailed dramatically. "I'm finished, I'm leaving! Atticus, take over. There's nothing this group doesn't know." Everyone laughed. "Amazing! Just amazing. I am left speechless!" Massimo began to clap his hands loudly, and the others slowly followed suit.

Evelyn grimaced, not liking the sudden attention. "It was a lucky guess, jeez. No big deal."

"Lucky guess?" Mary commented. "You've been studying up on that fountain and that palace ever since Atticus asked us to look into it."

Evelyn frowned. "All right, Mary, cool it."

"She's practically written a term paper on that fountain, Atticus," Mary continued, with a mischievous grin.

"Mary, I said lighten up. Nobody wants to hear it!" Evelyn was looking increasingly uncomfortable. Massimo diplomatically stepped in.

"Castor and Pollux indeed, also known as the *Dioskouri* in classical Greek, or 'sons of Zeus.' Leda, the mother of these two boys, was asleep with her husband, King Tyndareus, when she was seduced by Zeus, who was disguised as a swan."

This got a few snickers and raised eyebrows. Evelyn relaxed now that the attention was off her, but she still seemed angry with Mary.

"A swan? That's pretty kinky," Mark said.

Vanessa frowned. "Can't quite understand how that would be physically possible."

"A threesome with a swan?" Wayne said. "Can't say I've seen that yet on the internet."

"That's enough, Mr. Little, thank you," said Cynthia primly.

"Greek mythology, my friends. There's nothing, and I mean nothing, that you won't find there. It makes modern-day romantic scandals look like *Snow White and the Seven Dwarfs*. But now, getting back to our two friends here, Leda produced two eggs from her affair with Zeus."

"Who was disguised as a swan…," Vanessa said, still puzzling it out.

"Right, the *swan*, and out popped Castor and Pollux. And this is why they are usually portrayed with a piece of eggshell on their heads. Suffice it to say that they became two excellent horsemen, and that is why you also see this animal next to them or under them."

Massimo looked over at Evelyn, winked, and gave her a thumbs-up. There was no reaction. Evelyn was filleting Mary with her eyes.

"Before running off to take some pictures, let me just fill you in briefly on these three marvelous buildings you see forming a horseshoe around Marcus Aurelius." Massimo started to explain the origins of the Palazzo Nuovo, the Palazzo Senatorio, and the Palazzo dei Conservatori and how, over the centuries, they became what we were seeing now. I barely listened because I was puzzled by what Mary had revealed about Evelyn.

So it seemed that Evelyn had actually spent a lot of time, if Mary was telling the truth, undertaking the research I had asked for. That meant she was interested in at least some of the things she was seeing and experiencing on this trip. But this didn't fit with the "screw the world" and "I'm going to end it all" sentiments in her diary, to say nothing of her "Ha! Fat chance!" remark about me almost getting her interested in the history.

I needed to finish reading those pages that Michelle had given me to see if I could make sense of this. Something just wasn't adding up.

Massimo clapped his hands to get our attention. "I'll give you ten minutes to go and take some photos," he said. "Keep in mind once again that what you see here was designed by Michelangelo. Look at the facades of these buildings and how geometrically perfect they are."

The group started dispersing as Massimo was speaking. He came over to me and leaned against the stair rail where I was sitting.

"I never know whether I've said enough, said too much, or if I'm forgetting something or just boring these poor kids with all my chatter. They are such a sharp bunch, Atticus, so I really need to be on my toes."

He took out a brightly colored, collapsible fan from his small Versace shoulder bag, flicked it open, and began fanning himself vigorously.

"You could never bore them, Massimo," I assured him. "You've managed to keep each student involved and interested, even the more difficult ones."

"You are alluding to our Evelyn and her consort, James?"

"Yes. They've been a source of concern."

"I would say that our Evelyn has a hard time accepting and being accepted by others. I sense pent-up hatred and resentment. That can be troublesome for a teenager. She most certainly personifies the black sheep of this group, if not her entire class. Yet she knew who those two statues represented. She looked up and studied what you asked her to. I find that interesting."

Again, Massimo was spot-on. I was tempted to tell him about the diary entries but decided to hold off for now.

Massimo switched hands and continued fanning. "Have you noticed how she is always leaning against and wrapped around or in the arms of her beloved James?"

"It's been pretty much that way since they got here."

"Yet he appears completely indifferent to her. I am sure that you have observed that absent look in his eyes? Is he on some kind of medication, perhaps?"

I didn't reply at once. Massimo was truly astute, and I had found him to be a true professional, but did this allow me to go into personal details about the students? On the other hand, an outsider's point of view, someone who was not in contact with these students on a daily basis, might be helpful.

I looked Massimo in the eye. "James is taking an antidepressant. Protriptyline Hydro something. I think that's it."

"Hydrochloride, *Protriptyline Hydrochloride*?" Massimo stopped fanning himself. "Atticus, that's a very strong drug, and it has some nasty side effects."

"You know about this drug?" I was surprised at how fast Massimo had picked up on its tongue-twister name.

Massimo started waving the fan back and forth once again, but with more vigor.

"Let's just say that in my circle of lovers, there are a few overanxious, irritable, edgy, and depressed little girls. Protriptyline, in various doses, is just one of the many pills that are in high demand on the black market ."

For the first time since I had met Massimo, he seemed to be on edge. I had a feeling that one of the "little girls" who took this drug was Massimo himself.

"You need to watch that boy, Atticus" he warned. "In adolescents, these kinds of anti-depressants can increase the chances of suicidal behavior."

Oh great, exactly what I needed to hear, I thought. I raised a quizzical eyebrow at Massimo.

"Let's just say that I know what I'm talking about," he said.

"I believe you."

Massimo drew a deep breath. "In fact, I wanted to have a few words with you about another young man in the group. I believe his name is Anthony. He's the one who has an invisible umbilical cord with the other female teacher."

Before I could answer, Massimo pushed himself off the balustrade and advanced toward a small group of students who were coming our way.

"There's a great view of the forum from over there," Sabrina said, pointing toward the building where the statues representing the Nile and Tiber rivers were nestled alongside two elegant staircases that led up to the main entrance.

"A very enchanting view indeed. That, young lady, is the Palazzo Senatorio, and, as I explained before , it has held a dominant position on this hill even before Michelangelo completely redesigned it. Just imagine, the front of this building was actually in the back before Michelangelo's time. It's a pity that he was not able to see the completion of his work. Michelangelo died in 1564 and work on this particular building went on into the seventeenth century."

The rest of the group came up as Massimo was speaking.

"All right then, my friends," he said. "I do realize that museums can be, at times, a frightful bore, but I assure you that you shall see some veritable treasures in the one we are going to visit now. Is everyone with us?"

I took a rapid head count. Everyone was accounted for.

Before Massimo entered the museum, I told him that I would be waiting for them at the exit. I urgently wanted to get back to Evelyn's diary.

CHAPTER 38

I found a wrought-iron bench and sat down. I swiped my cell phone screen and again opened the memory card photos folder. I was back to that last line of text that Michelle had curiously erased. I hurriedly read on.

April 30, Friday

Strange start to a weird day. I got up about 5 this morning to go pee and noticed that M wasn't in the room. Then she comes sneaking back at about 5:30. What the fuck is going on.?? I pretended to be asleep. She's certainly not shacking up with anybody on this trip. No way! Not M! She's just been acting postal lately. Maybe I'll mention something to her later.

Atticus sure knows his music, but my darling J blew him out of the water this morning on the bus. A is a bit lame when it comes to Nickelback. J tore him up! I was a bit pissed to see how everyone was cheering it up for J, almost congratulating him. These people don't give a shit about him, they never have, or for me for that matter. What a bunch of hypocrites! God, I hope it'll all be over soon.

We went to see another bunch of boring ruins today, but I have to admit that our guide, as gay as they come, was pretty good. A real showman. Massimo is his name. He had a big old Coca-Cola flag so it was a synch to pick him out. Pretty clever.

V was looking like death and took a cab back to the hotel with none other than Ramsey.

Sitting in a car with that bitch would make me puke!

Lunch was pretty awesome. Got to say that the eating is good here. Makes up for the city which is falling apart. After lunch they served us these little glasses with this fruity tasting vodka. So good! I don't know if it was really vodka, but it was light years better than what Smirnoff or Burnett's has to offer up.

I wanted to go to the CD store with J this afternoon, but as soon as I found out that Mark was going, I backed out. I don't like that jackass. I went out with Cornwall instead. She asked me to go with her out of the blue, and for some stupid reason I said yes. Gotta say she's not all bad. I can see why A likes popping her. She's open but doesn't ask a lot of nosy questions. I never really got to know her in school. Didn't think it was worth it, I guess.

My J was acting really nitro this evening. I don't know what happened when he was out with Atticus, but some heavy shit must have gone down. He didn't want to talk about it with me which really hurt. It hurt a lot. He took his meds and went to bed early. What are we waiting for J?? Let's get this over with!!! In a few more days, this trip is over, and I am not going back!! Only in a body bag and with you next to me…

I closed the folder and put my phone back in my pocket. I agreed with Michelle that there didn't seem to be a red-alert situation with Evelyn, at least not yet. However, the line about "let's get it over with" made me uneasy. Was Evelyn writing all of this knowing that Michelle and others were possibly reading it? Was it just a means to get attention? Or was there a real danger there? The reference to body bags, which certainly would raise anybody's eyebrows, had me on edge.

I looked at my watch. It was close to two thirty. The group would surely be ravenous by now. And sure enough, when they came out of the museum, they were behaving more like a pack of wolves than a group of high school students.

"I'm starving, Atticus!"

"I'm gonna start chewing on someone's leg soon!"

"Pasta, Atticus! We need pasta!"

"Relax, everyone," I said, raising my hands. "Massimo and I will have full plates in front of all of you very shortly. Take just a few more minutes for some final photos. We meet in five minutes at the bottom of the stairs near the two Egyptian lions."

Most of the students bolted down the steps in anticipation of another tasty Italian meal, with just a few of the girls stopping to take photos. I walked over to Massimo, who was standing with the three teachers.

Cynthia was smiling blissfully. "My head is spinning like a top, Atticus," she said. "There was so much to see in there. Such beautiful statues, tapestries, mosaics. Breathtaking, just breathtaking!"

John was also rapturous. "I couldn't agree more, Atticus. *Overwhelming*, that's the only word that fits what we just saw."

Barbara nodded in agreement. "It was just beautiful, and Massimo did a fantastic job at keeping the group alert and interested." She turned to Massimo. "You're the best!" she said and gave him a kiss on the cheek.

Massimo blushed. "Oh my, my, my!" he exclaimed happily. "What to say? I am at a loss for words...and now I'm getting emotional!"

I was pleased to see someone else getting fire engine-red from embarrassment. Massimo took out a lilac-colored handkerchief from his back pocket and delicately dabbed the corners of his eyes.

"I'm happy that everyone enjoyed the tour," I said, "but if we don't get down those steps in a hurry and get these kids in front of some food, I believe they shall have *us* as their next meal. Massimo, I was thinking of taking them to Piazza Margana." I looked at the teachers. "There are lots of small restaurants and trattorias in that area," I explained, then turned back to Massimo. "I'm hoping that either La Trattoria Margana or Da Giuseppe will be open."

Massimo, who by now had gotten hold of himself, nodded enthusiastically. "I still have some time before I meet with my next group, so I can sit with some of them. I have been to Giuseppe's and know some of the waiters there. I'll threaten them for a table!"

"Great!" I said. "We'll probably have to split up into smaller groups. I doubt we'll find a place that can seat all eighteen of us. Let's go."

We reached the bottom of the stairs and met up with our ravenous students. There was a convenient set of zebra stripes that were practically in front of the two Egyptian lions. Once on the other side of the road, we made our way along a narrow sidewalk that led to Piazza Margana, a medieval residential area of Rome where the dwellings date back to the twelfth century. Standing in the middle of this piazza, one had the feeling that nothing had changed over the past nine hundred years. "Frozen in time" was an apt description for this part of the city.

A hush had fallen over the group, save for an occasional "Look at that!", "How old do you think that is?", "Must be cool living here." This was part and parcel of what it meant to walk the streets of Rome. Your hunger could be assuaged by absorbing the alluring, centuries-old atmosphere surrounding you.

We turned the corner and were now just a few steps away from one of the eating establishments. We were in luck—the

Trattoria Margana was open. So was Da Giuseppe, which was just up ahead.

Massimo read my mind. "Let me go in and see if, by chance, they can seat all of us, Atticus."

"Ladies and gentlemen, we shall be stopping here for lunch, I hope. Afterwards, if you would like to go out exploring on your own—"

Cynthia cut across me, "I don't think that's a good idea, Atticus. The group should not split up in a part of town that they're not familiar with. We've done this before, and we were fortunate that everyone got back safely. John, Barbara, do you agree?"

Her tone made it clear that her question was rhetorical. But some of the students spoke up.

"You cut us loose the other day, Mrs. Ramsey," Mary argued, "after we saw that funny-looking statue. We all got back to the hotel in one piece."

"I actually didn't agree to that decision, Mary," Cynthia replied. "Heaven forbid that something should happen to any of you."

"Oh, come on, Mrs. Ramsey," Mark objected. "We've walked this city day in and day out. We've even been out on our own after dinner."

"And know where the hotel is from here," Jeremy added.

Before Cynthia could answer, Massimo reappeared from the restaurant. "Atticus, they have a table for eight in here. I'm going to scoot up to Giuseppe's and see if they have a table for the rest of us there."

"That's fine. Okay, everyone, we'll talk about who is going where after lunch." I realized that I had practically ignored Cynthia's concerns but did not particularly care. "Who wants to eat here?"

Darlene, Vanessa, and Sabrina filed in at once. Jeremy, Mark, and Anthony followed.

"We can take this group," John said. I nodded, and they went in.

Massimo sprinted back and informed us that Giuseppe's had two tables for four, but not in the same room.

"Could you get them settled at Giuseppe's, Massimo? I'm going to handle the group that's dining here."

"This way, please!" Massimo took the lead with the remaining students behind him.

I walked inside the trattoria and was greeted by a young man who seemed to be expecting me.

"*Lei è il,* Signor Atticus?"

"*Si, sono io.*"

"*Mi segue per favore.*"

I did as I was told and followed him. We passed a long buffet table filled with a wide variety of mouthwatering grilled vegetables, variations of seafood salad, cold rice dishes, and cheese. He led me to the group's table, where menus, wine, bottles of water, baskets of bread, and green olives had already been laid out.

The waiter spoke English and had already taken the pasta orders.

"You look like you're all set here," I said.

I glanced at Cynthia, who was sitting opposite John and next to Anthony. She was nibbling a bread stick and appeared preoccupied. I wondered if she was still set on stopping the students from going out on their own.

"I'm just going to scoot over to the other restaurant and see how the others are doing."

"Hurry back, Atticus," Darlene said. "I have an empty chair waiting for you." Darlene patted the chair with her long, manicured nails, pushed out her chest, and gave me a wink. Luckily, the others, including John and Cynthia, were too busy devouring the bread, olives, and wine to notice Darlene's flirting.

On my way out, I informed the young man who had met me at the door that we were a group of students and that I was their chaperone. Most importantly, I told him that I would be handling the bill. But it only dawned on me when I was close to Giuseppe's that I didn't have any vouchers for these meals since the students were supposed to go out on their own today for lunch. Luckily, I had my wallet with me and a couple of credit cards that weren't maxed out.

Once inside Giuseppe's, which was not quite as full as the Trattoria Margana, I easily spotted the rest of the group.

"There you are, Atticus," Massimo called out. "Please, come have a seat. We managed to convince this wonderful man to let us sit all together. It just took a little persuading…" Massimo raised his eyebrows archly, then looked in the direction of the "wonderful man." I gathered from Massimo's expression that some seductive bonding had allowed all of us to be seated together.

I sat between Michelle and Bishop, with Barbara directly opposite me. Bread, pieces of a white pizza called focaccia, black olives, wine, and water were being rapidly consumed.

"Did you order already?" I asked Massimo.

"Ah yes, Atticus, I was given the honor of selecting the first course for everyone. I thought of you as well, my friend."

I nodded and turned to Michelle. "How's your headache?"

"Much better, Atticus," she replied. "I think this red wine is actually helping."

"Oh," said Bishop, "I was wondering why you chugged a whole bottle!"

"Have not, Bishop! What a pain you are sometimes!"

The joking and laughing went all around the table, and I was content to see that the group was relaxed and in such a good mood. At a certain point, my linen napkin began sliding down my leg. When I reached for it, my hand instead found Barbara's bare foot, which was sliding up my calf, then my knee and my thigh, before planting itself firmly between my legs. There was a rather large tablecloth that draped well over the sides of the table, so nobody was the wiser. Barbara's head was turned in Wayne's direction, and she was chattering a mile a minute. You would have thought that her foot had a mind of its own.

As I reached for the bottle of San Pellegrino, two waiters approached our table carrying large trays of pasta and rice. I saw the *rigatoni con sugo alla bolognese, spaghetti alla chitarra con funghi e salsiccia, risotto con carciofi,* and a very typical Roman pasta dish, *pasta alla Gricia.*

Everything looked mouthwatering.

Satisfied sounds went up all around as the contents of the trays were steadily being shoveled onto each one's plate.

"What kind of pasta is this?"

"Awesome meat sauce! Is it ragù, Atticus?"

I rattled off answers.

"This rice dish, Atticus, it's with artichokes, you said?" Barbara's foot had taken a break from ravishing my groin area and was now resting on my right shoe.

"That's right, Barbara, artichokes. They're in season right now and very popular in this part of Italy."

"What's the deal with this square spaghetti, Atticus?" Bishop asked.

"Good question, Bishop. This particular pasta is cut on a long board with strings, just like guitar or *chitarra* in Italian, and therefore the name, which gives it a square midsection instead of a round one. It goes with a thick, hearty sauce like this mushroom and sausage mixture that we have here. However, I don't know the origins of this pasta. Do you, Massimo?"

"Oh my, no," Massimo answered. "I just eat, don't ask me questions about food or cooking. I never step inside the kitchen at home. That's my partner's territory."

"What's his name?" Michelle asked without hesitation.

Massimo was uncharacteristically hesitant. "Sebastiano," he answered after a few moments.

"Maybe we can meet him before we go back," Wayne said at once, spooning down a forkful of pasta.

Massimo nodded, now back to his usual effervescent self. "I like that idea! I have told him all about this group, and I know that he'd just love meeting all of you." Massimo had quickly regained his composure, since nobody within earshot seemed the least bit bothered about this particular aspect of his personal life. I was, however, relieved that Cynthia was sitting at the other restaurant.

The pasta came and went, used dishes were replaced with new ones, meat and fish entrees crowded the table, and I didn't bother counting how many wine bottles had come and gone. I was neither sober nor drunk, but in that pleasantly mellow limbo between.

"Atticus, *Atticus?*"

"Huh?" I came out of my reverie. "Yes, Massimo?"

"I am happy to see you so relaxed, but it's past four o'clock. I believe we told the others that we would all meet at four thirty. Would you like me to go and see how they are doing?"

"Four o'clock? Already?" I had completely lost track of time. "No, thank you, Massimo, let me go show my face." I reached for my wallet and took out my MasterCard.

"Massimo, use this to pay, just scribble my name. And leave a nice tip. See you in about thirty minutes." I looked at Barbara and gave her a wink, not particularly caring anymore if anyone noticed or not. As I got up to leave, the dessert carts came rolling up to the table. What I really needed was a double espresso.

CHAPTER 39

As soon as I entered the Trattoria Margana, I met the young man who had taken care of our table. I asked him to prepare the bill and bring it to me. I then headed to the back of the restaurant.

Vanessa and Sabrina greeted me warmly, but it was a deep freeze with Darlene who got up as soon as she saw me.

"You can sit here, Atticus," Darlene said icily, shoving the chair next to her in my direction. "I saved it for you!" And off she went. I sat down slowly, not knowing what to do or say. Vanessa was drinking from a teacup. Sabrina was grinning.

"What was that all about?" I asked. "Can somebody fill me in?"

"She's upset because you didn't sit next to her. I think she's got a heavy-duty crush on you."

"Well, that would certainly be awkward, Sabrina, wouldn't you say?"

"That's just the way Darlene is, Atticus," said Vanessa. "She likes older men. Don't worry." Vanessa wasn't in the least bit phased and took another sip of black tea.

"How was lunch?" I said, getting off that delicate subject quickly.

"Too much and too good," Sabrina replied. "We must have tried five or six different pasta dishes." She sat back and rubbed her stomach.

"How is your appetite, Vanessa?"

"Getting better, Atticus. Sab can vouch for me."

"She did okay, Atticus, but I told her to order some tea and drink lots of it. She still needs to get that crap out of her system." Vanessa looked down at the cup in front of her and twirled the teaspoon between her fingers.

"Any urge to take more pills?" I looked at her hard.

"There are moments when I want to take a few Ritalins just to feel that buzz in my head again. But Sabrina's been really good at keeping tabs on me. She can tell when I'm getting an itch for the stuff and gets my mind off of it."

Nobody said anything for a few very long seconds. Finally, Vanessa spoke:

"How did it go after Stefano left? Do Ramsey and Seeward think something is up?"

I looked around to see if anyone was within earshot.

"Let's just say that he did an excellent job in fooling Cynthia and John into thinking that you went on a Tylenol binge."

I wasn't about to inform Vanessa or Sabrina that Stefano, in fact, wasn't a doctor. "But as he told you, Vanessa, he's worried and thinks you need some professional help when you get home."

Sabrina put her arm around Vanessa's shoulder.

"Nobody has a gun to your head. But two years is a long time to be hooked on stimulants, especially at your age."

Vanessa emptied her teacup and sighed.

"Okay, Atticus, when I get back to Atlanta, I'll check out some rehabs. I promise."

"Good to hear."

Wayne and the others came up. "Hey, Atticus, we're heading outside."

Vanessa got up. "I'm going to the lady's room for a second." She scampered off. Perfect timing.

"Sabrina, when we were at St. Peter's, we spoke a little about that statue of Mary with Jesus in her arms, remember?"

"Yeah, I do."

"Well, at the expense of making a fool out of myself, I would like to introduce you to someone who helped me a great deal when I was in a very dark place. She's close by. Right around the corner from here."

"Who is she, a shrink?" Sabrina wasn't convinced.

"No, no, nothing like that. I can't really explain until you meet her. Can you trust me on this? It won't take long."

"Okay, I'm good for it."

"Fine, I'll meet you outside."

Sabrina went ahead of me to the exit as I stopped to pay for lunch. The total was €390, about US$480, which wasn't bad considering that other than all the food, many bottles of wine had been opened, along with soft drinks and bottles of water. I paid with my Amex card and left €50 tip in cash—quite exorbitant, considering that tipping is not customary in Italy. As I left the restaurant, I realized that I had just spent over half of my chaperone pay on one lunch. Strangely enough, I didn't care.

Outside, I met most of the group sitting under large sun umbrellas. Several bottles of limoncello were on the tables with small shot glasses.

I was getting good at observing, almost immediately, who was and was not present. Raymond and James were gone. I wasn't worried about Raymond, but not seeing James around set off alarm bells.

"The waiter said it was on the house, Atticus. It would have been impolite to turn it down." John said, raising a shot glass full of the pale-green liquid and emptying it in one go.

"Can't disagree with you on that one, John."

Jeremy, in the meantime, filled one of the little glasses and handed it to me.

"Thank you, sir. By the way, do you have an idea how many people will be going to those movie studios, if Massimo can swing it?"

"It's kind of turning out to be a crowd. Mark, Wayne, and Bishop want to come. So do Darlene, Mary, Sabrina, and Vanessa. Is that going to be a problem?"

"Well, I'll have to run it by Massimo. Let's see if he can get us in there first."

Wayne came up. "Atticus, we'd like to split now and meet up at the hotel for dinner."

"You okay with that, John?" I asked.

"No problem with me," he answered. He turned to Cynthia and Barbara. "Any objection to the kids heading out on their own?"

Barbara gave John a thumbs-up, but Cynthia folded her arms and glared at him. "You know my view on that, John."

"They'll be fine, Cynthia," John said. "Don't be such a worrywart." He turned to the students. "Can I have a show of hands from everyone who's going off on their own?" John was now in control of the situation. Everyone raised their hands, except Anthony.

"Come on, Anthony, come along with us," said Mary. Cynthia stared hard at her, then shifted to Anthony. I couldn't quite read her expression, but she almost looked like she was in despair.

Anthony started to demur. "Uh, well, Mary, thanks but—"

Mary persisted. "Oh, come off it. Just have some fun for once."

Anthony was conflicted—*that* expression I had no trouble reading. But why? What was this power that Cynthia had over him? I recalled the last and only time I saw Anthony go off with a smaller group of students—at the Piazza Navona. Michelle, Raymond, Mary, and Anthony had teamed up, but then Cynthia had joined them.

I saw Anthony set his jaw. "Okay, I'm coming," he said.

He went over to Mary. I thought Cynthia would have a conniption fit as Anthony walked over to Mary.

Then Jeremy approached. "Atticus, Raymond asked me to tell you that he was going to stick around the synagogue for a while and that he would be back for dinner."

I nodded, but I was still concerned about James. I called out to the students. "Does anybody know where James is? Evelyn, where did he go?"

Evelyn's reaction was instantaneous and rage filled. "How the hell should I know? I'm not his friggin' keeper!"

Everyone stopped what they were doing and turned to watch Evelyn.

"To hell, she isn't…that weirdo can't take a piss without her strapped to his back." Sabrina had spoken in a low voice, but given the abrupt silence after Evelyn's outburst, the majority picked up on what she had said, including the subject of her scorn.

"Stick it, you sorry ass bitch!" Evelyn moved menacingly toward Sabrina, who held her ground.

"That's enough!" John bolted from his chair and stood in front of Evelyn, blocking her. Cynthia was also on her feet. "You are grounded for the next twenty-four hours, young lady! I won't accept that kind of language or behavior from anyone!"

Evelyn set her face, turned, and walked off. Michelle ran after her. They both turned the first corner and vanished from sight. I knew that in Michelle's company, Evelyn would get back to the hotel safely.

Cynthia turned to Sabrina. "I didn't hear what you said, Miss Hamlin, so consider yourself lucky for not being grounded as well!"

Sabrina rolled her eyes, but wisely kept her mouth shut.

Massimo and Barbara were at my side. "Are you worried, Atticus?" Barbara asked quietly.

"Not so much about the exchange between Evelyn and Sabrina, but I don't like it that any of the students, especially James, just goes wandering off without saying anything."

Massimo raised a reassuring hand. "My intuition tells me Atticus that the boy just needs some down time, on his own. I believe he's an intelligent individual. Mark my words, he'll be back at the hotel when you get there."

"That's what we need around here, Massimo," Barbara said. "Some positive thinking. You are wonderful." Barbara gave Massimo another kiss on the cheek and then went over to get a refill of limoncello.

"Atticus, if I enjoyed women in bed, that is one that I would challenge you for," said Massimo, watching Barbara.

I smiled, with a vision of Barbara in only high heels.

"By the way, Atticus, here is the credit and receipt. The total was two hundred thirty euros, and I left a twenty-euro tip. I hope you don't mind."

"Not at all. You should have left him more. I just hope everyone was satisfied with the food."

"Oh, most definitely! Plates were being filled and emptied at the speed of light. By the way, how much was the other restaurant?"

I told Massimo the amount.

"Did you have a voucher for the lunch today?"

"No."

"I thought as much. So three ninety and two fifty makes six hundred forty euros. Let's see, I've never been good with numbers, but if I have calculated correctly, you just spent your earnings for six days on two lunches."

"Yes, that's about right." Massimo obviously knew my daily wage. "Lunch was supposed to be on their own today, but I'm fine with it. I really want these kids to get the most out of this trip."

" I understand, but that's a bit *too* generous of you. You're a good man, you know that? And one hell of a chaperone." Massimo squeezed my shoulder. "I must be off now to escort a group of Hungarians. Oops! My dear Atticus, I was forgetting…my contact over at Cinecittà texted me and would be thrilled to take some or all of the group for a tour of the studios. The only problem is that he is only free tomorrow late morning."

"That's great news, Massimo. Tomorrow morning is fine. I'm glad to hear that they can accommodate the entire group. I think there will be at least eight or nine coming along."

"Shall we have the pleasure of your company, Atticus?"

"No, I have some things I need to do." I had promised Raymond some time, and I was also hoping to get Anthony alone for a chat.

"Very well. I shall be at your hotel tomorrow at around eleven, and we shall take the metro from there." Massimo looked at his watch and gave out a suffocated shriek.

"Attention, everyone, please! I would like to thank you once again for a marvelous day. I have truly enjoyed being in your company once again." Massimo was interrupted by a round of applause. "I must be off now to escort a group of Hungarians. If I am not mistaken, I believe your last full day in Rome is next Wednesday. I shall see some of you tomorrow morning, but for those that I miss, we shall certainly see each other before you leave. It's a promise. A warm hug to all of you in the meantime!" Massimo blew kisses to everyone as he scurried off toward the Capitoline Hill.

Barbara came up to me as soon as Massimo left. "You're worried about James, aren't you?"

"Yes, more than just a bit. Seeing Evelyn without him has made me apprehensive."

"Do you think we should split up and go looking for him?"

"That would be like looking for a needle in a haystack. Let's keep all eyes open for him, but going out of our way on a manhunt would be a waste of time."

"What are your plans now, Atticus?"

"I'm going to introduce Sabrina to a friend of mine."

"A friend of yours?"

"Yes, Miss Curiosity. I'll explain tonight."

"I also want to hear about Evelyn's diary."

"Well, I hope we just don't *talk* all night. By the way, you have some very talented feet."

Barbara came closer to me, pretending to brush something off of my shirt collar. "Just wait until tonight. I'll

show you what else they can do. See you later, Mr. Winterle."
She gave me a libidinous grin and trotted off.

I walked over to Cynthia, who was sitting next to John. I
was surprised to see a glass of limoncello in front of her.

"I'm heading back to the hotel, Atticus, after I've had
one more of these." She pointed to the fluorescent-green
liquid in John's glass. "I want to have a few words with Evelyn.
I don't know what made her fly off the handle like that."

"Well, all three of you told me on Day One that there was
no love lost between Evelyn and Sabrina," I reminded her.

"True, but to lash out in that way was totally inappropriate,
totally." Cynthia took a long sip of her limoncello.

"Keep an eye out for James on the way to the hotel. Don't
you both think it's a bit odd that he just left Evelyn high and
dry here?" I had opened my mouth before putting my brain
in gear.

Cynthia looked at me square in the eyes. "No, I don't find
anything odd at all. If the group is told that they can go off
on their own before lunch in a part of town they haven't been
to before, and then that they can go back to the hotel on
their own, why should it be out of the ordinary if somebody
is missing? But then again, it seems that I'm the only one who
comprehends this."

I got Cynthia's message loud and clear—if anything
happened to James, it would be my fault. John decided to
weigh in. "You need to relax, Cynthia. There's nothing wrong
with letting the students break out and do some exploring
on their own. I even overheard Anthony saying that he had a
great time on his own."

Too late when John realized that he had put his foot in
his mouth as well. Cynthia became rigor-mortis stiff.

"And what do you mean by *that*, John? Why are you
specifically pointing out Anthony?" "Why can't any of you
just leave that boy alone!"

Cynthia just glared at him, got up, and left us without saying a word.

"Damn it," said John. "I bet I'll get another earful about Anthony later."

"Well, you sort of asked for it."

"True." John shrugged." Who cares? This is too nice a day to worry about it."

Sabrina came out of the restaurant. "Atticus, did you still want to go? I'm ready if you are."

"Great. Off we go." I got up, then turned back to John. "If you're still here when I get back, I'll have another glass of that with you."

"You're on. I'll wait." John leaned back in his chair, flipped down his shades, and took in the warm sun.

Sabrina and I headed to our left out of Piazza Margana. I didn't bring up the incident with Evelyn. I wanted Sabrina to focus on something else now.

"We'll be there in just a moment. How's Vanessa? Anything we should be worried about?"

"No, she's good. I think she's feeling better about herself, and she knows I'm watching her. I'll beat her silly if she steps out of line."

We didn't talk again until we reached the Piazza di Campitelli.

"Okay, we're here," I said.

Sabrina looked around. "So where is this person?"

"She's in there." I pointed to the church of Santa Maria in Campitelli.

"In the church? Is she a nun?"

"No, she's not a nun. Let me explain. When I lived in Rome, my live-in girlfriend of seven years was diagnosed with terminal cancer. There wasn't anything anyone could do. The best prognosis was four to six months. I would come here on those days when I felt that the world was on my shoulders and just walk from one end to the other, praying for her. One day,

I noticed a statue on the right side as soon as you walk in. It was strange because in all those times I had gone there, I had never noticed it before. It was a statue of Saint Rita, who's patron saint of lost causes. How appropriate *that* was. What I found mesmerizing, Sabrina, were Saint Rita's eyes. Kneeling in front of her, I felt as if she was looking straight through me as if she was communicating with me. Call me foolish, superstitious, an idiot, whatever. I wouldn't blame you. Long story short, I came back to this church almost every day and sat in front of this statue and prayed. Those visits pulled me through a very difficult time in my life."

"What about your girlfriend?"

"I'm still in touch with her. She survived and is still in good health today. A miracle."

"Wow. That's kind of freaky. I'm glad it worked out for the two of you."

"Go in. Look at Saint Rita in the eyes, Sabrina, and let her look into yours. This probably doesn't make much sense now, but it may afterward."

"Just so you know, Atticus, I'm not a churchgoer. I mean, I'm a Christian, but I haven't gone to church since I don't know when."

"Makes no difference, no difference at all. Just try it and if you come away completely unmoved, you'll still have seen a beautiful church."

"All right, Atticus, I'll give it a shot."

"I'm heading back to the restaurant where I left John. When you're finished, you can come and meet up with us."

"Got it. See you later."

As I watched Sabrina go up the worn marble steps and enter the church, a worm of doubt began crawling through my brain. Perhaps I was taking this St. Rita thing a bit too far. Yes, visiting this statue and doing a lot of praying certainly had helped me in a particularly stressful period, but to involve someone else? Was it the right thing to do? Was Sabrina just going along with this to placate me? I would find out soon enough.

CHAPTER 40

When I got back to the restaurant, I found John seated comfortably under the rectangular shade umbrella, his socked feet up on an adjoining chair—so comfortable, in fact, that he had dozed off and was snoring rather loudly. I sat down next to him. A waiter in the restaurant came out and asked me if we needed anything else. The bottle of limoncello was almost empty, and the meager contents presumably warm by now. I ordered another bottle, an espresso, and two sparkling waters. As the waiter headed back inside, John snorted, yawned, and sat up.

"Oh, you're back," he said. He took off his sunglasses and stretched. "How long have I been out, Atticus?"

"I just arrived. Sorry I woke you."

"It's not like me at all to conk out like that during the day. This green drink packs quite a punch after a few glasses. What's it called again, *li-min -cel?*"

"Li-mon-cello. From *limone,* meaning lemon."

"That's right. Won't forget that anymore."

The waiter came back with my order, plus an ice bucket.

"Do you want an espresso, John? I only ordered for me."

"No, not just yet, Atticus."

I filled our glasses with the frosty-cold limoncello and put the bottle into the bucket. John raised his glass. "A toast to you, Atticus, for making this such an enjoyable trip."

"So far," I murmured.

"So far! I'll drink to that." John emptied the small glass in one go. "That's so smooth, like velvet going down your throat. Never would've thought that a lemon could be so, well, so *sexy.*"

That was certainly an appropriate and clever way of putting it. Limoncello could certainly be described as sexy.

John put his sunglasses back on and rested his head on the back cushion.

"Incredible art, architecture, and history all around you, wonderful food, and wine, the sun, and this green elixir. What else could one ask for, Atticus?"

The question was rhetorical, but I answered it anyway. "A beautiful woman?"

"I think that the puzzle is complete, Atticus. Where *is* Barbara, by the way?" John hadn't budged one inch, his head still comfortably reclined. I, on the other hand, felt as if somebody had taken a baseball bat to my chest. I wouldn't have been able to get a word out if my life depended on it.

John picked up on my total state of paralysis. He turned to look at me, grinning like a Cheshire cat.

"Weren't expecting that, were you, Atticus old buddy!" John then began to laugh and laugh and laugh, in total abandon. My total lack of motion, as if I was frozen to my chair, just added to his mirth.

"Oh, Atticus, man! You should see your face! Can't put a price on that! No way!" I just sat there and watched him buckled over in hilarity. I began to thaw out, slowly.

"Talk about being blindsided, John."

And again laughs, guffaws that filled up a noiseless Piazza Margana.

"Stop, Atticus, stop! I can't breathe, wow! Man, man, man…too funny."

"Glad to see that one of us is having a good time."

"Cheers, Atticus! Come on, drink up."

He filled our glasses to the brim. I drained the contents before John was able to place the bottle back on the table.

"Okay," I said. "I'm back on earth now. I'm all ears, John."

Even though more settled, he was still chuckling to himself.

"Did you really think that I and most of the others hadn't figured out how lovey-dovey the two of you have become?"

I opened my mouth, but nothing came out.

"Let me answer that for you: you did, correct? The two of you thought you had us all fooled. It was as plain as the nose on your face from day one that Barbara had taken a liking to you, and vice versa. Now since the cat's got your tongue, let me answer your next question for you." John settled back in his chair in a relaxed position, letting the sun warm his face.

"Yes, I was, Atticus. I was pretty pissed off, excuse my language. I've always liked Barbara, and I was hoping beyond hope that on this trip, she would also start taking a liking to me. But your charm, Atticus, it knocked her off her feet. You're a tough contender. I lost the duel." John took a sip from his glass and cleared his throat. "Are you just going to sit there, Atticus?"

"I don't know what to say John." I really didn't.

"Okay, Atticus, let's back up. I'm going to run my mouth now and let you in on several things that nobody knows. The time is right, the place is right, and I'm feeling the overwhelming urge to dump some heavy timber that I've been carrying on my back for years."

This was becoming a habit with this group—rocks, baggage, now timber.

John filled our glasses one more time. "Did you see the movie *Love Story*, with Ryan O'Neil and Ali MacGraw?"

"Many years ago. It came out in the seventies, didn't it?"

"In 1970, to be exact. Well, Atticus, you could say that my life, at least the first nineteen years of it, was almost a mirror reflection of that movie. My father came from old Georgia money, and so did my mother. And on top of a very large inheritance from both sides of the family, my father was like King Midas to boot. Everything he touched turned to gold. He had a knack for buying up failing companies, making them profitable, and then selling them off for huge profits. We had a twelve-bedroom mansion near Berkeley Lake. It had two swimming pools, tennis courts, an indoor basketball court, and stables for my dad's eleven thoroughbred horses..."

"Where's Berkeley Lake?"

"It's a rich suburb about twenty-five miles from Atlanta. A beautiful area with a lake, hence the name, huge houses, private schools, clubs of all sorts, and a good number of miserable people whose only preoccupation is how much money they have. That pretty much sums up my parents at least." John picked up his glass. "Cheers, Atticus, it only gets better from here."

Our glasses touched before we brought them to our lips.

"I was an only child because my father didn't believe in having more than one *male* child. Lucky thing for my mother that she gave birth to a boy on her first go. If I had been a girl, I'm sure he would have divorced her and tried elsewhere, if you get my drift." John wasn't joking. "Unfortunately, I didn't quite turn out the way he expected me to. He wanted me to learn horseback riding, but I didn't and still don't like horses. He wanted me to learn how to hunt, but I didn't and still don't like guns. He wanted me to excel in math, statistics, chart analysis, how to trade in commodities, the New York Stock Exchange, but I didn't care for any of that, especially not at ten years of age. I think the only reason he put up with me is that as I got older, I never drank too much, never got mixed up with drugs, and didn't get any girl pregnant like the majority of the rich kids in my community. I was a shadow for the most part of my child and teenage years, Atticus. A very rich, innocuous shadow."

"Where was your mother in all this, if I may ask?"

"My mother? She played the part, Atticus. Bridge games, fund-raising events, gardening competitions, lots of afternoon tea parties, preparing the weekly dinner menus with our cook and on and on. She was loyal to my father until the very end and never stood up to him or disagreed with him, heaven forbid. I say she *was* loyal because my dad passed away in 2001, just one week after 9/11. He hadn't been well for a long time, but I think the shock of that day pushed him over the edge."

John paused. "I know what you're asking yourself, Atticus."

"You do?"

"Let's just say that in all my life, I only remember my mother giving me a detached hug at my college graduation and the last time I saw her, about three years ago. Get up."

"What?"

"Get up."

I got up. John stood in front of me and placed the palms of his hands near my collarbones. He then moved closer to me, but not close enough to allow any other part of our bodies to touch.

"That's it, Atticus. That's been the extent of my mother's display of affection for me. In forty-six years, *forty-six godforsaken years. Sweet Jesus…*"

Despite his sunglasses, I knew his eyes had filled with tears.

"Did that answer your question, Atticus?" His voice was broken.

"Well, yes. I was asking myself if there was a more loving relationship between you and your mother, so, yes, you did answer my question."

"Good, very good, because I have no intention of repeating any of this ever again. Consider yourself lucky."

He wiped his face with his shirt sleeve and refilled the two glasses. Down the hatch they went. I was beginning to see triple.

"Now comes the juicy part, Atticus. My high school graduation. Obviously, I attended the most expensive, private college preparatory school in the Atlanta area and managed to get through with decent grades. It was 1982, the year Grace

Kelly and Ingrid Bergman died. I remember it well because my mother went into mourning for about a month. Anyway, graduation day was just two days before my birthday. After a long, boring ceremony, the three of us went out to dinner in a quiet, upscale restaurant not far from home. My father was in such a good mood, which was totally out of the ordinary for him. That should have warned me that something was up. In fact, the proverbial shit hit the fan when we got home. First of all, in the driveway, with a ridiculously large red ribbon on top, was a 1982 Mercedes 380sl. Do you remember those, Atticus? It was a two-seater with a V8, 155 horsepower engine. That was a seventy-thousand-dollar car back then. My father just turned and said, in a very matter of fact way, that it was my birthday present. He then ordered my mother and me to go to his private study, which until that moment, had been, and I quote, 'off limits to any living creature except me.' When the three of us were in his *sancta sanctorum*, he told my mother to sit on a small couch close to his desk before telling me to take the chair in front of him. I felt like the defendant at a murder trial. He opened the desk drawer and took out three A4 envelopes which he placed side by side on the table. They were numbered one to three." John shook his head. "Now get this, Atticus. He tells me to open the first envelope. There were ten thousand-dollar bills inside. Ten thousand bucks! That was a serious amount of cash back in 1982. Then I opened the second envelope and found a one-way first-class ticket from Atlanta Hartsfield Airport to Boston's Logan Airport. You should have been there to see the expression on my father's face. He was getting such a kick out of my total state of confusion. I do remember glancing at my mother, who only had an embarrassed smile on her lips. My dad kept on prodding me, 'Come on boy, open the third one, open it!' So I did. It was the thickest of the three, with a bunch of folded papers inside. But a quick glance at the very first page, and I understood immediately what my father had in store for me. It was an acceptance letter to the business management program at Harvard. Can you fucking believe it, Atticus? I had already applied, and had been accepted, by the skin of my teeth, to Duke University, and this guy, behind my back, used his influence and money to get me into Harvard! In hindsight, I should have figured it out. He never said a word when I spoke about Duke, which wasn't like him at all, given his very vocal opinions on everything I did and said. Duke obviously wasn't good enough. Only Harvard would do for a Seeward. So he just went ahead and decided to plan the next four years of my life for me."

Out of the blue, John glanced at his watch. "It's almost six o'clock."

"We have time," I said. "Dinner's at seven thirty. Please, go ahead."

"Something tells me you already know some of what happened next. Didn't Barbara tell you?" John took off his sunglasses and stared straight at me.

"Um, she did mention something."

He watched me intently. "Something?"

"Okay, John. She told me something about getting a girl pregnant, that you were living together until you came home one day, and the girl and baby were gone."

"Barbara told you exactly what I told her. I did indeed get a seventeen-year-old girl pregnant. She was from Guatemala. She was beautiful, Atticus. I thought I had found the love of my life. Our baby girl is named Izabella, with a z, but as I may have told you at the Pantheon, I haven't seen her since 1983." *No, she hadn't told me that.* "I came back from my daytime job one day, and she they were both gone. Ximena, that's her name, left me a note telling me that she was going back to Guatemala and to please not follow them or seek them out."

"So, wait a minute, I take it, then, that you didn't go to Harvard?"

"Hell, no! I left the house in the early morning, the day after my dad presented me with his version of what my life should be. Nobody saw me leave."

"Did you take the new car? The money?"

"Nope, nothing. I had about a thousand dollars stashed away in a drawer, a backpack with some toiletries, a change of clothes, a few books, and nothing else. I left all the credit cards my father had given me on my bedroom dressing table. I didn't want to have anything more to do with either of them. It was time to start a new life."

"Straight out of *Into the Wild*," I ventured.

"So Barbara also told you about that."

"She told me you were a big fan of the movie and that you practically did a Christopher McCandless."

"Oh, so you've seen it? It didn't really make a lot of noise when it came out. No sex, no violence, no special effects. But one kick-ass film, if you ask me."

"I enjoyed it. Especially the music and the photography. With Eddie Vedder from Pearl Jam writing the music, you couldn't go wrong."

"Impressive, Atticus. You're obviously a music expert, at least according to some of the boys."

"*Expert* is an exaggeration."

"Well, I don't know if it has to do with your music knowledge, but I can tell you one thing, you've been able to connect with these kids in what, four days, in a way that I haven't been able to in years."

"You're with them every day, John, and you're their teacher at their school. I'm with them for nine days in a special city like Rome. I'm part of the vacation package, if you will. But you certainly scored some points today with those Cleopatra comments. The kids loved it."

"You think?"

"I do. Nobody was expecting it. You threw everybody off."

John looked pleased.

"If I may ask, John, did you ever tell Barbara anything else about your background?"

"Nope, and I haven't told anyone else. Only you are privy to all this. Weird, huh?"

"Well, I'm honored."

John finished the last remaining limoncello, straightened up in his chair, and rubbed his eyes. "Ready to head back?" He had said all he was going to say, though I would have liked to hear more.

"I'm ready. Let's go."

This turned out to be easier said than done. In fact, we had to help each other up. Everything was spinning like a top. John was in a worse condition than me. Even so, my suggestion that we take a cab back to the hotel was met with disdain.

"A cab? No way, my good man. In Rome, one walks. Didn't you teach us that?"

"Yes, I did, but that pearl of wisdom is for sober people which we, at the moment, are not."

"Can't handle your lemons, Atticus? What a wimp! What does Barbara see in you anyway?" John smiled and put his arms out to hug me. In doing so, he tripped over the leg of the chair, tumbled against me, and we both ended up flat on the ground. Our faces were a few inches apart. We started to giggle like two schoolgirls. One of the waiters who witnessed our collapse rushed out to help us up, which was frightfully embarrassing.

We came to our feet rather quickly, considering the state we were in. I took out my money clip to pay but was told that the limoncello and the rest was on the house. I wondered if this act of generosity was due to the substantial tip I had left for at lunch or if the waiter just wanted to get rid of two drunks as fast as possible.

Once on our way, we both managed to regain some of our faculties. John, in fact, was walking at a pretty good clip, given the amount of limoncello in his system. You could tell that he was a hiker and fit.

Before long, we were back in the Piazza Venezia and in front of the garishly white monument dedicated to Vittorio Emanuele II.

"You know, Atticus, Massimo's right," John said. "That thing really stands out like a sore thumb. It has absolutely no connection with the history surrounding it. We should start a public referendum to have it knocked down. Pretty good idea, huh?"

"Hey! Watch it!"

John had inadvertently stepped off the curve and was about to fall into oncoming traffic. I grabbed him by the shoulder and pulled him back.

"Pretty fast reflexes there, my deal fellow," he said happily. "You may have just saved my life."

"That's a bit of an exaggeration," I demurred.

"Dying in Rome, that certainly would add a bit of pizzazz to my sorry-ass life."

I didn't comment. I did, however, put my arm around his shoulder to make sure that he didn't add any pizzazz to his sorry-ass life. At least, not on this trip.

CHAPTER 41

"Darlene! Are you ready? We've gotta go!"

No answer.

"Darlene! Goddammit! I don't wanna come in there and see you without that dress on!"

"I don't wanna go, Mama..." Darlene's voice was purposely low. She was, in fact, only speaking to herself. She knew that her mother would never be able to hear her anyway, especially with that Cleopatra DVD that was on again with the volume higher than usual.

But Darlene did pick up on those menacing, off-balance, creaking steps coming down the hallway, as she had countless times before. The scene was always the same. The door would soon fly open, and her mother would come in with that cigarette hanging from her lips and a glass of that smelly stuff she always drank in her hand. Then depending on how she judged Darlene's appearance, there would be a wide range of reactions—either a vicious pull of the hair and a slap across the face, not too hard though, since the judges would take away points for a flushed or splotchy complexion. Even so, things could go really bad with a hard shove to the floor and a few kicks to the upper legs and stomach. Judges couldn't see the bruises underneath the ball gown dresses. Once, her mother had gone too far and hurt Darlene so badly that they had to go to the hospital. She was six years old at the time and told the doctor that she had fallen down the stairs.

That's what Mama told her to say, so that's what she said. Darlene loved her mama more than anything else in the world. Now she was eight, but when it rained a lot and it was really hot and sticky outside, she still felt the need to rub her arm where the bone had broken.

"Just look at you, just look at yourself, Darlene!" Her mother took her by the back of the neck and shoved her towards the wall-to-wall, full-length mirror opposite Darlene's bed. Her mom almost tripped over Darlene, and the drink slipped from her hand. "Look what you made me do, you stupid little girl!" With both hands free now, her mother pushed her face hard up against the mirrored glass. Darlene's breath caused the surface to fog up.

"Do you think that any goddamn self-respecting judge would give you even one moment of consideration the way you're looking this morning?" A bit of ash from her mother's cigarette fell on Darlene's hair. Her mother shoved her to the other side of the room, where on the back wall were shelves and shelves of neatly arranged awards, trophies, and certificates for beauty contests that Darlene had participated in ever since she could remember. Darlene knew what was coming next.

"How much money and time have I spent with you to make sure you could win all of that?" her mother screeched. "You think I'm gonna let all of this go to waste just cuz you don't feel like meeting your goddamn obligations?" If she had a dime for every time her mother said "goddamn," Darlene could have bought those beautiful white rollerblades she had always wanted. Tears began swelling up in her eyes, and she was feeling nauseated from the smell of her mother's cigarette and Jim Beam breath.

"Now listen to me and listen good. I'm giving you an extra ten minutes to get your hair done, redo that make-up, and fix your dress. We've got a long drive ahead of us, and I wanna come

home with the first prize, do you understand what I'm saying?"
And then came the slap to the face, not too hard, but by no means
too soft. Darlene's mother then took a very long drag from her
cigarette and exhaled slowly. There was a momentary pause.
Darlene hated this part most of all. Her mother's voice suddenly
turned sweet and pleading.

"You're so beautiful, Darlene, and you make me awful proud
when you do what you're told. You know I love you, don't you?"

"Yes, Mama."

"I've got some good news for you. You know, Judge Perkins is
gonna be there today, and you know how he takes a liking to
you. Maybe after the show you can, you know, go backstage and
thank him personally for taking a special interest in you…"

Darlene felt sick to her stomach.

Oh, she would certainly bring home first prize today, but at a
price. Judge Perkins was always so enthusiastic when she came
to visit him backstage after the show. He always managed to find
a room, large or small, that had a door with a lock on it. After
he was through putting his fingers up between her legs and tired
of hearing her saying that it hurt, he would take down his pants
and underwear and ask Darlene to hold his "special friend," as
he called it, in her hands. This had been going on since she had
turned seven. Judge Perkins had promised her that they would do
some other fun things when she was a little bit older. She didn't
want to think about that now. Darlene had tried to tell her mama
what was going on, but Mama would never let her finish her sto-
ry. She wondered at times whether her daddy would have listened
to her. She didn't remember him very well, and Mama had told
her many times not to mention him. So she didn't.

"It's a good thing that Judge Perkins thinks so highly of you, and more importantly, a first-prize trophy is going to be a shoo-in today, young lady, if you just get your act together."

Mama picked up the whiskey glass from the floor and dropped her cigarette butt inside it.

"Ten minutes, Darlene. Be a good girl and get ready. Do it for your mama."

She stumbled out of the room, closing the door behind her.

I had forgotten about Sabrina.

Damn it! I had told her to meet up with John and me when she had finished her visit with St. Rita. Considering our state of inebriation, it was probably much better that she didn't. But where was she now? John and I had managed to stumble back to the hotel just a few minutes after seven thirty. Both Giovanni and Ludovica were behind the front desk. They nodded expressionlessly as we collected our room keys. I guided John to the elevator. Once he was safely in his room, I proceeded to mine. I immediately went to the bathroom and turned on the faucets. I couldn't get my mind off Sabrina. I also remembered that James had gone off somewhere right after lunch. Where was he now?

What I saw in the mirror wasn't particularly flattering, but I had to get down to the restaurant to do a headcount. When I did arrive in the dining area, I found what I had pretty much expected. Not everyone was present, and those who were looked like they had just come out of a cryonic freeze. The boys outnumbered the girls. I saw Anthony sitting with Mary. Wayne, Bishop, Mark, and Michelle were seated together. Then I saw Sabrina with Raymond and Jeremy. So one of my lost sheep was accounted for. I wanted to ask Sabrina about her church visit and to apologize for not having waited for her as promised, but I would have to do that later. I did not see either James or Evelyn for that matter. Then I realized that neither Barbara nor Cynthia was present. My group was going AWOL on me. "Hey, Atticus," Mark called out, "you're looking a little wasted, if you don't mind me saying so."

"No, I don't mind, Mark. Let's just say that the limoncello today got the upper hand. But looking around, I would say that most of you look less than a hundred per cent."

The excuses came thick and fast.

"Too much walking today, Atticus."

"We're bushed."

"Yeah, and way too much food."

I said, "And a little too much wine perhaps?"

"When in Rome do as the Romans do," Raymond replied. "Isn't that what you told us, Atticus?"

"Yes, Raymond, I guess I did. By the way, did all of you decide to liquidate the teachers and hide their bodies somewhere?"

"They're weak."

"Can't keep up the pace."

"Mr. Seeward looked pretty washed out after lunch."

"He's accounted for," I told them. "He just wasn't up to having dinner. But does anyone know where Ms. Ramsey or Ms. Cornwall are?"

At the word *Cornwall*, I received a few looks that clearly translated into *Don't you know, Atticus?* I feigned ignorance.

"Ramsey's back," said Mary. "I saw her about an hour ago. I haven't seen Mrs. Cornwall."

"What about Darlene and Vanessa?"

"They're both conked out in bed."

"And Evelyn, James?"

Nobody replied, which raised the nervous hairs on the back of my neck.

"Evelyn is in our room, Atticus," said Michelle, who was chomping on a large mouthful of rigatoni.

"Okay, good, and James?"

Please, someone say that they saw him.

"You can chill, Atticus," Jeremy answered. "I met him on the staircase when I was coming down here."

I tried not to reveal my overwhelming sense of relief.

"Aren't you going to have anything to eat, Atticus?" said Wayne. "The pasta is epic tonight."

"That's the problem, it's always epic. I've put on three pounds since we've been here." Michelle put her arms around her stomach and sighed.

"What's in this pasta, Atticus?" asked Mary. "It's too good."

"Looks like rigatoni with shaved ham and peas in a cream and butter sauce. I'm going to get some of that." I walked over to the buffet table and scooped up a large serving of the rigatoni. But there was an array of other tantalizing items that I also wanted to get my fork into. These included *orecchiette con broccoli e pepperoncino, mezze maniche con panna e salsiccia, paccheri ripieni con prosciutto e piselli,* and one of my favorites, *conchiglie con pesto.* There was a plethora of other meat, fish, and vegetable dishes on the buffet table, but just to finish what I had selected was going to take some doing.

When I went to sit down, I noticed that the students had turned their chairs in a more circular orientation so that everyone could talk to one another more easily.

"Sorry to see you aren't hungry, Atticus," said Raymond.

He was being sarcastic since my food was literally sliding off of my plate.

"How can you say no to this, Raymond?" I responded. "Look at these pasta dishes. You're not going to find any of this back in the States."

I started giving a culinary lecture about what I scooped up, from the concave-shaped pasta called orecchiette, or "little ears," with broccoli, garlic, and pepperoncino to the shell-shaped pasta with a basil, pine nut, olive oil, parmigiana and pecorino cheese sauce called *pesto al basilico.* The truly original and most sublime pesto can only be found in the Liguria region of Italy, in the north, given the specific type of Mediterranean basil that grows there, but average to good variations can be found all over the country.

Everyone seemed tuned in to what I was saying. Had I been speaking about any other cuisine in the world, I believe that I would have lost their attention. But Italian food is magical, just like the country.

Now it was my turn to get some information. I threw out a slew of questions: "What did you see? What struck you the most? What was the most enjoyable thing you did today?"

Comments, descriptions, rebukes were flying in all directions. Nobody stayed silent. The students had gone off in various directions, and I was genuinely surprised by the ground that some of them had covered. I was also very pleased to hear that they remembered what they had seen and could recite the names of places of interest that had particularly struck them. On the way back to the hotel, some of them had stopped in coffee bars, ice cream parlors, and takeaway pizza stands. The group was becoming familiar with their surroundings without the aid of a guide or translator.

"So what's your take on this trip so far?" I kept shoveling pasta down my throat but was taken aback by the dead silence that greeted my query.

"Come on, good or bad. I think it's important that you speak frankly. My feelings won't be hurt."

This, of course, was a blatant lie.

"Anyone want to give their five cents? Mary?" I persisted.

Mary screwed up her face. "Me, why me?"

"Because I know you'll enlighten me. Come on, nobody leaves the room until everyone has answered the question."

"What is this?" said Wayne. "A murder mystery, and we're all suspects?"

Chuckles ran round the room.

"If it were, you would be the victim, Wayne," I shot back, drawing even louder laughter. I turned back to Mary. "So, Mary, your thoughts?"

She cleared her throat. "Well, this will probably sound pretty corny, but so far, this is the best trip I've ever been on. Rome, honestly, just blows my mind every time we've gone out." She cleared her throat again. "Nobody should feel flattered, especially you, Wayne, but I'm also glad to be part of this group…" Everyone laughed, Wayne hardest of all. Mary waited for the laughter to subside, then continued, "Even the teachers have been pretty cool—"

"Except Ramsey," Wayne interrupted.

Mary shook her head. "Sure, but even she's lightened up a bit from Atlanta. Massimo has been awesome, and I've learned a lot of interesting stuff from him and you, Atticus." Mary sat back in her chair.

"Thank you, Mary," I said. "Anyone else?"

Sabrina raised her hand. "I agree with Mary about the city. I've seen a few things here and there about Rome on the History and Discovery channels at home, but I wasn't expecting any of this. This city gets under your skin. It's like being on a constant high. And the food…*sooo* good!"

"I didn't have any doubt that the food would be an eye-opener for everyone," I said. "When you get back to the States, you won't even be able to stand the food at most of the so-called Italian restaurants there. It's just not real Italian food. Jeremy, how about you?"

"Everything's pretty cool so far, Atticus. My only problem is worrying about getting hit by a car or scooter every time I cross a street, but that's Rome, I guess."

I nodded and scanned the group. "Anthony, how has it been for you so far?"

Anthony was looking down at his lap and seemed not to hear me. Mary gave him a hard nudge.

"What?" he said, blinking.

"How have you found the trip so far?" I repeated.

"Right, yeah," he said. "The place is pretty okay."

Jeremy threw up his hands. "*Pretty okay?* Is that the best you can do? C'mon, man, have you even *been* on the same tour with the rest of us?"

Anthony's cheeks were turning different shades of rouge at Jeremy's jab, but I stayed out of it.

"Yeah, sure, it's more than just okay. Today was really good."

"That's because you didn't have Ramsey breathing down your neck for once," said Wayne bluntly.

Anthony was now crimson red and rocking back and forth nervously in his chair. Nobody said anything. I looked at Wayne and inclined my head slightly in Anthony's direction. Wayne understood my message.

"Don't sweat it, Anthony. We just want you to break out with us more. The teachers don't need to be with us twenty-four seven. We've got your back, man."

Wayne's words had a stupefying effect on Anthony. Looking rather surprised, he looked up and smiled.

"Um, sure, I'd like that," he said. "Sounds great."

Wayne gave Anthony a thumbs-up, which was eagerly returned. *Home run, Wayne, bravo,* I thought. "Who wants something to drink?" I asked. "Espresso, cappuccino, a beer, Coke? It's on me."

Cheers went up all around.

After jotting down the varied requests on a napkin, I got up and headed to the front desk to see if Ludovica or Giovanni could supply us with our impromptu order. Ludovica was nowhere to be seen, but Giovanni was there, examining a stack of papers in front of him.

"Good evening, Giovanni." I asked him if someone could bring us the drinks.

"I will arrange it at once," he replied.

"Thank you, Giovanni. Put the order on my room, please." I gave him the napkin.

"As you wish." He looked up.

I turned to go back to the restaurant, but Giovanni cleared his throat tactfully. I turned back.

Speaking in Italian, he said, "I did not see any of the teachers come down to dinner tonight."

I switched to Italian as well. "Well, you may have noticed that Mr. Seeward was probably more in need of sleep than dinner."

"That was abundantly clear," he replied. "I was, however, referring to Mrs. Ramsey."

"Mrs. Ramsey?"

"Yes. I do apologize if I seem to be meddling, but when I saw her earlier, she seemed—how shall I put it? —distraught."

I leaned the desk and lowered my voice, even though we were still speaking Italian. "What makes you believe she was, as you say, distraught?"

"She was here in the lobby this afternoon, and I noticed some strange behavior."

"Such as?"

"Sitting on the couch one moment, standing the next, constantly clenching and rubbing her hands, as though she was rehearsing for the part of Lady Macbeth. And then the tears, a great deal of silent tears. I do not believe she even noticed me. She was so wrapped in whatever was tormenting her that she was oblivious to her surroundings. It was only when that very melancholy young man, the one in Room 10, came in the hotel that Signora Ramsey regained her composure and, I presume, went up to her room."

The melancholy student must have been James. "What time would you say that was?" I asked.

"It was exactly six fifty-two. I have a penchant for looking at my watch when someone leaves or arrives at the hotel."

This meant James had been out on his own for almost five hours. I wondered where he could have gone.

Giovanni turned the desk phone in my direction. "Would you like me to put you through to Mrs. Ramsey?"

"Yes, I think that would be a very good idea."

I took the receiver from him and listened to the phone ring on the other end. Giovanni had departed to the back office—the personification of discretion.

"Y-yes…hello?" Cynthia's voice was raspy.

"Cynthia? I'm sorry, did I wake you?"

"Atticus?"

"Yes, it's me."

"No, no, I wasn't sleeping, just reading a bit."

"I didn't see you at dinner, and I just wanted to check in to see that you were all right."

"Yes, I'm fine. Are the students all accounted for?"

"Yes, everyone is back. Some sooner, some later."

"That's good. I gave James his medication about an hour ago. He didn't tell me where he had gone off to."

"As long as he got back, we're okay. Just so you know, Cynthia, tomorrow is a free day, but Massimo is going to take a group of the students to Cinecittà, the movie studios of Rome, if you're interested."

"Thank you, Atticus, but I would like to go back to St. Peter's tomorrow. I want to spend some more time there and try to get back to the Sistine Chapel as well."

"That's fine. Well, some of the students are waiting for me in the dining room. We'll see each other tomorrow at breakfast. Good night, Cynthia."

"Yes…okay."

There was a long pause. I was about to speak when she said, "Remember you promised me some time at the forum?"

"Yes."

"Would Sunday work for you?"

Something in her voice made the question seem urgent.

"Sunday it is." I paused. "Is there anything else?" I tried to echo the underlying urgency I thought I had heard in her tone.

"No."

"Okay. Good night." I slowly put the receiver back on its cradle. I was so lost in thought that I didn't see Sabrina come up to the desk.

"Atticus?"

"Oh, Sabrina, sorry."

"I just wanted to get see you alone to thank you."

"Thank me?"

"Yeah. For introducing me to St. Rita."

"Oh! I wanted to ask you about that earlier in fact. How was it?"

"Let's say that I think I know how you felt when you visited with her. You really get a feeling that she's looking at you, that she's trying to tell you something. I must have sat there for thirty minutes just staring right at her. It was a good feeling. I don't know how to describe it, but I feel less stressed out. Like I've got a new perspective on things, if you know what I mean."

"Well, I'm very happy to hear that you made a connection. You're right. She does give you a good feeling. I'm also glad that you don't think I'm off my rocker."

"I kind of did before I saw her. But that changed in a hurry."

"Good. Oh, and I'm sorry John and I abandoned you."

"No worries, Atticus. I came back and saw that the two of you were deep in conversation, so I just headed back to the hotel on my own. It was a nice walk. This was definitely the best day of the trip for me so far."

She reached up and kissed me quickly on the cheek before turning to go back into the dining area. That was unexpected, but much appreciated.

I was about to go back into the restaurant myself when it dawned on me that I really had no idea where Barbara was. Nobody had mentioned seeing her. I picked up the lobby phone and called her room. After several rings, she finally answered.

"Barbara, it's Atticus. Are you okay?"

"Hi. No, not really…"

"What's wrong?" I was getting alarmed.

"Don't worry, it's not life-threatening. Well, maybe to other people." She began to giggle.

"What?" I said, now thoroughly confused.

"It's purely intestinal, my darling. Embarrassing, annoying, and smelly. I've just been eating and drinking too much, and now I'm paying for it."

I laughed. "Does that mean no visit tonight?"

"I'm afraid so. This is one side of me I don't want you to witness or get a whiff of. I have to maintain a minimum of self-dignity."

"I understand, but may I just remind you that I have become quite intimate with just about every square inch of your rather stunning body."

"You are a bad, bad boy, Atticus…and I love it! I do see your point, I really do. If I feel better later on tonight I shall most definitely come and sneak in bed with you, promise."

"All right, then. Just let me know if you need anything."

"Some air freshener would be appropriate." Barbara giggled again. "See you later, my dear."

I hung up and just stood there for a minute. Barbara had really won me over and in such a short period of time. I thought about Francesca for a moment and at how much time I had *not* spent thinking about her. I was beginning to consider that it would not be a bad idea if she accepted that New York job.

I headed back to the dining area and found Vanessa and Darlene had joined the group. I called over to Jeremy, who looked up.

"Good news," I said. "Massimo was able to get you a private tour of those movie studios. He'll be here tomorrow at eleven to pick you up."

"That's fly, Atticus! Thanks."

"Do we have a definitive count on who is going?"

"Eight of us."

"Okay, good. I'm leaving you in charge of getting everybody ready to go and be in the lobby tomorrow at ten fifty."

"I've got it covered," he assured me.

I plopped myself down on a chair and sipped on my now-lukewarm espresso. Everyone had brought out their laptops or iPods or mobile phones. Michelle got up from her table and grabbed a chair close to me. She looked around for a moment and then murmured,

"Did you get a chance to look at those images I gave you?"

"Yes, I did. Our Evelyn certainly has her fair share of bottled-up rage. You said earlier that she was in your room. Why didn't she come down for dinner?"

"She was really upset, to put it mildly, with Mrs. Ramsey. I don't think she wanted to risk running into her down here. I put some chicken and bread and cold pasta in a dish for her. I'm going to take it up soon."

"Did the two of you come back to the hotel together? I saw both of you walking off, but that's it."

"Yeah, we walked back together. She wanted to go off on her own, but I wouldn't let her." She saw my curious gaze. "Evelyn usually does what I tell her to do. She asks my opinion, and I give it to her. She listens to me. I think it because I've never made comments about her, her mother or father, before or after the fact."

"That's very wise of you, Michelle. You're probably the only one who knew about all that stuff and didn't pass judgement." I lowered my voice and leaned even closer to her. "Do you think she's going to do something stupid?"

"No. I agree with you that it's James we have to worry about. He's been separating himself from Evelyn lately, as you've probably noticed. She may have her share of problems, too, but she's his anchor. Now he seems to be more of a loner than before. I don't think that's good. Evelyn is really upset by his sudden cold shoulder."

We sat silently for a moment and just stared at the table.

"I'll keep my eye on her, Atticus, and if I can take some more pics of her diary, I will."

"Just be careful, Michelle. You're already going far out of your way on this."

She gave me another one of those beautiful, contagious smiles.

I snapped my fingers. "Before I forget, didn't you, Wayne, and Bishop want to have a chat with me? Tomorrow is already Sunday, and Thursday morning you guys are on the plane back."

"Don't remind me, time is going too fast. How about tomorrow? Maybe after dinner?"

"You're on. Sunday, it is."

"Great. I'm going to head up and give Evelyn this food. I'll let you know if there is something out of the ordinary."

"Call me at any time if you need anything. By the way, how's that headache?"

"All gone. I feel great. Thanks for asking."

As she turned to go out of the dining room, she bumped into Raymond, who was also leaving.

"Sorry," he said. "Did I step on your foot?"

"No, I'm fine." She shot him a quick smile, and Raymond blushed.

"Hi, Raymond," I said.

"What's up, Atticus?" he said without looking around. His gaze was still fixed on Michelle.

"Are you heading to the synagogue tomorrow?"

"Yup. There's a Shabbat service tomorrow at eleven thirty."

"Do you mind if I walk there with you?"

"Sure, you can even attend the service if you want."

"Oh, I didn't realize I could since I'm not Jewish."

Raymond smiled to himself.

"It always amazes me how many people think that a synagogue is only for Jews. When you tell them that of course they can attend a service, they give you that look that you just gave me."

"What look is that?"

"Total and utter surprise. As if the Jewish faith were some mysterious, obscure sect."

"You got me, Raymond. I'm guilty."

"Don't sweat it, Atticus, happens all the time."

"Right. If we don't catch each other later, we'll meet up in the lobby at ten thirty tomorrow morning."

"That's good. See you then. Good night."

A good night indeed, so far. Now I just needed to corner Anthony. But I needed a pretext. What could that be? I thought for a while, then the answer hit me—how terribly easy!

Anthony was still sitting with Mary and few others. As soon as I swung a chair next to him and sat down, he stiffened up, probably under the impression that I was going to quiz him once again on his supposed travel to Switzerland or the game of polo.

"What's up, Anthony, all well?"

"I guess."

"Listen, I need some advice, and I think you are just the person I need to speak to."

"Advice? About what?"

He was nervous.

"This is my problem. I have the opportunity to buy a handgun from a friend of mine who lives in Austria. He owns a small firearms shop not far from Vienna." Anthony's expression suddenly shifted from nervous to interested.

"He showed me—let's see if I remember correctly—a Beretta , a Glock and an HK, all .45 caliber. I must say I liked the three of them. What would you suggest? For home defense."

The metamorphosis was underway. Anthony was becoming another person. His eyes were now wide open. He sat up straight, and he began to speak with an authority that I had not noticed since his comments at St. Peter's about the pope's vulnerability to a well-trained sniper.

"Those three guns all have their pluses and minuses, as any conventional weapon, whether it be a revolver, a semiautomatic, a rifle, a shotgun, et cetera. But of the three semis that you mentioned, my personal favorite is the Glock, especially if you have a conceal-and-carry license. A Glock is probably the ugliest girl in the bar, but you can't beat it for dependability. You can run over it with a truck, throw it in the water, and cover it with sand, and it will still fire like it's out of the box. It's a gun that just won't let you down. Then you mentioned the Heckler & Koch—also a very good gun.. The recoil for a .45 is mild. It has a Picatinny accessory rail and interchangeable backstraps. It weighs more than a Glock, but I actually like that."

I was impressed with this new individual in front of me. It was almost as though Anthony had a split personality. He kept right on going, shooting off details of these firearms as if he had memorized the owner's manual.

"With a Beretta, you've got a high-quality firearm with an awesome design. This is the sexiest girl in the bar. You can tell that the Italians are behind the production process. It has the lines of an Alfa Romeo. What I especially like about the

Beretta , as well as almost all the others, is the large ejection chamber. You're not going to get a cartridge stuck in there. The only real issue with the Beretta is that I wouldn't want it run over by a truck or thrown in the water or in the sand and then depend on it one hundred percent to fire. It's like comparing a Ferrari with a Volvo. Which do you want in a snowstorm?" He looked at me and grinned. "Again, you have the choice between three great firearms, bit I would stick with the Glock. You can't go wrong, Atticus."

"Thank you, Anthony." I tried hard not to look dumbfounded. Barbara was spot-on—this kid knew his guns.

"Do you mind if we get together tomorrow afternoon when you get back from the tour with Massimo? I have a few questions about shotguns."

"I'm at your disposal, Atticus. I'll track you down as soon as I get back."

Mary appeared out of nowhere. "And what have the two of you been jabbering about? You look like two kids planning a candy store raid." Instantly, it was if the clock had struck midnight—the old Anthony reappeared, slouched down in his chair with his head hanging.

"Oh, nothing in particular, Mary," I said. "I was just asking our friend here about what he saw today and what he liked."

Now Darlene came up. "Hey, Atticus. Any problem if I go out and see Giacomo later on?" I had forgotten all about her new friend. "It's just going to be down at the fountain. He said he'd wait until I showed up."

"I would feel more comfortable, Darlene, if the two of you met in the lobby. So would your teachers."

Darlene rolled her eyes. "Everybody's treating me like a kid on this trip. I'm not, you know!"

"It has nothing to do with that. I don't really know who this Giacomo is, and neither do you, Darlene. What if he decided to clobber you over the head and drag you in an alley somewhere? What would any of us be able to do?"

Mary nodded. "Atticus has a point, Darlene. Can't you just ask him to come to the hotel?"

Darlene sighed heavily and proceeded to walk out of the restaurant, muttering, "I'm not a child anymore, and I'll prove it."

"I'll keep an eye on her, Atticus, don't worry," Mary said.

"Thanks, Mary. See you at breakfast."

"We're going to head up also, Atticus. See you in the morning." Wayne and Bishop waved and headed out of the restaurant.

Anthony, in the meantime, had snuck off. I sat back, took a swig of my now-lukewarm beer and thought about how these students, in a very short period of time, had managed to blend into the surroundings. They were coming and going with limited adult supervision and acting responsibly. On the other hand, the teachers, the ones liable for the students' safety, were shut up in their rooms suffering from a hangover, diarrhea, and God only knew what was wrong with Cynthia. I found it noteworthy that none of them had even bothered to check and see if all the students were accounted for. Hopefully, this was an overt manifestation of their trust in me.

After saying good night to the handful of students still in the room, I made my way upstairs, relishing the idea of some downtime of my own. I needed to check emails, read a few more of those student bios, and take a long, very hot shower.

Hopefully, there wouldn't be any surprises tonight…

I should have remembered that wishful thinking can be a boomerang.

Sunday
May 2, Day Six

CHAPTER 42

A real woodpecker? Or a dream-induced woodpecker?

Not possible. I hadn't quite fallen into the arms of Morpheus yet.

Tap-tap-tap in rapid succession, barely audible. I put on the bedside lamp and looked at the clock. It was 1:13 am.

There it was again. *Tap-tap-tap.* Still delicate but more insistent this time. Somebody was knocking on my door. It wasn't Barbara. She would have called me before coming across.

I had gone to bed in my briefs and my St. George's Island T-shirt, so I immediately went to the door and opened it. Although the gentle tapping belied a cataclysmic event involving one or more of the students, I was expecting some sort of emergency.

I turned the door handle, the person outside pushed the door open with considerable force, almost hitting me in the face, and a white clad figure dashed past me to the opposite side of the room, stopping at the window facing away from me.

"What in heaven's?" I started to say.

"Shhh! Close the door, Atticus," the intruder hissed urgently.

I shut the door, and the figure turned around. The light from the bedside lamp illuminated their features. It was Darlene.

She loosened the sash around her bathrobe. It had slid off her shoulders and down the length of her body to the floor. Other than a string-bikini bottom and a pair of black pumps with six-inch heels, she was there as Mother Nature had made her. Darlene's face was still in the shadows, but the rest of her stood out like a Penthouse centerfold. She began to stroke her full breasts. Her right hand slid down through her cleavage, over her tummy and belly button, her fingers stopping underneath that microscopic piece of cloth that only barely covered her pubic area.

"Atticus, I want you," she said in a low, throaty voice. "I've wanted to make love to you since the very first time I saw you on the bus. I'm not a *child* anymore, and I can *prove it*."

She came up to me in one swift motion, her breasts pressing into my T-shirt, then her lips zeroing in on mine. In the matter of a nanosecond, I had to make a choice—the right choice.

Option number 1, dictated solely by my groin area, was to screw the brains out of this Pamela Anderson look-alike and worry about the consequences later. Option number 2, dictated by the head on my shoulders, was to put an immediate stop to all this and go sit inside a walk-in freezer for a couple of hours. Flesh-to-flesh contact was imminent. If it happened, no reasoning of any sort was going to stop me from choosing option number one.

"Stop!" I said.

I grabbed Darlene's shoulders, squeezed hard, and stopped her in her tracks. I wasn't going to succumb to her sexual assault. She quickly removed her hand from between her legs, crossed her arms over her chest, and abruptly sat on the corner of the bed. Her face reflected a mix of hurt, embarrassment, and fury.

As I reached over for one of the two chairs in the room, swinging it between my legs in order to sit facing her, she shot up from the bed and started to unload.

"What's wrong, Atticus?" she said, her voice full of anger and confusion "This is so unfair. Why are you doing this to me?!"

"Darlene, what do you think is unfair, and what is it exactly that I am doing to you?"

"Why don't you want to make love to me!? Come one, let me show you, I'll give you a blow job that you'll never forget." She slid off the bed and got down on her knees and tried to push open my legs.

"Darlene, stop it. This isn't going anywhere."

I got up and retrieved her bathrobe from the floor. "Put this on, sit down, and listen to me."

"I don't want to listen to anything, goddammit!" She sat on the bed and glared at me. Tears began to run from her eyes. "You've been fucking Cornwall, so I know you're not gay. You mean to tell me that this isn't worth trying?" She opened her legs wide and pulled aside her panties. "It's all yours, Atticus."

Darlene's tears had smeared the excessive mascara she had applied to her eyelashes, creating jagged black lines on her face. She was the picture moral destitution.

"I want you to put your bathrobe on, Darlene, and listen to me. That's what I want." Realizing that she wasn't going to have sex with me, Darlene covered herself with the robe.

I sat back down. "Let me tell you why I'm not taking up your offer, Darlene. First, because I respect you. Secondly, because you could easily be my daughter, and I don't go to bed with teenage girls. Let me ask you something. If I had sex with you, would you still consider me a person you can trust, a friend, a shoulder to lean on, afterward? Or wouldn't I be then just another man who got into your pants?"

Darlene began chewing on her thumbnail. "I'm not a kid anymore, Atticus. I know what I like, and I know I can satisfy any man's desires. I'm a pro in bed. I just like fucking."

"Is that all you really want? Just to fuck yourself silly with every man that crosses your path? Is that all that interests you? I don't buy it. You wouldn't be on this trip if that were the case."

"That's what men want from me, so why not give it to them?"

"Because you don't strike me as being just a sex-starved girl. I think that you don't believe that anyone can appreciate you for who you really are, so you use your body as the answer for any situation. But I see a beautiful person behind the beautiful body."

Darlene was gnawing on her thumb with a blank stare on her face. "This is all that anyone's ever wanted from me, Atticus." She cupped her breasts through the bathrobe. "Ever since I was seven years old, Atticus, I've had men poking at me, feeling me up, and screwing me. I never wanted any of that!"

"It's called child abuse, Darlene."

"Yeah, well, call it what you want. It's all I've ever known. I even have women sticking their hands up my skirt or grabbing my boobs." Tears began to roll down her cheeks. "My mother never cared. I tried to tell her that the judges at all those beauty contests forced me to suck their dicks if I wanted first prize. She was drunk half the time and only wanted those trophies up on my wall. She didn't care what I had to do to get them. I was her money machine." She paused and rubbed her shoulders. "I paid for this trip, Atticus, with my money. I just had to get away."

I remembered what Barbara had told me the first day of the trip regarding Darlene's beauty contest marathon and was sickened once again by this barbaric practice. I searched for something to say to her, something positive.

"What plans do you have for when you get back to Atlanta, Darlene?"

"My dad wants me to model for him. Did I tell you that he's the proud owner of one of the sleaziest biker magazines in Georgia?"

"No, you didn't."

"Well, now you know. I wouldn't be surprised if he tried to get in the sack with me too. I haven't heard from him in years, and then a photo of me in a bathing suit was published in an auto magazine last month because I had modeled at a carwash show. That's when he called me, telling me I had what it takes to pose for him. Thanks, Dad, you really know how to make me feel important. What a prick!"

I didn't want to dwell on this either and changed the subject.

"Didn't you write in your student bio that you wanted to get into the fashion and beauty products industry? You certainly have a good understanding of the field. Have you ever thought about getting into a sales or promotional position for a big-name brand?"

Darlene didn't reply at once. There she was, practically nude, on my bed, with a body that the majority of men only see in their wildest fantasies, and all I could feel was sorrow for this fragile soul imprisoned in an X-rated body.

Finally, she spoke, "Yeah, I guess I'd like that. I'm good at beauty products, and I know what's good and what's trash for your hair and skin."

"You also wrote in your bio that you were going to a community college…was it Westwood?" Darlene flashed me a smile through the tears.

"You remembered that?"

"Let's say I have a good memory at times. More importantly, and I'm not promising anything here, Darlene, but I know some important people in the fashion business in New York, L.A., and Miami. Let's keep in touch when you're back. I'm going to make a few calls and see if I can get you to meet some of these people for a future position with a fashion accessories company. How's that?"

Darlene's eyes widened. "Would you do that for me, Atticus, I mean, for nothing? Can't I at least satisfy you tonight?" She began to disrobe once again.

"No, no. That's not necessary. And please, Darlene, do me a favor—try not to use your body as a vending machine.

You don't need to sell yourself for a favor. You've really got too much going for you."

She bit her lower lip. "You're not just saying that?"

"No, Darlene, I'm not. I know you'll go far. You just have to believe in yourself, what's in your head and what's in your heart. Let your body *follow* these instead of it *leading* them."

At this point, Darlene threw herself on me, hugging me with gusto. The robe had slid down her back, and my arms were around her bare back. Her skin was velvety smooth, and her breasts were pressing against my chest. *Good Lord, someone please shove a bag of ice between my legs*, I thought.

"Nobody has ever talked to me like this, especially no man I've ever known. You make me feel good about myself. Thank you. Can I give you a kiss?"

"Lips closed?"

Darlene giggled for the first time. "Lips closed, promise." She planted her mouth on mine and smacked her lips. She then rested her forehead on my shoulder.

"Darlene, what happened with Giacomo?" I asked.

"Oh, he's okay. Just really shy, which I think is kind of cute."

"So he hasn't tried to put his hands all over you?"

"No, he hasn't even tried to kiss me yet, which is really weird."

"Well, you see, that goes to show you that not all men consider you as just an object." Darlene looked thoughtful.

"Yeah, maybe you're right. There really is a guy, or *two*, out there who doesn't only think about getting me between the sheets. That's a nice feeling." She gave me a wink and then started to giggle.

"Something struck your funny bone?"

"Oh, I'm sorry." The giggling continued. "It just crossed my mind that there's a second guy right in this hotel who could care less about jumping between the sheets with me."

I raised an eyebrow.

"I mean Wayne," she explained. "Oh, don't get me wrong. I mean, I actually like him even if we do have our moments. He's usually real nice to me, but he doesn't like sex with girls."

"Well, Darlene, just because a guy doesn't want to go to bed with you doesn't automatically mean he's interested in men, does it?" But even I was having a hard time believing my own words.

"I didn't say he was gay. I just think he prefers hanging out with guys. Look at the way he's always all over Bishop."

"Okay, that's enough about Wayne now. I want you to tie up that bathrobe and get back to your room. By the way, didn't Mary see you jumping ship?"

"Nah, she was out like a light. If she wakes up, I'll just tell her that I needed to stretch my legs a bit."

"In your bathrobe?"

"This covers so much more than what I put on during the day."

"Good point. Now shoo!"

"You're really super, Atticus. I really mean it. I would've liked to make love to you, but now I think I like it even better that we didn't." She picked up her black pumps from the floor and darted out of the room.

I closed the door behind her. Standing there with my back firmly planted against the hard wood surface, I let out a sigh of relief. I knew I had done the right thing not giving in to carnal temptation. Darlene's last comment proved that it was the right choice.

Did I disappoint you, Derek? Didn't think that I'd be strong enough, right? Thought you had another video clip for your collection? Well, up yours, my friend.

"Atticus, let me in…"

What? Was Darlene back? I opened the door a crack, and it was again instantaneously pushed forcibly back in my direction with another bathrobe-clad individual walking straight into the room. This robe, however, was a dark color, and Barbara's Shalimar scent left a distinctive trail. She turned to look at me, opened her robe, and threw it on the floor, exposing her full curves. This was becoming an exceptionally pleasant routine.

"Okay, Mr. Winterle, I don't know who you were just speaking to now, and I don't know what Darlene was doing in your room with just a bathrobe on. What I do know is that I'm feeling much better, and more importantly, I'm horny as hell, and I want you to do something about it—*immediately*."

She certainly didn't have to explain herself twice. I pulled off my underwear and T-shirt in no time, allowing the overwhelming sexual urge I had put shackles on while with Darlene to be unlocked with Barbara. Nothing was going to stop me now, and once again, I knew that this was the right choice.

Half an hour later, Barbara was half-laughing and half-crying and catching her breath in between.

"Oh my God, Atticus, stop, please stop!" she begged. I had had two potent orgasms and was still the proud owner of a worthwhile erection. Not even a Viagra could accomplish this.

"Next time Darlene comes to your room, call me as soon as she leaves. That was as good as it can possibly get!"

We were both drenched in perspiration and wiped our faces with the bedsheet. I lay on my back, enjoying the pleasantly enervated feeling that follows a very energetic session of lovemaking. Barbara turned on her side and put her leg over mine. She looked at me seriously, and I knew what was coming.

"Go ahead, Barbara, ask."

"I will. Why was Darlene in your room at two in the morning with nothing on but a bathrobe and a pair of stiletto heels? I don't think it takes a rocket scientist to figure it out, but I would like to hear it from you."

"How do you know that she didn't have anything under that bathrobe?" Barbara raised her eyebrows.

"Stupid question, I take it back." I proceeded to tell Barbara everything that had transpired, and all that had not, with Darlene.

"Wait a minute, you are confirming that Darlene, totally naked except a bikini bottom and a pair of black pumps, was trying to have sex with you and you *didn't* give in?"

"I did not," I said, making it sound much easier than what it really was.

"I admire you, Atticus. I knew that sooner or later, Darlene was going to make a move on you, and I wasn't completely certain that you would be able to ward her off. In fact, I don't know of any man who wouldn't have taken her up on her offer, starting with my husband. And to be completely honest with you, if my husband had brought home a body like Darlene's at one of our orgy nights, I think I would have enjoyed experimenting with it."

It was my turn to look at Barbara with raised eyebrows.

"Did that surprise you, Atticus? It shouldn't. Don't get me wrong, I wouldn't touch a hair on Darlene's head. She's been my student. That's a relationship that I honor and respect." Barbara moved on from that topic. "Do you think that you can really give her a hand in finding a job? I'm afraid she's going to end up in porn if she doesn't get a helping hand."

But I wasn't listening anymore. An image of Darlene, naked and kissing Barbara passionately, had involuntarily formed in my visual cortex. I took Barbara's hand and led it between my legs.

"Oh, Atticus, not again!"

CHAPTER 43

Ringing, distant ringing.

"Hmm?"

I wasn't awake. But I wasn't asleep. *Ring, ring, ring.*

"*Atticus*, it's the phone."

I lifted my head a few inches and began to piece reality together. Barbara was in my bed, and we had been fast asleep, and the phone was most definitely ringing.

What time was it? I reached over and grabbed the receiver.

"*Si*, hello?"

"Signor Atticus, it's Giovanni, I am sorry..." There was another voice in the background—loud, angry, threatening.

"Giovanni, what's going on?"

"Can you come down immediately? There is an extremely rude young man here, and he is disturbing one of your students." Giovanni maintained an icy calm.

"*Eh, stronzo! Con chi parli?!*"

"Immediately, Mr. Atticus, please..."

"*Metti giù vecchio rincoglionito!*"

"I'm coming, Giovanni." The phone went dead. My pants and shirt were already on at the speed of light, and I was heading for the door.

"Atticus, what's wrong?"

"I don't know yet. It was Giovanni at the front desk. He's dealing with a very unpleasant individual and one of our girls is being bothered."

"One of our *girls?*"

I was already out the door and dashing down the hall toward the stairs. The ugly words the stranger had pronounced, one of my girls hassled, Giovanni's pleading, and the abrupt end to our phone call had my adrenalin pumping. I took the stairs three at a time. As I reached the lobby, I could hear someone cursing and threatening Giovanni and a girl sobbing.

I was on the ground floor and rounded the corner to the lobby with my fists clenched. The sight in front of me immediately put me in a fury.

Darlene was slumped half on the sofa and half on the floor, her hair disheveled and her right cheek aflame. Was that a drop of blood on her lip? My own blood was already past the boiling point. Giovanni was pinned up against the wall by a thin but well-built young man, who was filling the room with all kinds of vulgar epitaphs and insults.

And there it went.

That *snap.*

In the back of my head.

Snap! It had happened on two previous occasions, and the results had not been good. On one occasion, it had gotten me in trouble with the law for the use of excessive force. But that didn't stop me now.

I darted over to the man holding Giovanni against the wall. I grabbed his ears, pulling it outward and downward with a great amount of force. He came back like the puppet I had made him into, and I dug my knee into the small of his back, then twisted him face-first into the floor with my 210 pounds on top of him.

"*Ma chi cazzo sei?! Che vuoi?! Lasciami!*" His squealing just made me even more enraged. I released his right ear and savagely pulled his arm behind his back. A little more pressure, and he would have a dislocated shoulder or a broken arm. "*Stai zitto, stronzo,*" I snarled, "*o ti spezzo il braccio!*"

The asshole fell silent as I had ordered, not doubting I would break his arm as I had threatened.

"Giovanni, are you all right?" I said, still speaking Italian.

"Yes, yes. I'm fine." Giovanni's hair was tousled, and the skin under his neck was red from this punk's chokehold.

"Darlene? *Darlene!*"

"I'm okay." She pulled herself back up on the couch, rubbing her sore mouth with her fingers.

I turned my attention back to the creep below me.

"Listen to me carefully, you piece of shit. You and I are going outside, and you're going to tell me what you did to my friends here, or I will kick your balls up your fucking throat!" I was rather surprised and rather proud of my command of Italian curse words.

I grabbed him from the back of the shirt and pulled him up keeping his right arm pinned behind his back.

"*Mi fai male! Cazzo! Che stronzo!*"

I ignored his insults. I could easily have inflicted major damage, and he knew it.

As I pushed him through the opened glass doors, I caught a glance of Barbara who was leading Darlene out of the lobby. She had followed me, thank goodness. She would know what to do.

It must have been well after three in the morning, and the street was deserted. I kept tight hold of my prisoner, pushed him down the three steps, then slammed him face-first against the wall of the building in front of us. If his nose didn't get broken, it was his lucky day.

"*Il mio naso! Cazzo! Il mio naso!*" Yes, tell me about your nose.

"If you don't lower your voice," I spoke very matter-of-factly, "I'm going to break one of your ribs and then maybe one of your legs." He immediately piped down.

"First question. Who are you!?" Unfortunately, I already knew the answer to this question.

"*Sono…sono Giacomo—*"

"The Giacomo I met a few nights ago at the Trevi Fountain?"

"*Che cazzo ne so io?*"

He didn't remember, but I did. Darlene had told Barbara and me that he was a graduate student. At the University of Florence or Rome? Was it in *law*? Well, that was a joke. I pushed his head harder against the wall.

"That wasn't the answer I wanted."

"*Okay, okay, si, si, ero io. Che male, fanculo!*" Okay, so at least he fessed up. *Fanculo* is another one of those slang expressions that Italians employ in a variety of ways. The literal meaning is "taken in the ass" or, more explicitly, "fucked in the ass." This was definitely Giacomo's current state of affairs.

"And what exactly were you doing in there, Giacomo? Beating up an elderly man and slapping around a young lady! Is that how you get your kicks!? Do you know that they could both charge you with assault!? You see those round devices there at the entrance and on the ceiling in the lobby!?" I turned his head by jerking his hair. "Those are closed-circuit video cameras, you dickhead. I just need to make one phone call to some police buddies of mine, and your ass is grass. Is *that* what you want!?"

"*Cazzo no!*"

That word *cazzo*…you just couldn't get away from it.

"Then tell me what happened. If I think you're lying, I'm going to call the cops."

Giacomo started by telling me that he had seen Darlene that afternoon when she had returned to the hotel. He had told her that he was going to wait for her at the Trevi Fountain that evening—even until very late if necessary. He waited and waited, but she didn't show. Darlene had flirted with him that afternoon and led him to believe that there would be some "action" that night. I eased up on his arm, letting him turn sideways, but still kept him pressed firmly against the wall.

"What were you planning to do, stay out here all night?" Giacomo wiped his swollen nose with the sleeve of his wrinkled shirt.

"I've never had a woman with a body like that take any interest in me. This was a one-in-a-million chance."

"So she doesn't show. Then what happened?"

"I wait until two o'clock, then I come to the hotel and start walking up and down. I am still hoping that she will show up. I was about to leave, but then I see in the lobby, talking to the hotel guy."

"She saw you?"

"Yes. Because she says something to the hotel guy, but he looks at me as if I am a piece of shit."

"I'd say he was absolutely right." I shoved him against the wall again to remind him that I was light years from being civil with him. "Then what? You went in?"

"Yes, why wouldn't I?"

"So now you're in the hotel. Next thing I get a call from the hotel guy, and now here we are, and I'm still deciding whether you don't need a broken arm or not." Giacomo drew in a nervous breath. I was still angry, but that snapping sound in my head had subsided. Giacomo didn't know how lucky he was.

"We were sitting on the couch," he said, "and she got, you know, friendly. She started teasing when the old man left the desk to go in the back."

"Teasing?"

"Opening her legs, lifting her T-shirt, letting me put my hand in her *figa* then pushing it back. This is not a nice thing to do to a man, *sì*?"

Figa is an eloquent Italian word meaning "pussy" or "cunt." It comes from the Latin *ficus* or "fig tree." If you take a fresh fig and cut it down the middle and spread the halves open, it resembles a vagina. The ancient Romans, obviously, used to eat a lot of figs.

"And then what, Giacomo? What made you start beating up on Darlene and a man who could be your grandfather?!"

"She just stopped!" he said, his tone both outraged and hurt. "I mean, just like that! She covered herself up and said that I had seen enough. She told me I was a little boy and that she only fucked with older men. I could not see straight after that. I lost my mind, and I roughed her up. The hotel man tried to pull me off her and said he was going to call the police. I don't remember anything else until you came."

I stood there a moment, replaying everything that Giacomo had told me in my head.

"Tell me the truth, Giacomo, all that about being a grad student at the University of Florence, that's all bullshit, right?"

Giacomo lowered his head and started kicking the ground with the point of his shoe. Body language. It's amazing stuff.

"I am not a graduate student. I've just finished high school."

"How old are you?"

"Eighteen."

I let go his arm. He stepped back, rubbing it. His nose was swollen, and his cheek scraped from where I had pushed him against the wall.

"Get out of here, Giacomo. I don't want to see your face around here ever again. Understand?"

He nodded but didn't take off running as I had expected. He just stood there behind me and didn't budge.

"I would like to apologize to the hotel guy," he said.

"I will tell him. You've already caused enough trouble; you have no idea—" I cut myself off. "Go, before I change my mind about calling the police." I was suffocating my explosive frustration.

Giacomo hung his head and headed down Via dei Lucchesi in the direction of the Trevi Fountain. I sat down on the curb, thinking. After about ten minutes. I went back into the hotel.

Giovanni was back at the desk and, save for the red marks on his neck, looked his usual urbane self. He thanked me for coming down so quickly to take of the "overzealous young man," as he put it, and I told him that he had wanted to apologize, but I had sent him on his way.

"I see," he said, but I couldn't tell if Giovanni understood why the young man wanted to apologize or why I sent him on his way without letting him.

But as I headed toward the stairs, Giovanni launched one of his Latin proverbs at me: "*Exitus acta probat.* Good night, Signor Atticus." Telling me that the "result validates the deeds." He was letting me know that my actions were appropriate. I wasn't so sure anymore.

When I arrived in my room, I found Barbara still there, as I had hoped. She told me that Darlene was in bed and that, other than a sore cheek and a small cut on her lower lip, she was fine, at least physically.

I then filled her in on all that had happened.

"He didn't even run when I let him go. He wanted to come inside and apologize to Giovanni. But I told him to clear out."

"Maybe you should have let him."

"Not a chance in hell!" I burst out. "Damn it! I had just come from telling Darlene that not all men were only after her body. I actually used Giacomo as the example, who up until an hour ago, according to Darlene herself, had acted like a true gentleman. She left my room feeling good about this, feeling appreciated for more than just her boobs, and then this guy ruins everything! But you want to know the worst part of all this? I can't really blame him for his reaction."

Barbara looked at me inquiringly.

"He's an eighteen-year-old, hormone-driven young man in a hotel lobby with a flirtatious Playboy centerfold that suddenly throws up a stop sign saying that the game is over before it even started. That must have been like trying to stop a buffalo stampede with a white flag. I am not condoning his getting violent with Darlene, let alone Giovanni, but her behavior was the catalyst."

We sat there and just looked at each other.

"Why did she do that, Barbara? Why did she go downstairs in the first place? We talked a lot, right here, in this room. I thought I had gotten through to her."

"Atticus, listen, you can't expect to change a teenage girl in, what, a couple of hours? Darlene has grown up in a warped environment, been exposed to unhealthy sexual encounters at a very young age and hasn't had any guidance whatsoever regarding her body and self-esteem. I don't think that what you told her went over her head. I don't, but it's probably the first time she's ever heard something like that. Do you understand?"

I shook my head. "I'm trying to."

"She's still a kid, unfortunately packaged in a porn star's body. We can only hope that she'll make some right choices when she gets back home."

There was that word again—*choices*.

"You should have seen her, Barbara, sitting right here on this bed, crying so much that her mascara had run down her face. She was half-naked, but she just looked just like a broken doll."

"That's what I think we women are a good deal of the time, Atticus. Yes, we put on the expensive makeup, we rejoice putting on our Victoria's Secret panties, when we slip on those Jimmy Choo stiletto heels, pump up the old cleavage with push-up bras, paint those nails Chanel red, make our asses as round as we can, Botox those wrinkles, and then we go out to conquer the *man's* world. But take all of this away, put us alone in front of the bathroom mirror early in the morning after a shower, naked, with no makeup, and we return to what we are most of the time—fragile dolls in desperate need of a warm, innocent hug."

"I bet you wouldn't say that at a N.O.W convention."

"Oh, they're the worst. The majority of diehard feminists that I've met are only into pain and supremacy games with their sex partners who, for the most part, are other women. That's the way they cover their fragility and insecurity. I don't think they have any understanding of what it really means to be feminine."

"Well, Mrs. Cornwall, I believe you have an extremely good understanding of what it means to be a *woman*."

"Damn right, Mr. Winterle."

I leaned over and kissed her twice.

"I'm so tired," she said. "Can I cuddle up next to you and shut my eyes for a few hours?"

"Please do. Does the light bother you?"

"Won't...bother....me..." Barbara attempted to articulate while yawning with relish. She lay down, closed her eyes, and fell asleep almost at once.

I reached across the bedside table and grabbed hold of the stack of papers and books that had been leaning precariously to one side. I propped myself up against the headboard as gently as I could so as to not wake Barbara. Thumbing through the bios I had already looked at, I came to Raymond's.

It was of no surprise that he had put politics and history as his favorite subjects. His hobbies were tennis, travel, and music. For favorite foods, he listed several Jewish dishes that I was not familiar with: *charoset, holishkes,* and *lokshen kugel.* Under "Career Plans," he had written a substantial amount that confirmed all that John had told me on Day One of our trip. He closed that section by writing that the State of Israel was surrounded by mortal enemies and that everything had to be done, at whatever cost, to preserve it and strengthen it. No doubt he included violence and war as necessary methods to achieve this goal. I would be spending a good portion of the day with Raymond in a few hours. This was certainly going to be the main topic of our conversation.

Other than his political ambitions, I learned that he had lost a sister of two years when he was seven. He did not mention how. His parents were still married to one another, and even though he spoke lovingly enough about his mother, he wrote not a single word about his father. Interesting.

I looked over at the clock. It was almost four thirty. I would have to be up no later than seven, but I wasn't tired. Evelyn's bio was next in the pile. This I had to see.

I thumbed through the three stapled pages of the document and found very little content. Other than essential information such as name, place of birth, date of birth, address, etc., Evelyn had left everything blank. Everything. Definitely a hard nut to crack.

James came right after. I was expecting the same blank pages on his bio, but to my surprise, he had a lot to say about himself. Under "Favorite Subjects," he wrote music and art, especially Van Gogh, Rothko, and Basquiat. Music was a given, but art surprised me. I wondered about James's choice of favorite artists. Van Gogh was understandable for his legendary paintings and troubled, much-publicized personal life. Rothko was a question mark. I didn't care for abstract expressionism and therefore never studied up on his work. Basquiat I hardly knew at all, other than the fact that Andy Warhol had helped him in his career. One of his paintings came to my mind's eye, but I didn't remember the title. I did recall that he had died at a very young age by suicide.

Suicide…

Rothko…*suicide.*

Van Gogh…*suicide.*

Both of these artists had killed themselves. And I was pretty sure that Basquiat had died quite young, in his late twenties, from a heroin overdose. A sudden chill ran down my spine. These past few days I had been fighting the notion brewing inside of me that James was truly capable of committing this irreversible act. Reading this short list of artists was like a blow to the stomach. I read on.

James had not written anything under "Favorite Food" or "Sports," but under "Music," he had written a list of bands and singers. I knew most, but not all. There was nothing under "Career Plans" nor did he mention his parents. I knew he was an only child. A very troubled only child.

Under "Why this Trip?" James had written the following:

Get away from Atlanta.

Get away from people I can't stand.

Get away from all the mind games.

See some awesome art.

So there was one positive note there—an interest in seeing the millennia-old artworks that Rome had to offer. Along with his passion for music, art was a very noble and time-absorbing pastime. Hopefully, these two subject matters would turn out to be his lifelines.

I counted the remaining bios—eight in all. But I needed to get some sleep. I put the papers back on the table and turned off the light. I then curled up gently against Barbara's body. Her back was facing me, and her legs were pulled up in a fetal position. She was sleeping quite soundly, snoring a little. I would keep that observation to myself —women, in my experience, always became irate when you told them that, yes, they do snore. It isn't just a man's thing.

Barbara's soft skin and the warmness between her legs were calling millions of sperm to the battlefront. But I decided not to disturb her blissful rest. Instead, I would think about skinny-dipping in a Norwegian fjord in mid-January.

CHAPTER 44

The alarm rang reliably at 7:05 am. I felt as if I had just closed my eyes. I turned to find Barbara gone and a slip of paper on her pillow. Rubbing the sleep out of my eyes, I attempted to focus on what she had written:

My dear Atticus,

Hated to leave you but didn't want to risk being seen going back to my room. I was looking at you sleeping so peacefully and thought to myself how lucky I was to have met you and how absolutely spellbinding this trip has been so far. Rome is everything you said it was, and you have made it that much more special. You have managed to strip away a great deal of the pain that I had pent up inside me for so many years. I shall never be able to thank you enough for that. We still have three magical days and nights ahead of us! I am going to take it all in one minute at a time.

Love you, B.

I read Barbara's words a few times over. She had most certainly turned out to be an unexpected and delightful surprise on this trip. She was intelligent, witty, beautiful, and an electrifying bedmate. But I was certain of one thing: I was not in love with her, nor was she with me—not in the true meaning of the word. I was also very much aware that once these next three days were over, the chances of us seeing each other again were slim to none. Our meeting here—enjoying the time spent in each other's company, the lovemaking, the sharing of our experiences, our secrets, all under a Roman sky—was a hiatus from our everyday lives, responsibilities, and routines. I was certain that Barbara felt the same way. She was living this moment to the fullest, as was I, with the awareness that moments pass quickly. Carpe diem.

I glanced at the clock. It was already 7:35 am.

I folded Barbara's note and put it between the pages of my Moleskine notebook. I then quickly shaved and showered, got dressed, and made my way down to the breakfast area.

When I entered the restaurant, I was amazed to see everyone in the group sitting down or in line queuing for food. Not only that, but the tables had also been positioned into a large square so that everyone was facing each other or at a right angle to one another.

Mark noticed my goggling at the seating arrangements. "The waiters said we could do some interior decorating," he explained.

"Well, compliments for the initiative," I replied.

The other students noticed me and started calling out:

"Get some food, Atticus, and then join us."

"Yeah, go on, Atticus."

"Try the mushroom omelet. It's awesome!"

"And grab a few of those raspberry pastries."

"Look around, take your time, there's a lot to choose from today."

Why was everyone so insistent that I get something to eat? Something was up. Everyone was in the breakfast area for the first time in six days, even James, Evelyn, and Darlene (who looked fine even if she had piled on the lipstick on her lower lip.)

I looked over at Cynthia, John, and Barbara, who were all grinning like the Cheshire cat in *Alice in Wonderland*. Weird.

As I was spooning up some scrambled eggs onto my plate, it suddenly dawned on me that there was something else out of the norm. Practically all the students had pens and either notebooks or a piece a paper in front of them. *Now what was that all about?* I wondered.

Michelle came up behind me as I was between the croissants and the cereal bowls. "Morning, Atticus, did you sleep well?"

"Not much, actually, but I'm fine. And you?"

Michelle leaned closer to me. "I managed to get a few more photos, Atticus. This is recent. She wrote it before going to bed last night. I emailed them to you."

"And?"

"I think we can relax a bit. Something has changed, for the better, I think. Let me know what you think."

"Okay, Michelle, thanks. I will." She turned to walk off, and I said, "Oh, one more thing." She turned back, looking at me with wide eyes. "Um, is something going on here that I should be aware of?"

"No. I mean, we're working on our papers to submit back when we get back to Atlanta. Don't think you need to be aware of that." She gave me a big smile, then turned to go back to the table.

Well, that could explain it, I thought. I had read about that assignment when I was on the plane—a fifteen-page report they had to do. I had completely forgotten about it. I filled my glass with grapefruit juice and went to join the others.

Wayne reached over and pulled the chair out for me. "Here you go, Atticus."

"Thanks," I said, sitting down.

"What time is Massimo coming to pick us up, Atticus?" asked Jeremy. He had already been informed of the time the night before, but he was clearly anxious to get going.

"He said he'd be here at about ten thirty."

"Good, good. Did you know that *Once Upon a Time in America* and *The Passion of Christ* were filmed at this place we're going to today?"

"No, I didn't. I know that *Ben Hur* was produced there, but that was well before your time."

"Who hasn't seen *Ben Hur*, Atticus?" Mary piped out. "They've been repeating it every year around Christmas since the beginning of time."

"Really?"

"Not only *Ben Hur*, Atticus," Jeremy said, "but also *Cleopatra—*"

"What! *Cleopatra*?" Darlene practically shouted from across the tables. "That's a good enough reason to torch the place to the ground."

She got a few curious looks, but nobody responded. I recalled that Darlene's mother made her watch *Cleopatra* endlessly when she was a child.

"Are you going with us to this movie studio, Atticus?" Mark asked.

"No, unfortunately not. I have a few things I have to catch up on, as well as some paperwork. By the way, who *is* going? Can someone jot down the names for me? I see you all have paper and pens with you…"

Everyone looked on edge as I mentioned their writing materials. *What was really going on?* I asked myself.

"I'll take down names, Atticus," Sabrina offered.

"Thanks," I replied.

She quickly wrote out the list and handed it to me. I scanned it while I was eating. Other than the students, John was also going and, to my surprise, Barbara as well. A nanosecond of jealousy swept through me. Barbara saw my reaction, and I saw her grin at my reaction. Women can read men like books.

Everybody got up, most of them grabbing some fruit and water bottles on their way out. I still had to finish what was on my plate, but I had lost my appetite.

"What's wrong, Mr. Winterle? Are the eggs not cooked to your satisfaction?" Barbara had snuck up behind me.

"I was wondering if *I* am cooked to your satisfaction?" I said, attempting a joke but unable to keep the edge out of my tone.

"Do I detect a note of jealousy?" Barbara said, watching me with wide eyes.

"Are we still heading out later, Atticus?"

Barbara and I both jumped. Where the hell had Raymond come from?

"Sorry, didn't mean to give you a scare," he said.

"That's okay, Raymond," I said hastily. "Let's meet in the lobby at about eleven fifteen, okay?"

"Good. See you then. Are you coming with us, Mrs. Cornwall?"

"No, Raymond. I'm going to go see what an Italian movie studio looks like. But thanks for asking."

"Enjoy then. See you soon, Atticus." He turned and walked out of the restaurant. As I turned back to Barbara, I caught sight of Darlene who was filling a glass with fruit juice from the dispenser. I called her over. That was a mistake.

"Are you okay?" I asked. "Any pain from where he hit you?"

"No. It's happened to me before. I can handle it." Darlene was as cold as ice. I felt the hairs go up behind my neck. She glanced at Barbara, who was still standing very close to me.

"I guess your theory about men was wrong after all, Atticus." Darlene's gaze was a mixture of detachment and total apathy. She then bent down so that she could be eye to eye with me. Our noses were almost touching. "If you ever get tired of your MILF here, remember that I'm ready, willing, and very, very able."

"Darlene!" snapped Barbara.

"Take it as a compliment, Mrs. Cornwall. If the two of you want to try a threesome, I'm game."

"That's enough!" Barbara was enraged.

Darlene just turned and walked away, leaving us alone in the restaurant. Barbara was about to head after her, but I grabbed her arm.

"Let her go. I should've expected this. I let her down. I gave her false hope."

"That was unfair, Atticus, and plain rude. After all you did to protect her last night. And to call me a MILF!"

"Yes, um, what exactly is a MILF, Barbara?"

She looked at me, not sure if I was asking for information or teasing her. I just sat there, puzzled. Then Barbara started to laugh, uncontrollably. I had obviously lost something in translation because I didn't see what was so funny. The more I scrunched up my eyebrows, the more hilarity I generated. I started drumming my fingers on the table, waiting for this tidal wave of merriment to pass.

"You really don't know what a MILF is?"

"Obviously not."

That started round two of the hysterics. I was getting annoyed.

"Well, I have to go," I said.

"No…wait, no…" Barbara put her hands over her mouth. Her laughter was turning into full-fledged grunts.

"I don't have all day, Barbara."

"Mothers I'd like to—and do I really have to say what the *F* stands for, Atticus?"

"Excuse me?" I really had not made the connection.

"Mothers I'd like to *fuck*." She placed special emphasis on the last word. "Do I have to repeat it?"

The only reasons why my eyes did not pop out of my head is because there is a cord of some sort that holds them in place.

"She called you *that?*"

"Why do you think I wanted to go after her?"

"You should have given her a sound slap across the face."

"I was going to. Somebody stopped me."

I shook my head. "I can't believe she called you that."

"But, Atticus, if you think about it, that's what I am, isn't it? I guess the positive side of being labeled a MILF is that my body has weathered well. I am certainly happy that you seem to like it…"

"'Like it' is a gross understatement, but Darlene went well over the line this time. Who the hell does she think she is, anyway? She led Giacomo on, and now she's playing Little Miss Offended'? Somebody should tell her that when you play stupid games, you win stupid prizes!"

"Even so, she feels betrayed, and she's hurting inside all over again. And she wants to compete with me because I'm sleeping with the man who gave her some comfort."

I changed subjects abruptly; "Michelle sent me a few more pages of the diary."

"And?"

"I haven't read them yet. She emailed the images. But I'll let you know."

"What about James? I saw that he's not coming with us to the movie studios."

"We can't watch his every move. We just have to hope for the best."

Barbara glanced at her watch. "Oh, goodness, I have to get back to my room. Must make myself pretty for John."

I reached over to slap her bottom as she slipped away, giggling like a schoolgirl.

I was alone now. It wasn't even ten yet, so I had some time before Massimo arrived. I asked a waiter to bring me an espresso.

I opened my Moleskine notebook and looked at the last entries I had made on each student a few days back. An update was necessary:

1. Evelyn: No signs of real trouble so far.

2. Vanessa: Holding up pretty well after overdose. Sabrina is keeping an eye on her. Has promised me that she will check out rehab when she gets back home.

3. James: Don't know what to expect. Out on his own almost all day yesterday. Where to? I don't know where he's going today. I can't monitor him 24/7. Get a hold of him this morning if possible. Find out his plans.

4. Darlene: No comment. All wrong with her and Giacomo. Don't know if I should say or do anything else. At least now I know what a "MILF" is.

5. Mark: No more binges so far. Hoping for the best these next 3 days.

6. Wayne + Bishop + Michelle: powwow tomorrow night.

7. Cynthia: Meeting tomorrow. Will I finally see the light regarding this woman?

8. Raymond: Today's the day. Should be an interesting conversation.

9. Anthony: I had practically written him off. A lying, pathetically insecure kid. But there's another side to him—get him into what he likes (guns), and he becomes another person. Almost a split personality. I should remind myself of my miserable teenage years and try to help this kid out.

10. Barbara: Actions speak louder than words.

11. John: I'd like to have another limoncello with him.

12. Jeremy: Happy for him today. Cinecittà. He'll love it.

13. Mary: A good kid. Her opera knowledge is phenomenal.

14. Sabrina: St. Rita was certainly a plus. Pleased to see that she came away from that one-on-one so

positively impressed. I took a big chance. Sabrina could have labeled me an oddball, religious zealot.

15. *Remember: How many restaurant vouchers left, any other paperwork to fill out? Check in with Marco. Don't forget: check emails for job follow up.*

That was about it. What time was it? Ten twenty. Perfect.

As I made my way out of the restaurant area, I caught sight of Sabrina standing near the lobby desk.

"Any plans for the day, Sabrina?" I said, going up to her.

"Yeah. I've got a few things I need to do today. See you later and wish me luck!" She was out through the glass doors of the hotel before I could ask any questions. *Wish me luck… things I need to do? Okay.*

As I turned to go up the stairs, Cynthia appeared.

"Atticus, just the person I needed. Could you point me in the right direction to St. Peter's?"

"Sure, but it's quite a walk from here."

"That's just fine. Look at what a beautiful day it is!"

Ludovica had stepped out of the back office, and I asked for a felt marker. I drew a line on Cynthia's map of Rome from the hotel to the Vatican.

"That seems pretty easy. I may be at dinner tonight or I may not. I'm going to live every moment this day has to offer. And don't forget, you promised a tour of the forum tomorrow."

"I haven't forgotten. Enjoy yourself."

She also exited through the glass doors.

"Signor Winterle?"

"Yes, Ludovica?"

"I want to thank you for having helped Giovanni last night."

"Oh, he told you about that?"

"No, not really. I don't know what happened exactly, but he told me this morning that you came to his aid and that you were a brave and noble man."

"Well, that may be stretching the truth just a bit."

"Giovanni is not a man of many words, but when he says something about an individual, he's usually right. I know that for a fact."

"You do?"

"Yes. You see, Giovanni is my uncle."

"Really?"

"Yes, this hotel has been in our family for sixty-five years. It opened shortly after the war."

"Compliments to the entire family, past and present. It's a very comfortable and accommodating place to stay. And the location is optimum."

"Thank you, Signor Winterle. You are very kind."

"Ludovica, could you do me one favor?"

"Of course."

"Just call me Atticus, not 'Signor Winterle,' please."

"I'm sorry, but I cannot do that. When I am behind this desk or anywhere in the hotel, guests must be addressed by their last name."

I stood there and gazed at her for a long moment. She was most certainly an enchanting young woman.

Ludovica leaned forward and lowered her voice. "However, that is expected when I am in the hotel, not *outside*." She then retreated silently into the back office. How charming. Was that an indirect invitation of some sort? I was flattered and tickled at the same time. But now I needed to head to my room to pick up my wallet. I rounded the corner that led to the staircase and literally ran into Evelyn.

"Oh! Sorry about. Did I just step on your foot?"

"No worries, Atticus, these are steel-toed boots. I didn't feel a thing."

"Well, that's fortunate. Any plans for today?" I tried to sound disinterested so she wouldn't think I was being nosy.

"Yeah, there's something I really need to do. It's friggin' weird, but I have to do it. I really need to go now, see you."

Need to do? Again? Sabrina "needed" to do something, and now Evelyn "needed" to do something. *What was going on?* I wondered.

I took the stairs to my floor and ran into James coming in the other direction, carrying a notebook of some sort in his hand.

"Hey, what's up?" I asked.

"All's good, Atticus."

I looked more closely at what he was carrying. "That looks like a drawing pad."

"Yeah, sort of. I like sketching things sometimes. It clears my head. Everywhere you go in this city there's something to draw. It's pretty awesome."

"Sounds interesting, James. It's a perfect day for it. Enjoy yourself. I'd like to see some of your work when you get back if that's okay."

"You will," he said and took off.

Well, I was learning something new every day about this group. So James liked to draw. Nobody had mentioned this about him, and he had not brought along his sketch pad on any of our excursions. I was quite curious to see what he would come back with.

When I finally got to my room, I brushed my teeth, grabbed my wallet, and headed back downstairs. It was well after ten thirty.

As I entered the lobby, I saw Massimo talking with Ludovica. He had on a pair of tight denim jeans, ankle-length dress boots, a large Versace belt, a cream-colored button-down shirt with no collar, and, completing his ensemble, a Hermes scarf around his neck. He caught sight of me and stretched out his arms happily.

"Buongiorno, Atticus! What a glorious day to walk around Cinecittà, don't you agree? Where are my boys and girls? We mustn't be late now."

"They'll be here any moment. They're so excited about this, Massimo. It's extremely kind of you to have offered."

"The pleasure is all mine, my dear Atticus. I was talking to my partner last night about this very special group. He is delighted to know that they are such a pleasant surprise from the usually boring and judgmental people I deal with."

"Never a boring moment with this bunch, Massimo."

"Tell me, any new developments?" We were speaking in Italian. Ludovica had disappeared, and there was nobody else in the lobby, so I went ahead and gave Massimo a detailed account of Darlene's visit, although I omitted the aftermath with Giacomo.

"My, my! This is better than one of those 1980 American soap operas. I find it extremely honorable and practically a miracle that you did not succumb to that Aphrodite's offer. That must have required a series of ice-cold showers."

I did not inform Massimo of my immediate post-Darlene sex session with Barbara.

"What about our two boys?" I knew he was referring to Wayne and Bishop.

"We are having a meeting tomorrow night, together with Michelle. I told you that they wanted to let me in on something important."

"Let me know the outcome. If I am correct, and I think I am, I would like to propose something to you. Let's wait and see."

"Fine. I will let you know."

"Good. Ah! Here they are!"

In fact, the majority of the students going with Massimo seemed to come out of the woodwork. The only ones missing were Wayne, Bishop, and Michelle.

"Atticus, my dear fellow, are we complete?"

"No Wayne, no Bishop, and no Michelle," Mary noted.

"Where the hell are they?" Jeremy said.

"Don't worry, I'll track them down," I said. "Nobody else goes wandering off."

I turned and saw Ludovica, who was already on the phone, looking at me and shaking her head. She had called the two rooms. This girl was always one step ahead. I could only think of one other place they could be in the hotel: the restaurant. As soon as I entered, I saw that the situation was not good.

Wayne was holding Michelle up with an arm around her waist. Bishop seemed to be begging her.

He gestured to me as soon as he saw me. "Atticus, please tell Michelle she has to stay in the hotel and rest. She's got one of those headaches again."

"Bishop, stop mothering me," Michelle snapped. "I mean it. I'm going. I won't have this chance again!"

"She's in no condition, Atticus," said Wayne. "We know. We've been through this before."

"Michelle, what's the situation?" I asked.

"It came up all of a sudden. But I can't. I will *not* stay in bed! I'm in Rome, for God's sake! I want to see as much as I possibly can, and I won't let a headache get in my way. I just need these two macho men to help me a bit, again." She attempted a smile, but it was forced.

I looked at Wayne and Bishop.

"We'll always be here when Misha needs us, Atticus, both of us," Wayne said. "She's our princess."

Wayne was as serious as I had ever seen him. These two boys truly worshipped Michelle.

"All right. If the three of you are up to this, I'm not standing in the way. But you better get out to the lobby in a hurry. Massimo is getting worried about the time."

"I'm ready," Michelle said. "Are my two knights in shining armor prepared?"

"Ready, my lady." Wayne bowed.

"Hopefully, it will pass as fast as it cropped up."

I opened the restaurant doors, and the trio walked past me. I followed them into the lobby. Massimo caught sight of the boys and Michelle. Within a fraction of a second, he grasped the situation and avoided making any remarks that would have placed the spotlight on the new arrivals.

"Where the hell were the three of you? We've been—"

Massimo cut Mark off. "Off we go, my friends! It's getting late. Be aware that we shall be experiencing the Roman Metro today. I don't know if that is a positive or a negative, but if it is working properly, it shall get us to our destination quickly. Please take a ticket and do not lose it. Come, come now. We shall be back around five o'clock, Atticus."

He blew me a kiss and joined the group on the narrow sidewalk.

CHAPTER 45

It was close to eleven, so I decided to stay in the lobby until Raymond came down. Ludovica came out of the back room once again and started to type on the desktop Dell. Her lustrous auburn hair was brushed down and fell over her shoulders. She was wearing a peach blouse that was pulling slightly on an accentuated bosom that I had not noticed before. She had either put on one of those push-up bras that many women swear by or I had completely missed these two predominant features. She glanced up and caught me staring directly at them. Her head lowered, and she turned beet red instantaneously.

I had to say something, and fast, to break the tidal wave of embarrassment that had engulfed both of us. I cleared my throat. "If you don't mind me asking, Ludovica, do your parents work here in the hotel?"

"My mother runs the kitchen, Signor Winterle, as well as the housekeeping services."

"That explains why the food is so good here. There is a personal touch back there," I said, indicating the restaurant area. "And I bet that your father is the sommelier…"

The smile on my face rapidly shattered like a window hit by a baseball as I saw Ludovica's expression become pained.

"My father died less than a year ago. A car accident."

Fifty-four years old and still extremely capable of putting my foot in my mouth.

"I am so sorry, Ludovica. That's what I get for saying something inappropriate."

"No, not at all. You were actually very close. My father loved wine, red especially, and he handled all our alcoholic beverage orders. But he was mostly here, in the office, handling the financial side of the business. We had to hire an external company for all our accounting matters when he died."

"May I ask how old he was when he passed?"

"He was sixty-seven."

"Were the two of you close?"

"Very. I was his little girl, even when I turned forty."

Forty?! Not possible. Ludovica didn't look a day over thirty.

"You said when you turned forty…"

"Yes, that was two years ago. I will be forty-two this coming October." This girl must have found the eternal fountain of youth.

The office phone began to ring, and Ludovica excused herself to go answer it. There was still no sign of Raymond, so I took out my cell phone, connected to the hotel Wi-Fi, and checked my email. There was the message from Michelle. I clicked on the attached images and began to read:

May 1, Saturday

I don't know what's going on anymore. My J is ignoring me more and more and just wants to go off on his own. Then Mary doesn't keep her mouth shut, going on and on about me, reading up on those two stupid statues Atticus asked us about… like I give a rat's ass! And GET THIS, Sabrina, yeah, SABRINA, wants to talk to me, alone. I mean, what the fuck is going on????? Van comes up to me right before dinner and tells me that S wants to go out tomorrow for an ice cream, with me…yeah…. you heard that right, with ME!!! She'll probably have a knife up her sleeve to stab me in the back. V says that it's no joke, that S really wants this to go down.I told V that I wouldn't be seen dead with her. And then, get this, I mean really, come on!

> *V comes back to me an hour later and says that S understands.*
> *Understands?!? S said that if I changed my mind, she would*
> *be in front of the Trevi fountain at 11:00 tomorrow. What am*
> *I supposed to do? Part of me wants to go just to see what she*
> *wants, but the other part just wants to see her stand out there*
> *like some fool. This is really tooooo weird! I guess I 'll sleep on it*
> *and figure out what to do tomorrow. What do you want from me,*
> *Sabrina?? What!?!?*

Michelle was right. There certainly was a new development, perhaps a positive one. Why had Sabrina reached out to Evelyn? What was behind this gesture? The hatred between these two girls had been palpable since the day they had arrived in Rome.

But all that would have to wait. Raymond had come around the corner with a kippah on his head and one on his hand. For me, I assumed. "Ready, Atticus?"

"Of course."

We exited the building and took a left down Via di San Vincenzo. Raymond was confidently leading the way.

"I get the impression that you know where you're going," I observed.

"I walked back from the synagogue yesterday. It was fast and easy." Easy—perhaps. Fast—sure, if you're seventeen years old. I was struggling to match his eager pace.

Raymond handed me the kippah. "You don't have to wear this, but I would appreciate it if you did."

"How about I put it on right now?" I suggested.

Raymond looked at me doubtfully, then shrugged.

"Sure, if you want. Here take these." He reached inside of his pocket and handed me some bobby pins. I struggled a bit with my hair and the kippah, but eventually managed to secure it properly.

Raymond nodded his approval. "You look good, Atticus. Like a one hundred percent kosher Jew."

We both chuckled. Raymond took off again, with me lagging a few steps behind.

"So, Raymond, while you're making a marathon man out of me on the streets of Rome, tell me about your plans when you get back to Atlanta."

"Sorry, Atticus, I didn't realize I was walking so fast. You're keeping up, though."

"Yes. But I'll be crawling on all fours soon if we don't slow down."

Raymond began walking at a more sedate pace. "I'm enrolled at the Hebrew University of Jerusalem, and I start at the end of August. I'll be flying to Tel Aviv in July."

I nodded. "Let's backtrack a moment, Raymond, and if any of my questions bother you, just let me know."

"I doubt that'll happen."

I took that to mean he was certain in his convictions. "First of all, why did you go to a non-Jewish high school? I mean, it seems to me that you would have preferred to, how shall I put it—"

"To be with my own kind?"

"Well, yes. I know that may sound awkward and potentially bigoted, but that's not my intent."

"That was actually my own decision. My parents wanted me to attend one of the three Jewish high schools in Atlanta when I was fourteen. I refused. I wanted to mix with the others, be the butt of Jewish jokes, hear all kinds of racist slurs, be poked fun at, and get into more than an occasional fight which, by the way, I almost always won."

"Okay. My next question is, why?"

"To prove to everyone that I wasn't fazed by it. Sure, it hurt me at times, I had my down moments, but honestly, considering our history and all the hatred we have had to put up with for the last three thousand years or so, what I had to deal with was a walk in the park."

"So you endured it just to prove a point? To show that you were better than the others?"

"I don't know if *better* is the right word. Maybe *superior* to all the commonplace and stereotypical remarks that people make every day about Jews."

Raymond wasn't boastful, just matter of fact, in his attitude.

"So you entered Bradford High when you were fourteen?"

"Almost fourteen. I was a year ahead in school. I just turned seventeen in March."

"That's right. Your teachers told me the very first day."

"What else did they say, if I can ask."

"They told me that you were one of the brightest kids in the entire school, Ivy League material. The only other student they mentioned as being close to your academic level is Michelle."

Raymond smiled. "Yeah, Michelle's great. A one and only. Doesn't judge anyone, and I mean *nobody*! Always ready to lend a helping hand and really smart. Humble about it, too. She's going to go real far."

I could tell, not so much by his choice of words as by his warmth, that he was smitten by her.

"I see you have a soft spot for Michelle," I said, with a smile.

Raymond nodded slowly. "Yeah. But she doesn't give me the time of day. I mean, she's nice to me, but she's always around everyone else. I'm excluded from her little circles."

"Are you referring specifically to Wayne, Bishop, and Mark?"

"That's her primo group. She's probably good for all three of those clowns. God knows they need some supervision."

Despite his words, there was no animosity or ill will in Raymond's voice.

We had reached the far-right corner of Piazza Venezia and had the Vittorio Emanuele II Monument in front of us. Raymond didn't stop. Staying to his left, he entered the Via di San Venanzio. From here, there were various ways to get to the synagogue, and I was curious to see which direction Raymond would choose. He picked up the pace once again, but I was right alongside with him.

"Okay then, back to the university in Jerusalem. Any plans while you go to school there? Any idea yet which academic direction you'd like to take?"

"I've known that since I was a kid. Politics first and foremost, with a minor in journalism. I plan to join the Jewish Home party and climb the ranks as fast as I can."

So far, everything Raymond had told me fitted with the information John had given me during our first day together.

"Can you tell me a little more about this Jewish Home party?"

"It's rather small now, sort of a coalition of even smaller political parties that are right of center. I think it has incredible potential. We just need a strong leader who can keep the various factions focused on our objectives." Raymond's eyes were wide with excitement. He was already in Israel.

"And these objectives are…"

"No Palestinian State on the West Bank, maintaining and building more Jewish settlements all around Jerusalem, the protection of the Jewish State and all of its components at all costs."

"Including more wars and violence, if necessary?"

"No question. We will always fight for our right to exist as a state, and we shall eradicate those who want to harm us." Raymond had stopped dead in his tracks. His facial muscles were tense, and he seemed to be gritting his teeth. He stared at me, and it gave me a chill. One day, this young man would kill, with a knife or a gun or by pressing a button on a missile launcher.

"You said that you were also interested in journalism?"

"Political journalism."

"You know, there's a fine line between journalism, which describes the objectives of a political party, and propaganda."

"Yeah, I guess you could say that. As long as what you say and write serves a meaningful purpose, I'm fine with it."

We were now on the Via del Teatro di Marcello. We kept going at a fast clip.

"You want to be involved in journalism, Raymond, but I think that the saying 'The word is mightier than the sword' doesn't convince you very much."

"Epistle to the Hebrews, chapter four, verse twelve. It actually goes, 'For the word of God is living and active, sharper than any two-edged sword, piercing to the division of soul and spirit.'"

"That's very good, Raymond. I'm impressed. What I should have said is, 'The *pen* is mightier than the sword.'"

"Shakespeare."

"What?"

"Yeah, Hamlet, somewhere in the second act. Something about goose quills being more of a threat than those wearing rapiers."

"Remind me what a rapier is. Some kind of weapon, correct?"

"It's a long, pointed sword. Those with the real fancy hilts to protect the hand. I think they were used in the sixteenth and seventeenth centuries."

This kid is a walking encyclopedia, I thought.

Raymond continued, "Do you know that Napoleon was actually quoted as saying that the saber and the mind are the only true powers and that the mind will always vanquish the sword? This from Napoleon, can you believe it?"

All right, now you're showing off.

"Anyway, Atticus, no, I don't."

"You don't…what?" I had lost track for a moment.

"I don't believe that the saying the pen is mightier than the sword is pertinent when speaking about the State of Israel."

"I see."

"We're surrounded by people who want to see us back in the gas chambers and ovens. Sorry, been there, done that. Bring on the F-16s, bring on the Apache helicopters, bring on tanks and ground to air missiles, and blow the proverbial shit out of any our neighboring enemies who continue to harass us, threaten us, and kill us. My uncle was blown up on a bus by a suicide bomber in Tel Aviv. He was just going to see a good friend in the hospital, and he ends up at the morgue in about ten different pieces."

Raymond paused, taking a deep breath.

"I visited him a few times, and I'll never forget those days. He was strong man and lived for the State of Israel. A true patriot. He taught me so much. History, literature, politics. He was a good guy...I really looked up to him and loved him."

What do you say to a young man who has lost a close family member at the hands of a suicide bomber? Sorry to hear that? That's terrible? I can't imagine how you feel? Better to keep quiet.

"My uncle lived in Sur Baher, a neighborhood in south of Jerusalem. There are many Palestinians in that area. Probably some peaceful ones as well, but the majority just want to see us dead. It's so strange. These Palestinians, they speak Hebrew, they could go about their lives as we go about ours, but no, every once in a while, there's a knife attack, a car that rams into a group of Israelis at a bus stop, or a suicide bomber, like the one who killed my uncle and seven other innocent people. And, get this, when one of these Palestinians slashes an old Jew's face into a jigsaw puzzle with a butcher knife, what happens? The Palestinian newspapers praise him as a martyr. Even the Palestinian authorities go out of their way to visit the families of these murderers to honor them and give them money."

"Maybe these Palestinians don't feel that they're being treated as true citizens of Jerusalem?"

"That's their problem. If they don't like what we offer, they can go off to Rafah in the Gaza Strip. We certainly won't miss them."

There was already so much bitterness in this young man.

"You know, I've been to Jerusalem a few times, Raymond."

"You have?" Raymond looked surprised.

"Yes, for work. I had some good distributors in Tel Aviv, and when I would visit them, I would always ask to be taken to Jerusalem. I admit that the tension I felt in the air was like thick molasses. Walls, barbed wire, soldiers, tanks, guns, attack dogs, everywhere. Absolutely everywhere."

"I've spent a few summers in Tel Aviv and Jerusalem. I know what you're talking about, but I don't feel that tension. Instead, I see and appreciate a state which is doing the impossible to keep its citizens safe. At any cost."

This time, I stopped in my tracks.

"Raymond, you're a very intelligent young man. Part of that small group of young people that will probably make a difference in the world of tomorrow. I'm sure you see that all this loathing can't bring anything positive. How can a lasting peace be obtained and how can both sides educate their children not to have all of this hatred in their hearts—this is what you need work on in my opinion."

Raymond gazed at me, his expression combining both scorn and pity.

"What I need to work on for the rest of my life is the well-being of my people and the generations that will follow. Our history has been a plague. We've been hated, ridiculed, made fun of, banished, tortured, and killed for well over two thousand years. But we are still here. And we are still here because we are very good at what we choose to do in any discipline. We must be! We'd be crushed if we let our guard down. This won't happen. It may take even more centuries, but we'll conquer our enemies, and we'll show no mercy."

We had come to the end of the Via del Teatro di Marcello just before it turned into Via Luigi Petroselli. The magnificent Theatre of Marcellus was before us.

"Did you know that Julius Caesar had this thing built, Atticus?"

"No, I didn't."

"Yeah, but he didn't get to see much of it. Brutus saw to that in 44 BC."

Even though there was a glass-encased totem with a descriptive summary of the Theatre in four languages, I didn't need to look at it. Raymond was telling me everything. He seemed to have memorized the entire script, including dates.

"And it was finished in 12 BC by the emperor Augustus. After that, it was practically abandoned for centuries until it fell in and out of various big shot Italian families' ownership. Then this Orsini family took over this entire area and had this famous architect build their home based on the original theatre. This all happened in the sixteenth century. That's what we see now. Pretty spectacular."

Raymond then turned to his left and started walking off. It was a short way to a unique part of the city, composed of tangible layers of history. Portico d'Ottavia.

"Tell me about your parents, Raymond. Do they agree with your choices?" I noticed an almost indiscernible stumble in his step when I asked this.

"My mother doesn't discuss my decisions, but I know she's on my side."

"And your father?" Raymond had made no mention of his father in his bio.

"He's a loser. One of these progressive, civil libertarian Jews that believes we have to kiss everybody's ass and be lovey-dovey with our enemies. He's a pathetic pile of crap. He should have gotten blown to bits, not my uncle."

This was the first time I had heard Raymond use profanity and speak with such anger. I decided to change the subject and not press him further.

"Do you know what this is?" I pointed to the right of us at the corner of a temple composed of three, well over twenty feet, Corinthian columns placed at a ninety-degree angle from each other.

"A temple dedicated to Apollo. That's all I know." Raymond didn't stop walking. Bringing up his father had struck a nerve. A deep one.

I sprinted after him and grabbed him by his arm.

"Okay, no more questions," I said." I didn't mean to pry into your private life."

Raymond held his head low, and it was only then that I realized he was crying. He pulled away and wiped the tears with the sleeve of his shirt. He then began to pace back and forth with short steps. He was like a volcano right before an eruption.

"You know…you know what my *dear* father said to me when we found out my uncle, *his brother*, had died?! He said that he deserved it! Yeah, that's right, that he deserved being blown up! Said that my uncle was a warmonger and could only see as far as his Zionist nose. He then went on and on about how we mistreat the Palestinians and that this is the only way that these bastards can make their voice heard. By blowing up innocent people on a bus! Can you believe that? That's my father! A fucking waste of humanity. My dad is one Jew I wouldn't mind seeing in a gas chamber."

"Raymond, I think that's enough."

"No! It's not enough! What do you know about any of this!? I've always been an A-student. I've aced exams with a bloody nose, a broken finger, black eyes, busted lips—all luxuries I was granted if I went to the bathroom before class.

And what have I always gotten as a response from my dear father? That I was acting superior, yeah, that's the word, *superior.* That I should've blended in more with the others and get some Cs and Ds. What an asshole!" Raymond paused and caught his breath. "All my life I've had to endure insults, hatred, racist jokes, fights, and more fights, and yeah, I won almost all of them when there weren't three of them at a time. I've had countless swastikas drawn on my gym locker with shit and pieces of a pig thrown in my car and *always, always,* my dad would say that it wasn't the other guy's fault, that I must have done something to annoy these people!"

"But, Raymond, the group you're with now, everyone seems to get along with you. I don't understand." I was grasping at straws.

Raymond gave out a short laugh. "I'm a senior now, Atticus, and I have a black belt in Krav Maga." I knew that Krav Maga was an Israeli martial art, a deadly one at that. "If anybody gets in my face, and some sophomore juniors have tried, I kick their testicles straight up into their stomach. I'm talking about when I was in eighth through the tenth grade. And it was almost always the seniors that made my life miserable."

Raymond had stopped crying and pacing.

"This is a good group I'm in, Atticus. But don't be fooled—none of them feel comfortable being seen with me after school. I'm always a Jew boy. Michelle is the only exception, even if I hardly run into her. But that's no surprise. I think she would've given Idi Amin a hug." That made us both chuckle nervously.

I then stretched out my hand. "Are we good?"

Raymond reached out his and shook it. "We're good."

I was tempted to ask Raymond about his two-year-old sister who had passed away when he was quite young, but in consideration of his not bringing it up, I decided not to pry anymore.

"Great. Let's take a look at Octavia's Gate before we go to the synagogue."

"Fine by me. I studied up a bit on this place. Mind if I quiz you?"

"Go right ahead, but this is one of my favorite parts of Rome, so I think I'll be ready with whatever you throw at me."

We proceeded in silence for another one hundred feet or so and found ourselves in front of this magnificent gateway.

"Okay, Atticus, who built this and for whom was it built?"

"Emperor Augustus, and he built it for his sister."

Raymond raised his hand, and we high-fived.

"My turn," I said. "What was the purpose of this structure?"

"It was a walkway, formed by columns, and it enclosed two temples. Um, one for Jupiter and the other—damn, I don't remember."

"Neither do I. Skip it. We're still tied."

"Okay, when was it built?"

"Around 27 BC."

"Man, you've done your homework."

"Well, so have you. One last question for you. Why is there an archway there under the portico instead of columns like those on the left side?"

Raymond grinned. "I got this one. Earthquake. AD 400 something. That's when they built that arch."

"Spot on, Raymond." I gave him a friendly punch on the shoulder. Raymond was pleased. He put his hands in his pockets and looked around him.

"Look at all this history, Atticus. It's around us, under us, over us. And it's all in *our* backyard."

Raymond was hinting at something, but I wasn't sure what he was referencing.

"Oh, come on, you can figure that one out," he said.

"Okay, okay, don't tell me…give me a minute. 'Our backyard…'"

"*Our*, Atticus." Raymond pointed to his head. His kippah?

"Oh! You're referring to the ghetto, what used to be the Jewish Ghetto."

"That's right! That's where we are. Our little Jewish part of town."

I was about to ask Raymond what he knew about the history of this neighborhood when someone called out to him. He turned and waved to two young men dressed in suits, white shirts, and kippahs. "Hey! What's up? Good to see you guys again."

"Hello, Raymond, good to see you, too."

"Atticus, let me introduce you. This is Jacob, and this is Martin." Raymond explained that they had made each other's acquaintance the day before, after lunch.

"We heard a lot about you yesterday, Atticus," one of them said.

"Well, that's worrisome." I threw a glance at Raymond.

"No, no, it was all good. If we get to the States one day, maybe we'll have a chaperone as cool as you."

"Well, thank you. It's been a pleasure being with Raymond and the rest of the group. They're a great bunch."

"We didn't know you were Jewish."

They were staring at the top of my head.

"I'm not. I just decided to put it on before going into the synagogue. Raymond had one handy."

"Unfortunately, it's going to take more than that kippah to get you in today, Atticus. There's been another anonymous call, and security has been stepped up. Only Jews can go in today and until the alert subsides."

I was dismayed. "That's too bad."

"Not really," said the taller of the two. "I think it's much nicer outside than inside especially if being inside means getting blown to smithereens."

"Very funny, Jacob. Always the comedian." Martin gave his friend a shove.

"So tell me," I said. "I can just make out a hint of an Italian accent, but your English is impeccable. Are you both from Rome?"

It turned out that Jacob and Martin were actually Jacobo and Martino, that they were born in Rome, had lived in this neighborhood for all of their eighteen years, had studied English for the last eight, and were heading to Tel Aviv to go to the university.

"So the three of you will probably see each other again in Israel, and soon."

"That's right," Martino, the shorter one, said. "We'll be in Tel Aviv, and Raymond in Jerusalem, but there's no doubt that we'll meet up. I think God wanted us to run into each other yesterday."

"And we have a lot in common," Jacobo added. "All three of us want to get into politics and do our part for the State of Israel."

Two more firing rocket launchers, I thought.

"That is a coincidence," I said out loud.

"It sure is. Raymond here says he also wants to get into journalism, but he won't have time if he becomes a Jewish Home Party member. There's so much for us to do."

Jacobo's eyes were almost ablaze with anticipation.

"Will the three of you will be in the same party?"

"Martin and I are already members, junior members. Our fathers got us in."

At the word *father*, Raymond lowered his head and cleared his throat.

Got the message. Get off the subject.

"You know, just before you showed up," I said, "I was about to tell Raymond that there is a large Jewish community in this part of town. But he already knew that."

"Of course, it's the ghetto, or used to be." Martin spread out his arms as if outlining the area.

"It still is a ghetto," Jacobo interjected.

"Come on, Jacob, that's not quite true," said Martino. "More and more non-Jews are moving in, and many Jews are moving out."

"I wish we had moved out."

"Don't listen to Jacob, Atticus. He's just a rich, spoiled brat."

Jacob gave Martin a slight shove on the shoulder.

"I have always liked living here myself," Martino continued. "It's pleasant—you're in the center of the city, you have a wide choice of restaurants, everybody knows everybody else, we look out for each other—"

"Sometimes." Jacob interjected.

"All right, I'll give you that. Sometimes."

"Remind me, Martino, when it became the Jewish Ghetto and why." Some of the history of this place I remembered, but it was sketchy.

"That's the main reason why I like it here so much, Atticus. The history of the place. A history which is ours in more ways than one. I don't know how much you know about Pope Paul IV. A very holy man who had a distinct hatred for Jews. In fact, he's the reason why we were shoved into this eight-block space for centuries. In 1555, he passed the papal charter *Cum nimis absurdum,* which basically stated that because Jews were condemned by God to eternal suffering and slavery, they should be all be rounded up and put in a ghetto surrounded by high walls."

"Yes, I'm aware of that decree. I didn't remember the year."

"Oh, it's a great read, Atticus," said Martino "Google it and read through all fifteen clauses."

"Martino is absolutely right. We were born in it, and we shall die in it if we don't take action."

I looked at Jacobo, puzzlement etched in my face.

"I mean, living in a certain part of a city, all together, excluded from the majority and basically treated like scum."

"And *labeled*," Martino emphasized. "The Jews in this ghetto had to wear yellow caps or kerchiefs to be recognized as such. This was from 1555 to 1870 when the papal states ceased to exist, and Italy became a united country. Now you know where the Nazis got the yellow star idea from." Martino gave me a wry smile.

"So being Jewish certainly isn't easy," he continued. "We learn very early that we're different. It's especially tough when you're a child. As much as our parents would try to explain, I couldn't see any difference in those boys and girls that kicked and spat on me in the park. We both had two arms, two hands, two feet, two legs, and a great desire to run, scream out loud, kick a soccer ball, and laugh. We just couldn't do it together."

He had put his hands in his pockets, straightened his back, and tightened his lips. I could read Martino's body language like large print.

"But that's just the way it is," he concluded. "We do the best with what God has given us."

"And that's exactly why we must get politically involved, and fast!" Raymond added. "We will be respected one day, as a people, and our rights will no longer be trampled by anyone."

"That's an American Jew for you…a bit too much idealism," said Martino.

"Keep quiet, Martin," Jacobo replied. "Raymond is absolutely right. We're just wasting time here. We need to get to Israel and give ourselves to the state."

"Gentlemen, gentlemen," I interrupted. "May I ask you to reflect on one thing please?" I had raised my voice just enough to catch the three off guard.

"The three of you are what, seventeen, eighteen? You get that, right? Seventeen, eighteen?"

The three looked at me as if I had started speaking Pashto.

I shook my head. "Try to live and do things as teenagers while you can. It's admirable that you feel so politically motivated and patriotic, but enjoy yourselves a bit! You know, reckless abandonment every once in a while? Go out and party, or date some girls."

Both Martin and Jacob stiffened up.

"There's no time for that," said Jacob. "Between our school and religious studies, working in our parents' stores and chores at home, we don't have much time to even sleep."

"No girlfriend for either of you?" I asked.

"Martin has one."

"Not true! Besides, you know, and I know that you like that Catholic girl over there near the park." Martin pointed somewhere behind him.

Jacob shook his head. "I think she's cute, but that's it."

"It better be. Your father and uncle will cut your *schmeckel* off if you do anything stupid." I hadn't heard that word before, but it didn't take a rocket scientist to figure out what Martin was alluding to. There was a moment of uneasy silence before Jacob spoke up.

"Hey, Raymond, one of the chazzans is going to give a lecture on the Six Day War to a bunch of students in about ten minutes. That's where we were heading before we ran into the two of you. Want to come?"

Raymond attempted to quell his palpable willingness to go off with the two boys. "Yeah, well…thanks, but I promised Atticus—"

"It's no problem at all," I said. "Go ahead. You should get to know each other, considering your upcoming trip. Just one question, Martin—what is a chazzan?"

"He's the one who leads the congregation in prayer, similar to the ordained clergy in the Catholic Church. He's really cool. An incredible musician and a real history fanatic. The synagogue is always full when he talks speaks, especially about Israel."

"You're sure, Atticus? At least come inside—oh, wait, that can't happen today, right?"

"That's right, Raymond," said Martin. "Some screwball must have called saying there was a bomb somewhere or that they were going to spray machine-gun fire against the sons of pigs—that's us." Martin patted himself on the chest with a proud grin on his face.

"But if there has been a threat, why isn't the synagogue closed to everyone?" I asked.

Martin and Jacob began to snicker. "If the synagogue were to close every time there's a threat, they might as well tear the thing down and build a parking lot."

I nodded. "Okay, boys, off you go. Martin, Jacob, it was very nice meeting the two of you. Maybe we will run into each other again before the group leaves Rome."

"That would be great. Who knows?"

I shook their hands.

"Dinner is at seven, Raymond."

"See you later, Atticus."

I watched the three go off in unison. Three intelligent and engaging young men. What did the future have in store for them?

CHAPTER 46

I heard it. That unmistakable sound: stomach growls. I needed food. And what better place to find it than at Giggetto's?
All soft *g*'s, one of the most famous restaurants in all of Rome
and one of my go-to places when I was living in the city.
Founded in 1923 by a Jewish family from the area, it had re-
tained its status throughout the years as a source of authentic
Italian specialties. And what a location! The restaurant was
right next to the Portico d'Ottavia with outdoor seating in
front and back. It took me just two minutes to walk there.

I took off the kippah, went in, and selected a table in
the corner of the front room under a portrait of a lovely
woman with long dark hair. I sat down, and the waiter came
instantaneously.

I knew exactly what I wanted and rattled off my selection
in rapid fire: "*Un carciofo alla Giudea, un filetto di baccalà, due
fiori di zucca, un assaggio di puntarelle, due—tre funghi porcini
arrosti, una mozzarella in carrozza, due rigatoni con pagliata e per
il dolce vedremo.*"

"*C'è solo lei, signore?*"

"*Si, non si preoccupi. C'è spazio.*"

The waiter had asked if I was expecting someone else,
given the abundant order. I told him not to worry and that
I would be able to handle it. He turned and left with a look
of disbelief. I had, in fact, ordered enough for almost three
people. But I was starving, and this was Giggetto's!

Not even a minute passed before the waiter was back,
placing the expected bread and breadstick basket on the
table.

"*Mi scusi, signore. E da bere?*"

Of course, I needed something to wash all this down with.

"Acqua di Nepi, gassata, e una bottiglia di Amarone, forte e corposo."

"Si, signore."

There was a bottle of extra-virgin olive oil on the table, as well as red wine vinegar. Salt and pepper shakers sat behind them.

That was all I required.

I poured a generous portion of olive oil on to the plate in front of me, added just a dash of vinegar, and then shook some pepper and quite a bit of salt on top. I then took a piece of the oven-warm bread, tore off a piece, and wiped the middle portion of the plate with it, and gleefully shoved it in my mouth.

Heaven. Sometimes the tastiest food is the simplest.

I hardly had time to unfold my napkin and place it on my lap before my waiter was back. He put the Nepi sparkling water, named after a small town north of Rome where this bubbly water was collected from underground springs, on the table. He then uncorked the 2010 *Amarone* wine and poured a small amount of the dark-red liquid into my glass. I picked it up, swirled it, took a deep inhalation of the hearty aroma, then held a tiny sip in my mouth. Fabulous.

I paced my glass back on the table, the waiter filled it halfway, and headed to the kitchen. This time I took a proper mouthful, relishing the flavor.

I mentally went over the morning's events as I waited for my *carciofo alla Giudea*, a flattened, deep-fried artichoke, my *filetto di baccalà*, fried boneless dry cod, and my two *fiori di zucca*, deep-fried zucchini flowers stuffed with anchovies and mozzarella cheese.

Raymond and the other two boys were unique young men. I admired their drive and passion. They were fully dedicated to a cause, and they had a mission. Would they, however, be able to master the history of their people objectively? Would they understand where mistakes had been made? Would they be able to admit to these errors and let this knowledge guide their future decisions? Unlikely. This was almost a superhuman task. I doubted that their future endeavors in politics, journalism, or whatever else they decided to do would bring decades of hatred, acts of terrorism, and conflict between the State of Israel and the Palestinians even an inch closer to an end. The domination goal of both peoples was the destruction of the other. No ifs, ands, or buts.

How many had tried? Begin, Sadat, Carter, Rabin, Clinton, along with countless others far from the spotlight who had worked for peace to no avail. I had my own personal opinion about how a sincere dialogue could one day commence between the two camps but had not dared mention it to the boys. They would have thought me pathetically weak.

I momentarily suspended my thought process as my first dish was brought to the table—roasted porcini mushrooms and *mozzarella in carrozza*, mozzarella cheese sandwiched between two slices of bread, dipped in egg yolks and breadcrumbs, and fried in very hot oil. The waiter poured filled my wineglass. I tasted the mushrooms and the cheese and washed everything down with a healthy mouthful of wine.

Only then did I return to the Israeli-Palestinian situation and my Nobel Peace Prize solution to the problem.

It was actually very simple.

Somewhere on neutral territory, I would bring sixty women together inside a small, empty warehouse. Thirty would be Palestinian, and thirty would be Israeli. The one thing in common amongst these sixty women would be the loss of a son or daughter in war, an act of terrorism, an air raid, a missile strike, or any other violent action between the Israelis and the Palestinians. Beforehand, I would have collected pictures of those killed, enlarging and framing them. They would be placed on the walls surrounding the gathered women. The only things the women would be able to bring inside the warehouse would be more pictures of their dead children. They would all be searched for weapons or explosives before entering. Other than three or four translators to aid in any language barrier, there would be nobody else except a moderator, possibly of Asian origin, to avoid any signs of bias.

That was it.

After a few hours, food would be served. Israeli and Palestinian specialties. The doors would then be open, and shuttle buses would take the women back to their respective homes, on both sides of the wall, fences, and barbed wire.

I would repeat this at least six times a year slowly increasing the number of women to eighty, ninety, and more.

If anybody is going to bridge this chasm of hatred between these two peoples, it will be the mothers on both sides. The women, not the men.

My peacekeeping strategy was interrupted by a plate of *puntarelle*—a variant of chicory seasoned with olive oil, crushed garlic, anchovies, ground pepper, and a drop of balsamic vinegar. This was accompanied by the *rigatoni alla pagliata*, which is rigatoni pasta with unweaned calf intestines. I was about to dive into the pasta when my phone began to vibrate. It was Giorgio.

"Hello, Atticus, how are you?"

"Could not be better since I am at Giggetto's and eating practically everything they have on the menu," I responded.

"Lucky you! You didn't call me, so I am calling you to confirm."

"Um, confirm what exactly?"

"Oh my, I think that all that food and wine have gone to your head. We have our little surprise attack scheduled this afternoon at six. Your boy, Atticus, the one who got taken for eighty dollars?"

"Mark! Of course, but I wasn't expecting you to plan a raid."

"Oh, nothing too elaborate. Two cars, some officers, and a few guns."

I had a flashback of some of our manhunts and seizures that we had carried out together when I was stationed at the U.S. Embassy in Rome. Giorgio liked a good show of force.

"We'll be there on time," I assured him, "and we will hang back until you give us a thumbs-up."

"Good. Should be a nice ending to an otherwise boring day. See you soon."

I lowered the phone from my ear as the waiter appeared and started clearing some of the empty plates. My artichoke had also arrived, and I savored every bite. I was stuffed like a Thanksgiving turkey, but no earthly force was going to move me from my chair until I had one of *Giggetto's* exquisite desserts. I asked the waiter what was available.

He rattled off the list without pausing for breath: "*Oggi abbiamo tartufo nero, sorbetto al limone con vodka, torta di noci, torta di mela, tiramisù, profiterole, millefoglie…*"

"*Mille foglie per favore.*"

As soon as the waiter mentioned *millefoglie*, I stopped him. This was, by far, one of my favorites. Also known as a Napoleon, this elegant French dessert was principally composed of three strata of puff pastry with two alternate layers of *crème pâtissier*. What makes it so exquisite is the lightness and flakiness of the pastry. It's not an easy accomplishment to bring it to an airy texture, and I had been disappointed countless times in many European restaurants. But this particular dessert has always been a specialty of Giggetto's, and I did not expect to be let down.

As I waited, my thoughts now went to my children and how much I missed them. I thought about my ex-wife and at how difficult she and her lawyers had made my life since we had separated. I knew that my children were scarred, as are all children who grow up in broken homes. How deep that scar was would only reveal itself in time. I thought about

Barbara and her two children. Those weren't scars—those were hatchet wounds. I thought about Darlene's traumatized persona hidden inside her stunning physical self.

Parenting is, without a doubt, the most difficult job in the world. Most of us convince ourselves that we are doing the best we can. But are we? Where do we draw the line between what is more convenient for us versus what our children require? When do we stop focusing on our pleasures, habits, and wants and instead dedicate this time to our children?

Any discussion about our parenting successes and failures doesn't only depend on the here and now. Parents are not totally in control when it comes to how we manage the relationship with our children. Where did our parents draw the line with us when we were growing up? What skeletons do we all have in our closets?

I remembered reading about a nineteen-year-old in Texas who had been arrested after he raped and killed an eight-year-old boy. The child had been tortured with cigarette burns, had staple and thumbtack punctures in his arms and legs, had been fed only a can of dog food and a glass of water every two to three days and wasn't allowed to use the toilet or the bathtub save on days when his kidnapper was sodomizing him. On those days, which were frequent, the child was washed in expensive bath soaps and oils and his body rubbed with lotion. His teeth were brushed, and he was forced to gargle a cap of Listerine.

The child eventually starved to death. He would have died from extensive internal bleeding sooner or later. Those were the child's options in this world.

The perpetrator, during interviews with a psychiatrist, was almost surprised at how much "hubbub," as he put it, everyone was making about what he had done. He went on to describe in minute detail what *his* childhood had been like—how his father and uncle had raped and abused him since the age of six; how he would cry out for his mother, who always was so drunk when the raping started that she couldn't even stand; how he would pray to any God that would listen for his father to stop doing these things to him; how the pain and anguish began to slowly turn into numbness and resignation; how he began to accept it all...

Why had he tortured the kid with so many cigarette burns and pierced him with all those thumbtacks? What was the fucking big deal? What about that splintered broom pole his uncle would always stick up his ass!? And that nutcracker!? Always clamping down on his thumb if he didn't suck hard enough on his father's dick? What about that!? Where was anybody to stop and ask his father and uncle why they were doing this to him!?

The young man was given the death penalty. I had lost track after that and didn't know if he was still on death row or not.

"Excuse me, sir..."

The waiter had returned with my millefoglie in his hand. I hadn't noticed him standing there. I did, however, become aware of the tear running down my cheek.

I pushed an oversized piece of the pastry into my mouth attempting to exorcise the images in my mind. Closing my eyes, I concentrated solely on the texture and creaminess of the filling. I didn't want to think about anything else.

It was as good as I had remembered it, possibly even better. After that first excessive chunk, I broke off much smaller pieces and relished each of them.

My intensely gratifying lunch was topped off with a double espresso and the last glass of Amarone. I had, in fact, finished the bottle.

After paying the bill, which wasn't excessive, I wandered back in the direction of the hotel in a zigzag fashion along the maze of narrow, history-encrusted streets. I made it to the cigar shop that was closed the last time I had passed by and found the gold-plated Dupont lighter that I had wanted in the boutique's vast assortment. I bought it, experiencing that awkward bliss you feel when spending a good deal of money for an object that you don't need but must own.

When I finally arrived in the lobby of the hotel, it was just before three thirty. What immediately caught my attention was a breathtakingly large Murano vase with at least three dozen long-stemmed red roses on the counter of the front desk. I wondered who the lucky recipient was.

Neither Giovanni nor Ludovica had come out from the back office upon my entry, which I found a bit odd, so I proceeded up the stairs to my room.

Once inside, I kicked off my shoes and switched on my PC. As I waited for the internet provider to connect me to my email account, I walked into the bathroom to wash my hands and face. I looked at myself in the small oval mirror above the sink. I looked tired. More than tired. I looked, well, *old*. I had circles under my eyes and a series of wrinkles on my forehead that seemed deeper than just a few weeks before. I then pulled up my shirt, turned sideways, and took a look at my protruding belly. Not awful, but the makings of an inner tube were certainly in progress. Thank goodness for all the walking I was doing. With all the food and wine I was consuming these days, I would have been competing with the Goodyear blimp without a decent amount of exercise.

I left the bathroom and went to the desk, punched in my Gmail address on the keyboard, and looked at the emails waiting in my Inbox.

Other than a good amount of spam, I noticed an email from Francesca, one from my ex-wife, and a third from Mrs. Visconti, the headhunter I had spoken to on Wednesday.

I clicked on my ex-wife's email first, hoping for some news about the children. No such luck. As usual, it was short and to the point. She would be back in town on the eighteenth and wanted to know if I had deposited the alimony check in her account. Typical.

I then clicked on the mail from Mrs. Visconti, which informed me that after a meeting with the company in question, where she presented my curriculum, the decision had been made to interview two candidates. I was one of them. The next step was a face-to-face with the general manager. Mrs. Visconti would call me at the beginning of the following week to fix an appointment.

Well, it wasn't a shoo-in, but the news was auspicious.

I then took a deep breath and opened Francesca's email.

Atticus,

It has become abundantly clear to me these past few months that you are no longer interested in our relationship. Maybe you were, once.

I realize that the loss of your job was hard on you, but instead of letting me help you and be close to you, you decided to put me in the back seat, devoting 90% of your attention to your kids.

I am not a callous, insensitive person and fully realize that your children are important to you. I guess I was hoping to be as important, if not more. Well, that certainly wasn't and will never be the case. So, in a few words, let me tell you that I have accepted that position they offered me here in New York. I will, of course, have to come to Milan to get paperwork in order, go to the US Consulate, probably sell my car (do you want to buy it?) and pick up all my things in the apartment. If you are there when I get back, it's fine. If you're not, that's fine as well. Just let me know where you want me to leave the house keys in the case I don't run into you.

I don't care what you tell the children. They never liked me, and if I can say, you were no help here.

I did care for you, Atticus, and I could have fallen deeply in love with you. But it takes two to tango.

I wish you the best.

Francesca

I sat there a moment and came to the realization that I owed a big "Thank you" to Francesca. She had put into writing what I should have said months ago. Our relationship had been based, at least on my side, solely on sex, and I had been subconsciously aware of it from the beginning. I was just not willing to admit it.

Francesca had a body that would have put Wonder Woman to shame, and she knew what to do with it. Never a boring moment when she was only in stiletto heels and string lingerie. But could you really base a lasting relationship on a pair of breasts and a rear end? Granted, a pair of breasts and posterior that warranted an exhibition at the Louvre, but when the "exhibition" was over, then what? Most importantly, there had indeed never been a good feeling between her and the children, as she had said, and this was and would continue to be an insurmountable problem. There wasn't any other solution, and this was a solution I could certainly live with.

I was a free man.

And come to think of it, as far as satisfying sex was concerned, Barbara had certainly filled in all the gaps very nicely. And Ludovica…she had certainly jump-started a heart murmur. There was no denying that.

"Thank you, Francesca," I said out loud. "I shall toast to you and your success tonight." The words came out naturally and sincerely.

As I double-checked to see if there were any other emails of interest, the room phone began to ring. I answered it, hoping that there was not an emergency of some kind.

"*Signor Atticus, sono Giovanni.*"

"Yes, Giovanni, is everything all right?"

"Yes, yes, Signor Atticus. But I would like to show you something, if possible. At your earliest possible convenience."

"I'll be down right away."

I didn't even put my shoes on. I went straight out the door and headed rapidly downstairs. If Giovanni called me, it was for good reason, and I had no intention of making him wait.

As I arrived in the lobby, I saw both Giovanni and Ludovica standing behind the front desk looking in my direction. The impressive display of roses was still front and center on the counter.

"Is everything okay?" I asked, with some trepidation.

"Yes, Signor Atticus, but a very strange thing happened while you were out today. I was telling Ludovica in the office when you came back to the hotel."

"Yes?"

"That boy, Giacomo, he came to the hotel."

"When was *that*?"

"At about noon."

"I'm going to kill him."

"No, no, Signor Atticus," Ludovica interjected. "Look at the beautiful tie he brought to my uncle and take a look at this." She handed me a card, and Giovanni pointed to the light and dark-blue tie with a distinct pattern, neatly folded in an elegant gift box. I opened the card and noticed that Giacomo had written a good deal.

"He apologizes profoundly for his behavior and practically begs me to forgive him," said Giovanni. "I didn't have a chance to say anything to him. He just dropped them off and left. He was probably afraid of running into you, Signor Atticus."

"And look at these roses!" Ludovica's eyes were sparkling. "Aren't they stunning? They are for the young lady in Room 16, Miss Williams."

"You mean to tell me that Giacomo walked here with this huge vase of flowers?"

"Oh no. A florist's van showed up right after he left. The instructions were to leave the flowers here until Miss Williams could retrieve them."

I looked at the roses and then back at the tie.

"May I, Giovanni?" I pointed to the long rectangular box.

"Of course."

I took the tie out and looked on the back of the wider side at the keeper loop.

Marinella. I knew it. The pattern was unique to this well-known and expensive brand of ties from the city of Naples in southern Italy. A Marinella tie sold for about US$140, and there must have been at triple that amount sitting on the counter in the large handblown glass vase. Was Giacomo's apology sincere, or was he just throwing a good bit of money around to get a second chance with Darlene?

"There is a card for the young lady." Ludovica placed it near the vase.

"And, Signor Atticus, there is a card for you as well." Giovanni slid it across the counter. Looking at me straight in the eyes, which he rarely ever did, he practically whispered, "*Faber est quisque fortunae suae.*"

"A card *for me?*"

I was about to open it when I noticed some familiar figures passing by the large windows that led to the steps of the hotel. The Cinecittà group was back. I stuffed the card in my back pocket.

The glass doors slid open, and the students came in.

CHAPTER 47

"Hello, everyone, welcome back!" I was very glad to see them.

"Hey, Atticus!"

"Really good day…"

"Over-the-top place…"

"Sweet, really sweet…"

Most of the group walked past me heading to the stairs and to their rooms. Wayne, Bishop, and Michelle plopped themselves down on the lobby sofas. Mark was walking by me when I stopped him gently by the arm.

"What's up, Atticus?"

"I need you and the three couch potatoes over there down here in the lobby at six."

"Okay…everything all right?"

"Oh, yes. I think you'll get a kick out of what you're going to see."

"Cool. I'll be down later."

As Mark proceeded toward the stairwell, Massimo, Barbara, and John approached me, bringing up the rear of the group.

"My dear Atticus, what a lovely day!" Massimo gushed. "I thoroughly enjoyed myself, and I believe the group came away satisfied as well."

"*Satisfied?* "Barbara exclaimed. "It was exhilarating! Movie sets were up everywhere, Atticus. We even saw them shooting a scene of a film that's due out next year. It was incredible!"

John weighed in, "Massimo here was an incredible guide. He knew exactly where to take us and what to show us. He truly knows that place like the back of his hand." John slapped Massimo on his shoulder.

"It was awesome, Atticus. Massimo's the best," Bishop added from the couch.

Massimo blushed profusely, fanning himself with both hands.

"Well, thank you! What I won't do to be admired!" He giggled, letting out one of those high-pitched squeals that we had become accustomed to.

I said, "It was really good of you to offer this special visit to the students, Massimo. I'm sure they were all thrilled."

"As I have said to you before, when a group is as special as this, one my job becomes a veritable joy." Massimo glanced at his Rado watch and screeched. "Oh my! I must run, run, run! I have one more group before the day is done! Atticus, I shall call you tomorrow afternoon," he said all this as he quickly hugged Michelle, the two boys, Barbara, and John. "Look at those roses, to die for! Kisses to you, Atticus, kisses to all! Bye, bye." With that, he practically fled from the lobby.

"Well, I'm in desperate need of a shower," John said. "See all of you at dinner." John headed off. I turned around and faced the trio sitting comfortably on the couch. I told them to meet me at six.

"What for, Atticus?" Wayne asked.

"Curtail your curiosity," I replied, "and enjoy the moment when it comes."

"Okay. We'll be down at six."

"Can I come too? You've sparked my interest."

I had momentarily forgotten Barbara who was standing directly behind me.

"Sure, Barbara. Join us. Just be down here with the others."

As the four started out of the lobby, I asked Michelle to stay behind for a moment. I led her to the other side of the lobby to avoid prying eyes and ears.

"First of all, how's that headache?" I asked.

"All gone. They come and go, Atticus. I'm used to it."

"Well, good to hear you're feeling better. I wanted to let you know that I read what you gave me. I think that Sabrina and Evelyn, hard as it is to believe, actually met earlier today at the Trevi Fountain."

"That threw me off as well. There's been a lot of hate between those two since Sabrina's brother died."

"I wonder what caused this change of heart?" I said, musing.

Michelle looked off into the distance, through the hotel lobby glass walls to the street outside. "Don't think that I'm just a silly adolescent, but this city, well...this city, it's *magical*. It changes you. Maybe it's all the concentrated history. There's an energy here that I've never felt before, anywhere. It's as if you were living another *you* that's been hiding somewhere all your life. I find myself thinking of things and feeling emotions that are totally new to me. Pretty much the whole group feels the same way. We've opened up to each other, shared past experiences, especially the painful ones. We've told each other things that we would've never confessed to back home. We've removed some iron chains from our ankles, Atticus. Rome is where unbelievable things can happen. I think that its magic has rubbed off on Evelyn and Sabrina."

I thought for a moment about this, then nodded slowly. "You've summed up this city in a few powerful sentences Michelle." I rested my hand on her shoulder and looked into her eyes. "This is a special city, and you are a very special person." She smiled and lowered her head. There was a moment of embarrassing silence.

I gestured toward the front desk. "Speaking of magical, you see those?"

"Yes, you can't miss them. They're some of the prettiest roses I've ever seen."

"Take a wild guess who they're for."

Michelle looked at me quizzically but did not answer.

"Darlene," I said.

"Oh." Michelle didn't seem terribly surprised.

"Yes. Keep it to yourself, but she has an admirer."

"You mean Giacomo?"

I blinked. "Um, yes. How do *you* know about Giacomo?"

Michelle raised her eyebrows. "We *all* know about Giacomo, Atticus. Seems he roughed her up a bit last night. It was good to hear that you stepped in and took control of the situation."

Seeing the look of consternation on my face, Michelle began to explain:

"Darlene told Mary all about it when she got back to the room. Mary told Sabrina, Sabrina told Vanessa, then Vanessa told Mary, then—"

"Okay, okay, I got it."

Michelle displayed one of her brilliant smiles and laughed softly.

"I guess the roses are his way of apologizing to her," I said.

"I heard he was pretty rough with the hotel clerk as well."

"Yes. I see that part trickled down the grapevine too."

"Atticus, we have about eighteen hundred students in our school, and if somebody stubs their toe, everybody knows about it the next day. Can you imagine in such a small group as ours? A secret is impossible. It's lucky that I've been a*ble...*" Michelle cut herself off, turning pale.

"Able to what?" My question was a knee-jerk reaction, and I realized that I had suddenly placed Michelle in a very difficult position.

"Nothing. Just...uh..." She switched tack. "What time do we need to be down here?" Michelle looked at me, her eyes pleading that I do not ask any more questions.

I didn't press the issue. Later, I would wonder if I should have.

"Be down here by six latest, and make sure that the three musketeers are with you."

"Okay. I'm going to go upstairs now and see if Evelyn is back. See you soon."

"Oh, just one thing," I said as she turned to leave. "Given that the grapevine amongst all of you is so fruitful, could you try to find out where Darlene and James were today and if they are back? I totally lost track of them."

"Will do," said Michelle.

I leaned back onto the oversized cushions. Okay, then, Michelle was hiding something, too. Was it something pertaining to her or to Wayne and Bishop? I wondered what it could be. A secret, judging by her reaction. A well-kept secret.

It was almost five o'clock. I had an hour but didn't know what to do with it. I sat back a moment and remembered the Latin proverb that Giovanni had so aptly expressed: *Faber est quisque fortunae suae*—"Every man is the architect of his own fortune." Giacomo had taken the right steps in getting his name out of the mud, but I wasn't ready just yet to forgive and forget. There is never an excuse for slapping a woman around or roughing up the elderly.

I heard the familiar humming sound of the two glass doors sliding open but couldn't see who was walking in from where I was sitting. I waited a moment and then saw the backs of a young couple. He was tall and very thin with a rather large folder under his right arm, and she was a full-bodied blonde.

Wait a second.

It was Darlene with James by her side.

"Hey, you two." Both stopped and looked my way.

"Hey, Atticus," James said, giving me a half smile. Darlene just looked the other way.

"Good day today?"

"Yeah, pretty good. Dinner at the same time?" James asked.

"Yes, seven-thirty."

"Cool. See you later."

They both headed off, and I called after Darlene:

"Darlene, wait a minute."

She stopped but didn't turn around.

"I need to speak with you."

"I don't have anything to say to you," she said, with her back still turned to me.

"That's fine. But I have something to say to you, so get over here and sit down, I spoke firmly but calmly.

"James, go on up, Darlene is going to be here for a while." He glanced at me, then at her, and left.

Darlene turned, her arms folded over her chest, her eyes angry. She walked over, unceremoniously sat down on the couch in front of me, and crossed her legs.

I paused a moment, then said, "I want you to listen carefully to what I have to say Darlene."

"Don't lecture me!" she snapped.

Now I got angry. "Shut up!"

Darlene's eyes almost popped out of her head.

"Just who the hell do you think you are? Last night, you come to my room to seduce me, and instead of taking you up on your offer and treating you like a misguided teenage slut, what do I do? I try to explain to you why it isn't the correct thing to do, I try to give you some advice, I offer to help you in a future career when you get back home, I treat you with respect. And what do I get in return? That pathetic little show of yours this morning in front of me and Mrs. Cornwall. You were crude, ugly, and insensitive!"

I hadn't raised my voice, but my rage was no less heated for all that. Darlene folded her arms even more tightly across her chest, looking at me with poison darts flying with from her eyes.

"That was all bullshit, and you know it!" she said. "You had me thinking that I could be different, that not everyone out there just wants to screw my brains out! Well, get this, Mr.

Goody Two Shoes, I can tell a mile away when a man's dick is hard, and last night yours was rock solid!"

There was a certainly some truth to that.

"And then all that crap about Giacomo, how he was an example of a clean-cut guy who was interested in me as a person. Well, that was all bullshit, too!"

Darlene bent over and started to rock back and forth. She was almost in a fetal position. I wanted to point out that leading him on the way she had wasn't exactly conducive to gentlemanly conduct, but she was in her shell now. I felt sorry for her.

"Darlene?"

Just profuse tears now and rocking, back and forth.

"*Darlene?*"

"I'm sorry! I didn't mean to say those things to you!" Darlene cried out, taking me totally by surprise. "I didn't want to. I'm so…sorry! I just feel so dirty." Her words trailed off into an agonizing whimper.

I came off the couch and sat beside her, hugging her around the shoulders. The sobbing had almost become an anguished moan, and I knew that by now someone must have heard us.

"Listen, Darlene, there's something that you must see, but I need you to pull yourself together, okay?"

Giovanni and Ludovica came out of the office, saw what was going on, and went straight back in.

"I can't do this anymore," Darlene sobbed. "I'm so tired, tired of all the shit I have to put up with…from my mom, from all the perverts out there…I just want it to stop."

I hoped James hadn't been sharing his better-off-dead perspective with Darlene. That was the last thing she needed right now.

"Okay Darlene, I understand, but I just want you to look at something, okay?"

She raised her head, her face wet with tears.

"See those roses sitting over there on the counter?" She turned her head keeping it pressed hard against my chest.

"Kind of hard to miss. I've never seen so many roses all together like that before."

"Guess who they're for?"

"They're for a person? I thought it was the hotel doing some decorating."

"Nope. They're for *you.*"

She pulled away and looked me straight in the eyes.

"Is that supposed to be some kind of joke, Atticus?"

"No, no joke, Darlene. They are for you. They're from Giacomo."

"*Who?*"

"You heard me," I said, smiling.

The dawn of a smile began to creep across Darlene's tear-drenched face.

"He also gave Giovanni a beautiful tie," I said. "And there's a card for you, under the vase."

She got up and walked over to the counter, mesmerized by the sheer volume of red. She took the card and then slowly turned back in my direction.

"Well, wow." She paused, gazing at the roses in their large vase. "Do you think we can take them up to my room?"

I grinned. "Well, they may not fit, but we'll try."

Giovanni came out of the office and informed us that he would have the staff bring the roses up immediately.

"Go on up, Darlene, and enjoy your card," I said.

She was turning the envelope over and over again in her hands.

"I'm glad that Giacomo gave you a present, Mr. Giovanni. You deserve it."

She received a smile and a slight bow of acknowledgment in return.

"Thanks again, Atticus, and…and I'm really sorry for this morning. Really."

"Do me a favor, Darlene. When you see Mrs. Cornwall, try to patch things up, okay?"

"I will. See you at dinner, Atticus."

Ludovica and Giovanni looked me and smiled as Darlene went rapidly up the stairs. It was another good moment.

All this talk of Giacomo reminded me of the card he gave me. I took it out of my back pocket.

Sig. Atticus,

I do not know if this can or should change anything…but trying does not hurt.

I want to apologize to you, Darlene, and the hotel clerk for my behavior last night. It was unforgiveable. I don't know what got into me…you can ask people that know me, I'm really not the violent type.

I guess a little too much wine and what seemed to be a romantic evening "got me going," if you know what I mean. When Darlene abruptly put a stop to everything, I wasn't expecting it…not an excuse to rough her up the way I did, but I just saw red. And when the hotel clerk started threatening that he was going to call the police, I totally lost it. Again, unforgiveable.

I only hope that the two small gifts for him and Darlene can assist in erasing the worst of my actions.

To close, I must thank you, Sig. Atticus, for coming down hard on me. I needed it. I'm still aching everywhere, especially my nose, but I am thankful for the pain. It reminds me of what a jackass I was.

Well, I probably will not see you ever again. Please tell Darlene that was I truly fascinated by her and that my heart is broken for what how I behaved.

Thank you,

Giacomo

p.s. this is my number, just in case: 06/21324411

"We're here, Atticus!"

Barbara and the four students were right behind me. I had been so absorbed by Giacomo's note that I hadn't even heard them.

"Very good," I said, folding the card and putting it back in my pocket. "Are we all ready for a little surprise?"

"Don't know what you've got up your sleeve," Mark said, "but we're game."

"I think that you'll be pleased." I turned and headed out of the hotel.

CHAPTER 48

Once outside, we turned right and headed in the direction of the Trevi Fountain. Shops and kiosks were doing a brisk business, and the coffee bars, pizza parlors, and small restaurants with outdoor seating were full of tourists from all over the world.

"Let's keep moving," I urged them. "Can't miss the entertainment."

"Entertainment?"

"Hey, Atticus, come on, cough it up…what's going' on?"

"None of you are getting a word out of me."

Making a right onto Via del Lavatore, we were just steps away from the establishment where Mark had his encounter with the unscrupulous bartender.

I slowed down. "Does the place look familiar, Mark?"

"Hell yeah, sure does, it's where I…" He shot a glance at Barbara and then back at me.

"No worries, Mark," she reassured him. "I know all about it. It's water under the bridge."

"I think you were taken for a chunk of change, right?" I asked.

"Got that right, Atticus. I left the hotel with four twenties. I came back—"

"You mean you were *carried* back," Michelle corrected.

"Ha-ha! Okay, I was carried back, let's say, and the next morning, there wasn't any sign of the money."

"That's right. I checked your pockets before I handed in your clothes to the laundry, and they were empty."

"*That asshole,* excuse me…that guy in there took me for eighty bucks. Not even I could put down eighty bucks' worth of booze."

This got raised eyebrows from Wayne and Bishop.

"And that is why we are here, ladies and gentlemen! An abuse has been committed, and we must correct it! With a little help. What time is it, Barbara?"

"Six twenty-four exactly."

"Just a few more minutes."

"A few more minutes until what, Atticus?" said Wayne. "Did you put some plastic explosive in that place? Timer and all?"

"No, Wayne, but you're not too far off."

They all looked at me and stood very still. I was thoroughly enjoying myself. People were walking past our little group. We were on the corner of Via del Lavatore and Via della Panetteria with Mark's small bar just fifteen to twenty feet in front of us.

It was such a pleasant evening. The sky was still giving off an intense glow with strands of orange-laced clouds brush stroked against its sapphire blue canvas. The sun would be setting soon.

Then I heard it. Faint at first but steadily growing in strength. A siren, followed by another.

"My friends, it's starting."

"Huh?"

"What?"

"Where?"

Nobody had connected the sirens with our reason for being here. I moved behind Barbara and stood close to her and took her hand. It wasn't obvious, but neither was it covert. I didn't care. She turned her head and smiled at me.

The wail from the sirens was growing louder, but my small group still had not put two and two together. I saw heads beginning to turn in all directions and an opening starting to form between the crowds down by the fountain. Suddenly, two dark green Alfa Romeo 159s turned into the street where we were standing. Sirens and flashing lights were at maximum effect.

"What the…?" Wayne's jaw dropped.

"Is that…? Did you…? What!" Mark's eyes were wide-open.

Michelle just flashed one of her big, beautiful smiles.

Bishop looked like a zombie.

Barbara turned and gave me a kiss. "I don't know what's going on, but you are wonderful."

The cars came to a screeching halt in front of the bar where Mark, for all intents and purposes, had been robbed.

Six doors flew open. Guardia di Finanza operatives exited the vehicles fully decked out in their uniforms, body armor, Beretta 92 FS .40-caliber pistols and semiautomatic Franchi shotguns.

Giorgio had gone over the top.

I saw him get out of the first car, his driver sitting still behind the wheel. As he walked around the hood of the Alfa, he looked over in my direction and gave a thumbs-up. He then walked briskly into the bar with his small team right behind him.

"That was awesome! Just awesome!"

"How did you arrange all of this, Atticus!?"

"Is that Italian military or police?"

I answered Michelle's query: "They are a cross between our Drug Enforcement Administration, Internal Revenue Service and the FBI. I used to work with the guy who gave me the AOK. That was many years ago."

I knew that this was going to open up another series of questions.

"What did you do, Atticus?"

"Were *you* with the FBI? CIA?"

"I bet you were a spy, maybe you still are!"

"Okay, okay, enough for now. We're not finished here. We need to get Mark's money back. Come with me." We made our way through the crowd that had gathered around the two cars. The sirens had been turned off, but the lights were still flashing vigorously. I made eye contact with Giorgio's driver, who recognized me. He was still a young man, not a day over thirty-five, and still built like a double-door refrigerator. Getting out of the car, he walked up to me and warmly shook my hand.

"*Signor* Winterle! What a pleasure to see you again."

"The same for me, Pietro. I am happy to see as well. You look great."

"Can't complain. Life is always interesting."

"Your wife? Lucia, correct? How is she?" I could tell from Pietro's expression that he was pleased that I remembered.

"She's terrific, Signor Winterle. We have a twelve-year-old boy and an-eight-year-old girl now. We're very happy."

"That's great news! Spend as much time as you can with the family. It's precious, and we forget this sometimes."

"I will, I will."

"Do you mind, Pietro, if we go inside? This young man here is the reason why all of you are here." I put my hand on Mark's shoulder.

"Go right ahead. It was really wonderful to see you again." He gave me a military salute and went back inside the car, his large 45-caliber pistol with suppressor strapped to his side.

"This is all blowing my mind!" Mark exclaimed. "Who was that giant? I think you have some explaining to do."

"Yes "I'll clue you in on a few things later on. Now let's get in here."

I told the others to wait for us outside. They looked disappointed.

The bar was very small, and most of the space was taken up by the officers who had entered before us. The patrons had left in a hurry.

Two of the officers were behind the bar counter in front of an open cash register. From what I could tell they were checking the payment receipts with the cash and credit card payments to see if the owner was cheating on his taxable income. Giorgio, on the other hand, was interrogating a rather scruffy individual, who looked absolutely terrified. I didn't remember the last time I had seen such a deathly shade of pale.

The other two officers were close by, hands resting on their firearms. Giorgio was outlining a series of misdemeanors that the owner was presumably guilty of. You would have thought that he had broken into Fort Knox.

"And furthermore, Mr. Cassino, do you remember this young man?" Giorgio's enunciation was deliberately slow and almost flirtatious. He was enjoying himself toying with this guy like a cat playing with a mouse before the kill. The scene was straight out of the movie *Inglourious Basterds* where Christoph Waltz is interrogating a French farmer on the whereabouts of a Jewish family. Mr. Cassino took a look at Mark and shook his head nervously.

"*No?* You don't *remember?* Well now, that is unfortunate. You see, this young man, a student and tourist who came to our great country, unfortunately walked into this dump of a bar a few nights ago. You sold him a bottle of tequila, cheap stuff, and took one hundred and forty of his US dollars."

One hundred and forty? It was eighty. This was Giorgio going way over the top again.

"No, I don't remember…" You could barely hear Mr. Cassino.

"Speak up, please!"

"I…don't remember him."

There was a long and excruciating pause. "How interesting indeed. Because you see, Mr. Cassino, the boy here remembers you, don't you?" Giorgio turned and looked straight at Mark. I translated for him.

"Yeah, he's the guy all right, can't forget him. He sold me a bottle, said it was twenty dollars, but he ended up taking eight…" I kicked Mark's ankle harder than I intended.

"One hundred and forty dollars, right?" I said hastily.

Mark looked at me, bewildered.

"Isn't that right, Mark?" I looked at him intently.

"Yeah…that's right. A hundred and forty dollars."

Giorgio let the seconds tick away, grinning sadistically at the poor fellow. "Therefore, Mr. Cassino…one hundred and forty dollars. I doubt all the bottles in here are worth as much. Now we can do two things here. Either you give this gentleman back his one hundred forty dollars, or you can refuse. If you refuse, I will just add this fact to the very long list of fraudulent tax-evasion activities that you have been committing in this establishment." Another pause. Giorgio inspected the nails of his hand, looking very pleased at his manicure. "However, Mr. Cassino, if you do decide to give this boy back his money, I just may turn a blind eye to some of those unlawful pastimes of yours that my sergeant here is diligently noting down."

"Yes! Immediately!" Cassino replied. "But I don't have any dollars right now."

"Oh, oh. This is a problem. Mr. Winterle, do you think that our friend would accept euros instead of American dollars?"

"I don't see any problem with that," I said.

Mr. Cassino reached over to the open cash register and hurriedly took out two €50 notes and two €20. That was about US$175 at today's exchange.

"Take, take it!" he said, almost pleading with Mark.

Mark took the notes, knowing it was almost double of what had actually been stolen from him. I sensed that he wasn't feeling good about it. Giorgio saluted us and turned back to his victim. Mark and I were done in here.

The crowd had subsided, but there were still a good number of people around the two Alfa Romeos. The rest of the group were standing exactly where Mark and I had left them.

"What happened in there?" Bishop asked.

"I got my money back." Mark held up the euros gripped in his hand.

"Well, ladies and gentlemen, we're finished here," I said. "I'm hungry, let's go get dinner."

I started off toward the Trevi Fountain with what sounded like a pack of baying hounds behind me. All four of them began reeling off questions about my past and how I had managed to set up the "shakedown," as they called it. However, I noted with interest that they also wanted to know what was going to happen to the bartender, with Mark and Michelle especially concerned.

"Are they going to throw him in jail?"

"Is he going to lose his business?"

"Does the guy have a family?"

I turned and faced my demanding followers.

"Now how could I know if he has a family, Mark?"

Mark cocked his head. "Well, you seem to know a lot of things, Mr. Secret Agent man."

"If it will make all of you feel better, I can assure you that this guy won't go to jail and won't lose his business. He'll probably be fined, but that's it. And I wouldn't feel so damn sorry for him. As soon as those officers leave and the dust has settled, he'll probably rip off another tourist. I can assure you of that."

"When are you going to spill the beans, Atticus?" Wayne asked. "How did you manage to pull that stunt off? You can't leave us hanging like this."

"All right already. Before all of you head back to the States, I shall let you in on a few secrets. Now stop and look at that and take it all in. It's a spectacle to behold." I pointed at the Trevi Fountain, which was enveloped in various degrees of suffused pastel lighting. The cascading water threw alternating shadows on Oceanus standing majestically on his open-shelled chariot, pulled by his two-winged horses guided by proud tritons.

Other questions were thrown at me about my past, but I avoided answering them.

Finally, Michelle intervened. "Since we can't squeeze anything else out of you, do you mind if we don't go straight back to the hotel? I'd like to walk around a bit and maybe just grab some pizza later. You guys with me?"

Mark, Bishop, and Wayne nodded.

"It's fine by me," I said. "Mrs. Cornwall? What do you say?"

"Of course. Enjoy yourselves. Just try to be back no later than ten thirty."

"Okay. Done deal."

We watched as the four disappeared into the crowd around the Trevi Fountain. Barbara turned and faced me.

"Well, that was certainly exciting. Promise me that we'll go out together tonight, even if late. Just the two of us."

"You don't have to ask me twice."

"You must tell me how you pulled off that police dragnet. You obviously have a few connections in this town."

"Just a few, from the old days."

We were now in front of the hotel.

"I'll catch up with you after dinner then."

Before I could answer, Barbara did a rapid 360-degree scan, then zoomed in, and gave me a soft kiss on the lips. So much for discretion. She went up the three steps and entered the lobby, the sliding glass doors closing silently behind her.

Before going in, I decided to stop at the *Tabacchi* (literally, "Tobacco Shop") a bit further down the road to buy another box of Toscanello cigars. As I exited with my purchase, I encountered Mary, Anthony, Raymond, and Vanessa passing right outside.

"Well, where are the four of you headed off to?"

"We're just going out to some more exploring," said Vanessa. "We wanted to walk around a bit and then go to one of those trati...tratta...tratto—"

"Trattorias?"

"Yeah, that's it. Like the one we went to after the Sistine Chapel."

"Sounds like a great idea. Enjoy yourselves and don't get back too late. Do you have enough cash with you?"

"We're fine," said Mary. "We have credit cards if we need them."

"Okay, then. Remember to order dishes you've never had from the menu. Also, look closely at the bill. I don't want you to get taken."

"No worries, Atticus," Anthony assured me. "We've learned about that with you. See you later!"

I was pleased to see him out and about without Cynthia hovering like his personal mother hen. I strolled back to the hotel and decided to head to the dining area. I caught a glimpse of Barbara as she was sitting down at her table with a plate already full of food. I went over to the short line of hotel patrons, who were waiting to serve themselves at the buffet. There was a particularly rich array of items this evening. The three double boilers had the pasta dishes: spaghetti in a rich tomato sauce, butterfly pasta with peas, diced ham and a cream sauce, and in the third tray, pappardelle with mushrooms and what looked like crumbled sausage. I took some of each and decided to come back afterward to fill up with many other dishes covering the length of the buffet table.

We were a much smaller group this evening. But what really caught my attention was the seating arrangement. Four tables had been pushed together, and at the far end, I saw James and Jeremy sitting across from Darlene. Closer to where I was standing was Evelyn, with Sabrina sitting directly across from her. I did a double take. I had never seen these two so close to each other before.

"Well now, it seems that we have quite a few absentees this evening."

"I wanted to go out," said Jeremy, "but Massimo walked us to death today at the movie studios. Not that I'm complaining. It was really terrific."

"I'm glad you enjoyed it, Jeremy."

"I'm bushed, too," Sabrina said. "I'm going upstairs and Skype a few people back home." Sabrina did look very tired. Where had she been all day?

"Anybody seen Mr. Seeward?" I asked. I knew that Cynthia was out for the day, but where had John gone?

"No clue," Barbara answered. "Last time I saw him was in the lobby when we got back from the movie studio."

Darlene cleared her throat. "Mrs. Cornwall?"

"Yes, Darlene?" Barbara replied, looking at her expressionlessly.

"Can I speak to you for a moment, out in the lobby? Maybe in ten minutes?"

"Come up to my room instead." Barbara made it clear from her tone that she hadn't forgotten that morning's episode.

"Okay, thanks. See you in a bit." Darlene quietly got up and left the restaurant.

I was still hungry and went back to the buffet as the waiters were beginning to take the serving dishes back to the kitchen. When I got back to my seat, I noticed that Jeremy had also left the room.

James and Evelyn, strangely enough, had moved directly in front of me and Barbara.

"Hungry, I see," James said, eyeing my overflowing plate.

"Most definitely. Walking all day in this city can build an appetite, and you know in this city, an appetite is never disappointed."

Evelyn also glanced at my plate. "Yeah, the food was great tonight," she said. "Those beans are good. What's mixed up with them?"

Something was different about Evelyn. I wouldn't have gone so far as to say that she looked cheerful, but there was color in her cheeks, and her eyes were wide-open and receptive.

"You may not like the answer, Evelyn," I said.

She gave me a crooked smile. "Try me."

"Black pepper, vinegar, thyme, salt, red onions, garlic, olive oil and…" I paused for dramatic effect.

"*And?*"

"Crushed anchovies, bones and all."

"What? No way, you're messing with me, Atticus."

"That's the recipe. You liked it though, right?"

Evelyn giggled. "Maybe I shouldn't have asked you, after all."

Evelyn giggling? Really?

I saw that Barbara was just as awestruck as me at this transformation. But both of us continued looking and acting as if nothing was out of the ordinary.

I glanced at James, who was also observing Evelyn. I could tell that he also puzzled by her sudden mutation.

"The chicken is good, too." Evelyn continued, eyeing my chicken filled with bell peppers.

"Really well made. They do a good job in this kitchen."

Evelyn looked across at the buffet table. "Isn't anyone getting some dessert? There are some great-looking ones." Evelyn looked at James, who just shrugged his shoulders.

"Well, I'm going to take a look. Come with me, J." She nudged James. They both got up and headed toward the desserts. Barbara and I turned to each other simultaneously.

"Unbelievable!" Barbara exclaimed, but in a low voice. "Evelyn must have a twin living here in Rome."

"I'm certainly surprised."

"Oh, it's more than just a surprise. I haven't seen Evelyn so, let's say, social, since well before Derek died and all that mess with her parents."

"Even James was looking at her as if she were an alien." I took a quick look over my shoulder to make sure that they were still far from earshot.

"I wonder if Sabrina has anything to do with it. I noticed that she was sitting right across from Evelyn when I came in. That was also unusual."

"I noticed that, too."

"All very curious, but now I have to see what Darlene wants with me."

"I'm pretty sure I know. Oh, that reminds me, those roses were for Darlene."

"Darlene? All of them?"

"From Giacomo."

"You're kidding!"

"Nope. He also gave Giovanni an expensive tie and a card. Darlene and I both got a card as well. I thought you'd better know before meeting with her."

"Which is about right now. I'm off. Call me in my room in about forty-five minutes."

She leaned over and gave me a kiss on the cheek just as Evelyn and James were seating themselves. I could feel a tidal wave of blood engulfing my capillaries as Barbara left.

"Well now," I jabbered, "I see you guys have made a very good selection of sweets. I mean desserts…" I tried to stray away from that kiss on the cheek and my consequent ruby-red complexion, but to no avail.

"You and Mrs. Cornwall are really an item, huh?" Evelyn said.

I almost choked on my garlic sautéed spinach. *Didn't these young people believe in discretion?*

"I thought that the two of you were just in it for the sex, but I can tell now that she really likes you," Evelyn said, daintily cutting open and eating her profiterole. "I gotta say, you make a nice couple."

I looked over at James, who had a satisfied grin on his face.

"Don't look at me, Atticus. She said it, not me."

"You're not offended, are you?" asked Evelyn.

"No," I said. "I guess that we haven't been too discreet lately."

"Discreet? We all knew the two of you were an item the second day we were here. Can't pull a fast one on us." Then she did it again, giggled.

I shrugged. "Okay, yes. I admit it. I like Mrs. Cornwall a lot, and I think she likes me. There, I said it. So let's pour some of this"—I reached over for a half empty bottle of red wine—"and make a toast."

I filled our glasses and raised mine.

"To Mrs. Cornwall and Atticus," said Evelyn.

We clinked our glasses and took a big sip.

"Enough about me and Mrs. Cornwall," I said. "I haven't seen the two of you all day. Did you do anything fun?"

"I had a good day, Atticus. Let's leave at that for now." She nodded, but as if at her inner thoughts. "It was good day."

I didn't ask her anything else.

"James? Anything worthwhile? Did you get to do any draw—"

"I did a lot of walking," James said, cutting across me. "Took some notes. I ended up in a museum up near the train station. That's all."

So James didn't want his drawings mentioned. Why not?

"There are quite a few museums in that area," I said. "Do you remember the name?"

"No. I do remember that from the second floor you could see a humongous train station."

"Ah. That's the main station. You must've been in the National Museum of Rome. I haven't been in there in years."

I paused a moment, wondering if I had ever really been in there after all. "Did you see anything that sparked your interest?"

"Yeah, I did. I saw something mind-blowing."

James was staring right above my shoulder as if whatever had captivated him in the museum was now right behind me.

"Um, what was it?"

"This." James reached for his cell phone and turned it toward me. The photo was of a bronze statue, in a sitting position, its head turned up with an indescribable expression on its face. I knew exactly what I was looking at.

"The *Boxer at Rest*. It's a famous Greek statue from about 300 BC. Imagine, it was found around 1885 not very far from here, and it was so perfectly buried that the only damage to it were the eyes, which were probably made of painted glass or ceramic. I can understand why you found it interesting. It's a powerful work of art." I was looking down at my plate, stuffing my mouth with last forkfuls of spinach.

"No, you can't." The three little words came out from James's mouth like slow-motion bullets.

I stopped eating, realizing in a split-second that I had made a big mistake. What I had just said about this statue would not have made waves with anybody else, but this was James, and James was not like anybody else.

I looked up at him. He was glaring at me. Evelyn felt the sudden electricity in the air and attempted to lighten up the moment. It backfired.

"Hey, J, it's all good, Atticus was just trying—"

He put up his hand but didn't even look at her. "Don't you have something better to do?" That was worse than a slap in the face for Evelyn. She got up, shoving the chair behind her violently.

"Yeah...anything is better than being here with you!" Tears were welling up in her eyes. She rushed out of the room.

James had never taken his eyes off of me even when addressing Evelyn. I knew that my next words would either get him back on my side or permanently rupture any bonding that I had managed to slowly create between us these past few days.

"Okay, James. You're absolutely right. I don't know why you found that particular statue awesome. I apologize." I was now staring at him just as intensely as he was at me. He didn't say a word. I was profoundly apprehensive that he would get up, tell me to stick it or worse, and leave the room. Finally, he spoke:

"Have you ever really looked at it, Atticus, observed it? Or do you just know the hard facts about it? Things that I can fucking google up if I wanted to?" He paused a moment, and then his gaze went back over my shoulder.

"I must've stood there an hour, looking at that face. I couldn't stop looking at it. It was his expression. You knew he had been defeated. But he looked more than defeated. He was tired, like, tired of life, in total despair. I don't think he ever had eyes. I think the sculptor made him with those empty spaces where his eyes should have been. That was part of the statue's power."

I kept my mouth shut, my eyes still fixed on his. I thought about Sabrina and her positive encounter with the statue of St. Rita. This was a different story.

"I remember seeing this statue, James, and reading up on it years ago but, no, I didn't spend any time studying it the way you did."

James sat back. I relaxed a bit. He wasn't going to leave after all.

"You should," he said. "I've never felt so drawn in by a piece of art in my life. Never."

"Think you may go back and see it again before you head back to the States?"

"Yeah, maybe. Why?"

"Well, if you do, and if you don't mind the company, I'd like to go with you and get a second look at it." James looked down at his hands and scrunched up his lips as if in deep thought. Had I put my foot in my mouth again?

"I guess so. As long as you don't act like that jerk guide we had at the Pantheon."

"Comparing me to that jerk is like putting my balls in a vice, James."

"'Balls in a vice?'"

"Yeah, that's exactly what I said." I looked at James. Had I gone over the top?

He grinned at me. "The lyrics of a famous 1970s song," James was talking to himself. "Okay, Mr. Music Man, can you answer this one? Give me the name of the song with 'balls in a vice' in the lyrics and who wrote it. I'll even give you a hint: released in 1979. I'm waiting."

"Hey, give me a break, let me think a moment." I tried to buy some time, but I didn't have the slightest idea who James was alluding to.

"The Scorpions?"

"No, you're way off."

"Um, Def Leppard?"

"You don't have a clue, do you?"

"Wait a minute, Metallica. That's it!"

"Metallica didn't get together until 1981. You're killing me."

"All right already." I was annoyed. "Who are we talking about?"

"Zappa, Frank Zappa. One of the best songwriters and musicians of all time."

"Can't say I really ever followed any of his work."

"Don't know what you're missing. Listen to 'Bobby Brown Goes Down,' that's where you'll hear about your balls in a vice."

"I'll do that. Now, can you do me a favor?"

"What favor?"

"I think you may have been a little rough with Evelyn."

He began to fiddle with the only remaining fork on the table.

"If you don't mind me saying so, it's obvious that she cares about you a great deal."

"Yeah, I guess so. But she's like a leech sometimes. Today was the first full day that I was able to get out on my own without her hanging all over me. And did you catch how weird she was acting tonight? All happy and shit. Talk about bizarre."

It wasn't opportune to mention anything about Evelyn's encounter with Sabrina. Instead, I asked if he had any plans for the rest of the evening.

"No, I'm going back to the room," he replied. "I walked my ass off today. You happen to know where Ramsey is? I need to take my pills." This was the first time that James had mentioned anything to me about his medication. I ventured with a risky question.

"Do they help you any?"

James locked his eyes on me again. "Let's say that they keep me from falling into a deep, black hellhole." He got up from his chair.

"Sorry about earlier," I said. "I need to learn to shut up sometimes."

"Chill, Atticus. I still consider you one of the handful of people I can stomach."

"I'll take that as a compliment." James turned at the door of the restaurant and looked back at me. "Take it any fuckin' way you want. I could care less."

James walked out the door, and I just sat there a moment, stunned. There again, in a split second, was that chilling aloofness in his voice that left me numb. *My God, what's wrong with this kid?*

It was almost nine o'clock. I needed to make a phone call before tracking Barbara down. I tapped the numbers on my phone and got Giorgio on the line after two rings.

"Pronto?"

"Giorgio, it's me, Atticus."

"Atticus, I was expecting a call from you. How did I do? Are you pleased?"

"You went overboard, Giorgio. You really put on a show. My group was incredibly impressed. You can't imagine the questions I was hit with when we left." There was a slight pause at the other end of the line, and I immediately deciphered what Giorgio was thinking.

"Don't concern yourself. You know my lips are sealed. They know I worked for the justice department and was stationed at the embassy, but that's it." I could feel Giorgio relaxing at the other end.

"That's very good, Atticus. Some things are better left unsaid. I know it's still an open wound for you…"

Now it was I who fell silent.

"You know me very well, Giorgio," I said, after a bit. "Very well." Another silent interval. I returned to the topic at hand. "By the way, what happened to our friend there at the bar?"

"I slapped him with a three-hundred-euro fine for all the errors we found in his bookkeeping, but nothing more. I could have shut down that rattrap. Tonight, he'll be back at screwing tourists out of their money. That's not going to change."

"You know, Giorgio, my kids, especially Mark, the one who got taken by that guy, were particularly concerned that he would lose his business."

"He doesn't have to worry about that. It won't happen."

"Thank you once again for all you did."

"You know where to find me if you need me."

"Speak soon." I tapped my phone, and the line went dead.

Giorgio was truly a special person. He had been there for me in the very good times, in the horrible ones and, lastly, the more "covert" times. We had been through a lot together.

But now I wanted to concentrate on Barbara and a lovely evening stroll in this captivating city.

I looked at my watch. It was almost nine thirty.

CHAPTER 49

I left the table and headed for the lobby. Barbara was waiting for me. She was absolutely stunning. She had on an off-turquoise dress that accentuated her abundant curves, with three-inch open-toed sandals. Fingernails and toenails matched with the same brick-red nail polish. Her makeup was captivating, subtle but sensual. And of course, I could smell the Shalimar when I reached out to take her arm.

We exited the hotel like two giddy schoolkids. I guided her down all the charming side streets that would lead us to our destination—the home of the gods.

Once there, the evening became even more special. The Pantheon was still open! I knew that one day a month, this monument remained accessible to the public until eleven. We had managed, unknowingly, to be at the right place at the right time.

Needless to say, she was awestruck the moment she set foot inside. I proceeded to take her around the building, pointing out the unique details, explaining how it was built around AD 120, and generally seducing her with my historical knowledge. However, her gaze magnetically strayed upward to the large space in the center of the dome.

"There is something enchanting about that opening up there, Atticus" she said. "Don't you almost feel a special connection with the sky, the universe?"

"I do. I suspect that the main purpose of that opening was for the Romans to experience a closer relationship with the gods."

We strolled randomly through the Pantheon, holding hands. It couldn't get any better than this. When we exited, we headed to the fountain in the middle of the piazza.

As usual, there were throngs of tourists going in all directions, admiring the sights, enjoying a gelato or an *aperitivo* at one of the many outdoor restaurants and bars.

"Atticus!" Barbara was pointing and bobbing up and down like a child in front of a toy store window.

"Let's go sit over there, close to where we went the other night."

We made are way over to the table that Barbara had indicated and made ourselves comfortable. A waiter came within seconds. I asked Barbara if she would care for some champagne, as on our previous night out together.

She gave me a brilliant smile.

"*Una bottiglia di Moët, freddissima, grazie,*" I told the waiter.

"How wonderful to be able to speak more than one language," Barbara said, admiringly. "Let's see, I got the bottle of Moët, but what does *fredd…ii…si* mean?"

"*Freddissima.* It means 'very cold.' There is nothing worse than a lukewarm bottle of French champagne."

"My little snob."

"There are just some things in life where there can be no compromises. Ice-cold Moët is one of them."

"I'll remember that."

"See that you do." We leaned over and kissed each other warmly. This was heaven. I reached in my pocket for my Toscanello cigars and my brand-new Dupont lighter, setting both on the table.

"May I see that?" Barbara asked.

"Sure, I bought it today."

"It's beautiful." She examined it and then flicked the flame on and off a few times. "Sometimes I think it's worth smoking just for the gadgets…the lighters, the silver cigarette cases, and those gorgeous outrageously expensive Louis Vuitton ashtrays."

"Well, you don't have to smoke to buy those ashtrays, and you can always play with my lighter…"

"Oh, is *that* how you call *it* now?"

I realized my unintended double entendre, and we both had a good laugh.

Barbara cast her gaze upward. "My goodness, Atticus, look at how magnificent the Pantheon is lit up that way."

She was right. The lights were positioned in such a way to allow the monument an aura of grandeur. High-beam bulbs were placed at the base of the portico columns and around the central portion of the circular structure. The intensity of the light would reach a crescendo and then fade back to almost pitch dark, in continuously alternate patterns.

The Pantheon had a soul.

I turned back to Barbara. "Question for you before I forget. Did you know that James draws?"

"Draws? Draws what?"

"That's just it, I don't know. I ran into him this morning as he was heading out of the hotel with a sketch pad under his arm."

"All news to me, Atticus. Are you sure?"

"He told me as much and mentioned that drawing cleared his head."

"Maybe he has a new interest. With James, anything is possible."

The waiter arrived with the ice bucket stand and the bottle of Moët. He skillfully tore off the aluminum foil around the very top and undid the wire caging that held the cork firmly pressed inside the rim of the bottle. He then tilted it to one side and slowly pushed the cork upward until it made the harmonious popping sound that only comes from a quality bottle of champagne. He proceeded to pour the bubbly liquid into two goblets that another waiter had placed on our table.

I raised my glass. "I would like to make a toast."

"I'm all ears," Barbara said, looking at me with wide eyes.

"To this group, that each one finds their path to happiness when they get back home."

"I will most certainly drink to that."

Our glasses clinked, and we both took a deep swallow.

"By the way, I have some reading material for you," I said.

I took out my cell phone and opened the folder where I have saved Michelle's emailed photos.

"This will help explain Evelyn's change in behavior this evening. It came as a bit of shock to me, a positive one." Barbara skimmed through the text, her eyes becoming wider with every line.

"Well now, that is surprising!" she exclaimed. "I definitely wasn't expecting to see Sabrina in the equation." Barbara scratched the back of her head. "I never thought that those two would ever end up speaking to each other again other than a truckload of profanities. And it seems here that Sabrina made the first move. I wonder what sparked that."

I told Barbara about how I had suggested that Sabrina go take a look at the statue of St. Rita, inferring that it may have had a positive effect on her.

"Oh, come on Atticus," said Barbara. "That's all well and good in la-la land, but it's 2010. You're telling me that a teenage girl sits in front of a statue for a few minutes and then sees the light? Far-fetched, wouldn't you say?"

"I understand where you're coming from. I didn't put any worth into it at all until I started going to see her on a regular basis."

"*Her?* It's a statue, Atticus, at least that what you said."

"Yes, it is. Very true. Tell you what, you're still here for a few days. Go over to that church and take a look."

"No, no, no, that's not me. I don't believe in any of that. If it really did have some positive affect on Sabrina, then good for her but leave me out of it."

Barbara had stiffened up a bit and seemed uncomfortable. I decided not to press the matter.

"I think that Evelyn decided to meet with Sabrina today at the Trevi Fountain. I don't know this for a fact. They didn't bring it up at dinner, obviously."

Barbara cleared her throat. "I really am surprised they didn't throw themselves into the fountain and try to drown each other. It will be interesting to see how they act these next few days."

I poured more champagne into our empty goblets.

"How did your meeting with Darlene go?"

"Oh yes, I was going to tell you about that, but we got on that statue thing…"

Barbara's words and body language made it abundantly clear that invoking a religious explanation for Sabrina's change in behavior was ludicrous.

"She was already in front of my door when I got upstairs, looking like a helpless stray dog. I don't know how much of that was an act."

"What did she have to say for herself?"

"Nothing at first. We went into my room, but she just stood by the door."

"And?"

"She apologized for calling me a MILF and all the rest. She blamed it on that incident with Giacomo, which she said shook her up."

"Understandable, I guess, but there was no need to take it out on you. She didn't say anything about the flowers and Giacomo's card?"

"Oh yes, I think she was quite taken by all of those roses— what woman wouldn't be? But she wasn't in my room to talk about Giacomo. She wanted to talk about you."

"Me?"

"She really admires you, Atticus, you know that don't you?"

"Oh, brother…"

"Come on now, this is serious. Not succumbing to her female attributes hurt her. She understands and respects you for not giving in, but it crushed her."

"Did anything else come up, or was I the only star topic?"

"Not really, other than asking me if I was in love with you."

The sip of my champagne I was taking instantly went down the wrong way. Barbara gave me a few slaps on the back.

"Hey, everything okay?"

I finally stopped coughing. "Yes. All's well." I coughed again, covering my mouth with my fist. "I just wasn't expecting that."

"She was very tactful about it and apologized for putting her nose in my business."

I studied Barbara a moment and then asked her the obvious. "Did you give her an answer?"

"I did. A rather profound one if I must say so myself. But I'm not telling you what it was, not now at least." Barbara picked up her glass and clinked it against mine. "To you, Atticus Winterle, the collector of women's hearts and bodies."

"Oh, please."

"Well, you've conquered Darlene, you have pretty much bulldozed me, and then there is that attractive young lady at the front desk. She eats you with her eyes every time you pass by. You've got her smack dab in the palm of your hand."

"Ludovica?"

"So you know who I'm talking about." Barbara grinned.

"Well, she's the *only* girl at the front desk."

"Never mind that. She would be all over you in a second if you let her. Trust me. You're just a lady killer, Atticus, and you know it." She leaned over, kissed me quickly on the lips, and took another big swallow of champagne. I noticed that our glasses, and the bottle for that matter, were nearly empty.

"One more?" I said, pointing to the ice bucket.

"Why not? I'm having a great time."

I signaled to the waiter with the empty bottle of Moët in my hand. He acknowledged my request with a nod of the head and disappeared inside the bar.

I said, "The group seems to have enjoyed themselves over at the movie studio today. I'm sure John was particularly interested." I glanced at Barbara with a raised eyebrow.

"He was actually on his very best behavior today and really sociable with the kids, which is unusual for him. He even offered me his arm when we were waking on some unsteady ground around the set of *Ben Hur*. Yes, John was a charmer today." Barbara turned her head slightly attempting to strangle a smirk of satisfaction.

"You said that on purpose."

"Oh, Atticus." She chuckled and put her arm around my neck. "John can't compete with you, and you know it."

That made me feel a little better.

"John's closet has demons in it," said Barbara, "but I think this trip is helping him shed a few." Barbara had unknowingly hit the jackpot.

"Speaking of demons, any idea where Cynthia may have run off to this evening?"

"No clue."

"There's a lot of pain stored up in that woman."

"Maybe, but I'm not very sympathetic. She can be very hard to put up with at times. She has her own agenda and careful if you mess with it."

"I didn't tell you that Cynthia and I are going to the forum tomorrow, alone?"

"Oh really? No, I don't think that you brought that up." It was now Barbara throwing a raised eyebrow in my direction.

"She didn't get to see any of it the other day, remember?"

"That's right, Vanessa wasn't feeling well."

"Correct." I swallowed a salubrious mouthful of Moët. "She wants to speak to me in private. I don't know about what."

"A lady killer *and* a therapist. What's next, Atticus?"

"Father confessor?"

"Father confessor…hmm. I like that idea. I can just see you all dressed in black with that white collar on…I wouldn't let you out of the confessional with your clothes on." Barbara began toying with my earlobe.

"Continue doing that and I won't be liable for my actions," I said.

"I'm waiting." She put her left leg on my right knee. Then she took my hand and led it straight down into her panties that were, undeniably, moist. I began working my fingers.

Nobody was paying attention to us, thank goodness. It didn't take a rocket scientist to figure out what was going on, even if the tablecloth was long enough to cover up our libidinous moment.

"One bottle of Moët."

The abrupt appearance of our waiter almost made us jump an inch off our chairs. My hand, which was nestled so delightfully between Barbara's legs, came up, slamming against the underside of the table. Our glasses would have toppled over had we not grabbed them with our free hands.

So much for going unnoticed.

"*Si…grazie…*I'll open it, thank you."

"*Si, signor…*" The waiter attempted to suppress a roguish grin as he walked off. We would very soon be the talk of the establishment.

"Oh my God! I was about to have an amazing orgasm—damn that waiter!"

"He's just doing his job. We're the naughty ones."

It took us a few minutes to regain our composure and act as if we had been sitting there innocently admiring the Pantheon.

"I would like to make another toast." I filled our glasses with the bubbly elixir.

"Yes?" Barbara said.

"To Francesca."

Barbara raised an interrogative eyebrow. "Your girlfriend?"

"*Ex*-girlfriend as of today. I want to toast to her future, her health, her happiness, and, most importantly, for having had the proverbial balls to tell me that this relationship is over. Something I should have done time ago and never did."

"Well, a few days back, you mentioned that she wasn't the right woman for you and that there was no chemistry between her and the children."

"No, she wasn't the right woman for any of us, but I led her on for almost a year. That was unfair."

Barbara saw that I was tethering on a morose reverie and quickly changed the subject.

"So, Mr. Secret Agent Man, after that brilliant performance with your Italian police buddies, I want to hear all about that part of your life. If you won't have to kill me after, that is."

I laughed. "No, but I might have to tie you up and do unspeakable things."

"I have no objection to that," she replied with a mischievous grin.

"It's been a good fifteen years since that chapter was closed," I told her. This wasn't entirely true, but there were certain details that only a selected few were privy to. "What is it that you would like to know exactly?"

Barbara took my hand in hers and looked straight into my eyes. "All of it."

"In that case, we have to go back to 1985. That's when I graduated from college."

I explained that I had applied to the FBI shortly afterwards and was accepted to the foreign intelligence division, mainly because of my Italian and French language skills.

"You worked for with the bureau right after college?"

"By the time all the security clearances were conducted, it was closer to end of 1986."

"Then what?"

"After a few months in Washington, I was sent off to the Defense Language Institute in Carmel in California. I spent eleven months there doing Russian language training."

"That sounds exciting."

"Didn't seem so at the time. Ten hours a day, six days a week, with only every third weekend off. Students dropped out of the course every week. We started with forty-eight people and ended up with nine. But, get this, at the end of the course, which I did rather well in, what does the bureau do? They send me to the U.S. Embassy here, in Rome."

"I guess you were expecting somewhere in Russia."

"Or at least any, at the time, one of the Soviet Republics, like Uzbekistan or Kazakhstan."

"Well, Mr. Bond, I don't think that you could have gotten a much better assignment than this." Barbara spread out her arms and looked admiringly at her surroundings. I had to agree with her. She took a large gulp of champagne and continued the interrogation.

"Okay, so you get to Rome, then what? We haven't gotten to the hardcore stuff yet."

"Before we get to the hardcore, as you call it, I have to introduce you to Clara, a very important piece of the Atticus Winterle puzzle."

"It's always a woman who holds the key—that's what you men never admit."

"Well, if so, Clara had a ring of keys, not just one."

"I like her already. Who was she? Another spy like you?"

"No, she was my landlady while I was stationed here. But she also happened to be one of the foreign national administrators at the U.S. consulate, which is next to the embassy. She was the daughter of a duke and duchess from the region of Emilia-Romagna and inherited a great deal of money and land when her father passed away.

"How old was she when you met her?"

Odd question, I thought.

"She was exactly twenty years older than me. I was twenty-five, and she was forty-five."

Barbara studied me a moment. Her next question showed that women are always one step ahead of men.

"And was this relationship the two of you had just landlord-tenant, or was there more to it?"

"I'm getting there. Let's just say that, after a few weeks of getting acquainted, well, one thing led to another and…"

"You were on top of each other, right, Mr. Toy Boy?"

I frowned. "I wasn't a toy boy," I almost snapped.

Barbara was taken aback at my reaction. "I'm sorry Atticus, I didn't mean to—"

I placed my hand on her arm and squeezed it gently.

"No, I'm sorry. It's still a sensitive issue. We did start up a physical relationship, but it soon became an emotional one as well. Clara and I were together for almost eight years even though she would frequently repeat that it would all end one day with me going after a younger woman."

"Which you did."

"Yes, I left Clara for my first wife, which, in hindsight, was a mistake of monumental proportions, with the only exceptions being my two children."

"She sounds like a very special person."

"Oh, she was. Clara was instrumental in getting me to know many influential people. Her contacts ranged from high-ranking officials in the Italian Secret Service, the police, the Italian and American armed forces, and the Guardia di Finanza, one of which you had the pleasure of seeing in action this evening. Then there were her contacts in the banking industry, those in the Ministry of Finance and Foreign Affairs. She even hobnobbed with high-ranking prelates in the Vatican. When Clara threw a party at her home, it was a *Who's Who* of the rich and powerful."

I paused and took another sip of champagne. Barbara broke the momentary silence:

"You've been speaking in the past tense the entire time. Is Clara still alive?"

"No, she isn't, unfortunately. And that's another story. She came down with a serious form of skin cancer back in 1987, melanoma, fourth stage, on the underside of her foot. To make a long story short, after three operations where the practically ended up taking her foot off in chunks and four grueling cycles of chemo with a new product that had just hit the market, Clara made it until 2007."

"She must have been one tough cookie."

"That's an understatement. That woman had a backbone made of titanium. She handed Death a raincheck and said, 'Come back in twenty years.'" She regained about ninety percent of her strength and never missed a day at work. We were optimistic about the future and lived each day to the fullest."

I paused. Barbara didn't say a word.

"And then I made a mistake, a very big mistake. In the spring of 1989, I got it in my head that the bureau wasn't enough. I wanted to work for the CIA. There were colleagues of mine in the embassy who were egging me on, who thought I would be a great addition to the 'farm,' as it's called."

"Sounds like a reasonable next step if you wanted to stay in that line of work."

"True, but I made a fatal error. The timing, talk about timing..." I mumbled these last words to myself. I drained my glass of the Moët and poured some more for both of us.

"Clara, as I told you, had many contacts and friends in high places. One of these was Liam Brewster, Liam W. Brewster. Does that name ring a bell?"

Barbara furrowed her brow.

"Wasn't he the head of the FBI?"

"Bingo! Head of the FBI and then the—"

"CIA…," Barbara finished, with hesitation. She frowned. "This sounds like it's all going south and fast. How *friendly* was Clara with Brewster?" Again, a woman's intuition.

"Well, she was pleasant with him, found him interesting, but he wanted much more than that. And then comes to find out that a twenty-five-year-old bureau analyst is the obstacle to his desire."

"Wait a minute, you're telling me that while you were applying for the CIA, the big boss is making a move on your girlfriend?"

"That's it in a nutshell."

"That couldn't have been helpful to your career."

"No, it certainly wasn't. I don't have any tangible proof that he was directly involved, but let's just say that, during my screening process, those farm boys interrogated me as though I were a Jihadi militant. The process took four days, and the report said that I was a heavy drug user, active in promiscuous sex with both men and women, and that I was a possible security threat."

I stopped to take another mouthful of champagne.

"That must have been devastating."

"I almost laugh about it now, but I certainly wasn't laughing then. I had nothing but excellent performance appraisals at the bureau with actual letters of commendation from guess who? Brewster himself when he was still the director. Needless to say, I wasn't accepted at the CIA, and the bureau advised me that they no longer needed me in Rome or anywhere else for that matter."

"What did you do and what about Clara? Wasn't she able to pull some strings with all of her contacts?"

"Well, I jumped on the next available plane and came back here. Clara became ice-cold with you-know-who, and he realized quickly that his romantic overtures were futile. Fortunately, he did not create any problems for her, as he easily could have."

701

Barbara stewed for a moment.

"Isn't there anything at all that you could have done? This all seems like a gross injustice to me and borderline criminal. I would have gone on a rampage!"

I smiled at Barbara, who looked genuinely furious.

"I don't hold a grudge, Barbara. It's part of the game. If you want to play hardball in Washington, you better accept the rules, *their* rules. What stings to this day is that Brewster shot down my career in the intelligence field, which I truly loved."

"For a woman."

"Yup, in this case, Clara was the innocent cause of my downfall."

I reached for my empty glass for the third time. "Would you care for another bottle?"

"I'll pass, because I'll probably pass out if I have any more."

I called our amused waiter over to the table and paid the bill. We got up from the table, both unstable to say the least. "Should we get a taxi?" I suggested.

"I'd prefer to walk, if you don't mind," Barbara said.

I put my arm around her waist, and we made our way through the crowds of people who were out and about enjoying an enchanting Rome evening. We headed down Via dei Pastini, commenting on the countless restaurants, wine bars, and curio shops that were bustling with people from all nationalities. Grand palazzi and churches were interspersed everywhere, majestic with their centuries of history.

As we were heading toward the Via del Corso, Barbara began leaning a little more heavily on me. I didn't mind. After a while, she resumed her questions:

"What I don't quite understand, Atticus, is your tight connection with the Italian Police, I mean, after what, fifteen years?"

"Let's just say that when I came back to Rome, the various foreign intelligence agencies I had worked with were upset with how I had been treated. Suffice it so say that they gave me some opportunities to get back into the business."

"Covertly, I take it?"

"Absolutely."

"Very good. Something to blackmail you with, Mr. Winterle."

Barbara gave me a very wet, champagne-scented kiss that ended up on my lips, cheek, and nose. It was most definitely time to get her back to the hotel. I was practically holding her up at this point. Quite suddenly, I stopped and hustled Barbara into one of the centuries-old, recessed doorways that punctuated the cobblestone street. Her back was up against the building, and I was pressed against her body.

"Oh my," she breathed, "can't wait to get back to the room, huh?"

"Quiet," I whispered, "keep your head down."

Fortunately, she did what she was told. We waited as a familiar voice grew louder, passed by, then faded out of earshot.

"Did you see that?" I said, pointing to the left. She peered over my shoulder.

"It's him, all right. But who is *she*?"

"No clue, but I don't know anyone in our group that wears that kind of heels and short skirts except Darlene. But that's a brunette, not a blonde."

John, hand in hand with a young lady, had exited the hotel and walked right by us.

"Well, it seems that our John has found a little excitement," said Barbara.

"Well, if her front looks anything like her back, I would say that 'excitement' is an understatement."

We came out of the recess and resumed our short walk to the hotel. I was practically carrying Barbara at this point.

"How are you holding up?" I asked.

"Just get me upstairs," she answered. "It's all I can do to stand up."

I led her through the sliding doors of the hotel. As we entered the lobby, I noticed Ludovica standing behind the counter. She shot a quick look at me, then at Barbara, before lowering her head and disappearing into the back office. There was an entire script in that shifting of the eyes. Barbara squeezed my arm but didn't utter a word.

I opted for the elevator since the stairs would have proven a difficult challenge in Barbara's state. As soon as the door closed behind us, she let out an uproarious laugh.

"My, my Mr. Winterle, you have royally pissed off that young lady! Did you notice that look she gave us? She *shish-kebabbed* me with those eyes."

"You're exaggerating," I remonstrated. But I knew Barbara was right.

"Ha! Well, she can try to get her claws into you, but only after I leave Rome. You're all mine until then."

The elevator door opened, and Barbara, stumbling a bit, got out.

"I'll be up in a minute, Atticus. Need to do a few girlie things before I disrobe and—" The elevator shut and lurched upward before the end of her sentence.

CHAPTER 50

The first thing I did when I got back to my room was shower. I put on a clean T-shirt and pair of shorts, and after smoothing out the bed sheets, which looked as if they had been chewed on by a Rottweiler, I set the alarm for 6:30 am. I wanted to be the first down for breakfast.

Cynthia was still out on the town for all I knew; John had left the hotel in the company of an unknown female; and I didn't have the faintest idea where any of the students were. I was particularly concerned about James. Had he taken his medication? I was also worried about Mark. Was he with Michelle, Wayne, and Bishop? What about Evelyn?

I knew what I had to do.

As I reached for the door, intending to go downstairs and do a quick room-by-room check, the handle turned, and the door opened toward me. Barbara came in, wearing the same bathrobe from two nights ago, plus flip-flops. A black lacquered pair for stiletto heels were dangling from her left hand.

"No worries, dear Atticus, I checked up on everyone."

"What?"

"Yes, before getting into my robe. Isn't that what you were about to go off and do?"

"In fact, it was. How perceptive of you, Mrs. Cornwall."

Barbara sat on the corner of the bed, kicked off the flip-flops, and slid her beautifully pedicured feet into the stilettos.

"Nearly everyone is in their rooms. Some of the boys and a few of the girls are in the restaurant area. No sign of John, of course, but Cynthia was in her room."

Barbara stood up, walked a few steps away, and turned, letting the bathrobe fall to the floor, once again.

"What do you think? The shoes do make a difference, don't they?"

My eyes were locked on to her completely nude body and those provocative heels. The sperm factory was at full capacity.

"So glad to see that you approve. I couldn't let an eighteen-year-old upstage me. I picked up these Louboutin pumps today." Barbara lifted a foot. "Expensive as hell but, oh, so sexy Italian." Barbara got on the bed on all-fours, the six-inch heels pointing straight up in the air.

I launched my T-shirt and shorts across the room.

"Ready to do your duty, Atticus?"

I was now kneeling on the bed behind her as she teased me by rubbing her behind against my groin. My hands were on her sculptured posterior as I took aim. What this woman did to me was like nothing I had ever experienced before. Just raw, physical pleasure. No foreplay this time. Here I come, Mrs. Cornwall!

Tap, tap, tap.

I didn't hear that.

Tap, tap, tap.

"Atticus? Mrs. Cornwall? Are you in there?"

It was a whisper but sufficiently loud enough to bring a bacchanalian carnal feast to a screeching halt. Barbara turned and glared at me, her expression horrified.

Tap, tap, tap.

"Coming, just a second," I called.

Barbara shook her head violently, attempting to stop the unstoppable. I gestured to her that the door wasn't locked. We grabbed the closest available garments, including the bathrobe, and threw them on. We both tried to regain our composure at lightning speed. Barbara sat up straight, crossed her legs, and grabbed a book from the night table. I admired the effort, but no matter how fine a writer he was, nobody would believe she had come to my room to peruse Wilkie Collins.

I opened the door.

Michelle, Wayne, and Bishop came in. I closed the door and turned to look at them. Barbara closed the book and put it back on the table. There was a moment of absolute silence.

"Okay, well, this is rather unexpected," I said.

Michelle looked at us with a nervous smile. "Sorry, Atticus, Mrs. Cornwall, for barging in like this, but I needed to get these two up here. It's about what we started talking about at the restaurant the other day. Remember, Atticus?"

"Sure, of course I do."

Barbara cleared her throat. "Maybe it would be better if I left the four of you alone."

"Oh no, Mrs. Cornwall, don't go. We wanted to see both of you and thought this was a good time."

Oh, great. No use feigning ignorance. Barbara and I were officially an item as far as the students were concerned.

"Well, I guess I feel privileged," Barbara said. "Michelle, come and sit next to me then. Boys, grab a chair." Bishop sat, but Wayne remained standing, leaning against the door.

Michelle looked at the boys. "All right, you two, I know how much it took for you to come up here. Let's get it out in the open."

Wayne's ankles were crossed, his hands buried in his pockets. Bishop was seated, seemingly fascinated by the hotel rug. Nobody spoke. Finally, Wayne, after clearing his throat nervously, spoke up.

"Yeah, well, it's not that easy. But there are a few things that Bishop and I really need to get off our plates. We think the two of you can give us some good advice." Wayne walked over to Bishop and before I could register what he was doing, he took Bishop's hand in his.

"Bishop and I like each other," he said. "I mean, as more than friends. We've been together for over a year now."

Barbara looked as though two thousand volts of electricity had gone through her. Bishop, noticing Barbara's total shock, tried to walk things back a bit.

"Don't get us wrong, we still like girls. I mean, we don't have problems with girls and, well, sex. But Wayne and I just prefer being together."

Wow! Massimo had been right after all. He had it all figured out at the forum—and only after a couple of hours in the boy's company.

Barbara ran her hands though her hair. "Oh my God, I can't believe it…not about how you two feel for each other, but how on earth you were able to hide this for so long? Does anyone else know about this?"

"Only Michelle and now the two of you," Wayne answered. "There's one more person, that's why we're here."

Wayne had let go of Bishop's hand and was now sitting on the floor.

"Mark?" It was only natural for me to ask considering how close the three boys were.

"No, Mark hasn't figured it out, though I think he has his suspicions."

"So who are we talking about?" Barbara enquired.

All three exchanged glances.

"My stepmother," Wayne said.

"Your stepmom? Janice?" Barbara asked.

"You know her, Mrs. Cornwall?" Wayne asked in surprise.

Barbara shook her head. "No, not really. I saw her picture in the paper after the wedding and recognized her at school one day. Your dad was there with her. I introduced myself as one of your teachers. It was pretty much hello and goodbye. How is she mixed up in all of this?"

"Come on, you guys," Michelle interjected impatiently. "Spit it out, or I will."

"Okay, okay." Wayne looked like a caged animal.

"About six months ago, Bishop and I were shooting some hoops in my backyard. We had had more than just a few beers, and we were sweaty from the workout. So we went upstairs and took a shower—together. Nobody was supposed to be home except the two of us, at least that's what we thought. Come to find out later that Janice's car was at the shop and that she was asleep in the pool house."

"Pool house?" I asked with curiosity.

"Yeah, it's actually a guesthouse, separate from where we live. It gets used for large pool parties." Wayne looked at both Barbara and me. "I guess you can figure out what happened next…"

Barbara nodded. "Janice caught the two of you doing… well, in the shower."

"Bingo."

"And then what happened?" I asked.

"She just stood there and looked at us for a moment. Then she began to laugh, saying to herself that she'd hit the jackpot.' I didn't understand what she meant. Not till later. Anyway, I tried and tried to grab some towels, but she beat me to it and threw them behind her. Then she took off her bathing suit right there in front of us. To cut a long story short, she made it crystal clear that, if we didn't do everything she wanted, she would tell my dad and Bishop's parents about us. That's when she held up her phone. She had taken photos."

Barbara remained as cool as a cucumber. "Let me guess, you had sex with her, together."

"Yeah…right there is the bathroom. I was hoping that it would be a one-off, but she kept on threatening us afterward. I can't count how many times we've had to meet up with her. She'll text me that she needs me to go to Publix and buy some fruit. That's the code. I have to hurry and get Bishop wherever he is and meet her at the house, in a hotel, in the back of her SUV, Christ, we did it in a cemetery one night! Sometimes, my dad will be right downstairs watching TV, and she's upstairs giving me and Bishop a blowjob...sorry, Mrs. Cornwall."

Barbara shook her head, her face full of sorrow. Tears welled up in Wayne's eyes. "This is my friggin' stepmother! Can you believe it?"

"And if your dad did find out about you and Bishop?" I said, tentatively.

"He'd kill me," Wayne said, as though stating the law of gravity.

"So no joy there," I said. I looked at Bishop.

"They'd kick me out of the house for good," he said, then paused. "At the very least."

I rested my chin on my hands and looked at them quizzically. "Boys, not that I want to contradict either of you, but aren't you both being a bit extreme?"

Wayne stared at me. There was such terror in his eyes that I was momentarily taken aback.

"You don't know my dad," he said. "He goes hunting in Africa, fishing in Alaska, skiing in the Swiss Alps with his multimillionaire buddies. He bought a new Ford 350 and started a club. Most Saturdays, my dad and these guys will take off in their souped-up trucks and go to one of their thousand-acre properties in South Georgia to race and sling mud."

Barbara tried to reassure him. "None of that means he'll be violent to you, Wayne, let alone kill you."

"You haven't heard these guys talk in private, Mrs. Cornwall. They basically think that if a man isn't white, straight, and Lutheran, he shouldn't exist. And if someone brings up the subject of gays, butch lesbians, and transgender, they make jokes about beating them up and hanging them from the nearest tree."

"You've heard your father say these things?" Barbara asked.

"Oh yeah. So has Bishop. It was like a big indoctrination for both of us when we turned sixteen. My dad really did take Bishop and I to a lap dance club, Atticus, and paid for the dancers to have sex with us. He said that this was what real men did." Wayne paused wrapped his arms around his chest. "He really would kill me if he ever found out, and he wouldn't care if he spent the rest of his life in jail for it."

Michelle gazed at Wayne, her expression mixed with tenderness and sorrow. "They've tried to convince Janice to stop, but she just picks up the cell phone and threatens to call Wayne's dad.

Wayne nodded. "She'll probably end up telling him one day, anyway. Once she finds another rich guy willing to spend big bucks on her."

"Maybe your dad will get tired of her first?" I suggested.

"She'd be even happier to tell him if that happens."

I saw his point.

"I doubt that he'll dump her anytime soon, though," Wayne continued. "She's like a big game trophy for him. My dad is pushing sixty-five. He must have ten Viagra bottles in his bathroom. He gets a huge kick showing Janice off at the club in Vegas when he goes gambling to all his friends. And as long as Dad keeps her supplied with Porsche Cayennes, diamonds, and uncapped credit cards, she's going to be good with it."

I turned to Michelle. "Do you know Wayne's dad?"

She nodded. "I've been to Wayne's house tons of times. Janice usually isn't around, though, or she disappears if she sees me."

"Wayne's dad loves Michelle," Bishop offered.

"You can say that again," said Wayne. "He thinks Michelle is the best thing next to sliced bread."

Michelle shook her head. "I don't know if I'd go that far. I just tell him what I think when he asks me a question, and there are many times I tell him he's dead wrong. He just likes that I'm straightforward, I think."

"Rich people don't get that a lot," I put in. "Everyone just wants to kowtow to them or stab them in the back, or both. Maybe that's why he likes Michelle."

"Remember that time the two of you got into it over Knowshon Moreno?" Wayne said.

Michelle smiled. "I do! He was really upset with me that time."

I raised my hand. "Um…a little background, please."

"Knowshon Moreno was a running back for the Georgia Bulldogs," Michelle explained. "Wayne's dad is a big fan of college football, and he thought Moreno was a god, even though he has a Puerto Rican father and an African-American mother. We were talking about football in the kitchen, and he was going on and on about Moreno. I asked Wayne's dad how he could be so racist and still think Moreno was so great."

"You should have seen my dad, Atticus," said Wayne. "He just froze. Then he said something about that being different and that it was the team that mattered, not the individuals on the team. He didn't talk to you for a while after that, did he, Michelle?"

"For about a week. But then everything went back to normal. I think he's got a good heart, basically. He just plays the tough macho guy because, well, that's what people expect of him."

Barbara and I glanced at each other. We were both on the same wavelength.

"Michelle, has it crossed your mind that maybe you could speak to Wayne's dad about this situation?" Barbara suggested. "It seems like he really listens to you."

Michelle shrugged. "We've discussed doing that. It might work, or it might go horribly wrong. No matter how he finds out, he's going to have a negative reaction at first and probably a violent one. You know what I mean?"

Barbara nodded. "Crystal clear, Michelle."

"All right," I said. "Here's what I think we should do right now. Let Barbara and I think all of this over, see if we can come up with anything. It's past one, and we all need some sleep. We'll regroup before Thursday's departure. How does that sound?"

The boys nodded. "Thanks for listening to us," Wayne said.

"Yeah, thanks a lot." Bishop looked a lot more at ease now than when he had come into the room.

Barbara watched them, her puzzled expression once again on her face. "I still don't get how you pulled this off. Everyone at Bradford thinks the two of you are partying jocks with nothing but boobs in your brains."

Both boys smiled faintly.

"Well, we do love basketball, we do party, and we still like girls, just not having sex with them. The macho jock act is to stop anybody from wondering why Bishop and I are so… close."

"Darlene may have suspicions," I ventured, remembering her outburst at the forum.

Wayne shrugged. "We're not really worried about her or anybody else at school. We'll all be going our separate ways once we're back in the States. The real problem is my stepmom."

I clapped them on their shoulders. "Leave it us. We'll see if we can't find a way out for you two."

They all looked hopeful. As they left the room, my hope was that I wouldn't disappoint them.

CHAPTER 51

I had set the alarm for six o'clock but was already awake shortly after five. As soon as I had opened my eyes, I reached over and touched Barbara's warm skin. Her breathing was heavy but rhythmic. She was still fast asleep.

After Wayne, Bishop, and Michelle had left the room, Barbara and I had no desire to pick up our interrupted carnal session. We spoke at length, instead, of Wayne's and Bishop's predicament but saw no easy way out. This Janice was going to let the cat out of the bag sooner or later, no matter how sexually gratifying her on-call threesomes were.

"It's a power game," I said. "She snaps her fingers, and two good-looking young men are at her beck and call. She's also got a guarantee that Wayne won't criticize her to his dad. Obviously, she could care less about him, but the money and the social standing must outweigh any other options she may have, at least for now. I'd say that she's got a solid insurance policy in her hand."

Barbara sighed and raised her head from the pillow.

"What those boys need is something to blackmail *her* with."

As soon as she uttered these words, I knew that she had cracked the code.

"That's brilliant! You just found the solution! There's got to be something in this woman's past that would make Wayne's dad's stomach churn."

Barbara rubbed her hands in glee. "Do you really think it could work? But who's going to poke his nose around Janice's past?"

"That's the easy part, but I am going to need some basic data on Janice to get the ball rolling. Such as her full name, age, place of birth, date of birth, parents' names, social security number, where she's lived. The more the better."

"I think I can get some of that info, and I bet that Wayne can find a way to get the rest when he gets back to Atlanta. There was a lot of information in the local press, Facebook, and gossip magazines about her and that wedding."

"Perfect. Get all you can and as fast you can, and I'll start pulling strings with my intelligence connections. Barbara, you may have just found the ticket out of this mess."

After that, we had kissed and embraced, quite satisfied with our action plan. I didn't remember anything after that. Now it was five fifteen, and I was anxious to get the day started. I quietly slipped out of bed without turning on the bedside table lamp. Using my cell phone as a flashlight, I located my underwear, pants, and shirt, along with my Moleskine notebook from the desk. I took everything into the bathroom, shut the door, and turned on the light.

Within minutes, I had washed my face, brushed my teeth, shaved, and combed my hair. I sat on the toilet seat and opened my notebook. The days remaining were few, and I still had many loose ends to tie up. I jotted down what came to mind. I went over my list and felt that I had covered just about everything. It was now six fifteen. I needed to get downstairs.

Slowly opening the bathroom door, I saw that Barbara was still sound asleep. I had no intention of waking her. Instead, I wrote her a note and put it on the pillow.

Leaving the room key on the desk and the door unlocked, I headed downstairs. Ludovica was behind the front desk.

"Good morning, Mr. Winterle." There was a tangible chill in her voice.

I remembered that transitory yet piercing stare she had given Barbara and I when we had entered the hotel the night before.

"Good morning, Ludovica. You're here early this morning."

"No, my day usually starts at five. You have just been too preoccupied to notice."

Hell hath no fury like a woman scorned, I thought.

Ludovica was busy making notes in a large blue ledger. I didn't know what to do. Stand there like a lamppost or head out through those sliding glass doors.

"When are you checking out, Mr. Winterle? I have you scheduled to depart from here Thursday afternoon." She looked up at me with an expression that was difficult to interpret. Resentment mixed with hurt and battered pride was mirrored in those eyes.

I stared right back at her. "I shall be staying Thursday night, Ludovica, and checking out on Friday morning. That is, of course, if there is a room available."

"I will have to double-check. Just one moment please." She shifted her body in front of the computer screen and started to energetically tap away on the keypad. I waited a few minutes, and then a few minutes more. I had a distinct impression that she was making me wait just to get under my skin. I just stared at her with a condescending grin.

"Yes, Mr. Winterle, we have a room for this Thursday night. Should I book it for you?"

"Yes, please, and there is a very good chance that I may be checking out late on Friday as well. Any problems with that?"

"I...yes, well, I need to check and see, I mean, for availability. Could you come back shortly?" Her cheeks were suddenly flushed.

"I'm on my way out for an espresso and a brioche. Can I get you anything, Ludovica?"

"Oh no, no, I mean thank you, but no." She turned quickly and darted to the back office. I was pleased to see that I had hit a nerve.

Skipping down the four steps of the hotel and veering to the right, I managed to barge right into someone.

"Apologies!" I said, looking up.

It was John.

"Wow there, Atticus! Where are you running off to with your eyes closed?"

"I'm so sorry about that, John."

"No harm done." We both looked at each other for a long moment. He knew in a heartbeat that I was wondering where he was coming from.

"Yes, I've been out for the night," he said, nodding happily. "Suffice it to say that I had a wonderful time. Probably one of the best that I can remember."

"I'm glad to hear that."

"Her name is Rhea."

I feigned ignorance. "Who?"

John rolled his eyes. "You and Barbara were probably terrible at hide-and-seek when you were kids."

I was about to play dumb but realized it was foolish.

"She's from Greece," he said. "A visiting professor at the University of Rome. A Greek linguist. I literally bumped into her in the English language book section of a bookstore down the street. *Felti, Felri…*"

"Feltrinelli."

"Yeah, that's it. We just started a conversation, which snowballed into a lot more. Let's just say that I'm walking on cloud nine right now."

John did, in fact, have an aura about him. He almost glowed.

"The two of you looked awfully detective-like, pretending to make out up against that wall last night. If it hadn't been for your eyes bugging out in my direction, I probably wouldn't have noticed you."

"All right, all right, I guess we weren't terribly discreet, but I am happy for you."

"I feel better than I have in a very long time, Atticus. Letting me vent the other day, meeting Rhea, this city…let's just say that I have a new perspective on life. I want to thank you for this."

John took my hand and shook it. Before I could respond, he turned back in the direction of the hotel, whistling to himself. He was in a very good place.

After having savored an espresso with a touch of whipped cream on top and my raspberry brioche, I headed back to the hotel. Ludovica wasn't behind the desk, so I continued to the breakfast area.

Granted it was Sunday morning and relatively early, I was expecting to find more than just one lonely soul amongst all the empty tables. The woman had her back to me, but I knew it was Cynthia without looking twice. I came up behind her, clearing my throat so as not to startle her.

"Good morning, Cynthia."

"Oh, good morning, Atticus. Very nice to see you. Please have a seat." She glanced over her shoulder to see if there were others behind me.

"Gladly." I signaled to the waiter for a cappuccino. "Did you sleep well?"

"Like a rock."

"Wonderful. Are we still on for our forum visit?"

"Most certainly. I have been waiting for this moment for a long, long time."

I found her response a bit intense. Her eyes, glistening, were locked onto mine. She seemed to almost vibrate with nervous energy, reminding me of a jack-in-the-box about to shoot up through its lid.

"We can head out at eight thirty if that suits—"

"The sooner the better," she said, cutting me off.

I heard footsteps and then a string of students filed in— Mark, Wayne, Bishop, Michelle, Raymond, Vanessa, and Sabrina.

I nodded to them. "Did all of you get up at the same time?"

"Just about," said Raymond. "We're on our own today, right?"

"Um, yes, but only until I get back from the forum with Mrs. Ramsey. Then if any of you would like, we can go somewhere together."

"I think we're good today."

Okay, I thought. *Long live youthful independence.*

The doors opened, and the remaining students all walked in, with Barbara and John in tow. Good mornings went all around.

"Any of you need some suggestions on what to see today?" I asked diffidently.

"No thanks, Atticus, I mean, not for me." Mary looked around at the others. "I've got a game plan."

"Yeah, so do I."

"We do, too."

"You can chill, Atticus."

Cynthia cocked her head closer to me to get back my attention. "I'll be down at eight thirty." She seemed unaware and disinterested in anyone or anything around her. She got up and walked out without acknowledging a soul.

"She okay?" asked John.

"I think so," I said. "She's looking forward to going to the forum today."

Both John and Barbara sat down with me as the students were filling their plates. Barbara placed my room key on the table in front of me with absolutely no concern about what John might have thought.

"Everyone seems to be on some sort of schedule this morning. What's up with that?" I said, genuinely curious.

"Nothing out of the ordinary," said Barbara. "I just think they know what they want to go out and see. Time is running out, and there is so much to explore in this city. Right, John?"

"Couldn't have said it better, Barbara."

Listening to these two gave me the impression of a scripted dialogue.

"And the two of you? Already have a blueprint for the day?" I asked.

They glanced at each other. Yes, something was most definitely out of the ordinary.

"I'm meeting Rhea soon," John said.

Barbara didn't change expression, so I imagined that John had found the time to fill her in on his encounter.

"And I've got a plate full," Barbara said. "I have a date with Google Maps today."

Huh? I would have liked to press these two as to what the hell was going on, but it was almost eight thirty, and I had to meet up with Cynthia.

"We're off, Atticus. Have a great day!"

And with that they were both gone.

Monday
May 3, Day Seven

CHAPTER 52

Flash Back

"Just get rid of it, you hear me!"

She heard him loud and clear.

"What the hell's wrong with you, anyway? How many times have I told you that I don't want any snotty little kids? You deaf or something?"

"No, Buck, I'm not deaf…"

The sting on her face from the back of his hand felt like the bites of a thousand red ants.

"Didn't I tell you to be careful, you stupid bitch?" Buck took another large swig of beer and began muttering to himself. "Jesus Christ, I go to bed with your sorry ass because you fucking beg me, and you get knocked up! Fucking unbelievable!"

Yes, she remembered. How she had enticed him before he drifted off into his usual drunken stupor. No, no Buck! Stay with me! She remembered.

She remembered pulling off his pants, she remembered fondling him aggressively so he would stay awake, she remembered giving him oral sex, and finally, she remembered getting his semi-erect penis inside her. She remembered his foul odor, rank breath, and his drool on her face. Come on, Buck! Give it to me! Make this fuck one you'll never forget!

It had been the most nauseating thing she had ever done in her life.

"Me and the boys are going hunting. I'll be gone for a few days. Get rid of that thing while I'm gone. Do you understand what I'm saying, or do you need me to slap you around a bit more?! I swear to God I'll kill your ass along with that thing inside you if you don't do what I tell you!"

Cynthia nodded.

She was pregnant, but it wasn't Buck's child. Had he ever found out how the child had been conceived, it would have meant certain death for her and the baby she was carrying at the hands of the man she married fifteen years ago. She had to act and quickly.

As soon as she found out about her pregnancy, she devised her plan. Buck would believe that the child was his. He would never know the truth. She was going to have this child, no matter what the cost, even if it meant planning and carrying out her own rape.

The blow came unexpectedly.

She fell to the kitchen floor, banging her head against the stove as she went down. She had no concern for herself but was terribly worried about the baby inside her. She prayed to God that he wouldn't kick her as he had in the past.

"What the hell are you staring at? Get off the goddamned floor and get my eggs and bacon ready. It's the only fucking thing you know how to do right."

Good, very good, no kicking this time. She got up as fast as she could and stumbled to the refrigerator.

Concentrate, Cynthia, concentrate. Only one objective. Just one. Bring this child into the world.

***

It was only when the door shut behind John and Barbara that I realized I was the only one left in the room. The students had also left without my noticing. I felt abandoned, strangely enough. Obviously, I was no longer indispensable to this group. Everyone knew what they wanted to do, where they wanted to go, and with whom. I took my room key and went upstairs to get my wallet and notebook before meeting up with Cynthia. I was melancholy, to say the least.

There was an unnatural silence in the hotel as I walked down to the front desk, as though everyone had been evacuated. When I got to the lobby, I was pleased to see a familiar face.

"Good morning, Signor Atticus."

"Good morning, Giovanni."

"I noticed that your students left the hotel rather early and with an, how can I say, abundant amount of energy. Did they leave you on your own?"

"No, not really. I will be escorting Mrs. Ramsey to the forum today."

"Ah, I understand." Giovanni paused. "You must be very pleased."

"Pleased?"

"Why, yes. Your students, they are like foot soldiers on a reconnaissance mission. Going off on their own, sightseeing, dining out, just getting around this most chaotic of cities. Unquestionably, you have instilled a great deal of confidence in them."

It was mind-boggling how this man was able to pick up on and be one step ahead of either what I was feeling or thinking.

"And remember, Signor Atticus, *Exercitus sine duce, corpus est sine spiritu.*"

With that sally, Giovanni excused himself and vanished into the back office. I was about to call after him when I felt a hand on my shoulder. "Hello, Atticus. Ready when you are."

Cynthia was not an attractive woman. I had come to that conclusion when I had first laid eyes on her at the airport. But this was a different Cynthia in front of me now. Hair up in a chiffon bun, a pleasant amount of makeup, a colorful scarf tied loosely around her neck, and a sober yet elegant knee-length beige dress. But it was the light shining from her face that struck me. First, John this morning, and now Cynthia. I began to wonder if by nightfall they both would be glowing in the dark.

I inclined my head. "Let's go, then," I said, holding out my arm, which she took without hesitation.

"Shall we walk to the forum?" she suggested. "I know it's not that far."

"Of course," I responded. "It's a beautiful day for a stroll."

We exited the hotel and made a left. In less than fifteen minutes, we were in front of the much-maligned Vittorio Emanuele II Monument, alias the wedding cake. About one hundred yards before reaching the Colosseum, we made a hard right and entered the forum area through the main entrance gate. Surprisingly, we did not have to spend too long in the ticket line.

"Here we are, Cynthia—the Roman Forum." I headed to my right and quite automatically began spewing out dates, the names of various ruins that I remembered and that Massimo had elaborated on. Cynthia just nodded here and there. We walked for another fifty yards or so, passing various temples and shrines on our left and right. I felt as if I were talking to myself. And then I discovered that I was.

Cynthia had stopped dead in her tracks behind me. For a moment, I thought she was feeling poorly.

"Cynthia? Are you okay?" I asked, walking quickly back in her direction.

She peered straight into my eyes and, without any preamble, simply said, "Anthony is my son."

I think I can forgive myself for not understanding what she was saying at first and thinking she was speaking metaphorically rather than literally. "I realize that Cynthia," I said stupidly. "Your sun, your moon, your shining star, that's not a secret."

Cynthia put her hand over her mouth and gave a gasping laugh.

"Not my *sun*, Atticus! She pointed to the sky and shook her head. "*He's my biological son!*"

She began to cry and laugh simultaneously. Unrestrained grief intertwined with frenzied hilarity shook her slender frame. I just stood there, an upright, embalmed corpse, attempting to interpret what she I had just heard. *Her son? How in heaven's name?*

She sat down on the corner of a large chunk of a Corinthian column, head bowed low in this awkward mix of suffering and mirth. I sat beside her, and she clenched my hand with surprising strength and drew me near. I was still in a confused stupor. Then she sat up and rested her head on my shoulder, pulling several Kleenex tissues from her tote bag. She had come prepared.

"Atticus, I need a drink. And I don't mean a coffee."

"Yes. Even the best espresso isn't enough for this."

We got up from that piece of granite that had been witness to millions of passersby over the centuries. Cynthia did not let go of my hand. We headed to our left. I was looking for a small pathway that few, if any, tourists were aware of. This would lead us out of the forum.

Shortly afterward, I found a coffee bar with outside tables. We sat down under one of the large patio umbrellas, taking advantage of the shade.

A young man with a varied display of piercings through his nostrils, and ears approached and asked us what we wanted to drink.

"Cynthia?"

"JW Black, double, no ice." Her succinct choice contrasted with her empty gaze into the distance.

The waiter gave me a thumbs-up, indicating that he understood.

"Two of those, please," I said.

The waiter left. Cynthia said nothing, still staring at nothing. I followed her lead.

The young man returned in no time and placed our drinks on the round, weather-beaten table. Cynthia took her glass and drained it in one swallow. She looked at the waiter.

"Another one," she said, rapping the table decisively.

He nodded but gave me a quick glance before heading back inside the bar. I took a swig of the Johnny Walker and felt embers sliding down my stomach.

"Nineteen years," Cynthia said, her voice low.

I remained silent.

"Nineteen years. Christ Almighty."

I still stayed silent. Cynthia needed a listening ear now, not a talking head. She put her elbows on the table and rested her forehead on the heels of her palms. The waiter returned with what seemed more like a triple scotch. I took it from him, nodding in approval, and placed it on the table.

"What's the longest you've kept a secret to yourself, Atticus?" The question was sharp and abrupt. "I mean, a really deep, dark secret?"

I could have answered with a few secrets that I had kept for a number of years, but this was Cynthia's moment, and it made no sense to bring my person into the discussion. "I really wouldn't know off the top of my…" I was cut off abruptly.

"I've kept my secret for nineteen years. My son was conceived nineteen years ago, and nobody, *nobody*, has ever known. Not even his biological father. Jesus Christ, I deserve some kind of goddamn medal!" She took up the fresh drink and emptied half in one go.

I had never heard Cynthia swear or use any profanity, but I was also aware that the person beside me had just been released from many years of solitary confinement.

"That son of a bitch, yeah, I really pulled the wool over his eyes. I did that!" Cynthia began to rock back and forth. "You remember, Atticus when we were in front of the beautiful statue of Mary with Jesus in her arms, at St. Peters?"

"Yes, *La Pietà.* You seemed to be quite moved by it."

"Well, Atticus, let me begin by telling you why I was so moved. I have a lot to unload here, so bear with me."

"I'm all ears, Cynthia."

She took a large swallow of her scotch and sat back. "My husband was stationed on the *USS Independence* in 1976. The ship stopped in Naples during a Mediterranean exercise at the NATO base. It was April. We were to be married in July. He wrote me saying that he was going on this two-day trip to Rome with a few of his lieutenant friends to see the sites. I was so thrilled. It was as if *I were* going to Rome, the city that I had read about in books, seen in photographs. I was so anxious to get a letter, postcards, anything, and I was so excited to see all the pictures he would show me when he came back to the naval station in June. To make a long story short, I never got any letters, any postcards, or any pictures. That should have rung an alarm bell in my thick skull. But the wedding came and went, completely overrun by my father's and husband's navy buddies. On my first night as a married woman, as I was heading back to my hotel room, alone. Buck, my knight in shining armor, was with his pals in one of the lounges, drunk as a skunk. I heard them and sharing stories about all the Italian girls they had managed to take to bed in those two days in Rome."

I remembered Cynthia's harsh comments about the drinking and flirting by Wayne, Bishop, and Mark. Now I understood her bitterness.

Cynthia continued, "In that instant, but *only in that instant*, did I realize what kind of man I had married. But I was stuck, Atticus. I came from a military family, I had married into a military family, and there was a price to pay. And I paid dearly. On my wedding night, Buck went out whoring with his army buddies. Can you believe that?" Cynthia took another swallow of scotch.

"You started telling me something about your husband when we were in St. Peter's."

She looked at me, squinted her eyes, and tilted her head to one side. The tears came without warning. "All I wanted, all I ever wanted was a family. That's all." The rocking motion became more accentuated. I reached out and placed my hand on her shoulder.

"I need you to listen to me, Atticus, please. Just listen to me."

I sat there and watched this frail woman being torn up on the inside by invisible claws.

"I'm here, Cynthia, and I am listening."

In the next fifteen minutes, I learned a great deal about Cynthia Ramsey. When she interrupted her story to ask for another drink, you could have shocked me with a defibrillator, and I probably wouldn't have moved an inch.

I heard that she came from an abusive family. Her father was an alcoholic, and her mother had been diagnosed with borderline dementia when Cynthia was only ten years old. She told me about her marriage to Buck in 1976 and the continued abuse that reared its ugly head shortly after her wedding. I heard about her overwhelming desire to have a child, even with Buck if absolutely necessary. But he had his group of whores, and he didn't want the responsibility of children. She was only useful as a punching bag. He relished telling her over and over that just the sight of her naked made him want to puke.

I heard about how happy she was on her twenty-eighth birthday when she was accepted at a local junior high school as an assistant teacher. I also heard about the busted lip and black eye Buck had awarded her with when she gave him the news. Who was going to do all the housework during the day? Furthermore, the money wasn't enough. How was she going to buy his booze and cigars on that shitty salary?

I heard that Cynthia at one point didn't care anymore. The days began, and they ended. The weeks came and went. Months were just words on a calendar, and the years a series of four digits. Buck was either drunk, or violent, or away fishing, hunting, and chasing skirts with his pals.

They lived in a low to middle-income neighborhood near Fort Benning in Georgia surrounded by active duty and retired military personnel. Rarely did she converse with her neighbors, ashamed of the frequent black and blue marks on her face, neck, and arms. She did know a rather young mother down the street who had told her once, out of the blue, to just get up and leave. But you couldn't just get up and leave! It just wasn't done. And furthermore, Buck would have found her and killed her.

In fact, the thought of dying at times seemed rather appealing to Cynthia. A bottle of pills, a warm bath, a large glass of Buck's 101 Wild Turkey. Oh yes, she had read up on the best way to end it. But as perverse as it seemed, she knew that there was something of importance out there. Something that one day would make her life worth living.

These were the highlights. As she finished her repertoire, Cynthia also managed to drain the last remaining scotch from her glass. The amount of alcohol she had consumed began taking its toll. She was now sitting back with her legs outstretched. She had released the hair bun and taken off her neck scarf.

"I haven't even spoken about Anthony yet, have I?" she said.

"No. But what you've been telling me seems to be leading up to him."

She smiled at me and took my hand again, gently this time.

"I was thirty-five. It was 1991."

"And you were still living with Buck?"

"Oh yes, I did until his liver exploded in 1996. Amazing, isn't it?"

"That took an overwhelming amount of courage, Cynthia."

"Courage? You mean an amazing amount of stupidity! I wanted to kill that man. Every day of every month of every year—I wanted him dead. What he did to me..." Cynthia lowered her head and paused. "What have I already told you about Anthony?"

Mr. Johnnie Walker was systematically taking over his host. Cynthia wouldn't last long, and I really wanted to hear about Anthony.

"That Anthony is your son, Cynthia. Who else knows about this?"

"No one!" she snapped. "And no one must ever know!" There was a sudden look of terror in her eyes. "You mustn't ever tell a soul, swear it to me."

"I swear. Nothing will ever come out of my mouth."

"Not even to Barbara!" So she had also put two and two together.

"Nobody, Cynthia. That's a promise."

That helped to clear tension that had momentarily enveloped us. Cynthia closed her eyes and continued with her story.

"I was thirty-five. Still teaching at that school near our house, but now full time. I'll never forget that day, the second of March. One of the teachers was celebrating her birthday at a local bar. Buck was away on one of those hunting trips, so I decided to go. It was particularly cold and rainy, but I remember being in a very good mood for no apparent reason. There weren't many at the party—five teachers, a few of the back-office staff, and two of the maintenance workers."

Cynthia picked up her empty glass, looked at it, and put it back on the table.

"I won't lie. I had been searching for an opportunity to go to bed with a man and get pregnant. But it wasn't easy. I wasn't bad-looking back then, but I already had that frumpy ol-maid teacher look about me. The very few times I had a chance, I was either on my period or Buck was home. When I walked into that party, I had no idea that I was finally going to put my plan into motion. One of the maintenance workers was named Daniel. He was young. He had just turned twenty-one and was an electrician at the school. He had only started there a few months before the party. Well, I drank too much, way too much, which was very unusual for me. But I was focused, nonetheless. I knew what I wanted, and I knew what I needed to do. The situation was perfect. Daniel was tall and thin, extremely shy, and a bit clumsy. But he was a gentle soul. Anyhow, the party was coming to a close, and I had to make my move. I waited until the teachers had left, as well as the office staff, with the excuse that I was going to grade some papers. Daniel was shooting pool. He had also had a good amount to drink and didn't seem to be in hurry to leave. When he came back to the table to get his beer, he saw me sitting there. This was the moment. I mustered up the nerve to ask him if he would take me home since I didn't feel I could drive. For a moment, I thought he was going to say no. He was so flustered!"

Cynthia giggled like a schoolgirl, lost in her memory. She stretched her legs and arms out once again and closed her eyes.

"So did Daniel take you home?"

"Oh, yes. We left in his pickup truck. I felt just like a spider in the heart of her web waiting for my victim. When we were out on the open road, I began to pull up my skirt just enough to get him thinking. Daniel's eyes were darting from the road to my thighs. My legs were actually pretty good back then, Atticus." She slapped the sides of her knees gently. "I had Daniel drive in the opposite direction of my house. I just kept fidgeting and playing with my skirt. Beads of perspiration were forming on his brow as well as a prominent lump between his legs." Cynthia paused once again and looked straight at me. "The power that I felt in that moment, Atticus! Here was a young man, obviously very excited about little ole Cynthia. That's when I decided to strike. I put my arm on his shoulder and asked him to pull off into the woods somewhere. My skirt now was above my panties. I then placed my other hand just below his knee. He couldn't believe his eyes. I thought he was going to drive that truck into a telephone pole. We went into a dirt road through the forest and parked in a clearing behind some trees. It was almost romantic, in a way. I began to undo his pants. He just sat there, frozen, panting like a dog with his eyes popping out of his head. Daniel was actually nervous. I had to reassure him, telling him that everything was going to be okay and that this was our little secret. Once I had his pants down to his knees, I mounted him. He was well endowed, but I hadn't had sexual intercourse in years so it took time before he was able to penetrate me. I was worried that he would ejaculate prematurely, which would have ruined my plan. However, after just a few seconds, voilà! Mission accomplished."

Cynthia paused. "Can we get a bottle of water?"

"Right away."

It took a minute, but I did get our waiter's attention. Cynthia drank a full glass, then another.

"So, after practically raping a twenty-one-year-old in his truck, I asked him to drive me back to my car, assuring him that I was sober. We didn't say a word to each other on the way back. When I did get home, I didn't wash up until late that night. I wanted everything inside of me to stay inside of me. What a nutcase I was."

"When did Buck come home from his hunting trip?"

"Two days later. And now I had to put part two of the plan in motion. Buck had to think that this child was his. It took everything I had, Atticus. I managed to seduce him and managed to make him remember it." Cynthia grimaced. "I'm still sickened by it, years after the fact."

"When you found out you were pregnant, how in the world did you manage to keep it a secret?"

"It was the most difficult thing I have ever done in my life. When I did find out I was pregnant, which wasn't a given, I was overjoyed, dancing on cloud nine. I was so positive about everything that I went as far to think that Buck might accept the child. My God, was that ever a mistake! He beat me silly when I told him. He wanted me to get rid of it while he was away hunting. I told him I would, and that was the end of that. I knew from Buck's doctor, who felt sorry for me and my marital situation, that he had cirrhosis of the liver and had two years max to live. That was music to my ears. In two years, that monster would be dead, and I would be able to live and be a real mother to Anthony. Or at least I thought…" I didn't pick up immediately on Cynthia's last words.

"But how in the world did you hide the pregnancy, physically, I mean?"

"Tight underwear and very loose garments. I've never been much on the breast department and only went from a size A to a double A. And I didn't have much morning sickness, which made the pregnancy much easier to manage."

"And Buck, he didn't suspect anything?"

"I kept him drunk. When I thought he would become violent I would throw a few sleeping pills in his glass. Christ, I spent my entire monthly salary on beer, bourbon, and pills, but it was worth every penny. He was getting weaker and sicker as the weeks went by, so I was able to avoid his punches most of the time. I was getting stronger, eating healthy foods, and exercising. My only concern was bringing this child safely into the world."

"What happened to Daniel?"

"He was *so* apologetic. I saw him the next day, and you would have thought that *he* had taken advantage of *me!*" Cynthia shook her head and laughed. "We actually met a few more times during that first month of my pregnancy. Always in the pickup truck, in the same wooded area off Route 165, right over the Georgia/Alabama line. Then one day, he just disappeared. I found out later from the other maintenance guy that he had gone to North Carolina for a better-paying job. I was fine with that even if it would have been nice to say goodbye and good luck. Daniel had given me what I wanted, and I was truly appreciative."

"When was Anthony born?"

"December 16, 1991. He'll be nineteen this year." Cynthia hesitated for a moment, fiddling nervously with her bottle of water.

"I gave Anthony up for adoption on the twentieth of December. I thought about going to one of those battered women homes, maybe moving to another state, but this wasn't realistic with Buck alive. One of his best buddies was a particularly violent younger man. This guy would do anything for Buck, including searching for me and maybe even killing me if Buck said so. So instead, I went to an adoption center in Columbus, Georgia, which was about fifteen miles from my home. I told the head there everything about my situation, though I left out Daniel. I told her I wanted to take back Anthony as soon as Buck died. She was really kind. What this woman didn't do for me. She was an angel." Cynthia finished the water left in her glass. "She found a family for me that was willing to keep Anthony for a two-year period. All I had to do was pay to cover the necessities for him. She even drew up a contract for the arrangement, which I wouldn't even have thought of. It had seven pages about what I could do and not do for the two years Anthony would be with them. The only real problem is that this couple lived about three hours and forty minutes from my home."

I must have let my puzzlement show because Cynthia picked up on my bewilderment right away. "I know what you are thinking, Atticus. Why did I go through all of this just to give the baby up for adoption, even if temporarily, correct?"

"Well, yes. You've pretty much nailed it."

"Selfishness. Selfishness at its worst. I came to this realization only a few years back. After a horrible childhood and an even worse marriage, I needed a motive, a justification if you will, of why God put me on this earth. I knew that I could be a caring and loving mother, I was sure of it. That's a love that I had never experienced, and I wanted a piece of it. I knew there would be huge obstacles, and I knew that the child wouldn't be with me in those formative years if Buck didn't die, but this didn't stop me. I had to do it, Atticus, I just had to. You understand, don't you?" Cynthia was pleading with me. "You know, the first two years of Anthony's life, I actually got to see him once, twice a week. I babysat for Richard and Carol, the caregivers. This was part of the agreement. I will never forget those moments. I was the happiest woman on earth. But God knows it wasn't easy. All that driving, timing things so Buck would not become suspicious. I would buy Buck new fishing equipment and ammunition for his guns so that he would leave the house more often. He was getting weaker, but nothing would stop him from going fishing and hunting."

"What happened at the end of the two years?" I asked. "Isn't that when the contract expired?"

Cynthia's next words were barely audible. "That's when reality set in." She sighed, an exhalation that seemed to come from the depths of her soul. "Buck just wouldn't die. In hindsight, I should have just poisoned him. It would have been easy. I could have used bootleg liquor. Anyway, he didn't die after two years, so I called Carol to set up an appointment to discuss extending the contract. We scheduled a meeting at their house on a Friday afternoon. I hadn't been able to come see Anthony in over a month because of work, Buck, and car trouble, so I was super excited to get to their house. I reached by them really early that Friday, so I decided to wait in the car instead of going up to the house before they were expecting me. Then I saw Richard pull up in the driveway. He got out of the car just as I was about to. Carol opened the front door with Anthony. She put him on the ground, and he…"

Cynthia paused and drew a deep breath.

"He started walking in Richard's direction! I had never seen Anthony walk. Richard got on his knees and stretched out his arms, and Anthony managed to walk right up to Richard. I saw how Carol and Richard hugged and kissed him, and I knew that I had lost my son."

Cynthia took a sip of water and wiped her face with the back of her hand. "I didn't even get out of the car. I just drove straight back home. Lord knows how I made it. All those large trucks coming in my direction. I really wanted to drive my car right under one."

At that point, my phone buzzed. I looked at the screen.

"It's the hotel," I told Cynthia.

"Go ahead, answer it. I've got to go pee, anyway." She extracted herself from the chair easily and appeared relatively stable on her feet. I watched her enter the bar as I answered for my phone.

"Yes?"

"Signor Atticus?"

"Yes, it's Ludovica. One moment please."

There were some muffled noises as the phone receiver was passed on to someone else.

"Atticus? It's Michelle."

"Tell me," I said, knowing it had to be a problem.

"We can't find Mark…"

"Can't find as in he's not with you or not in the hotel?"

"Not with me, not in the hotel, and not with anyone else that we know."

"And you're sure he hasn't just gone out on his own somewhere?"

"We were supposed to meet up in the lobby at nine thirty. When he didn't show, Ludovica was kind enough to look at the security video."

"And?"

"The footage shows that Mark left the hotel at about nine twenty. In a hurry, from how he was walking."

"All right, Michelle, listen to me. I am here at the forum with Mrs. Ramsey. We'll hop in a taxi and be there shortly."

"We'll be in the lobby."

"Not a word to you-know-who when we get back."

"Clear."

We ended our conversation just as Cynthia made her way back to the table.

"Atticus, I think I better get back to the hotel," she said. "I really need to lie down for a bit."

That solved one problem.

"Sure thing. I'll get us a cab." I paid the waiter, left a disproportionate tip, and asked him to call us a taxi.

"The cab will be here in five to ten minutes. Tell me, when did Buck die?"

"Not until 1996, unfortunately. He managed to hang on one more whole year longer than expected. I felt almost as happy when he died as I did when Anthony was born. Do you know what his last words to me were, Atticus? He said, 'You really fucked up staying with me all these years.' Then he looked me straight in the eyes and said, 'But I do want to tell you something important before I croak…I never ever liked your sorry ass, you dumb bitch.'"

Oh well, so much for redemption, I thought. *If there really was a Hell, that man deserved a VIP pass.*

Cynthia continued and told me that Anthony's adopted parents still allowed her to babysit Anthony until he was almost eleven years old.

"Carol and I understood each other, and she knew in her heart of hearts that I would never do anything to interfere with her and Richard's relationship with the boy. It was evident that Richard wasn't comfortable with this arrangement at first. He told me years later that he actually thought that I would abscond with Anthony, never to return. Not that it didn't cross my mind on a couple of occasions, to be honest. With time, however, Richard became my biggest supporter. He saw that I would never do anything to harm Anthony, no matter what sacrifice I had to make."

Cynthia explained that Anthony came to see her as a favorite aunt.

In 2005, Carol and Richard moved to the outskirts of Atlanta for Richard's work. Anthony was enrolled at Bradford in 2006. It was Carol who informed Cynthia that the school was looking for two high school teachers. Cynthia applied and got one of those two positions for the 2007 academic year. She moved to Atlanta, found a small but comfortable house in the southeast part of the city, and began a new life.

"Excuse me, but your taxi is here," the waiter informed us.

I took hold of Cynthia's arm and guided her to the car. She had drunk quite a bit of water, but all that scotch was still navigating her system.

Once in the taxi, I just had to ask Cynthia a few more questions, even though Mark's disappearance was hammering away at the back of my mind.

"So, Cynthia, what's the plan? Are you ever going to tell Anthony that you are his biological mother?" The question was direct and perhaps tactless, but I had to ask.

"For the time being, I've decided not to tell Anthony anything. As I've said, he sees me as a favorite aunt. You might have noticed that I tend to smother him with attention. That's a weakness on my part."

"Actually, Cynthia, everybody's noticed. It doesn't particularly matter anymore, but if Anthony had still been at Bradford next year, I would have suggested that you control your doting."

From the look Cynthia shot me, I thought she was going to tell me to mind my own business, but instead she said, "I know, I know. But put yourself in my shoes. For nineteen years, my child, who was the only thing I ever wanted in life, is with me every day, just as if I was his mother on a trip with her son. But he doesn't know I'm his mother, I can't tell him, and for all my doting, as you put it, I can't interact with him the way my heart wants me to." She shook her head. "It hasn't been easy for me."

"I would say that you have done the impossible, Cynthia. And I mean that sincerely. I truly don't know how you did it." Our taxi was getting near to the hotel. I had to ask a question that had hounded me since meeting Anthony.

"Cynthia, all these stories Anthony tells about living in Switzerland, playing polo, wanting to be a heart surgeon…"

"All lies. Anthony has a very good heart, but he *is* a compulsive liar. I noticed it as soon as I started teaching at Bradford. But I am not in a position to question him about it, except on rare occasions. I've talked about it with Carol and Richard, though. Carol has some distant relatives who live in Switzerland, that's true, but Anthony has never seen hide nor hair of them. I really don't know what to think or do about it, and neither do they. It's a real problem. The one thing that he knows a lot about, and so he has no need to lie on that topic—guns. And yes, before you ask, I *am* very worried about that."

The taxi was now within a stone's throw of the hotel.

Cynthia brushed her hands through her hair. "Atticus, many children fall out with their parents during their teenage years or when they're older. The relationship I have built with Anthony, this aunt-nephew rapport, is special. He talks to me in a way that he doesn't talk to Carol. I just want to be in a position where I can advise him, help him. I want him to know that he will always be able to count on me. I could live with that and be at peace with myself."

The taxi stopped in front of the hotel. It was time to bring this story to a close, at least for now, and focus on finding Mark.

CHAPTER 53

Cynthia hugged me effusively, thanking me over and over for having listened to her story. Once inside the lobby, I waited for her to head for the stairs before turning to Michelle and Jeremy, who were at the front desk with Ludovica "Any updates?"

Michelle shook her head. "We walked to the Trevi Fountain and back, but we haven't seen him. Wayne and Bishop are still outside looking around."

Ludovica gestured for me to come behind the front desk. She hit a few buttons on a console and a video of the lobby area appeared on the screen. She pressed the rewind button, then stop and play. The footage showed a young man quickly crossing the lobby and exiting the hotel. The time on the display read 9:28 am.

"Any idea who he was talking to before he left the hotel?" I asked Michelle.

"He told me he was going to be on the computer for a while," she replied.

"What time was that?"

"This morning at breakfast, maybe around eight forty."

"Did he say anything else?"

"Nope, and he didn't tell Wayne or Bishop anything either, because they were with me."

I had an idea. "Jeremy, can you get into Mark's computer? I mean, hack into it?"

"Well, yeah, I guess. I need to check the security level of his password, but I should be able to bypass it."

"Okay, we didn't hear that, but it's music to my ears. Ludovica, I need to get into Mark's room. I'm sure Raymond is out and about."

Ludovica opened a drawer and gave me the master key. "It is Room 10."

"Thank you, Ludovica. Let's go, Jeremy. Michelle, stay down here and stall Mark if he comes in. I'd be greatly relieved if he walked through those doors, but I wouldn't want him to see us messing with his computer."

Jeremy turned to me. "I'll meet you there. I have to go to my room to get some cables."

We both headed upstairs. When I got to Room 10, I knocked. No answer. I knocked again, louder this time, just to make sure Raymond wasn't inside asleep. There was still no answer, so I used the key, and the lock clicked open immediately. Jeremy came up behind me carrying a black satchel.

The inside of the room was a study in human psychology. Raymond's side was orderly, with the bed made and most all of his clothes folded and put away in the closet. Mark's side of the room looked like a home invasion. The mattress was at an angle to the frame of the bed. Bedsheets, clothes, half-opened bags of nuts, chips, and candy were interspersed between empty cans of soda and beer. There was a large stain, which looked fresh, on the wall right above Mark's desk. A rather large perforation in the wallpaper was at the center of the stain. Something had been thrown with a great deal of force. Mark's computer was shut, but there was an orange LED blinking on the left side.

"All yours," I said.

With the speed and efficiency of a cybercriminal, Jeremy opened the laptop, switched it on, and started rattling away at the keyboard. It made absolutely no difference that he had only one human arm. The fingers attached to his prosthetic hand tapped away at the keys at the same speed of his normal one. He then opened his satchel and took out something that looked like an oversized memory stick, which he inserted into one of the USB ports. Then more typing before he took out a cable and a modem-type box from that same black pouch. I felt like I was in a *Mission Impossible* movie.

"Okay, let's see what Mark was up to before he hightailed it out of here." Data was streaming vertically across the screen. Every few seconds, Jeremy would stop the flow of information and analyze what was in front of him.

"So between 7:28 and 7:57, he was cruising back and forth between porn sites. He was up on Facebook since last night. He didn't log off. He visited a few travel sites for what seems to be airline tickets this morning as well. Atlanta to San Francisco and back. No activity between 8:30 and 8:52. Then he logged on to Skype at 8:53, logged off after seven minutes, and then logged back on again at 9:06. He pulled up Google Maps at 9:17 and didn't log off."

"You said Skype?"

"Yeah, the second time he logged on; he was talking with someone for about six minutes.

"Can you tell who he was speaking to?"

"Hang on a minute." There was much more key tapping.

"I have a Skype name. It's Tracy1907. It's a US-based Skype address, but...wait." Jeremy peered at the screen. "That's weird."

"What?"

"I wanted to see if there was any messaging or any calls made to this address before this morning." That made good sense. "But there's nothing here...it's like...yeah, look at that. Mark deleted everything. I'm only picking up this Skype address because Mark paid for the second call with a credit card. Something must have really set him off to delete this address and its messaging history from his directory."

"So he's on Skype with someone from the US. At what time was it, Jeremy?"

"Between 9:06 and 9:12 am. The second time he logged on."

"The second time he logged on…so he must have felt the need to speak with this person again, right after he deleted everything. That's odd. It was 3:00 am on the East Coast. Too early to be speaking with his parents unless it was an emergency."

"Mark has a sister, but I don't remember where she lives."

"That's right! His sister lives in California, and it was just after midnight there.

He could have been speaking to her."

"Midnight?" Jeremy looked puzzled.

"There's a nine-hour time difference between Italy and California."

Mark had told me, with notable enthusiasm, that he was going to go visit his sister when he got back to Atlanta. *Where did she live? San Francisco? Sacramento?* I couldn't remember. I thought about sending a Skype message to Tracy1907, but I wasn't one hundred percent sure that that user was, in fact, his sister. Furthermore, I didn't want to alarm anyone quite yet, given that there was still a possibility that he had just gone out to blow off steam.

I nodded to Jeremy. "Okay, now unplug everything and make it look like we were never here."

In less than five minutes, we had closed the door behind us and locked it. When we got downstairs to the lobby, Wayne and Bishop were back. We told everyone what we had found on Mark's laptop.

"It looks as though something happened during those Skype calls that set Mark off," I said. "Does anybody know his sister's name?"

"Theresa," Wayne answered. "Mark's always talking about her. She lives in Sacramento."

"That's important, Wayne, thanks."

Bishop snapped his fingers. "I just realized there's one place we didn't check out yet,"

"You mean around here? Which one?" I asked.

"That bar where we found him the first night."

I thought long and hard for a moment. "Could be. Why would he go back there, though? Not to drink himself stupid again because the owner wouldn't make that mistake twice."

"He was really worried that the owner was going to have to shut down," Michelle pointed out.

I nodded. "True. Jeremy, I still need your help."

"Sure, what can I do?"

"Stay here in the hotel lobby until we return. If anybody from the group comes back, let them know that we're all looking for Mark. Don't make a big deal of it, though."

"Will do."

I asked Ludovica to give me a call if she saw hide or hair of Mark. She said she would and wished us good luck. The four of us walked out of the hotel.

"Has anyone noticed anything out of the ordinary in Mark's behavior these past few days?" I asked.

"Not really," Bishop answered. "He was just going on and on about this trip to go see his sister and how he can't wait to start at the University of Georgia. He just wants out of the house."

"Amen to that," Wayne said.

I looked at him with an interrogative eyebrow.

"His dad is never home, and his mom, at least the times I've been to his house, is either sleeping or stumbling around drunk. His parents call him 'shot baby' because he was conceived during some wild party in the Bahamas while they were doing tequila shots. They think it's a joke."

"Tequila? That's what he was drinking that night you found him hammered."

"That's his drink of choice, Atticus," Michelle said in a subdued voice.

We had turned the corner onto Via del Lavatore and were homing in on the Pappagallo Bar. Michelle continued, "Mark's told us that he's overheard his mom say that he should have been given up for adoption, that it was too much trouble having a kid so many years after the first one."

Well now, that will do wonders for one's self-esteem.

"The sister seems to be the only saving grace in the family," I said.

"He adores his sister, even though she's lived in California since she was like twenty-six. She's the one that really looked after Mark when he was little."

This reinforced my conviction that something was said in those Skype calls that caused Mark to vanish without a word.

We had arrived at the bar, and it was, as I expected, open for business.

As soon as we walked in, I saw the owner, Mr. Cassini. He looked at us, started to say something in English which sounded like "Welcome, come in!" before he froze up. He had recognized me.

"No, no! I didn't do anything wrong!" he said, starting to panic. I told him to stay calm and that I only needed some information. He forged ahead with his "I don't know anything" rant. He was hiding something. I could feel it. I turned up the heat.

"You will tell me what I want to know, or I make a phone call to my friend who was here with me last time." My Italian was cool and collected but with a menacing undertone. He turned very pale. Rushing to the cash register, he counted out several twenty-euro notes and thrust them in my direction.

"Here, take it! And go away, all of you!"

"What are you doing?" I said, frowning. "I don't want your money."

"He came in here, he put this money on the bar, said it wasn't his!"

I knew who he was talking about, but I wanted to make sure. "You mean the young man I was with the other day?"

"Yes, yes, him! He came in and left this money. All he wanted was a bottle of tequila." That, I really did not want to hear.

"Shit!" Wayne said. He didn't know Italian, but he knew I was talking about Mark, and he heard "tequila."

What direction did he go when he left here?"

The owner pointed towards Vicolo Scavolino, which was a crossroad of the street we were on.

"And do you remember the time?"

"It was ten, that's when I open, and he was already standing outside."

"Okay," I said. "There won't be any more trouble."

"And the money?"

I gave him back half. He had, after all, taken Mark for about eighty dollars that first night in town. We left and regrouped outside.

"Listen up now," I told them. "I have to make a few calls to people who may be able to help us. What I need all of you to do is to go around looking for him. Wayne, you go down that street," I pointed in the same direction that the owner had. "Bishop, you go west, in the direction of the Pantheon, and, Michelle, head back in the direction of the hotel and go look around the Vittorio Emanuele Monument."

"You mean the wedding cake?"

"That's it. Look in any parks you may pass and alleyways. By this time, he's probably passed out somewhere. It's one thirty. Let's meet back at the hotel no later than three. All of you have your phones on?" Everyone nodded. "Okay, off you go."

The three of them took off in their respective directions. I ducked into a coffee bar and ordered a double espresso with a shot of Sambuca. I pulled out my cell phone and dialed the first number. It was Marco's.

I explained the entire situation and told him what my next steps were going to be. This time, I was the boss speaking to my subordinate.

My next call was to Ludovica, who said that no one from the group had come into the hotel since we had left. I gave her an update and gave her a message to relay a specific message to Barbara and John if she saw them but warned her not to say a word to Cynthia.

The third call I made was the most important—Giorgio. After giving him a rundown on the situation, he asked a few questions. I could tell he was taking notes.

"Let me put in a call to the hospitals in the area. Do you know if he had any identification on him when he left the hotel?"

"No, I don't."

"In order to be thorough, Atticus, I will run his name and description on the recently deceased database. I know this sounds pessimistic, but we must eliminate all the possibilities."

I swallowed hard but knew he was right.

"Do what you think is best, Giorgio."

"I'm also going to get his description out to all the mobile units. I have a good image of what he looks like in my old brain cells."

Giorgio asked me where Mark was last seen, and I gave him the name of the street. He offered to have the tapes from the outside city surveillance cameras, situated at the corners of many streets in Rome, reviewed. This would be of immense help to see in what direction Mark went and possibly where he was now. "Thanks, Giorgio. I'm sorry about all this, but you're the only person I could turn to."

"It will cost you a lunch at Giggetto's." Giorgio chuckled.

"Done deal."

"We can also celebrate my promotion yesterday to full colonel."

"Full colonel? What great news, Giorgio. You truly deserve it!"

Even in the midst of my worry, I was truly pleased for Giorgio.

"Thank you, my friend, I am also very happy. You know, Atticus, that kid has got a good heart."

"What do you mean?"

"Well, he went back there to give that rat the money. Stupid, but a good kid."

"I guess you're right. Let's hope for the best."

I placed my phone on the counter and threw back the expresso in one go. I wasn't sure what I should do next. After a bit of thought, I decided to go back to the hotel and wait in the lobby for any news.

I proceeded to the Trevi Fountain, turned left in the direction of the hotel, and almost immediately spotted Mary and Sabrina doing some window-shopping.

"Hey, you two," I called out.

They looked around. "Hello, Atticus," Sabrina said as I came over. "What's up?"

"We've got a problem, and I need your help." I told them about Mark's disappearance but didn't mention the bottle of tequila.

"Any idea where he could have gone, Atticus?" Mary asked.

"None whatsoever. That's why I need everyone's help to backtrack the places we've been these last few days."

"It's a big city," said Mary.

"I know, but the more eyes out there, the better the chance of finding him."

"Knowing Mark, he probably got his hands on some booze," Sabrina said.

I didn't respond.

"Do you have my cell number and the number of the hotel?" I asked.

They both nodded.

"Okay then. Let's meet back at the hotel at three."

With that, they took off.

I found Jeremy in the lobby with James, Evelyn, and Vanessa.

"Didn't find him?" said Jeremy.

"No, not a sign," I answered. "And obviously, he hasn't come this way."

"Nope. I told them about Mark." Jeremy gestured to the other three.

"Unfortunately, the situation has become more serious," I said. "We went back to that bar where Mark had a few drinks the first night he was here. We found out from the owner that he bought a bottle of tequila at about ten thirty this morning."

"Damn," said Vanessa, "he's probably passed out behind a garbage can somewhere."

"Did he have any meds with him?"

I looked hard at Evelyn. "What do you mean exactly?"

"I mean meds, pharma, drugs, you know!"

I couldn't help but glance at Vanessa. She gave a quick shake of the head.

"Hate to ask," said James, "but has someone checked the morgue?"

That's when I lost it.

"Christ Almighty, James! A little bit of optimism here, please! Nobody is dying under my goddamn watch, is that clear!?"

My outburst shocked them. I quickly got hold of myself, realizing that I was a bit of a hypocrite. When Giorgio had mentioned that he would be checking the recently deceased database, I not only agreed but understood where he was coming from.

I raised my hands. "Sorry about that. I overreacted. I'm just trying to find a silver lining somewhere, anywhere."

Before anyone could respond, my phone began to vibrate in my back pocket. I reached for it and looked at the incoming number. It was Giorgio. "Stay here," I said, then went outside to take the call.

"Giorgio, ciao, tell me."

"We have him on video, Atticus…"

External surveillance cameras, one outside of a bank and the other on the corner of the Italian Parliament building, had recorded Mark's movements after he had left the bar. He had reached Via del Tritone, a major thoroughfare cutting the city from West to East and entered a bookstore on the corner of Via del Corso. When he left the store, he crossed the street and headed to a bus stop. Eight minutes later, he boarded a city bus, Number 684, which headed all the way the Via del Corso and ended its route just behind the Roman Forum. Another security camera then captured Mark waiting at another bus stop before getting on Bus 84 this time.

"Where does that bus stop, Giorgio?" I asked.

"At Piazzale Ostiense."

This is where Rome's the third largest train station is located. My mind was racing. Did Mark leave the city? Where would he have gone?

"One more thing, Atticus. The boy can be seen holding a brown paper bag with what looks like a bottle," said Giorgio. "He may not have drunk anything yet at the time of these recordings."

This was indeed good news. It seemed as though Mark was planning to go some specific place before hitting that bottle. He had probably gone to the bookstore to buy bus tickets, and if we were lucky, get directions to wherever he was heading.

"The problem is that he did not get off the bus at terminus," Giorgio continued. "He must have gotten off somewhere on Viale Aventino where we don't have cameras. This must have been between 11:55 and 12:10. I dispatched patrol cars to the areas. I think we shall find him soon, hopefully sober."

"Patrol cars? I appreciate it, but don't stretch yourself too much on this."

"The rank of colonel has its privileges, my friend."

I thanked Giorgio profusely, asking him to call me back with any other news. I then went back into the hotel and updated the others.

"So at noon, it seems, Mark was still sober," I concluded. I glanced at my watch. "But that was nearly three hours ago."

"But where on earth was he going?" said Vanessa.

"That's the million-dollar question."

"Where is the street that he took off on when he left the bus?" asked James.

"It's south of the city, past the Colosseum, in the direction of that pyramid that we saw coming in from the airport."

"Evanescence…."

I glanced at James. He was staring off into the distance.

"What?" said Jeremy.

"Evanescence," James repeated.

Jeremy frowned. "Hey, man, not the time for music trivia."

James continued staring. "Mark's pissed at the world, something his sister said to him really fucked him up. He gets a bottle, but instead of drinking it in the bar or just outside, he has a location in mind, a place he identifies with."

"Here in Rome?" I said thoughtfully. James was on to something.

"You don't get it, do you?"

"Get what?" asked Vanessa.

"Evanescence. First album. What's on the cover?" James was looking straight at me. "You've got the answer right in front of your eyes, Atticus. You're the one who told Mark where to go."

What? I didn't understand what James was referring to. Then a light bulb went off in my cobweb filled memory.

On the tour bus, heading to the forum. *Evanescence*, the band. The first album, on the cover. The angel kneeling on the tombstone. The very same tombstone in the Protestant cemetery next to the Pyramid of Cestius…

"James, you really think, that?" I began.

"It's his favorite band, and he's in love with Amy Lee, the lead singer."

"James, you're a genius! I'd kiss you, but you're not my type."

The others clapped him on his back. But James didn't react. He got up slowly, said he was tired and was going to his room.

"That's where I would go if I were Mark," he said, getting up. "But then again, I'm not Mark, am I?"

He left the lobby, walking as though the weight of the world was on his thin shoulders.

CHAPTER 54

The rest of us just sat there a moment, speechless. My mind was racing. "Okay, listen up. Jeremy, you're coming with me. Vanessa, Evelyn, when the others come back, let them know that Jeremy and I may now know where Mark is. If Mr. Seeward or Mrs. Cornwall come back, give them the rundown on what happened. I'll take care of Mrs. Ramsey."

I got up and went to the front desk and asked Ludovica to call me a taxi and to connect me to Cynthia's room. She passed me the receiver. Cynthia picked up on the second ring.

"Yes?"

"Cynthia, it's Atticus. I need your help."

"Tell me."

"Stay in the hotel for the next few hours. We may have to go somewhere together."

"Certainly. May I ask what this is about?"

"Not yet. You have to trust my judgment for now. If I do call you, I will require the Cynthia I met today, not the Cynthia of yesterday."

I paused, waiting to hear her response.

"I understand," she said calmly. "I'll be here when you call."

"Thank you." I passed the receiver back to Ludovica.

"The taxi is outside," she told me.

"Great, thank you." I gestured to Jeremy to come with me.

We entered the cab, and I told the driver where we were going and that we were in a hurry. Then I punched a number on my phone.

"Giorgio, I think we know where he is…" I gave him the exact location.

"I'll send a squad car and ambulance immediately."

"Wait, Giorgio, I'm not one hundred percent sure of this."

"Better safe than sorry, my friend. That boy of yours is just one year older than my son. I feel better knowing that I may be able to help him." Then the line went dead.

The taxi driver had taken my request to hurry to heart. Jeremy was holding on to the handle above the door and clutching the seat with his left hand.

"Is this guy trying out for the Indy 500?" he almost shrieked.

"Relax, he knows what he's doing."

Famous last words.

Jeremy relaxed a little. "Do you think the teachers are going to flip when they find out about Mark?"

That was a good question.

"I hope not." I didn't want to call Barbara and John just yet. The one person I was relying on was Cynthia. This would have been impossible twenty-four hours ago. Suddenly, I found Jeremy flung against me as we took a corner at about fifty miles per hour.

"This guy's out of control!" Jeremy yelped.

"Just hang on and close your eyes."

"Do I need to slow down?" the driver asked in Italian.

"*No, no. Vai!*" I replied. "Go!"

At this speed, we would be at our destination in under ten minutes. But Jeremy was stressing out. I decided to talk to him to distract him from the taxi's breakneck speed.

"Jeremy?"

"Yes," he said, his eyes still fixed on the buildings speeding by in a blur.

"Look at me, Jeremy," I said insistently.

He tore his eyes away from the car window.

"Are you going to college, Jeremy? I haven't read your student bio yet."

"Yes, I mean, I think so. I've gotten some job offers from software houses, but I want to do four more years of school." He glanced outside again. "If I live."

His little joke told me he was calming down.

"Where are you going?" I asked.

"It's still a toss-up between the University of Washington and the Georgia Institute of Technology. Both have awesome computer programming departments, and I have a full scholarship at both."

"That's phenomenal! Congratulations."

"MIT admitted me as well, but only with a fifty percent scholarship. My mom and dad don't have the money to foot the rest of the bill."

"What's half of the tuition, if you don't mind me asking?"

"About thirty thousand with room and board."

I nodded somberly. "That's a big chunk of change."

"Yeah. Even if I worked and studied, I'd just make seven or eight K a year, but that's just a dent."

I had often marveled at the outrageous tuition fees at so-called institutions of higher learning and questioned the value proposition.

"Two more minutes," said the driver, barreling down Viale Aventino, a four-lane city street, at almost 110 kilometers an hour, or 68 mph. My distraction had only partly worked. Jeremy was now turning green.

"It's okay, Jeremy," I assured him. "These guys know how to maneuver in traffic."

We passed the pyramid and pulled into the main entrance of the Protestant cemetery. The gates were closed, but there was an elderly gentleman standing in front as if he were expecting us. I paid our racing driver, and we exited the taxi.

I introduced myself, and the caretaker just nodded his head, turned to the gate, and unlocked it. I asked him what the opening hours were.

"We open at eight, close at twelve thirty, and reopen from four to six," he informed me.

Had Mark made it here before the gates closed or had he jumped the fence somewhere along the perimeter? As I pondered this, I heard two sirens approaching. One was that of an ambulance and the other a Guardia di Finanza squad car.

"Can you tell me where the *Angel of Grief* is located?" I asked.

"Follow that path, always straight, you can't miss it."

As the caretaker walked off, both the ambulance and squad car pulled up close to where Jeremy and I were standing. I did a double take when the passenger side door of the car opened. It was Giorgio.

I went forward and shook his hand. "Very good to see you, my friend," I said, "but you didn't have to bother yourself."

"Never a bother for you." I introduced Giorgio to Jeremy.

"Do you know where we're going?"

"I do. Let's move." Every minute was important.

The three of us, along with two ambulance attendants pushing a stretcher, headed down the gravel pathway.

The cemetery had been built in the early eighteenth century and showed its age. It was far from properly maintained, either because of lack of funds or inefficient city officials. Many of the imposing monuments and tombstones were in desperate need of repair. The granite and marble structures were chipped and stained in many instances, ledgers and slants were at an angle, flower vases were broken or missing, and the invasion of weeds and shrubbery was substantial.

I observed all this as we proceeded at a fast clip, in silence.

Only a few minutes passed before I caught a glimpse of the angel. The monument was larger and whiter than I had expected. The angel itself was draped over an altar of sorts with one arm dangling down the front and her head buried in her other arm across the top. The rest of her body and wings were not visible due to the angle we were approaching. The grass and weeds were tall, but there was no sign of Mark. As we came closer, it was apparent that the lower half of the angel's body was hidden by the top of the altar. It was when I circled the front of the monument that my heart stopped.

CHAPTER 55

Skype call, outbound, Rome, 8:53 am

"Hey, sis, hope it's not too late."

"No, no...it's fine. I'm still up finishing a project for work. How are you?"

"I'm good. I've been up for a few hours. Can't shake off this jet-lag even after a week of being here."

"Yes, I remember the feeling when I went to London."

"You okay, sis? You sound a bit off."

"Yes, I'm fine...just fine."

"I just wanted to let you know that I found a great flight out of Hartsfield that leaves on May 28 and gets into San Francisco at about two thirty in the afternoon. The return flight is for June 14—that is, if I really have to go back to Atlanta. Super cheap too, round trip five hundred sixty-five bucks. Not bad, huh?"

"Mark, I'm glad you called. I wanted to talk to you about this trip."

"Yeah? What's up?"

"I'm afraid that time period isn't going to work."

"Hey, that's cool. I can push it back. Just tell me the dates that are good for you."

"I'm afraid that there aren't any dates that will work, Mark."

"What do you mean, no dates?"

"Mark...Adam and I are getting married. Mark? Are you there? Did you hear me?"

"I heard you."

"Mark, you should be happy for me. I mean, I'm pushing twenty-nine. It's time for me to settle down. And the really good news is that you will be an uncle soon. I'm pregnant."

Skype call disconnected.

Skype call, outbound, Rome, 9:06 am

"Mark? What happened? The call dropped."

"Why didn't you tell me any of this before, Theresa!?"

"Tell you any of what? About my pregnancy, you mean?"

"Everything. Being pregnant, getting married—"

"Mark, not even our parents know about the baby."

"Who cares about those assholes! You needed to tell me!"

"Mark, calm down. Why are you so angry? I didn't—"

"I've been waiting for this trip all fucking semester, and now you tell me I can't come, that you're getting married to that dickhead, and you're pregnant!"

"What the hell is wrong with you, Mark?! Who do you think I am? Your frigging girlfriend? I'm your sister, for Christ's sake, and what I do with my life is my goddamn business!"

"I don't want to hear this bullshit."

"Well, listen to this then: I was always there for you when you were just a snotty little kid. I changed your diapers, I fed you *most of the time, I took you out for walks and to the playground, and I played with you in your room when Mom was too drunk to even stand up. But that was a long time ago. You're eighteen now. I'm not your babysitter anymore. Got that!?"*

"You split when I was eight years old!"

"I left the house because I was going insane with Dad always gone for work or at the golf course or screwing some girl my age and Mom always hammered drunk. But I was only thirty miles away just because I didn't want to abandon you, you, ingrate! Who took you to the movies on the weekends and to most of your after-school activities? It was me, Mark! Remember?"

"Then you went all the way to California."

"That was three years ago. You were almost sixteen. (pause) Mark...Adam and I are going to Australia after the wedding. He's got family there and a great job offer. You might as well know. If you can get over all this anger, maybe one day you can come...Mark? Are you there? Shit!"

Skype call disconnected.

***

Cynthia leaned over and said quietly, "So that's how you found him?"

"Yes."

"Because of James?"

"Absolutely. He put the pieces of the puzzle together."

We were sitting in Room 321 on the third floor of the San Camillo Hospital, which was about three miles from the cemetery where we found Mark. He was now asleep after getting his stomach pumped, vomiting induced, and IVs stuck into his arms to restore hydration, blood sugar and vitamin levels, plus a catheter for urination. A monitor, humming softly in the background, tracked his vital signs with colorful numbers and graphs.

I had told Cynthia everything that had transpired since we separated after our long talk. What I had not yet told her was the condition we had found Mark in.

"I have rarely been so scared, Cynthia," I said. "I walked behind that angel and the first thing I saw was a limp arm and hand resting in the grass. Mark's skin was deathly pale. I thought we had lost him. Thank God the ambulance attendants were there."

"Was he conscious?"

"No. He was sitting with his back against the altar, and his legs were tucked under the angel's wings, almost in a fetal position. He had a bad gash on his forehead. He was covered in vomit and urine. The bottle of tequila was on its side and completely empty. He was barely…barely breathing, Cynthia."

My voice cracked. Cynthia reached over and took my hand.

"We had him on the stretcher and in the ambulance at the speed of light."

"And after that?" she asked.

"Giorgio drove Jeremy and me to the hospital, sirens on, with the ambulance right behind us. Jeremy thought the drive with the taxi driver was rough. You should have seen his face when we arrived at the hospital. Giorgio actually had me worried. We were going between seventy to eighty miles an hour and on the wrong side of the road half the time. It was brilliant driving."

Once all the paperwork was filled out and Mark was settled in his hospital room, Giorgio offered to take Jeremy back to the hotel and pick up Cynthia. I called her as soon as they had left and asked her if she would come and sit with Mark and to bring a few things for his stay. She didn't ask any questions, only saying she would be ready when Giorgio arrived.

"You will have to explain a few things when you get back to the hotel, Atticus. Almost all of the students were downstairs asking about Mark, as well as Barbara and John. I just told them that you would fill them in as soon as you got back. You should have seen their faces when they saw me getting into that police car with the lights flashing." She smiled. "I got a kick out of that."

I had asked Jeremy to inform everyone to be at dinner at eight and that I would be there to explain the situation. It was now close to seven.

"As a matter of fact, I've got to go now," I said. "Are you going to be okay?"

"Absolutely. I have a change of clothes and a good book. I plan to stay here by Mark's side, if the hospital will allow it."

"No worries about the hospital, but I was planning on coming back after dinner."

"No, Atticus. I've never given this boy any quality time. This is the least I can do for him. You do understand, don't you? Especially after today?"

I looked at her and smiled. "I do. And thank you."

There was a soft knock on the door. A young man walked in wearing medical scrubs and a white jacket. He asked us if we were next of kin. I explained the situation and who we were to him in Italian, letting him know that Cynthia only spoke English. I asked him about Mark's status.

"Let's say that your auspicious discovery and the warm weather prevented what could have been a permanent trip back to a cemetery." I was about to ask how he knew about Mark's whereabouts.

"No, I'm not a mind reader, I had a chat with Colonel before he left the hospital."

Okay, all clear. Giorgio had brought the doctor up to speed.

Hypothermia had not set in yet, and miraculously, he did not choke on his vomit. There was nothing in his stomach except the liquor, which on this occasion was fortuitous, considering the large amount ingested. He was dehydrated from all the alcohol in his bloodstream, and he may have suffered some damage to his liver, but it is too early to tell at the moment."

I explained to the doctor that Mark's parents lived in the US, and the group was scheduled to go back stateside this coming Wednesday morning.

"We shall need to inform his parents to obtain an authorization for whatever other procedures we may have to adopt." He noted our reaction and said, "Not that I foresee any invasive action, but just in case."

"If the boy's condition does not get worse, will he be able to leave here by tomorrow afternoon?"

"That's a possibility. I shall have a better understanding of his overall status tomorrow morning. Is one of you staying the night?"

Cynthia nodded. "I am."

"That's fine. I shall arrange for a more comfortable recliner."

He went over to Mark's bedside and checked the monitor and the drip bags, then took Mark's pulse and listened to his heart.

"His pulse is getting stronger, and his heartbeat is more rhythmic. What he needs now is lots of rest."

When the doctor left the room, I made sure that Cynthia was comfortable before heading downstairs. Luckily, there were several taxis in line outside the main entrance to the hospital. After settling in and once again repeating that I was in a great hurry, I was back on the phone with Marco.

"ASA Atlanta is attempting to get in touch with the boy's parents, but no luck so far. Did you give the hospital my number?"

"Yes, as soon as we checked Mark in. I didn't have the office number so I gave them your cell. Sorry about that."

"You did the right thing, Atticus. I informed ASA here, and they've started the process with Atlanta."

"We almost lost him, Marco."

"Almost. You probably saved his life."

"Not me. One of the boys came up with the idea of where he could be, and he was spot-on." I briefly explained James's reasoning concerning Mark's whereabouts.

"Hopefully, he'll be released Tuesday afternoon. He should be able to take the flight back on Thursday." Marco and I went over a few more odds and ends regarding the boy's hospital stay.

As soon as I got off the phone, I pulled up Massimo's number. I had promised him a call.

"Ciao, Atticus! How are you?"

"Next question, Massimo."

"Why, my friend? More problems with our boys and girls?"

It took a good ten minutes to explain everything to him. There was an outrageous amount of traffic, so I had time to elaborate.

"My God, Atticus, what else is going to happen in these next forty-eight hours?"

"I don't know. I really don't know."

"What about our two boys, Wayne, and Bishop, correct? Did you learn something?"

"You bet." I summed up what the two had divulged to Barbara and me.

"How interesting and tragic at the same time. My companion, Sebastiano, was almost killed by his father when he came out of the closet. In a moment of rage, his father threw a kitchen knife at him which struck him right below the collarbone. A few inches, and he would have been hit in the throat."

"Well, according to Wayne, his dad is capable of something similar."

"Atticus, I would like to propose something, but I want you to be honest and tell me if you believe it to be appropriate or not."

"Okay, I will."

"Sebastiano and I wanted to invite the two boys and Michelle to lunch. We thought it would help them unwind a bit. I was certain at the forum that there was more than just friendship between those two. And now that you bring up Wayne's father, I think that chatting with Sebastiano would help him and the other boy immensely."

"I see no problem with this. If it can help Wayne and Bishop, I am all for it."

"I just didn't want you thinking that I was planning an orgy of sorts…"

"With Michelle?"

"Well, yes, that would be awkward."

We both laughed.

"Very good then, Atticus. We can speak about the details tomorrow morning."

"Tomorrow morning?"

"Yes, tomorrow we go to Castel Sant'Angelo and the Spanish Steps. It's the last scheduled tour for your group."

"Thank you for reminding me. So you will be our guide?"

"Absolutely! I would not miss it for the world."

"Great news. The students will be delighted."

The taxi had pulled up to the hotel without my realizing it. I ended the conversation with Massimo, paid the taxi driver, and rushed inside the hotel. Barbara and John were in the lobby pacing like tigers waiting to be fed. Ludovica was behind the front desk with thinly veiled curiosity showing behind her professional poise.

"Where are the students?" I asked.

"In the restaurant," Barbara snapped.

John thrust himself forward. "How is Mark? Why weren't the two of us informed about what happened?"

I was in no mood to start explaining everything there in the lobby. "I have answers for you, but right now," I said. "I need both of you to come with me."

"I'll let everybody know what the situation is and give the two of you more details later." I turned and looked at Ludovica. "Thank you for all your help today. You were extremely valuable."

Ludovica shot me a brief smile and gave Barbara a brief but distinct leer. I proceeded to the restaurant with John and Barbara right behind me. As soon as I walked in, the students erupted with rapid-fire questions.

I walked over to a center table and pulled out the chair, facing the students. I waited for John and Barbara to seat themselves next to me, then started explaining what had happened. I did not know what Jeremy might have said, so I skirted over the details of how we entered Mark's room and hacked his computer. I was hoping that Jeremy had been discreet about this.

More questions were shot at me:

"You found him in a cemetery?"

"How much did he drink?"

"Were the Italian Police really there at the cemetery?"

"What the hell did his sister say to him?"

(So much for Jeremy's discretion.)

"What is it that got under his skin?"

"Did they pump his stomach?"

"Where did Mrs. Ramsey go in that badass police car?"

"When is Mark getting out of the hospital?"

"Mrs. Ramsey is with him?" was Evelyn's contribution. "That may just kill him." I was tempted to give her a cutting reply but opted against it.

For the next twenty minutes or so, I answered, or tried to answer, all of the students' questions. When their remarks petered out, I stood up.

"I want to sincerely thank Jeremy and James. I think it is safe to say that without Jeremy's computer skills and James's astute reasoning, Mark could very well have not made it today." That got everyone's attention. I turned to the two boys. "The two of you probably saved a life today." I began to clap my hands, and the whole group followed suit. Jeremy was blushing profusely, but James just sat in his chair, expressionless.

"Okay, listen up. This trip isn't over yet. We have one more tour tomorrow, and I want all of you to take advantage of it. We need to leave the hotel at nine. Our guide will meet us here."

"Do we know who it is this time, Atticus?" somebody asked.

"Not yet." I wanted the group to be surprised. "Can I see a show of hands of those who are going out tonight?"

"Can we go see Mark?" Wayne asked.

"I shook my head. "He's not going to be ready for visitors until tomorrow."

The students started grouping together, with some saying that they were going out for an ice cream or just to walk around. John and Barbara didn't budge from their chairs.

"Remember, everyone," I said. "Breakfast is at eight o'clock, and we leave at nine. Have a good night."

I sat down, signaled one of the waiters, and ordered an espresso and a Sambuca. Although I had not eaten anything substantial for the day, I wasn't hungry. As soon as the students were out of the restaurant, John started in on me.

"Was it really necessary to have Jeremy break into Mark's computer?" he said.

"I think it helped save Mark's life. I don't know if Jeremy told you about the two Skype conversations?"

"He did, supposedly with his sister."

"That's the verdict. And something was said in one of those two conversations that had a devastating effect on Mark."

Barbara weighed in, "But what does that have to do with James figuring out where Mark possibly was?"

"It was the key, Barbara. If we hadn't found that conversation, we wouldn't have known that this was what set him off, and James probably wouldn't have put the pieces of the puzzle together."

Barbara shook her head. "I still can't believe that you didn't tell us, Atticus," she said. "We are responsible for these students, just as much as Cynthia is. But what I really can't fathom is that, of all people, you ask her to go to the hospital to sit with him. Cynthia has always been contemptuous of Mark, as well as Wayne and Bishop."

Barbara's voice had risen in anger. I could understand this, but she was beginning to get on my nerves.

"Obviously, there is a reason why I felt Cynthia was the right choice," I said. "I had a very long talk with her this morning, and let's just say that her attitude has completely changed. I am not going into more detail, so don't bother asking me."

Both Barbara and John looked surprised at this. I folded my arms. Barbara's eyes narrowed.

"Well, I think that John and I need to go to the hospital to see what the situation is," she said.

I shrugged. "Feel free. But not tonight. You can both go in the morning."

"Are you actually prohibiting us from going tonight?" John said disbelievingly.

I gazed at him icily, now thoroughly fed up. "Yes, John. The boy is sleeping. He mustn't be disturbed. Cynthia and the doctors know to call me or the hotel if there is any development during the night."

They were both clearly unhappy with me. But they said nothing more, which was all I wanted. After a few long seconds, John and Barbara got up and left the restaurant area. I just sat there and kept sipping my Sambuca. They were obviously upset with me. *But why had Barbara become so aggressive?* I wondered. She should have known that I would have told her everything once we were alone together. I was bothered by her behavior and also hurt.

"Atticus?"

Sabrina was standing in the doorway of the restaurant.

"Do you have a minute?" she asked.

"Sure. Come in."

"Not here," she said, glancing at John and Barbara in the corner. "I need to talk with you in private. Maybe we could meet in your room if you don't mind?"

I looked at Sabrina carefully. She seemed calm enough, but I could see it was a façade put up to hide dire stress. And I suspected I knew what was causing it. I didn't like being alone, again, with a female student in my room, but I consented.

"Wait down here for a few minutes. I'll go up and unlock the door. You know where my room is?"

"Yes."

I got up and left with Barbara's behavior still fresh on my mind.

CHAPTER 56

Once in my room, I left the door ajar. Sabrina came in after a few minutes. I sat in the armchair, and she pulled one of the straight-backed chairs in front of me.

"So what's up ?" I asked.

She clasped her hands in her lap. "I just wanted to thank you."

"Thank me?" I was surprised. "For what?"

"We—I mean, the students—we've all seen how you care about what's going on with us."

"Okay," I said, not seeing where this conversation was going. "I think you're all good kids. All of you have impressed me in one way or the other."

"That's what I mean. We see that, and it's a good feeling, you know."

"Well, I don't believe I've done anything out of the ordinary."

"You have," she said. "Like, you took the time to speak with me at St. Peter's. Then you told me about that statue in that church. You helped Vanessa and now saved Mark's life…"

I realized that flattering as all this was, Sabrina was really trying to persuade herself to talk to me about her real issue. "I appreciate all that very much, Sabrina," I said. "So tell me, is there anything in particular that you would like to talk to me about?"

She took a breath, then let it out slowly. I could see the tension easing in her as she made up her mind.

"You know about my brother, right?"

I nodded. "Derek. He died about a year ago in an accident."

I didn't reveal that I knew anything more. To do so would have meant revealing James's secrets. Also, Sabrina needed to tell me what she wanted me to know, in her own way. I felt that if she had an inkling that James had talked about her brother with me, she would close off.

"Yes. He rode his bike into a truck." She paused, biting her lip. "Derek and James were friends. But Derek kept that secret. Turns out, my brother had a lot of secrets."

I didn't let my surprise show.

"What kind of secrets?" I asked.

Sabrina's deep sigh was equal parts grief and regret. "My brother was evil, Atticus. I only found out when it was too late to do anything about it."

"How do you mean?"

"My brother wrote two letters before he was killed. One for me, one for our parents."

"Go on."

"Stuff he wanted us to know after he died. Or, rather, after he killed himself."

"Killed himself? I thought he died in an accident."

"Accidentally or on purpose, maybe. I don't know."

Sabrina began fidgeting with her necklace and was having difficulty getting the next words out.

"Basically, Derek had a double life. To the outside world, he was Mr. Perfection, the best at everything. Our parents were so damn proud of him. But in his own world, Derek was some kind of devil worshipper, had been since the age of fifteen! That's one of the things he wanted us to know in his letter. Can you believe that? My *I-can-do-no-wrong* brother worshipped Satan."

What Sabrina had told me so far was a carbon copy of what James had opened up to me about. However, I continued to be the picture of complete surprise.

"Devil worship? At fifteen? That's unusual. Did he give any explanation in the letter as to why?

"Sort of. He wrote that he had studied up on Satan, satanical masses, something about their commandments and that eternal darkness was the only possible option for salvation. He was really into that crap."

"I see."

"Here's the kicker, though. He wrote that everything he did had just one purpose—to inflict as much pain as possible on our parents. And me. He made sure he was the best at everything he did so it would be that more devastating when he killed himself."

"So he did intend to kill himself?"

"Yes. But maybe not in that way. Who knows what somebody like that was thinking."

"He must have had a great deal of hate in him to plan something like that."

Sabrina began rocking back and forth. I was reliving my morning with Cynthia, minus the scotch.

"Yes. My loving brother was full of hate. He despised our parents more than me, Atticus. Our mom, for example, is the biggest slut I know, and our dad is a borderline pedophile. Derek tore them both up about this in the letter. He laid into me too."

"Into you?"

She hesitated, then looked at me with tear-bright eyes. "Only two people know what I'm going to tell you, and one is my therapist."

"Don't tell me anything you feel uncomfortable with, Sabrina."

"That's just it. I do feel comfortable with you. I really would like to tell someone else I trust."

"You can rest assured what's said in Rome stays in Rome."

She gave me half-smile.

"Okay, then, you need a little background. And I'm not making excuses, but by the time I turned sixteen, I was lost. I was feeling really feeling shitty about myself, my life, everything. There just wasn't any meaning to anything. So, to stop feeling like shit, I began drinking, smoking dope, and hanging around the wrong crowd. Because that's the way stupid teens deal with feeling shitty, by doing actual shit. Anyway, I got involved with some people on the south side of town and started some heavy-duty partying. There were a few black men in this bunch who were older than me…"

"How much older?"

"In their late twenties, early thirties."

"And you were sixteen?"

She nodded.

"Long story short, I slept with these guys, sometimes with one but usually with two, and well, what we did would make a regular porn flick look like a Disney movie." There was a long pause. "One of these guys was really violent. He ended up dislocating my right shoulder and breaking my left arm while we were having sex." Sabrina pointed to a spot on her left arm where some scar tissue was still evident. "I just felt that this was all I was good for. I gave them what they wanted, and they gave me what I thought I wanted. I think I enjoyed the pain. I know that's sick, and I understand it now, but for pretty much one year, that was my life after school. My parents never noticed anything, but Derek did. I think he followed me a few times and figured out what was going on."

"What made you finally stop?"

"I got tired of getting beat up…I mean, I really liked the rough stuff in the beginning, thought I was a real badass being able to handle these big, and I mean *big*, black guys. But the hitting, slapping, choking, and other shit they did to me just got to be too much. Guess who helped me pull out of that mess."

"Who?"

"Michelle."

My jaw dropped. "*Our* Michelle?"

"Yup. She got me out of a very bad place. It took a lot of time and patience on her part. She's a saint. Then when I finally broke free, those two black guys came looking for me. That's when Michelle's brother stepped in."

"Her brother?" I remembered that Michelle had mentioned having an older brother in her student bio.

"Yeah, her brother, Jack. He's an ex-marine. He actually confronted those dudes with three of his marine buddies and told them that if they ever caught sight of them anywhere near me, they'd be dead, floating in a lake somewhere."

"Did this have the desired effect?"

"Not really. Michelle's brother did time, because of me." Sabrina lowered her head.

"Time? Prison, you mean?"

"Yeah. One of those black guys cornered me one day in the parking lot of a mall. He slapped me up pretty good, tried to push me into his car. Michelle was with me but hid behind a car and texted Jack before coming to help me. She managed to stall by talking to that asshole, telling him that maybe we could have a threesome—she was awesome."

"Let me guess, then Jack shows up."

"Yup. And a buddy of his. They beat the shit out of that guy, literally. Both Jack and his friend got a year for excessive force. They could have gotten much more, but because they were ex-military, no previous record, and the guy they beat up had a rap sheet as long as your arm, the judge was lenient. They served six months."

I looked at her, frowning.

"You just said that Michelle is a saint. Yet I don't think I've seen you and her share more than a few words on this trip. Is there some bad blood now between the two of you because of the prison time?"

"Oh no! I love Michelle to death, and she loves me, but you've got to understand Michelle. She's on a mission to save people. It's how she is. She's helped some of the others with serious issues in their lives. Now she's hanging around Wayne, Bishop, and Mark. I'm hoping that she'll be able to help Mark a bit before we all split from Atlanta. He's got a serious drinking problem."

This reminded me that I had to call the hospital. I glanced at my watch, then turned my attention back to Sabrina. "Tell me, did your parents read the letter Derek left for them?"

"No, I got my hands on their letters after I found mine. Derek had put a copy in my dad's bar cabinet and another one in, get this, my mom's collection of vibrators that she had in a shoebox. I don't think he left other copies. I would've found them by now."

"That was good of you, Sabrina, not to put your parents through that."

Sabrina shook her head. "I didn't hide those letters out of goodness, Atticus. I plan to give it to them once I've milked them for everything they have. I hate them just like Derek did. I don't know why they even had us. All they've ever thought about is themselves. But my dad's filthy rich, and there's nobody that phrase doesn't apply to more. I plan to take advantage of that."

I took Sabrina's hand. "I wish I could say or do something that could make all the wrong right. But I don't have a time machine."

Sabrina squeezed my hand. "You know what really helped a lot, Atticus? This is really crazy…that statue. I felt at peace just sitting there in front of it and staring into her eyes. I know it's just a piece of plaster or concrete, or whatever, but it felt like she…what's her name again?"

"Saint Rita."

"Yeah, Saint. Rita. I felt like she was trying to tell me something."

"That's the same feeling I had, and I've seen hundreds of religious statues. None of them has touched me like that one."

"It really was a good feeling. I even told Mrs. Cornwall about it today, but I could tell she thought I was off my rocker." Sabrina chuckled. "And maybe I am, a little," she added, "because I've started to patch things up with Evelyn, can you believe it?"

I smiled. "No, I don't believe a word of it."

"Well, it's true. We're talking now at least. That's a start. I was really shitty to her. She didn't deserve it. We're actually going shopping together tomorrow after the tour."

"The ultimate female bonding experience. I'm glad, though. Evelyn has issues of her own to deal with."

"You can say that again, but that's another volume."

There was a short silence. Sabrina came to her feet.

"Thank you, Atticus." She leaned over and hugged me. "I want to go out for a walk. This city is so awesome, and I only have a few more days to enjoy it."

"Thank you, Sabrina, for sharing so much with me. I appreciate it."

"Don't tell Mrs. Cornwall about this, please."

"Not a word will escape my mouth."

"Thanks. The two of you make a nice couple." She gave me a wink and left the room.

I don't think that I moved from my chair for at least ten minutes. I was truly pleased that Sabrina considered me a trustworthy listener of her innermost secrets. But what she told me saddened me tremendously.

I looked at my watch. It was almost ten. I reached for the phone and dialed the number the hospital had given me before leaving Cynthia. The nurse who answered assured me that everything was under control. Mark was sleeping soundly, and his vital signs were improving. Cynthia was fast asleep as well. I put the phone down and wondered if Mark's parents had called Marco or the hospital.

The ringing startled me. For a moment, I didn't know what it was because I had just placed the phone receiver on the cradle.

"*Sì?*"

"Signor Atticus?"

"Yes, Giovanni?"

"Everything is fine, just fine, but I wanted to let you know that Signor Giacomo is here and would—" I hung up on Giacomo and bolted from the room at the speed of sound.

It was only as I was racing down the stairs that I remembered the flowers, the tie, and the cards. I unclenched my fists, took a deep breath, and entered the lobby calmly.

Giacomo was standing very close to the glass entrance doors of the hotel. Darlene was next to him.

"Everything is under control, Signor Atticus." Giovanni, for once, was looking at me straight in the eyes.

I stared at Giacomo. "What are you doing here?"

"It's okay, Atticus." Darlene moved in front of him, defensively. "We've cleared everything up. Giacomo wanted to wait here to make sure that you were okay with him coming to see me." She looked at Giovanni imploringly.

"*Sì, sì,* Signor Atticus, the young man did not want to enter the hotel without your permission."

"Signor Atticus, I just wanted to see Darlene one more time before she left."

I drew a deep breath. "Listen to me, young man, I saw the flowers and the other items. That was all well and good, but you are not off the hook yet. I'm still very upset about what you did to this gentleman and to Darlene. I am still suspicious of you, to say the least."

"Yes," he said, nodding. "I mean, I understand, I understand completely."

Darlene clasped her hands, as if in prayer. "There's a group of us playing cards and listening to some music in the back. I'd like Giacomo to join us."

I considered her request. Finally, I said, "Okay. But the two of you stay in the hotel, not one foot outside. Got it? Or Giacomo we will have a rerun of what happened the other night."

Giacomo nodded fervently. Then he and Darlene walked out of the lobby in the direction of the restaurant.

I turned to Giovanni. "If you hear, see, suspect anything out of the ordinary, call me."

"*Suspecta dona hostium recipienda.*" Giovanni glanced at me and grinned. "The power of words, Signor Atticus, especially when in Latin."

I opened my eyes wide when I saw Ludovica come out of the front office. "Good evening, Signor Winterle," she said, apparently oblivious to my goggling. "I wanted to let you know that there is a room available all of next week—that is, if you plan to stay with us that long."

She looked absolutely stunning. Her hair was brushed down, makeup sober yet appealing, her fingernails manicured and painted bloodred polish. Her white button-down shirt gave just a peep of her well-sculpted cleavage.

"Thank you, Ludovica, I think I will stay until Saturday morning."

She nodded. "May I ask, Signor Atticus, how is the boy in the hospital coming along?" I filled Giovanni and Ludovica in on my last phone call with the nurse's station. I asked Giovanni to give me a wake-up call at five thirty, just in case my alarm didn't go off. Then I said good night and went back to my room.

Even though I was disappointed by Barbara's behavior and absence, I was looking forward to getting some sleep. The entire week had been eventful, but these last two days had really taken a toll on me. But I still had one thing to do.

Once in bed, I grabbed the student bios from the night table. I read through Wayne's and Bishop's, but now I knew that what they wrote was just a front. The real Waync and Bishop had come to my room the night before.

Before letting Hypnos, the god of sleep, envelop me in his arms, I made a mental note of everything I had to do the next day: go to the hospital, meet Massimo and the group to Castel Sant'Angelo, confirm Massimo's lunch with Wayne and Bishop, plus I needed to get everything ready for…

Tuesday
May 4 , Day Eight

CHAPTER 57

"Atticus...Atticus, wake up."

"Hmm...huh? Okay...I'm awake, I'm awake. Barbara...? What time is it?"

"It's almost one."

With my track record of late-night alarms, I sat up immediately.

"What's wrong? Is somebody hurt? Mark?"

"No, nobody's hurt."

"Evelyn, Vanessa?" My mind was agitated.

"I said nothing is wrong with any of the students."

Barbara was sitting on the bed, but with a space between us, both physical and emotional. She was obviously not happy.

"So, Atticus, do you feel good about your day today? Did everything go as planned?"

"Well, it was most certainly an intense day, with Mark and—"

"You don't *care*, do you?"

"*What*?"

"You don't care about anybody but yourself!"

I shook my head. "I don't quite understand."

Barbara got up and started pacing back and forth. "I thought we were a team—you and me, a team—but now I see how you really are. It's all about you. You call the shots. You decide who to involve and who to leave out regarding matters which you deem important or not. You don't want any advice, anyone to share your ideas with, do you? You're just a one-man show!"

"Barbara, is all of this because of today? Because of what happened to Mark?"

"Let's just say that the situation with Mark was the straw that broke the camel's back!" She was almost yelling at me now. I had never seen her like this before.

"You left this morning with Cynthia and told me it was just a tour of the forum. Well, it's a different Cynthia that came back to the hotel, Atticus. It was more than just a tour! Then all this mess with Mark. Everyone and their mother knew what was going on, including that sidekick of yours at the front desk. I didn't know a damn thing!"

I said nothing, only hoping that this confrontation would be over soon.

"Then you come back for dinner and treat John and me like foot soldiers under your command! Well, I'm not your goddamn foot soldier! Is that clear, Mr. Winterle?!"

Her pacing had become more and more pronounced.

"Barbara, I never intended to—"

She cut across me again. "I've been with you since that first night, and I've done everything you've asked," she snapped. "I've tried to be helpful with Vanessa, with Evelyn, James, then Darlene, and yesterday, with Wayne and Bishop. I've shared my thoughts and concerns with you. I've told you my most personal secrets, things that nobody else knows. And what do I get? I get a day like today where you just blow me off! You made it crystal clear today that I am only useful when you want something, especially a good screw!"

This last assertion crossed the line. It was becoming harder for me to hold my tongue.

Barbara didn't pause in her rant. "And then I meet up with Sabrina today. Even she tried to convince me about that stupid statue, saying that spending time with her—not *it* but *her*—had changed her perspective. You just say and do what you want, even if it means filling these kids' heads with superstitious garbage!"

"You don't know what you're talking about," I said rather curtly.

"Oh yes, I do. I—"

"Barbara, shut up and listen to me!" I was out of patience.

Her face became a mask of fury. "I'm leaving! I have no intention of staying here one minute longer!" She started toward the door, but I was there before her. I was like a gazelle off of that bed and kept the door shut with both hands.

"Sit down!" I said brusquely.

"No."

"Sit down!" I growled. "I listened to you. Now you're going to hear me out. Then you can leave. Or not."

This had the desired effect. She reluctantly sat down in the armchair, her arms tightly folded against her chest.

"What the hell has gotten into you? First of all, I don't accept your accusations. They're completely unjust and false, and I think you know that. You've been part of every problematic situation that's arisen this past week. Yes, today I didn't communicate with you, but you have no idea what took place, especially with Mark. As far as Cynthia is concerned, I gave her my word that I wouldn't reveal what we talked about, not even to you, who she specifically mentioned. Suffice it to say that the Cynthia of today is not the Cynthia we knew yesterday and that, if you knew what I knew, you wouldn't be wondering why I trusted her to stay with Mark."

I was now pacing up and down furiously.

"I dropped Cynthia off at the hotel, and the Mark situation exploded in my face! I believe I did the best I could, considering the circumstances. Wasting precious moments looking for you and John just wasn't an option. Maybe it hasn't hit home yet, Barbara, but if Mark had been in that cemetery even a half hour longer, he might have become a permanent resident there! To cap the day off, Sabrina comes to my room and opens up to me about her home situation, including why her brother killed himself."

Barbara gasped.

"Yes, Barbara, that's what I had to deal with today on top of Mark. All delightfully tragic and heartbreaking, of course. And as far as Sabrina is concerned, since you brought her up, I only shared with her an experience that made me feel better in a time of need. The fact that it involved a religious statue should be neither here nor there. What's important is whether it helped a troubled young person or not. So don't accuse me of brainwashing anybody! Finally, don't give me this crap that I have only thought about myself on this trip. I haven't had a spare moment for me, myself, and I because I've been constantly dealing with this group's problems, including yours! If I were a psychiatrist, I'd make a fortune off you people! And yes, you are a good screw, by the way! Does that make you feel *better*!?"

This was crossing the line too, but she had broken that ribbon first.

Barbara just sat there, staring at the floor. I stopped pacing and took a seat on the chair near the wall.

Barbara looked across at me finally. "My husband wants to start divorce proceedings as soon as I get back to Atlanta," she whispered without any emotion.

Did the drama never stop with this group? I wondered. I didn't know whether to roll my eyes or commiserate with her. Luckily, my better self won out.

"When did you find out?" I asked, trying to speak gently.

"He called this afternoon."

Barbara was subdued now. I was still angry, but I also felt terrible for having shouted at her.

"Didn't you say things were satisfactory at home, considering all that happened?" I asked.

"That's what I thought, but I guess I was wrong. Seems like I'm alienating everyone these days, even from a distance." Barbara was crying softly, wiping her tears with the back of her hands. I was still sore at her words, but my temperature level was stabilizing.

"So what do you plan to do when you get back?"

"I really don't know. He said he was willing to discuss things. He doesn't want the house. He says that he wants to make this as easy a transition as possible for me."

"Well, maybe he'll have a change of heart when you sit down and talk it out."

"I don't know if I care anymore, Atticus. That call was a shock to me. But I don't know why I was so surprised. I've lost my two children, I lost having a normal husband some years ago, and in two days I will lose you. Then I will go home and lose the man that has loved me, even if in a very peculiar way."

I rested my head in my hands and tried to offer some comfort.

"You have your house, and you have your job. Maybe living with a man who sleeps with just about anything that walks on two legs isn't the best you can do. Maybe the time has come to find a new, healthier relationship?"

Barbara was silent for a moment.

"It's always been about convenience for me, Atticus. I've never had to struggle for anything. I accepted my husband's desire to sleep around and joined in only because I didn't want to disrupt my comfortable life. I've never put my fist down and said 'No!' I've never been a fighter. That's why Jeff's call came as a shock. It interfered with Barbara's sheltered little world where Barbara usually gets what she wants. I'm hollow inside, Atticus, absolutely hollow."

I took her hands in mine. "I don't believe that. That's not the woman I've been with for the past week. Listen, we've got two more days here in Rome. I want you to stop thinking about all of this now. Rome is your bubble where nothing can hurt you and life is perfect. Live in the moment for the next two days, just like you've been doing. When you get home, you can deal with that situation. I'm sure you will make the right decisions, the ones that are best for you. But that's outside the bubble."

Barbara smiled at me through her tears. I handed her a Kleenex.

"Do you know what I told Darlene when she asked me if I was in love with you?"

"What?"

"I told her that you were like a magical potion that freed me from a prison of pain. I told her that I wasn't in love, but in a state of ecstasy, which always has a finite lifespan." Barbara chuckled softly. "Darlene looked at me as if I had lost my mind, but you know exactly what I mean, don't you Atticus?"

I did. I knew that any attempt at a serious relationship between the two of us would have fizzled out quickly.

"I don't want the magic of these nine days to ever disappear. Do you mind if I stay here tonight?"

"Of course not, but my alarm goes off in three hours. I have to go to the hospital."

"Can I please come with you? I'd like to switch out with Cynthia."

"That's fine with me. What about John? I think he wanted to go as well."

"He can come later and trade with me."

Barbara stood up, went to the bathroom, and came out shortly afterward in nothing but her panties. She got into bed, but both of us knew there would be no sex tonight. We ended up talking for almost an hour about almost everyone in the group and just about everything that had happened over the past few days. I went into great detail about Mark and Sabrina but said nothing about Cynthia. I did imagine, however, what Barbara's reaction would have been if she found out that Anthony was Cynthia's son. It was, after all, earth-shattering news.

I also told her that Giacomo had shown up at the hotel and I had not beaten him to a pulp.

Barbara was beginning to nod off when I reached the part where Massimo and his partner wanted to invite Wayne, Bishop and Michelle to lunch.

"I think it may be therapeutic for Wayne and Bishop to unload their concerns and share their experiences, especially with Sebastiano," I explained.

There was no answer. Barbara was out like a light.

I glanced at the clock. It was close to three thirty. The alarm would go off in two hours. I thought about turning off the light and getting some sleep, but I knew it was futile. Instead, I got up, took a leisurely shower, dressed, and turned on my laptop.

As soon as I logged on to my email, I saw a communication from the ASA office in Atlanta. I opened it and noted that it was addressed to me with Marco and another Italian name that I did not recognize, in copy. There was a PDF attachment that opened up as a five-page document. It was titled "Accident and Hospitalization Incident Report," and I had to fill it out as chaperone. This was no surprise. There wasn't much I could do to hide the facts, given that the police and hospital records had officially recorded the incident. I did not, however, mention Mark's sister or the Skype calls.

It took me about an hour to complete the report. I saved it and sent a copy to Marco. I still had a half an hour before I would have to wake Barbara up. I clicked on Wikipedia and typed in Castel Sant'Angelo. The amount of information and links to other websites were substantial. I read through as much as I could.

"Hmm…Atticus?" Barbara's eyes were closed, but she was stretching under the sheets.

"It's close to five thirty, Barbara, but you don't have to get up. You can sleep in another two hours before breakfast."

"Hmm," she yawned. "Are you going to the hospital?" Her yawning was contagious.

"Yes."

"Then I'm going with you."

Suddenly awake, she practically bolted out of the bed and went straight to the bathroom. Within minutes, she was out with a smile and ready to go. The phone alarm rang sharply.

"Thank you, Giovanni, I'm up. Could you call me a cab please?"

"Immediately, Signor Atticus."

"By the way, Giovanni, what time did Giacomo leave last night?"

"It was a little past midnight. Miss Darlene stayed in the hotel. Your 'Beware of enemies bearing gifts' remark, however, was appropriate. One can never be too sure."

I didn't understand what Giovanni was referring to until I remembered my Latin quip.

"We'll be down momentarily. Mrs. Cornwall will be going with me to the hospital."

When Barbara and I arrived in the lobby, our taxi was waiting for us. I told the driver where we needed to go and that we were not in a great hurry. It was early and half of Rome was still asleep, even it was a Monday morning.

"I wonder if Mark is awake?" said Barbara.

"Good question. He may be sedated but, then again, maybe not."

"If he opened his eyes and saw Cynthia sitting there, he probably had a stroke."

I put my hand on Barbara's shoulder. "It's a different Cynthia. Mark will have picked up on it."

"What is it that you did to that woman, Atticus?"

"Absolutely nothing. She did everything on her own." Which was the God's truth.

"I'm a little jealous, to be honest, and am burning up with curiosity. I can't fathom what the two of you discussed."

"It's better that way. She may tell you one day, Barbara. I wouldn't be surprised."

Our taxi driver was not a Mario Andretti this time, but he had quite a knack at finding just enough space to wedge his taxi through a crescendo of early morning traffic.

"Atticus, what should I say to Mark when I'm alone with him?" Barbara asked.

"That's a good question. It's the second time he's pulled this stunt here, and there have been other times in Atlanta, as you know."

I sighed and looked out the window. "These kids, Barbara. There must be a huge void, an enormous hurt, somewhere in their timelines. All this drinking, pill popping, Sabrina's masochistic sexual encounters at sixteen—all cries for help."

"What about Wayne and Bishop? Do you think they are sincerely attracted to each other, or is that also a form of rebellion?"

"If they were younger, maybe twelve or thirteen, I'd say it was curiosity or a way to get attention. At eighteen, I think it's different. But you heard them, they still like girls, even though Wayne's report card in bed seems poor to failing, according to Darlene."

The taxi had pulled up in front of the hospital entrance. I paid the driver, and we entered the foyer area where several elevators were going to the lower and higher floors. We hit the second-floor button. Room 321 was just off to our left. Barbara stopped me just outside of the door, which closed.

"Atticus, I apologize. What I said to you back in your room wasn't fair. I've just been overwhelmed by you, this city, these students' problems, and my husband's phone call. I'm also upset that this truly magical time here is about to end."

I put my arms around her and gave her a hug. "We'll make these two days special. Let's focus on that."

She nodded, sniffling a bit. "Yes, let's do that."

I pushed the door open, not knocking in case Mark was asleep. Sure enough, he was. Cynthia was sitting close to his bed, holding his hand. As soon as she saw us, she signaled to step back into the hallway so as not to disturb him, then came out herself. Once the door was shut behind us, I told Cynthia that Barbara would be staying with Mark until the afternoon. She thanked both of us for coming so early.

"You should've seen the expression on that poor boy's face when he turned and saw me sitting there." Cynthia was a bit amused, and out of the corner of my eye, I saw Barbara almost do a double take. "It took me a while to reassure and calm him down, to convince him that I was on his side," Cynthia continued. She shook her head sadly. "The things that boy told me. He had me in tears for almost two hours. I told him a few things about my past, none pleasant, which I think helped us bond. When he started talking, he didn't stop until he fell back asleep. That was around four this morning."

I was neither surprised, after our long talk near the Colosseum, at Cynthia's new attitude nor her words of concern for Mark. Barbara, on the other hand, was still gazing at Cynthia as if she was an alien creature pretending to be human.

"So his relationship with his parents is a total mess," Cynthia revealed. "They're both alcoholics. But that's the least of their problems from what Mark said. His father constantly travels for work, so he's never really been in Mark's life. And when he is home, he prefers to be on the golf course or at the club with his friends. It's just as awful family situation." Cynthia shook her head, then looked at her watch. "Atticus, I think we should try to be at breakfast this morning. I'm sure the group will want to know how Mark is doing. Is John at the hotel?"

"He should be, but you're right. We need to get back."

Barbara was still staring at Cynthia. Cynthia turned to her. She took Barbara's hand in hers and looked at her straight in the eyes.

"I'm sorry, Barbara."

Barbara blinked in surprise. "Sorry? Sorry about what?"

"I'm sorry I lost so many chances to get to know you better. I'm sorry I've been so judgmental about you over these past three years. I hope you can try accepting my apology and that we can make up for lost time."

She patted Barbara's hand. Barbara smiled, then they both hugged. Both women had tears in their eyes, and I feared I wasn't far behind myself.

Cynthia stepped back and looked at the both of us. "Let's go and see how Mark's doing."

We went back quietly into the room. Mark was still asleep. His bed and been slightly elevated, and his head had a large bandage covering the deep laceration he had sustained when he fell on the gravestone. He was still sound asleep. Considering what he had been through, he looked well, peaceful. I thought for a moment what his childhood must have been like with absent and alcoholic parents. In my mind, I could hear my nightmare Derek giggling, chanting a perverse tune where the only word repeated, over and over, was *choice*.

Cynthia and I left Barbara sitting comfortably in the recliner and managed to get a cab right outside of the hospital. It was rush hour, and the traffic was bumper to bumper. As soon as we got settled into the back of the Fiat Punto, Cynthia told me the rest of Mark's story.

"The only person Mark had was his older sister. She has been a dominant figure in his life. But not a healthy influence, in my opinion."

"How so?"

"It took a while for him to tell me this. I didn't want to bring it up with Barbara, but Mark trusts you. I know you'll keep this to yourself."

"Absolutely."

"When Mark was thirteen, his sister came into his room one night, and there was, let's say, all kinds of sexual acts, short of intercourse. And she did that, too, when Mark turned sixteen." Cynthia shook her head in disbelief. "He told me that he had fallen in love with her. She was his friend, confidant, sister, and lover."

"Talk about unhealthy…"

"Yes. She left for California a few months after his sixteenth birthday, but this absolutely devastated him."

"Did he tell you if this drinking binge he went on had anything to do with his sister?"

"Oh yes. They spoke this morning." Bingo! "He was supposed to go out and see her in California, but she cancelled everything. She's getting married, is pregnant, and to top it off, she's moving to Australia with her husband. All this sent Mark over the edge."

"I can understand why he felt betrayed. His world must have collapsed around him."

"But there's one positive coming out of all this. Mark understands that he's at fault. He realizes that those sexual encounters were unnatural. He called it for what it was— incest. It's good that he acknowledged it."

"I guess that's a silver lining."

Cynthia nodded, then asked, "How are Wayne and Bishop?"

That question came out of the blue. "They're fine, I guess. Why?"

"Those are two boys I must also make amends with," said Cynthia simply.

The taxi had arrived in front of the hotel. We entered the hotel lobby. Nobody was around, except Ludovica behind the front desk. We greeted her, explained that Mrs. Cornwall was with the student, and updated her on his condition.

"Most of your group is already in the breakfast room," Ludovica informed us.

As soon as the students saw us enter, we were deluged with questions. John was also there, but Cynthia immediately took control of the situation. She asked that everyone be seated. She then gave them a synopsis of Mark's condition.

"Will he be able to check out of the hospital today?" asked John.

"No, but the doctors are aiming for tomorrow afternoon."

I looked around, hearing some commotion. Mary, Vanessa, and Raymond had entered the dining area and immediately huddled around Cynthia.

"Ladies and gentlemen, Mark needs our help. I would request that you not to badger him with too many questions when he's released from the hospital. He needs our support, but we also have to give him space and time to recover from what happened."

Darlene raised her hand. "Mrs. Ramsey?"

Cynthia looked around at Darlene.

"Are you feeling all right? I mean, I thought you couldn't stand Mark."

A hush fell over the room. Darlene had said out loud what everybody else was thinking. Cynthia bowed her head and sighed.

"I am all right, Darlene. I understand why you asked, though. Let's just say that things have changed for me over the past two days. This city, and being all of you here in Rome, have opened my eyes. I'm not the person today that I was yesterday. My real self was buried under layers of mud. I think some of you know what that's like."

You could have heard a pin drop.

Cynthia looked around at all the students. "The truth is I haven't been there for most of you when you needed me. I see that now. It's too late for an apology, but I do plan to do my best to get to know all of you better before graduation."

Another silence, which Michelle broke, "It was awful nice of you to sit with Mark all night long, Mrs. Ramsey."

Cynthia shook her head regretfully. "Too little too late, I'm afraid."

She looked directly at Wayne, Bishop, and Darlene. "You three I owe a special apology. I've been unfair, prejudiced, and downright mean. I am sorry."

Darlene turned to Mary. "Did she just say what I think she said?" Darlene thought she was speaking quietly, but with the dead silence in the room, everyone heard her.

The new Cynthia was amused, just as the old one would have been furious. "Yes, you're not hearing voices that aren't there, Darlene. And I meant every word."

Wayne cleared his throat. "It's all cool, Mrs. Ramsey. Bishop and I needed a good slap down sometimes, anyway."

"Well, you make a good point, Wayne," Cynthia replied.

This got some chuckles.

"Now we have two days left together here in Rome," Cynthia continued. "I'd like to make the most of it with you. Hopefully, you'll give me a second chance."

Then to everyone's surprise, if not shock, she got up, went to the students, and started hugging them, shaking their hands, or patting them on the back.

There weren't many dry eyes in the house. I stepped forward to give everyone a chance to regain their composure.

"Okay everyone," I announced, "today is the last tour before you all head back home. You will be visiting the Castel Sant'Angelo and the Spanish Steps. I need all of you to be ready in the lobby in fifteen minutes."

I was wasting my breath, though. Very few of the students budged or even heard me. Most of them was still wrapped around Cynthia. I walked over to where John was standing.

"Talk about a metamorphosis," he said with a flabbergasted expression on his face. "Did you give her some mind-altering drug, Atticus?" I shook my head. "As she said, her time here in Rome has opened up some new vistas for her."

"Well, whatever the cause, I'm totally floored."

I wanted to get off the subject of Cynthia in case I inadvertently revealed too much.

"Didn't something similar happen with you, John?" I said with a grin. "Speaking of which, how's Rhea?"

John ducked his head in acknowledgment. "Touché," he said. "Rhea's fine. I only get to see her in the evening given her schedule."

Before I could answer, we heard a commotion behind us.

"And, *voila*! Here I am! Surprise, surprise!"

Massimo had come through the dining room doors like a Hollywood star. Applause and hurrahs went up from the students who realized that he was going to be their guide for the final tour.

"Are we all here and ready to go see one of the most fascinating castles in all of Europe?" he trilled.

"They just need ten minutes, Massimo, to get their things for the day," I said. "All right, everyone! Let's get moving." I motioned everyone to leave the room.

When Massimo and I were alone, I gave him a quick summary of Cynthia's change. I did not tell him about Anthony, but only said that she had confided in me, and it had seemed to help her see things from a fresh perspective.

"My, my, dear Atticus…you are in the wrong business." Massimo chuckled. "You should be a psychologist. You would make a fortune!"

"I think it's more Rome than me."

"Speaking of which, how is our young man in the hospital?"

As we both walked toward the lobby area, I updated Massimo on Mark's condition. Ludovica and Giovanni were at the front desk. While they chitchatted with Massimo, I approached Michelle and told her about Massimo's lunch invitation.

"I think that's a great idea," she said.

"I'm keeping this hush-hush."

"Of course. Not a peep out of me."

"No headache this morning, I hope?"

"None, and I slept like a rock. Oh, by the way, Evelyn's diary was nowhere to be found last night. Not on the floor, not on her desk, nowhere."

Before I could respond, Massimo's voice thundered over all the others:

"Time to be off! Everyone follow me please!"

As the group made its way up the narrow road, I marveled at how the students were paired off. What a change from eight days ago. Cynthia was between Wayne and Bishop. Evelyn was next to Sabrina with Vanessa right behind them. Anthony was next to Mary, James was with Darlene, and Jeremy. Raymond was in the back with John, and the discussion was once again about Israel. Massimo was leading the way between Michelle and Barbara.

When we arrived at the bus, Riccardo and Massimo greeted each other profusely. Not a surprise, given that he had driven many of Massimo's groups around Rome. Once on the bus, Massimo asked me if he could have the microphone and take a few minutes to describe where we were heading.

"Ladies and gentlemen, again good morning! Now who can tell me a little something about the Castel Sant'Angelo?"

Jeremy piped up. "Well, I know it was an emperor's shrine or memorial, or something like that before it became a castle."

"Riccardo! Stop this bus, Stop this bus now! I'm getting off, off I tell you. Atticus, you don't need me here anymore! You are surrounded by scholars!" Massimo had gone off on one of his exuberant theatrical displays, which greatly

804

entertained and energized the group. Someone in the back then started chanting "Mas-si-mo, Mas-si- mo!" Everyone joined in, including the teachers, with Cynthia screaming the loudest.

When the commotion died down, Massimo started going a mile a minute, filling the bus with informative and humorous anecdotes regarding the castle and the plethora of famous individuals who had graced its quarters throughout the centuries.

I had already decided that I would escort the group to the entrance but would wait for them outside. I had too many phone calls to make, the first going to Barbara for an update on Mark.

CHAPTER 58

"Ladies and gentlemen, we have arrived! Please follow me and keep to the right side of this small road. Look out for the cars and motorbikes."

Once we passed through the imposing entrance to what was originally Emperor Hadrian's mausoleum, I gave Massimo the voucher for the tickets and told him that I would be waiting outside. As Massimo stood in a short line waiting for one of the attendants, Mary approached me grinning like the Cheshire cat.

"So, Mr. Music Man, what does this castle remind you of?" she asked.

"Um, give me a second." I didn't have a clue as what Mary was referring to.

"Don't think about James and that awful stuff you two listen to. You've got to go back to 1899."

"1899? Mary, you've stumped me."

"*Tosca*, Atticus, where does Tosca leap to her death? From the terrace of this building. That's pretty cool. Check out the third act when Cavadorossi sings '*E lucevan le stelle.*' Absolutely sublime. Seems you need to brush up on your operas." She winked and rejoined the group.

In fact, in the opera, Tosca, the female protagonist of the same name throws herself off this building when her lover is executed. I had forgotten this. Touché, Mary!

Massimo and the group were going up a sloped embankment leading to the papal apartments and the top of the fortress. I headed to the right and made my way to the grassy area off to the side of this imperial structure. I found various wrought-iron benches and chose one that had the least amount of pigeon poop. I started making my phone calls.

First, Barbara, who told me that Mark was doing much better. He had had eaten solid food for breakfast, and his blood pressure, temperature, and electrocardiogram were normal. The doctor had informed Barbara shortly before my call that Mark would probably be released the next morning.

"He'd like it if Wayne, Bishop, and Michelle came by today, but he'd rather see everyone else after he checks out."

"That should work, Barbara," I said. "Let's see how long their lunch lasts, and then I'll get them over to the hospital. How are you holding up?"

"I'm fine, very relieved to see Mark feeling better."

"Can you speak freely? Did he give you a clue as to why he almost did himself in?"

"I'm on the phone at the main desk. No, he didn't go into great detail, just complained about his mom and dad, all things that we pretty much knew already."

"Anything else?"

"Not really. He wants to get out of the house as soon as possible and go to college. He mostly spoke about the future."

Mark had not shared anything about his sister with Barbara. I wondered if this was because he trusted Cynthia more, or if he was afraid that Barbara might let the cat out of the bag.

"Atticus? Are you still there?"

"Yes, sorry. Just lost in thought for a moment."

I told her that I would let her know when Wayne, Bishop, and Michelle would be heading over and ended the call.

My next calls were directly linked to something I had in mind for the group before they left Rome. I had been thinking about a farewell event for the past couple of days. It was going to be costly, and now since Francesca would no longer be there to contribute to daily expenses, probably not the best of ideas. However, I was rather confident (possibly, naively so) that the Baines & Courtney job prospect would come through, which would greatly improve my financial situation. More importantly, money aside, I really wanted to do this for the students and the teachers. There was no getting around it—I had grown very fond of these sixteen people and knew I would miss them.

Luckily, I managed to get a hold of the two individuals who were pivotal in making my plan a reality. After lengthy salutations and complaints from them about how I had disappeared from the face of the earth, I explained my intentions. We spoke at length, and I was satisfied with the outcome. I made arrangements to meet with one of these gentlemen later that afternoon.

The sun was resplendent today, and there was a delightful breeze coming from the west. I sat there contemplating the massive structure in front of me, which had been an integral part of so many far-reaching historical episodes. I thought about all the sites that the group had seen and how I had asked them for feedback on some of them. Nobody had gotten back to me except Jeremy and his report on the Caserta Palace, but I wasn't the least bit concerned. As long as they came away from these nine days with something they would remember and cherish, that was sufficient.

"Hey, Atticus!" I looked in the direction of the main exit of the castle and saw the group waving at me. It was time to move on to the Spanish Steps.

As everyone was boarding the bus, I gestured to Massimo, and we walked some distance away from the others. I wanted to briefly describe to him what I had in store for the group and extend the invitation to him and his partner.

"*Tomorrow* night?" he exclaimed.

"Yes, I hope it isn't a problem. It wouldn't be special without you there."

"Well, yes, we will certainly be there, I just need to adjust a few things." Massimo looked momentarily flustered. Then he gazed at me with a concerned look. "My dear Atticus, it's none of my business, but how much is all of this going to cost you?"

"Let's say, a tidy little sum."

Massimo patted my knee.

"Quite a change in your attitude considering what a little bird told me just a week ago."

A six-foot bird, on the plump side, with loose lips to boot, I thought.

Massimo guffawed. "I refuse to reveal my sources."

"That bird was correct eight days ago," I admitted, "but he is completely off the mark now. This has been an eye-opening experience for me in more ways than one. This group deserves a memorable send off."

Massimo nodded. "If this is your wish, my friend, Sebastiano and I will be overjoyed to attend."

We went back to the bus. Massimo took a seat next to John as I walked to the front and switched on the microphone and shared the news about Mark's health status and that he would be released from the hospital tomorrow. As expected, a round of cheers went up from the entire group.

Riccardo was skillfully maneuvering the bus down narrow streets, negotiating tight curves, continuously watching out for kamikaze motor scooters. In short order, he managed to bring the mechanical mastodon into a small parking area in front of our destination. I handed the microphone off to Massimo.

"Ladies and gentlemen, straight ahead you shall find the Spanish Steps. These steps, one hundred thirty-eight in all and built back in 1723, were intended to link the Spanish Embassy with the Trinità dei Monti Church up above. In front of this staircase, you shall find three of the most beautiful and ludicrously expensive shopping streets in all of Italy. Be sure not to miss the Via Condotti where all the most luxurious fashion brands are to be found." Massimo sighed ecstatically.

"On a more down-to-earth note, take the time to go into the McDonald's that you see right here outside the bus because it is like no McDonald's you have ever seen before. I am at your disposal if you would like to group up. If you want to go exploring on your own, but want a ride back to the hotel, Riccardo will be here until…" Massimo turned to look at our driver.

"I can stay a couple hours, Signor Massimo."

"So back here at two thirty if you want a ride back."

Darlene spoke up, "Atticus, Massimo, can we just walk back to the hotel? Some of us have been here already. It's not far at all." This came as a bit of a surprise.

"Sure, Darlene," I said. "I would just prefer that you go back in twos or more."

Darlene rolled her eyes but smiled. No protesting this time.

As the group got up and started leaving the bus, I stopped Michelle and whispered to her to wait for me outside of the bus with Wayne and Bishop. She nodded.

Cynthia and John were at the bottom of the bus's stairs waiting for me.

"Atticus, should one of us plan to go to the hospital and switch with Barbara?" asked John.

"No, I don't think so. I plan to go there in about an hour. I'll call you if I need you."

"Please give Mark our best," Cynthia said.

"I will. Enjoy this part of Rome. It's beautiful here."

By now, most of the students had grouped up on their own and were off leaving Massimo and me alone. Wayne, Bishop, and Michelle were near the back of the bus. I signaled to Massimo to come with me. We approached the three, and I explained that Massimo and his partner, Sebastiano, wanted to invite them to lunch. The three eagerly accepted.

"By the way, Mark really wants to see the three of you today if you'd like to go.

They beamed with satisfaction.

"He may not be so happy to see us after we beat him silly for what he did," Bishop said.

"Let's hold off on the beating until he's out of the hospital," I replied.

"My dear Atticus, I have a wonderful idea!" Massimo interjected. "After our lunch, Sebastiano and I can escort them to the hospital."

"That's far out of your way, Massimo. Don't you have other tours today?"

"I would not have offered if I had not deemed it possible. Enough of this silly chitchatting. It's decided. Do not concern yourself, dear Atticus, these three members of your entourage are in good hands."

"I have no doubts."

"Come, come my lady and gentlemen, there is so much to see, and we don't have that much time."

Massimo was already walking toward the Spanish Steps, calling after the three to catch up with him. Michelle and Bishop trotted in Massimo's direction. I held Wayne back for a moment.

"The three of us have to meet up after dinner, Wayne. Barbara and I have some suggestion on how to deal with your stepmother."

Wayne's eyes widened. "That's awesome, Atticus! Thanks a million."

"Okay, go now, go."

I looked around and realized that I was alone. It was close to twelve thirty. Time for a good espresso and a bite to eat.

I walked past the front of the bus and noticed that Riccardo had reclined the seat and was dozing like a baby. The doors of the bus were shut, and I certainly wasn't going to disturb him.

I walked past the top of Via Borgognona, one of the fanciest shopping thoroughfares in Rome, surpassed only by the Via Condotti, which ran parallel. Then I stopped and did a double take. *Was that Anthony?* Yes, it was. He was standing alone in front of a shop window. I went closer and saw the name of the store—Beretta. Well, if any store was going to catch Anthony's interest, it would be one of the most famous Italian brands for rifles and handguns in the world. One of the large windows that had Anthony hypnotized displayed a large range of hunting rifles and shotguns.

I went up to him. "Quite an impressive selection," I murmured.

He nodded. "Yeah, not bad at all. Beretta has been making weapons since 1526. It's the oldest-surviving manufacturer of weapons in the world."

Anthony had mutated into another person again. He was citing dates, manufacturing techniques, wars where Beretta firearms were decisive, and the pros and cons of their hunting rifles, shotguns, and pistols.

I wasn't really listening; instead, I was observing this young man who had suddenly become so mature, cool, and collected. Anthony had a split personality.

I cut across his lecture. "Listen, if you don't have anything planned, I thought we could go get something to eat and drink while I ask you about shotguns."

"Sure, I'm going back to the hotel on the bus so there's plenty of time."

"Great. I have a good place in mind."

I led Anthony around the corner and to the beginning of the Via Condotti, where the leading brands in fashion, fine watches and jewelry, and home furnishings brands have their exclusive boutiques. These are not merely stores but also small historical centers of luxury goods. And tucked between Cartier and Prada was the Caffè Greco—the oldest bar/patisserie in Rome, established in 1760.

We entered and were ushered to a table for two. The selection of teas, coffees, and pastries were exceptional.

Anthony settled for a Coke and a piece of *Sacher torte*, an Austrian chocolate cake specialty that I recommended to him. I ordered a double espresso and two Nutella macarons.

Anthony wasted no time returning to his favorite subject. "So what kind of shotguns are you interested in, Atticus?"

Actually, I could have cared less, but I knew that this topic would help get me answers to some pretty hard questions that I would soon be asking.

"Something for home defense, short barrel, pistol grip. Any suggestions?"

The floodgates opened again as they had in front of the Beretta boutique and when we had discussed handguns at the hotel. Remington, Mossberg, Benelli, and Hatsan Arms were named and described with all the pluses and minuses of each brand and the models they produced. I let Anthony rattle on until our orders arrived. As Anthony bit into his Sacher torte, I launched my first series of ground-to-air missiles.

"You've never played polo, have you, Anthony? And you've never been to Switzerland, correct?"

Anthony grabbed his napkin, placed it in front of his mouth, and began coughing violently. I just sat there, watching him.

It took a few minutes for Anthony to regain his composure. When he did, he just sat there, not saying a word. I then unleashed a second missile.

"I know all about your compulsive lying, and I know for a fact that in those rare instances where you're not lying, you're exaggerating everything out of context."

"But…but I have been to Switzerland."

"The closest you've been to Switzerland is when you have a map of Europe in front of you. Having distant relatives in that country doesn't mean you've been there."

Anthony's eyes widened. He had realized that I had more information at my disposal than he imagined.

"Why do you do it, Anthony? Why do you lie to the point that you don't know what the truth is and what is bullshit?" I was relentless, but I knew what I was talking about. He started to perspire and almost hyperventilate. Time to ease up a bit.

"Listen, Anthony, take a bite of your cake and relax. I'm not here to criticize you or belittle you. I'm here to give you some advice."

"Advice? Why do I need any advice? You don't even know anything about me."

"You're right. I don't know that much about you, but I bet I can make some pretty safe assumptions. For example, I bet you had a happy childhood and that you were a very good student in elementary and junior high. Probably one of the most popular kids to boot. Then all of this changed when you arrived at Bradford."

Anthony froze when I mentioned his high school.

"Something must have gone terribly wrong during your first year. Let me guess, your classmates thought you were a loser, and they ignored you and made you the butt end of all their jokes. In no time, you went from being number one in everything to being a loser in everything."

Anthony was turning red.

"Go ahead and swallow before you start choking again."

He did so and took a large gulp of his Coke.

"To add insult to injury, your grades fell off the charts, and you probably only managed to pass freshman year by the skin of your teeth."

"How…how do you know all that?"

"Not finished yet," I said. "Therefore, to compensate for this total train wreck of your self-esteem, you began to lie, with one lie leading to the next. You made up stories about your past that were always bigger and better than the real-life experiences of your peers. This make-believe world you were living in actually put you on the map for a while, so you kept on. But then you couldn't keep up with what you had lied about—you couldn't remember. That's when the bubble burst. People began catching you at your lies, and your classmates began making fun of you again. No matter what you said, nobody listened to you anymore."

I gazed at Anthony for some very long seconds.

"Would you say that I'm pretty close?"

Anthony didn't look at me but nodded his head slowly.

"Would you like to know how I figured this all out?"

No answer. No movement from my table companion.

"Well, I'm going to tell you. 'It's simple. It takes one to know one.' You know the expression, right? You see, when I was your age, I also lied, twenty-four seven."

Anthony jerked his head up.

I gestured to the bar section. "Do you want something a little stronger to drink?"

"Yeah," he replied.

I ordered two rum-and-cokes and another piece of Sacher torte. I paused a moment before telling my story. It wasn't a chapter of my life that I relished thinking about.

When the drinks arrived, I took a large gulp, as did Anthony. We both commented on the generous measure of rum in the Cokes and how delicious the chocolate cake was. For a moment, it didn't appear that we were in the middle of a problematic and uncomfortable discussion.

I sat back, took a deep breath, and began telling Anthony about my freshman to senior year experience in high school. How I had transferred from a modest junior high school as a straight-A student and ended my first year in my new school, a college preparatory institution well above my scholastic preparation, with a C minus to D average. How from the most popular kid in eighth grade, I had in ninth grade become the dunce of the class with no redeeming qualities. That I began to make up stories and lie every time I opened my mouth. I would wake up in the mornings physically sick at the idea of going to school. Finally, how my lying had completely blurred my awareness of the truth to the point where my lies *were* the truth.

"Does this sound familiar, Anthony?" I asked. "You don't have to answer me. Just think hard about what I just shared with you. I wish somebody had sat me down and confronted me with all of this when I was your age. You know, I didn't stop my wholesale lying until I was out of college. Talk about residual damage."

I fiddled with my fork thinking about those dark years. "It was like a category-five hurricane that had torn through New York City. It took me years to regain the trust of my family and the few friends I still had." I looked into Anthony's eyes. "I just don't want you to go through what I did. Understand? You still have time to correct all of this if you want to."

I was certain that Anthony had paid close attention to my confession. But how much importance did he attach to my words? That was a different matter altogether. "And remember, Anthony, what Quintilian said."

"Who?"

"Rome's most famous teacher two thousand years ago. He said, 'A liar must have a good memory.'"

Anthony scrunched up his eyebrows a moment before giving me a tepid smile.

"The next time you're involved in a conversation, and you don't know anything about the subject, keep your mouth shut. Learn to say, 'I don't know.' These can be three powerful words. Do we have a deal?" I stretched my hand across the table. He hesitated, but then shook it.

I was fully aware that what I had confessed to Anthony would only serve to put a small dent, if any, into his habitual lying. It had taken me years to stop even after it became abundantly clear that I was just hurting myself. The temptation to aggrandize everything I did or invent situations out of the blue was just too strong.

We had finished our cake and drinks, but I wanted to ask Anthony another question.

"Mrs. Ramsey thinks highly of you. Did you know that?"

Anthony wasn't surprised at my change of subject.

"Yeah, she's always been nice to me. Did you know that she used to babysit me when I was little? We met up again at Bradford. It's like, well, like she's been following me around all my life. Pretty bizarre."

If you only knew, Anthony, I thought.

"Has she ever spoken to you about your lying?"

Anthony shrugged. "She mentioned it a few times, but I...well, I told her it wasn't such a big deal."

"And now that I've spoken to you, do you still think it isn't a big deal?"

"I've...I've got to get my head around it. You know what I mean?"

"Yes, I think so. One thing's for sure, you certainly don't have to lie or exaggerate when you talk about guns. It's like you're an expert."

Anthony smiled for the first time since we had sat down.

"It's my one and only hobby. I've always been into guns, warfare, and all the history behind military and civilian combat weapons. When the Chinese invented gunpowder back in the year 1000, it changed the way people developed new methods to kill each other. Not that swords, spears, the longbow, clubs and maces, crossbows and all those other weapons disappeared between the Middle Ages and the eighteenth century, but with the matchlock gun, the road to the high-powered, fully automatic weapons of today was just a matter of time."

As Anthony carried on about armaments that were decisive in winning battles throughout the centuries, I just sat back, dumbfounded. Anthony's knowledge didn't just encompass guns as hardware but included a detailed history of warfare. With uncharacteristic self-assurance, he named battles, foreign armies, generals, and weaponry that I had never even come across. *Remarkable*, I thought.

"What I don't understand, Anthony, is why you mentioned such bogus hobbies, like polo and human anatomy in your student bio instead of guns and military history. This is obviously where your passion and knowledge are."

"I try not to talk much about guns when I'm around people, especially at Bradford. They already think that I'm weird and a loser."

"And a liar."

"Yeah, I guess so." Anthony lowered his eyes to his hands that once again were engaged in a wrestling match. "If I talked about guns, they'd probably all think that I'd come to school one day and shoot up the place."

I was sure this had crossed the minds of many people at Bradford.

We sat for another five minutes before going back to the bus. Anthony wanted to get some sleep.

"I hope you'll think about what we talked about," I said.

"I will," he replied.

Somehow, I felt he wasn't lying.

CHAPTER 59

I saw Anthony back to the bus, then got on the phone, and called Barbara. She told me that Mark was doing fine and was eager to get out of the hospital. He would be released in the morning. There was still no word from his parents, which, I thought, was very odd.

I informed Barbara that Wayne, Bishop, and Michelle would be arriving soon with Massimo and Sebastiano. I didn't mention my tête-à- tête with Anthony.

"I'll be there shortly to switch out with you," I said. "I just have to run an errand first. Is there anything I can bring the two of you?"

"Mark and I would love a slice of pizza, if it isn't too much trouble. You choose the toppings. They're all tasty.

"Consider it done."

We ended our call as I made my way down Via Condotti toward Franco's record store where I had taken James and the others the day before. He was an integral part of the plan for the following night, and I was glad to have reached him on the phone earlier on.

Upon my way to the store, I saw Darlene and Vanessa practically frozen in front of a Louis Vuitton display window. I made my way over to them.

"I see you have expensive tastes," I said.

They both turned. Darlene said, "Oh my God, Atticus, just look at those handbags! Aren't they to die for?"

Darlene was practically salivating. I looked at the impressive display area behind the large glass panel. Various LV handbags were hanging from almost invisible nylon threads, descending and ascending off of an abstract airport runway. Background panels with multicolored clouds slowly interchanged, creating a striking visual effect.

"That one over there is forty-five hundred, and that one over there is fifty-eight hundred. We went inside and asked. Atticus, I'd do anything to get my hands on one of those!"

Vanessa said, "Come on, Darlene. The bags are nice, but fifty-eight hundred bucks? I can buy a used car with that kind of money!"

Vanessa's feet were obviously closer to the ground. But Darlene didn't even hear her. I wondered, for a moment, how far she would actually go if someone dangled one of those bags in front of her eyes. The power certain brands yield can be hallucinogenic.

"I have to go, ladies. Do you know how to get back to the hotel?"

They both rolled their eyes.

"Yes, Atticus, no worries."

I grinned. "Well, women and directions mix as well as oil and water. Just making sure."

"Get outta here!" The girls chased after me for a few steps, laughing as I took off running. After another ten minutes walking, I was finally at the record store. Once inside, Franco, who this time was behind the counter, noticed me and came over and embraced me. He had aged, but well. We reminisced for a few minutes about the old days. I volunteered some information about my current situation without going into details, and he didn't ask me any questions. Franco had always been very discreet.

He seemed quite pleased to be involved in my small event. We migrated to the bar next door to drink espressos and review the equipment and albums I wanted him to bring. Franco was planning to be at the location at four in the afternoon to set up. After we had confirmed all the details, I left him at the bar and went outside to hail a cab for the hospital. On the way, I just sat back and closed my eyes.

Traffic was awful, as usual. At least the driver was in no mood to strike up a conversation.

I didn't really want to think about anything weighty, but my subconscious had other ideas. No sooner had I rested my head on the back of the seat than Derek and my nightmare came rushing back, knocking on that part of the brain that deciphers visual stimuli. It was quite unbelievable that large chunks of it all were still so vivid—even that putrid smell of decay and rot. Some of those cruel scenes displayed on the monitors were back. I wasn't in the mood to relive all that. Opening my eyes, I turned my head to look outside the window.

We were going to down *Viale di Trastevere*, which cut through one of the oldest sections of the city. I had spent many an evening in this section of town when living in Rome. As usual, the sidewalks were filled with people coming and going. Tourists were mixed with residents in the neighborhood, which had existed here for over two thousand years. I observed the young, the old, and the middle-aged walking purposefully, everyone with something to do, everyone with something on their mind.

All of them had their own story to tell. Whether young, older, or old, each one of these people was the product or the consequence of choices made by others and, at the same time, each one of these individuals was shaping others by their own choices. Thirteen students and three adults had been with me for almost nine days. How many stories and experiences had I been privy to? And I hadn't even scratched the surface with some of them. There are almost seven billion people in the world, each with their share of emotional baggage. That's a hell of a lot of suitcases.

"Excuse me, sir, we're here."

"Oh, yes, I'm sorry."

The cab was idling in front of the hospital entrance. I hadn't even noticed.

After paying the driver, I crossed the busy street and looked for the omnipresent pizza kiosk. I found one in no time. With my purchase carefully wrapped in some wax paper and aluminum foil, I made my way into the hospital and up to Mark's room. Once on his hallway, I ran into Massimo and a man who was, I assumed, his partner.

Massimo introduced me, and I shook hands warmly with Sebastiano. He was taller than Massimo, probably five to six years older, and at first glance less flamboyant.

"We had an absolutely fabulous lunch together, Atticus, but I will let the boys and Michelle fill you in. Mark looks wonderful, by the way, like nothing ever happened."

I thanked them for their time with the trio and reminded them about tomorrow night.

"We are truly looking forward to it. Now go, go! Mark and Miss Barbara will be happy to see you, especially with what smells like a savory selection of pizza. By the way, she looks absolutely ravishing."

Massimo winked at me and took Sebastiano by the arm as they headed toward the elevator.

***

"Hotel TeRovami please, close to the Trevi Fountain."

Barbara was sitting next to me on the taxi. Another cab directly behind us was carrying Wayne, Bishop, and Michelle.

Barbara took my hand. "I'm so glad all of you made it over," she said. "Mark was so happy."

"Yes, he seemed pleased. Did anybody say anything about what he did before I arrived?"

"No, nobody said a word. After a few questions about how he was feeling, most of the conversation was about this summer and college. At one point, I thought Mark was about to say something, but he didn't. Massimo and Sebastiano were very discreet and just kept complimenting Mark on how well he looked. Do you know anything about how their lunch with the boys and Michelle went?"

"Just that Massimo said it went very well. Maybe they will fill us in tonight. I did have a long and interesting discussion with Anthony, though."

"Anthony?"

"Yes, indeed. I'll tell you about it later. What I need to let you know now is what I have planned for tomorrow night. But keep it a secret."

"Tomorrow night…"

"Yes. I'm actually quite proud of myself." I went ahead and explained what I had in store for the group. "We just need to be ready to leave the hotel at six sharp."

"Oh, well now…that sounds…like fun."

I looked at her. "Is something wrong? I feel as if I've just invited you to a funeral."

"Oh no, no, it's a wonderful idea. The kids will love it, I'm sure."

She was out of sorts, but I chalked it up to her being tired. The drive back to the hotel was faster than expected, and we were presently on the street of the hotel.

"Any plans for this evening?" I asked Barbara.

"I'm game for anything, as long as it's with you."

I squeezed her hand. "That's the answer I was looking for."

"We'll need to get a hold of the trio and tell them about our little scheme for dealing with Wayne's stepmother."

"As long as they don't show up at your room while I'm sitting on top of you."

I saw the taxi driver give me a wide-eyed glance in the rearview mirror. He obviously understood English. I smiled to myself but didn't let Barbara in on it.

"I still can't believe that Mark asked for Cynthia to sit with him again tonight. Those two really created a bond in no time. But then again, Cynthia is another person. What did you do to her at the forum, Atticus?"

"Nothing at all. I told you, she did it on her own."

We were now on the street to the hotel, but the traffic was virtually standstill. I paid the taxi driver, and Barbara and I exited, and I went to the second cab to pay the driver.

"Thanks, Atticus," Wayne said. "I had money for the fare."

"No worries," I replied. "Keep it for something else."

When we walked inside the hotel, I saw John at the front desk speaking with Ludovica and Giovanni. Cynthia was across the hall chatting energetically with Jeremy, James, and Sabrina. As soon as they caught sight of Barbara and me, all chatter immediately ceased.

Cynthia called out to us, "Hey, Atticus, Barbara. How's Mark?"

Despite her breezy tone, I noticed that she seemed nervous about something. When I looked around, John had vanished, along with Jeremy and James.

Wayne, Bishop, and Michelle left in the direction of the stairs and elevator.

Barbara touched my arm. "I need to freshen up myself, Atticus. See you in a bit." She went off as well, with Sabrina in her wake. That left Cynthia and me. Ludovica and Giovanni had already disappeared into their back office. I was beginning to wonder if I had started to emit a bad odor.

I turned to Cynthia and narrowed my eyes. "What's going on?"

She blinked. "What do you mean?"

"I mean, I walk in here, and everyone shuts up and disappears like I'm carrying the Black Plague. There's something up, and I would…"

"Atticus! Enough! Stop asking questions," Cynthia snapped. I felt like one of Cynthia's students caught disrupting class. She saw my startled expression and grinned.

"I'm sorry, but just stop...okay? Everything is just fine. Don't spoil things."

"Spoil what things?" I was super curious.

She shook her finger at me. "Didn't I just tell you to stop asking questions? Just enjoy your evening, take Barbara out, and have a good sleep. Tomorrow is our last day together, unfortunately."

"Yes, these days flew by much too fast. I'll do as you say, Cynthia."

"Good. Now tell me about Mark."

"Well, he actually would like you to sit with him tonight, if that isn't a problem."

Cynthia swallowed hard. "Me? He asked for *me?*"

"Just for you."

"Oh my, that makes me so happy! I'll be ready to go right after dinner, Atticus. If you could just call me a cab."

"Of course."

She squeezed my hands hard and walked out of the lobby. Ludovica had come back out of the office, so I went over and told her about tomorrow night. "I hope that you and Giovanni can come, but just keep it for yourselves until I announce it at dinner tonight."

"Thank you, Mr. Winterle, but I have to be here at the front desk tomorrow. But I think Giovanni would love to go."

"Oh, okay. Well, I am sorry you can't make it."

"No, but I..." She paused. "But I am off Thursday night."

This time, Ludovica looked straight at me.

"Are you..." I said, trying to sound casual. "Well, maybe we could plan a dinner or something of that sort?"

"Gladly. We can talk about it when you come back from the airport." She smiled at me and retreated to the back office.

I had already come to the conclusion that it would have been awkward to have both Ludovica and Barbara at this going-away event that I had planned, especially if Ludovica was harboring feelings for me, which Barbara was certain she was. I, as well, was experiencing emotions that were new to me. On the one hand, I wanted to enjoy Barbara's company to the fullest before she left. On the other hand, I was already looking forward to Wednesday evening with Ludovica. I chalked this up to women being fascinating creatures with unparalleled and diverse powers of seduction. There wasn't much more to say on the matter.

Ludovica came back out. "Mr. Winterle? Excuse me, are you all right?"

"Ah, yes, yes" I stammered. "Um, just thinking about something."

She smiled in a way that made me think she was reading my mind.

"Ms. Farling just called and asked if she could meet you in your room," she said.

"Evelyn?"

"Yes, Ms. Evelyn Farling. I do not think it is an emergency."

"Let's hope not. We've had our fair share of those."

I turned and headed toward the stairs, trying to figure out what Evelyn wanted to talk to me about. I would soon find out.

She was already standing outside my door waiting when I arrived on my floor.

"Evelyn, everything okay?"

"Yeah, I just wanted to speak with you for a few minutes, if that's okay."

"Sure. Come right in." I unlocked the door, not remembering if I had at turned up the bed and hoping that Barbara's lingerie wasn't hanging from one of the bedposts. As it turned out, the bed looked like a cluster bomb had gone off in it. I pulled up the sheets and sat down quickly, as if nothing was out of the ordinary.

Evelyn hesitated. "Do you mind if I sit on the floor, Atticus? It relaxes me."

"Go right ahead." She plopped down and brought her knees up to her chin.

I waited without saying anything.

Evelyn cleared her throat. "I feel like I have to apologize to you."

I raised my eyebrows. "Why?"

"Well, I've been a bitch pretty much this whole trip, and I wanted to fess up. You deserved better."

Talk about being hit by a tsunami.

Evelyn fiddled with her bootstraps. I noticed that the nails of her hands were chewed almost down to the cuticles.

"A lot has gone down these past eight days. Things I wouldn't have ever dreamed possible if it wasn't me experiencing them." She wrapped her arms even more tightly around her legs. "Nobody knows this except James."

She paused. I continued saying nothing. Evelyn sighed.

"I was seriously considering ending it all. The only question was whether I would do it on this trip or when I got back to Atlanta."

I managed to hide my surprise that Evelyn was confessing to what I had read from her diary. "I'm sorry to hear you had reached that stage," I said. "Can I ask why? You don't have to tell me."

She peered off at the window. "It's hard to explain. It wasn't any one thing, you know. I just felt empty. Like, every day I woke up wondering, what's the point of living? There just isn't any purpose to my life, Atticus. Look at me. I'm eighteen years old, my dad's a religious nutcase and has been all his life. My mom's a weak, pathetic woman who ends up in bed with a butch dyke and becomes a hero with all the queers in town. I'm sure the teachers told you what happened. Seems like everyone in the state of Georgia knows about it."

Evelyn watched me to confirm that I knew what she was talking about. I nodded.

"You don't know how much shit I've had to put with recently, Atticus, as well as my entire sorry-ass life. Ever since I can remember, I've had Bibles and prayer books stuck in my face, always getting the lecture that I would burn in Hell if I wasn't a good little girl. There was always a reason why I couldn't have a toy, why I couldn't sleep over at a friend's house, and why my few friends, when I had them, couldn't ever come over to my house. I've never had a Christmas tree. I've never gone trick-or-treating because my father said that Christmas and Halloween were just money-sucking traps run by the Jews. Can you believe that crap? The *Jews*? What the hell do they have to with it? My parents are so fucked up." Evelyn sighed heavily. "Do you know that my mom never talked to me about menstruation until after I had my period? Did you ever see the movie, *Carrie*?"

"Yes, many, many years ago. That came out before you were born, Evelyn."

She frowned. "It came out in 2002. I was ten."

Now it was my turn to frown. "No, it came out some time in the '70s."

"Maybe there was a remake. In the movie you saw, did it end with Carrie using her telekinesis to squeeze her mother's heart till she dies?"

"No, but that scene was in the Stephen King novel the movie's based on."

"Then the remake was better."

"I'll see if I can find it on DVD."

"I must have seen it twenty times. As far as the religious part goes with Carrie's crazy mother, my life wasn't very far from that movie. Stephen King should have paid me royalties." Evelyn's voice cracked. "Do you have any water here?"

I handed her a bottle from the mini fridge, and she emptied it in one go.

"All I've ever wanted was someone I could talk to, someone who I could share my feelings with, someone who would just listen to me. You can't get through this shit life if you don't have somebody who can catch you when you fall, without someone to pump you up when you feel like dirt. The only person who's ever given me the time of day has been James, but I only got to know him about a year ago."

"You said that James has also thought about taking his life?"

"Yeah. More than me. I'm actually a little surprised that he hasn't done himself it yet."

"But why does James want to kill himself? Is it a family situation, like you?"

"Not really. I mean, his parents are pretty normal. Much more than mine, that's for sure. They're just absent, like ghosts. James doesn't exist for them."

I just sat there hoping for more information.

"His dad is always buried in his books. He's a writer for some scientific journal, and he's never given James the time of day. His mom is a nice-enough lady, but she's out in left field half the time. All she does is work in the garden from morning to night. You'd think they had a twenty-acre estate. I think she's on happy pills half the time. She's always got this stupid little smile on her face that I would love to slap off of her." Evelyn gazed down at the floor and then straight at me. "Why do some people have kids, Atticus? Why can't they understand if they're going to be decent parents before they start screwing each other? If my mom, if James's mom, had just gotten their tubes tied, we wouldn't be here! We wouldn't have put up with all this shit! It's just not fair, Atticus, not fair…"

She buried her head in her arms. I went over to her and sat on the floor. I put my arm around her as her tears streamed down her cheeks like rain on barren ground.

Wednesday
May 5 , Day Nine

CHAPTER 60

"What time is it, Atticus?" Barbara asked.

"Close to one."

"I thought I'd be out like a light by now, but I'm not sleepy at all. I can't stop thinking about what you told me about Anthony and Evelyn."

I had, in fact, filled Barbara in on my lengthy discussion with Anthony at the bar as well as Evelyn's visit later in the afternoon.

"Did Evelyn really say that she and Sabrina were now— what was it?—*tight?*"

"That's what she said. She's having a hard time believing it too. They were together for most of the day today, shopping and sightseeing. The initiative was totally Sabrina's to connect with Evelyn."

"And of course, you're going to give all the credit to that church statue…"

"Did I say anything about the statue? No, so let's not go there." I wasn't about to get into another argument with her over this.

Barbara started doodling on my chest with her index finger. We had both given an above-average performance of sexual prowess shortly after Michelle, Wayne, and Bishop had left the room. That was close to eleven thirty.

"Do you think Wayne and Bishop were pleased with our little sink-the-Janice-bitch plan?" I asked.

"Absolutely," Barbara replied. "I need to look up a few more things on the internet. I'll give you what I can find tomorrow. If Wayne can get her social security and driver's license numbers, will that be enough to get some dirt on this woman?"

"I'm sure of it. I still have a few contacts with the Bureau stateside. With what you can find and those ID numbers, I should be able to find out everything about Janice from the day she was born."

"That's wonderful if it can help those boys, even though I don't like the idea that it's so easy to find out so much about someone so easily."

"Privacy is a thing of the past. With the FBI, CIA, NSA, State Department, Department of Justice, and God only knows how many smaller covert agencies, there is no such thing as privacy anymore. People are so naïve, putting all their lives out there on Facebook, for example. Just you wait, a scandal is going to hit one day when we find out that all that information is getting sold or traded with other high-tech social websites, political parties, Amazon, Google."

"Oh, come on. That sounds a bit extreme."

"Maybe it is, but I wouldn't be surprised." I shifted gears. "Question for you, speaking of being surprised, I had the air taken out of my balloon at dinner tonight."

"Why? What are you talking about?"

"Well, when I informed everyone about tomorrow night, a special place, dinner, a going-away party, everyone gave me the same look that you gave me when I told you about it in the taxi. Like if I was inviting them to a funeral."

"Oh, come on, Atticus, we're all excited about it. They just didn't expect it. You pulled the rug from under their feet."

"You think? I wouldn't have organized this if I thought the group wasn't interested."

Barbara pulled herself up and looked straight at me. The problem was, her breasts were bare, and they were looking straight at me as well.

"Atticus, stop. These kids love you, they really do. The fact that you went out of your way to prepare something special for them on their last night here is greatly appreciated, more than you think. Take my word for it. Atticus, are you listening to me?"

My hands were underneath her breasts. I hadn't heard a word she said.

"Oh, Atticus, not again…"

"What am I going to do without you when I get back to Atlanta, Mr. Winterle?" she panted afterward. "I'm getting accustomed to all of this."

We were once again drenched in perspiration and out of breath.

"I'm concentrating on the here and now, Barbara. I'll deal with your departure when we're at the airport."

I stroked her hair as she leaned over and kissed me on the cheek before getting up and going into the bathroom. I turned on the bedside lamp. The alarm clock display was showing 2:05 am.

I called out to Barbara. "I wonder how Cynthia and Mark are doing?"

"Probably fast asleep, as we should be. Cynthia was so proud when she got into that cab to go to the hospital."

I had asked Ludovica to call a taxi for Cynthia immediately after dinner. I told her that I would be with them in the morning around seven to bring them both back to the hotel.

"Could you do me a favor?"

"Just ask, my knight in shining armor."

"Try to get everyone up and in the breakfast room by eight thirty. I think it would be good for Mark to walk in and see everyone already waiting there."

"Well, we have some sleepyheads, but I shall do my best."

Barbara came out of the bathroom with a negligée-style bed jacket that made her look even more sensual than she did wearing nothing at all.

"I didn't tell you about the latest news from the home front," she said.

"From your husband?"

"Yup. Seems like he's now open to the idea of talking things out and possibly not moving away. I just don't know any more if that's what I want. A few days ago, when he said he was leaving me, it was like a kick in the stomach. But now I think that it would be best for both of us that he vacates the house. What do you think?"

"I don't know how much I can help you here, Barbara. I guess there are some pluses and minuses for him staying or going. You told me once that he has treated you well and that he's a good companion, but I don't think he has any intention of stopping those sex games. That means that you either go back to that or that you end up looking at porn and handling things on your own again. Do you really want to go back to one of those scenarios?"

"No, I certainly wouldn't be part of the wife-swapping scene anymore. That's done and over with. He is good company, and I think he really cares for me. That's a few points for him. The house is actually big enough that we could partition it off and each have our own private space. That could be an idea, but I'm just not—"

The phone rang, and we both jumped. Who was calling at half past two in the morning?

"This can't be good." I reached over quickly and grabbed the receiver.

"Yes?"

"Mr. Winterle? It's Giovanni at the front desk. All is well and there is no emergency, but I do have Miss Michelle here who would like to speak with you."

I put my hand over the receiver and turned to Barbara whose eyes were almost out of their sockets.

"It's Giovanni downstairs. Everything is fine, but Michelle wants to speak with me."

"Michelle? At this hour?"

"Atticus? Are you there?"

"Yes, Michelle. Are you okay? You've got me worried."

"I'm sorry to bother you and Mrs. Cornwall, but I really need to speak with both of you if at all possible."

"Did Evelyn do something stupid?"

"No, this has nothing to do with Evelyn. It's about me."

About her?

"Sure, Michelle, just give us a few minutes and come right up."

Barbara shot out of the bed as if she had sat on a nail. I hung up the phone.

"She wants to speak with both of us, Barbara, and it has nothing to do with Evelyn."

"Did she seem anxious?"

"No, not at all, but it's about her." I put on my shorts and a T-shirt. Barbara put on the bathrobe over her negligee and brushed out her hair.

"I'm concerned, Atticus. It must be very important for Michelle to come and see us at this hour."

"Well, we're going to find out soon enough."

As I spoke, there was a light tapping on the door. I got up and opened it.

Michelle came in, looking at us apologetically.

"I'm really, really sorry about this, but I really needed to speak to both of you, and it just couldn't wait."

"Sit down, Michelle. Do you want some water, a Coke?"

"Do you have anything stronger?" Michelle glanced at the open bottle of red wine that was on the table. I poured her a glass, and she quickly downed half the contents.

"Thanks, that helps."

Barbara and I glanced at each other, not knowing what to expect.

"I just got back from a long walk. Sorry, I know that I shouldn't have snuck out." She cocked her head back. "There's really something magical about this city. It speaks to me. When I walk by all these century-old buildings and churches, it's as if the spirits of the dead surround me and give me advice. I know that sounds like I have a screw loose, but it's how I feel."

She looked at the dark window, then turned to us. "Now I know it's the right time, the right thing to do. You see, Atticus, Mrs. Cornwall—"

"*Barbara*, Michelle, please call me Barbara."

"Okay, thanks, Barbara." She paused to take another big gulp of wine.

"Nobody knows this, except my mom and dad. Not even my brother knows."

I began to feel uneasy.

"Lately, I've found it too hard to keep it to myself any longer. This trip, Rome, meeting you, Atticus, and getting to know you better, Barbara…well, it's just the right time."

"Michelle, you're scaring us just a bit here," I said.

Barbara took my hand and squeezed it hard.

Michelle's voice was steady, as was her gaze. "I have a brain tumor. I'm not going to make it to the end of this year."

I felt as if a bunker-piercing projectile had just hit the room. Barbara gasped, and her hands flew to her mouth. I buried my face in my hands.

Michelle came over and put her arms around both of us.

"Please, don't be upset. I know this caught you off guard, but don't worry about me. I've accepted it."

"Oh my God, Michelle…how long?" Barbara asked. "When…when did you find out?"

Barbara began to cry, and I felt the tears prickling my eyelids.

"I've known since January of this year," said Michelle. "At first, the surgeons were going to go in and get it, but then the tests showed that it was too big. Plus, it has already metastasized to my lymph nodes and liver."

I was reliving snapshots of the past few days: Michelle's headaches, Marco's pharmacist brother-in-law noticing something strange about Michelle when she passed us in the stairwell, Massimo's preoccupation with her being so pale when we were at the forum, nothing in her student bio about school or future plans—I just hadn't put two and two together.

"I wasn't going to tell either of you. When it happened, you would have found out. But then, getting close to both of you on this trip, I decided that I preferred, and I thought you might prefer to hear it from me before…well, before."

Barbara held Michelle's hands. "We're glad you told us."

She glanced at me, and I nodded.

Michelle said, "It's been hard on me keeping everything inside. It's been tough on my parents."

"You said that your brother doesn't know?"

"No. Jack did two tours in Iraq. He came back fine physically, but he struggled for years with PTSD. He's better now and has a good job. Life is finally looking up for him. I don't want to hit him with this until I really have to. We're very close. He's my protector, my Superman."

I remembered what Sabrina had told me about Jack doing time for dealing with her attacker. Michelle looked at me, and I awkwardly wiped away the tears that were now rolling down my face.

"The headaches are getting worse and more frequent," she continued, "but I knew that was going to happen. My parents were the ones who insisted I come on this trip. They knew how much it meant to me. I'll be on a steady stream of morphine and other painkillers when I get home. I've been able to stay away from that stuff so far."

I had to draw a few deep breaths before I could speak. "Are you going to tell Wayne and Bishop?"

"Not yet. I'll have to soon, like I'll have to tell my brother, but I've got to keep tabs on those two clowns as long as my strength holds. I hope we can resolve this problem with Wayne's stepmom before, well, before I go."

Barbara was now sobbing.

"There was a line, Michelle, from Evelyn's diary that you redacted in your photo. Did Evelyn suspect something?"

"Yeah, I thought you'd catch that, Atticus."

Michelle flashed me one of those beautiful smiles. "She had mentioned I wasn't looking or feeling well. I had a bad headache that night and threw up forever. I told her it was just a stomach bug, but I don't think she bought it."

"No mention, as well, on your student bio about school or the future…" I was now a teary mess.

Michelle edged herself in between us.

"Well, I guess I could've written that I was going to Harvard and that I wanted to study medicine, but it seemed like a waste of good ink."

She let out a giggle, but Barbara and I just gushed like Niagara Falls.

"Okay, you guys, I think that's enough now. I need you both to pretend that you didn't hear anything about this. I don't want to see pouty faces tomorrow. It's our last day in this fantastic city, and you've planned something great for us tomorrow night, Atticus. We're all looking forward to whatever it is, so no more tears and no more sad looks, please."

Barbara and I both held on to Michelle while attempting to compose ourselves. Michelle gave both of us a kiss on our cheeks.

"I feel much better now that the two of you know. I feel lighter inside." She hugged us both again, then got up and headed towards the door. "We all need to get some sleep now. Last day in Rome today. It will be a day to remember, I'm sure."

She let herself out.

***

The alarm sounded like a jackhammer banging against my head. In that phase of grogginess bridging sleep and consciousness, Michelle's late-night visit came to mind, sending a shiver down my spine. *Was it a nightmare, or was it true?* I thought, before realizing it had really happened. Barbara and I must have fallen asleep shortly after she left us. We were still wrapped around each other with our legs hanging off the bed when the clock started blaring. Barbara did not wake. I managed to disentangle myself from her, get up, dress, and head down to the lobby in a very short period of time. I wanted to get to the hospital as fast as possible. Mark was being dismissed, and this was a wedge of good news.

As soon as Giovanni saw me, he called a cab, which arrived within minutes. When I arrived at the hospital, Mark was already up, dressed, and ready to go. Cynthia looked rested and serene. As much as I attempted to act delighted to see Mark looking so well, Cynthia kept eyeing me in the taxi on the way back to the hotel. Several times she asked if something was wrong. I said everything was fine, but a good actor I was not. I just couldn't stop thinking about Michelle.

When the three of us arrived at the hotel and entered the breakfast area, Mark was met with cheers, a standing ovation, and warm embraces. I shot a glance at Michelle, who was standing close to Wayne. She looked buoyant and happy. To think that she was doomed at such a young age was agonizing.

Looking around the room, I saw that everyone was present. Barbara had done well getting everyone down from their rooms. It was the right time to say a few words on this last full day in Rome.

I clinked a spoon against the water pitcher. "May I have everyone's attention for a moment, please?"

Everyone quieted down.

"Well, ladies and gentlemen, this is it, our last day together, and I can't think of a better way to get it started than having Mark back with us." Applause and cheers erupted once again.

"Today is open, but I need all of you in the lobby a little before six this evening. I'll have taxis ready outside."

"Where are you taking us, Atticus," Mary asked. "Can you tell us now?"

"Hopefully, it will be a nice surprise, that's all I'm going to say. Try to get your bags packed before we head out. I don't think we'll be back here at the hotel until late. Breakfast will be at six thirty tomorrow morning."

This initiated a cacophony of guttural sounds and boos.

"Okay, okay, I get it, but we have to be on the bus no later than six thirty. Your flight leaves at ten, and we have to be at the airport a good two-and-a-half hours before ten."

I don't know what came over me, but my voice suddenly became shaky, and my eyes were beginning to water. Silence fell over the room.

"I would like to say that it's been an incredible experience for me. I'm not going to forget any of you…" I saw that I wasn't the only one who was getting emotional. This just made matters worse.

"Now get out of here…enjoy every minute of this day. Just be back here at six." I grabbed a few napkins from a table, turned quickly, and headed out to the lobby. I needed to go outside and get some air.

***

The rest of the morning and early afternoon flew by like a fiery comet. I took care of the last invitations to the *soirée*, telling Darlene she could bring Giacomo, Raymond his two Jewish friends that I had met at the synagogue, and suggesting to John that he invite Rhea. Luckily, I managed to see all of them before they all headed out for one last day of exploration. Cynthia left the hotel with Vanessa, Sabrina, Darlene, and Evelyn. I found out later that Anthony and Mary had gone out with Barbara and that James had teamed up with

Jeremy and Raymond. The last students that I saw leave the hotel were Wayne, Bishop, Michelle, and Mark. I asked Mark if he felt up to going out on the town, having just checked out of the hospital. Michelle immediately said that she would be watching him like a hawk.

I was hoping to have a chat with Mark, a one-on-one to get some firsthand information on why he did what he did. He certainly had unloaded a good deal of information on Cynthia, including the Skype call to his sister. Thinking about it a bit more, however, I decided not to pursue that conversation After all, in less than twenty-four hours, I would probably never see Mark again. I just hoped that he had learned something from his experience.

I called Marco around noon and recapped the schedule for tomorrow morning. So far, the American Airlines flight was on time, and Riccardo would be at the usual spot with our bus at seven thirty. He then informed about something that I had forgotten to follow up on.

Mark's parents had finally called. They said they had been on a golfing vacation in the Bahamas and had only found out that something had happened to Mark when they got back home. I thought that sounded rather unlikely. ASA had the cell phone numbers of all the parents directly involved in this trip. Marco told me that once Mark's mother found out that he was being released in twenty-four hours, she practically ended the phone conversation asking whether anyone needed a credit card number for any hospital charges. Her very last words were, "You know, boys will be boys." Marco was stunned. I was not, considering what I had learned about Mark's parents from Barbara, Cynthia, and Michelle.

Before we ended our call, I extended that night's invitation to Rosanna, our tour guide at St. Peter's. Marco said that he would try to get in touch with her, but he couldn't promise her attendance. After I ended this call, I called Massimo's number. He answered after the first ring, sounding more exuberant than usual.

"I just wanted to remind you about tonight, Massimo. Six o'clock, you know where."

"Oh yes, yes, certainly. We would not miss it for the world. Oh my, so much to do, so much…" He was mumbling to himself.

"Are you all right, Massimo?"

"Who, me? Oh yes, of course…just, just, oh goodness, where do I start? Oh! My, my, Atticus…. yes, you were saying?"

"Nothing, nothing Massimo. I'll see you and Sebastiano tonight."

"Of course, you will, silly man! Oh, the time, so little time! Kisses, bye!"

After going out to a trattoria near the hotel for a very pleasant lunch, I walked back to the hotel and ran into Cynthia and her group of girls. I tried to start some light conversation and even invited all of them for an espresso or cappuccino, but they all hurriedly excused themselves and dashed off to the lobby. Only Cynthia accepted my invitation.

I chose the very same coffee bar where Cynthia and I had gone just a few days ago and where I had prodded her about Anthony's student bio. How much had changed in such a brief period!

"So where did you head off to this morning?"

"Oh, nowhere in particular. We had a very pleasant walk, and the girls did some last-minute shopping. I managed to have some nice conversations with all of them."

"You had an interesting following. Weren't you stunned to see Evelyn tagging along? Especially with Sabrina?"

"Yes, that did take me by surprise. But I eventually figured out that they had managed to talk things out." Cynthia looked at me and opened her eyes wide. "Stranger things have happened on this trip, haven't they?"

"And what have you been doing so far today?" she asked. "Relaxing a bit, I hope."

"Nothing much. All of you abandoned me so I've been rather lazy so far. I do have to go to tonight's venue soon to check up on things."

Cynthia shot me a brief but nervous glance. A forced smile only emphasized her sudden uneasiness.

"When, Atticus? I mean, is it necessary? What is there to check up on?"

I leaned over the table stared at her, "I don't even remember if I filled you in on tonight's soirée, Cynthia. What I do know is that everyone has been acting a bit odd ever since I brought it up. Is there something going on that I am not privy to?"

She drew back.

"Nonsense, Atticus! What in the world would I be hiding?"

Interesting choice of words, I thought. I had not said that anyone was hiding anything.

Cynthia blabbered on, "It's just that, you've done so much already just by setting this evening up for the group, why go check up on something that you've obviously already taken care of?"

There was no logic in in Cynthia's argument, but I wasn't going to exacerbate the situation any further.

"Well, thank you for your concern, Cynthia, but I will have to drop by. Don't worry, I won't be long."

We hadn't finished our coffees, but Cynthia was clearly anxious to get back to the hotel. Something was up, but I had no clue what. I walked back with her.

As soon as we entered the lobby, Cynthia excused herself saying that she had to pack. Giovanni was at the front desk and confirmed that he would be attending our get-together and was very pleased with the invitation.

"I'm going to head out and make sure that everything is set up for tonight, Giovanni. Could you call me another cab?" This question prompted another of the rare times that Giovanni lifted his eyes from what he was doing to look directly at me.

"Excuse me, Mr. Winterle, but won't you just be tiring yourself? You have had a grueling week, with little sleep. Why not go upstairs and rest an hour?"

Now Giovanni was behaving oddly. Was there some sort of virus infecting everybody?

"Listen, Giovanni," I said sternly. "People have been either avoiding me or suddenly concerned about what my plans are this afternoon. Could you enlighten me please? I do believe you are aware of something."

Giovanni lowered his stare and continues trafficking with papers in front of him. "*Forsan et haec olim meminisse juvabit…*" Giovanni was practically whispering.

"What was that?"

"The taxi will be here in three minutes, Mr. Winterle. Now you must excuse me. I have much to do before joining all of you tonight." And off he went into the back office.

I was still trying to come figure out Giovanni's and everyone else's strange behavior when I heard a car horn outside the glass doors. The taxi was here.

CHAPTER 61

When I arrived at the restaurant, I was greeted with hugs by almost all the waiters, some of whom had worked in the establishment for over thirty years. Dino, the head cook, and Matteo, the restaurant manager, were the most effusive in their salutations. I couldn't count the times I had been to this restaurant during my years living in Rome. Located in a section of the vaulted basement of the Theatre of Pompey, completed in 55 BC by the Roman general of the same name, the cuisine, the exceptional choice of wines, and the ambience made this restaurant one of the most famous in Rome.

Matteo led me to a large backroom that had already been set up for our group. The tables were pushed together to form a large *U*. I counted the place setting: thirty-two. Matteo also informed me that Franco had come a few hours earlier to set up his equipment. I saw two turntables, an amplifier, and a mixer. Four large speaker units were up against the front wall. On the ceiling were what looked like spotlights and one of those 1970s disco balls. Franco had really gone all out.

Dino joined us after a few minutes and went over the menu with us. There would be four pasta dishes, various roasted meats, and grilled fish, as well as an open salad and appetizer bar. I was confident that all the guests would be pleased. Mario further informed me that a group of waiters who had served me throughout the years had volunteered to stay as long as the group wished to stay. There would be no closing hour tonight.

***

I looked at the clock on the bedside table. It was almost a quarter to six. After leaving the restaurant, I had decided to walk to the hotel. Once back, and seeing that nobody from the group was around, I went to my room, showered, shaved, and picked out some comfortable clothes for what I was hoping would be a long, enjoyable night.

I grabbed my wallet, Toscanello cigars, my new Dupont lighter, and was ready to head downstairs when a distinctive series of knocks sounded on the door. Opening it, I was a bit taken aback to see many smiling faces looking back at me.

"Can we come in, Atticus?"

"Um, sure, but we have to—"

"Yeah, we know, we've got to go, but this will just take a minute."

Sabrina, Vanessa, Mary, Evelyn, Darlene, and Michelle all walked in and sat down on the bed and the floor. "Yes, um, make yourselves at home," I said. I looked at all the bright faces smiling at me. "So to what do I owe this pleasant surprise?"

"We haven't seen you all day, Atticus," Evelyn replied. "We just wanted to come and say hello and see how you were doing."

I wasn't buying it, but I decided to play along.

"Well, I had a nice walk and good lunch. I packed a few things and then headed out to check on our location for this evening. Speaking of which girls, the cabs are probably outside waiting for us."

They all exchanged glances.

"Yeah, well, um, don't you want to know what we did today?" Vanessa sounded desperate.

"Of course, but you have all night to tell me." I motioned toward the door.

"Right, that's right!" The girls on the floor got up, blocking the doorway.

"We went shopping," Sabrina interjected. "We got some really cool stuff."

I put my hands on my hips. "Okay, girls, what gives? It's ten past six, the cabs are surely outside, and you're keeping me prisoner in my room."

In that instant, the phone rang, and I noticed Michelle and Mary give out a short sigh, as if relieved. I reached for the phone.

"Yes? I thought so, Giovanni. We'll be down immediately."

The girls all looked at one another in unison.

"Okay, Atticus, we're ready to go," said Darlene. "Looking forward to whatever you've got planned," Darlene said, winking at me.

And as fast as they came in through that door, they left just as suddenly. I smiled to myself, realizing how much I was going to miss each of them.

Once downstairs, I found the lobby full and bustling. I first saw Raymond, who was speaking with his two friends, Jacob, and Martin. I walked over and greeted them.

"I'm really happy the two of you could join us," I said.

"We wouldn't have missed it for the world. Thank you for inviting us," Martin answered.

Looking around the room, I saw Darlene standing close to Giacomo. I deliberately approached them surreptitiously from behind. When Giacomo realized that I was practically standing by his ear, he almost jumped off the ground. I controlled my laughter.

"I'm not going to bite you, Giacomo. I wanted to thank you for your card and say that I'm glad that you could make this evening."

Giacomo cleared his throat, nervously. "I'm glad you liked it and thank you for inviting me."

I patted him on the shoulder and made my way to the front desk. Ludovica was behind the counter and looked absolutely gorgeous. She wasn't going to be able to join us this evening, but she was dressed as if she were going to an upscale event.

"Mr. Winterle, there are five taxis parked a bit farther down the road, ready to go when you are."

"Thank you, Ludovica. I am sorry you can't make it tonight, but we shall see each other in the morning."

"Yes, yes we will…and tomorrow evening as well."

Her smile spoke volumes.

As I made my way to the sliding glass doors, I encountered Barbara, who was speaking to John and a woman.

"Atticus, I'd like to introduce you to Rhea." John was blushing a bit.

"It's a pleasure to meet you, Rhea. I'm really glad you could join us this evening."

"Thank you, Atticus. You have a very interesting name, by the way. Greek origin."

"I believe John told me that you are from that country."

"Yes, I am originally from Athens. But I have been in Rome for two years now, teaching at the university."

"Atticus, I need to speak with you just a moment." Barbara placed her hand on my arm and tugged it gently. I excused myself.

"I just wanted to ask you if you noticed how gorgeous Ludovica looks tonight." Barbara was staring straight at her. She leaned closer to me. "That's all well and good, but just remember that you belong to me these next twelve hours."

"She's not coming tonight, Barbara."

"Oh, really? Well, I think that was a wise decision on her part."

"By the way, where have you been all day?"

"Here, there, everywhere. It was a busy day. I needed to occupy myself with as much as I could and try not to think of what Michelle told us. I still can't believe it."

"You and me both."

I stroked Barbara's shoulder, marveling once again at how soft her skin was. Glancing around, I saw Mark sitting in one of the lounge chairs.

"Let me go check on, Mark."

He nodded as I sat down beside him.

"How are you feeling?" I asked.

"Pretty good, considering. Just a bit tired."

"Do you really want to go? Nobody is going to have an issue if you decide to call it a day and get some sleep."

Mark looked at me as if I had lost my mind.

"I wouldn't miss this for the world, Atticus. I'd also like to speak with you before tomorrow morning, just the two of us."

"You're on. We'll make time tonight."

It was now almost six thirty. We really had to get going.

"Ladies and gentlemen, the taxis are waiting for us outside," I announced. "I hope all of you enjoy yourselves this evening. I am looking forward to a good time together."

I stood by the open glass doors as everyone filed out. As I turned to exit the building myself, Ludovica called after me:

"Atticus, I wanted to let you know that Giovanni will be arriving in about thirty minutes."

"Thank you, Ludovica. See you in the morning."

"I'll be here."

Ludovica flashed me a mesmerizing smile. She really did look exceptionally beautiful this evening. As I made my way to the waiting taxis, I realized that she had called me by my first name for the very first time. I liked it.

As I reached the area where the cabs were waiting for us, I saw that two had already left and a third was pulling away. Ludovica must have told the drivers where to go. James, Anthony, and Jeremy were in the last taxi waiting for me.

"You're dragging tonight, Atticus." James grinned.

"Okay, wise guy, take it easy. Without me, you wouldn't even know where to go."

I told the driver the name of the restaurant in Italian.

"Yeah, right," Jeremy muttered.

I turned and looked at him. "Jeremy, do you know something I don't?"

"Who me? No, no, I mean…what are you talking about, Atticus?" He was as red as a fire hydrant. It was abundantly clear now that almost everyone was hiding something from me, but I let it slide.

Our driver was very talented at handling the Rome traffic and got us to our destination in a very short time. Once out of the taxi, we made our way up a gently sloping stone pathway that led us to the entrance of the Trattoria Costanza.

Two waiters at the door greeted us. The three boys, who were slightly ahead of me, turned to their right and went down a short hallway. They then made a left and walked through one of the rooms filled with restaurant patrons. Reaching a set of wooden doors, they opened them and entered what would be our dining area for the rest of the evening. Only then did I realize that they had made their way without any directions from me or the waiters. Before I could wrap my head around this mystery, I was overcome by the music, the guests, and the overall jovial atmosphere.

I saw Marco and his brother-in-law, Stefano, with their respective consorts; Riccardo, our bus driver with a woman I assumed to be his wife; Giorgio and his driver, Pietro, decked out in their Guardia di Finanza uniforms; and Rosanna, our wonderful tour guide at St. Peter's. I spotted Sebastiano, Massimo's companion, but Massimo was nowhere in sight. Franco was off to the left side of the room behind his stereo equipment, orchestrating the music. Other than Massimo, the only person that was missing was Giovanni.

Waiters were bustling in and out of the room, bringing baskets of bread and a variety of antipasti ranging from olives, artichoke hearts, stewed mushrooms to sliced ham, salami, mozzarella cheese, ricotta, and fried cod tidbits. Many bottles of wine were already on the table, as well as bottled water.

After greeting all the guests and sharing a few words, Barbara motioned to me to come sit beside her. I did so and found myself at the head of the horseshoe formation of tables with Cynthia on my left. At a certain point, I felt two warm hands on my shoulders. Looking up, I saw Massimo's smiling face.

"My dear Atticus, my, my, my! What an absolutely exquisite evening this is going to be! I am so excited! Oh! I am saying too much, much too much…enjoy, enjoy!"

With that, he leaned over and gave me a quick kiss on the cheek. He was just as excitable as he had been on the phone earlier that afternoon. I wondered if he had popped one too many happy pills.

I was already beginning my second glass of wine and knew that this was the right time to stand and make a short speech, which I had been rehearsing in my head all day. I was the host, after all. I turned to Barbara. "I'll just address the group, and then we can start dinner."

To my surprise, she shook her head firmly. "No, Atticus. It's not the right time." She placed her hand on my arm with a certain amount of force. A split second later, I had Cynthia's hand on my other arm. *What in the world?*

Suddenly, the lights dimmed, and a soft spotlight came on right above me. Michelle got up from her chair and walked to the middle of the room. A single beam of light fell on her as well. I was bewildered.

"Dear Atticus, welcome to our last night in Rome together!" Michelle began clapping her hands, and everyone followed suit. "We have a little surprise for you that all of us have been working on. So sit back, pour yourself another glass of wine, relax, and enjoy. You deserve it."

The light over her head switched off, as did mine. All the students quietly got up and made their way out of the room, just to come back almost instantaneously, each carrying something concealed by a sheet.

I turned and looked at Barbara, then back at Cynthia. They both smiled at me with a great amount of satisfaction.

As soon as these covered objects were positioned around the room, in front of the tables, the students took positions behind each of them. The guests and teachers at the table were dead silent. Even the waiters had stopped trafficking back and forth.

Then I heard the music. Franco kept the volume low, but it took me a split second to recognize the voice of Maria Callas singing "O mio babbino caro" from the opera *Gianni Schicchi*. This had Mary written all over it. A spotlight overhead suddenly switched on above the first mysterious object to my left as the other lighting in the room faded out. The sheet was pulled off by someone I could not identify.

There stood an easel with a canvas, probably close to three feet in length and two feet in width. The brushstrokes were matte black, strong and almost violent. It was a surreal image even if the subject matter was abundantly clear: It was a representation of the fountain, the statues of Castor and Pollux and the obelisk in front of the Quirinale Palace. The monuments that I had asked Evelyn and Mary to research for me on our first day in Rome. In fact, the voice coming from behind the canvas was Evelyn's.

A concise but informative explanation of what this specific canvas represented came streaming through hidden speakers. Evelyn's voice was bold and unwavering. When she had finished, the spotlight above her faded out with another one switching on above the next easel displaying another canvas. Maria Callas had now rolled into Mirella Freni singing "Che gelida manina" from the opera *Tosca* as I admired another abstract yet forceful image. It was a drawing of the column in Piazza Colonna, dedicated to the Roman emperor Marcus Aurelius. The symmetry and perspective of the buildings wrapping around the column were impressive. Whoever had sketched this knew what he was doing. Mary came into view and gave a brief but informative description of the column's history, describing the two battles that were represented in the spiral relief. I remembered asking someone to get back to me on the history of this column when we were heading to the Pantheon but didn't think anyone was listening. I was wrong.

The show went on with Mark giving us a description of the Knights Templar. The canvas portrayed a knight with a white mantle and a red cross on his chest, which was their distinctive vestiary.

Surprisingly, the spotlight then brought Anthony into view who, with just a bit of timidity, was able to give us a portrayal of the prime minister Benito Mussolini and his tenure from 1922 to 1943. The canvas portrayed a rough sketch of Mussolini standing on the balcony of Palazzo Venezia, where we had stopped for a moment before heading to the Vatican. It was a remarkable drawing, again only in charcoal and pencil.

The next canvas was presented by James. When he took the sheet off, various elongated designs seemed to jump off the paper. He had depicted the most important Egyptian obelisks in Rome, most of which we had seen during our walks. His description was brief, yet informative. His voice was a monotone, and he kept his eyes on the floor as he spoke. *But this was James.* I was thrilled that he had taken a subject that had spiked his curiosity since Day One and had actually researched it. And the drawing, again, was exceptional.

The information that I had asked for was now presented to me in art and in words. The fulfillment these students were giving me was beyond description. I was particularly touched by the last canvas.

The music had changed once again to "E Lucevan le Stelle," one of the most moving aria's ever written, from the opera *Tosca*, which is set in Rome. The same black accentuated brushstrokes were visible, but this was not a monument or a place. It was the impressionistic bust of a man. At the top of the canvas, a large letter *C* and the Roman numeral *V* were visible. It was Charles the V. As if in a time machine, I was suddenly back to Day Two, after our lunch close to St. Peter's. We were walking back to the bus and had passed the portico that leads from the Vatican to the Castel Sant'Angelo. I had made an offhand remark about how Charles, the holy Roman emperor at the time, and his army had laid waste to Rome, destroying everything and everyone in their path. I was certain at the time that no one had even heard what I said, let alone wondered why a Roman emperor would destroy his own kingdom. How wrong I was! It was Michelle's voice I heard behind this last canvas: "A smashing victory over the French at Pavia, Italy, in 1525 practically made Charles the V, the holy roman emperor, dominant in Italy. In 1527, these forces stormed the city of Rome and started an orgy of destruction and massacre, terrorizing the population and humiliating Pope Clement VII. And why was this? Had Charles lost his mind? No, Rome was not attacked on Charles' orders, but by his imperial troops who were angry at not being paid. These ragged and hungry soldiers, including German mercenaries and Spanish infantry, mutinied and marched on Rome, destroying everything in their sight and killing everyone they encountered. So, in the end, Rome was sacked primarily for money, not because of Charles commanding them to do so."

At this point, the light above Michelle switched off. We all clapped our hands with enthusiasm while I was making a valiant effort at the same time to hide my tears.

The lights in the room came up slowly as the students all moved to the center of the room. Michelle was in the middle, holding three gift-wrapped objects in her arms.

"I would like to start by saying thank you to everyone who participated in our show," she said. "Atticus, you certainly didn't make things easy for us with your surprise evening. This was all going to be set up at the hotel."

Now I understood why everyone was scrambling and acting downright weird these past few days. In fact, Cynthia, Marco, and Giovanni all looked at me and grinned.

"A special thanks also goes to James, whose artwork made this all possible. And for your efforts, James, we have a little something for you."

Michelle handed James one of the gift-wrapped packages. His look of surprise made it clear he wasn't expecting this nor was he going to say anything.

"Another special thanks goes to Massimo," Michelle continued. "We could not have had a better tour guide these past nine days. This is a small something to show our appreciation."

She gestured to Massimo to come to the center of the room. Just like James, you could tell that Massimo had not expected this. But unlike James, Massimo was going to make his voice heard.

"Oh my! I wasn't expecting this…I'm just so overwhelmed! Let me just say that you have been the best group that I ever have had the honor to escort in this enchanting city. Please, we must remain in touch…I am sure that we will see each other again either here in the eternal city or in your beautiful Atlanta."

At this point, Massimo was overcome with emotion and rushed back to his seat to crushing applause.

"Atticus, could you please come here?" said Michelle.

The music had changed once again: "*Torna a Surriento*" sung by Luciano Pavarotti. I took a quick glance at Franco standing behind his sound equipment. I had told him once, many years ago, that this was one of the few songs that brought me to tears. He obviously remembered. By now, I was a sniveling mess.

I got up from my chair, trying to maintain some form of dignity, but it was useless, especially when I stood in front of Michelle. She handed me the third gift.

"To the best escort, tour guide, listener, and friend. We will never forget you."

She hugged me, with all the others coming forward. I noticed that there weren't many dry eyes. There were handshakes, hugs, kisses, tears, and laughing. This was certainly a magical moment.

CHAPTER 62

I was on my second Toscanello cigar and halfway through a well-chilled bottle of limoncello. I had been sitting at a small outside table on the portico, which wrapped around the restaurant, for well over an hour now. It was close to one thirty in the morning, and nobody had gone home yet.

After the tear-filled hug fest, where Michelle presented James, Massimo, and me with our gifts, a conveyor belt of food and beverages arrived with everyone *ooh*-ing and *aah*-ing at the assortment of pasta, meat, fish, and vegetables. I had gone back to my seat between Cynthia and Barbara and was egged on to open my gift-wrapped item. After battling with the scotch tape and all the multicolored tissue paper, I unearthed a beautiful Louis Vuitton ashtray. I shot a glance at Barbara.

"Turn it over, Atticus," she said.

All the names of the group were engraved on the back with the dates of the of the trip, as well as a two-line dedication:

To a wonderful human being who took the time to listen and advise. Not a bad tour guide to boot! We love you!

Once again, I felt the tears threatening to spill. "This is beautiful," I said. "I'm speechless."

"Well, good," Cynthia said. "Barbara and I had to almost tear off the head of the LV store manager to get that engraving done on time."

Barbara touched the ashtray. "Now you have something to remind you of all of us when you have your little Italian cigars."

"I have a feeling I won't be forgetting any of you for a very long time." I reached over and hugged both of them. A sudden squeal of delight interrupted us:

"Oh! It's just exquisite! I can't believe it! Priceless, just priceless!"

Everyone looked in Massimo's direction as he proudly held up an Atlanta Falcons leather bombardier-style jacket. He then turned it around so we could see all the names of the group embroidered on the back.

"Now how did you manage to pull that one off?" I asked in genuine astonishment.

"This was Wayne's and Bishop's idea," Barbara explained. "With Wayne's father's clout, the jacket was purchased, personalized, and FedEx-ed within seventy-two hours. Piece of cake."

"Well, you could not have made him any happier," I observed.

Massimo had gotten up and was hugging and kissing everyone. I then looked over at the far corner of the *L*-shaped table and saw James quietly opening his gift. I couldn't really make it out, save that it came in a good-sized wooden box. James slowly opened the hinged lid.

Barbara leaned over. "It's a box of Swiss drawing pencils and charcoal with a sketch pad. He really has a lot of talent."

"That's an understatement," I said. "Those sketches tonight were gallery material. Did anyone know about his drawing skills?"

"He certainly did a good job keeping it secret," Cynthia said. "I didn't have a clue until we started talking about this surprise for you. That's when he offered to handle all the designs."

As much as I was delighted with James's skill, I remembered the artists he had mentioned in his student bio who had all committed suicide. But it wasn't the place or time to dwell on this.

As the eating and drinking progressed, Franco became more and more creative with his choice of music. From the best of the '80s to country to classic pop and now disco. When he put Donna Summer's "Hot Stuff" on, almost everyone got up to dance. From that point on, nobody really sat down anymore, other than to stick a fork in a dessert or try one of the numerous *digestivos* that the waiters had placed on the tables.

After a good bit of dancing myself, as well as a decent amount of chitchatting with just about everyone present, I slid out the back and with a bottle of limoncello and my new LV ashtray. I had been looking forward to my Toscanello and some time on my own to enjoy the moment.

A movie projector in my brain was continuously exhibiting flashbacks of everything that had transpired these past nine days. I also thought very hard about how I had changed in such a brief period of time—from my unwillingness to get involved with these people to finding myself completely intertwined in their lives.

I was realizing that as much as I needed a well-paying job to cover the financial responsibilities I had toward my children, the trade-off was for a more superficial and less caring attitude toward my fellow man. I had always given importance to the title, position, and responsibilities as well as the perks of my previous positions. These last few days were an eye-opener, and I had come to the realization, in a very short period, that for a large portion of my life, I had missed out on everything that makes life truly special.

I had just snubbed out my Toscanello and was thinking about lighting a third, when someone tapped me on the shoulder. It was Mark.

"Do you mind if I sit with you for a minute?" he asked diffidently.

"Of course not. How's it going in there?"

"It's great, really good. Everyone's having fun. Don't know how we're going to catch our flight in the morning. You're going to need some wheelbarrows to get us on that bus."

He fidgeted a but with the glass of red wine he was holding. "Wish we didn't have to go back."

"All good things come to an end, Mark. That's what makes them special."

"Yeah, I guess."

I waited for him to continue the conversation. I knew why he was here.

"Atticus, I think I owe you an explanation."

I shook my head. "You don't owe me anything. But if there is something you'd like to tell me, I'm ready to listen."

He sighed. "I really screwed up. I know it. I guess there isn't any real excuse. I just really felt like shit, you know?"

"Well, something must have been bothering you. It could have—"

Mark cut across. "Did Mrs. Ramsey talk to you?"

I wasn't expecting this question, but I should have.

"She told me that she had some long conversations with you and that she was heartbroken by what you told her. That's about it."

Mark looked into his glass. "I knew she could keep a secret. Turns out she's really cool. I was so wrong about her."

"Sometimes our first impressions are not spot-on."

"Do you mind if I tell you what I told her? If you've got some time?"

"I'll stay here all night if it helps."

With that, the faucet opened up, and I got the whole story, probably word for word what Cynthia had been told.

"Well, Mark, that was a lot to get off your chest," I said when he was finished. "I'm honored that you decided to share all of this with me."

"It felt good unloading on Mrs. Ramsey, but doing it again with you makes me feel, well, stronger, more in control of myself. Does that sound weird?"

"Not at all." I lighted another cigar. "By the way, Mark, now that I think of it, did anybody tell you how it is we found you?"

Marks eyes squinted a bit and his lips pressed together as if he were reviewing the entire sequence of events since he woke up at the hospital. "Now that you mention it, Atticus, no, I don't think I even asked."

"It was James."

"James?" This wasn't the answer he was expecting.

I went ahead and explained how we had made mention of the Evanescence album on the bus and the angel on the cover. "James remembered me mentioning that this angel was in that cemetery by the pyramid. He's the one that put two and two together. He may have just saved your life."

"Wow, I guess I should thank him."

"No, Mark. As odd as this may sound, I wouldn't bring it up unless he mentions it. It's James we're talking about. You catch my drift?"

"Yeah, I guess so. I'll do what you say. Makes sense."

I patted him on the back. "You make sure to keep in touch when you get back. Just an email occasionally, okay?"

I knew that this wouldn't happen or, if it did, maybe once or twice before I would become one of those memories stored away in the dust-filled attic of the brain.

"Atticus?" Mary popped her head out of the door. "Some of our guests are leaving."

"Be right there, Mary, thanks."

I could tell Mark wasn't quite ready to get up yet.

He shifted uncomfortably. "Do you think there's something wrong with me? I get it that my behavior with my sister wasn't normal. Do you think I've got a problem? Something to worry about as I get older?"

Mark had a desperate air about him. I could tell that he was going to hang on to every word I was about to say.

"I'm not a psychiatrist, Mark. What I can tell you is that now that you've admitted what happened and understood that it wasn't appropriate, you're way ahead of the curve. I think you feel genuine remorse. Therefore, in a nutshell, I would say, no, there is nothing wrong with you. If it makes you feel better, though, maybe a chat with a professional family services counselor when you get back could help."

He looked relieved. "Thanks for that, Atticus. It helps more than you think."

"Okay, then, let's get back inside and see who the cop-outs are."

We both smiled and headed back to our room.

When Mark and I walked back to our private dining area, the spectacle in front of us was something out of the Delta Tau Chi fraternity house in the movie *Animal House*.

I couldn't even begin to count the number of empty wine, beer, and limoncello bottles on the tables and on the floor. Shoes were scattered everywhere, as well as certain items of clothing. Some of the students were playing cards in small groups on the floor, others were still attempting to dance after a more than generous amount of alcohol, and still, others were speaking with the adults in the room, who were also looking worse for wear. Rosanna, our tour guide at the Vatican, came up to me and gave me a hug.

"I can't begin to tell you how much fun I had tonight, Atticus. These students are so special, and I had some very interesting conversations with the three teachers, and with Marco, and Giovanni…well, everyone! I would stay if it weren't for a group I have at eight this morning."

I looked at my watch—it was two o'clock!

"Glad you could make it, Rosanna," I said. "I will keep in touch via Marco."

"Please do, and if you ever need a guide for the Vatican, remember me." She gave me a kiss on the cheek and made her way out of the room.

John and Rhea then came up to me, looking quite disheveled.

"What a night, Atticus," John said. "I don't think I've danced this much since my senior prom."

"And what a special group of people," Rhea added. "So glad that you invited me."

"What time do we have to be at the bus?" John asked.

"In less than four hours, I'm afraid."

I saw Rhea wince a bit at this realization. John looked at her and said, "Well, let's make the best of the time left." He was obviously very much taken by this woman. There was sweetness in his voice instead of a "Let's go pound our brains out" undertone.

Giorgio and his driver Pietro were the next to leave. "Atticus, my dear friend, what an enjoyable evening. I don't remember the last time I was out so late. I am sorry for Pietro here, but I think that he also enjoyed himself."

Pietro nodded. "Not only did I have a wonderful time, but I learned a great deal from that young man over there." He pointed to Anthony. "I thought I knew a thing or two about firearms. Well, let me tell you, I am an amateur compared to him."

I promised Giorgio that I would keep in touch and that I would take him to Giggetto's restaurant on my next trip to Rome. We embraced, and they took their leave.

As I reached for a glass of limoncello on the table behind me, I felt a tap on my shoulder. I turned to see Stefano and his wife. "So glad you invited us, Atticus," he said. "We had a marvelous time." Stefano took me under the arm and leaned in a bit. "I'm happy to see that our drug-addicted young lady looks so well. Have you had any issues since I visited her?" I explained to Stefano that there had not been any surprises. "And the other young lady, the one we met in the staircase, she's looking much better." It took everything I had not to wince. These last hours had been so carefree, and Michelle had looked so wonderful this evening that I had temporarily forgotten the limited time she had left.

"Are you all right, Atticus?" Stefano sensed my shift in mood.

"Yes, yes, just fine. Just a little concerned with the condition of the students. We need to be at the airport in less than five hours."

"Don't worry, they are young." With that, Stefano and his wife exited.

Giovanni was the next to go. We would see each other back at the hotel because he wanted to give once last goodbye to the group. He shook my hand and looked me straight in the eye, "*Forma bonum, fragile est.*" Everything good must come to an end. How true!

The group was thinning out, but the students hadn't really noticed. Some were occupied with card games, others were laughing and reminiscing about the trip, and still, others looked in bad shape, sitting on the floor and slouching on each other's shoulders. The limoncello had taken its toll.

"Atticus?" I turned to Raymond standing there with his two Jewish friends, Jacob and Martin.

"Gentlemen, glad to see you're still standing," I said.

"Well, that's easy," said Jacob. "We don't drink. Just Sprite and Fanta for us."

"The three of us are going to head back to the hotel, Atticus," said Raymond. "They'll drop me off and head home from there. I still have to pack up all my stuff."

"That's fine but let me get a waiter to hail a cab. Don't need the three of you wandering the streets of Rome at three in the morning."

"Yes, dad," Raymond grinned.

I gave the two boys an index card with my email address on it. Luckily, I had remembered to prepare a bunch of these before I left the hotel. I asked them to please keep in touch, especially when they were in Israel. They said they would.

I asked one of the waiters to wave down a cab for them. As I watched them leave, I wondered what the future had in store for all three.

It was now almost three o'clock. It was time to get back to the hotel. As I was approaching Cynthia and Barbara, Marco and his wife approached me.

"Well, my friend, what can I say, a glorious ending to an eventful nine days."

"You're right, Marco. Looking back, I wouldn't have missed this for the world. I owe you an apology for being so uncooperative in the beginning, and I owe you more than just a thank-you. These people, this entire experience, has opened my eyes in so many ways."

Marco stretched out his hand and squeezed my shoulder. "I'm happy to hear this. It's going to be hard on you to say goodbye to these people in just four hours." He shot a glance around the room. "Just make sure they get on the bus. By the looks of some of them, you're going to need some help."

We embraced and promised to hear from each other very soon.

Now it was only Massimo and his partner who had not taken their leave and did not seem in the least bit interested in doing so. They were speaking with Wayne, Bishop, Mark, Jeremy, and Michelle and the conversation seemed lively. In the corner of the room, I saw Evelyn, Mary, Anthony, and James. James was sketching Mary's portrait. I approached gingerly and peeked over James' shoulder. The resemblance was flabbergasting. James was beyond just talented. However, I checked myself this time and did not come out with a sudden flattering statement regarding his skill. This was James, and I had learned my lesson.

"He's really good, Atticus." Anthony opened the door for me.

"I would say more than just good. Rarely have I seen such attention to detail in a pencil sketch. Compliments, James. I hope you keep this up when you are back in the States."

I walked away at once, avoiding any unexpected reaction from our artist.

I made my way toward Cynthia and Barbara and their small group. "Ladies, I don't know if you are aware that it is now four in the morning. We must be on the bus in two and a half hours."

It was as if I had said that a nuclear warhead was about to strike Rome.

"What! Four o'clock?" Darlene shrieked.

"No, it can't be!" Cynthia was in disbelief.

"Can the bus just come here and pick us up?" Barbara was borderline hammered. "Oh, I guess not...our luggage is at the hotel." She started to giggle and then laughed, which got everyone else roaring. Marco was right, getting my group back to the hotel was going to require assistance. I turned and looked at Massimo and Sebastiano. As soon as they locked eyes with me, I tapped on my watch and pointed at the door. They immediately understood and got up out of their chairs. Massimo, in his inimitable theatrical style, hopped on his chair and gave the marching orders.

"My dearest friends, the time has come to leave this comfortable abode. We must get back to your hotel, pack up, and get ready to go the airport."

"Thank you, Massimo," I murmured to myself.

The next hour was action-packed.

Between getting everyone on their feet, getting all their belongings together, saying goodbye to the staff that was still in the restaurant at this very late hour, taking care of the bill, calling six taxis to take us and the thirteen canvases back to the hotel, and finally, getting everyone back to their rooms to slap some cold water on their faces and grab their suitcases.

By six, we were all sitting in the restaurant area of the hotel, ready to head out to the bus.

I had managed to spend about fifteen minutes alone with Barbara. We hugged each other and shed some tears.

She held my face. "My dear Atticus, we may never see each other again, but I want you to know that I will never, ever forget you."

"Nor I. This trip would not have been the same without you."

"Oh, I don't know about that. You certainly had your hands full with Cynthia, John, let alone most of these kids. Of course, I can still show a man a thing or two in bed."

"Take the prize for the understatement of the year."

Barbara laughed.

"Keep me informed about Michelle, James, Evelyn—hell, all of them." This is where I became emotional. "These kids, you know, they mean a lot to me, as awkward as that may sound."

"I will, no worries. As soon as I have any news, I'll drop you an email."

We hugged once more and realized that it was probably for the last time.

Back in the breakfast room, Giovanni and Ludovica came in to give their farewells, as well as the cook and the rest of the kitchen staff. This group had left their mark.

Massimo, who was still with us, began saying goodbye to each student and teacher. He was a teary mess by the time he got to me.

"I won't forget them," he wept. "They are all so special. This has been a magnificent journey for me. And you, my special friend, don't you dare disappear on me. I want to know your whereabouts and what is going on in your life. Please, stay in touch."

"I will Massimo. Milano is close, and I plan to come to Rome frequently."

I didn't add that Ludovica was in the back of my mind. Instead, I glanced at my watch for the umpteenth time. It was six twenty-five. Time to go. I asked Barbara, Cynthia, John, and Massimo to round up the group, making sure that no one and nothing was left behind. We formed a line and sloppily made our way to the hotel lobby and exit. Ludovica and Giovanni were waving and blowing kisses to everyone. Quite unexpectedly, from the back of the line, I saw Barbara walk up to Ludovica and whisper something to her. Ludovica blushed and gave Barbara a sincere smile. That was a surprise.

We trudged along the same exact road that brought us here just nine short days ago. The suitcase wheels were still snagging in the San Pietrini, motor scooters were zipping back and forth, and the smell of fresh pastries was everywhere. Just another day in the Eternal City.

We arrived at the bus. Riccardo was standing at its side waiting for us. He looked fresh as a rose.

"How is it that you stay up all night Riccardo and look like a movie star?"

He gave me a sly grin. "Practice, Signor Atticus, practice. I do this a lot."

At a slower-than-desired pace, everyone got their suitcases tucked under the bus and got comfortable in the reclining seats. The teachers sat up front, as did I.

Once Ricardo got the Mercedes bus rolling, I knew the time had come to say a few last words to my group. I got up from my seat and took the microphone from the center consul.

'Hey, just a few last words, and then I'll shut up and let you get thirty minutes of shut eye." I had everyone's attention. "Just nine days ago, we were sitting on this very same bus going in the opposite direction. All of you were trying to figure me out, and I was asking myself why in the hell I had accepted this job."

"Best decision you ever made!" Wayne said, getting cheers.

"Yes, Wayne, you're right. We've been through a lot, together. You opened up to me, and I opened up to you. We did what human beings do. We shared experiences, we listened to each other, and we tried to help when help was needed. Now, as much as we promised each other last night that we will keep in touch, in a month or two, we probably won't. That's just the way life is. We go from one experience to another. What I do hope, however, is that all of you remember little pieces of this nine-day adventure as you get older, as I hope you remember me."

I had thought I was going to get through this as cool as a cucumber, but that wasn't the case. "I...I love you all. You're all so special in your own unique ways. Thank you for an unforgettable experience. Now get some sleep before we get to the airport."

I hurriedly put the mike back and sat down.

CHAPTER 63

I spoke to Cynthia, Barbara, and John the rest of the way to Fiumicino Airport.

John revealed that he was planning a trip to Greece to see Rhea at the end of August. Cynthia wanted to get back to prepare for the new school year as well as "make up for lost time," as she put it, with the students on this trip and the ones who did not participate. Barbara was vague, but I knew what she had to deal with as soon as she got home.

I stood up a moment and looked behind me. There wasn't a set of eyes open.

"It's going to take a team effort to get this group off the bus. I'm amazed at the three of you. No sleep in twenty-four hours, and you're not that badly off."

"Same can be said for you, Atticus," Cynthia noted. "Other than a five-o'clock shadow, which looks rather sexy if you ask me, you look well rested."

The three of us looked at Cynthia.

"You don't mind the observation, Barbara, do you?" she asked.

We all laughed.

I turned my head and noticed through the bus's large windshield that we had off-ramped onto the airport service road. We would be at the departure hall in just a few minutes.

I saw Riccardo fiddling with the stereo system, and after just a few seconds, Nat King Cole's voice came over the speakers singing "*Arrivederci Roma.*" What a classic touch!

The teachers and I struggled less than we thought to get everyone off the bus, suitcases in hand, and into the airport. I shared a few words with Riccardo before he left and promised to check in on him every once in a while. The truth was that I would probably never see him again.

The American Airlines counter had an employee dealing solely with group check-ins, which was truly fortunate. In no time, the students and teachers were processed with tickets in hand. It was approaching eight, and the flight was boarding at nine twenty. I wanted the group to have some time to buy some last-moment souvenirs once they passed passport control.

This is where everything became awkward. We didn't know what to say to each other. We were in that limbo right before a definitive goodbye where words are sparse and inadequate.

I decided to break the ice by going to each student and sharing a few last words.

I began with Mary, thanking her for the opera lessons.

I then turned to Vanessa and Sabrina, hugged them both, and told them I was only a phone call or an email away if they ever needed to unload.

I shook Anthony's hand and asked him to remember our conversation at the café. I also told him to follow his passion and make a profession out of it. There were plenty of arms manufacturers in the United States that he easily could work for.

Next was Jeremy, who I thanked profusely for his help in finding a certain someone.

Mark followed. We had made our peace hours ago. I told him to give me a holler if he needed anything.

Raymond and I hugged. I told him to let me know what he was doing in Israel and to not forget that he had a friend in Italy.

James and Evelyn were next. "Look after yourselves, please. You've got a pair of ears here in Italy twenty-four seven if you want to discuss anything at all."

"Why would we ever want to speak with you again?" James was as serious as I had ever seen him. My temperature went down a notch. Then he punched me on the shoulder. "Can't take a joke, can you? Here, this is for you. I don't care what you do with all those canvases. Trash them if you want."

He handed me a long-rolled paper with a black ribbon tied around it. "Open it when you get back to the hotel."

Evelyn gave me a quick but tight hug. "Thanks, Atticus. You've been cool. I'll be remembering you for a while."

Now I was standing in front of Darlene. She gave me a bear hug and a big kiss on the cheek, which made me go fire-engine red for a moment. "You've taught me a lot, Atticus. And remember, you promised me some connections when I get out of the community college."

"Just say the word, Darlene," I replied.

She winked at me and walked over to Sabrina and Vanessa.

Wayne and Bishop were next. "Thanks, Atticus, for everything. We'll get to work on that "project" you and Mrs. Cornwall talked to us about as soon as we get back." I gave them a thumbs-up. "Just tell me when you're ready, and I'll get the show started."

Last was Michelle. It took everything I could do not to start crying like a baby in front of her. She watched me directly in my eyes and said, "It's all going to be okay. I'm ready. You and this city have been the best thing that has ever happened to me. I'll remember you now and afterwards That's a promise."

She gently pulled away from me, knowing that I was about to lose it.

As soon as I regained a minimum of composure, I went up to say goodbye to Barbara, Cynthia, and John.

When I hugged Barbara for the last time, she whispered in my ear, "I went to see St. Rita. I asked her for something that is very important to me. Let's see if she is as magical as you say."

I looked at her and smiled. "May I ask you what you said to Ludovica on the way out of the hotel?"

"Just woman's talk. I told her to take good care of you and that you were a very special person." She hesitated a moment. "I'm going to go now, Atticus. This isn't easy for me." She leaned into me one more time. "I love you." Then she turned and headed toward passport control.

I shook hand with John and wished him all the best with Rhea. "Who knows, Atticus, I may just move to Greece." He embraced me and then rounded up the students.

That left Cynthia and me. Her eyes were wet, but she had a beaming smile. "I have no words, Atticus. You are my savior. I will never be able to thank you enough." We hugged for a long time. She backed away a little and told me that she would keep in touch, and that I would not be forgotten.

"Thank you, Cynthia."

I watched her head in the direction of the group. As they went through the metal detectors, they all turned and waved at me. I waited until they had cleared customs and turned the corner to the departure area. My group was going home.

I made my way back down to the arrivals hall and stopped at the café where I had met with Marco just nine days ago. I found a small table in the corner that faced outward, in the direction of those sliding glass doors where I had first met the group. As usual, they were opening and closing, streaming human beings of all nationalities. I remembered how Cynthia and Barbara had been the first to come out with John and the students arriving shortly afterward.

How much had transpired in just nine days? I wouldn't be able to fit it into a book even if I tried.

My cappuccino and cornetto arrived, and the fragrance of both reminded me of Filippo's bar. I knew that Filippo and many of the bar's patrons were waiting for some juicy tidbits upon my return. Of course, I would have to tell them something, but most of what had come to pass with these sixteen people was going to be kept to myself. In retrospect, I had treasured every moment of this excursion and greatly respected each of the students and each of the teachers. I wasn't going to make light of any of them or of any of the situations that only I was privy to.

Now, however, I had to force myself to think of the future. I would be receiving news about that job offer shortly. I had to get back to Milan and clear out Francesca's belongings, and most importantly, I would be able to see my children next week. Thank goodness I had decided to stay in Rome a few more days. I needed some rest. I was also looking forward to my time with Ludovica that evening and wondering if the closing of a very special chapter in my life had given impetus to a new one being opened.

Amidst all these thoughts, I had completely forgotten the tubular piece of paper that James had given me. I pulled on the ribbon, unrolled the drawing paper, and gasped. In front of me was a photo-likeness pencil drawing of *The Boxer at Rest* that statue that James had been so enthralled with. Down in the bottom right-hand corner, he had written: "We didn't get to see this together, so I made you a copy. Keep it or burn it. I don't care."

Typical James.

EPILOGUE

Email from Barbara (01/16/2011)

My dearest Atticus, it's been some time since I last wrote or heard from you, but I just had to tell you about some earth-shattering news. My boys! They got in touch with Jeff and me! They will be stateside in May and asked to come over to the house! I am besides myself with joy! What makes this news even more incredible has to do with something I never told you. When I went to see the statue of St. Rita, I asked her for one thing: to see my boys again! You know me. I try to be levelheaded about these things, but I must say, Rita came through! Jeff and I are counting the minutes. We are so nervous and agitated. I just can't stand it!

Let me change subject, or I'll just go on and on about this. I do have some news for you about the group. Some good, some bad, unfortunately. Michelle's brother: after Michelle's funeral back in November, he went over the deep end (by the way, Michelle's mom and dad still bring up how much she spoke so highly of you when she got back home. She really loved you). He just snapped! We don't know if it was due to PTSD or Michelle's death. Long story short, he got drunk and had a fight with two individuals in a seedy part of town. He almost killed one of them. He was sentenced to four years. The family is devastated.

Darlene: I lost track of her. I know she didn't go to Westwood Community College, as she said she was, and we think she may have left town. Cynthia has been trying to call, text, and email her, but no answer. Have you heard anything?

James: Last time I saw him was at Michelle's funeral. He did have some back-and-forth text messages with Cynthia, and it seems that he went to NYC (he has a distant cousin who lives up there). The good news is that someone up there has taken an interest in his art (news always via Cynthia). He may even get a gallery show. That's exciting for him!

Evelyn: Don't know much other than that she moved out of her parent's house. I think she has a roommate, but not sure. Has she been in touch with you lately?

Wayne and Bishop: Well, our little plan worked, as you know. The stepmom is gone, but Wayne did not come out unscathed. The photos Janice had taken reached Wayne's dad. No violence, thank goodness! But Wayne has moved out of the house and Atlanta. He and Bishop got an apartment in Athens, GA. Wayne has just started at U of G, and Bishop is in a technical apprentice school for mechanics. They keep in touch with Cynthia almost weekly (remember how she used to rag on them all the time when we were in Rome?).

Mary: I have lost touch with her, but I know that she's at Marquette University in Michigan. I'm sure she is doing well.

Vanessa and Sabrina: After Vanessa checked-out of rehab back in October, she seems to have kept clean. I know that Sabrina and Vanessa are really tight—to the point that I think they may be a couple. Some of their photos on Facebook are a bit "revealing," if you know what I mean. They seem happy. I don't think they have money issues. Sabrina's parents are loaded.

Raymond: As you know, he came back for Michelle's funeral. It was terribly hard on him. He must have had a soft spot for her that nobody was aware of. I have had no news from him since then. But I think you have a connection with him? Is he doing well in Israel?

Jeremy: No clue. I think he went up north to a tech university. He was our hacker, as you know.

Mark: Bad news here. When Michelle passed away and then Wayne and Bishop moved away, Mark went into a deep state of depression. Cynthia was speaking with him almost every day up until the end of December. Then he just vanished. We have no clue where he is. Cynthia even confronted his parents, who didn't seem terribly concerned. She went to their house and told me that they were already drunk out of their minds at two in the afternoon. I'll keep you updated. Let me know if you hear anything.

John: As you know, he left for Greece way back in August and never came back. Not even for his mother's funeral, which was in late November. A lot of family "history" there, I bet. I know he's in touch with you, so nothing to add here. I love his postcards! What a beautiful island he's on—and running a B&B! That fits him to a T. Do you think he will be tying the knot with Rhea soon?

Cynthia and Anthony: I think you are also very much aware that Anthony moved to Springfield, MA, and is working as an apprentice at the Smith & Wesson headquarters. I am very proud of him. Did he or Cynthia ever tell you how he got the job? He wrote a paper on how the S&M semiautomatic pistols could have better precision by modifying some thingamajig in its mechanical parts. S&M was so impressed that they invited him up to MA immediately. What you may not know, fresh off the press, is that Cynthia accepted a job at a high school close to Springfield! You know, Atticus, you never told me what she told you in Rome, and I respect that. One day, she almost spilled the beans with me. She said that she wanted to tell me something about Anthony. But she never did. She leaves Atlanta at the end of February. I guess it will just remain a mystery for me.

What about you, Atticus? Last time we communicated, you were going to Barcelona to a boat show. Are you enjoying your new employment? You sounded awfully happy back in June when you accepted. Must be nice going in and out of the ultraexpensive yachts. You also mentioned that you were seeing Ludovica. I'm happy for you, jealous but happy. I think I had mentioned that I had gone in great detail about you with Jeff. He wasn't upset, maybe a bit hurt, but he knows he can't say anything. He's actually been very quiet in his "extracurricular" activities ever since I got back. I know he loves me in his own way, and I guess I still love him. Maybe with the boys coming back, we will be able to mend some of the deep wounds between all of us.

Please pray for me. Yes, I said "pray." I can't screw things up again with my children. I just still cannot believe that they are actually coming, after all these years. I'm a nervous wreck. Well, that's it, Atticus. Sorry I was so long-winded. I think about you often, and I won't forget you. I hope it's reciprocal.

Speak soon,
Love,
Barbara

ABOUT THE AUTHOR

First attempt at writing a book;
Seasoned business executive with over forty years'
experience in sales,
Marketing, and general management;
Lived and worked abroad for thirty-four years;
Married with three children;
Residing in Florida and Milan, Italy.
Hobbies: writing, cooking, and reading.

ACKNOWLEDGEMENTS

Many direct and indirect experiences, in the course of a rather lengthy lifetime, have culminated in the production of this book. However, a special thank-you must be shared with a group of individuals with whom I passed a considerable amount of time back in the late '80s as well as another group of individuals who I never personally met.

After my tour of duty at the U.S. Embassy in Rome, Italy, I found myself in a predicament that closely resembles that which our protagonist, Atticus Winterle, finds himself in—to wit, the need for employment. The job market in Italy back then was not a compassionate one, and my hands were tied when interviewing, considering that my security clearance did not allow me to speak about my past "experiences" or "professional background." Long story short, I found myself escorting groups of US-based high school students to various European destinations: Berlin, Paris, Rome, Florence, Athens, Istanbul, and Moscow from the beginning of 1988 to mid-1990. Even though *Nine Days in Rome* is considered a work of fiction, I can honestly say that many of the experiences that our protagonist finds himself involved in, have a basis in fact.

I shall never forget those now nameless individuals who filled my life with such memorable experiences. Just like our friend Atticus, I was not particularly interested in teenagers any more than most ordinary adults. But as time passed, especially during the trips to Rome, Paris, and Athens, I came to realize that these individuals had a voice and that it needed to be heard. An awkward "thank-you" also must be extended to the parents of these students, whom I never met. Awkward in that these so-called "parents," in some cases, were a fountain of information from which I was able to develop the storyline of *Nine Days in Rome*. Parenting is the most difficult employment that the job market has to offer.

How our parents nurtured us depends, to a large extent, on how they were brought up, and on and on back through time. There are parents who do the best they can, there are those who fail their children, and then there are those individuals who should never have had the word *parent* attached to them in the first place. In this book, I hope I have exposed situations that will make all parents reflect upon their relationship with their children. For the younger adults who may pick up this book or download it, may it be a helpful guide in making the best choice when confronted by a fork in the road. Life is a journey, with a beginning and an end. This journey is punctuated throughout by the choices that we make. In this book, my objective was to bring some examples of these choices to light, as well as their sometimes-devastating effect. I hope you enjoy reading it as much as I enjoyed writing it.

I would like to thank Leaders Press and Simon & Schuster for all their assistance in getting this book published. It has been a long, arduous road that would never have seen an ending without the skill and dedication of the team of people who worked with me from day one. I look forward now to starting a new project, *Nine Days in Paris*, with them in the following months.

Milton Keynes UK
Ingram Content Group UK Ltd.
UKHW020627220124
436466UK00020B/1180